THE BALLAD OF SIX:
ICARUS

CONTENT WARNING

While this book is Fantasy, it contains scenes and subject matter that will be triggering for some. If you are sensitive to heavier topics, please see my website (www.JessicaJeannine Author.com) for a complete list of content, and continue at your own discretion.

For everyone that has been unsafe in a place they called home.

CONTENTS

THE ORDINEM CREED

We are the one of many.
We are the protectors and the destroyers.
We are the creators of the world to come.
We are the true Order, void of error.
We are our ancestors and our children.

We stand on the words of our prophet, Holy and Right like no other.
We walk in the steps of the heroes that died for our cause.
We follow the light of our Guide— The Chosen One.
We trust the wisdom of our Counselor, The Most Gracious of All.
There is no other way.
There are no other vessels.
There is no better Code.

We will not rest until the lower world's righteousness mirrors that of the higher.
We will not rest until the light is too bright for any darkness to remain.
We will not rest until every soul is granted mercy,
And the powers of Assecula reside with us no longer.
Until the Veil between realms has been sealed,
And Grim have been expelled from this world they long to destroy.
We will not rest until Terra is safe.
May the Wind grant us strength.

May we always fight fairly, and in the name of justice.
May we act with integrity, and treat every soul with the mercy we have been shown.
May no lie ever fall from our lips.

May our hands never do harm.
May our souls be kept in the light.
May the mark of our allegiance never fade.

All obeisances to Nathaniel Warnock.

PROLOGUE

The boy was seven the first time he entered Inanis.

Blond hair, blue eyes, his father's jacket wrapped around him— he sat on his bedroom floor with his knees to his chest and his hands over his ears, trying to silence the thunder.

Then, it was always thunder, but that day it was more.

He lifted his head from his knees, his teeth chattering, and took one last look at his window before closing his teary eyes tight, struggling to breathe.

Desperation is a strange thing.

Icarus didn't know if he believed the stories; he had only heard a few. He knew only that he could still hear the voices of the Council members in his living room, and that he wanted to make them stop.

He knew that the people he was supposed to trust claimed that there was some place where things wouldn't hurt and that if he tried hard enough, he might be able to find it. So he folded his shaking hands and prayed to anything listening that he could go somewhere else. Anywhere else.

And he did.

When he opened his eyes, he was alone. He could see nothing but darkness— hear nothing but the wind.

"Heh...Hel... Hello?" he asked the nothingness. "I-is there an-n-anyone..."

Silence, but the wind still blew. It wrapped itself around him and lifted him.

His eyes widened as his feet left the ground, but for once, he didn't feel afraid. There was no malice in the darkness, and as he rose, the void began to come to life.

He couldn't understand how, but it was as if he could feel the place's breath, its heartbeat— and another's.

He blinked quickly, jumping a little at the feeling of being watched, but when he turned around, there was nothing but the same blackness in front of him. Then, like

fireflies, little sparks of light spread themselves across the sand, blown about in the win
d.

He moved to pull himself loose from whatever held him, and it lowered him, dulling the ache of his legs when his feet collided with the ground.

He stepped forward without thinking, knelt, and reached for the golden shards; when the light finally met his skin, it burned him. Surprised, he closed his eyes, and when he opened them again he was back in his bedroom.

The boy stared ahead in shock, his breath fast, and didn't move until there was another knock at his door. Startled, he jumped out of the way and ran over to his bed, pulling the covers up around his shoulders.

"C-come... Come in," he said, and the door opened, his mother stepping through it with soft eyes.

"Icarus," she said, tucking her brown hair behind her ears. "You look as if you've seen a ghost."

"A M-Mortum," he said. "They... they aren't called ghosts, they're the Mortum."

She closed the door behind her, sat on the bed, and offered a tired smile.

"Right, the Mortum. Too many stories for me." She leaned back against the wall and folded her arms, sighing deeply. "I say you're ready to join the Ordinem now."

"I'll n-n-never be..." The thunder interrupted him, and he stopped, shaking his head. "N-not like this."

"Like what, baby? Don't tell me you think a little trouble with your words will hold you back."

"They w-won't... Won't want m-m-me like this," he said. "I'm too... too s-s-slow, and..."

She shook her head, her face becoming more serious.

"No, no. You're not too slow," she began, and the boy crossed his arms. "If anything, you're in too much of a rush. Speak slowly, visualize the words in your mouth as you say them... Be silent, if you must. You do not always need to speak."

He didn't want to be silent.

"There are things in each of us that the Code takes issue with, but that is a part of it," she continued. "Learning to do away with the bad. Expelling those things that are unsuitable. It's a journey— for all of us."

He continued to stare ahead but nodded again. "Yes, Myon."

She smiled a little, but the term of respect weighed heavy on her heart.

"Mom works, too."

"Yes, Myon—" he paused, reddened. "M...mom."

She ruffled his hair but remained otherwise serious.

"You're young, but I think you deserve honesty, and I believe you're mature enough to handle it."

"I... I am."

"It's not going to be easy," she said, and he fell silent again. "It may be harder for you than some of the others, but it will also be harder for others than it will be for you. You must not allow yourself to feel..." She struggled to find the words. "Life is many things: A journey, a dance, a battle, but it goes lightly on no one."

His eyes fell to the bed— to his hands, and he turned them over, noting the black dirt smudged across them with a quick beating heart.

"You must work, and you must fight," she said, and he listened carefully, even with the rumbling in the background, hanging onto her every word. "But you were not born to be conquered, Icarus."

He dusted his hands on his pants, looked back up, and nodded without believing her.

"I know that," she said, "and your father knows that, and you're going to make all of them know it too, one day."

"B-but I—"

"No buts," she said. "You can be anything you want to be, Icarus. You're not what you come from."

PART ONE: THE REAPER

"The fault, Dear Brutus, is not in our stars."
-William Shakespeare

CHAPTER ONE

"Don't you think you've done enough, Icarus?"

Jack's voice is the only sound in the quiet of his study, pulling his son's eyes up from the book in front of him. It is sometime between too late and too early to be awake, the sun not yet risen, and Icarus has not slept. He sits in front of his father's cluttered desk with dark circles and messy hair, which is pulled back haphazardly behind his head.

"No," he responds. "Not yet. I'm still not confident."

"You're never confident," Jack says, and he frowns, his blue eyes sharp. "You've not failed a test since you came here, and yet, here we are; you've not even slept."

"I'm not tired."

"Yes, you are."

Books and papers are spread all around him, and he lets out a heavy sigh as he looks at them. Sure, he's tired, but he could be worse. He sees no reason to rest *now*.

His father turns out the light, leaving only the lamp in the corner, and he feels his body sink into the chair beneath him.

"Rest," the man says, and Icarus rubs his face, shaking his head.

"I can't," he responds. "Anem...m...mos will be here soon, either way. There's no point in s...sleeping now."

"Why is *Anemos* up? He's right next to the school already. It doesn't start for hours."

"I don't question him," he sighs. "He's nervous. He wants to... to be-be on time. I don't know."

"When will he be here?"

Icarus leans his head back, checking the clock behind him, and fights a groan.

"Within the hour."

"Rest your eyes until then, kiddo."

He nods reluctantly, his breath already becoming heavier. But before his father can leave the room, Icarus takes one of the many papers from the table, holding it in the air.

"Can I practice the vow, at least? Just run through it once? I'm having a hard time..."

Jack sighs and walks back to the center of the room, sitting on the sofa across from the desk.

"Alright," he says. "Let's hear it."

"With m-my... With my voice, I vow to honor the..." Icarus starts and then stops, shaking his head. "Not off to a great start, am I?"

"You're fine," Jack insists, and Icarus nods, continuing with tight fists.

"I vow to honor the words of this scroll," he rehearses, and his father closes his eyes, listening silently. "To dedicate my m-mind to those things which are worthy, according to the... to the wisdom of our ancestors. To align my soul with those wh...who... Can I ask you a question? I'm sorry."

"Of course you can, Icarus."

"Does it hurt?" he asks. "When they cut you, I mean. I kn...know it's a small thing to be worried about, but... I'm just so nervous, you know?"

"Stings like a wasp," Jack answers. "Why are you so nervous?"

Icarus leans his head back, yawning. "I don't know."

"I mean, don't get me wrong. You've plenty of reason—"

"That doesn't m-m...make me feel better."

"It's just a big day," the man says. "That's all. I'm not trying to make you more nervous than you are, I'm just saying I understand."

He doesn't, Icarus thinks, closing his eyes.

The darkness is making him so *heavy*.

"I just don't want to fail," he whispers. "And I know my scores are good, but... This is different." He opens his eyes again, squinting at the fan above him, and runs his hands nervously over the arms of the chair he sits in. "You know this one's different."

They are both quiet for a moment, letting the morning settle around them, and then Jack stands up, putting his hands on the boy's shoulders.

"When you get on that stage, you look at me and your mom and ignore the rest of the crowd. Ignore all of them, and you'll be fine."

It isn't just the vow. It's everything. Everything else. But Icarus nods anyway, forcing a fragmented smile.

"Okay."

"Now rest," the man says. "I'll wake you when your friend gets here. You don't need to wait up."

"You'd think I was s-s...still a child, the way you're having to reassure me."

Jack laughs quietly, mussing his eighteen-year-old son's hair.

"You are," he says. "Now go to *sleep.*"

A minute later— once Icarus leans forward on the desk, folds his arms, and closes his eyes— Jack leaves the room. Subsequently, Icarus rises again, pulling a penlight from the drawer under the desk. It *is* futile, he thinks— studying like his predicament is one with answers. There is no guide for passing the test he'll be facing, because it shouldn't be a challenge. All he has to be is a good Ordinem student and a good person. He only has to hold the right ideals, profess them the right way, and not be anything his government considers a threat.

But then, he was born outside the wall. That alone is enough of a reason for them to suspect him.

"I vow to honor the words of this scroll," he repeats. "To dedicate.... Mind, to those things which are worthy, and to align my soul with those who came before me."

He has read all of the books in front of him countless times. There is nothing else to learn from them. He turns around sharply in his chair, looking at the high cabinet behind him. It is his mother's cabinet, where she keeps the books and objects that should not be left lying around. He stands and approaches it slowly, trying to keep as quiet as he can.

Behind the dark wooden doors, on the middle shelf, sits a heavy bound copy of The Code. Beside it is a painted image of Nathaniel Warnock: the man who wrote it. He has seen his mother praying in front of it on several occasions— for a bit of the wisdom the great man was blessed with, or guidance, or even strength. Perhaps he would be better off if he joined her on occasion, or even approached the image alone. Maybe he could find mercy at Nathaniel Warnock's feet.

But the saint, he thinks, was just a man. Now he is a dead man. And the dead have been in no place to help men since the tearing of the veil, if they ever were.

Still, he bows to the image, muttering a pointless repentance for being in its presence. He takes The Code in his right hand, pulls it to his chest, and walks back across the room.

There is no life here, he reads, upon opening it. *No goodness.*

He lets out an exhausted sigh, flipping through several pages and silently praying that he will land on something helpful.

A man who ceases to fight is like a man who has already died. He moves nothing, in that action-less state. But a man who, faced with adversity, refuses to back down? That man's every movement reverberates in the air around him, inevitably affecting everyone else, whether he wins or loses. Perhaps it does not always breed success, but it makes a space for it in a way ceasing never will. Therefore, in every war, we must continue to do what is right, even when it seems we will lose...

The words ache in his chest, along with the others.

So then, Icarus supposes he should move forward despite the inevitable failure in front of him. He should continue to battle the darkness within him, even if he knows he will never rid it from his spirit. There has to be some merit in trying. There *has* to be, or he is hopeless—

The light in his hand dies, leaving him in darkness once more.

Hopeless, he thinks, setting The Code aside. That's what the book says, but his mother has always told him differently. He was not born to be conquered, he remembers, resting his head on the desk.

A decade later, he still clings to those words like they might save him.

Chapter Two

"Icarus," a voice says. *"Icarus."*

Icarus lifts his head from the desk in front of him, rubbing his eyes before opening them to a room that is still dark, save the early morning light passing through the curtains. Anemos stands next to him, resting one hand on the Code, which still lies o pen.

"Morning, sunshine," he says, and Icarus leans back, stretching.

"I'm sorry," he groans. "M...my dad said he would wake me—"

"Did you sleep?" Anemos interrupts, and Icarus stops, quiet settling in his chest.

"No," he answers, even though the opposite is apparent; he knows what Anemos means well enough. "Did you?"

His friend shakes his head, pushing a strand of dark, curly hair out of his eyes. "No."

Icarus looks down at the holy book in front of him, his heart pounding, and swallows hard. Exhaustion pulls his shoulders down.

"It'll only take m...me a... a second, to get ready. Then we can go."

"We could have some coffee first, if you want," Anemos responds. Then, when Icarus is silent: "Your dad was offering. Said he's already brewing a pot."

A moment later, they are seated at the kitchen table, Icarus pulling his jacket tightly around him, fighting a chill.

"And for you?" Jack asks, sitting a large mug in front of Anemos, who flashes a tired smile in response. "Cream?"

"No, that's fine," he says. "Thank you, Myon."

"Of course." Jack nods, turning to Icarus. "I know you want all of it, yeah?"

"He drinks his coffee *white*," Anemos remarks, and Icarus lets out a quiet sigh, nodding with his eyes half closed.

"Yes, please."

While his father makes his coffee, Icarus watches his friend uneasily. He tries to imitate his posture and the air of confidence around him, even though he questions its honesty. He can't imagine Anemos can be as unfazed by everything as he seems, but his steadiness is convincing enough that he wouldn't question it if he knew less.

That's what Icarus needs. He needs to be convincing.

"Here you go," his father says, and he takes the coffee in his hands, bringing it to his lips without waiting for it to cool.

"Thank you," he replies, and Jack puts a hand on his shoulder in response, moving to sit down beside him.

Icarus tries to ground himself in the man's presence— that, and his feet on the floor, and the warmth of the mug in his hands— but it does little to halt the anxiety already returning to his body.

This close to ceremony night, he isn't sure anything is capable of quieting his fear. But he concentrates on his breathing anyway, listening to Anemos and his father talk silently.

"So many of them are buzzing with excitement," Anemos says. "I think they'd skip today, if they could. So eager to take their vows. I think most of them have forgotten the burden they'll be accepting when they do."

"Oh, certainly. That's the way it always is."

"I understand it's our duty, but I can't imagine that thought ever bringing me as much joy as it brings them. I guess that's a moral failing, on my part, but battling creatures that aim to rip my soul from my body is hardly my idea of a good time..."

Icarus' father gives his shoulder a gentle squeeze, and he tries to focus on the feeling, his anxiety pushing him out.

He finds some comfort in his friend's words, but not much.

"That's a long way in the future," Jack says. "Nothing you need to be worried about today, or tomorrow."

"Oh, I know. It's just...." Anemos' words trail off, and then he clears his throat, tapping his fork against his plate. "What's bothering you, Icarus?"

Icarus' eyes shoot up from the table, his hands finding his pockets.

He shakes his head.

"Nothing. It's nothing. I just have... I have a lot on m...my m-mind."

"Like what?"

"Like... I don't know." Icarus shakes his head again, running his fingers along the rim of his mug. "Just...The usual."

"What's the usual?" Jack asks, and he shrugs, trying not to feel cornered.

He isn't being interrogated *yet.*

"I've been thinking about the Code," he mutters, unsure of what he will say until the words fall from his lips. "About... This notion of... Expelling th...things that are unworthy; exorcising the darkness within yourself, d-doing away with the bad. I guess... I guess I've been-b-been wondering if it's always possible."

Anemos lowers his eyes, takes a sip of his coffee, and stays silent.

"Aliya would certainly say it is," Jack responds, and Icarus laughs quietly.

"Yeah, well, Mom think's *everything* is possible—"

"I'd have to say it's a little more complicated."

Anemos looks up at that, and Icarus questions his father's choice to utter those words in front of him. It's not an opinion he's sure the man is allowed to have. But Anemos doesn't question him, instead turning to Icarus, keeping his voice low.

"What about you is unworthy?" he asks.

How can I respond to a question like that? he wonders. *How can I not?*

The first step of repentance for any sin is confessing it, but he can't; not even to his father. If it were his best friend asking, he might consider being honest enough to admit the smaller crimes he is committing: Missing his home, spending too much time in his head... But Anemos isn't Cole. He isn't close enough with him to admit something like that, even after all the years they've passed together.

Ask your parents what about me is unworthy, he wants to say. *They'll tell you.*

"I don't know," he says, instead. "It's just... been on my mind. I guess because tomorrow we'll know for certain. Everyone *thinks* there's something. I've just been trying to figure out how to rid myself of it before..." He shakes his head, wringing his hands under the table. "I just don't want to fail, that's all."

They reassure him, and he nods along, trying and failing to listen.

The conversation moves slowly after that, never going deeper than the surface. Anemos says he isn't nervous about any of it, but it is strange to think that tomorrow will be their last day as kids. He cracks his knuckles as he says it, and Icarus understands why he suggested they have coffee before leaving.

He is trying to make it all last as long as possible, he thinks, and he can't blame him.

Soon, though, they leave the warmth of the boy's house and step out into the cold of the early morning.

Anemos falls silent as soon as they are on the road, and Icarus isn't sure whether he should speak or not, but his head is too full to produce good conversation either way. So, they walk without it, neither of them uttering a word until they stand outside the shelter where Cole lives.

"He should be out by now," Anemos mutters, and Icarus sighs, leaning back against the building.

"There's a l...lot of kids in there, and not-not a lot of bathrooms. It's the last day of school, I'm sure there's chaos."

"That's why we're here so early. Everyone should still be asleep."

"I *agree*," Icarus yawns, and Anemos shoots him a disappointed glance, folding his arms over his chest.

"We're already running late," he notes. "He's had enough time. Now we're going to be later."

"We're two hours early, An."

"It's the day before the ceremony. Two hours early is late."

Icarus closes his eyes, fighting off a wave of annoyance.

"W...why don't you just... go in and get him, if it's so important?"

Anemos is quiet for a minute, but even without looking, Icarus knows he is gnawing on his lips and fidgeting with his hands.

"Alright," he says finally, and Icarus' eyes shoot open, just in time to see Anemos open the door to the shelter.

"I wasn't serious."

"Well, I am."

With a groan, Icarus pulls himself from the wall and follows Anemos through the door.

"You're gonna wake everybody up," he whispers.

"You notice there's no chaos? Icarus?" Anemos scans the rows of sleeping teenagers and children with no obvious effort to quiet his footsteps before stopping next to the place where Cole lies, his eyes closed. "I told you everyone would still be asleep."

Despite his frustration outside the shelter, when Anemos kneels beside his sleeping friend, none shows.

He does not make a single sound— only places a hand on Cole's shoulder and waits for him to open his eyes.

When he does, regret instantly floods the boy's face.

"Oh, no," he mumbles, only half awake. "I didn't wake back up."

"No," Anemos confirms. "You didn't."

"Are we late?"

"We're t-two hours early," Icarus whispers.

"But that's late the day before the ceremony," Cole groans. "Anemos, will the school even be open?"

"It doesn't need to be."

"I don't get it," he says, pulling himself up. "But give me five minutes, and I'll be ready. You should get out of here, it's bad for your reputation. Both of you."

"You realize m...my reputation can't get any worse."

"It can always get worse, Icarus," Anemos breathes, and Cole laughs sleepily, rubbing his eyes. "Always. I can think of at least six ways I could soil my reputation without so much as standing—"

"Alright, you walking scandal," Cole interrupts. "Stay here if you want, go if you want, I've gotta get dressed."

Once they're all outside, they continue their walk, but much less silent.

"Are you guys nervous?" Cole asks, and Icarus looks down, watching his shoes.

"No," Anemos says. "Not one bit. Icarus is."

Cole looks over at the boy, his brows furrowed. "Are you?"

"I'll be fine," Icarus answers, and Cole gives him a reassuring pat on the back.

"Well of course you will."

"I have stage fright, you know. Getting up in front of people, testing..." He shakes his head like maybe the fear will fall from his shoulders. "Are you? Nervous?"

Cole looks up at the sky, considering, and puts his hands in his back pockets, letting out a heavy sigh.

"Not really. I'm just ready to be done with *this,* start doing something interesting, you know? I've spent *years* learning the rules of the game. I'm ready to play."

"I think the rules are pretty interesting," Anemos mutters. "And we've learned more than rules. We've been prepared for a whole way of life."

"But we haven't entered Inanis, have we?"

Icarus' chest tightens, and he looks away, toying with the hem of his shirt.

Yeah, well, neither have *most* of the Ordinem," Anemos remarks.

"Your point?"

"My point is that you don't just say your vows and enter Inanis. It takes years—decades— of training, and still, only a few people are ever permitted to go in. Entering Inanis is not a fair comparison to *school.*"

Icarus forces a small smile but stays quiet. His mind is on the darkness, the wind, the silence, and the gold flecks of fire he so often found in his path.

He thinks of the place he *used* to visit so frequently, and his chest aches.

"Let him dream, An," he jokes. "M...maybe he'll be a quick learner."

"Yeah," Anemos laughs. "Maybe."

CHAPTER THREE

The walk from Icarus' home to his school is a sort of ritual for him.

Every day, he looks at the city around him with yearning in his stomach, shuffling through different aspects of himself in his mind. He tucks away the bits that are not suitable for this home of his and tries to present the best of himself.

Whatever is most digestible.

It is a makeshift metamorphosis, every morning, but his friends make it harder. They don't let him sink back into himself as much as he likes to, making him feel safer than he should with their reassurances and words of comfort.

Nonetheless, when they arrive at the University, he is not the same boy he is at home. His face is neutral, his hands are steady, and his head is held high.

Of course, a confident outsider within the Ordinem capital is hardly easy to digest for most of the Higher-class, but it is better than coming across as *guilty*. He may not know his place, but at least they have no reason to question him; at least they will not notice the fear he carries.

Not that it is much of an issue, at the moment.

"This place is *vacant*," Cole says, and Anemos nods, widening his eyes as if to say that is the whole point.

"I like it b...better like this," Icarus mutters, and Anemos agrees before Cole can rebuke the anti-social sentiment.

The boys follow Anemos without questioning where he is leading them. Through the bushes to each side of the still-locked gate— Icarus enjoys this part, picking leaves off and folding them in his hands— past the statues on the front lawn, and back around the main building.

"Will he find a door?" Cole muses, sighing as they pass another that is locked.

"I always find a door," Anemos says. "Or..."

They stop in front of a small window, and Anemos walks up to it, pulling it open from the bottom.

"Perfect," he says.

"Breaking and entering, on the final day of the year?" Cole questions. "Where'd you get this grand idea? Brekka?"

"Is it really breaking and entering when you're nephew to the Guide?"

They would both resent the words if they came from anyone but Anemos, who has, prior to this moment, never made a single positive reference to his somewhat royal status.

"Couldn't tell you," Cole remarks. "It is when you're from the Outskirts."

"Or *beyond the wall,* in Jakara,"Icarus adds.

"Hell, that's right. Icarus is breaking and entering just by being here."

The joke forces a laugh from Icarus' lips, but he quickly recovers, folding his arms over his chest in mock reluctance.

"Well…" Anemos groans, one leg already inside the building. "It's not like there's a camera, lads."

"My word," Cole mutters. "If you get us caught—"

"I *won't.*"

The window, it turns out, opens to a library that has gone almost completely out of use. Icarus didn't even know it was in the building. Anemos and Cole seem to be familiar with it, though, not even bothering to look around as they shut the window behind them.

The ceiling is high and arched like those in the main halls, decorated with a single pale gold chandelier and an unreasonable amount of cobwebs. It smells like dust, and has books stacked erratically up the walls.

Icarus stumbles as he pushes away from the window, trying and failing to fight a sneeze.

"Ah, so dust is what defeats the great Ordinem warrior," Cole remarks, getting an eye roll in response. "I'd think this place would be right up your alley."

"It is," Icarus says, sniffing.

"Why don't you give us a word before we go?" Anemos asks, and he sighs, picking up the book closest to him. "Ah, that's a classic. I'm sure there's something useful. Whatever you land on first."

"He crossed th…the hall with a-a disgruntled sigh, a portrait of melancholy," Icarus reads. Then, skimming until he lands on something better: "How about this one? N…n-no one can end this war, but the beasts… that set it in m…motion. That's interesting."

"A little heavy, this early," Cole remarks, and Icarus nods, laughing as he sets it aside.

"I agree."

"Come on," Anemos mutters. "This way. Follow me. Don't trip."

It all feels absurdly typical— following Anemos and Cole through the University, talking about things that don't matter while they do. Icarus is almost able to pretend it's a typical morning.

If only it weren't for the terrible pit in his stomach.

He looks over the building as they walk through it, thinking of all the time he has spent here. The last few years, it has been a second home to him.

Once they make it to the main area, he can almost find the chips in the stone walls by memory— running his hands along them, as he always has.

"I wasn't sure I'd m...make it to the end," he confesses, and Cole chuckles in response.

"I don't think most of us were sure we'd make it," he says.

"If only there was security in it being over," Anemos remarks, and Icarus looks away.

Anemos has always been vocal about how little he enjoys time spent at the University and the Palace. Icarus has hoped he would feel some relief at not attending one of the two as frequently, but also knows that the next part of their journey will be harder in many ways.

For Icarus, there will be some security in having taken his vows. No more testing, no more exams or being watched with the eye of a hawk. But for Anemos, he imagines the tension will only grow.

There is so much expected of him. There will be so little time for moments like *this,* which seem to be the prince's main source of joy. He will be watched *more* closely and held *more* accountable when he is no longer a student— if that is even possible. He will marry some Higher-class woman when the time comes.

"Trading one hell for another," he remarks, and Icarus shakes his head.

"There will be good things," he insists, and Cole nods, letting out a heavy sigh.

"Lots of them. We'll move into the Compounds, get you out of that house for a while..."

Anemos pulls a sad sort of smile, but it is obviously forced.

"There will be good things," he agrees.

It is not long before the building begins to fill with students and instructors— an hour at most— and when it does Cole and Icarus cannot help but wish Anemos had forced them to rise earlier than he already did, even though they have done nothing but talk and cast farewell glances at all of the places they have frequented. They listen to the noise of everyone coming in for a long time before preparing to leave the abandoned corner of the University they have been haunting, no longer able to ignore what the clock tells them.

"We've gotta go," Cole insists. "They'll be blowing the horn any minute."

Icarus ties and unties his shoes, killing time.

"Look who's punctual now," Anemos scoffs. "If only you'd been so precise when waking up."

"Wow, that's a lot of attitude for such a small vessel."

"I'll have you know I'm of perfectly average height—"

"That's what all short people say."

Icarus drops his laces and looks up, eyebrows raised.

"Forget armed combat testing, show the instructors how much v-violence *words* can carry."

"I've got some that will really pack a punch, before we go," Anemos says, standing up.

Icarus and Cole both fall silent, waiting, watching as the boy cracks his knuckles. He emits a nervous laugh and drops his hands to his sides.

"Guess who's making a guest appearance for our morning lecture?"

Again they wait, but he does not continue, waiting for them to force him.

After a moment, the horn blows, and he turns toward the hall. "Ah, well, I guess you'll see on your own then—"

"You're not going to tell us?" Cole asks.

"You were supposed to guess."

"Nathaniel Warnock," he scoffs. "I don't know. How would I know? Who is it?"

Anemos turns around again, but only for a moment before he continues walking in the other direction.

"My uncle," he says. "Come on, now. We're late."

Chapter Four

The Ordinem's Final Year children all crowd into the large auditorium at the center of the University, buzzing with excitement and anxiety. Anemos, Cole, and Icarus try to get lost in the mass of people but are unfortunately pushed to the front, left with no one to hide behind.

Icarus takes a step forward so at least his friends can find some shelter behind him.

"A warning would have been nice," he whispers, and Anemos grimaces.

"I gave you a warning—"

A horn is blown for the third and final time, and Icarus flinches at the sound.

"*Silence,*" the man at the center of the auditorium calls, but his voice is not loud enough to do much good.

Icarus sighs, shaking his head in an attempt to clear his mind of the anxiety which in an instant has become too strong to ignore, but he still has to close his eyes when the door to the auditorium is pulled open. It is a terrible, thundering sound, and he knows it will be followed by the even more thunderous sound of the audience blessing the man who will walk through it. He has only a few seconds to find some peace before he is expected to speak.

In that moment of silence, broken only by questioning whispers, Icarus takes Anemos' hand, giving it a tight squeeze.

"You good?" he whispers.

Anemos looks over, a little surprised, but doesn't shrug him away.

"Yeah," he says. "Yeah. I'm..." *Fine,* he means to say, but the word dies in his throat.

The Guide steps into the room, heavy boots like drums against the floor, and every head bows in honor of him— even Anemos', though his friends know he doesn't mean it

"Rise," the Guide says, and they all straighten, hands at their sides.

"*Long live the Guide,*" they say.

Icarus' eyes follow the man as he walks, staring in awe. His hair frames his face in dark waves, unhindered by the crown which— again— he has chosen to leave behind. His suit, made for battle, covers almost every inch of his skin, and a dark cape follows him; the inner fabric is red as blood.

His every movement is powerful, his head carried high and his eyes wide. He is the portrait of a warrior— a king.

It is still hard to think of him as just a man, even after every flaw Anemos has aired in his presence. He is a living saint. He is *worshiped,* and it is not hard to see why.

"Long live the Code," he says, turning toward the crowd. He pauses, looking over them a moment before letting a smile spread across his face. "I trust you're all well, and assume you're all anxious."

The crowd laughs, but Anemos does not so much as exhale.

"It's normal," the Guide insists. "The life you've lived up until now is ending tomorrow, and a new one is beginning. That's worth a little bit of discomfort."

His eyes rest on Icarus for a second, and then move on, skipping over Anemos entirely.

"If you're experiencing any serious uncertainty, of course, that's different, and I would strongly recommend seeing the Counselor before tomorrow to straighten it out. Please, know there's no shame in doing that. I assure you, he will handle you graciously."

"*The most gracious of all,*" the crowd recites, and the Guide nods, pleased.

"I've come to talk to you all about what comes next. First, with the trials, and then beyond that. Understood?"

"*Yes, Myon.*"

"Very well," he nods, and then, pulling a sword from the hilt on his waist and swinging it nonchalantly: "The trials— It will be a long day and a longer night, so you should come rested and fed. Time is of the essence: Do not arrive less than an hour before trials begin..."

Icarus steals a glance at the floor, taking a shallow breath and scraping at his palms with his fingernails, trying and failing to focus on what the man is saying.

"...It *will* be exhausting, but you will not be doing anything you've not done previously, so there's hardly any reason to be nervous..."

Hardly. It's what his mother keeps telling him too. It's what everyone is telling him, and he is starting to think it is little more than a script.

They have fought before, but not for a ranking that will help to dictate the rest of their lives. There has never been pressure like that or stakes that high. They have been tested on their knowledge, but never with their Ordinem identity on the line. They have never had their words and mannerisms privately analyzed, looking for signs of deviation—

"Icarus?"

His head snaps up, and his eyes focus on those in front of him— cold and blue as ice. He blinks once in disbelief, but before he can speak the Guide repeats his words, his voice steady.

"You," he says. "Icarus."

"Yes, M...Myon?"

The Guide takes a few steps closer, his boots thumping against the floor, and looks the boy over carefully, having not seen him in some time.

Still, almost, seeing a child.

"I've been told you're the most advanced in almost every class," he says. "Is this true?"

Icarus swallows hard, wishing he had been listening more closely.

"Yes," he responds, his chest tight. "It's true."

"Well done," the man muses, taking a step back. "Very well done. And... You." He points to a brown-haired, freckled boy near the back. "I've been told you're the *least.*"

"Yes, Myon," the boy replies, his voice a little sick. "I am."

"Come," he says, and then, seeing the hesitance on their faces: "Come here, both of y ou."

Icarus steps forward, no more comfortable than the other boy, and watches as he walks to the front, his eyes on the floor and his hands clenched beside him.

"Chase," the Guide says, pacing as he speaks. "I have a question for you, and I want you to answer honestly."

"You have my word."

"Did you try?"

Chase falls silent, clears his throat, and shakes his head.

"No, Myon. Not at first."

"Why not?"

"Because I didn't think I had to," he says, and then: "Because I was distracted."

"But you shouldn't have been,"

"I know," he says. "I apologize, I did seek counseling."

"Chase," the Guide says again, and he stops, shoving his hands into his pockets. "You said you *have* been trying, yes?"

"Yes," he breathes. "As hard as I... I got behind, so catching up has been difficult."

"But you're here," the man says, and Chase nods. "Why? Why are you here?"

"Because I'm Ordinem," he says, casting a sideways glance at Icarus as he does. "*Born* Ordinem, and this system has protected me since the day I was born. I want to serve it. It's my *duty* to serve it."

"And what about you?" the Guide asks, turning to Icarus with eyes he cannot read. He waits for the crowd to quiet its sudden cheers for the other, and then continues. "Did you try?"

"Yes," Icarus says, and the crowd is silent.

"Yes," he repeats. "Why?"

Icarus is quiet for a second, and the man continues, his tone unchanging.

"Because you thought you—"

"Because... I love it," he interrupts, and the Guide falls silent, his jaw tightening.

"Because you love it?"

"Yes... M...Myon."

He could hear a pin drop on the other end of the school, he thinks.

"Why?" the Guide asks him, and he falters.

"Why..?"

"Why do you love it?" the Guide asks. "You say you love it, I'm asking why."

"M...more reasons than I can—"

"Give me one," he says, and Icarus sighs nervously, shaking his hands.

"Well, I'm... I'm lost without it."

"Ah," the Guide breathes, pointing at him. He nods with approval and turns back to the crowd. "And there is the heart of it."

Icarus lowers his face.

"We all are," the man says. "And that is why *this*," he gestures to the room around them, "doesn't mean anything. The ranking, the classes you've formed? Worthless, tomorrow morning. Your advantages and disadvantages will be considered for position, and that is *all.*"

Cole shifts from one foot to the other, sighing in frustration, and Anemos squeezes his hand a little tighter, watching with hard eyes as the Guide beckons the headmaster forward.

"Chase," he says. "How confident are you in your ability to fight?"

"Confident that I don't have much ability, Myon," Chase answers, and the crowd laughs, but the Guide waves them off.

"Icarus?" he asks, and Icarus clenches his fists, swallowing nervously. "How confident are you?"

"Confident," he mutters hesitantly, "within the context I have been—"

"Give him your sword," the Guide says to the headmaster. Icarus' eyes widen in surprise, but he reaches out and takes the silver blade being offered to him without question. "Chase, you're released, thank you for your time."

"What the hell is he doing?" Cole mumbles, his voice barely a whisper, and Anemos shakes his head.

"I don't know," he says.

Icarus casts a sideways glance at them, trying to keep his face blank, and then turns back to the Guide with uncertain eyes, watching as the man steps toward him. Then, without so much as a word of warning, the Guide raises the sword over his head and brings it down toward Icarus in one fell swoop, stopping only an inch from his face, striking his blade; it is raised haphazardly in defense, steadied by hands that are not entirely steady themselves.

There is a question in Icarus' eyes, unmoved by the stunned gasps of the crowd, and the Guide nods but does not answer.

"Good," he says. "That's very good."

The sword swings again, lower this time, and Icarus blocks it again, taking an uncertain step back.

The fight continues this way for a few seconds: almost predictable swings from the Guide, who hardly tries, and unsettled blocks from Icarus, who does not try much harder.

He sees no reason to when he doesn't know what he is fighting for.

But then the energy in the room builds, uneasiness grows, and the Guide moves in a little closer. He forces their blades into collision, a loud ringing sound piercing the room when Icarus pushes him back, a little out of breath.

He pushes him back, and then meets eyes with the headmaster, who is watching— he thinks— a little too closely.

The Guide swings again, leaving an opening on his right side, and Icarus does not take it; he does not take *any* of the openings left for him as their leader grows distracted and uncertain.

Their swords meet again, and he loosens his grip without thinking twice about doing it, knowing better, being too smart to win.

The weapon falls from his hands, knocked away, and the Guide's blade rises to cut him across the face, just under his left eye, leaving a long bleeding line in its wake.

He is too startled to wince and instead only stares ahead, struggling to catch his breath until the older man lowers his blade.

When he does, Icarus lowers himself to his knees, bowing his head in a posture of respect as The Guide returns his sword to his hilt.

The man begins to talk again, but Icarus does not hear him; only the murmuring of the audience, and his own uneven breath.

"The best fighter among you," he says, and the whispers do not cease. He waits for them to stop, waits for the words to sit, and then shakes his head. "You will, *most* of you, fight things far greater than *me.*"

Blood drips down the boy's face, and he lifts one hand to wipe it away, staining his shirt.

"I have seen and heard much of you all," the Guide continues, "and I have *been* you, and I know the way it is. You look at each other as competition, challenge... You idolize those greater than you and judge those you deem lesser. You judge each other based on where you're from, and how you *speak,* and I have expected nothing more because you are children, but that ends *tomorrow.*"

Someone in the back of the room claps, and the rest of the audience joins— some grudgingly.

"If you think that you have made it," he says, "you are wrong. This has been child's play, and it has served its purpose, but it is only one small step in a very long journey: one much more easily traveled when we do not put ourselves on pedestals. If you think that your pride, your individual strength, will hold a candle to the strength of those we face— Grim and all others belonging to that force that so threatens us— you are a fool. If you believe that *any* of us have the privilege not to try, you are naive, and I suggest you correct that now before someone corrects it for you."

The words are enough to silence them all, and he lets them rest a long moment before picking them up again, his voice hard, but not unfeeling.

"It is good to have a safe place," he says. "But there is a danger, here, of forgetting what lies outside; of growing stagnant, and comfortable. I fear that even the best of us have become accustomed to dismissing the urgency and the danger we still face, inside and outside of these walls. We have not had one moment of absolute safety since the Grim tore into this world four decades ago and brought their hell with them— something that might have been avoided had those who came before us been more proficient, and spent less time dividing, bickering, and othering."

Icarus lifts his head, his breath strained, and watches the man with heavy eyes as he lifts his right hand in the air, showing the long, white scar across it.

"When you bear this mark," he says, "When you sign your name into that book, you are Ordinem, and that is *all* that matters. Whether you love it, like this boy on the floor, or you call it duty, like that boy on his feet, your individual wants, needs, and accomplishments are *dust*. You attempt to build your worth upon them, and it will crumble."

Another round of applause, and the energy in the room changes, the pressure almost suffocating.

"Your freedom is here," the Guide says, and Icarus wipes his face, blood smearing across his hands.

CHAPTER FIVE

The rest of the day moves slowly, minutes like hours.

There is not much time to talk, with everything that has to be done, and even if there were, Icarus and his friends spend most of their time separately.

No one else says a word to Icarus, but they do look at him. Their glances make the cut on his face burn more than it already does. It hardly matters, he knows that, but humiliation and fear are already making his stomach turn. He does not want their eyes on him, on top of everything else.

Either way, he cannot afford to keep his head down, so he continues.

By the time the day comes to an end, he is exhausted from the act. He sits at a table in the dining hall and picks at his food without eating it, looking around the room in an attempt to find the only person he does not wish to avoid.

In the end, it is Cole who finds *him*.

A hand is placed on his shoulder, and his friend circles in front of him, a heavy sigh escaping his lips.

"I have been looking for you everywhere," he says. "Are you okay?"

Icarus smiles softly, nodding without hesitation.

"I'm fine."

"I don't know how that's possible." Cole slides onto the bench across the table, and Anemos follows suit, looking considerably more tired. "That was awful. I think I almost had an aneurysm."

"It was fine," Icarus insists, laughing quietly. "It was just... a spar. W...we spar all the time. A few stitches won't kill me."

Neither of them respond to him, but Anemos' brows draw closer together, his eyes dark. He's angry. Icarus knew he would be.

"I'm really fine," he restates, shifting awkwardly in his seat. "I'm just tired. It's been a long day..."

Across the room, a group of shadowy figures burst through the door, speaking with loud and aggressive voices. It startles Icarus so badly he has to look away, forcing himself to eat in an attempt to look natural, but no one around him even notices.

All the noise echoes off the walls, bouncing off of the high, arched ceilings. He thinks he could drown in it. The dim lighting of the room mixing with the blurriness of his vision makes it feel a little like he imagines it would be underwater. The air is thick enough.

"He shouldn't have put you through that, Icarus." Anemos' voice cuts through his thoughts, and he looks up, his heart in his throat. "I don't know what he was thinking."

"He was trying to prove a point, and he did. That's all—"

"Let me rephrase that, I don't *care* what he was thinking. Exactly what point did he prove? It was a show of power against you because they hate that you're doing well."

"Anemos," Cole cautions, and Icarus looks away again, his jaw tightening. "You're not helping."

"Why would you let him have it?" Anemos asks, ignoring the boy beside him.

Icarus shakes his head, taking another distracted bite of his food. "I didn't."

"I know you didn't miss those openings he was leaving. You're too good for that—"

"*Anemos,*" Cole repeats, and he falls silent.

The shadowy figures in Icarus' peripheral vision pass through the room without quieting, and he does not even attempt to respond until they are far behind him. When he does, his voice comes out quiet, but it is steady enough.

"I was caught off guard. It wasn't my best performance, but I did try. Why wouldn't I try? I don't wa-a-want... anyone to m...make an example of me, either."

"But—"

"What else should he have done?" Cole interrupts Anemos, his voice sharper than he means for it to be. "Put the Guide in a position of surrender? That would have been worse. You see how that would have been worse."

"Can we talk about something else?" Icarus asks. "I'm really... done w-with this—"

"I'm just so sick of them getting away with stunts like this..."

Icarus groans, letting his face sink between his hands as Anemos continues to talk.

He gets it. He knows that his friend's anger comes from the right place. Anemos' eyes have returned to the cut on his face with every other word. He cares, but as much as Icarus appreciates that—

"I think I'm going to head home."

The two arguing boys stop, looking over at him with wide eyes.

"Oh, don't do that," Cole pleads. "We'll stop. I swear."

"I'm r...really tired. I'm not hungry. It's loud here."

His friend's shoulders fall. He shakes his head.

"I'll walk you home, then. It's going to be dark now."

"There are lights everywhere. I'll be okay. You guys... You probably want some time alone anyway, don't you?" Neither of them respond to that, but he knows well enough. He stands, taking his plate with him. "I'll see you both tom...m...morrow m-morning. We'll spend all day together. I'll be okay."

"You're sure?" Cole asks.

Icarus forces a tired smile, nodding.

"I'm sure. I'm not a child. I'll m...make it home."

"And you'll rest when you get there? You won't stay up all night rehearsing that damn vow?"

"I'll rest."

"Promise."

"I promise." Icarus laughs softly, turning and waving goodbye as he walks away. "Goodnight."

They both raise their hands in farewell, and a moment later, he is gone.

Anemos and Cole do not talk for a long while after he goes, sitting and eating in silence. It's funny how it can get harder to talk the more there is to say. It is only when almost half the room has cleared that Cole finally leans forward onto the table and clears his throat, having quietly watched Anemos long enough.

"You want to go somewhere else?" he asks. "Somewhere we can talk?"

Anemos continues to look elsewhere, chewing the inside of his cheek, but eventually, he nods in response. They both push their plates to the center of the table and stand up, making their way to the most vacant edge of the room, Anemos quickly taking the lead like he usually does.

Cole follows him down a series of dimly lit hallways, not rushing to break the silence his friend is so dedicated to maintaining.

He has grown comfortable enough with it by now. He cannot count the hours he has spent like this, walking through the less populated halls of the University with Anemos. Whether they speak or not doesn't matter all that much anymore. Still—

"I'm sorry if I was sharp with you," Cole says, and Anemos sighs, shaking his head.

"You realize this might be the last time we do this?" he asks.

Cole's lips tighten with his chest. He nods.

"Yeah."

"What an ending," Anemos remarks. "The end of an era."

"It's not the end of anything." The words are pointless, and Cole realizes this as he says it, but he doesn't rescind the statement. "You're not losing half of what you think you are. You don't have to be so afraid."

"No?"

"No," he says. "We'll have the Compounds to explore, and the city... And we'll have each other. We're going to be fine."

Anemos doesn't respond to that. He only continues to walk, his steps heavy.

"I'm going to see Zahra in the morning," he says, when another minute has passed. "To say goodbye. I don't think it will be safe, once we're sworn in. They'll start keeping a closer eye, and we'll be expected to focus on the Order without much exception."

"Do you think it'll be safe tomorrow?"

"I think I'll risk it," he says. "I'll just avoid the main path. You should come."

"I've spent enough time on the Outskirts for the rest of my life, Anemos—"

"We could be free there. I think about that often."

Cole stops in place, his chest tight.

He feels his jaw clench but forces his face to soften as Anemos turns toward him, eyes somber with the little bit of hope he still carries.

Cole shakes his head.

"They would look until they found you," he reminds him. "If they didn't find you, something would: hunger, or violence, or sickness—"

"Maybe a short life is better than a long life that suffocates you."

"There's *no* life there, Anemos. It's different when you're not just visiting. It's hopeless."

"Zahra doesn't seem hopeless."

"Zahra's not exactly a fair example," Cole says. "But still, she's more brave than happy, isn't she? You're going to see her tomorrow, ask her if she feels free."

Anemos looks away, toying with the ends of his sleeves. He looks more distressed than he usually shows, and the sight makes Cole's chest hurt.

It's a shadow of what Anemos went through before, he thinks: Asking for someone to get him away from this place, only to be dismissed. He doesn't want to be or do that to h im.

He drops his shoulders, trying to gentle his voice.

"Are you asking me?" he asks. "If you ask me to go with you, I'll go. I'm with you no matter where that takes me, but I've lived out there, and I'm telling you, we'll be no better off than we will be here. You know if I thought there was peace beyond the city wall, I would've taken you in a second, Anemos."

"I know."

"And you know I have more allegiance to you than I'll ever have to this vow?"

Anemos hesitates, his eyes darting around the boy's face anxiously.

"Yes," he whispers, and Cole takes a step forward, putting a hand on his shoulder.

"Then don't be afraid," he says. "Why are you so afraid?"

Anemos' eyes fall to the floor, and he steps away, walking to the window on the other side of the room. It is large— more than ten feet tall, and half as wide. The ledge beside it is big enough that when Anemos slides up onto it, there is still room for his friend to sit down across from him, watching him as he looks at the sky.

"My whole life," he says, when a minute has passed, "I've watched my family serve this Order I'm about to pledge myself to."

There are footsteps somewhere off in the distance. He waits for them to fade before speaking again, lowering his voice.

"I have my father's eyes and my mother's way of speaking. I like to think I'm different from them, and this won't kill me the way it's killed them, but I have their blood in my veins, Cole."

Cole listens with heavy eyes, his knees pulled up to his chest.

"I don't want to become what I hate," he says. "It's nothing new."

The words sit between them, and Cole considers them carefully. There is nothing he can say to ease his fear— he knows because he has been trying for five years. He holds out one of his hands, and Anemos takes it, his eyes distant.

Again, they return to silence. They look out the window at the sky, polluted by smoke and the city's lights. It might not shine with stars like it once did, but it is still the sky, and they still look to it for answers it can't give.

"Icarus' face will scar, won't it?" Anemos asks, and Cole nods, his stomach sick at the thought. "We couldn't leave if we wanted to. He'd never come with us."

"You think he loves it as much as he says he does?"

"Oh, definitely." Anemos rests his head back against the wall, closing his eyes. "I think he'd die for the Code, if he could."

"I'm not sure I'll ever understand that," Cole admits, and Anemos shakes his head, a long sigh escaping his lips.

"We're lost without it," he repeats.

CHAPTER SIX

The streets are different after sundown.

Icarus looks over his shoulder as he walks, his feet carrying him quickly toward home. He tries to avoid walking alone on empty streets, but tonight, he wishes he had less company.

The shadowy figures from inside the University are here, too. There are more of them than there usually are, and they are frantic tonight. It makes him nervous, and the dark makes him nervous enough on its own.

Together, they make him feel sick to his stomach.

It doesn't matter though, because soon he will be home, and he will curl up on the couch with a book, and his father will be there. Everything will be okay again for a few hours. He won't even look at his studies—

A sharp scream splits the air around him and he swallows hard, picking up his pace.

He hasn't yet decided what he will tell his parents when they ask about his day and the cut on his face. The Code commands truth, but he is too tired to manage their concern—and it *will* concern them; there is no doubt in his mind about that.

He could tell them another student got carried away when they were sparring, but then, they will probably find out the truth on their own, and they will be concerned about the fact that he lied to them. He looks up at the sky, letting out a long exhale, and groans at the permanent clouds above him. He would give his life to see the stars he used to see back home again. They would bring him comfort, surely.

Not a moment later, his thoughts are interrupted by the feeling of a cold hand taking hold of his wrist. All of the shadows pale in comparison to the sensation. It freezes him in place, making his face go white with dread as he draws in a sharp, uneven breath. He glances around him nervously, looking for any eyes that could find him before closing his own, shaking his head.

It's difficult to handle at the best of times, but being on a public street makes it far worse. He can keep walking, but then the hand will remain on his wrist, and he wants it gone desperately. If he were in his room, he would turn and address the thing. If he were truly desperate, he would dull his senses so at least he wouldn't have to feel it, but it makes him sick when he resorts to that.

It is best he addresses it, he decides, but he can't do it here.

Hesitantly, he walks forward, turning into the first alleyway he can find with a quick beating heart. As he moves further into the shadows, he tries to prepare himself for what he might see. The shadows that follow him are usually distorted— often violent— but the grip on his wrist is not one of aggression. Its touch would be light, if its nature were not so heavy.

Once he is completely hidden, he turns and looks at the figure across from him, ready to fight if he has to; instead, his shoulders fall, his heart sinking into his stomach.

It is just a girl— six or seven, with pale eyes and graying hair.

He swallows hard, and she shakes her head, letting his hand go.

"I scared you," she says, turning to run from him. "I'm sorry—"

"No, don't go..." The words fall from his mouth before he can stop them. He curses himself in his head, but kneels in front of her, speaking as quietly as he can. "I just didn't expect you. It's too... late, for a kid to be out alone."

She stops, wringing her hands in front of her.

"I lost my parents." The words make his stomach turn, but his face doesn't change.

"Are they in the city?"

"We're not allowed in the city," she whispers. "I don't know how I got here... No one else has seen me. I've been lost a long time..."

Icarus watches the girl with careful eyes, his chest tight. Her frame is thin. He could have guessed she lived outside the city walls.

He wonders what happened, and shudders at the thought.

They are alone. The chances of being seen are slim, but not none. He doesn't want the risk so close to the ceremony, but what choice does he have? He doesn't hear anyone nearby. Most of his fellow students will not be out for another hour, and the Higher-class is busy with preparations for the day ahead.

"I can help you find them," he forces, the words like tar in his throat. "Come... Come here. Take my hand... What's your name?"

The girl takes a step closer to him, shaking with what he assumes is fear.

"I don't remember," she mutters. "I don't know where it went. I don't remember a name."

"Don't worry," he assures her. "I forget mine too, sometimes."

At home, Jack and Aliya sit in the living room waiting for their son to come home. Dinner is already made, and Jack has taken his place in the chair by the door, reading a book that the Ordinem has all but forbidden. He looks up only when Aliya sits down in front of him, sighing heavily.

His mouth curves into a soft smile, understanding.

"He'll be home soon," he says. "He's probably just spending a little extra time with his friends. Don't worry."

"Those kids are mean to him. I don't like when it gets late like this, thinking about him walking home on his own."

"He's not seven anymore," he reminds her. "He can handle himself, but I'll walk down there if he's not home within the hour."

Aliya nods reluctantly and sits back in her chair, staring off into the distance.

It is quiet for a moment, the only sounds the fire in the hearth and Jack flipping the pages of his book, until she speaks again.

"Do you think he'll be okay tomorrow, Jack?"

He looks up again, blinking slowly.

"Why wouldn't he be?"

"I don't know. He's always been…"

The front door cracks open, and the words vanish.

Icarus steps inside, his hair hanging in his face, and smiles softly, taking off his shoes.

"Sorry I'm late," he says. "I took m…my time getting home. Long day."

"That's fine," Aliya says. "Dinner's ready."

She catches a glimpse of the cut on his face, so brief she thinks she might have imagined it, and her stomach tightens.

"I'm going to get changed really quickly," he says, turning away before she can get another look. "I'll be right out."

"Okay. Don't be long."

When he has left the room, she turns back to her husband, finding concern just as visible on his face.

A few minutes later they are at the dining room table, and the boy sits down across from them with heavy eyes but a light expression. His hair is tied back behind his head, so there is no hiding the mark across his cheek, but neither of them addresses it immediately; instead, his mother hands him a plate and his father puts a hand on his shoulder.

"How was your day?" he asks. "Feeling better about tomorrow?"

"A little bit," Icarus lies. "My day was okay. What about you guys? Bus...B-b-busy?"

"Very," Aliya responds.

"I'm glad to be home," he says, taking a bite. "I don't know how m...much I'll sleep, but it... it f...feels-feels good to be able to sit, and... breathe."

"I bet," she nods.

"Maybe... Maybe I'll work on that story I was writing tonight, do something other than rehearse the vow. You guys b-*better* not throw my notebooks out, when I m...move into the Compounds."

"Worse," Jacks says. "We'll finally get to read them."

"Mm... Maybe burn them, actually."

They both laugh, and Aliya looks down at her plate, her shoulders raised.

It is only another minute before she decides she can't wait any longer.

"What happened to your face?" she asks. "Spar?"

Icarus sighs, then, shaking his head.

"Sort of," he forces. "It was... *really* weird."

"Weird?" Jack asks. "Weird how?"

"So, first thing today, the Guide came in to talk to everyone..." Icarus does not look up from the table, his words slow. "And he called on me and this other kid... It's k-kind-kind of a long story, but he ended up challenging me, and... Well, I lost, obviously."

Aliya's brows furrow, and she begins to question him— concerned despite his casual recounting of the story. Jack doesn't hear much of what she says.

They were trying to scare his son, he thinks, but he isn't sure why.

To startle him to the point of unmasking a deviation they expect him to possess, or to put him back in the place they think he belongs? Perhaps it was all a dramatic way to embarrass him.

Surely, though, the Guide would not participate in that.

"*Mom.*" Icarus' voice breaks through his thoughts. "I'm f-f...fine. It's just a cut. It's okay."

"It's absolutely not okay," Aliya responds. "A spar is one thing, harming you is another. Does it hurt?"

"I m...mean, yes, it hurts, but—"

"I'll be speaking with him tomorrow."

"*Mom.*"

"What was the point of challenging you to this spar, do you think?" Jack asks, and Icarus hesitates, picking at his food.

"I'm the most well-performing," he says. "He was making a point that... Things are going to be hard. We'll be fighting Reapers, and Saenks, and... You know, the war between Trellis and Brekka is getting really bad. He was demonstrating how easily even the... b-best of us is defeated. He made a lot of good points. And I don't think he meant to hurt me. Afterward, he told m...me how well I did, so... You know, very little harm was done."

His body language suggests otherwise, but Jack doesn't draw attention to it.

There is an uneasy quiet that settles over the table, only disrupted by the clinking of their silverware. Icarus hates it, and hates that he has caused it, so after a minute, he laughs.

Aliya looks up.

"What?" she asks. "What else?"

"Nothing else," he replies, shaking his head. "He's just not as good as I expected. I think I could have beaten him if I'd been less nervous."

She stares at him long and hard, and he knows he has done it; he has managed enough audacity to distract her from her worry. Jack chuckles beside him, lowering his face when Aliya shoots him a halfhearted glare.

"Imagine if we did it again, when I'm sworn in. The Ordinem could have a Jakaran Guide."

"Alright, that's enough," his mother says. "Let's get through tomorrow before we challenge a saint."

"He started it," Icarus jokes, and Jack pats his shoulder again, a wide smile on his face.

"You are my boy, aren't you?"

The words still make Icarus' throat tight, after more than a decade of hearing him.

He smiles in his father's direction, another laugh escaping his lips.

"Hopefully I don't drive M...Mom *as* crazy," he says, and Jack laughs again, giving his arm a tight squeeze before letting him go.

Say it again, he wants to ask. *Tell me I belong here.*

"Hardly," Aliya says. "And for what it's worth, Icarus... We wouldn't have a Jakaran Guide. We'd have an Ordinem Guide, just like now. It'd be just as good and just as holy."

His stomach sinks, but he pushes the feeling aside, forcing a thankful smile in her direction.

"M...might be a stretch—"

"No," she insists, shaking her head. "That's the whole point of tomorrow. You take that vow, and you're Ordinem."

Her words are meant as encouragement; they *are* encouragement.

It's not her fault he misses his home.

CHAPTER SEVEN

Despite the face he put on for his parents, Icarus was not well. Upon going to his room and realizing he couldn't rest, he continued to rehearse his vow, trying to make the words fit in his mouth. It was almost dawn when exhaustion finally took him.

He woke this morning with his hand still resting on the cut below his eye, and he didn't experience peace for even a moment.

When his eyes began to flutter open, finding the light on the ceiling, he found that he was not alone. A shadow wrapped itself around the structure above him, staring down at him with its teeth bared.

Instinctively, he kept his eyes all but closed. He hoped that he might be dreaming, or that the stress had caused his mind to play tricks on him. He waited for it to disappear, but it didn't.

It is still there now, and Icarus does not know what to do but lie very still.

It is nearly half an hour before he opens his eyes, speaking through gritted teeth.

"Go away," he whispers. "Be gone from here."

"No," it spits, the word emerging from its throat as a strangled cry, sending chills down his spine. *"You go, Icarus. You don't belong here."*

It is impossible not to notice how pleased the thing is that it has been noticed. The mere thought of it makes Icarus' chest tighter.

"I can m...make you go," he says. "I won't let you torment me. You can't. I'm s-stronger than—"

The thing moves and Icarus jerks back against the bed, cursing himself for trembling.

"Strong," it laughs. *"You can't even s-s-speak, you fool."*

"I-I can—"

The shadow drops down from above him, onto his chest, resting one leg on each side of his body and leaning forward into his face.

He has to close his eyes and bite his own tongue to keep from screaming.

"*You can what, Icarus?*"

He opens his eyes, and the thing is gone.

There is no blood on his shirt, no spit on his face, and no smell choking him, but he knows that he can't hold it long.

He pushes the hair out of his face with trembling hands, gasps for air, and tries to think past a quickly forming migraine, but his thoughts are scattered. If only he could live in one world instead of being caught between so many.

He pulls himself up, shaking violently, and presses a hand against his nose. It's bleeding, just as he feared it would be. He can only hope his parents trust him enough that it won't be a dead giveaway. Either way, he cannot remain in his room.

Trying and failing to act as if nothing is the matter, he steps quickly out of his room, across the hall, and into the bathroom, locking the door behind him.

There is no guarantee that the shadow has not followed him, but his vision is growing dark. Having no choice, he lets power flood his body once more. It is like air, rushing into his lungs and steadying him.

Opening his eyes and finding that he is alone again, he leans back against the wall, putting his face in his hands. A sob works its way through him, and escapes his lips no louder than a whisper.

Of all days, why today? *Today,* when he most needs to appear human.

It is several minutes before he manages to straighten and approach the sink, his face hot and tear-stained— blood smeared across it.

He meets his own eyes in the mirror and shudders. His throat is tight, but a cry escapes it all the same, anything but silent.

"God..." he whimpers. "What do I... What do I do?" Frantically, he scrubs his hands, watching the blood-stained water as it drains. First his hands, and then he will handle his face. He will have to get a new shirt. He didn't realize how much he had bled—

There is a knock at the door, and it turns him to stone.

"Icarus?" A voice asks, and he grips the sink, fighting the urge to vomit. "Icarus, are you okay?"

"Yes," he forces, his voice catching. "I'm fine."

"Are you sure?"

"*Y-yes,*" he repeats, knowing how unconvincing his voice is. "I'm... I'll be out in just a m...minute. It's not time to leave already, is it?"

"No," his father replies. "It isn't. Can I come in?"

"I'll be out in just a minute."

"There's blood on the floor." Icarus shuts his eyes tightly. His father's voice is calm, but it is the type of calm that suggests effort. He is afraid, Icarus thinks. There will be no getting him away from the door. "Do you think you could go ahead and come out?"

He takes a long, shaky breath before nodding to himself and reaching for the handle. He pushes the door open with one hand, still holding a rag to his face with the other, and tries to avoid Jack's eyes, not wanting him to see that he has been crying.

"I'm sorry," he says quickly. "I'll clean it up. I j-just... The auditorium was so dry, yesterday. I stood up and m...my nose just started."

Jack does not respond for a long minute, only looking at him. Then, stepping into the bathroom and shutting the door behind him:

"You need to tip your head forward."

If the door is shut, that means he does not plan to walk away quickly. Icarus swallows the anxiety that realization causes him.

"I think it's stopping," he says. but he leans forward anyway, watching out of the corners of his eyes as his father grabs another rag, helping to clean the blood off his neck. "It better be stopping, and it b...better stay away. They'll brand me a demon if it starts in Karneji—"

"You're not a demon," his father interrupts, and he nods, finding it an odd response.

"Sure, but I'm from Jakara. They'd jump at the opportunity to get rid of me."

Again, Jack's voice is that calculated calm.

"Is that something you're afraid of?" he asks, and Icarus shakes his head, lying.

"No, I'm sure it'll be f-f...f-fine."

"They need reasonable evidence before they can *get rid of you,*" Jack reminds him. "A nosebleed would make them suspicious, though. I don't deny that. As long as it doesn't happen in Karneji, it shouldn't be enough to brand you as anything."

Icarus' heart beats unsteadily, hearing his fears confirmed by someone else. If it happens in Karneji, it *will* be enough to brand him. That is what his father is implying, and he already knew it, but it feels so much worse this morning.

"It's an awful trick," the man continues. "Taking Grim to a place so infested with death that they make themselves ill to avoid seeing it."

"Smart," Icarus remarks.

"I think it's a horrible thorn in the argument that the Grim aren't human. The only thing more human than love is fear, and that's an act of fear if I've ever seen it."

The words hang in the air. They make Icarus' stomach twist.

His father has said lots of things the Ordinem wishes he wouldn't, but this is the first time he has uttered words as deadly as those. Even suggesting the things are human is grounds for a charge of blasphemy.

"Everything feels fear," Icarus says. "It doesn't change what they are, and you shouldn't suggest otherwise."

"I'm not the first man of the Order to suggest it, and I won't be the last."

It's as if the words are a fire, the way they burn under his skin.

"Why are you saying these things?" he snaps, tightening his hands in an effort to hide the way they shake. "You know if I reported you they would—"

"I know," Jack interrupts. "I know what I say, and when I choose to say it."

Icarus grits his teeth, keeping his head low.

"In Karneji, tonight, there will be dead, and cursed-dead in every corner, along every wall. For Grim, it will be a minefield— but so long as they don't avert their eyes, or react, or tremble... They can pass through. That's what they look for, Icarus. They look for nosebleeds, illness, and anxiety. "

His heart is like a drum in his chest. He can feel it all the way up his throat and into his temples.

"Why are you telling me this?" he repeats, and his father lifts his face, pulling the rag away from his nose.

The bleeding has stopped. Jack does not reply.

"Should you need anything," he says, instead. "You come to me, immediately. Not a teacher, not your mother. You come to *me*. Do you understand?"

No, Icarus thinks, but he stays silent, too afraid to speak.

"I'll be in Karneji tonight, after the ceremony. If I don't make it home before you leave for the Compounds in the morning, I'll visit you as soon as I'm back in the city. And of course, I'll be watching you tonight, so if you get nervous on stage, just look at me and pretend everyone else is gone."

He couldn't know, Icarus thinks; even if that's what it seems like. It's impossible that he could know and speak as kindly as he is speaking now.

His father pulls him into a tight embrace, and hesitantly, he wraps his arms around the man's back, resting his face on his shoulder.

"My son," Jack mutters.

The words fill Icarus' chest, even while his heart is breaking within it.

When his father finally lets him go and leaves the room, he stares after him a long moment, feeling every word he said like glass in his skin.

CHAPTER EIGHT

Anemos opens his bedroom door, looking out into the darkness of the hallway.

He hasn't slept much, but he can't be sure whether or not his parents have come home. They were in Karneji when he came in the night before, but he knows they will be back before the ceremony, so he listens for them.

He doesn't hear anyone moving downstairs, so he tiptoes out of his room and to the edge of the staircase.

The lights aren't on—sometimes his father, Alastor, does not turn them on, but if his mother was up they would be, and his mother does not sleep when she has been to Karneji.

All in all, the odds are in his favor.

Anemos makes his way downstairs into the living room, feeling around blindly until he reaches the front door.

The morning air is cold and damp, and the sun has not yet risen. It's his favorite time to go walking. It feels like he can move through the city without a single soul seeing him. Today, though, it brings him very little joy.

He squeezes his hands into fists as he walks, taking heavy breaths even as he curses the air. He tries to forget what day it is, and the night he has just suffered, but to very little avail.

Every tremor makes him remember the way his body shook with panic while he read over the vow he will take in a few short hours. He has regained control now, but it still feels as if it could slip away at any moment.

Zahra knows what to do if that happens, he tells himself. He is going to a safe place.

He wishes he could pretend he didn't have to return.

Despite the fullness of his mind, he walks with steps as light as a shadow's, moving quickly around every building—down every street and alley; he has memorized it all. By the time he reaches the wall that separates the city from the Outskirts, his legs are aching. It isn't a good sign for the day to come, but he expected as much.

He runs his hand along the long marble pillars beside him, looking for the one space wide enough for him to slide through.

Anemos has always considered the wall an unnecessary cruelty. It is not quite ten feet tall— easy to scale— striped like a picket fence so that both sides can see the other. It is more of a slap in the face than any kind of defense.

The first time he came to it, he was shocked by the difference a few feet could make. Still, he notes the way the pavement cracks, splits, and stops a couple of steps from the barrier. Weeds grow wildly, untrimmed, and there are none of the Ordinem's trees.

It is the truth of this territory his people have claimed, without any of its falsified order. He clings to it the way Cole clings to the city.

The sky is moving from blackness to an eerie shade of gray, signaling the light's return, so Anemos makes his way quickly along the path he has made through the grass, careful not to be seen.

Almost an hour passes before he sees something like civilization, and it looks worse than it did the last time he visited. There must have been an attack, he thinks as he approaches. The majority of the few houses that stand have been damaged. Roofs are strapped with tarps, and windows are boarded.

Anemos approaches the first familiar face he sees, and the man turns toward him with furrowed brows.

"An?" Benji questions, leaning against the railing of his porch. "On Ceremony day?"

He has grown thinner, Anemos thinks, but he still looks well. His eyes are still bright, if a little bloodshot. His short blond hair is unkempt, turning a pale gray, but his clothes are clean.

Anemos ignores his question.

"Did something happen?" he asks, gesturing around them, and the man nods, stifling a cough.

"Blood dogs," he says. "Whole pack. Six or seven of them."

Anemos' chest tightens, but the man quickly shakes his head.

"Don't worry, your Zahra is fine."

"Did they send any aid?" he asks, a relieved breath escaping his lips with the words.

Benji shakes his head, chuckling. "They never send any aid, but that's hardly your concern today, son. You've got plenty on your mind already."

Anemos lets his eyes fall, kicking at the stones beneath him.

"Is she home?" he asks.

A moment later he is at her door; it is something like a door, the large slab of wood sat against the structure she built for herself. She is just down the road from the man she grew up with and the perfectly good house they built together, but she explained that she needed her own space, and Anemos can understand that.

He would abandon the Palace in a second for Zahra's little tent.

He knocks twice against the wood, and her voice rings out like a song.

"Who is it?" she calls. "State your intentions."

A small smile tugs at Anemos lips. He clears his throat.

"Disgraced Prince. My intentions are to see my sister..."

There is a loud rumble of things being knocked over inside, and then the door is pushed to the side, tossed to the ground. Almost before the boy can make her out, Zahra pulls him into her arms, burying her chin in the crook of his neck.

He fights back the wave of anxiety he feels at being touched and relaxes into her embrace, wrapping his arms around her back. *Safety. Finally.*

"Have you decided to run away?" she asks. "Say you have."

"Zahra..."

"Oh, Inanis," she mutters. "It's today, isn't it? You've come to say goodbye."

He wants to deny it. He wants so *badly* to deny it, but only shakes his head, not moving from his place in her arms. After a minute though, she pulls back, taking his hands.

"Are you feverish? You're warm."

"So are you," he says, looking down at her hands.

Her gaze follows his, and she lets out a heavy sigh, her palms instantly growing cooler.

"I guess I'm a little anxious."

"Am I making it worse?"

"I can feel you, is all," she whispers, her dark hair falling into her face. "You're more afraid than you were last time."

"It's closer," he admits.

Her eyes hover over his for a minute, and then she turns, gesturing for him to follow her.

Soon he is sitting on a rug on the ground, watching as she starts a fire in the corner of the room. It is one of his favorite parts of visiting, watching her work her magic. He can remember when she was too shy to share it with him, but now she does not think twice. She spins her hands around quickly, steadies them, and a small ball of light appears above them, only to be passed onto the wood in front of her. Her confidence fills him with a quiet sense of pride that he knows is rebellion.

She stokes the fire with only her hands, holding them just a little too close to the flames. Her hands look better than they did the last time he was with her. The burn scars have faded, leaving only faint reddish blotches on her deep bronze skin—reminders of all the times the fire has come too close.

"Does it hurt?" he asks, again.

She turns around, shakes her head.

"No, not from this distance, it's only warm."

He doesn't respond, and she watches him carefully, noting the way he fidgets with his hands.

"Talk to me, would you?"

"I don't know what to say."

"Whatever seems most pressing," she suggests, and he lowers his eyes.

He cracks his knuckles, shakes his head.

"I had another seizure last night," he says. "I was rehearsing the vow, and it was like the world closed in around me. I started thinking of all these things, and then I couldn't stop, and the next thing I knew I had lost control."

"Anemos... I'm sorry."

"It's happened so many times now, Zahra," he mutters, but he does not dismiss the trauma of it like he thought he would. He can't. "It's just... I feel so out of control. And it's going to get worse, now. I don't know how I'm going to make it."

"The way you always do." She knows the words are unhelpful, but it is the best she can manage.

He lets out a quiet sigh, looking back up at her.

"I'm tired," he says.

Zahra looks back at the fire so he cannot see her eyes. He hasn't been to Inanis, and doesn't possess the abilities it has given her, but she thinks anyone could read her face now.

She thought she had already decided to follow through with her plans, but she is more certain now than she has ever been. And she *cannot* have him realize them, because if he does, he will stop her. She can't blame him. She knows breaking into the city is a bad idea. She knows the punishment for treason is execution, and crossing through the wall as a

Deviation is enough to justify the charge, but she doesn't know what other choice she h
as.

"I know," she says. "I know you are."

"I don't want to worry you, Zahra. God knows you have enough to worry about."

"I would worry about you anyway," she sighs. "You're my little brother, after all."

He smiles a little at that, but his chest grows heavy. She may not be blood, but she is
the only family he claims, and he can't bear the thought of not seeing her again.

"I'll be alright," he insists. "This is what I was born for, after all. It won't kill me."

Zahra doesn't respond, but after a moment, she stands and crosses the room, sitting
down across from him.

"You *have* come to say goodbye, haven't you?" she asks. "I won't have it."

"Zahra..."

"I won't have it," she repeats. "I've had enough goodbyes, and I'm not having another
one. I know it won't be safe for you to visit, but we'll find a way. We'll meet and talk
through the gate if we have to."

He wants to argue with her— to point out the obvious issues with her plan, but he
doesn't have the heart for it.

"Okay," he says instead.

"Are you sure you're not ill?"

"I'm fine, Zahra—" A loud whistle interrupts him, and he sits up a little straighter.
There is a rattling noise outside the tent that they have both come to recognize.

"The train," Zahra confirms.

Anemos nods, dusting his hands on his knees.

"It'll be my parents," he says. "I should be heading home."

"Stay a little longer," she insists, and again, he does not argue.

When Anemos makes it back to his house the sun is fully risen, though the clouds do not
show it. The first thing he hears when he opens his front door is his parents yelling.

He steps inside, but keeps a grip on the handle when he shuts the door behind him.
He does *not* want to get in the middle of them.

"Charles has enough to handle," his father insists, his voice gruff. "It's ceremony day,
for Inanis' sake. I can deal with it myself."

"You're not dealing with anything, Alastor. You should have reported it the moment you found it. I should have reported you."

"Try it," the man threatens, and Anemos' chest grows impossibly tighter. "I tell Charles, he'll rule in mercy and the thing will be executed. The war is getting closer every day and if we don't get a leg up, we'll drown in it."

"The Code forbids using E.D.T.s for war—"

"Don't preach the Code to me, you damn waste."

Silence. Anemos lowers his face.

His mother's voice comes again, finally, but with much less volume.

"I'm telling him," she says. "You can't stop me."

There is the shuffling of footsteps, and Anemos goes to open the door again, but before he can his mother is standing in front of him.

She wears a long black dress and black gloves, her dark hair falling in waves around her face, framing her onyx eyes. She looks like a woman in mourning.

"Anemos," she whispers, her eyes darting over his face. "I don't know where you've been, but you best get ready for the day. You're horribly pale."

"I'm fine," he mutters.

"Put on the makeup then, either way. You need to present yourself well today."

He's tired, but he nods anyway, stepping to the side so she can reach the door.

Still, she doesn't move.

"I found your dinner in the trash," she says. "I won't have that. There isn't enough food going around for you to be wasting it."

"Yes, Myon."

"Don't repeat a word of what you just heard," she adds, and he nods, sick.

"I know."

She leaves without saying anything else.

CHAPTER NINE

Far from the Outskirts, in a room high above the rest of the city, the Guide opens his eyes. He has fallen asleep on top of the covers again, and he shivers as he pulls himself up. His hair hangs in long, tangled waves around his face and shadows drape themselves around his shoulders. Shadows drape themselves over the whole room, even though there is no light to cast them.

A knock at his door startles him and he looks toward it, pulling a robe from the table beside him as he stands. It's not unheard of for someone to wake him early on ceremony day, but he doubts it's for anything good.

He clears his throat before he speaks, his heart pounding in his chest. "Yes, who is it?"

"Elise, Myon." The young assistant's voice is tense enough he can tell through the door. "I'm sorry to bother you—"

"Come in. Please."

The door slowly opens, revealing a short young woman with cropped brown hair and sharp cyan eyes; she keeps her eyes low.

"I'm sorry to bother you, Myon," she repeats, bowing a little in a show of respect. "Council Member Ursula has requested your presence."

The Guide's stomach twists inside of him. "She's here now?"

"She's asked me to prepare a carriage for transport to Karneji, Myon. She's waiting in the entry hall."

A dozen questions move through his mind, but he doubts Elise has answers for any of them. He forces them back, painting a mask of calm on his face. "Thank you. I'll be right there."

It isn't often Ursula visits him here. That is the thought on the forefront of the Guide's mind as he scales the Palace stairs. He can't imagine what brings her here, unless something has happened with Anemos.

He is supposed to be calm. He shouldn't be panicking over something he doesn't know. There shouldn't be frantic prayers falling from his lips, and *yet...*

His eyes find the woman standing like a shadow in the hall, her hands folded in front of her, and he softens at the sight of her.

"Ursula," he says, and she turns toward him, her eyes afraid.

"Charles," she breathes; then, correcting herself: "Myon. I'm sorry to bother you, especially so close to the ceremony."

He stops in front of her, cracking his knuckles at his side, and shakes his head.

"It's no bother. Is everything alright?"

"There's been a failure on my part, Myon." She lowers her gaze, keeping her voice low. "I seek to rectify it, albeit at the worst time."

"A failure?"

"We've failed to report a finding, in Karneji. A girl, no older than seventeen. My intention was always to inform you, once we were sure, but more time has passed now than I'm comfortable with." Ursula pauses, the words seeming stuck in her throat. "An E D.T."

Charles pales. He tilts his head to the side, unsure he heard correctly.

"An E.D.T.?"

"It has no apparent deviation, aside from healing. It's posed very little danger, even when it's turned..."

An *Exercitum de Tenebris*— a possessed soul, within Ordinem territory.

If it were any more uncommon, it would be completely unheard of. Fifty years ago, it might not have come as such a shock, but E.D.T.s are found so rarely now that he is completely stunned.

There is one E.D.T. in Trellis: the Changeling, a key weapon in the war between the southern countries, but he knows of no other.

He knows what he is meant to do with this one, but his curiosity is louder than that knowledge.

"How long have you had her?" he asks, and Ursula pauses, swallowing hard.

"No more than two weeks, Myon."

"Two *weeks?*"

"Alastor has been hesitant to report it, given the mercy clause. He thinks it's too great an asset to destroy. That's why I've come to you—"

"Take me to it," he interrupts. "Please. At once."

"The carriage is already prepared, Myon. I requested Alastor's attendance, but he was resistant."

"Request it again," Charles says, and Ursula nods, never lifting her eyes from the floor.

No one speaks on the journey into the desert. Charles stares out the carriage window with heavy eyes, too many thoughts spinning in his head.

Alastor has not offered so much as a word in defense of his decision to withhold information about the E.D.T., but it isn't necessary. Charles knows his brother well enough to understand his reasoning.

Most of it.

The war between the countries south of them seems to escalate every day, and the threat of it reaching them is always present, even if it is Charles' responsibility to assure his people it isn't. An E.D.T. could've offered them some protection, if it was as powerful as Alastor likely expected; even if using it as a weapon would violate the very Code they have sworn to uphold.

The carriage jolts to a stop, and Ursula shifts in her seat, uneasy.

"I hate this place," she mutters. "Bloody wasteland."

Alastor's jaw clenches, but he doesn't respond, his eyes distant, *guilty*.

"I'll certainly feel better about things when we're inside," Charles says, but when he looks back at her, he finds that her expression suggests otherwise.

Elise opens the carriage doors abruptly, a set of keys in her right hand, and nods with a sense of urgency.

"There were a pack of blood dogs— Acthens, along our path. I'm unsure of whether they followed us, so it's best you proceed as quickly as possible. I'll keep watch at the door, once I've gotten you inside..." They're all ushered out. Charles grimaces at the sound of the gravel under his feet, afraid of being heard. "Permission to shelter in the carriage if necessary, Myon?"

"Yes," he says, squinting against the sand being blown about in the wind. "Of course."

The Facility looms in front of them like a shadow, stretching deep into the rocky mountain behind it. It has always felt like a living thing. Ever since Charles was a child.

He has seen so many horrors inside its walls.

Elise feels it too, he thinks, watching as she struggles with the keys. There is an inhuman cry somewhere in the distance, and it startles her so badly that she drops them.

"I'm sorry," she says quickly.

"The place does a number on your nerves. You're fine. Try to stay as calm as you can—"

The door swings open, and Charles falls silent, his throat tightening as he looks at the concrete hallways stretching out in front of him.

Alastor shoves past him and Ursula follows in his footsteps, her hands still folded together.

It is quieter today than it usually is. Most of the prisoners have been moved to cells far from the main building in preparation for the exams in the evening. Despite knowing the reason for it, the calm makes Charles uneasy.

He doesn't remember why.

"We'll have to take the lift," Alastor says, finally. "The E.D.T. is several floors down. It's on the lowest level, where we keep the Reapers."

"You're keeping the E.D.T. with the Reapers?" Charles asks. "That's absurd."

"None of them have enough strength to wield any power over the thing. The enthroproxan has made that certain. Besides, they're behind bolted steel..." The door to the lift slides open, and Charles steps inside, glancing up at the ceiling.

"No light?"

"It went out. There's a lantern just right of you, when you step into the hall. The E.D.T. is twenty paces forward and eight to the left, behind door seventeen. You should find it with ease."

Alastor slams the door shut, and they are in pitch darkness. The lift lurches beneath them and then moves lower into the Facility. Charles' stomach sinks with it.

He hasn't been to this level since shortly after it was built, and he had hoped he wouldn't have to return. He hated it even when it was empty— the cold, damp air and uneven halls. He hated the darkness and the unseemly quiet.

Now, with Grim imprisoned in its stone rooms, he would rather be anywhere else.

When the door opens to the same darkness of the lift, it is a struggle to keep his eyes open with the fear he feels in his chest.

"Will you go alone?" Ursula asks, and he nods, still unable to see her.

"I should. Twenty paces forward, eight to the left."

"Door Seventeen." She has already stepped around him and lit the lantern Alastor spoke of, and now she hands it to him, her hands steadier than his. "It's defenseless. It won't hurt you."

Defenseless. The word leaves a bad taste in his mouth in a place like this.

He can't manage a response, so he turns and goes without one.

Twenty paces forward, a dozen doors with no sound of life behind them. Reapers, injected with enough enthroproxan and paralytic they are likely unable to move.

He is *still* afraid of them.

Eight paces to the left and he tugs on the large metal rod keeping the door to the E.D.T. closed, willing his legs not to fail him. Thick, coppery air hits his face just as the dim red light left in the room reaches his eyes. He looks only at the floor as he steps inside, letting the door close behind him. When he looks up again, pain explodes in his chest.

The E.D.T. is kneeling on the floor, and the ground beneath her is stained a deep red. Her skin is raw, and her arms are tied up above her head, littered with scars. Her clothes— torn and stained with blood— barely even cover her.

She's no older than Anemos.

She lifts her head just an inch at the sound of the door, her movements weak, and sobs past the gag between her lips. There is a futile attempt to pull her hands free. She pulls against the ropes so violently that they tear her skin—

"Don't be afraid," Charles says. "I'm not here to hurt you."

He steps forward as she pulls back and retrieves the dagger from his waist. She starts to scream when he cuts the ropes, but he doesn't hesitate.

When she's free, she throws herself back against the wall, gasping for air and pulling her hands to her chest. Her knees are two busted ulcers, red and purple and trembling.

Hesitantly, Charles reaches forward and pulls the gag from her mouth.

"Please," she cries. "Please, no more."

He nods, holding his hands up in a quiet gesture of peace.

"No more..." She sobs. "I'm not... I don't want to hurt anyone. I don't want to hurt you..."

"I know," he whispers, almost to himself. "Please..."

The girl falls silent, crying quietly into her arms, but he doesn't push her to speak. He only watches in horror, his stomach burning with the anger he feels.

When she finally opens her mouth, minutes later, her words are a broken plea.

"Are you going to kill me?" she asks. Her blue eyes are stained with red, her lips busted. "Show m...me mercy?"

"No," he replies.

"Is that *man* going to kill me? Or the woman? Is she..."

His skin burns like *fire*.

"No. No one is going to kill you, love."

She lifts her face slightly, looking at him with doubtfully.

"Then what are you going to do?" she questions, and he presses his lips together, letting out a short sigh.

"I'm going to talk to you," he says. "Just talk. If you're willing to do that"

She takes a shallow breath, familiar with routines like this one, and nods. She knows she can't refuse—

"You don't have to," he continues. "I won't force you."

"I have nothing to hide. I've never had anything to hide. I'm useless."

"Oh, no. I don't believe that."

"I've no reason to lie to you. I have nothing to lose. I explained that to him, but he didn't listen, and now they've already done everything they can to me."

Charles shakes his head, pale as a ghost.

"No, love, I believe you. I just don't believe that you're useless. Have you a name?"

"Will you take that too?"

"No." His voice breaks, and he pauses, shaking his head again. "No, I won't take that."

The girl is silent for a long moment, her rage palpable, and then, her voice almost a whisper: "My name is Rosemarie."

"Rosemarie," he repeats. "Okay, Rosemarie. I'm Charles."

He holds a hand out in her direction, knowing he shouldn't, and she takes it hesitantly.

"I'm so sorry I didn't come sooner, I wasn't informed... I'm going to help you. Let's just... get you clean, get you somewhere less..." He gestures to the darkness around them, and she feels a bit of unwelcome hope rise in her chest. "Then we'll talk, alright? Just a conversation, none of this. We'll help each other."

She nods, disbelieving.

"Okay. Very good. I'll speak with Alastor, and—" She tenses, her eyes darkening, and he pulls his hand back. "I won't let them touch you. Don't worry about that."

"Thank you, sir."

"I'll have a nurse with you soon," he finishes, bile rising in his throat. "If you don't mind my asking, Rosemarie, how long have you been—"

"I don't know anymore. It's all the same." Her teeth chatter, her eyes never lightening. "It's been worse than *Trellis*. It's like this darkness is all that exists."

"Trellis," Charles repeats. "You came from Trellis?"

"I told you I have nothing to hide."

When Charles leaves the room, his heart is in his throat.

His brother and Ursula are still standing in front of the lift, hidden in darkness, no doubt speaking of him. He takes a deep breath, the weight of the shadows around his shoulders almost heavier than he can bear, and moves toward them in long strides.

He stops a few feet away from them, fighting to remain composed, and wraps his fingers back around the hilt of his dagger, silent.

"Charles," Alastor says, his eyes darting down to the hand.

Ursula looks at his eyes instead, and when she does, her chest hollows.

"She's just a child," Charles says. "A *child*, Alastor."

"There are no children—"

What Alastor *means* to say is that Assecula— hell, evil, wickedness— has no children, and in a way, he is right; but the words are stolen from him.

He is slammed back against the wall behind him before he can realize what's happening, and the dagger is pressed to his throat.

A gasp escapes Ursula's lips, but she makes no effort to pull Charles away.

"*This*," he says through clenched teeth. "This is wrong, brother."

"You are not the man to be speaking on right and wrong."

The dagger is pressed closer, leaving a thin line of blood on the older man's neck, and he falls silent, trying and failing to back away from the pressure.

"You've seen what they do," he says. "You've seen what they *are*. How could you possibly defend them?"

"I have seen *Grim*," Charles interrupts. "I have seen darkness take form. I have *killed* it. I have vowed to destroy it and fight against it just as you have. But this?" He points down the hall. "This is a child. This is a soul, sick as it is, and if it must be extinguished in the end you know I will not hesitate, but now? What you've done?"

"Charles," Ursula says, her voice pleading. "You—"

He pulls another dagger from his left hip, sick, and holds it in the woman's direction. She falls silent.

"This is darkness," Charles says. "Was all of this necessary? To be sure of what she was?" The woman shakes her head, but can't manage anything more. "I'm sure you've pleased your masters. Both of you."

"Damn you," Alastor mutters. "You take your child of night—"

"You don't command me!"

There is a moment of noisy silence, and then he steps away, holding the daggers loosely at his side. His brother gasps for air, and Ursula stands in something like shock.

"I want Elise to come assist the girl in getting cleaned. You are not to touch her— either of you. Do you understand me?"

"Yes," Ursula mutters, stealing a glance at her scowling husband. "We understand."

"I will return to speak with her tonight during the exam. She is to be kept safe until I arrive. If she is not..." He puts the dagger in his left hand away, swings the one in his right, and wipes off the blood with his bare hands. "Be prepared to face the consequences."

The lantern flickers and Ursula glances over at it, uneasy.

"I, and I alone, will decide what we do with her from there. I want a carriage ready here tonight, in case I decide we need to cross the wastes."

"Cross the wastes?" Ursula asks. "Why would we need to cross—"

"That is information that I would hardly trust with either of *you,*" he says coldly. "I will be informing Jack and Aliya of the situation."

"Jack?" Alastor laughs. "You would trust *Jack?*"

"Sooner than I would trust you."

He reholsters his blade and turns back toward the lift.

"Please know that I have not threatened you idly," he says, and with the words, he returns to the shadows.

CHAPTER TEN

A heavy fog has fallen over the Outskirts. To Zahra, it makes loneliness a tangible thing. She does not bother to warm herself as she sits beside the dying fire; she only stares into it, trying not to feel so much.

She is used to being alone but doesn't realize how lonely she is until she is visited and then left again. The little house she has built is quiet, even though she can hear noise beyond it.

She wonders if she will miss it, once she is somewhere else, but she can't imagine she will when she has so little love for it now.

Slowly, she pulls herself up from the floor and outside, wishing for sun and finding only haze. She has been debating with herself over how to do this for weeks. She wants to tell the people she loves goodbye, but then they will ask her to stay. They will *beg* her to stay, and try to dissuade her by reminding her how foolish and rash she is being.

But Zahra doesn't want to stay.

Even if it weren't for Anemos and her desire to protect him, she would not want to stay. It's not that she hasn't found something worthwhile where she is, but she is bored with her struggle. It is going nowhere, and she is doing nothing.

Athena, who is like an older sister to her, has reminded her on numerous occasions that there is work to be done here. But Zahra is not a revolutionary like her friend. She is not selfless enough to spend her whole life helping the people around her survive.

There is shame that comes with knowing that, but she has been trying for years, and she still feels empty. She is tired of living here— fighting off threats, and sickness, and starvation. She hates the Guide and his Ordinem, but that doesn't change the fact that she craves the safety the city brings.

It's betrayal, and she realizes that, but she is tired.

Besides, she is telling herself that that isn't why she is going— even if she knows it is only half true, her desire for comfort probably wouldn't have been reason enough. It wasn't enough when she was thirteen and offered *legal* entry. Zahra is going because Anemos needs her there, and she will spend every moment she is there fighting for him, because *he* is worth the effort it will take. He can do more than survive, and if she gains that from the city too, why should she be scorned for that?

It is her life, and she has the right to risk it for what she sees fit, doesn't she?

Her steps fall heavy on the gravel beneath her, the feeling rattling through her whole body like it usually does when she is near panic, but she continues toward her friend's house, readying herself for a goodbye she will not speak. Within a minute, she is knocking at his door.

"Let yourself in." Athena's voice greets her instead of Ghost's, and she swallows hard.

Two goodbyes, then. She saw Athena yesterday and had already started at an attempt to distance herself, not expecting to see her until after the ceremony was over. The thought of having to start over makes her chest hurt, but she forces a smile, cracking her neck nervously before she opens the door. Athena and Ghost are sitting in the center of the small living area, playing some game with a small pile of wooden dice. They are always inventing new games— ways to escape the tension that is living on the Outskirts. It worked, for a while. Zahra thinks back over the nights she has spent with them, doing pointless but fun activities, and feels her stomach sink.

She will miss some things.

"Zahra," Ghost exclaims, pulling himself up from the floor. "I was hoping you would come by. I've found something you're going to *love.*"

"Oh?" she inquires, her voice sounding more forced than she expected. Luckily they don't notice.

"Close your eyes," he says, and she does, shaking her head.

"You're building it up now."

"Open your hands."

She cups them in front of her, and hears Athena let out a sigh riddled with laughter.

"You're going to frighten her," the woman says. The warmth of her voice makes a wave of sorrow pass through the girl, but she forgets it when something is placed in her hands— warm, moving, and *alive.*

"Alright, open them," Ghost commands, and when she does, her heart skips a beat. The thing is nearly the size of her hand, with small hairs covering its entire body, a cluster of eyes, and eight legs.

"Oh God," she exclaims, her brows furrowing. "A spider? Is it a spider? This big?"

"We looked in one of Attie's encyclopedias and determined it's a tarantula."

"Is it poisonous?"

"Oh... A little. But as long as it doesn't bite you, or shoot hair in your eyes..." She looks up at him, frightened, and he shakes his head, laughter erupting from his chest. "It's been very friendly. You'll be fine."

"*Ghost.*"

"Do you want me to take it back?" he asks.

Zahra looks at the thing, which has started to crawl toward her wrist, and lets out a heavy sigh. This is what it has always been like with Ghost. Ever since they made it out of Karneji, he has been finding things and bringing them home. They are little treasures—signs that not all life from before the Six has passed away; and they're Ghost's pets, now. He has three snakes he has kept with him, keeping them fed with smuggled food and what insects he can find. Feeding slithering beasts when he can hardly feed himself has gotten him many questioning glances, but Zahra loves him for it. She loves him like he is her own blood.

"No," she replies, a soft smile creeping over her lips. "I'd like to hold him a minute longer."

"That's what I thought," Ghost says, and Athena shakes her head.

"Why do you find nothing pleasant? A bird, or a butterfly, or something else that doesn't *bite.*"

Zahra spends almost an hour with her family, talking about things that matter very little, and the ceremony, and everything else. Then, she realizes how high in the sky the sun has gotten and turns toward the door, handing the tarantula—which Ghost has named "Little Wolf", in her honor—back to him.

"I need to go," she forces. "I have a lot to get done before the sun goes down again."

Ghost looks surprised, but nods, sitting the spider on his arm.

"You must, if you're leaving this early."

She stands and nods in reply, avoiding both of their eyes.

"I do," she says, but then she stops, taking a moment to look at them a little longer.

Her little family. The only family she has, other than Anemos.

She tells herself that she will see them again; she can sneak out through whatever gap in the wall she sneaks in through.

But then, she can't know for certain.

"I love you both, though," she says, and Athena smiles, scooting away from Ghost as she casts a glance at the creature moving closer to her.

"We love you too," she says, and Ghost shakes his head.

"You're alright," he jokes, and she laughs, nodding with her eyes on the floor.

"Alright," she says. "Bye, now."

She is amazed at her ability to hold herself together as she walks away from the home with nothing but the clothes on her back.

She takes in the place around her for what might be the last time, but speaks to no one as she passes through it, walking with a speed that suggests she is going nowhere important.

Soon, she is in the field between her cluster and the city wall— where she met Anemos for the first time. She picks thorns from her pants as she walks, pushing the high grass out of her way.

She would come here all the time when she was smaller. It was like a little forest— or the closest she could find to one. She would lie on the ground and pretend the weeds were trees. She thinks there are trees in the city.

She hopes there are. In truth, though, all that she knows about the city is what Anemos has told her, and what lies before her now: The wall.

Zahra has thought about crossing it many times but has held herself back because she has always been aware of the danger being caught could bring. Today is no different, but she is hoping the chaos of the ceremony will be enough to let her slide through.

Once she has the mark, they will have no reason to question her; so long as she does not let her power show.

It's an ugly wall, she thinks, passing through the same gap Anemos has always used. It's a waste of money, building something so easy to breach, just so you can make a statement about who is allowed where.

As soon as she is on the other side of it, there is pavement beneath her feet.

She looks down at it, and back up at the city in front of her, and her stomach twists.

It is a short walk to the nearest building, where Zahra cleans herself up and scolds herself for her foolishness. It is a shorter walk to the bar stool she claims for herself when she vacates the washroom.

"What'll you have?" the man in front of her asks, and she stares at him, wondering if he can tell she is not welcome.

"Just give me the strongest thing you've got," she laughs, and he shakes his head.

"It's nine in the morning, Myon."

The term of respect catches her off guard. She is not sure why would use a term meant for a superior, until she remembers what she wears: a stolen higher class uniform, in a Lower-class sector.

She shrugs, biting her bottom lip.

"I've not slept," she admits. "And it's ceremony day."

"A coffee, then?"

She squints at him, the strangeness of the situation seeping into her. There is not much money in her pocket, but she can't imagine she will need much, if she makes it to the Compounds. If she doesn't, money will hardly matter.

"A coffee would be perfect," she says. "Would you mind adding cream and a shot of whiskey?"

CHAPTER ELEVEN

"Highest score in the exams goes to..." The blonde woman flips through several sheets of paper, adjusting her glasses as she goes. "Icarus, again."

"Of course," Charles replies. He looks up at the ceiling and rubs his face, already hearing the outrage the results will bring.

"Of course?" she asks.

"Pardon me, Cindy. I've had a long morning." He sighs. "But then, he is always first, isn't he? It's hardly a shock."

Cindy laughs bitterly, her lips tight.

"Yes, he is. Doesn't that embarrass you? Having an outsider pass all of our children?"

"No. Physical exams, please."

She fights the urge to roll her eyes, picks up another stack of papers, and repeats the routine.

"Icarus," she says, sometime later, not bothering to elaborate.

Charles begins to laugh, running a hand through his hair.

"How high was his score?"

"It was the *highest* score, Myon."

"I understand that Cindy, but how high—"

"No, *Guide*. You don't understand. It was *the highest score.*"

His eyebrows draw together, and he holds out his hand.

She passes it to him and watches as his eyes move over the words.

"I'm surprised you beat him in that little ordeal yesterday," she says. "It seems you'd make a fair match."

The boy's numbers are higher than the man's were at the same age. He cannot deny that, but he also does not acknowledge it.

"Oh, please don't remind me of that," he breathes. "The showiness of it all? My word. It was awful."

She doesn't respond. She only continues watching him read until he sits down the report a few seconds later.

"Well," he says. "The child is stronger than he looks."

Someone bangs on the door before she can respond and they both look over at it, startled.

"Yes," Charles calls. "Please, come in."

The door opens, and Cindy looks down at her hands.

"Jack! Lovely. I was just about to come find you. You ought to let Cindy read you your son's..." A girl follows Jack into the room, and as Charles' gaze falls on her, he falls silent. Her skin is a deep bronze, a few shades lighter than her eyes. She has scarred hands, poorly cut hair, and an Ordinem uniform.

"As much as I'd enjoy that, Myon, I'm afraid this is a visit with a purpose," Jack says, and Charles nods, his chest tight.

"I see," he says. "And who is this?"

"This is Zahra," the girl says. Then, more respectfully: "*Myon.*"

A smile pulls at the edges of Charles' lips, even as Cindy stands to express her indignation.

He holds out a hand in her direction and waves her back down, but keeps his eyes on the girl.

"Zahra," he says. "It's nice to meet you. Care to sit?"

Zahra clenches her jaw, forcing a tight smile. "No, thank you."

"Very well."

Jack closes his eyes for a moment and rolls his neck, managing a tired grin.

"Myon," he begins. "Perhaps we could speak privately?"

Charles nods, fighting a smirk, and follows Jack out of the room, leaving Cindy and Zahra to stare at each other in very different forms of disgust.

"I like her," Charles says, once the door is closed. "She reminds me of you. Where'd you find her?"

"Arguing with the headmaster at the University," Jack says. "She didn't bring any identification."

"Didn't bring it?"

"Didn't have it."

"And the headmaster?"

"Claims he's never seen her before in his life."

"Delightful," Charles sighs. "We'll never see a Ceremony day without some drama, will we?"

"It's doubtful, Myon."

Charles paces back and forth a moment before leaning back against the wall, folding his arms over his chest.

"What's her story?" he asks.

"She's lost her papers," Jack replies, searching the other man's eyes. "Is there something else—"

Charles furrows his brows and laughs, disregarding the question.

"That's all?"

"Yes," Jack says. "That's all."

"And how does she explain the headmaster?"

"She doesn't," he breathes, shaking his head. "She said, and I quote: *I don't know what to tell you about that, ask the headmaster.*"

"What a day we're having. She's lying, I assume?"

Jack hesitates a moment before shaking his head, uneasy.

"I can't tell, Charles. Not like I usually can. If she's lying she's doing a damn good job. I'd believe her if her story weren't so..."

"Completely unbelievable?"

"Yes, exactly."

"Does she seem to be hiding anything else?" Charles asks. "Have I any reason to be suspicious?"

"You have every reason to be suspicious," Jack says. "But no, Myon. I don't believe she's dangerous."

"From the Outskirts, though?"

"Almost definitely."

"Mhm." Charles nods, his eyes distant. "Reminds you a bit of Ursula when she was younger, doesn't she? She has the same scars on her hands."

"I noticed that, myself," Jack agrees. He folds his hands behind his back, letting his gaze drift out the window beside him. It's a gray day, and it's reflected in Charles' posture. His eyes are the same cloudy gray as the sky. "Charles?"

"Jack?"

"Is there something else?"

The Guide raises his eyes to meet his, his lips pulled tight. He doesn't speak for a long moment, and Jack would be willing to swear on his life that he has some battle waging in his mind for the entirety of it.

"Ursula and Alastor have been holding someone in Karneji," he says, finally. "An E.D.T., from Trellis."

Jack's eyes widen at the words, letting his hands fall.

"*The* E.D.T.?" he asks, and Charles quickly shakes his head.

"No, not the Changeling. A girl. She's about Anemos' age, and... Powerless, aside from the healing." His expression is dark—troubled. "I want to find out what we can about her tonight, during the interrogations. I want you with me."

"Of course, Charles..."

Zahra tries her hardest to listen through the door, but her effort is futile.

She pulls her gaze from Cindy, bored with the stern-looking woman, and redirects her attention to the room around her.

It's big, she thinks, bigger than they need. Big enough to shelter at least a moderate sized portion of the cluster she lives in, but instead, the space is almost empty.

Of course it is.

She takes a deep breath and stretches, groaning a little as she does. She is too stubborn to sit but too tired to keep standing, so she settles on leaning back against the wall.

She hopes that her shirt stains it.

It is only a couple of minutes before the Guide returns to the room, but to Zahra it feels much longer. Of course, *almost* everything has gone according to plan, so she has little reason for the insecurity building in her stomach, but this?

This will be the hardest part. This is where the danger lies, and she is most at risk of herself.

She has so many things that she would *like* to say to this man she has come to hate.

When the door opens and Charles walks through it, his smile sends chills down her spine.

"Zahra," he says, sitting back behind the large desk he came from. "You've gotten yourself into quite a situation. How exactly did you go about losing *all* of your identification?"

She blinks slowly, forcing her lips into a tight smile.

"With all respect, Myon, if I knew the answer to that, it wouldn't be lost."

"Fair enough," he breathes, putting a foot up on his desk. "I would think, though, that someone else would remember you."

"Well, I'm hardly social, but I'm sure someone remembers me. Jack only asked the headmaster."

"Yes, and in all the years that man has been headmaster, he has never once forgotten a face— until now."

"Well, that's just my luck, isn't it?" she laughs. "Please, you must have *some* record of me. Something saved somewhere."

"Yes, we should, but we don't," he says. "All signs point to you lying, Zahra."

"I'm not—"

He stands again, suddenly, and points at Cindy. Zahra falls silent.

"You're excused," he says. "I'd like to speak with her alone."

Cindy gives him a look of something between concern and irritation, then stands, bows, and goes.

He's more intimidating alone, Zahra thinks. He seems taller. His shoulders seem broader. His eyes seem harder.

She cannot believe she wants that woman and her pompous expression to come back.

"Sit," the Guide says sharply. "Now."

Zahra fights every single instinct she has and crosses the room, her hands warm at her sides, to sit in front of him.

He looks at her for a long while, silently, and then sits once more.

A cloud moves in front of the sun, and the room dims.

"The Ordinem has no tolerance when it comes to liars," Charles says quietly. "But you are not of the Ordinem, so I will bend the rules, this once."

She stays still as a stone, willing her eyes not to betray her.

"Tell me the truth," he says, "and I will forget the lie."

His head is lowered, and his eyelids hang heavy. His hands rest on the table in front of him, far away from the daggers on his waist. His posture has shifted to one of submission, vulnerability, and openness.

A wolf in sheep's clothing, she thinks.

It is something she has mirrored before.

She weighs her options in her mind— all of them— and then looks down, anxiously feigning regret.

"There is... shame, in admitting you have lied," she says, and he nods, keeping his voice low.

"Shame, yes. But also mercy."

I don't want your mercy.

She isn't sure where she pulls the grief from. Maybe it is for something long gone—from a wound long ignored or a secret buried deep in her chest. Maybe the tears are for her family, or for Anemos.

It doesn't matter. It only matters that they replace the scowl wants to respond with.

She takes a deep, shaky breath, wiping her eyes with trembling hands.

"I... I didn't know what else to do," she says, her voice cracking. "If there had been some other way... It's no excuse, Myon, but if you've ever visited the Outskirts, surely you can understand my fear, being there."

"Of course," he says. "You are from the Outskirts, then?"

She nods, her breath catching in her throat— becoming a sob.

"Yes. I'm sorry, I..."

"Don't apologize," he says firmly. "Not for the truth. I suspected as much, given your behavior this morning."

"I'm sorry," she says again. She isn't.

"No more shame," he says. "Why are you here?"

She takes several deep breaths before attempting to explain, grabbing tightly to the sleeves of her shirt, but making sure to keep her chest open.

Submission, not defense.

"I failed the test," she says. "The first one, when I was younger. I didn't understand yet how important this is. I didn't understand the Order. I didn't understand the darkness..."

Charles' eyes dig into hers, even as they rest, but she doesn't flinch away.

"I was young," she breathes. "Young, and stupid, and deceived, but... I thought that if I worked, maybe I could... I thought that maybe it wasn't too late. I didn't expect they'd need my papers, and then I panicked, and... Well, I'm hardly better than I was at thirteen, am I?" A broken laugh escapes her chest, and she shakes her head. "I've only added to my shame, but then, I suppose that's all I've ever done."

He watches her carefully, searches for the lie, and finds none.

"You came prepared, then?" he asks. "To test?"

"Yes," she whispers. "I did."

He takes a deep breath— stretching his neck.

"Well then, you'll test."

Her eyes widen, and she lifts her head.

"Myon?"

"You've already missed the time slot for the knowledge and physical exams, but I will allow you to test here, privately. I'll have the combat testing pushed back an hour, which should allow you to participate, and in the meantime Cindy will work on getting your papers in order. Do you understand?"

"...Yes. Yes, I understand."

"Good," he says, standing up.

"That's all?"

"Were you expecting something more?"

"No. It's just... I lied. I thought—"

"I don't recall." He is already across the room, already opening the door, but he pauses before leaving. "Do well, Zahra," he says. "And do try not to lose your papers."

CHAPTER TWELVE

"If I had done three less push-ups they would have failed me," Anemos says, stabbing at a pile of mashed potatoes on his plate. "If I die in combat, please, feast on this soggy ass meat in remembrance of my struggle."

Cole takes a bite and puts his hand over his mouth.

"Oh, that is vile."

"I can't believe you even put... put it on your plate," Icarus remarks. "They didn't even tell you what it was."

"It's beef," Cole says.

"No, it's *meat,*" he laughs. "It... It m-might be beef, but it *said* m-m-meat, which is... a little... disconcertingly vague, in my opinion."

"Wait, seriously?"

"That's why I didn't take any."

Cole looks down at the pile of thick, gray ground on his plate, and then up at Anemos.

"Hold on," Anemos sighs. "I'll get to the bottom of things."

"You don't have to."

"No." He stands up— puts out a hand to silence him. "I do."

Icarus starts to laugh as he walks away, and is still laughing when he returns two minutes later.

"What?" Cole asks. "What's the verdict?"

"It's... meat."

"I t...t-told you."

"But I asked the cook to specify," Anemos continues, clasping his hands together. "And she said..."

"Stop." Cole leans forward on his elbows, rubbing his temples. "The anticipation is killing me."

"Classified. She's only the cook."

The boy lifts his plate into the air, and Anemos takes it, scraping the meat onto his own.

"Are you still going to—" Anemos takes a bite, and Cole falls silent.

"What?" he asks, his mouth full. "I'm hungry. Did you forget that I'm like, literally dying right now?"

"I bet you could get...get out of the... combat test, if you went to the nurse," Icarus says. "Everyone knows you can fight."

"And I'll fight through the death," Anemos says, raising a fork in the air. "Straight on cap—"

Cole presses his hand to Anemos' face, and he stops abruptly.

"Take me to dinner first, Cole."

"You're warm," he says. "And... clammy."

"Keep the compliments rolling, please."

"You need to rest."

"He's right," Icarus says. "You look exhausted."

"I'm *fine*. Seriously, the self-torment gets me—"

"I'm going to the nurse," Cole interrupts.

"Fine." Anemos sits back in his seat, sweat beading his forehead. "Screw you, though."

Cole stands up, stretching as he does, and pats his tired friend on the shoulder.

"You're welcome."

When he leaves, Anemos turns to Icarus and puts a hand over his, pulling him from whatever train of thought he had previously been on.

"How are *you* doing?" he asks.

"Better," Icarus says. "I've been— been... been distracted."

"Yeah, apparently. People are talking, you know."

"Are they?"

"Yeah, you bloody titan. How well did you do?"

Icarus smiles a little, laughs, and shakes his head.

"I don't know. They should be giving the results s...soon, yeah?"

"Yeah, yeah, but, I mean, surely you have *some* idea—"

"I was," Icarus interrupts, "very, very tense."

"Yeah?"

"I think I just... I had a lot of pent-up energy, you... you know? So, I mean... I don't know *what* happened."

"How well did you *do*?" Anemos laughs. "You don't need to sugarcoat it, sweetheart, I already know I'm pitiful."

"You are *not,*" Icarus says firmly.

"I'm telling you, I've accepted it, it's okay. What did you do?"

He takes a deep breath and exhales loudly, keeping his eyes on his hands.

"I think... I think I-I... You know, The Guide's score was the highest."

"Was the highest?"

"It was," he says, "but, I'm... not *sure* it still is."

"Icarus. Are you kidding me?"

"The results will be out soon, yeah?"

"Dude. You—"

Cole walks quickly up to the table, followed by a still-young but slightly older man with glasses and short, straight brown hair.

He points at Anemos, and Cole nods.

"Open your mouth," the man says.

Anemos turns around, bewildered, and Cole shoots him a look that begs him to please, *please* watch himself.

"Pardon me?" Anemos says, trying not to laugh.

"Your temperature," the man says, holding out a thermometer. "Please."

He sighs, a bit melodramatically, and opens his mouth, letting the man stick the thermometer under his tongue.

A long minute passes, and then the man's wrist watch begins to beep, and he takes it back.

"One hundred-point-five," the man says. "Have you had anything to eat or drink?"

Anemos points at his plate and the man squints, shaking his head.

"Don't eat that."

"My word. Is it human meat?"

"What?" The man's eyes widen. "No. It's just... Probably everything else."

Icarus drops his head into his hands.

"Thank you for sharing," Anemos says. "Am I out of commission, Myon?"

"I'd like to keep an eye on you."

"And the combat test?"

"You'll be docked some points, but you'll get through; excused absence. Your overall grade is fine. You'll just have a lower ranking."

Anemos goes to argue his desire to stay, but then glances at Cole and forces a smile.

"Ah, well, I'm already a disappointment," he laughs, patting the man on his shoulder.

The man takes a step back, shaking his head again, and Anemos scrunches his nose.

"I'm sorry," he says. "I'm sleep-deprived."

The man sighs, nods.

"Yeah. Just... Come with me."

Anemos nods in response, pulls himself from the chair and begins to follow the man away.

"Oh, wait," he says. "Icarus?"

Icarus lifts his head and raises his eyebrows.

"Kick their asses for me, yeah?"

"Anemos," Cole starts.

"Sure," Icarus says, drawing Cole's eyes, and Anemos' smile, before lowering his voice. "I mean, I'll... I'll try."

It's another hour until the horn is blown and everyone is called back into the auditorium. When they're inside, Icarus turns to Cole and laughs.

"It's so *weird,*" he says.

"What?" Cole asks. "The smell? Because... Wow."

Icarus rolls his eyes and shakes his head.

"All of it," he says. "It... It... It's all weird. Even the smell."

"Especially the smell," Cole laughs. "But yeah, I get what you're saying."

"And I'm, like... I'm not uncomfortable."

"See? I told you. Nothing to worry about."

"I mean, at... At least the Guide isn't trying to *kill* me."

Cole blinks a few times and rubs his face.

"I still haven't processed that at *all.*"

"M-m...me neither." A door off to the side of the auditorium swings open, and Icarus stops.

"Eh, speak of the devil," Cole says, laughing nervously. "Still comfortable?"

The Guide enters the room and slides off to the side, Zahra following close beside him. He makes no effort to draw any attention to himself, but of course, even in the chaos that is ceremony day, he draws attention anyway.

Dozens of eyes find their way over to Charles as he catches the attention of the headmaster, beginning to explain the situation.

Icarus' eyes fall on the girl next to him, and she notices *before* she looks in his direction.

"Icarus?" Cole asks.

"Yes, sorry. Very... Very comfort— comfortable," he replies, his mind elsewhere. "W-what do you think he's d...doing?"

"No idea," Cole says, and then, a moment later: "Hey, do you recognize her?"

"I don't think so." He pauses. "No, no. Definitely not. I'd rem...mem-member her. Do you?"

One by one, almost every eye in the room turns to Zahra, and the crowd begins to chatter, asking the same *mostly* well-meaning questions. She could imagine without hearing any of it, but she doesn't have to— not with the headmaster in front of her.

"But, Myon—"

"Please, tell me something I don't know," Charles says, irritation rising in his voice.

"She's just not..."

"No, she's not from here," Icarus says. "I would remember her."

"I'm telling you, she looks familiar. Maybe you missed her, before. Do you honestly think you could pick out everyone in this auditorium in a crowd?"

"...Yes? Maybe. I don't know."

His eyes fall to her hands— to her scars, and she instinctively pulls them to her chest.

"Are you sure you remember her from... from here?"

"You think she's from the Outskirts?"

"I m-mean, it would make sense. The headmaster looks pretty—"

"Oh, he's *pissed.*"

Zahra pushes her hair behind her ear, her throat tight and her face warm.

Stay silent, she reminds herself, fighting the urge to defend herself and her people with everything she has.

"She has proven herself capable."

"But has she proven herself trustworthy?" the headmaster asks. "You know why we get them early, Myon. Eighteen years on the Outskirts is too long. The people are filthy..."

She tries to send her mind elsewhere—tries not to hear the words. She focuses on the room instead. On the stares. On the weight of them.

His eyes seem to cut through the rest. They seem to cut through her.

She focuses on the feeling entirely, for a moment, and then twists her head around, meeting his eyes.

It is strange, seeing him *here*, now. She wonders if he ever noticed her.

His eyes, like hers, are the eyes of someone caught between two worlds. A friend? An enemy? A threat?

She can't be sure anymore.

She lifts one hand slightly, hoping the hello serves as a peace offering, and the blond-headed boy lifts his in response.

Like two criminals catching a glance of each other, she thinks. If nothing else, she takes comfort in the mutually assured destruction.

"Your top student is from *Jakara*," Charles says, his voice cutting through her thoughts. "Six years beyond the veil does more damage than eighteen years on the Outskirts, no?"

"Well, I'm not particularly comfortable with him either..."

The man continues speaking, but Charles stops listening, rubbing his face and groaning in exasperation.

"Headmaster," he cuts in, eventually. "Let's just drop the formalities, okay?"

The man falls silent, turning a little pale.

"You will let her compete, you will treat her fairly, and you will cause me no further trouble on the matter."

"But—"

"If she is dangerous, we will know tonight. She is taking the same test as everyone else, and assuming it is designed efficiently," his eyes narrow, "no one who is a threat will get through, isn't that correct?"

"Yes, Myon, but—"

"If you would like to argue your point further, please, join us in Karneji tonight. If you are unable to side with me on the issue, I'm sure Alastor could make a much more *compelling* argument."

Icarus brings his hand back down, folds his arms in front of him, and decides to look anywhere else.

"I wonder what they're saying," he says, but Cole does not seem to be listening. He continues to look at the girl, his eyes squinted. After a minute, though, he shakes his head, clearing his throat.

"Yeah, I don't know."

"I can't imagine."

"Damn it. How much training do you *need* before you can shift into Inanis?" Cole asks, laughing under his breath.

"Why?"

"Because," he says. "If we could just..." He gestures to the space around him wordlessly. "Like, hypothetically, we could totally listen in on them."

"You can eavesdrop without shifting into another dimension, Cole."

"Yeah, but it would be easier if I *could* shift into another dimension, wouldn't it?"

"It'd still be... kind of invasive."

"Come on. Tell me you wouldn't be interdimensionally eavesdropping right now, if you could."

"I really, really wouldn't be."

"Fine, play the moral card, that's fine."

Icarus laughs and takes a deep breath.

"It took Mom twenty years," he says. "But I... I don't know if that's... typical."

"Twenty years," Cole breathes, pushing his hair out of his face. "Damn. That's a lifetime."

"Hopefully not," Icarus breathes. "Does the headmaster look... a little pale, to you?"

"Oh."

The headmaster turns away from Charles with a white face and sweat beading his forehead. He walks into the center of the room with his hands squeezed tightly together in front of him, and clears his throat.

The crowd slowly becomes silent and turns to face him, even as their eyes dart over to Charles—who stands in the corner of the room like a hawk, watching the man's every move.

He forces a bright smile, claps his hands together again, and begins a long-winded introduction that almost no one pays any attention to.

"So," he says, sometime later. "On that note, you'll be split into two groups, and then..." The man swallows, seeming to lose his train of thought. "Well, we'll take it from there. Please understand that this is purely for ranking, and that if you are last today, that will not in any way exclude you from the ceremony tonight; it may, however, exclude you from future combat-related assignments. So, please, do not take it lightly."

He waits, and after a few seconds of confusion, the crowd collectively nods.

"Good," he says. "Now, we'll have group one on the left, and group two on the right.When I call your name, please move in the correct direction."

"Easy enough," Cole mumbles. "We better be in the same group. I don't want to hurt you."

"Oh. You.. you wouldn't hurt me," Icarus says, fighting the urge to laugh.

"Wow, thanks."

"I'm *kidding.*"

"Now," the headmaster begins. "In alphabetical order."

Zahra sighs, tucking her arms together in front of her and preparing to wait.

"Anemos." The headmaster looks up. "Is Anemos here?"

She tries to look unbothered—tries not to panic at the silence of the crowd, but when Cole raises a hand in the air he almost flinches away from her gaze.

"Anemos is... The nurse wanted to keep him for a while. He was sick this morning."

"Sick?" the headmaster asks. "How?"

"He had a fever—" Charles stands, walks silently out of the room, and a shudder passes through Cole and Zahra in the exact same instant. They both want to bolt out of the room after him, but instead, they stay completely still, avoiding each other's eyes.

"That's all I know," he finishes, his voice unsteady.

The man pauses a moment before nodding, scratching a pen vigorously against the paper in his hand.

"Very well. Excused absence. Brody?"

Time begins to move more slowly. Cole moves right, Icarus stays left, and then, finally:

"Zahra," the headmaster says. "Move to group one."

She looks up and then back down, moving as quickly as she can across the room.

For all of her confidence, for all of her resentment, she can't help but feel out of place as she walks across the floor. It's only a survival instinct, she reminds herself— wanting to fit in. She knows deep inside that she doesn't really want their acceptance; but at this moment, she just wants them to stop looking at her.

"Do you mind if I—"

"Yes," the young woman she is attempting to stand with spits. "I do."

Before she has a chance to respond, another voice speaks up.

"Z-Zahra?" he says.

She looks back, catches the blue eyes, and drops her hands.

He doesn't *look* like a threat.

"You can st-stand... here," he says, and his voice does not show all of the hesitance he feels.

She is hesitant, too, but she approaches him anyway. She is far too alone in the Ordinem to refuse the act of kindness, even if she can't trust it. He is Anemos' friend, and that makes him better than the rest of them.

She holds out her hand.

"Icarus, right?" she asks.

He takes it, shakes it firmly.

"Icarus, yeah. It's nice to m... It's nice to meet you."

"It's nice to meet you too," she says, keeping her voice low enough that the headmaster won't be bothered. "Thanks for..." The words trail off, and she shakes her head. "Just, thank you."

"You don't need to—"

"First round!" The man calls, interrupting both of them. "Icarus and Jeff, to the center."

Zahra pulls her hand away and forces a small smile.

"I think that's you," she says. "Good luck."

"Thanks."

"To the center *now*," the headmaster snaps. "Time is of the essence."

Icarus steps to the front only a few seconds before his opponent, and the headmaster hands him a staff. He looks it over quickly, tosses it a few inches up, and catches it again as he watches the other man make his way there.

Jeff is—by no means—bad with a staff. If he were to encounter some other enemy, perhaps some creature in Karneji, his odds would be better than most. He is a little taller than Icarus, a little thicker, and undoubtedly more intimidating—to anyone who has not seen them fight.

He approaches with a heavy sigh and takes a staff from the headmaster.

"This is bent," he says dryly. "You expect me to fight with a bent staff?"?

Icarus leans forward, looks it over, and then holds out his own.

"I'll trade you," he says. "I don't m...mind."

Jeff looks at him for a moment, considering, and the headmaster grows even more impatient.

"Time—"

"If you're sure," Jeff says.

"Yeah, it's no problem."

They switch staves, and the headmaster takes a step back.

"Alright, begin."

Icarus holds the slightly bent staff in his left hand and blocks the almost instantaneous swing at his chest without moving anything above his wrist. Jeff takes a swing at his ribs, but Icarus crouches underneath the weapon, pops back up behind him, and sweeps his feet out from under him in one swift motion, snatching the staff from Jeff's startled hands as he falls.

He hits the ground with a thud and looks up with wide eyes.

"Are you serious?"

"And that's how we do things in a timely fashion," the headmaster interrupts, taking both staves from Icarus. "Very good. You'll begin group three. Next to the center..."

Icarus leans forward, holds out a hand to help the other man up, and he shakes his head.

"I don't take help from your kind," he says, coughing as he pulls himself from the ground. "Go back to Jakara."

Icarus freezes for only a second—less time than Zahra does, hearing it—and then rises once more, nodding with the hint of a smile on his face and turning away. He crosses the room with his head no lower than it was before, and leans back against the same wall the Guide stood by only moments before, watching the little spars with a very similar posture.

His eyes only really wander when her name is called.

"Zahra and Mitchell, please come forward."

Zahra takes a deep breath and nods, stepping forward with much more confidence than she feels.

The crowd begins to murmur, but by the time she arrives in front of them, she has almost stopped caring.

Mitchell approaches slowly, laughing under his breath.

"Hand to hand," the headmaster says. "Unarmed."

"Are there..." Zahra starts, and they both turn to her like she's committed a crime. "Sorry, are there any... rules?"

The headmaster only stares at her, no doubt needlessly insulted by her lack of knowledge on the matter.

"If you want out," Mitchell says, "you tap. If I tap, let me out."

"Is that all?"

"Yeah, basically. Think you can take it?"

Zahra forces a small smile, but doesn't bother responding.

"And..." The headmaster takes a step back. "Begin."

Mitchell takes a fighting stance, his legs parted slightly, his knees bent, and his hands raised as fists in front of his face.

It makes his strategy too obvious, Icarus thinks. Mitchell is more of a defensive fighter. He'll throw a punch he doesn't plan on landing just to provoke her into hitting back; just to grab her hands an inch from his face and twist her to the ground.

She suspects as much, and consequently stays in her place, her hands hanging casually at her sides.

He throws the traditional punch, and she leans to the side, swatting his hand away like a fly, and then returning to her previous position.

"What are you *doing?*" he asks. "Do they not teach you Karneji kids how to fight?"

"No one teaches us anything," she breathes. "We teach ourselves."

"Hardly."

"Oh?" She laughs. "And yet I'm still standing. Please, show me how it's done."

He grimaces slightly, his eyes bright, and glances over at the headmaster like he might do something to help.

"*Well,*" he says. "Show her how it's done."

Mitchell steps forward with a loud sigh, and swings his fist again; again, she dodges the blow.

"Is that the only move you have?" she asks. "*Come on.* Show me how it's done."

He steps forward again, aims his fist directly for her stomach, and she grabs him by the arm— one hand on his wrist, the other on his elbow— twisting him around so that he isn't facing her.

He winces slightly, swats back at her with his other hand, and she pushes his elbow just a *little* too far, kicking hard into his other side, bringing him to his knees.

"I understand it might be hard for you to tap in this position," she says. "So please take this as an offer."

He jerks his head back, trying to pull free, and feels his arm begin to tear.

A loud swear breaks free from his lips, and he shakes his head.

"Yeah, let me out," he says, his voice rough.

She releases his arm and takes a step back, raising her hands in the air.

"Sorry about that," she says.

"Yeah, sure you are."

She walks away from him with a smirk tugging at the ends of her mouth, and joins Icarus in group three, standing close beside him.

He glances at her out of the corner of his eyes, fighting a smile.

"So," he says. "Karneji?"

"Jakara?" she responds.

"How did you hear that?"

"I hear everything," she answers, and then, a minute later: "I spent some time in Karneji, yes, but I don't live there, and I wasn't born there."

"Where... Wh-where were you born?"

She hesitates— looks down at her hands.

"Jakara," she says. "But I don't remember it. I was only one or two when we left."

"You crossed... your family crossed the veil?"

"Didn't yours?"

She is met with silence, and her chest tightens.

"I'm sorry," she says.

He shakes his head.

"Jakara was destroyed," he says softly. "Jack, my father, he found me and brought me back."

"Jack?" she asks. "I know Jack."

He turns to look at her, eyebrows raised.

"It's a long story," she says. "Anyway, I didn't think they could bring people in from outside."

"They can't," Icarus says. "I'm a bit of a red flag."

"Well, so am I," she breathes, "Seeing as I got here this morning."

"R-Really, how *did* you manage that?"

She smiles a little, clenching her fists.

"I suppose," she says, "that I was shown *great mercy*."

A flash of light goes through the room, and a minute later thunder rumbles overhead, so loud that it causes the lights hanging from the ceiling to sway and a shudder to run through the building.

Icarus' body tenses, and he grabs the bottle of water on the floor by his feet.

"Well then," he says, taking a long drink before holding the bottle out in Zahra's direction. "H-here's to mercy."

Remembering her thirst, she takes the bottle and takes several swallows with her head tipped back, hesitating only a second.

"To mercy."

CHAPTER THIRTEEN

A nemos is in the nurse's office, staring out the window as the storm begins to roll in. It's quiet here. He can think.

But he doesn't want to think.

He *wants* to rest.

The sky seems to be darkening with every minute that passes.

When brought back to the nurse's office, Anemos was given a quick, useless examination.

"*Do you have any other symptoms?*" *he was asked.*

"*I had a seizure this morning.*"

The nurse—Ian, going by the letters on his workbench—began to write on the clipboard he held.

"*Did you have a fever before your seizure, or did it appear afterward?*"

"*I don't know,*" *Anemos said.* "*This has happened before, so—wait, no, don't write that down, just...*" *He sighed and rubbed his face with his hands.* "*I've had them before. It's fine. I'm fine, I just—*"

"*Seizures are, usually, a pretty good sign that you aren't fine,*" *Ian said.*

"*Well, I am. I don't know what to tell you.*"

"*Are you epileptic?*"

"*They're psychogenic. I've had them before.*"

"*Psychogenic...*"

"*Yes.*" *Ian began to scribble again, and Anemos stood up, ripping the clipboard from his hands.* "*What did I say?*"

"*Not to write it... Look, this is my job. I have to do my job.*"

"*Yeah? I have to keep the skin on my back. Just...*" *He realized he was yelling and tried to rub the heat out of his face.* "*Look, I'm sorry, just... Please don't.*"

"*I didn't realize it was so serious.*"

"Yeah, I know. It's fine. I'm fine. Just, please, let me rest. I came here to rest."

Ian stood, shocked, for a long moment before speaking.

"I'm going to take your blood pressure," he said, finally.

Anemos took a deep breath, forced himself to soften, and nodded.

"Okay," he said. "That's fine."

"I'm going to get the cuff."

"Okay."

"Just, stay where you are."

"Sure, yeah, of course."

"Okay, thank you."

Ian walked quickly, hesitantly, into the other room, and Anemos glanced down at his hands.

Trembling, again. He is still trembling now.

He cracks his knuckles as he watches the wind blow through the trees. He can see, from this room, that there is already rain falling over the Outskirts. It will be raining here soon, he thinks. It hardly ever seems to rain anymore. He's missed the thunder.

He's always liked the thunder.

It rumbles through the room again, and at the same moment, there is a knock on the door behind him.

He turns his head, suddenly aware of how alone he is, in this room; aware of how weak his body feels.

Ian is long gone, somewhere else in the building, doing something else for someone else. Maybe this is him returning, he thinks, as if he doesn't recognize the rhythm of the man's hand against the wooden door, as if he doesn't know immediately—

"Come in," he says, before he can think any longer, and the door swings open, the hinges creaking.

"Anemos," Charles says. "I heard you were ill."

Anemos is silent for a long moment, only looking at the man. He hopes the disdain he feels shows on his face.

"I am ill," he says.

"Too ill to compete?"

"Stage two hypertension, apparently." He pauses, his breath shallow. "I've been told that that's cause for concern."

Charles stands still for a second before stepping into the room, going to shut the door behind him.

"No," Anemos says, his voice firm. "Leave it open."

Charles looks at him with troubled eyes, and then cracks the door back open.

"You're safe," he says. "You know that."

"Do I?" Anemos asks, looking back out the window. "What do you want?"

"Was it another seizure?"

The words make Anemos' stomach twist. He shakes his head.

"No," he mutters. "It was a fever. The seizure was last night. I don't remember you caring."

"Do you know why it—"

"Eighteen years of torment," Anemos interrupts. "If I had to guess."

"Anemos—"

"Can you just—" His voice comes out strained, and it cracks on the last word. "Can you just go? Please, just leave me alone."

"Anemos."

His hands are still trembling. His hands are still trembling, and he's still trying to crack his knuckles.

What?"

"Were you with your parents?"

"No."

"Where were you?"

"Am I *required* to tell you that?"

"Yes."

"I was with Cole, then."

"Cole?"

"Yes. Cole."

"Did he know how to handle it?"

"He knows how to handle everything," Anemos says. "Stay away from him."

"*Anemos.*"

"*What?*"

"I've not done anything to—"

"And you've not done anything to stop it either, have you?" Anemos says the words loudly enough they hurt his throat, and then stops, shaking his head. "No, I'm not doing this. I'm not talking about this."

Charles' hand moves instinctively to rest on his dagger, but he quickly corrects himself.

"I won't make you," he says, "But you should."

"Should I?" Anemos scoffs. "Well, thank you for the advice, but... You know, I think I'm approaching a hypertensive crisis. Could you get Ian?"

"Please, listen to me. Just for a minute."

"Leave me alone!" He snaps. "I don't *want* to listen to you. I don't want to talk to you. I don't even want to look at..." His breath catches in his throat, gagging him. "*Please,* go."

"No."

Anemos looks down at his hands. They're trembling. He can feel that he's going to cry, and it makes him feel pathetic. Pathetic. He's pathetic. He needs to be quiet. He didn't mean to snap. He doesn't mean to cry. His hands won't stop trembling.

"I think I deserve," Charles says, "Just a *minute* of your respect."

"You will *never* have my respect," he says. "You've never done anything to earn it."

"I don't *have* to earn it."

"Stop," he interrupts. "I want you to go."

"I—"

"Go. Now."

Charles stops, pale, and after a moment, he reopens the door—listening, despite his words.

"I have removed your absence," he says. "Your *parents—*" the word is harsh— "will never know you were missing."

Relief fills the boy's chest, but his face doesn't change.

"Okay," he says dryly, his chest starting to cramp. "Could you please get Ian on your way out?"

Charles shuts the door without a word, leaving Anemos staring numbly at the floor, but Ian arrives in the room a few minutes later.

Cole is trailing behind him, a wet towel held to his face.

"My word." Anemos stands up, wiping his eyes. "What happened?"

"I'm fine," Cole mumbles against the towel. "Got somebody to beat the shit out of me. Wanted to check in."

"*Cole.*"

"I'm fine, Anemos," he groans. "Don't turn this around on me..." He pauses, turns to Ian. "Yeah, you're not hearing this."

"What else am I here for?" Ian laughs, tired. "I'll be in the other room. You want meds?"

"Strong meds. Thanks."

Ian gives a weak thumbs-up and walks into the other room.

"The ranking," Anemos says, when he's gone. Cole shakes his head, rolling his eyes.

"I ranked fine. Don't worry."

"You're getting a black eye."

"Anemos." Cole takes his face in one of his hands and pats the side of his head. "I am *fine.*"

"You're an *idiot.*"

"Yes, but I'm your idiot. Am I still bleeding?" He lifts the towel away from his face, and Anemos puts it back.

"Yeah, you need to tip your head forward."

"Alright."

"I'm going to kill you," Anemos says, resting the hand that isn't on the towel on the back of Cole's neck. "You know that?"

"Yeah," he sighs. "I know."

"I swear."

"You haven't rested," Cole interrupts. "I can tell just looking at you, and I think my eyes are swelling shut."

"I tried."

"I know." He pauses. "Did Charles come up?"

"Yeah, he did," Anemos replies. "How did you—"

"Are you okay?"

"Sort of." He looks into the distance for a minute, and then back at Cole, letting his shoulder fall. "Better with you here, stupid."

"You're such an asshole."

"Exactly why you shouldn't take a fist to the face for me."

"First of all," Cole says, raising one finger in the air. "It was a staff."

"*A staff?*"

"I had no other choice, okay? I was dying of concern down there."

"My temperature was one-hundred-point-five."

"And your crazy uncle was walking up here like a man on a mission. What's your point?"

"What's my point?" Anemos asks, taking a shaky breath. "I don't know. I'm like, right in the middle of an anxiety attack."

"And that's why I'm here. You need *someone* to remind you to breathe."

"I'm too anxious to breathe, just let me yell at you."

"Fine."

"If you ever put yourself in harm's way again–"

"What are you gonna do? Tickle me?"

"Oh, screw you."

Cole laughs, a tear running down the left side of his face.

"I'm sorry, I'm sorry. You're very intimidating. Continue."

"Tickle you to *death*."

"Oh, have mercy."

Ian walks back into the room with three pills, a glass of water, and an ice pack. He hands them to Cole with concerned eyes, glancing back and forth between the two of them.

"Take these as soon as the bleeding stops," he says.

"Okay." Thunder booms outside, again, and they all flinch. "Say, you don't have a blanket in there, do you? I need something to coax my friend to sleep with."

"We have the weighted one. We usually use it to calm people down, but..."

"That's perfect, thanks."

"Yeah, alright," Ian says, walking back out of the room.

"Alright," Cole breathes. "When he comes back, you're resting."

"I'll try." Anemos pulls the towel away from his face and dabs it a few times with the clean edge. "I think it stopped."

"Am I horribly disfigured?"

"Horribly." He folds the towel once and rubs it gently around the boy's nose. "No, you'll be fine. I don't even think it's broken."

"Alright, well, I suppose I should drug myself. Hopefully it doesn't knock me out for too long."

"How long till the ceremony?"

Rain beats down, and the room darkens.

"Oh, like five hours? We've got time."

Ian opens the door again, hands Anemos the heavy blanket, and starts to look at Cole's busted face.

"Go lay down," Cole says. "You don't need to watch."

Anemos nods, lets out a long sigh, and moves to the corner of the room, making the floor a bed.

"Does it seem broken, to you?"

"I'm not sure. It'll be easier to tell when the swelling goes down. Here... Just keep pressure here."

"Ouch."

"Yeah, it's going to hurt for a while. Keep your hand there for five minutes, then apply the ice."

"Alright, thanks Ian. You're the real MVP, you know that?"

"I appreciate it."

Anemos laughs softly, watching from the corner with tired eyes until Cole is free to collapse on the ground beside him

He feels sick, terrified, and a little hopeless, but his body has relaxed. He knows he's safe, and that is far from nothing.

He can breathe. His trembling hands can hold to something. He is okay.

Lightning strikes something, out beyond the city.

"I'm feeling pretty drowsy," Cole mumbles, his eyes already closed.

"Does it hurt less?"

"I can barely feel it."

"That's good," Anemos whispers, glancing up again at the locked door. "You can fall asleep, I don't mind."

"*You* need to sleep," Cole says, positioning the ice between his face and Anemos' chest.

"Yeah, well, I'm working on it."

"Are you feeling any better?"

"Better with you here."

"I don't regret it, then."

"You're an idiot," Anemos mutters. It isn't an insult.

"You're still warm," Cole yawns, and the wind blows rain against the windows. "It's cold in here."

"Do you want the blanket?"

"No." He moves his head slightly, wrapping an arm around Anemos' waist. "I'm okay."

"Okay."

"Anemos?"

"Yeah?"

"What do you think they'll do, if they find us out?"

Anemos is silent a moment before answering, his voice tired.

"Nothing today," he says. "We're just kids."

"Tomorrow?"

"They won't."

"But if they do?"

"They won't," he says.

Cole sighs, barely shaking his head.

"Okay," he whispers. "It doesn't matter, then."

"It wouldn't sway you anyway."

"Death wouldn't sway me," he breathes. "Actually, could you share the blanket?"

"Oh." He pulls the blanket out from between them, and wraps it back around them both. "Yeah, of course."

"It's so cold in here," Cole shivers.

"You already said that."

"Did I? I'm drowsy."

"Sleep," Anemos whispers.

"If you need anything, wake me. Don't go anywhere without me."

"I'm not going anywhere."

Cole falls asleep before he can respond, and the rain beats down harder—harder, it seems to Anemos, than it ever has; maybe harder than it ever will again.

But Anemos is still young, and for all of his cynicism, he is still optimistic.

He still believes, deep inside, that if *he* is good, and careful, and with the people he cares for, things will turn out alright. Much like Zahra—much like Jack.

In a better world, he might be right.

"I'm not going anywhere," he whispers again, and with the words, his eyes close, not realizing how lightly the rain falls.

CHAPTER FOURTEEN

"Icarus! To the front," the headmaster calls, raising his voice above the sound of the rain.

Icarus takes one last swig of his water, wipes his mouth, and walks to the center of the room, his steps uneven. His skin is shining with sweat, his arms littered with cuts and scrapes, and a deep, purple bruise lies under his eye, not far from the slice the Guide placed on him the day before.

It's been a long day.

Zahra watches him as he walks forward, wipes blood from her lips, and grabs his bottle of water when she's sure he isn't looking—taking a long drink, rinsing the iron from her mouth.

She can feel her pulse in every inch of her body, and the heat doesn't help. It feels as if all of the air has been sucked out of the room, and replaced with *sweat;* sweat and blood.

"Begin!"

This man lunges at Icarus *instantly*, not bothering to take any stance or any time to prepare. He rams into him, wrapping an arm around his torso, trying to throw him back onto the floor. He almost succeeds.

Icarus stumbles back a few feet before regaining his footing and reaching around to his opponent, grabbing his shirt and yanking him backward, only to be punched square in the jaw.

The crowd has, at this point, lost any formality it had at the start of the day, shouting and hollering over the action.

One punch, two, and Icarus begins to lean forward, looking understandably dizzy.

His opponent thinks, for a moment, that he might fall, and raises his fist a third time, but before he can land it, Icarus jerks his elbow upward, hitting just under the other boy's jaw.

He stumbles backward, and before he can catch himself, a hard kick lands in the middle of his chest and knocks him off of his feet.

He stays bent over on the floor for several seconds, trying to regain the air that has been knocked out of him, and Icarus crouches beside him.

"Do you..." He gasps for air, blood running from his mouth. "Do you want... Do you want out?"

"You *fucking*—"

Icarus doesn't hear the rest of the insult; he has heard enough, in these last few hours; he had already heard enough before them.

He stands up quickly, his muscles heavy, and kicks the man to the ground.

"*Tap,*" he says.

The man on the floor lets out a long groan and pulls himself up, leaving a deep red stain in his place.

"Not," he spits, "To *you*—"

Another blow lands in his stomach, and he falls forward again, coughing blood onto the tile.

Icarus turns to the headmaster, wiping his face.

"Do you need me to *kill* him?" he asks. "He's... H-he's out."

"If he can still stand, it's not finished."

"But he's—"

"If he wants out," the headmaster says. "He will *tap*."

Icarus has to bite his tongue to keep from cursing, but he keeps his face almost neutral as he turns back to his enemy.

"Can... Can you s-stand, Regis?" he asks, his voice heavy.

The man pulls himself to his feet, spitting on the floor.

"Duh-Duh-Duh-Damn you."

Icarus stares at him with a sick feeling in his chest, clenching and unclenching his fists, stretching his neck.

He doesn't want to hurt him, he tells himself. He's just a man. He doesn't want to hurt him, but he does. He can feel the hatred rising behind his eyes, the anger surging through his veins.

He knows what he could do, if he were to allow himself, and he hates himself for wanting it.

He hates them for making it so *easy*.

"Come on, hit me," Regis growls. "Don't just wait around."

"Why d...don't you try and hit *me?*"

Thunder rattles the window panes. Regis steps forward.

Icarus looks at him through squinted eyelids. He doesn't flinch as the man raises his fist—as it collides with his face—but Zahra does.

Lightning flashes through the room. Icarus spits blood.

"Try... Try it again."

Regis, who only seconds earlier was so full of pride and confidence— ready to become a martyr to a cause he doesn't even understand, looks suddenly hesitant.

Zahra stands and watches with a lump in her throat, scratching nervously at her arms. She can feel Icarus' anger.

A second punch slams into his face.

"A...a-a-again. Come on. Do it. Send me back to Jakara, Regis."

Zahra closes her eyes, struggling to breathe. She tries to let it all fade away, but he is there *still.*

Darkness draws itself to him like a moth to a flame. She sees it. She sees *him*, in the void that has become the room, and she wants to scream. She wants to run across the floor and pull him away before—

She doesn't see it happen; she only hears the man hit the ground with a scream. She hears the crowd murmuring, and she can feel Icarus wanting more, even as he hates himself for wanting it.

He takes a step toward the man as he writhes on the ground, and—

"Icarus."

She opens her eyes, and at the same moment, he whips his head around to look at her, his eyes dark.

A single thought, a word, passed through the darkness in a telepathic plea. It isn't much, in the scheme of things, but it's enough to bring him back.

It's enough to terrify him.

He holds her gaze, and she shakes her head, casting a pained glance at the man on the ground.

It's enough to destroy her, she realizes.

Icarus' eyes are hard with something worse than hatred as he walks away, something that she doubts anyone else in the room can recognize.

It is something like what she's seen in Anemos' eyes, and something that she's seen in the mirror, but it is stronger, here. Deeper.

He does not return to her side.

"Josh and Zahra to the front."

"He broke..." Regis screams. "He broke my fucking leg... He..."

Icarus stares from his place in the crowd, blank-faced, breathing hard.

"Josh and Zahra to the center. Could someone get a stretcher?"

Zahra walks forward slowly, making awkward eye contact with Josh across the room.

The man continues to scream, but the headmaster seems unbothered.

"He... He really..."

"You should have tapped." The words leave Zahra's mouth almost of their own volition, but she doesn't take them back.

The headmaster nods in unwelcome agreement and hands her a staff.

"To repeat the rules," he says. "The match ends when one of you loses your weapon, surrenders, or is unable to continue fighting."

The door to the auditorium swings open once more, and the Guide re-enters, his head low.

"Otherwise..." the headmaster resumes. "It is beyond my power to intervene."

Josh swallows loudly, nods.

"Understood?"

"Understood," he mutters.

A man and a woman run onto the floor, pull the still-screaming man onto a stretcher, begin to cart him away, and Zahra's world starts to spin.

"Understood," she forces.

She glances back at Icarus and holds the staff a bit tighter.

She'll have to fight him, if she wins.

He looks at her wordlessly, and when she reaches out for him in her mind, she can't find him.

"And," the headmaster says, "begin."

She dodges Josh's first swing unsteadily, nearly tripping on her own feet as she swings around behind him, slamming the staff against his back.

Her mind is elsewhere; *everywhere* else, it seems.

He lets out a quiet, pained grunt, and his staff strikes her hard in the shoulder.

"Are these the last three?" Charles asks, his hands pressed tightly against his lips.

Cindy, who stands at his side, nods stiffly.

"Yes, they are."

He lets out a long sigh, watching as one staff strikes the other, again and again.

"You ought to pray she loses," Cindy says. "It won't look good for you if she doesn't."

"I like her," he says.

A snapping sound splits through the room, and Josh steps back, his staff split in half.

"Yeah, no," he says. "I'm out."

The broken staff is dropped to the floor, and Zahra stands, just trying to catch her breath, as the spirit in the room changes.

The crowd seems to swim around her, and her vision goes in and out. There are hundreds of voices, and she can hear all of them.

"I'll be damned," Cindy mutters. "Look. Look at what you've done."

"I've done nothing."

"You've done *everything*. It's practically an act of war."

"Oh, stop it."

"They won't have it, Myon. They were already unhappy with the boy, but this?"

Zahra turns around, struggling to breathe in the humid air, and looks at Charles.

An unlikely defender, she thinks, but his words do not calm the fire that rages in her chest when she looks at him. His words do not lighten the shadows that drape themselves around his shoulders, or those that hide— *barely* hide— behind his eyes.

He meets her gaze, and ice seems to fill his body, weaving its way through his bones.

"I didn't think she would make it this far," he whispers. "If I had known..."

"You should have known."

She stretches her arms, her neck; she thinks of Anemos, as she looks at him.

"Icarus, back to center..." The headmaster's voice is more hesitant, but Icarus is not. The crowd is not.

"You will fight unarmed, and then with the blades."

"Blades?" Zahra asks.

"The last two always fight with blades, and, *anyway,* seeing as you destroyed the staff."

She lets out a shaking sigh, still unable to catch her breath. She doesn't know if it is the crowd, or the anxiety, or...

"She needs..." Icarus starts, clearing his throat. "Do... Do you n-need to get some water, or—"

"There's no time for that," the headmaster interrupts. "The ceremony will already need to be pushed back."

"But—"

"Begin. Now."

A tired laugh escapes Zahra's lips, but she forces herself to straighten, even as panic begins to choke her.

"Catch... C-catch your breath," Icarus says. "We'll s-start when you're ready."

"You'll start *now.*"

He looks at her and nods, ignoring the man beside him.

"When you're ready."

She lowers her head slightly, fighting back the tears forming behind her eyes.

"I'm ready," she says.

"Are you sure?"

She looks back up—looks him in the eyes.

"Are you?" she asks.

"Now!" The headmaster's scream seems to rattle her body, and she steps forward without even thinking.

She raises a fist in the air and strikes him—weakly— in the chest. She can feel the impact in her wrist, and for some reason, this time, it seems to paralyze her.

He snatches her by the forearm, twists her around much like she did to the first man, but holds her differently. Her arm is bent up, the only pressure in her wrist and her shoulder— she has to stand on the tips of her toes to relieve it— and she is pressed back against him.

A move used to interrogate, she thinks: to threaten, but not to defeat.

She uses her free hand to grab back at him, but she struggles to reach.

"This," she whispers, "is so much worse than being hit."

She jerks her head backward, almost hitting him in the chin, and he tucks it into her shoulder in response.

"Well," he breathes, "You can tap-tap... tap out."

"I *could.*"

"But you *shouldn't...* You... you can get out of *this.*"

"I know I can."

"And yet you aren't." She can feel his breath on her neck. "Why?"

"Because," she says, exaggerating her struggle. "I'm trying to figure out why you haven't thrown me to the floor."

"I'm-m-m trying to figure out w-why...why you threw such a w...weak punch."

"Because I'm afraid of you," she says, and with the words she wraps her right leg back around his, sweeping it out from under him and causing him to tumble to the floor. "Or because I like you."

She lands on top of him, scrambles for his hands, and manages to pin one to the ground behind his head; the other grabs onto hers and tries to pull it loose, leaving her clinging to both of his wrists, trying to keep her grasp.

"I think you like m-me," he says. "Given our pos...position offers very little r...reason for you to worry."

"Oh, surely you can get out of *this.*"

He abandons his effort to pull her hand loose, and instead pulls himself—and her—over with it, reversing their position.

"I can," he breathes, fighting with her hands in the air between them.

"Oh?" She pulls herself back over him, but this time with only one knee pinning his body to the ground, and his hands around her wrists. "So can I."

He pries himself out from under her, yanks her up by her wrists to meet him in standing, and she punches toward his face, only actually skimming his jaw, her wrist still held.

"Close," he says. "Better."

She pulls herself back, kicks him in the hip, and knocks him back to his knees; sadly, she goes with him.

"You're like a *leech.*"

"I'm n-not sure," he grunts, wrapping an arm around her neck, "that-that that's really a fair comparison."

His elbow closes around her throat, and when she tries to break free she falls backward onto him.

"Shit."

"Sorry," he says. "I win."

"You're not even choking me."

"Do you *want* me to choke you?"

She grabs onto his arm, tries to pull it loose, and lets out a long sigh.

"I am going to *stab* you."

"You're go... go... You'll try," he says, squeezing a little tighter, if only to make the violence more believable. "Who *are* you?" he whispers. "How did you..."

"Time is of the essence," she chokes out.

She taps his shoulder and, being released instantly, stands up.

"Give me the sword."

The thunder booms again, reminding her where she is.

"Please," she adds, half-heartedly.

Icarus arrives at her side, holding out a hand for his own blade, and the headmaster hands one to each of them.

"Should we try not to kill each other?" Zahra asks, never moving her mouth.

It's a strange thing, having another person's thoughts pop into your head.

"I suppose," Icarus replies. *"So you* can *hear me."*

"And... Begin."

They swing their swords at exactly the same moment, and the blades meet between them.

Zahra pushes him back, and the fight begins; almost effortless, almost like play.

"How can you hear me?" Icarus asks, in between slashes. *"I've never—"*

Her sword grazes his side, leaving a long red gash, and a slit in his shirt.

"How can you hear me?" she asks.

"Who... what are you?"

Their swords collide again, and he almost loses his grip.

"What are you?" she asks.

A wave of fear comes off of him, suddenly—grief. It seems to travel the entire room. She wonders if anyone else can feel it.

There is a word, amidst the pain.

"A Reaper?"

To Zahra, it is just a word. Of course, she is not so naive as to think it is an easy one— she knows of the weight it must hold, inside the Ordinem— but for all of her good intentions, she doesn't understand. She can't.

The word is a living thing, to Icarus: a living threat. It is the barrel of a gun pressed to his forehead, and the finger that pulls the trigger; a bolt on the door that leads to Inanis.

It is the word his parents mumbled as they decided they didn't want him, before he even knew what it meant. It is the word he heard when his home was destroyed. It is the word all of the adults used while they decided whether or not a scared, starving child was worth pulling from the rot and the rubbish and the ash that was left behind.

It is a death sentence. It is the thing that he hates the most.

The thing that he is.

He twists his hand without even thinking, twisting the two swords— not even noticing as Zahra's slices his arm— and knocking hers away.

He doesn't realize what he's done, how close he's come, until the blade is already against her throat; until she speaks.

"Icarus?"

The room quiets, and the darkness falls away from him, leaving only a boy, horrified by the thin red line on her throat. She stares at him, her heart like a hammer in her chest. He startled her with his movements, but not as much as he startled her with what caused it. She has never experienced fear that felt so like death, and it has not left him.

"I'm sorry," he whispers. "I—"

She drops her weapon and takes a step back, raising her hands in surrender.

Icarus is declared the winner, but he doesn't hear it.

The noise returns, and he doesn't hear it.

"Zahra—"

"Your arm is..." She interrupts him without meaning to, and he stares at her in confusion. "You need a bandage. I didn't mean to cut you."

The headmaster approaches her, and she turns toward him, shaking.

"He's going to need a doctor, too," she says pointlessly. *"Icarus?"*

"He's not your concern."

Anxiety is taking the little bit of air she has been clinging to. It's making her head spin.

"No, you don't understand, he's bleeding—"

A hand is placed on her shoulder, and she whips around quickly, ready to fight again.

"Zahra," Charles says. "I need you to come with me."

The room is loud. It's dim. It's too hot and too big and she is suddenly much too small because she can feel all of it. She can see the darkness in the eyes of this man she is supposed to be trusting. *Something is wrong.*

"Now," Charles emphasizes, and she lowers her face, terror coursing through her.

She follows him away, too afraid to do anything else.

CHAPTER FIFTEEN

"Keep your head down," Charles says. "Don't look at them."

"There's... Something's wrong. Isn't it?"

Charles lets out a long sigh, keeping his hand on Zahra's shoulder and guiding her through the crowd. Her head is spinning.

"You're going to be fine."

"Did I hurt him?"

"He's going to be fine, love. He's gotten much worse before." He opens a door that leads them out through the side of the building, and she only realizes that they're leaving when the cold night air hits her skin.

"I'm sorry... I..." Her voice trails off.

She is aware enough to realize she is dissociating, but hardly well enough to pull herself back.

"Are you sending me back?" she asks. Then, when he does not respond: "I'm afraid."

"You have nothing to be afraid of."

"You're lying to me," she breathes. "Why are you..."

Her head begins to swim, and her vision blurs. Every sound is magnified. It's like the rain is drowning her.

"You're tired, love," Charles says. "Why would I lie to you?"

His voice is so soft; *so* soft, and so gentle, but her legs are telling her to run.

The Wind is telling her to run.

"Zahra, did something—"

A carriage pulls around the street corner, and Charles falls silent.

Run.

"They wanted to hurt me," she says, "and *him.*"

He stays quiet, and watches with his jaw clenched as the carriage stops in front of them. The door opens, and a woman in all black steps into the rain.

Run. She tries, but she can't. She is so dizzy she can hardly stand.

"I'm sorry," the woman says quickly. "We were caught up, for a moment. You know how the rain brings them out."

"You have nothing to apologize for, Myon," Charles says. "Zahra, this is Ursula."

Ursula steps forward and holds out a gloved hand, but Zahra cannot make herself reach for it. There is something off about the woman, though she cannot say what.

It makes her skin crawl.

"She's having an episode," Charles says softly. "I had to give her something. She became very frightened, inside."

"Oh, silly girl. Frightened of what?"

Zahra's mouth has sewn itself shut. *Give her something?*

Ursula shakes her head, but when she goes to grab Zahra's hand again, the girl steps back.

"Please," she whispers. "Please don't touch me."

"Oh, don't be—"

"Ursula," Charles interrupts. "Give it to me, please."

Ursula hesitates, her face blank, and then passes a small syringe to Charles, who steps back from Zahra very slowly.

He takes her hand, and she doesn't fight.

"Can you look at your hand for me, child?" he asks, holding it up in front of her chest.

She looks down at her open palm and her chest fills with regret.

"Metal," she whispers. "Did I..."

"It would appear that when you became too afraid, you melted the handle of your sword."

"I didn't mean to."

"I know," he says. "It's alright. I'm going to assume that things like this have happened before?"

She stays silent, staring down at the ground.

"It's alright, love. Deviations are common, and yours is only elemental, so it's... It's nothing to be afraid of."

"I'm not afraid of *it*," she says, her voice quiet and shaking. "I'm afraid of *you.*"

"She speaks so freely with you—"

"And I have not commanded her otherwise, so she has no reason not to," Charles interrupts, and Zahra's hands begin to tremble. He turns back to her. "Listen to me, will y ou?"

There are dark spots in her vision. She feels like she might be sick.

"Yes, Myon."

"You understand the Ordinem. You proved that well enough today."

"Yes."

"Then you understand why Deviations may not serve."

"Yes..." *Shit.*

"And yet you attempted to join us anyway," he says, keeping his voice low. "Why?"

She stays silent, fighting the urge to cry. She will *not* cry here. Not now, not in front of *him.*

"I need you to tell me," he reiterates, after a moment, "or you'll have to tell someone else, and neither of us wants that."

"Because I was afraid." Her voice breaks. "Have you not visited your Outskirts, Myon? You've left us to die out there."

He stands still, pale, only looking at her for a moment before speaking again. She could swear she sees guilt in his eyes.

"I'm going to have to give you an injection," he says. "It's... It's not..."

She looks him dead in those guilty eyes, and he thinks he might crumble under the weight.

"What will it do to me?"

"It's just going to calm you. Just to keep you from... You understand."

"What did you give me inside?" she asks. "Where are you taking me?"

He shoves the needle into her arm as gently as he can, and forces the serum into her veins.

"Where are you—"

Run.

Charles steps back, and Ursula steps forward.

"Where are you taking me?"

She falls forward, her body limp, and Ursula catches her, draping one of the girl's arms around her shoulder.

"What did you do to me?" she cries.

Charles avoids her eyes, and instead, looks at Ursula.

"She won't be harmed," he says, but it sounds more like a question than a command.

"No," Ursula breathes. "Of course not."

"Make sure she's on to leave tonight." He watches as Ursula guides her weak body into the carriage. "I don't want any room for error."

"I understand."

Zahra barely manages to twitch her fingers, and feels her heart drop into her stomach at the cold sensation in her hands.

"What did you *do* to me?"

"Okay, okay, you've got it," Anemos laughs. "I swear, Icarus. If you forget this vow, I will... What am I betting?"

"How about you start going by Annie," Cole suggests.

"Alright, deal. You forget the vow, I'll start going by Annie."

Icarus forces himself to laugh past the weight in his chest. They are just behind the stage they will soon take their vows on, but they are clean, and no one is swinging at them, so breathing comes a little easier.

"That's... Which way are you trying to m-motivate me, An?"

"Oh, so you *want* me to suffer. I see how it is," Anemos shakes his head in mock disappointment, and starts to stomp out of the room.

"Hey, no, get back here drama queen," Cole demands. "You're taking it easy."

"You won't let me *walk?*"

"Fight me and you'll *sit.*"

"Did you guys ever think we'd be such a m-mess tonight?" Icarus asks. "Look at us."

"Pardon me?" Cole asks, his voice slurred. "I am the epitome of grace and health, Golden Boy."

Anemos snorts.

"I think you took too many pills, sunshine. But yeah, honestly Icarus? Pretty much tracks for us."

"How bad is that cut looking?" Cole asks, and Icarus sighs, laughing under his breath.

"Which one?"

"Either. Both."

"W-well..." He takes a deep breath, pulls up his sleeve, and Cole flinches. The bandage wrapped around his arm is stained a deep red. The few emergency stitches he was given have not sufficed in the *slightest*. "N-not good."

"You need to get that stitched, like, as soon as this is over."

He drops his sleeve, lifts up his shirt, and reveals his side.

"I think... I think this one is w-worse."

"Oh my... Okay, forget I asked," Cole says, cringing. "Does that not hurt you?"

"Oh, n-no. It hurts," he says. "But I don't feel like I can complain, when I... By the dragon, I feel horrible about it."

"Stop it," Anemos waves him off. "It was a fight. So, you snapped someone's leg, so you almost cut someone's throat—"

"*Anemos*," Cole groans.

"I'm *serious*. I've seen people *die* sparring. It gets intense. You can't beat yourself up over it."

"Oh, but I... I can," Icarus breathes.

"Well, sure you can, but you shouldn't."

"As much as it pains me to say it," Cole sighs, "he's right. Don't be too hard on yourself, man. Someone had to break Regis' legs eventually."

"I-I'll try."

"No." Anemos walks over, circles behind Icarus, and rubs his shoulders. "No trying, only doing."

"What are *you* doing?"

"You're so damn *tense*," Anemos says, shaking him a little. "Relax, breathe, close your eyes, imagine a beach."

"Maybe I did take too many pills," Cole yawns, and Icarus starts to laugh. "Last I checked the only ocean either of you has seen is over the edge of that cliff."

"Ignore him," Anemos says. "He's bringing bad energy. This is a *peaceful* beach, very flat."

"Oh, you know how I love a flat beach—"

"Quiet, Cole," Anemos snaps. "Icarus, you are... a seagull."

"A... a s-seagull?" he laughs.

"Try not to fly too close to the sun—" A muffled voice cuts through the room, drawing their attention, and Cole stops cold. "Did the Ceremony just... start?"

Anemos releases his grip on Icarus' shoulders and walks just out of sight, returning a minute later.

"Yeah, looks like it. We should head on over."

Icarus takes a deep breath, nods, and stands up at the same time as Cole, who walks up to the space between them and takes their hands.

"I guess we're doing this," he says. "Good luck, both of you."

"Th-thanks, good luck to you."

"We'll meet up inside, yeah?" Anemos asks. "Just by the entrance. I don't want any of us getting on that train alone."

"Y-y-yeah, for sure."

"Okay, okay. Well, my name is pretty early on, so..."

"Yeah," Cole gives his hand a tight squeeze. "Break a leg."

Icarus chokes slightly at the words, and Cole laughs under his breath.

"Thanks. I'll see you guys soon."

Anemos goes onto the stage a few minutes later, and Cole follows soon after him, leaving Icarus alone.

He looks around at the crowd of people waiting to have their names read, and can't help but notice that one is missing.

She could be anywhere, he thinks; he would be hiding from the crowd too, if he were in her situation, but he has not seen her all night. Every minute that goes without her arrival causes the anxiety in his chest to grow.

After all, the Guide did take her *somewhere,* and that is reason enough to worry.

There is a thought tugging at the back of his mind, begging to be paid attention to, and as much as he tries to fight it back, quieting his own mind is a skill he is far from mastering. He could reach out to her, but he shouldn't. She *knows*, and the knowing makes her dangerous, especially considering she may have been taken.

He knows better than to take a risk like that.

And yet, his eyes still search over the crowd, and with every name that is called, his mind grows louder.

Zahra lies motionless against the carriage window. She can feel the cold glass against her face and the pain in her neck from the awkward position, but she can only barely feel her hands.

With every bump they hit, every crack in the pavement, her head pops up and then bangs back into the glass. Her forehead is bleeding now. It's hardly the worst injury she's sustained, but there is an added pain in the fact that she cannot do anything to help herself; and in the fact that Ursula is doing nothing to help her.

"We'll be leaving the city in a moment," the woman says softly. "Perhaps we'll pass your home."

For a moment, she wants to say that she doesn't have a home, that she has *never* had a home, but as soon as she thinks it she knows it is a lie.

There was a time, many years ago, when it might have been true. After her parents died—never making it far enough to feel safe, never leaving Karneji—before Ghost found her. *Then*, she was alone.

She can still remember it all so clearly. Almost a year there, alone in the wilds of Karneji. A year of long nights and poorly slept days. There was so much death, so much decay. She said that she would never return, but it's out of her hands now.

She was only eight years old when Ghost found her there the first time. She wishes he would find her again.

He was home. Him, Athena, and that little village that always tried so hard, even when trying seemed futile. All of the people that welcomed her without questions, that treated her with respect even when she was young, that saw the little innocence she had when she arrived as something to nourish instead of something to exploit or take advantage of... That was home, and Anemos was home, too.

She wonders if she'll ever see any of it again.

Ursula leans over toward her, pushing the hair out of her face.

"Do you know where we're going, Zahra?"

Zahra tries to pull away from the woman's touch. She tries to speak, but it's impossible. The serum is too strong, and her body is too weak.

"Have you been to Karneji?"

How unfair, she thinks, that her useless body can still feel fear.

Ursula takes back her hand and looks out through the window.

"You're going to get what you deserve, you know that?"

How pitiful that her body can still cry.

Her tears stream down her face, onto the window and onto her neck and her chest, and she cannot even wipe them away.

Swallowing is the one action she can still force, but it is a struggle to do so past the lump in her throat.

"I promise you—"

"Zahra?"

Her heart skips a beat. Ursula's voice fades into the background.

"Icarus?"

"Where are you?"

His voice is so soft, so warm, compared to the one of the woman sitting beside her; but he can't save her, and she wouldn't risk him, even if she thought he could.

She swallows back her tears.

"Where are you?" she asks, hoping the thought is as light as she wants it to be.

"The ceremony. I'll be on in a minute. Are you here?"

A sob breaks free from her lips, but if Ursula comments on it, she is too distracted to hear.

"Are you okay?" he asks, a few seconds later.

"They sent me back to the Outskirts," she lies, pleading with everything that he will not fall silent.

"Why? What happened?"

"I melted the handle of my sword," she says. *"I'm a Deviation."*

Icarus takes a sharp breath, but before he can respond—

"Icarus," a woman says. "They're calling for you."

He looks up, torn away from her, and nods, trying to steady his mind as he walks onto the stage.

Hundreds of eyes find him; he fights the urge to shrink under the weight of them.

It is different than he thought it would be.

The wood creaks under his feet as he walks, only stopping when he reaches the large book at the stage's center.

His name is written in large, red letters across the top of the page in front of him. He remembers writing them at fourteen, but that is far away now.

It all seems so far away.

They sent Zahra back to the Outskirts. He wonders if there is anyone in this room who would not cast him away if they knew his secrets. He wonders how many *already* wish him ill.

He shouldn't be thinking about this. Not now. Not here. But there are so many souls, and they are all watching him, and he is too weak to push the thoughts away.

His breath is shallow and his chest is tight, and he is barely paying attention as he holds out his hand to the man standing beside him.

With all of the things he *should* be doing, he is instead searching the crowd for his father's face; for the only set of eyes that he *knows* he can trust, but he can't find them.

He cannot find his mother.

The loneliness that has been lying in his chest for so long seems to come to life, standing in front of this crowd. It seems to weave its way through his veins, wrap around his throat and choke him. It is *fear* that chokes him as he looks back down.

His blood on this paper in front of him: it could be his best chance at survival, yes, but it is just as likely a death sentence. He could die *tonight,* if they find him out. But perhaps it isn't about him; perhaps he should not even think of his own, worthless life. Perhaps he should not feel fear as the cool metal of the blade touches his hand. After all, this is the right thing to do. A last-ditch effort to bring salvation to a world headed for fire.

And yet, he is afraid.

He presses his left hand down onto the scroll bound tightly in front of him: The Code, the Order, the rules and the plan and the solution. He thinks of all the time spent studying it. He thinks of how much sense it used to make.

"With... My voice," he begins, keeping his voice slow. "I vow to honor the words of this scroll..."

Which words? he wonders. He realizes, for the first time, that the words do not fit; he is lying. To honor the words bound up in front of him would be to take a knife to his own chest.

"To dedicate m...my m-m-mind to those things which are worthy..." Can they see him trembling? Can they hear the breaking behind his voice? "According to the wisdom of our... Ancestors. To align my soul with those who..."

More lies. They feel thick in his throat. He is swearing to *their* ancestors, swearing to bind his soul to those that murdered Grim en masse. That swore to destroy his own kind.

He does not know his own ancestors.

"With those wh...who came before. I put aside the-the personal." His voice has an edge now— is brimming with anger that the crowd might perceive as passion. He speaks as if maybe he can drown out the voices in his head if he only repeats the Ordinem's jargon a bit louder. "The... The indulgence, and the attachment, and I embrace the road which leads to life. I t-take this role without b-b-burden, and accept it with responsibility."

He glances at the man beside him, but keeps his head lowered, looking only at their hands as the man drags the blade through his skin.

It hurts. More than a little. He fights the urge to flinch away.

"With this blood..." He holds his hand over the book, watches as his blood begins to spill around his fingers, and thinks, for the first time, that he doesn't *want* it. "I commit my life."

Red drops onto the paper, and he bows his head, eyes burning.

"*Welcome*," the crowd says.

He doesn't believe them.

He walks quickly to the other end of the stage, and Ian meets him there, bandaging his hand as the next student steps on.

"You did well," he says. "Good job."

"Thanks," Icarus breathes. "I appreciate it."

"*I'm sorry they sent you back there, Zahra.*"

"Have a safe trip tonight."

"Thank you, M...Myon."

"*I thought I'd frightened you away,*" she says.

"*No. I was taking the vow. I'm sorry.*"

Ian tears the gauze, forcing a small smile.

"You're good to go."

"*Will you be heading to Karneji, then?*"

"*Yes. Soon.*"

"*You know about the Mortum, there?*"

"*Yes.*"

"*Please, be careful.*"

"*I will.*"

Zahra closes her eyes and tries to relax into the feel of the carriage. It might seem futile, looking for peace in a situation so dire, but she has learned to look for peace everywhere. It has kept her alive more than once.

At least she is not completely alone. At least she has her mind. At least she will regain her voice and her body with time—

"*Zahra?*"

"*Icarus?*"

"*I'm sorry. I didn't mean to come so close. I didn't mean to frighten you.*"

She opens her eyes again, watching the dark landscape outside the carriage in her peripheral vision.

"*I didn't mean to frighten you either.*"

It doesn't make sense. That is all Icarus can think, talking to her. It's as if what he is doesn't matter at all.

"Why aren't you afraid of me?" he asks.

"Should I be afraid of you?"

"I don't know. I'm afraid of myself."

"Because you're..."

"A Reaper," he says; it is the only time he has said it, even to himself. *"Yeah, Zahra."*

"Icarus?"

"Yes?"

"That doesn't frighten me. It doesn't matter. It's different, on the Outskirts. I'm not saying it's safe— not by any stretch of the imagination—but people don't all think the same thing like they do in the city."

Icarus leans back against a wall, pressing his bandaged hand against his lips.

He has no idea how to respond, drowning in the sound of his own heartbeat. She's the *only* person he has ever heard suggest it is okay to be what he is— at least the first person he's known. It's an opinion he's only heard in the context of execution.

Sympathizers have been like a myth in his life, only encountered in stories.

"You terrify me," he says, after a minute.

A hint of a smile appears on her face, but it's quickly wiped away by the lights of the Facility, just coming within view.

"I should," she says. *"I have to go, Icarus. But I want to talk again, okay? When we're both safer?"*

"I'd like that."

The carriage pulls to a stop, and a distant shriek sends a shudder through her body.

"It'll happen then. Promise me."

"I promise."

Bright light floods the carriage, and she squints her eyes, unable to turn away.

"Pray for me," she pleads. *"Okay? It's not been an easy trip. It's not easy being back here."*

"You think I can pray?"

"Of course you can pray."

"What do I pray for?"

Ursula steps out of the carriage and walks quickly around to Zahra's side. She opens the door and lets the girl fall out onto the sharp, wet ground.

Zahra takes quick breaths, blinks away rainwater, and tries to spit the dirt from her mouth. For a minute, she thinks she has been abandoned.

"Over here, please," she hears Ursula say, and two sets of footsteps come within earshot. "Solitary confinement for now. Keep her unharmed. She leaves tonight."

A pair of hands grab her by the shoulders, yanking her gracelessly from the ground, and she is draped between two men, one arm held around each set of shoulders, her head hanging down on her chest.

"Strength."

"Icarus!" Cole calls from somewhere across the room. "Come on, we've got to go, Anemos is waiting at the entrance."

"Come-coming," Icarus calls back, but he mutters a quick prayer before he goes.

Little does he know what is actually happening, or that Cole is praying for her, too.

CHAPTER SIXTEEN

Anemos is standing at the entrance of the University, looking at the crowd outside through the window. His fingernails are digging into the palms of his hands, and sweat is gathering on the back of his neck.

He has been trying not to think about it, but it's too close now.

"Found him," Cole says from behind him. "Let's go."

He turns around, and when he meets eyes with Icarus, he sees some of his own fear reflected there.

At least he isn't alone, he thinks, but it hardly helps.

He nudges his friend in the side, forcing a weak smile.

"Did you fall asleep back there?"

"No," Icarus laughs. "I just needed to b...breathe for a second, An."

"*Breathing* is for the weak," Anemos responds. "I know *I'm* not breathing."

Cole glances at him out of the corner of his eye and tries not to let all of the concern he feels show.

No one has the energy to laugh, but Icarus lets out a long sigh, hesitantly tapping the back of Anemos' hand with his own.

Anemos' eyes fall down to it, and he takes it, his whole body softening as he does.

It's enough to remind him that he's safe, and that is far from nothing.

"Hey," Icarus says. "You're headed to the Compounds tom-m-morrow too, yeah?"

"Assuming they don't decide to keep me," Anemos responds, and he doesn't bother to pretend it's a humorous statement. "Yeah."

"Well, assuming they don't," Icarus says slowly. "Do you... Do you want to come back to m-m-my place tonight?"

"Are you sure you wouldn't mind?" he asks. "It's the last night there with your family. I don't want to intrude on that."

"You... are family," Icarus says. "I'm sure."

Cole breathes a heavy sigh of relief, and grabs Icarus' other hand, squeezing it gently, trying to thank him without speaking.

Icarus squeezes back, and Anemos nods.

"Thank you," he breathes. "You don't even... Thank you."

"I'd love to join," Cole says, "But the shelter wants everyone out by seven, and seeing as we might not be back until... late."

"Early," Anemos says, and then, rubbing his face: "My word, I'm so tired."

They walk through the door, and the cold air sends a chill over Icarus' arms. It is still raining, but it is not raining enough.

"Too tired for Karneji," Anemos continues. "By the way, am I the only one here who's *terrified* of this place? Because, I feel like we're all being really casual, and..."

Cole keeps his eyes on the ground.

"...like, I'm trying not to have a fit."

"No," Icarus says. "I'm... Yeah. I... I don't... love it."

"Cole?" Anemos asks.

"What?"

"How are you feeling about all of this?"

"Oh, I feel okay," he says. "Just trying not to think about it, I guess."

"I swear, if any of us get executed..."

Cole lets out a long sigh and rubs his face, but Icarus just laughs.

The laugh is soft, and light, and nothing that anyone would ever imagine holds the fear that it does.

"An," he says gently. "Ev-everybody is going to be okay."

A man begins to yell in the distance, announcing that the train is loading, and they begin to walk a bit faster.

"People *will* be executed tonight," Cole says, keeping his voice quiet. "Won't they?"

Icarus watches the puddles on the ground. He watches all the little ripples each drop of rain sends through them.

"Yeah," Anemos responds. "Mostly Reapers."

"In Karneji?"

"In Karneji."

It's strange, he thinks: the impact something so small has, as it collides with the water.

"Shit," Cole breathes. "I don't want to see that."

"Me neither. I'll never get why so many people do."

"It's..." Icarus' voice comes slowly. "They hate them."

Them.

"I don't think I could ever hate anyone enough to want to see them burned alive," Cole says, a shudder running through him. "That's... That's disturbing no matter how you cut it; no matter who— or what—"

"Agreed," Anemos interrupts. "I appreciate the fear factor, but I wish they would just deal with them inside like they do with everyone else."

"Yeah—"

Icarus stops, raising a hand to his mouth. Bile burns in his throat, his whole body shaking.

"Hey," Anemos says. "Are you okay?"

"I'm.." His voice catches, and he shakes his head. "I'm f...fine."

"What's wrong?" Cole asks.

"I'm j-just... I think... The noise. I'm feeling kind of sick."

"Oh, okay. Let's... Anemos, go find out when the train is leaving. I'm gonna get Icarus out of the crowd."

"Yeah, alright."

Ten minutes later, Cole and Icarus are alone, over on the side of the University, away from the train and all of the people.

Fighting the nausea well enough, but too panicked to stand, Icarus falls back against the pavement, skinning his hands on the ground.

"You're okay," Cole says softly, putting a hand on his shoulder. "Come on, try to breathe."

He takes deep, strained breaths, so dizzy he can hardly hold his head up.

"I'm... I'm sorry," he says. "I—"

Deal with them.

"No, you're fine," Cole whispers, moving his other hand lightly over his back. "It's been a long day."

Stop touching me.

"I don't... I don't know what's wr-wr...wrong with m-me," he trembles, bringing his hands up in front of his face. "I..."

His breaths turn into quiet, strained sobs, and Cole moves in closer.

"Icarus," he says. "You're exhausted, in pain, and you're right in the middle of one of the most stressful days of your life. I would be doing this too if I wasn't high off my ass on pain meds."

You don't understand, he wants to say, but the words don't come.

"Come on," Cole whispers. "It's... You're alright..."

A door opens a few feet away, but they don't hear it. They don't even notice as Charles walks through it, approaching from behind them.

"What's the matter?" he asks, not bothering to announce his presence.

Cole turns around, startled, but Icarus doesn't move. It takes him a few seconds to recover from the shock of seeing the man.

"He isn't well, Myon," Cole says. "I think it's just been a long day."

"Does he need a nurse?" The Guide's voice is smooth— unconcerned, but not unkind.

"I don't know..."

Anemos turns the corner, and Cole falls silent. The boy meets eyes with his uncle for only a second before looking away but does not allow his face to change.

"Myon." He tips his head in respect and then turns to Cole. "The train leaves in forty minutes. Is he alright?"

"We don't have time, then," he sighs. "I don't know."

"If the boy needs a nurse, we will make time," Charles says. "He can ride with his parents when he's well."

Anemos looks at the ground, cracking his knuckles.

"Are you sure that—" Cole starts.

"I'm sure," Charles nods. "I'll take him to the nurse. You two head to the train, don't miss it."

A threat lies just behind Anemos' teeth, but he bites it back.

"Is that what you want, Icarus?" he asks instead.

Icarus keeps his eyes on the ground, his jaw clenched.

Not a teacher, not your mother. You come to me. Do you understand?

"Would it be possible to j-just call for m..my... my father, instead? Tell him what's happened, and... I should be able to make it back from the nurse before the train departs, but that way he'll be here in case?"

"That'll be fine," Charles nods. "Can you make it to the nurse without aid?"

"Yes," Icarus forces, turning to his friends. "I'll be fine. I'll meet you on the train, I promise. Go find a seat before it's crowded."

His friends look at each other with equal degrees of concern before nodding and turning away.

Icarus does not hear them go; he only becomes aware again when Charles kneels beside him, putting a hand on his arm.

Jack is just across town, standing on the bottom floor of a small weapons base when he gets word.

It is only a single sentence at first, and upon hearing that whatever he is needed for involves Icarus, all of the blood drains from his face. He keeps his voice steady as he asks what's happened, but only regains his breath once the story is finished.

He places a sword in the sheath on his left hip and straps a bow onto his back before turning sharply around, tipping his head in Alastor's direction.

"I have to go," he says. "It seems Icarus is ill."

"Ill?" Alastor asks. "Did something happen?"

"I've no more information than that," Jack says. "Only that he needs a nurse and requested my presence."

"Kind of my brother to allow you to go," the other man says, but there is no warmth in the words.

Jack forces a smile, but it is strained.

"Yes, very. Blessings be upon him." He walks to the doors of the lift and taps a button in the wall. "I imagine I'll see you later this evening?"

"Possibly, but it isn't likely." Alastor looks down at his hands, flexing them. "Executions tonight."

"*Tonight?* While the children are in Karneji?"

"Best prepare them for the real world," Alastor sighs, pulling on a pair of thick, leather gloves, similar to those Jack is wearing. "They can't stay children forever."

"Perhaps," Jack says, exercising a considerable amount of restraint in keeping his voice low. "But breaking a child is hardly the best way to help them mature."

"I think they can live with seeing the death of a few devils, don't you?"

Jack looks at Alastor with a face that shows none of the emotion— none of the *hatred* that he feels; he looks at his posture, as he speaks, and the way he absentmindedly covers his hands. He's always done that, as if trying to hide a weapon.

Jack doesn't remember what he thought of Alastor when he first met him anymore. He only remembers how he has felt since he has known Anemos.

Anemos, who leaves every door open, pales at every unexpected sound, flinches at every sudden movement, and winces at the feeling of his own clothes upon his skin.

Jack is one of the few who have bothered to notice. He sees the anger and fear in the boy's eyes, just as he sees the darkness in his father's.

"They will live with it," he says. "But they shouldn't have to."

When he arrives at the nurse's office, Icarus is sitting on the examination table, looking down at his feet with hazy eyes. His hands are clasped together, but even so, Jack can see that they are still trembling.

He turns to Ian, who is sitting across the room in a small, black chair, scribbling down notes.

"What's happened?" he asks, and Icarus looks up, apparently not noticing his father before.

"Oh," Ian says. "He's fine. Lost too much blood during the combat test, ate too little food, drank too little water, but he'll be okay. He should have come in for additional stitches earlier, though."

"Stitches?"

"I..." Icarus' voice comes out choked. He clears his throat. "I didn't think I had t-time," he says slowly.

"Well, it's all alright now," Ian says, and even though he's wrong, Jack nods. "Gave him a low dose of medication. Have him take more when he gets back from Karneji."

"Very well," he says. "We can go, then?"

"Yes, yes. Free to go," Ian nods. "Icarus?"

The boy looks over with tired eyes.

"Water," Ian says simply.

He forces a tired smile, nods.

"Will do."

Jack nods toward him, and he stands up, stretching a little bit, but not enough to pull the stitches in his side.

"Thank you for taking care of him," Jack says, already returning to the door.

"My pleasure, Myon. Be safe."

"Thank you."

Jack and Icarus step out into the hall, and as soon they're out of sight, Jack wraps an arm around his son's shoulders.

"Are you alright?" he asks, as if he doesn't already know.

"I'm fine," Icarus lies. "I'm... I'm fine. I'll be fine. I'm sorry for calling you."

"No," he says. "Don't be sorry. It's alright."

Icarus looks at the floor, his breath shallow, and stays silent.

"Do you want to tell me what happened?" Jack asks. His voice is quiet, but still seems too loud in the empty hall they are walking through.

"I panicked," Icarus says.

Jack doesn't ask why; he doesn't need to.

"I'm with you now," he says, instead. "You're safe."

Thunder rolls through the building, quieter than earlier, but no less threatening.

"I d-don't... *feel* safe," Icarus whispers. "I'm...m...m n-not sure I can—"

The sound of footsteps appears in the distance, and they both fall silent.

There is always something ominous about the University at night, when everyone has gone home and the space goes quiet. Some would say that the building itself seems to breathe. Some would say the same about the whole city— but it is different, tonight.

Tonight, the place seems to be *holding* its breath, as all of the children who have spent nearly half a decade within its walls board the train.

The footsteps pass, and they walk more quickly, not daring to speak. It is only when they make it outside, and their voices are drowned in chaos, that he turns to Icarus once more. When he does, his heart grows heavy.

He is only a child. He should not look as afraid as he does, or handle that fear as calmly as he does. He should not be boarding a train into the desert when he is ill, and he should not have to receive the warning he is about to.

"Executions will be held tonight, likely along the path you're taking," Jack says, and Icarus' face does not change even a little.

"Anemos mentioned it," he says.

Jack grits his teeth, wishing he could protect him and knowing that he can't.

"If I could end all of it and give you a world that was safe, I would," he whispers. "If I could just shield your eyes, and protect you from all of it, I would do that too."

Icarus keeps his eyes low, trying not to let the words slip through his fingers.

"I would do anything in the world to convince you you don't deserve what you're about to see, Icarus. I would give my life to speak love over every part of you they have condemned."

"I would give my life to give yours back," Icarus mutters, and Jack falls silent. "I don't... know how long you've known, b-b...but I'm sorry. I'm sorry for what I am, and I'm sorry that I've m...made you love me."

"Icarus—"

"I never should have asked anything of you, Myon," the boy forces. "But I'm going to again, because I'm terrified, and you're all I have."

Jack quiets, listening, and Icarus shakes his head. He closes his eyes, fighting back a sob.

"Tell me something I can hold to, when I see the fire," he whispers. "Just tell me something good, please. Just tonight."

Chapter Seventeen

"*Tell me something good,*" *Jack said, lying back on the grass in their backyard.*

"*S-s...s-something good?*" *Icarus asked, plopping down on the ground beside him. "Like what?*"

Jack looked over at the child— his son, who was much smaller then; eight years old and full of spirit.

"*Like anything, kiddo,*" *he said, trying to rub the day behind him from his eyes. "Anything at all. Something that makes you happy.*"

"*Something that m-m...makes me...*" *The blond boy folded his arms and looked up at the sky, thinking. "Grass.*"

"*Grass?*" *Jack asked.*

"*Yes, grass,*" *Icarus laughed. "It's... It's... It's lovely.*"

"*I suppose I've never really thought about it,*" *Jack laughed, pushing his hair back out of his face.*

"*Well... In Ja...ja...*"

"*Jakara?*"

"*Yes. In... There, it was all sand. But here...*" *He lay back beside his father and tugged at the ground. "Grass! And flowers.*"

A smile spread across Jack's face, lighting up his features.

"*And you,*" *Icarus said. "You m-make m-m...me happy.*"

"*You make me happy,*" *Jack said. "You're my best little friend in this world.*"

"*I thought-thought m-m-mom was your b...best friend.*"

"*Shhhh,*" *he laughed. "She's my other best friend.*"

"*Well, m...mine too.*"

"*Your other best friend?*"

Icarus started to laugh— the way he still does— with his arms folded around his chest, and his eyes almost closed.

"*Does that mean I'm your* best *best friend?" Jack asked, poking him in the shoulder.*

"*Don't... Don't tell.*"

"*I won't," he laughed. "Hey, why don't we bring her some flowers? I bet she would like that.*"

"*Okay," Icarus sat back up, stretching his arms up above his head. "Th-that sounds n-nice... nice.*"

Two years later, he woke up to the sound of something at his window.

He slid quickly out of bed and crept over to the glass, trying not to slip in his socks.

He pressed his still small hands against the cool surface and then reached up— standing on the tips of his toes— to open the window, just enough to stick his head through the crack and look around.

Nothing, again.

He put his arms on the windowsill, leaned against it, and sighed heavily, still sleepy.

He woke up many nights to sounds he couldn't find, but it had been more frequent those last few months.

He tried not to let it frighten him, and he told no one. Loved as he was— loved as he felt— he still feared that if he became too much of a burden that love might be lost.

He didn't have the words for it, then; he didn't understand the neglect that marred his young life. He only knew that he didn't want to be left alone again.

It was too early to wake up, but he was too frightened to sleep, so he shut the window, grabbed a small flashlight from his nightstand, and grabbed a book from under his bed, but just as he turned the first page—

"*Icarus.*"

His head whipped up, his eyes wide, but he saw nothing.

"*Hello?" he whispered. "Is... Is something there?*"

For a minute, there was no response, no movement, but then, slowly, a shadow crept out from around the side of the dresser.

Almost before Icarus could process what he was seeing, he was on his feet and out the door, running into his parents' room.

He cracked the door open and, quietly as he could manage—

"*M-m-m..." He took a deep, shaking breath. "Dad?*"

Jack stirred, lifted his head from his pillow.

"*Icarus," he asked. "What's the matter?*"

"*I... I... There's...*"

Already hearing the panic in his son's voice, he slid out of bed and moved quickly to the door, pulling Icarus out into the hall with him and kneeling to his height.

"What is it?" he asked. "What's the matter?"

Icarus' breaths were fast, and his eyes were afraid.

"There's... There's a... a..."

"Hey," Jack said, taking his hands. "It's alright, you're safe. What's going on?"

"There's..." His voice was hesitant. "There's a boy... in m...my-m-m-my room."

"What?"

"A... A boy, but his face is... It isn't right."

Jack stood up quickly.

"Let's go see," he said.

"B-b-be careful."

"I'll be careful."

He walked Icarus back to his room, and when they entered it, they found it empty.

Jack looked around every corner, anyway.

"I don't see anything, kiddo," he said, his voice still raspy from sleep. "I think it was just a bad dream."

Icarus felt his chest tighten and shook his head.

"It... It wasn't a dream. It was real."

Jack took a deep breath and sat down on the boy's bed.

"Well, the room seems to be empty," he yawned.

It was hardly the first nightmare the boy had had— hardly the first time he had run terrified into his parents' room, and Jack was too familiar with the situation to suspect— yet— that anything might be different.

"What exactly did you see?"

Icarus pulled himself up on the bed beside him.

"A boy," he said again. "But his face was... his f-face was all f-f-fuzzy. And he... he knew m...my name, and I think he was tapping on the window..."

Jack rubbed his eyes, still trying to wake himself.

"Tapping on the window?" he asked. "Perhaps it was a moth... Or..."

When he opened his eyes again, Icarus had gone white, staring into the corner of the room with wide eyes.

"Hey," he said softly, putting a hand on his son's shoulder. "You're okay..."

Icarus pointed shakily into the corner, and then toward the dresser, as if his hand was following something.

"R-right... Right there," he whispered. "Do you not..."

Jack looked into the space his son was watching, but saw only space, and a dresser, and a bed.

"You see him now?" Jack asked, his voice tinged, suddenly, by something Icarus did not recognize. "Right there?"

Icarus' hands began to tremble, and he nodded, shakily.

"Don't... Don't you?"

Jack looked over at his son, confusion muddling his mind, and then back at the empty space.

"Do you... Do you not s-s-see him?" Icarus asked, his voice becoming more shaken, more afraid, with every word. "How can you not..."

Fear exploded in his father's chest, so quickly and so intensely, that for a moment, it felt like something close to dying.

No. No. Not Icarus.

"What does he look like?" he forced, trying not to let the terror come through in his voice.

"He... He just looks like a b-boy," Icarus said, his voice choked. "A... A little boy... He looks lost..."

It was a warning sign he had been prepared for, but he was not prepared; nothing could have possibly prepared him.

"If any signs manifest," Charles had said, "you must bring him in immediately."

It sounded easy, then. Mostly because it had seemed impossible. A hypothetical he would never have to encounter.

But then, he was encountering it, and everything he had been told seemed suddenly unhelpful.

This was a child.

"I'm... I'm— I'm sorry, I..." Jack looked at his son, and watched as he struggled with his words. "I don't understand. Is there some-something wrong with m...me?"

He should have been afraid, but he wasn't; he couldn't be.

He only shook his head in response.

"No, no..." he said softly. "No, don't worry..."

"Something's wrong, isn't it?"

"Nothing's..." His voice broke, and he closed his eyes, bringing his hands up to his lips.

He wasn't sure if he was even making a decision. He didn't seem to have any choice, in the moment, as he put a bounty on his own head.

"I'm s-s-sorry," *Icarus said again.* "I don't..."

Jack shook his head, fought back his own tears, and wrapped his arms around his son, willing himself not to tremble.

"Child," *he whispered.* "You're okay, you needn't apologize."

"Are you sure?"

"I'm sure," *he answered.* "I'm sure, baby."

"Why don't you s-sound..."

He pulled back and shook his head again, grabbing the boy's hands.

"Listen to me," *he said, and his voice, although kind, was firm enough that the boy knew he needed to.* "You... There's nothing wrong with you."

It was the truth, but it felt like a lie.

Icarus' eyes darted back and forth, doubting.

"But this... You can't tell anyone else about this, do you understand?"

"Why?"

"I just... I need you to trust me. Not this, nothing like this."

"Can I tell you? If it happens again?"

"Not if anyone else might hear."

"Can I tell mom?"

"No, no."

"Why?"

Jack didn't respond, and tears rose to Icarus' eyes.

"Will it hurt me?" *he asked.*

"No," *Jack said.* "It can't hurt you, as long as you ignore it."

"What is it?"

A sudden migraine split through the man's head, and he let out a long, frightened sigh. He was only a child.

"You just... treat it like a dream," *he said.* "Just like a dream that you have while you're awake."

"J-just a dream?"

"Just a dream," *Jack said,* "And then you come and crawl into our bed, if you need."

"Can I come with you tonight?" *Icarus asked, hesitant.* "I don't want to be alone with him."

"Yes," he said. "Yes, of course. Come on."

So father and son crept back across the hall, and the terrified boy climbed into the middle of the bed.

"Mm." Aliya rolled over, only half awake. "Is something wrong?"

"Another dream," Jack said.

"Aw, baby," Aliya yawned. "I'm sorry."

"It's... I'm okay."

Jack lay down beside them, pulled the blanket up over himself, even though he knew he wouldn't rest, and Icarus wrapped one arm around his chest.

"Dad?" he whispered, a few minutes later.

"Tell m-m-me something good."

Jack took a deep breath, and forced himself to answer past the lump in his throat.

"I love you," he said. "More than everything."

Icarus pulls himself up onto the train and looks out over the quickly filling seats. There are so many faces and voices, all shouting over each other. It's like the anxiety he feels is manifest in front of him.

He looks for Cole and Anemos, and eventually spots them toward the back of the section. When he makes it to them, Anemos stands to let him into the row.

"Are you okay?" he asks, and Icarus nods, struggling to breathe.

He takes his place between them and clears his throat, flush with panic.

"Yeah, so... The nurse gave me some drugs, some stitches, and a glass of orange juice. It's just been a long day, and..." His voice trails off, but they wait, listening. "I'm scared. I'm really scared."

"We're all scared," Cole insists, and Anemos nods in agreement, sweat glistening on his forehead. "It's scary."

You don't understand, he thinks, but he stays silent; he knows they're trying.

"There's nowhere in the world I want to go less than Karneji," Anemos adds, his voice tired. "I get it. But we're together, and we're gonna be fine."

Icarus' breath feels caught in his chest. He is not sure he is able to speak, but—

"M...my dad said the executions are taking place on the-the... the path we're taking. I'm n...not sure I can handle that. My whole family died in fire, I... I-I can't..."

Both of Icarus' friends' chests grow heavy at his words. They don't feel it the way he does, but they feel it. Cole's stomach turns inside of him so violently he thinks he might be sick.

"Look at me," Anemos says, and the boy does, finding his eyes red. Icarus has never felt as close to Anemos as he does Cole— because of their families, and their past, and everything else— but when Anemos takes his hand, something inside of him stills. "You look at me, or Cole, or anywhere but out that window. We'll hold you through it, I pr omise."

"But if I fall apart," Icarus breathes, his knees starting to shake. "What if they think... What if they think I'm..."

"Icarus," Cole interrupts, holding his other hand tightly. His face is red, but his voice is steady, unshaken by the emotion beneath it. "You don't honestly think we would let *anything* happen to you?"

It isn't long before the train groans and begins to move. The whole thing rattles in a way that makes Icarus feel sicker than he already does. He has to close his eyes and lean his head back against the seat to feel anything close to steady. Anemos and Cole are talking over him, but their voices are low enough that they fade into the background with everything e lse.

The only thing Icarus manages to focus on is the dull throb of his hand. He can feel the cut on his palm sticking to the bandage. It's going to be an awful scar, just like the one on his face.

When he was seven or eight, he respected the mark. He would see it on an outstretched hand and think that the person in front of him was a hero.

He doesn't feel like a hero, bearing it. He doesn't even feel like a sinner with something holy carved into his skin. He just feels like he is going to bleed through his bandage.

He feels like if he makes it to his father's age, he will still shudder when he looks at it, even when it is dull and white. He will not think of his loyalty, or a great cause, or the saints he has pledged to walk in the path of, but of a dagger piercing his skin, and lies spilling from his mouth.

Some time has passed when a cough escapes the lips of the boy next to him, interrupting his thoughts. He opens his eyes to find Anemos leaning forward, his eyes watering.

"Are you okay?" Icarus asks, and his friend nods, clearing his throat.

"Yeah, I'm sorry. It's... It just stinks. I mean, it's making my throat burn."

Icarus takes a sharp inhale, and then lets his breath fall shallow. He didn't even realize, he was so in his head, but Anemos is right. The smell is faint, but it's hard to ignore once noticed. Smoke.

He looks over at Cole instinctually, craving some reassurance that he is going to be okay, but finds him staring out the window with an expression that says otherwise.

He is pale as snow.

"Cole?" Anemos asks, and he shakes his head in reply, making a visible effort to stay calm.

"There's fire on the horizon," he mutters, and the words make Icarus' throat so tight he fears he might choke. "It's all I see. Just... fire."

There's a bump in the track, and when the train jolts Icarus nearly comes out of his seat. Cole turns away from the window and looks over at him, putting a hand on his arm.

"Breathe," he instructs, and Icarus shakes his head, folding his trembling hands together in his lap.

"I don't think I can."

It isn't just him. In the next few minutes, coughs and uncomfortable grumbles fill the train cart, becoming the main source of sound as the air grows thicker.

"They say Reaper smoke is worse," someone remarks, and Icarus leans a little closer to Cole, who pulls him under his arm in response. "Smelling the fires of *hell*."

"Smells great," someone else says, taking a deep breath of the smoke which now fills the cabin. "Let those fuckers cook."

A strained laugh escapes Icarus' chest as the train hits another bump, but by the time it reaches his lips it is something like a cry.

Light begins to flood in through the windows, and he shuts his eyes tight, trying to stay quiet as sobs start to shake his body. Cole leans over him, holding him so tightly that Icarus thinks he must be afraid too.

"Don't look," he insists, running a hand over his hair in an attempt to soothe him. "Keep your eyes closed, okay?"

"They're screaming," Icarus whimpers. "I... I can hear them..."

"Shh..." Cole looks up at Anemos, and finds him looking around the cabin and outside of it in disgust. "It's going to be okay. I promise. Everything is going to be—"

Either way, Icarus thinks, he deserves the fire. If he does not deserve it for being Grim, he deserves it for being Ordinem. Either way, he is wicked. He wishes he could open a door and step into the flames himself, just so he would not have to hear the screams any longer.

He wishes for death, and yet, the thought still terrifies him.

It is like he can feel the flames, now. He can feel his skin burning, and his lungs collapsing under the weight of the panic and the smoke surrounding him.

Still, for all his fear, there are dozens around him that cheer on the suffering. Holy, they call it. It is *holy,* and he would be angry if he was not too busy being afraid. He can see the light of the fires burning through his eyelids, blinding.

"Calm down," Anemos whispers, putting a hand on his back. "Icarus, you have to calm down..."

He can't *breathe,* and yet, he gasps for air so quickly that he starts to hyperventilate. His cries begin to muffle the voices of those around him, despite his best attempt not to be noticed—

"Is something the matter?"

The voice does not manage to pull him from his panic, and despite the realization that it means danger, he does not open his eyes.

A guard is standing beside them, one hand resting on the hilt of a sword. He eyes Icarus cautiously, but addresses all three of them.

"No," Cole says. "We're fine, he's just—"

"Yes, something's the matter," Anemos interrupts. "You see what we're driving through?"

The guard's face doesn't change, but Cole's runs paler. He keeps his arms around his friend and tries to soothe him, but to very little avail.

"The executions," the man replies blankly. "Traitors, criminals of the highest order, and agents of a realm I dare not speak of."

"You dare not speak of it. You dare not speak of it? We can't handle the mention of the place but we're supposed to sit through *this* without flinching?"

"Is something the matter, Myon?" The guard redirects the question to Icarus, ignoring the boy to his right. "I'll need a reply at once."

"M...my family..." Icarus stutters, still not opening his eyes. *Myon.* They refer to him like he is one of them. He's going to be sick. "M...my..."

So what if he is taken? He has always been destined for fire. He escaped it once, and has spent his whole life carrying the guilt of it. Perhaps it is best if this time he lets it take him.

"His family died in the fire that took Jakara," Cole says quickly. "He's traumatized, and this is too much like it—"

"This is the Jakaran boy?" the man asks, and Cole bites his tongue. "Icarus, that's your name, isn't it?"

Icarus cannot make himself respond. Despite the noise of the train, and the fact that most of the Reapers beyond his window have already fallen silent, he can still hear them crying out. They are louder than the shouting, or the engine, or even the bombs that fell on his country. They are *deafening*.

"Your cries are indicative of greater sympathies," the guard says, and he shakes his head, his lips betraying his will.

"I have no sympathies," he spits, the words forming as if by their own volition. "Curse them. All of them. Let them die. I don't mourn for them." The cut on his hand is like fire, and the words are acid on his tongue. Lies, all of them.

"I'm going to ask you to come with me anyway," the man replies, and his grip tightens on his sword as he does. Anemos sees it, and Icarus does not have to. He knows what awaits him if he goes with the man.

He wonders if they can kill him purely on the grounds of a Jakaran boy not being worth the risk.

Still, he begins to pull himself up from the chair, but he does not make it far.

Anemos puts a hand on his shoulder and pushes him back down, rising from his seat to put himself between the two of them.

"You're not going anywhere with him," he says firmly. Then, he turns back to the guard, his jaw clenched tight. "The place you *dare not mention* seems to have you in a tight grip, *Myon.*"

The man's eyes flash with anger, and he stands up straighter, puffing up his chest the same way Anemos' father does when he wants to be intimidating to his mother.

"I will not tolerate—"

"Don't then," Anemos interrupts, his voice low enough that only the guard can hear it. "But you're going to have to run me through with that sword before you take him anywhere."

The guard only stares at him, baffled, and pulls the sword an inch out of its sheath.

"You drive us all through a grotesque scene of death— portraits of people, burning up to nothing, and you tell us not to flinch. You find the only one of us brave enough to feel it and seek to intimidate him, hand on your weapon as if you're not talking to someone who was a child this afternoon. You learn of his trauma, and the reason he cries, and instead of expressing sympathy, you jump at the opportunity to pain him more. Do you think they'd reward you for ridding the Ordinem of the Jakaran thorn in their side?"

The hand falls away from the hilt, and Cole breathes a sigh of relief, still holding Icarus' hand tightly in his own.

"I see through you," Anemos continues. "Whether you want power, or fame, or money, it doesn't matter to me. What matters is that there's nothing honorable about you. You're disgusting. And if you don't back away now, I will tell my father, and our Guide, and even the counselor of the sickness you suffer."

The man lowers his face, and Anemos raises his eyebrows, leaning closer.

"Is that understood, Myon?"

"Yes," the guard mutters, and Anemos nods, returning to his seat.

Before a minute has passed, the guard has returned to his station, and Anemos has turned back to his friend, whose face rests on his hands.

"Icarus," he whispers, placing a hand on his back. "He's gone."

He receives no response, and he didn't expect to. He looks up and finds Cole's eyes— red and cast in shadows. He doesn't need him to say anything to know what he is thinking: that he wishes there was someplace to run away to, as Anemos suggested the night before.

There is an apology on his lips, but Anemos stops him before he can utter it, shaking his head.

They stay silent until the light from the fires has faded, and the students around them have calmed. It is only once there is some semblance of peace that they try to reassure Icarus again.

"It's over," Cole whispers, his voice frayed. "You can open your eyes."

Still, Icarus does not reply.

"The fire is gone," Anemos adds, moving his hand over Icarus' shoulders as another sob shakes them. "It's gone, Icarus. You're safe—"

"I d...don't want to do this anymore," he whimpers. "I don't w-wa-w...want to b...be here. I should've gone with m...my sister. I..."

"Please don't say that," Cole pleads, his voice soft. "You're so important to me, Icarus."

"I'm not even supposed to be alive—"

"Yes you are," Anemos interrupts, taking his hand and squeezing it as tightly as he can. "Look at me. Yes you are..."

Icarus looks over at him, and he falls silent, his voice catching in his throat. He has never seen eyes that look as heavy as Icarus' do now.

He will feel the weight of them as long as he lives.

"Think of what your dad would say," he forces, searching for anything that might make those eyes plead less. "If you told him you weren't supposed to be here. He risked his life to save you from that place. Doesn't that make you worth something?"

"I don't *know...*"

"Well, I do."

"You b-barely even know me, Anemos."

"But he does," Anemos says, desperate. "What would he tell you, if he were here?"

"I love you more than everything," Jack said, and Icarus looked up, his voice a sleepy whisper.

"Everything?" he asked.

Everything, kiddo."

Without a word, Icarus falls into Anemos' arms, and Anemos holds him all the way to Karneji.

Chapter Eighteen

The hall the Facility has opened is packed, students almost shoulder to shoulder as they anxiously await examination. A quiet, static hum fills the space around them, and the room is lit only with dull generator lighting. It makes them feel that their senses are dulled, lowering their defenses even further.

Icarus and Cole stand against the wall, trying and failing to put some distance between them and the crowd.

"I wish he would just come out already," the latter mutters, but Icarus does not respond.

He has hardly spoken a word since they got off the train; he's only followed his friend expressionlessly, his eyes vacant.

Cole cannot take the weight of them much longer.

He can't take the weight of any of it much longer— Icarus' suffering, or Anemos' fear, or the knowledge of Zahra's appearance earlier that day. He has been looking for the girl all evening, hoping to find her before Anemos can so he can soften the blow of anxiety seeing her in this awful place will bring him; instead, he has not found her at all, and that is *much* worse.

She is missing, and Icarus is falling apart, and now Anemos is alone in the exam room. He is only managing not to vomit because he doesn't have enough space to do it.

"I'm... sure he'll be out soon," Icarus forces, when some time has passed.

"I'm sure you're right," Cole echoes, his eyes resting far off in the distance.

He wants to add that he is afraid anyway, but he doesn't. He knows everyone is heavy enough without him adding to it.

"I'm glad I have you," he says, instead. "I hate that you have to be here, but I can't imagine doing this without you."

"You've spent all n...night trying to hold me together, Cole. I'm more of a burden than anything else—"

"I don't want to hear you say that again," he interrupts. "You're *burdened,* yes. But I shoulder what I do of the weight you carry by choice, because *you* are one of the only good things about this place. *You* make me feel safe, and like I'm not going through all of this alone."

Icarus looks over at him with teary eyes but struggles to form the words he needs to respond.

He wants to drift away, Cole thinks. He has seen it before. Icarus does not want to matter as much as he does, no matter how much love he has in his heart. He wants to be a burden so he can justify *going.*

The worst part of it is that Cole suspects it would be easy for his friend to go, here. He does not know every secret Icarus carries, but he doesn't doubt it could be enough to warrant his execution.

Where he is afraid Anemos will slip and get himself in trouble, he is afraid that Icarus will do exactly what he intends to do and never make it back from the exam room.

Icarus looks toward the door and clears his throat, wiping absentmindedly at his nose.

"Anemos is back," he mutters, and Cole's head snaps around to look for him, finding him lost in the middle of the crowd.

"I'm going to go grab him," he says. "Don't move, okay?"

"Okay," Icarus agrees, and Cole nods, stepping away.

He weaves through the crowd as politely as he can, muttering apologies as he shoves his peers out of the way to get to his friend. When he gets to him, he places a hand on his shoulder.

Anemos turns around with a gasp and then places a hand on his chest, shaking his head.

"You scared me," he breathes, and Cole gives his shoulder a tight squeeze, but doesn't take the time to apologize.

"You good?" he asks, and Anemos shakes his head.

He stands with clenched fists, drenched in sweat with his arms hanging awkwardly at his sides.

"No," he says. "I mean, yes, I'll be fine, but…"

"Was it bad?" Cole asks, and Anemos shakes his head again, swallowing hard.

"No, not bad, just…"

The sound of the overhead speaker interrupts him, a ring so loud that it makes Cole's ears hurt, followed by words that choke him: *"Cole, to the exam room."*

"Just what?" he asks.

"Be careful," Anemos says. "Don't be afraid, or they'll see it."

He takes a step closer, closing his eyes in an attempt to fight the vertigo in his head, and lowers his voice.

"If you have to lie, don't think twice."

"Will I need to lie?" Cole asks, and Anemos hesitates, cracking his knuckles at his side.

"I don't know," he says. "I did."

"Cole, please, to the—"

"You'll be here when I get back?" Cole asks, interrupting.

"Of course I will," Anemos whispers. "Good luck."

"Thanks. Thank you. I'll..." Cole lets him go, and for a minute, in that dark, buzzing room, Anemos thinks that nothing could be worse than watching him walk away.

"Soon."

"Soon," Cole responds. "Icarus is right over there, by the wall—"

"I'll find him," Anemos says, and Cole nods, stepping away.

Within seconds, Anemos is alone. Alone, with nothing to distract him from the thoughts beating their way into his mind. With no clocks on the walls, and a head too fuzzy to be keeping track, he has no idea what time it is, and that only adds to his anxiety. That made everything worse, when he had to stay here: never knowing if it was day or night, if he could rest or if the horrors of the day were waiting for him. Even in the more made up parts of the Facility, there are no windows. There is no sunlight. You never know where you are in the massive building—

His eyes find Icarus in the distance, and the sight of him interrupts his thoughts. The boy's skin is pale, and his eyes are vacant, red around the edges. He stands completely still, as if all of the energy has gone out of him, and doesn't even seem to notice the surrounding crowd.

Anemos pushes through the people toward him without a word, only stopping when he reaches the wall. Icarus looks over at him and forces a tired sort of smile.

"You made it," he says, and Anemos shakes his head, letting out a long sigh.

"I don't make it until we all make it," he says. "Cole is back now."

Icarus nods and looks up at the ceiling, his breath shallow. "Was it... How was it?"

"It was fine," Anemos insists. "You shouldn't worry. Just tell them what they want to hear, pretend you mean it, and you'll be golden."

The words seem to catch Icarus off guard, making his brows furrow, and Anemos wonders if perhaps he spoke too freely. He assumed Icarus would hate the place as much as he does, if not more.

"You shouldn't say things like that," Icarus says, instead; but the words have very little spirit behind them.

Anemos doesn't bother replying to them, choosing to change the subject instead.

"Speaking of which," he says. "I need to apologize to you for what I said earlier, by the train."

"Oh, I don't even rem...member—"

"About the executions."

Icarus falls silent, and Anemos knows his words are necessary, even if he does not want to admit them.

"I'm an ass about things that scare me," he says. "The scarier they are, the more I tend to trivialize them. It's something I don't like about myself, because it hurts the people around me, just like it hurt you tonight."

Icarus goes to interrupt, but Anemos doesn't let him, putting a hand in the air between them as he continues.

"I don't want anything to go through that, inside or outside. I hate all the death, and I want it to stop. I don't take suffering like what we saw tonight lightly, whether it's necessary or not."

"I... kn...know you don't," Icarus forces. *Necessary.* "You don't... need to apologize. You did nothing wrong."

"Icarus, to the exam room."

The words ring through the space like an alarm, and Anemos cannot help but feel like everyone turns toward them upon hearing it.

"I guess this is it," Icarus says, pulling himself from the wall. "See you somewhere."

"Icarus."

"An?"

Anemos only looks at him for a second— the careless way he holds himself, and the exhaustion on his face. He looks at the bandages on his arm and hand, and the cut on his cheek.

"Make it back, okay?" he asks, and Icarus doesn't say anything. He only nods, his lips pressed into a tight smile, and turns away.

———— ✵ ————

Not far from the hall Icarus stands in, a similar smile lights up another face, and fails to reach another pair of tired, frightened eyes.

Rosemarie's smile is forced, but it is only for herself— standing alone, almost safe, in a bathroom. It is hardly a privilege, but to her it feels like one. She was able to shut the door, shower, and dress herself on her own; that is an independence she hasn't felt in a long time. So, she takes the opportunity to smile in the mirror, just to remind herself that she is human.

She is human.

She stares into her own blue eyes and pushes her short, gold-blond hair off of her forehead, only to let it fall back down onto it; it is damp, clean. *She* is clean. The shower was cold, but it washed away the sweat, and the blood, and it soothed the burning in her skin. It was good, feeling something other than pain for a few moments.

She is not naive enough to believe that the reprieve will last, but she is hopeful enough to savor every second of it as best she can, so that she can hold to it later.

"Rosemarie?" Elise asks, just beyond the door. "Are you almost—"

"Yes," Rosemarie responds, a little too quickly. "Yes. Just... Just a minute."

"Time is of the essence, love."

Rosemarie takes one last glance at her fragile form in the mirror, and then moves quickly, checking all of the drawers for anything that might be of use to her. She finds only a small silver lighter, but it isn't nothing, and she finds solace in stealing back anything that she can, so she shoves it into her pocket before opening the door. Elise greets her with a smile brighter than she knew she was capable of receiving from anyone but her friend in Trellis. It disarms her, seeing it. She was starting to think no one could be kind to her if they weren't profiting from it in some way, but she can't imagine how Elise could benefit from this; unless she is being kind out of fear, which is always a possibility.

"Feeling better?" the woman asks.

It takes Rosemarie a considerable amount of effort to respond, but she manages a weak nod.

"Yes. Better."

It's a stupid question, she thinks. Of course she is better than when she was locked in Karneji's basement. Of course having a shower is better than torture.

"Good," Elise says. "I'm glad to hear it."

Her eyes fall over the girl's body, and she shakes her head.

"Are you sure you want to wear that?" she asks. "Something... Something shorter or lighter might be more comfortable, with the burns."

Rosemarie looks down at herself— her thick, too-big black sweater, and her too-clingy black pants— as if she has not noticed any discomfort, and nods.

"Yes, ma'am— Myon, sorry, this is fine, thank you."

"If you're sure."

Other clothes would undoubtedly be more comfortable; they would rub against the burnt, raw patches on her skin less. But *these* will provide a barrier between her and whatever floor, car, or wall she might be thrown into next. *These* clothes cover her, letting her hide the parts of herself she has not been allowed to protect thus far.

"I'm sure, thank you."

Elise nods and opens the door behind her. "On our way, then."

Rosemarie is guided down the hall with her hands tied loosely behind her back. It's ridiculous. She has no place to run to, no place where they will not find her. She would die trying to escape Karneji. She has no reason to resist.

Revenge, maybe, but she is too tired for that.

Eventually, they come to a small, steel door, and she is ushered into the room behind it.

"Wait here," Elise says, as if there is any way she could leave. "The Guide will be in to talk with you soon. Alright?"

"Yes," Rosemarie responds, keeping her voice quiet. "Thank you."

Elise tips her head in response and then leaves, shutting the door firmly behind her, making the room feel much smaller. Rosemarie slowly makes her way to one of the chairs and pulls it out from the table with her foot. She sits awkwardly, trying not to put too much pressure on her hands as she leans back against them.

It's all been too much, she thinks casually; too much to ever really recover from, probably. The closed door makes any brief sense of peace she had slip away, reminding her that she is a captive. The man, Charles, seemed kind enough, but she doubts that he will do anything so radical as free her. She knows what it means for the Ordinem to have mercy on E.D.T.s, and even if he claimed that he wouldn't execute her, he never told her what he *did* intend for her.

She doesn't understand why she still wishes for freedom when she has never tasted it, but her heart races at even the thought of it being handed to her. She has always been captive. She doesn't even know what she would do, if not for locked doors and handcuffs and men barking commands at her.

She thinks, probably, she would keep looking for her brother. She would look until she found him, and then they would go to the ocean and look at the stars like they did back home. Everything would be okay, then. Rosemarie looks up at the concrete ceiling above her and laughs as she comes back to reality, her heart heavy in her chest.

It is a silly fantasy, but it is better than this world— where the boy is dead, and the stars cannot be seen, and the ocean is unreachable. She closes her eyes and goes there for a little longer.

CHAPTER NINETEEN

Icarus stands in front of the cold, steel door to the exam room. His legs are barely holding him up, as unsteady as they are.

He is trying to decide whether he should even try to stay calm or just accept his fate. Reapers are not supposed to make it past tonight. Reapers are not supposed to be Ordinem. They are not meant to *be* at all.

He swore to uphold the Code, and this might be the only way he can. As much as he has tried to convince himself he can change his nature and exorcise this darkness he carries, he knows it is impossible. He knows the burning bodies he just passed did not choose their fate. He heard their screams, and he knows their pain. If they were wicked, and they deserved their deaths, then he is wicked too. If he is wicked and unable to do anything about it, he should die with them.

If they were innocent, that is something he isn't sure he can live with.

"S...straight back?" he clarifies, desperate for any reason to stall, and the guard nods, exhaustion visible on his face.

"About a hundred paces, then you take a left. It's the only open door."

Darkness seeps out from the hallway like blood, escaping through every crack it can find. When Icarus touches the handle, chills scatter over his arms.

It would be an easy decision if not for his father, his friends, and the cowardice he feels. He's not sure how he can still fear death when he spends so much time longing for it, but he does. He is afraid of what comes next and the pain it will take to send him on. He is too tired to go through all of it tonight, he decides. He can always turn himself in. He can do it tomorrow, if that's what he wants.

He doesn't want to do it tonight. But then, he isn't sure how much that matters.

No matter how badly he *might* want to live, he will be the first Reaper to make it through the exams, if he does. The odds are against him.

His hands are shaking.

He closes his eyes as he turns the handle, but it doesn't do anything to help. As soon as the door opens, what sounds like a hundred voices call to him, all at once, and his chest begins to cramp. His eyes shoot open and find the hall in front of him filled with dead. Malemortum cover every wall, hang from the ceiling, and writhe on the floor.

To shut himself in with them feels like a death sentence on its own, but there is no better option.

He steps forward, and one of the things slides out in front of him, so close that he can hear its breath.

"Finally," it snarls, and Icarus looks away, swallowing hard as he shuts the door behind him. What he does next surprises even him, but it is all he can think of, here. He has nowhere else to turn but toward her, seeking for her in his mind and finding her with ease he does not expect.

"I don't think I can do this," he says.

In Karneji, Zahra lifts her head from the floor of the cell she was placed in. She is just starting to regain feeling, but the space around her is dark and silent.

The last thing she expected was to hear anything. But there it is, popping into her mind so clearly it is as if Icarus is in the room with her. Her chest becomes impossibly tighter at the words, and she can feel her heartbeat quicken.

She is almost too exhausted to breathe, but she responds anyway.

Where are you?"

"It's too much. There are too many of them." Zahra can feel the fear behind the words, hot as fire and heavy as tar. *"I can't do this."*

The girl blinks a few times, trying to clear her head.

"Breathe," she tells him, fearing the reminder to be pointless, but having little else to comfort him. *"Don't look at them. Keep your eyes ahead of you."*

"I'm going to die."

"They can't hurt you. They're only half here, half in Morta. They have very little power and they're terrified of you."

"Terrified of me?" Icarus asks. *"But we're the same. Why would they be terrified of me?"*

The words baffle Zahra, even with where she is, and the day that has passed. She knows what the Ordinem says about Reapers, but she hardly thought there were Grim who believed it. The realization makes her stomach sink.

"You're not the same," she says.

If Icarus were somewhere else, he would've stopped in place, but he keeps moving, shaking his head in disbelief.

"Darkness is darkness. It doesn't matter what form it takes."

"No." With every step he takes, the shrieking around him grows louder. The Malemortum are beating against the walls like they might be trying to escape.

"No?" he asks.

"You aren't darkness, Icarus. You're not evil. They're deceived, and they're deceiving you."

He doesn't know what to do with the words. He hardly believes them, but he is too afraid to argue against the statement.

He doesn't want to argue against it.

"Say something," Zahra says, and he clears his throat, swallowing hard.

"I can see the door," he says. *"I'm almost there. I want to believe you, but—"*

"Listen to me."

One of the things pulls itself up from the floor, and his whole body tenses, begging him to run.

"I'm listening."

It reaches toward him, running its hand over his shoulder and whispering things in a language he does not recognize, but he continues to move forward, keeping his eyes on the door.

When he enters the room, he finds a man already there, shrouded in darkness, waiting for him.

The man looks at him with the same eyes that everyone else in the Higher-class has, and that turns the fear in his chest into something else.

He is grieved. He is angry. He is tired of being deemed worthless before he even speaks. This man has no reason to suspect him, and still, he knows by the look in his eyes that he is already being judged.

They hate him even without knowing what he is.

He isn't sure he can blame them, when he has shared the sentiment most of his life, but he cannot help but wish for kindness now and then. Surely there is something about him that does not instantly inspire disgust and dismay.

He can accept that he is an abomination, but he can't help but be crushed every time he is reminded that that's *all* he is.

Every part of him.

"You are good," Zahra says, and the words pour over his aching shoulders like warm water, wrapping themselves around his tired body like the embrace of a long-lost friend. They contrast so sharply with the expression of the man across from him. *"You're human, just like the rest of us, and you're exactly who you're meant to be."*

She is the only person to have ever spoken the words to him, knowing what she knows, and he doesn't know what to do with them.

As much as he longs to believe them, he can't. Not now. Not this easily.

Not for more than a moment.

For a moment, though, in the darkness of the examination room, Icarus rattles the chains that The Ordinem— and the darkness itself, have placed on him. He questions the lies he's been told and if he really deserves all of it.

He wonders if being born is really enough to damn him, or if perhaps he might be worth more than he has been told. The thought barely lingers a second, but while it does, the light hits his eyes differently. The darkness catches a glimpse of the spark he holds within him— the spark which, although smothered, buried, and beaten down, has never quite been extinguished.

It sees it, and it recoils in horror.

Icarus moves across the room casually, sits down in front of the man, and tucks his shaking hands into his pockets.

"Let's... l-let's get this... over with."

CHAPTER TWENTY

Rosemarie sits quietly, chewing on the neck of her shirt. She pulls nervously at the fabric on her back with her bound hands. She has brought her feet up onto the small seat— which still looks rather large, with her sitting in it— and curled up so her knees nearly touch her chest. She does not bother to sit more politely when Jack and Charles enter the room.

The Guide looks less kind now, she thinks. He just looks tired.

"Rosemarie," he says calmly. "You look like you're doing better now. I'm glad to see it."

"Much better," she says, but she doesn't thank him. He has already told her he doesn't want her thanks, and in truth, she has very little desire to give it.

"This is Jack," Charles says, pointing to the other man, who is already standing just diagonal from her. He nods in her direction as he sits down at the table. "I hope you don't mind his being here."

She rolls her head slightly, looking him over with tired eyes.

She does not particularly like being alone in a room with her hands bound and no company save two men she doesn't know, but this one looks kind. There is no disdain in the way he looks at her, but he doesn't seem much happier than she is to be here.

A gentle smile paints its way across her face, and he returns it.

"I don't," she says simply. "Nice to meet you, Jack."

"It's nice to meet you, too," he says. His eyes dart over hers like he is looking for something— like he thinks perhaps they have met before, and is trying to put a name to her face. "Are you doing alright?"

"Yes," she says. "All things considered, I'm doing just fine, I think."

"That's wonderful," Charles says, the kindness returning to his face like something he conjures with every word he speaks. "So, I'd like to explain what we're doing, if that's alright with you."

It's very strange, the way this man acts. From his behavior, she would gather this is a normal situation for him. She wants to say it isn't alright with her, just to see what would happen.

"Aren't we talking?" she asks, instead.

"Yes," Charles says. "We're just... I'm going to ask you some questions, alright?"

"Alright."

"And Jack here..." Jack's eyes are still searching, but she is sure she doesn't recognize him, so she looks away, her chest tight. "Jack is just going to ensure that we're being honest with each other."

"How is he going to do that?"

The Guide hears the fear in her voice and quickly shakes his head.

"Very easily," he says. "It's a skill he's had a long time. It's very rare that a lie will slip past without him noticing—"

"That's what you get, living in Brekka," Jack interrupts. "If you don't know when you're being lied to, you won't make it through the night."

Rosemarie laughs a little at that, but keeps her face low.

"Okay," she whispers. "That's fine."

"Good," Charles nods, clasping his hands together. "Let's start with some simple questions, then. Do you know how old you are?"

"I'm seventeen."

"And what is your—"

"Name, please," the man across from Icarus says, tapping a pen on the table between them.

Malemortum cower in every corner of the room, but Icarus fights the urge to look at them, keeping his eyes locked on the man.

"M-m...my name is Icarus."

"Odd name," the man responds. "Never heard it anywhere else. How did your parents settle on that?"

"They didn't..." He shakes his head, his throat tight. "I did. I chose it. There's a story I loved, when I was—"

"*You* chose it?" The man sounds like he might laugh, but Icarus cares very little.

"Y-y...yes."

"When?"

"F-five or... six?"

"What's your real name, then?"

"I'd rather not say, M-Myon."

The man shakes his head from side to side, debating on whether to press him on it, and then shrugs.

"Well enough. Age?"

"Eighteen."

"And where were you born?"

Rosemarie blows the hair away from her eyes.

"I was born in Jakara," she says. "But... I don't remember that time very well."

She has answered these questions more times than she can remember; it feels like she is reading from a script.

"Why don't you remember it well?" Charles asks.

"Because I was five."

"Why else?" Jack asks, drawing both of their eyes. "There's something more, yes?"

She looks at him, and then back at her knees.

"It's because I was five," she repeats. "But I don't remember much of anything, really. I don't know. Kieran is the same way. He says the pain does it, makes things..." She is not telling them the whole truth, but she isn't lying. She hopes that is good enough for the man across from her. "Makes them blurry. Makes them go away."

Jack's face falls, but Charles' remains the same.

"What do you remember?" he asks softly.

She hesitates a second, waiting to see if Jack will interrupt and point out her dishonesty, but he doesn't, so she continues.

"Of Jakara?" she asks.

"Yes, of your life there."

She looks up at the ceiling, thinking before speaking.

"What do I have to tell you?"

"Whatever you feel comfortable with, love." Jack glances over at Charles, surprised by the sincerity in his voice, but Rosemarie only sighs, closing her eyes as she begins to speak.

"Life was fine in Jakara," Icarus says. "N-nothing eventful, until it was burned... burned down."

"And the monsters?"

"The lights kept them out."

"The Reapers?"

"I was young. We were afraid, but I don't remember m...much."

"You were afraid," the man says. "But you tell me life was fine?"

"Yes," Icarus laughs. "Well, I'm... I'm alive now, aren't I? No need to dwell on it."

"I had a family," Rosemarie says. "I... We had a little house. The walls were... Yellow."

"Do you remember them?" Charles asks. "Your family."

"Mm." She smiles, and a tear streams down the side of her face. "Yes."

"Did you..." He clears his throat. "Did you have any brothers or sisters?"

"None like me," she says. "That's what you want to know, yes?"

Charles stays silent, and Jack looks down at the floor.

"A brother. Michael," she says, letting her feet slip from the chair. "He's dead. I'd like to talk about something else."

"Where were you before you came here?" Charles asks, not even pausing. "Where did you come from?"

"A Facility outside, in Trellis."

"Trellis?" The Guide laughs. "You came a long way, child."

She doesn't laugh with him. For a moment, she cannot even make herself respond.

"I did what I had to do," she says finally, and the man leans forward, digging.

"And what is that?" he asks. "Why did you come here, Rosemarie?"

She looks at him silently, her eyes swelling with tears, until a broken laugh escapes her lips.

"Because you promised safety," she says. "Because you're all liars."

She can see some change in the Guide's demeanor when he hears those words, but still very little.

"Why else?" Jack asks, again.

She looks at him, her lips tight, but doesn't respond.

"Did you think you'd find them here?" he asks. "Your family?"

"No," she mutters. "But I've got nothing else. I thought I ought to try."

"I'm sorry," he says. "That you lost them."

Charles looks down, visibly uncomfortable, and she tries not to hate him for it. She tries to focus on the man closest to her, who speaks to her as she imagines he would speak to anyone else.

"Thank you," she forces. "You know, you're the second person to say that to me in my whole life. No one else has cared."

She turns back to Charles, failing.

"Do you tell your people we're so inhuman, sir, that we cannot feel?"

"I tell them very little about you," the Guide replies.

"What little *do* you tell them?"

"You're a victim of the same tragedy as the rest of us, dear—"

"I'm not dear to you," she interrupts. "You don't love me. My name is Rosemarie, and I'd appreciate it if you used it."

Charles pauses, his jaw tight, before nodding in submission, clearing his throat.

"You're a victim, Rosemarie. Not a monster. Nothing evil—"

"Useful?" she asks, and he stops again. "Out there, they see us as useful."

"We stand against them," Charles responds, steady. "We have always stood against them."

"And yet you're going to deliver me back into their hands."

Jack's eyes widen, and he looks over to see Charles with his fists clenched, sweating like a man on the wrong side of an interrogation.

"Killing me," she whispers. "You would see that as merciful, no?"

"Do you wish to die?" the Guide asks.

"Sometimes," she admits. "But that's not what matters. You don't care what I want. You don't even care what I've suffered, and yet, you've kept me alive. Why, Myon?"

His eyes dart over her face, but he remains expressionless. Jack watches him with stress building in his stomach, having no idea what the man is thinking. When he speaks, his voice is blank.

"You will not be harmed. I can promise you that."

"You're lying," Rosemarie observes, and the Guide shakes his head.

"I will do everything in my power to keep you from being harmed."

"You will protect me here, then?" she asks. "No?"

Charles continues to look at her but doesn't respond.

The silence is an answer on its own, and it causes her to break, quietly, not even moving as tears fall from her eyes and laughter rattles her chest.

"Child," the man says softly. "I would, if it were in my power, but this is bigger than you. It's bigger than both of us."

She shakes her head, unable to wipe her eyes.

"I've known people like you before," she whispers, her voice choked. "You're the kind of man who... Who whispers words of comfort as you kill your enemies. As if you think your kindness absolves you."

She stands up, and he places a hand on the dagger at his waist, watching carefully as she walks around behind her chair, pacing nervously.

"I hope it helps you sleep, but I don't want it, sir. Do what you will with me, and let it b e."

"Please, love, I understand how you must—"

"Do you understand?" she asks. "Do you understand how afraid I am?"

"Rosemarie," Jack says, holding a hand in her direction.

She doesn't acknowledge him; she only looks at Charles, and as she does, her voice changes into something like a scream.

"Do you know how easily I could *make* you understand?"

"Are you nervous?" the man asks Icarus.

"Not... not really."

"Speak more clearly, then. Quit stuttering."

Icarus bites the inside of his bottom lip, glances up at the ceiling, and then— seeing what hangs above him— looks back down.

"I... I have a stutter, M-Myon, I can't—"

"Have you tried?"

His throat tightens, his eyes burning.

"Yes," he says. "I've tried."

The man sighs, shakes his head, and scribbles on his notepad.

"You know, kid, I'm going to be honest. You've always given me some red flags."

"Have I?"

"I mean, Jack found you in Jakara, yes? No family left. They leave you there?"

The question jars him, enough that the other man can see it in his eyes.

"Ex... Excuse me, Myon?"

"You were abandoned. Why?"

"Nothing," the being beside him growls. *"Worthless."*

Icarus looks at the man like he is the only ghost in the room, his eyes dark.

Shadows leap from the creature at his side, drape themselves around his shoulders, and he fights the urge to lean back into their embrace.

"I've wondered that m...myself."

"And then Jack brings you here," he continues. "I remember that, you know— You being brought in."

"You could be more than this."

"I... I d-didn't."

"You were so... Well, there's always been something wrong with you. Fucking weird kid. Thought you might be an E.D.T...."

The hair on his arms begins to rise, and the darkness holds him more tightly.

He should cast it away, he thinks.

"Reckon we would have figured that out by now, but, you know..." The man leans forward in his seat, tapping his pen on his lips. "Reapers... Reapers will make it this far, sometimes."

"We want you, Icarus."

"Will they?"

"Not often, no, but sometimes, one will manage to slide through." He lets out a long sigh. "Hardly think you're clever enough to hide it that long, though."

"We could be more than this."

"M...Myon..?" Icarus gasps, baffled by the words.

"Then, your tests say differently," the man says, looking him dead in the eye. "So, tell me, Icarus— or whatever your name is... How does a stupid, slow..."

The boy's vision begins to blur, the voices around him growing louder, and the darkness presses in, wrapping itself around his throat— his hands.

"...orphan from Jakara, end up excelling beyond so many more..." He gestures wordlessly at the air, and as Icarus watches, rage begins to burn in his chest. "*Worthy,* people?"

He could break him so *easily.*

He swallows past the lump in his throat, shrugging before he can tremble. "I... I guess I had to," he forces. "I wasn't given much of a choice."

"Had to?" the man asks. "Why?"

"Had to earn my place somehow, yeah?" he breathes, then, laughing under his breath: "Or... or perhaps I'm a Reaper."

The man laughs, looks down at his notepad, and when he does, the Icarus' eyes change.

"You want to," the darkness wines. *"You know you—"*

"Reaper or not," the man says, still looking down. "You have earned nothing."

"Silence." Charles snaps, and thunder rolls in, as if it is summoned by the word. "Sit, now. No more of this."

"Charles," Jack mutters. "You shouldn't—"

"*Both* of you."

Rosemarie closes her eyes and presses her chin to her chest but doesn't move.

"Rosemarie," Charles repeats, and when she remains silent, he turns to Jack. "I'll go for Ursula," he says, and the words shatter any hope the girl had left. "Can you handle her?"

"Yes, Myon," Jack responds. "Please—"

Charles is out of the room before he can finish, and when he leaves, the girl crouches down on the floor, leaning over like she might be ill.

Jack pulls the sword from his hip and places it on the table before kneeling in front of her, his eyes heavy.

Neither of them speaks for a long time, but after a few minutes, she lifts her head.

Jack's heart falls into his stomach, and for the third time this evening, he feels real fear.

The girl's face has gone pale, and thin black veins stretch themselves across it. The whites of her eyes are stained with gray, and blood drips from her nose.

"I'm sorry," she whispers.

He shakes his head, holding out an open hand.

"You don't need to be sorry," he says.

She glances at his hand and swallows hard.

"Are you... Are you sure?"

"I'm not afraid of you," he responds.

A quiet sob escapes her lips, and she reaches out one cold, vein-covered hand, taking his.

He shudders, but not enough for her to notice. "Does it hurt? Controlling it."

"Not always," she replies, gripping him tightly. "What is he going to do to me?"

"You're safe right now. I promise. I need you to breathe for me—"

"I don't f-*feel* safe," she says, and Jack's heart sinks into his stomach.

That's what it is, he thinks.

She reminds him of Icarus.

CHAPTER TWENTY-ONE

"Something's wrong," Anemos says. It is the first time he's spoken in a while, trying to save his breath. The air in the hall has grown thicker. "He's been back there twice as long as everyone else."

"I'm sure he's fine," Cole says. "He'll be back soon."

He chokes on the last word, and Anemos looks over at him with soft eyes, placing a hand on his shoulder.

"You're right," he insists. "You're right, I'm just being paranoid. Don't let me scare you. Don't pay me any mind."

"No," Cole breathes. He looks down at the floor, feeling like the noise might drown him. "It's been a long time. You're right."

Anemos just looks at him, his throat tight, until he speaks again.

"I'm scared," he says. "I'm terrified. I know there are things he's not telling us, and I don't want them to come out in there—"

The steel door opens again, and Icarus walks through it. His eyes are dark, but they still search for his friends in the crowd.

Relief floods both of their chests and Cole falls silent, a weary sigh escaping his lips. He shoves his way through the crowd, stepping on several feet to get to the boy faster.

"Hey," he says, pulling him into a tight hug. "What happened?"

Anemos follows close behind, but stays quiet, only watching.

"Nothing," Icarus breathes. "N-n...nothing worth m...mentioning. When did you get out?"

"I don't know. Time doesn't make sense here. It's been a while."

"By the dragon," he mutters, pressing his fingers to his temples. "It's so loud."

"It's hell," Cole says. "I never thought I'd miss the shelter."

"Do you think they'd let us outside? I know it's Karneji, but—"

"I think we can do what we want," Anemos interrupts, and Icarus smiles at him, pale as snow. "As long as none of us get killed."

"I'm not dying in Karneji," Cole mutters. "Lead the way."

"Finally, fulfilling my family duty and stepping into the shoes of the Guide—"

"Alright your highness, get us outside."

Anemos turns around, gestures for the other two to follow him, and begins to weave through the crowd, and the building, like he's taken the route a thousand times.

They arrive at a door in no more than a minute.

"Oh, sweet air," Cole breathes, stepping outside.

A shiver runs down Icarus' spine.

"I think you're probably the first person to say that in Karneji," Anemos coughs. "It smells like shit."

"Better than whatever the hell was in there."

Icarus forces another small smile, but his eyes are distant, staring off at nothing in the darkness.

His silence is felt by both of them.

"Icarus," Cole says, his voice heavy despite his attempt to lighten it.

He looks over, eyebrows raised.

"Everything went okay? You're okay?"

Icarus takes a deep breath, tucking his hands into his pockets, and shrugs.

"It's over. The hard part is over. We're done."

"We're done," Anemos repeats, raising his hands to the heavens. "Praise the void."

Cole laughs under his breath, shaking his head, and Icarus leans onto the rail in front of him.

"I'm ready to go home. I think m...my dad said it would be a long night for him, so... I'm glad you're coming over, An. I think I'd have a hard time being alone."

Anemos nods, joining him along the rail.

"I would, too. Cole, are you sure you can't escape the shelter tonight?"

"Yeah. Unfortunately."

Icarus reaches into his pocket while they're talking, pulling out a small, see-through packet of pills. He takes two and swallows them without water.

"Still hurting?" Anemos asks, and he nods.

"Yeah, I barely felt the first few. Hopefully these help."

"What's the dose?"

"N...no idea," Icarus says, and Anemos pats his back.

"Be careful, then."

"I'll be careful, An," he says, putting them back in his pocket. "Anyway, how did things go for the-the-the... both of you?"

"Oh," Cole sighs. "Hardly a joyride. A bunch of weird, cult-ish questions."

"Hey," Anemos hisses. "Let's not get charged."

"Sorry, sorry. A bunch of beautiful, meaningful questions about if I really understood what I was doing in signing. Like, if I was really willing to sacrifice—"

"Romance," Anemos finishes. "And at such a young age!"

Icarus laughs under his breath as he listens, but another ache springs up in his chest; a familiar one.

"Luckily," Anemos says. "I am a cynic, who cares naught for things of this world. That being said, I was about... Eh, five seconds from a breakdown when we finished."

"Are you..." Icarus' voice stalls, and this time, his neck heats. "I'm sorry. Are you okay now?"

"Sorry for what?" Anemos asks. "And I'm alright now, yeah. Will be, anyway."

"Th- that's... that's good."

"Suppose so," he nods. "Got more worried waiting for you, golden boy."

"I'm sorry."

"Sorry?" he asks again. "Icarus, you don't need to apologize because I care about you."

"I'm s..." He stops and shakes his head, and Anemos laughs, taking his hand and saying nothing else.

With great effort, Zahra manages to pull herself up from the floor of the carriage she has been placed in— if it can be called a carriage. There are no windows, save a long, narrow slit along the top of each wall, and only one door in the back, which cannot be opened from the inside. She was placed here by a man twice her size, who carried her over his shoulder and tossed her into this box like luggage.

She is used to small spaces but still struggles to catch her breath. Her head is spinning, and tears fall hot and fast from her eyes.

She knew the risks. She knew them, and yet, now—

The large door on the back of the transport is yanked open, interrupting her thoughts, and she turns her head to face it.

Another man approaches, with another girl at his side. Her hands are tied behind her, and connected to a long chain that the man holds.

Her eyes widen at the dark space in front of her, and she turns toward him, quivering with fear.

"Please," she whimpers. "Not in there, not in the dark..."

Zahra has to squint to see her clearly. A blonde girl, younger than her, with a delicate frame and baggy clothes. Veins stand out, dark, under her eyes.

"No light to give you," the man says, pulling her into the transport against her will, but having the decency to untie her wrists and let her sit upright. "My apologies, Miss."

"Please... I... I'm terrified—"

"The lighter," Zahra suggests.

They both look over at her, and she swallows hard.

"The lighter, in your pocket," she repeats. "Will that be enough?"

The girl blinks a few times, her eyes darting wildly over Zahra's face, and then manages to nod.

"Yes," she says. "I... I suppose."

The man squints and shakes his head, muttering something about witches as he pulls a syringe from his belt. He drops it in the blonde girl's lap and steps back quickly, exiting the carriage again.

"In your wrist," he says, and the girl picks up the needle with shaking hands.

"What's it going to do to me?"

"I don't have time for this. If you want your hands to stay untied, I'm going to need you to give yourself the shot."

She looks at it a long second before pressing it into her skin, not wincing as she injects the poison into her bloodstream. The moment the syringe is empty, the man slams the door shut again. They're both quiet for a minute and then the younger girl reaches into her pocket, pulling out the lighter Zahra mentioned, even with the heaviness in her arms.

"Scared of the dark?" Zahra asks, pointlessly.

The girl nods, pressing her head back against the wall.

"I used to be too," she continues, breathing slowly in an effort to keep her sobs subdued. "You get... Your eyes will adjust. It hardly looks dark to me, now."

After several tries, the girl flicks on the lighter, and then lets the flame die.

"How..." Her voice is frail. She clears her throat. "How did you know I had it?"

It isn't an easy thing to explain, but Zahra doesn't have the energy to spin a good lie, either.

"The Wind told me," she states, at the risk of sounding insane to this prisoner she does not know— the only person who will be with her for the most terrifying journey of her life; but the girl just laughs under her breath, keeping her eyes low.

"Does the Wind speak in Karneji?" she asks.

"It speaks everywhere," Zahra replies. "Everywhere I've been, anyway."

"You have not been to Trellis, then. The only god Trellis has is Commander Hawkins."

"Trellis?" she asks, trying not to let fear creep into her voice. "Is that where they're taking us?"

"It's where they're taking me." The girl squeezes her eyes shut. "What are you?"

"A Deviation. Elemental."

"That's all?" she asks. "Is that a crime?"

"Not on the Outskirts," Zahra breathes, and the girl lets her head fall to the side.

"What have you done, then?"

Zahra looks out through the thin slit in the wall, squinting in a futile effort to see through it.

"I tried to join the Ordinem. So... Treason."

"Why?"

"Because I was afraid," she answers, her breath caught. *Trellis.* "What are you?"

"An E.D.T.," the girl says. "But don't worry. I'm *subdued.*"

"E.D.T...." Zahra breathes. "That's... Exercitum de..."

"Exercitum De Tenebris. Host of darkness." She flicks on the lighter again, trying to find comfort in the flame. "I'm not particularly fond of the name."

"What's your name, then?" Zahra asks, and the girl falters.

She looks at Zahra like she has said something baffling, confusion heavy in her eyes.

"I've been asked my name more times today than I have been my entire life in Trellis," she says. "Are you kind, like the second man? Or lying, like your Guide?"

"It's not really... kind, to ask you your name," Zahra mutters. "It's just decent. But I'd like to spit on the *Guide,* so I guess I'm more like the second."

"You don't have any reaction to what I am?"

A man yells outside, and they both fall silent, trying to listen.

"...finished!" Charles calls. "Start loading the train. I want them out of Karneji before we open the veil. Make sure the boy is on it. Has anyone gotten to him about his parents?"

"No, Myon, not yet."

Charles descends the stairs of the Facility almost as if he is floating, skipping over half of the steps out of habit.

"Jack," he calls. "You've got the girl?"

"Yes, Myon."

"And where is Aliya?"

"Here, Myon."

Aliya steps out from behind one of the carriages, and Jack fights back something of a smile at the sight of her.

She is dressed much the same as him, but with two daggers placed across each other on her back, and several smaller blades strapped, with a sword, onto her waist. Her hair flows across her shoulders in brown waves, as she hasn't bothered to tie it back, and her gloved hands rest— somehow alert— at her sides.

Charles swallows hard, lowering his voice as he approaches her.

"Are you busy?" he asks.

She looks around her— at the several carriages preparing to leave their territory, at her husband, Ursula, and the blades a few inches from her hands.

"No," she says. "What do you need?"

"Find your son," he says. "He's had a troubling night. He shouldn't return home to missing parents."

"Troubling how?" she asks. "Is he alright?"

"I haven't the time to explain. He should still be at the Facility now, but they'll be loading the train soon. Let him know that the path has changed, and his journey home should be easier."

Confused, Aliya nods, clenching her fists at her sides. "I'll be quick, Myon."

She goes to pass him, but he grabs her wrist before she can, and she turns back to face him.

"Charles?" she asks.

"Give him my apologies, Aliya," he says, and she quiets.

"For what?" she asks.

"He'll understand." He releases her. "Thank you."

She hesitates a few seconds, trying to read his eyes, and then goes on her way.

"Just finished the last exam," Cole says, walking back out of the building. "They're going to start loading the train. Seems like they're rushing it this time."

"Should we go, then?" Anemos asks. "I don't want to be left behind."

"I mean, we can, but I'm sure we have a minute."

"Let-l-let's wait a minute, then," Icarus says, looking pale. He is sitting on the pavement, his back against the wall and his knees pulled to his chest. "I'm not ready for the... the noise—"

The door opens beside them, and they all look over. Instantly, Icarus scrambles to stand up.

"Mom?" he asks. "What..."

Fear passes over her face at the sight of him and his red eyes, but she keeps herself firm. "Icarus. Are you alright?"

"I'm alright," he lies. "What are you... doing here?"

She debates whether to press the issue for a few seconds but settles on letting it be.

"Charles sent me," she says. "We're crossing tonight, and he wanted to be sure you knew. We may be gone well into tomorrow evening."

"But I'll be..." Icarus' shoulders fall. He shakes his head. "Okay, thank... thank you for telling me."

"Anemos?"

He looks up.

"Yes, Myon?"

"Your parents will be crossing as well, if you'd like to stay together."

"Two steps ahead of you, Myon."

"Good," she says. "Icarus, Charles wanted me to give you his apologies for earlier. He didn't elaborate, but he said that you would understand. He also wanted me to inform you that the train's path has been changed, and this journey will be easier."

The words make Icarus' shoulders fall. He hates that what happened has already made it back to the Higher-class, but he has never been more relieved to hear something in his life.

"He's forgiven," he forces, and the words make Anemos' stomach turn.

"Very well," Aliya nods.

They are all quiet for a moment, and then, a bit hesitant:

"Myon?" Anemos asks. "Am I permitted to ask why you're crossing?"

"We're returning something to Trellis," she answers. "That's all that I'm sure I can tell you."

"Trellis?" Cole asks. "Isn't that—"

"Please be careful," Icarus breathes.

Aliya forces a small smile and pulls her son into a hug.

"I will be, don't worry."

Anemos stretches, his arms raised above his head, and laughs under his breath.

"Bring me home an Acthen's spine, would you?"

Aliya smiles, laughing as she pulls herself away.

"We'll see," she says, reopening the door, but before she can leave, something stops her. She looks back at Anemos and lets her face fall.

"Anemos," she starts. "Will walking back to the train through the main Facility be an issue for you?"

All of the remaining blood drains from his— and Cole's— faces, instantly.

"What?"

"The way you came in has been blocked off for the crossing. They're walking all of you back through the main Facility," she says. "If that is an issue for you, I can walk you along another route before I head back."

"Yes," Cole answers, standing up before Anemos can even respond. "It would be greatly appreciated, Myon."

"Very well," she says. "Come with me, all of you."

Anemos stands, slowly, and they all follow her away.

It is a short walk back to the train, but he keeps his head down, and he keeps his hand in Cole's, and he tries his best not to pay attention to anything but the steps that he is taking. If he were alone, walking anywhere on the property would be enough to bring him to his knees.

He isn't alone, though. He's safe. He keeps reminding himself that he's safe, that this isn't even the same building, and that he doesn't need to be afraid. He keeps glancing over at their hands and telling himself that, if nothing else, he can count on the man next to him; that at least Cole will keep him safe, even if that idea isn't foolproof.

It's just Karneji, he tells himself. He passed the exam, he is here as an innocent. They don't know how many times he's betrayed them.

He needs to focus on his steps.

One foot after the other. His shoes crunch down on the rocks under his feet.

"You okay?" Cole asks, giving his hand a squeeze.

"I'm okay," he replies, adding, in his mind, that he would *not* be okay if they were walking through the main Facility.

He glances up at Aliya and wonders how she could possibly know. Charles wouldn't tell her; Charles doesn't even *know*— not really, not all of it.

His parents would do nothing to lessen his suffering, and even with all of Jack's unexplained knowledge... Surely he couldn't know *that.*

He tries not to dwell on the question, but then, there are worse things to dwell on.

"You're my hero, you know that?" Cole asks, his voice barely a whisper.

Anemos checks to see if Aliya is distracted, and only responds when he sees her talking to her son.

"Why would I be your hero?"

"Why wouldn't you be?"

"You know how many ways I could answer that?"

"I know how many ways you could try," he says. "I don't think any of them would be very convincing."

Anemos swallows hard, reminding himself to breathe as his feet meet the now-solid concrete. He is outside. He is safe. He is not—

"You're the strongest person I've ever met. Probably the strongest I ever will," Cole says, and Anemos shakes his head.

"I'm not strong."

"Yes you are, and I don't think I tell you that enough, but I always think it. Every day."

"Cole," Anemos breathes. "Why are you saying this?"

"Because I want you to know it," he responds. "Because... I don't know. We're in it now. Things are real. It's been a hard day, yeah? Days like this make me feel a little... less invincible?"

"None of that," Anemos says. "You *are* invincible."

"Sure. Sure I am, but I'm not feeling it, and there's just... There are so many things that I don't say enough."

"You don't have to say anything."

"But I should. I want to. I—"

A whistle blows, and they both look up.

Neither of them had realized how close they were to the train, but now it stands looming in front of them.

Icarus hugs his mother, and then walks over to Cole, saying something that Anemos doesn't hear.

He approaches Aliya hesitantly, shaking her hand as a show of thanks.

"Myon?" he asks, his voice barely audible over the noise around them.

She nods, a gesture for him to continue.

"How did you know?" he asks.

She takes a deep breath, shrugs, and lowers her voice.

"I suppose that Inanis wanted me to know."

Anemos blinks a few times, shaking his head.

"Inanis?"

"Is that so shocking?"

He laughs under his breath, baffled.

"Can a place know a person?" he asks.

"The spirit of a place can," she responds.

"But why would it..." He stops, looks down, and cracks the knuckles on his left hand. "Thank you, anyway," he says.

"Of course," she says gently. "Take care of Icarus for me, tonight. Will you?"

"Yeah, of course I will."

She squeezes his hand— releases it.

"You're a good friend, Anemos. Thank you."

"I appreciate that, Myon. Be safe out there tonight."

"Will do," she nods. "Have a safe trip home."

Anemos joins his friends on the crowded train, and they stop in front of an empty row of seats.

"You want the end?" Cole asks.

"Yeah, thanks," he says.

Cole nods and slides into the row, letting Icarus in after him, and when the last boy sits down, Icarus leans toward him without even meaning to.

When he realizes he has, perhaps in an attempt to distance himself from the window, he nearly moves away, but before he can, Anemos' arm has already wrapped itself around his shoulders; the embrace is too comforting for him to fight, or even question. He only glances over at him, forces a small smile, and wonders when his friend became family.

"I'm so tired," Cole says, gazing out the window at the darkness stretched out in front of them. "I don't want to pack when we get back. I want to sleep."

"We could help you," Icarus says, his voice even softer, even sadder, now that they're on the train.

"Thanks, Icarus, but I don't think they'll let you guys in this late."

"We could sneak in," Anemos suggests, half-heartedly.

"No, you two need to rest. You're pale as death, and anyway, I can handle it. I just don't want to."

"Think we'll be b-back be-be-before sun up?"

"Yeah," Anemos breathes. "I don't think it's that late. Maybe one or two."

"This has been the longest day," Cole yawns. "Surely they won't all be this long, now that we're in."

"That's im...possible," Icarus says. "D-don't even suggest that."

"Sorry, sorry." Cole wraps his arm around Icarus' shoulders too, not even thinking, and the latter boy smiles, laughing under his breath. "What?"

"We're just..." Icarus leans his head over onto Anemos' shoulder and starts to laugh, if only to keep the tears behind his eyes. "Look at us. What are we doing? *Cuddling?* On a train, in Karneji, at two in the morning. And we're all s-such a m-m-mess."

Anemos starts to laugh, too, and Cole follows suit, and suddenly, for a moment, they are okay; even with the darkness outside, and the sadness that hangs around them. For a moment, they are still young, and they are almost innocent, and the darkness looks weak compared to the light they hold together. They feel almost invincible, and the fear that clings to them all seems to cower in the corner.

But moments are not lives, and they do not last forever.

The train engine grinds back to life, and soon it begins to move, taking them sleepily back to their home; just as a carriage lurches forward across the plot, pulling Zahra away from hers.

On the Outskirts, Ghost sits awake, staring into a fire, too broken to reach out to her and too fearful to sleep. He can almost feel her pain, distantly, just as Aliya— hardly realizing— can feel her son's rest.

She squeezes her husband's hand, and wonders if she should be more afraid of the journey than she is. His eyes tell her that she is safe, even if he can't really be sure himself.

Across from him, Charles sits with eyes less present, his hands restless, staring into some other place; Trellis, perhaps— his mind in the same city as the girl whose trust he does not *want* to betray.

She flicks on the lighter again, now, and keeps the flame burning as long as she can. This time, when it dies, it does not return.

The darkness falls over them all.

Chapter Twenty-Two

"I lost my parents," the girl said, and the words made Icarus' stomach turn.

"Are they in the city?" he asked.

"We're not allowed in the city," she whispered. "I don't know how I got here... No one else has seen me. I've been lost a long time..."

Icarus watched the girl with careful eyes, his chest tight. Her frame was thin. He could have guessed she lived outside the city walls.

He wondered what happened, and shuddered at the thought.

They were alone. The chances of being seen were slim, but not none. He didn't want the risk so close to the ceremony, but what choice did he have? He didn't hear anyone nearby. Most of his fellow students would not be out for another hour, and the Higher-class was busy preparing for the day ahead.

"I can help you find them," he forced, the words like tar in his throat. "Come... Come here. Take my hand... What's your name?"

The girl took a step closer to him, shaking with what he assumed was fear.

"I don't remember," she muttered. "I don't know where it went. I don't remember a name."

Icarus shook his head, forcing a tired smile as she took his hand in hers.

"Don't worry," he assured her. "I forget mine too, sometimes. I'm sure it'll come back to you."

"I hope so." She stopped and stared into the distance. "You're the only one who's stopped to talk with me, you know?"

He knew. He knew because even if there was another Reaper in the city, he was the only one foolish enough to talk with a Mortum in the open.

"You said you've been lost a while," he said, changing the subject. "How long, do you think?"

Her eyes wandered as if she was watching something that he couldn't see, but he knew she was listening; he knew she was trying.

"I don't know," she said. "It just feels like a long time."

Too long, either way, but at least he knew it hadn't been long enough for her to forget entirely. At least she hadn't started to fade, and distort, like the little boy in his room so many years ago.

"Do you remember where you live? Was it the Outskirts, or Karneji?"

"Yes! We have a little house on the Outskirts."

"Far from the city?"

"Very far. Things were horrible—" She froze, her eyes afraid, and turned back to him. "I don't want to remember. I'd forgotten."

"No, no, you don't need to rem-m-member anything," he said quickly, and a bit of distress left her eyes, but a little color left with it. His stomach turned. "Let's get you to your parents, yeah?"

"Yeah," she responded, nodding fervently. "Are they far?"

He swallowed hard, past the lump in his throat, and forced away the grief rising in his chest. It was useless, wishing he could give her more time, but he wished it anyway. He wished he could cross the barrier into the Outskirts and return that child to a family that was still waiting for her.

"Farther than you've ever been," he answered honestly. "But I can take you to them. You'll have to be brave—"

"I'm the bravest!"

A smile broke across his face again, and he nodded.

"Well, of course you are. Just... take m-my other hand, okay? And we'll go."

She hesitated, looking around at the town, and Icarus wondered, for a moment, if maybe she knew she was gone.

His chest was tight when she took his other hand in her own.

"Okay," he whispered. "C-close your eyes. You can trust me, I'll still be here when you open them."

She closed her eyes without hesitation, and he closed his.

Within a few seconds, the city around them faded away, leaving only the void Icarus had become so familiar with. This time, though, he knew he had to go further.

He didn't do it often, so it didn't come easily to him, but slowly, the darkness began to fill out. First, the ground under their feet, dark red dirt, pale grass that was high enough to tickle the girl's knees. The field they were in seemed to go on for miles before the scenery changed, sloping up into hills, then mountains in the northeast, and filling out into a glowing civilization in the west.

He asked himself, once again, why this world had been designed to look so much like his home; perhaps this was his home.

There were differences, of course. One being that so much of the beauty that still lived, here, had been burned away in the other. The sky was a deep blue at night, instead of the blackness that hovered over the streets there, and it had a light purplish tint in the day.

It was beautiful, he thought; beautiful, if not good.

"Open your eyes," he said softly, and she listened.

Her eyes opened, and she looked around, panicked for only a few seconds. "This isn't... We aren't on the Outskirts. We aren't..."

"N-no," he said. "But I d...don't think your parents are on the Outskirts, either."

"Where are we, then?" she asked.

He took a deep breath, tucking a loose strand of hair behind his ear as the wind pulled it toward his face.

"M...morta," he said. "We're in Morta."

"Morta?"

He forced a small smile, nodded, and let her look around for a moment without speaking.

"Do you remember their names?" he asked. "It m-m-might help—"

"Have her call for them," the voice was gentle, nameless. "They will hear her."

"No," she said. "I don't. I'm sorry."

"It's... It's okay," he said, and then, not entirely understanding: "Just... Call for them."

"Call for them?"

"They'll hear you."

A cloaked figure stood watching, hidden in the shadow of a large tree just east of them, as the child began to call for her parents, but he remained silent; not for fear of frightening her, but for fear of frightening the boy.

She called for them quietly, too timid to raise her voice any louder, but it was enough. In Morta, so close to the end, the Wind carried her small voice to the woman waiting for it.

Her soul crossed the grass at a speed no living woman ever could, and took her child into her arms without hesitation, her chest heaving with sobs.

"Baby," she cried. "Where have you been?"

"Looking for you," the girl said.

"I'm right here, baby. I'm right here."

"Where's daddy?"

"Daddy's not here," the woman said. "He's gone on already."

"Gone where?"

The woman stood, taking the girl up in her arms, and turned to Icarus, her face stained with tears.

"Thank you," she said, reaching out and touching his shoulder. "Thank you for bringing my girl back to me. I thought... I thought I'd lost her."

Icarus nodded, his chest heavy, and met the woman's eyes against his own will.

So afraid, the cloaked man thought; so afraid of himself, and them.

"Of course," Icarus said, anyway. "You... You don't n-need to thank me—"

"I do," she interrupted. "I do. I know it's dangerous, doing it."

"Y...you don't need to worry about that, m...ma'am, I..." His voice broke. "I'm sorry."

"Oh, no, it's alright," she said. "I've processed it, love. I just didn't want to let go without her."

Her hand felt heavy on his arm, even though she was all spirit. Her eyes still looked like they must have in Terra, heavy and cast in wrinkles. She must not have slept much, before. He was surprised she managed to hold on, here, being as tired as he suspected she was.

"That's dangerous too," he said, and she smiled a pitiful smile, holding her girl close to her.

"One day you'll have a child, and you'll understand what little choice I had."

He nodded at those words and lowered his head, finding nothing to say in response.

"Perhaps you could help us," she said, when a moment of silence had passed between them. "Help us let go?"

The cloaked man watched as Icarus nodded— as he took their hands and spoke gently to them, even in his fear, and eventually, as they both faded from his vision; as they left Morta and the rest of their world behind, crossing into whatever was next.

Icarus knelt on the ground when they were gone and rubbed his face with his hands, his breath heavy.

He did not even hear as the man approached from behind him— not until his voice cut through the night air like a blade.

"Michael."

The name sent chills down his arms, and he turned around before he could even think, a silver dagger raised in the air— one he hadn't had before.

The cloaked man only stood, staring at Icarus with icy blue eyes, the wind blowing his dark hair into his face as he lowered his hood.

"Lower your weapon," *he said calmly.* "You won't be needing it."

"You're Grim?" *Icarus asked, his voice trembling.*

"As are you," *the man said.*

Icarus hesitated, just a moment, and then lowered the dagger to his side, running his hand across his eyes.

"You don't trust your people," *the man said.* "Why?"

"Why?" *Icarus laughed bitterly, his eyes burning.* "W-why do you..."

The man nodded, knowingly.

"The Six," *he said, and when Icarus stayed silent, he held out his hand.* "My name's Cyrus. I assure you, I am not one of them."

Icarus reached forward unsteadily, shook the man's hand, and tipped his head in respect that he was not sure either of them deserved.

"Am I the first you've met?" *Cyrus asked.*

"Y-y-yes..."

"But you have been here before?"

"A few times."

The man's eyes narrowed.

"And you've had no teacher?"

Icarus hesitated, and then shook his head slowly.

"Not a Reaper."

"Inanis, then?"

The boy looked at the man in front of him carefully, his head tilted to the side.

"How do you know me?" *he asked.*

"The same way you know how to do* that," *Cyrus said.* "I am given the information I need."

"You... you've been—"

"Come back to town with me," *the man said.* "We can talk there. It's cold, here."

Icarus looked up at the sky, and the town behind him, considering the proposition a moment longer than he thought himself capable.

"I can't," *he said, finally.* "I have to be getting home."

Anemos still has his arm around Icarus when they arrive back at his house, and Icarus pushes the door open sleepily.

They step into a house that feels too empty, and too silent; it is too dark for either of them to see.

Icarus detaches from his friend and moves across the room, switching on a lamp in the corner and flooding the room with warm light.

Rain taps down on the roof, and Icarus collapses back onto the couch as Anemos walks into the kitchen.

"Any claim on the biscuits?" he asks, a few seconds after opening their fridge.

"Help yourself," Icarus yawns. "B-bring m-m...me one, while you're at it?"

A minute later, Anemos sits down next to him, a plate of biscuits in one hand, and a jar of jam and a knife in the other.

"A feast," Icarus laughs weakly.

"Precisely. Now..." Anemos smears jam across the bread, takes a large bite, and wipes crumbs off of his shirt. "Screw this day."

"Yeah."

"This has been *the* shittiest day of all time, I swear. I am *enraged*."

"M-me too."

"And now Cole has to go back to that shitty shelter—" Icarus takes a biscuit off of the plate and picks at it awkwardly before taking a bite. "—And your parents have to be gone on that shitty ass journey—"

"Anemos?"

"Mm?"

"Can I talk to you?" he asks. "Like, r...really, t-talk to you?"

Anemos' eyes soften, and he sits the food on the table, cracking his knuckles as he sits back. "Of course you can. What's going on?"

The question is impossible to answer.

Icarus looks ahead, avoiding his friend's eyes, and his silence makes Anemos' chest tighten.

It would hurt less if he wasn't so familiar with the look of fear in his eyes, but recognizing it, his skin begins to crawl.

"Hey," he says softly. "You can trust me. Whatever it is. I promise."

Icarus nods, even though he is unsure, and swallows hard before speaking.

"I think... I think m...my exam was... Was yours very personal?"

"Personal?" Anemos asks. "No. Pretty standard. Why? Was yours..." His voice trails off. "Did something happen?"

"Shut your mouth," the darkness whispers, and Icarus wonders where it is, if he can't see it; in his soul, perhaps.

"Icarus?"

"Yes," he whispers. "Yes, something happened."

"Okay."

"He... He started asking about m...my family— m-my *other* family, in Jakara, and why they..." His voice cracks. "Why they *abandoned* me."

"What?" Anemos asks. "That's... No. That isn't permitted."

"He told me I was s-stupid, and s-slow, and was v...very bothered by my speaking."

"You speak fine," Anemos says, shaking his head. "You aren't stupid or slow..."

"He said he thought I might be an E.D.T...."

He looks at his friend with his brows furrowed, his eyes narrowed, and his hands on his knees.

"Or... or a *Reaper.*"

"If he thought you were a Reaper," Anemos says, "he wouldn't have told you. He was screwing with you."

"You think?"

"Yeah, man. They're terrified of The Grim. If they suspected you they would have tranquilized you, not provoked you."

Icarus sniffs, rubs his eyes, and nods, picking nervously at the skin on his wrists.

"It really freaked you out," Anemos says, almost to himself. "I'm sorry. It would have scared me too. That shouldn't have happened."

Icarus looks down at the ground, bouncing his knees.

"It..." He clears his throat and looks back over at Anemos. "It did scare me. I was terrified."

"But?" Anemos asks, and Icarus shakes his head, his breath shallow.

"It made me..." Thunder rattles the window panes, and lightning flashes through the kitchen, sending a shudder down his spine. "I'm so *angry*. I m-mean... I really... I wanted to *hurt* him. That's... That's what happened earlier, in combat... With Regis. He... H-he started on me, and I just..." He shakes his head, pressing his hand to his forehead. "I think there's something wrong with me."

"There's nothing wrong with you," Anemos says, but Icarus only continues to stare forward. "Icarus."

"Yeah?"

"There is only so much a man can take peacefully," he says. "I would know."

Icarus looks over at him, his eyes hazy. "Are you afraid of yourself too, then?"

Anemos hesitates a moment, and then looks down at his hands.

"I used to be," he says, "but, no. I'm just afraid of everyone else."

Icarus stays silent, the words heavy on his chest, but Anemos leans back with a small smile.

"Everyone but you and Cole, anyway."

"Do you talk to him?" Icarus asks. "About... Whatever it is? Whatever happened?"

Anemos nods, his hands clasped tightly together in front of him.

"Yeah. I mean, you... I think you know, yeah? I know word spreads around the Higher-class like wildfire."

"Some of it," Icarus replies.

"Enough of it, I'm sure." Anemos sighs. "We don't need to talk about me—"

"Are you safe, An?" The words are hesitant. They make the hairs on Anemos' neck stand on end. "Have things gotten any better?"

Before Anemos can answer that it hasn't, they are interrupted by the sound of something crashing against the kitchen window.

They both look up, and the lamp beside them flickers with the wind.

"Wh-what was..."

"I'll go look," Anemos says, eager to get away. "Stay here."

He walks back into the house a few moments later with wide, sad, hopeful eyes, and his hands cupped in front of him.

"You won't believe this," he says softly, approaching the couch and stopping to kneel beside the table.

Icarus leans forward, hears the quiet chirping sound coming from the other boy's hands, and raises a hand to his mouth.

"H-how—"

"He must have flown in while they were crossing," Anemos says, holding the small, brown bird carefully. "He flew into the window."

"Do you think he's hurt?"

"He was stunned when I found him," he says. "I thought he was dead, at first, but... I don't know. I'd feel better if he was moving a bit more."

Icarus bends closer to his hands, squinting to see.

"His wing," he says. "It looks broken."

"You think?"

"Yeah-yeah, see? It's hanging lower than the other one..."

Anemos looks down at the bird, and then back at Icarus as he watches it.

Afraid of himself, he thinks; it seems impossible.

"What should we do with it?" he asks.

Icarus thinks for a few seconds before responding.

"Get it comfortable," he says. "Let him recover from the shock, then wrap the wing, I guess."

"You guess," Anemos laughs. "Okay, you know..." He glances at him again— the paleness of his face, the darkness under his eyes, and forces a gentle smile. "I can handle this, you should rest."

"You don't need to."

"I'll be fine," Anemos breathes. "I have gone much, much longer than this without sleeping. I'm hardly tired already."

Icarus presses his lips together and nods, too tired to fight him on it.

"Okay, w-well, let... let me hold him, while you get what you need, at least."

"And then you'll sleep?"

"I'll sleep out here," he says. "Just... Just in case."

"Okay," Anemos says.

"Okay."

Soon, Icarus is lying on the couch with heavy, sleepy eyes, curled up in the same blanket he has been using since he was twelve years old. A light smile graces his lips as he watches Anemos— who is equally tired— tucking a soft towel into a small wooden box.

"There you go, little guy," he says, placing the bird inside of it as gently as he can. "I'm sure that's more comfortable."

The bird settles down in its place, stretches one wing, and once again begins to chirp.

"You came a long way," he whispers, wrapping a bandage around it, holding the wing to its small body. "How did *you* brave Karneji?"

Icarus laughs under his breath, but closes his eyes before Anemos looks over at him, pretending to be asleep until eventually, he is.

Anemos lies down on the floor, facing the bird, and keeps one hand on the box as if maybe its presence will provide some comfort.

"I have a friend," he whispers, watching it, "who would think you were the most beautiful thing in the world."

The bird blinks, as if acknowledging the statement.

"She's always hoped that there were still birds, out there."

The light flickers again, and he glances over at it before resting his head once again.

"I don't think you'll meet her but I imagine that Cole will be here soon enough."

He is so certain that he waits up, even when his eyes start to ache from exhaustion. He sits awake, keeping watch, until he hears the front door creak open.

He lifts his head and meets Cole's eyes with a soft smile, gesturing for him to sit his packed bags in the corner of the room.

"Took you long enough," he says, and Cole lets out a heavy sigh, dropping his luggage to the floor.

"I'm sorry for barging in, I didn't want to wake you guys, but I couldn't sleep. It all just keeps... replaying in my head." He casts a glance over at Icarus, who is still sound asleep. "I thought we were going to lose him for a minute, An."

His voice is so tired it makes Anemos' heart sink.

"I just couldn't keep thinking about it alone. I needed to see you both here, okay—"

"Come here. Lie with me," Anemos whispers, tapping the floor beside him. Cole looks back over with red eyes and nods, crossing the room and kneeling beside him. He does not even notice the bird, too focused on Anemos' eyes. "We're all okay, now. You can rest, I'll watch out for you."

"I don't think I can. I see the fire every time I close my eyes. I took a shower as soon as I got back and I still feel like I smell of smoke."

"Come here," Anemos repeats, and Cole lets out a heavy exhale, lying down beside him.

As soon as he does, his eyes fall on the wooden box, and he stills.

"What is that?" he asks, and Anemos slides the lid further to the side, showing him. "Where did you—"

"It flew into the window," Anemos says. "It's got a broken wing."

"Poor little guy." Cole reaches forward, running two fingers over the injured bird's back. "I don't remember the last time I saw one."

"Me neither. I hope he makes it."

He moves his hand over the creature's wing as discreetly as possible. Warmth flows through it, like it did when he ran it over his injured face at the shelter.

Anemos won't notice on a night like this, he thinks. He has never noticed before.

"He'll make it," he whispers, pulling his hand back.

"I hope so," Anemos says again. He slides the lid back into place, just in case the little bird tries to fly, and rolls onto his side.

Cole watches him, letting a quiet smile find his face.

"They made me commit to so many things tonight, in that exam room," Anemos whispers, and he nods, his throat tight.

"Me too."

"They've planned our whole lives out, haven't they?"

"They think they have," he admits. "I'll still run away with you, if you ask."

Anemos smiles, at that, his eyes sparkling in the dim lamplight. He lays his head on his arm, and Cole mimics his posture, only a few inches from him.

"Don't tempt me," Anemos whispers, and Cole laughs, closing his eyes.

He reaches across the space between them and rests his bandaged hand on the side of Anemos' face, brushing the hair from his eyes.

"You told me to lie without hesitating," he says, when a minute has passed. "I did. I didn't mean a single vow I took."

INTERLUDE: AFTER THE FIRES HAVE DIED

The sky hangs heavy over Morta— as if the clouds themselves are mourning, and the wind blows just hard enough to bring some comfort to the hot, tear-stained faces of the grieving.

Hundreds of Grim gather in the cool twilight, lighting up the space around them with the glow of hundreds of candles. Their cloaks do very little to warm them. The cold seems to ache down to their bones.

Cyrus passes through the crowd with his head lowered, one hand in his pocket and one rubbing his face. He cannot handle their eyes today; he cannot handle their questions, but he will.

He steps to the front of the crowd with heavy eyes, his short black hair hanging loosely in his face, and uses one of the candles around him to light the torch at his side.

He clears his throat and looks at the group of people in front of him hesitantly; mostly Grim, but a handful of ordinary persons, all red-eyed.

"The fires in Terra have ceased," he says, his voice only loud enough to be heard. "It was... A long night—"

A strangled cry breaks free from the lips of a woman in front of him, and it rattles his chest.

"There was... The rain ceased in Karneji early on, so it didn't matter in the end. But..."

"Were there any survivors?" a young man asks, his voice heavy.

"No," Cyrus forces. "Not one."

Tears fall faster, every eye in the crowd burning. Quiet sobbing fills the air.

"I know the pain everyone is in. I feel it in my chest," he continues. "No one here has gone without some loss. No one here is without grief, but it is worth stating that the number of men lost during this year's executions was the lowest it has been in almost a decade—"

"Because there are less of us," a younger woman cries. "Less of us in Terra, less of us surviving the year..."

"I have to hope," Cyrus forces, "that that isn't the case."

"Hope will only take us so far, sir."

"I know," he responds heavily. "I know. Please, do not think me naive. We will be consulting on what steps to take as soon as we commence here. You may join— any of you— if you believe you have something to offer."

Several members of the group nod, and Cyrus clasps his hands together tightly.

"This is the moment before that," he says. "We must take a moment to grieve this loss before we can continue. We must rest for a few hours. I believe that is what..." His voice cracks. "I believe that they would want that. I believe that they deserve to be honored peacefully, given their struggle."

The torch flickers in the wind, and he lets his eyes fall to the ground.

"That said, I want to apologize, before we begin, that my blood has brought such great agony to our people..." He swallows hard, running a hand through his hair. "And I want to assure you that that blood will not influence the actions we take. *You* are my brothers, my sisters..."

An older man steps to the front, approaches him slowly, and puts a hand on his shoulder without speaking.

"We are, all of us, family, and my loyalty lies here." He wipes his eyes, too tired to fight the tears forming in them. "If anyone else has something to say—"

A young woman steps forward, and Cyrus steps away.

Two men hold him in the crowd as he breaks.

Part Two: Trellis

"We are all in the gutter..."
– Oscar Wilde

Chapter Twenty-Three

S un has started to seep through the slits in the carriage. It wakes Zahra from her sleep, and when she opens her eyes, her chest fills with anxiety. At first, she doesn't know where she is, but then she remembers, and that's worse.

As soon as she realizes what's happening, pain floods her body anew, and a wave of nausea passes over her.

She squints against the sun.

"Good morning," Rosemarie says, and Zahra lets her head fall back against the wall. "You slept so well I was starting to think you'd passed."

"I don't feel like I slept well," she mutters, and Rosemarie smiles softly, still fidgeting with the dead lighter. "Where are we?"

"We're somewhere between Karneji and Trellis," Rosemarie says.

Zahra rolls her eyes, tired. "Well I know *that.*"

"There aren't a lot of names out here. It's just space. I don't know what else to tell you. There haven't been many trees, so I doubt we're close."

In the dim light of day, Zahra can see the girl better. It makes her a little sad, looking at her. She can't be more than seventeen, but her eyes are much older. She holds herself a little like Ghost does— like she has been through too much for her body to carry.

It makes sense, with what she is.

Zahra knows very little about E.D.T.s, but she knows the basics: Rosemarie is host to something from another world; a spirit of darkness that doesn't compare to anything from their realm. Every moment is likely a struggle to keep the spirit under control, and even if she has mastered that game, it has undoubtedly taken a toll on her.

Most deviations don't live through an attempt at being possessed. Many argue that no one *should* live through it, and that if someone does, their life is not worth living.

Rosemarie looks over at her with tight lips and furrowed brows.

"What?" she asks.

Zahra shakes her head.

"Are there a lot of trees in Trellis?" she asks, changing the subject.

Rosemarie relaxes a little, nodding with wide eyes.

"*So* many trees. They're everywhere. You can hardly see the sky."

"You're exaggerating," Zahra says.

"Maybe," Rosemarie admits, a smile tugging at her lips. "Yes. I am, but it is wooded. And everything is covered in moss, and fungus. It's humid. A lot different from the Ordinem, although I never saw the city."

"Do you like it there? In Trellis?"

She folds her arms over her chest, grimacing. "I don't know. It's not my home. Of course nowhere is, really, but... Can you like a place when you're imprisoned there?"

Zahra thinks of her little home, nestled between two locked gates.

"I don't know," she says.

The carriage hits a rock and jolts, sending another stab of pain through her chest. The night before is a blur now, but the feeling brings a memory to the surface.

She doesn't understand why the guards in Karneji had to handle her so roughly— why they had to drop her on the wet concrete and pull her up by her hair. She doesn't remember why she was hit so hard between her shoulder blades, but she can't imagine they had a good reason. If Rosemarie sees Trellis as a prison, she wonders what type. She wonders if it is like the Outskirts, or like Karneji. She never thought she would yearn for the former.

"I don't think you can," Rosemarie continues, when the carriage has steadied. "I don't think *I* can. But you might like it—"

"I'll probably be a prisoner too, won't I?"

"I don't know why Trellis would keep you over treason against the Ordinem," she shrugs. "They're separate territories. I don't know why they're taking you there."

"Maybe they just want to dispose of me somewhere they won't have to clean me up," Zahra mutters.

Rosemarie's eyes darken at the words. She shakes her head.

"You don't think they're going to *kill* you?"

"I'm a traitor."

"I hate your country," she remarks. "They don't have any way of dealing with things without violence, do they? Kill the Reapers, kill the E.D.T.s, kill the Deviations if they enter the city, torture the prisoners... But they're warriors for peace and justice! Bull. Shit."

"Yeah," Zahra forces.

She would usually respond with more enthusiasm, but she can't muster it. She's too tired, and in truth, she doesn't feel much better than the people Rosemarie criticizes. She offered her allegiance to them for something as pathetic as comfort.

She thinks of Icarus and her stomach turns.

This is deserved. She bowed to the people who made him fear execution, and now she is in his place.

"I'm sorry, that was rude. A country isn't its government—"

"No." Zahra shakes her head. "Don't apologize. You're right, I'm just... scared."

Rosemarie braces herself against another bump in the road, suddenly quiet, and Zahra slumps back further against the wall. She can feel the weight of the other girl's gaze in her chest, and she wants to cower away from it.

Finally, Rosemarie shakes her head and looks away.

"People have wanted me dead my whole life," she says. "It doesn't mean anything, whatever they've planned for you. You can survive it if you try hard enough."

Zahra isn't sure about that.

"Can you move?" Rosemarie asks. "Feeling is starting to come back for me. I can move my arms, with a good deal of effort."

"Just barely."

"We might not reach Trellis before the evening. If it's barely now, it'll be more by then. What's your element?"

"Fire," Zahra mutters.

"Burn them and get out."

"And go *where?*"

"Anywhere," Rosemarie says. "It's going to be hell, but you can make do—"

"I don't want to make do anymore." The words come out sharper than Zahra means for them to, but she doesn't retract them. "I'm tired of surviving. I'm *tired.*"

"You think I'm not?" Zahra looks away when Rosemarie says it, a little embarrassed. "I'm about to walk into the thing I hate the most in the world, and there's *nothing* I can do about it. My whole life I've suffered, Zahra. But it's worth it, isn't it? Wouldn't you rather survive than die?"

Zahra feels like her own throat is choking her.

"I'm not saying you'll make it long, or that you won't die over and over again," Rosemarie continues, her voice cracking. "You're going to suffer, but you don't need to suffer this; this helplessness? You're not helpless. You're fighting, and you're just going to have to keep fighting. That's all it is. That's what I tell myself every day, and you're much freer than I am. I think I'll hate you if you give up."

Zahra shifts her weight slightly, the action taking all the strength she has.

"What are you going back to?" she asks. She is desperate to take the spotlight off of herself. "What do you mean when you say you're a prisoner?"

"I mean that Commander Hawkins wants a weapon, and every time I fail to become one for him, he takes my life away from me. The Ordinem is taking me back to him—"

"What do you mean he takes your life away?" Zahra asks, and Rosemarie shakes her head.

"My past, my memories, my name... They leave what serves them and take the rest. That's what they always do. At least, that's what Kieran's explained to me."

"So you don't remember anything from before?" Zahra asks. "You don't even remember that they've done it? Who's Kieran?"

"Kieran's my friend," Rosemarie mutters. "He's the only one I have."

Zahra struggles to process everything she has been told. She chews on the inside of her bottom lip, anxiety coursing through her. She can't imagine going through that. She can't imagine the girl across from her going through it *again*. She can't bear how casually Rosemarie explained it all.

"I'm sorry," she forces, unable to shake the feeling that the words mean very little.

Rosemarie shrugs, peering through the slit in the carriage wall.

"It's just my life."

"It's horrible," Zahra says. "It's not fair."

"Of course it isn't. There's not much right and fair in this world. Does that still surprise you?"

She lets her eyes fall, heat burning behind them.

"I can't imagine a day when I'll cease to be shocked by something that cruel."

"You're lucky, then," Rosemarie replies. "I hope no one ever takes that innocence from you."

Zahra looks down at her hands, her chest tight.

There is a certain insanity to what she is about to say, she thinks, considering that she is in the back of this carriage, drugged and terrified and alone. Still, she speaks, her voice frail.

"There is good," she says. "I've seen it."

"I know there is," Rosemarie replies. "*That's* what surprises me; every time I find it. It's always in the darkest places, isn't it?"

Chapter Twenty-Four

They don't arrive in Trellis until after dark.

Zahra looks out the windows as they are transported through the capital. There are trees everywhere, just as Rosemarie said there would be. Moss hangs from the branches, blowing in the wind.

It feels different here. The air is warmer. She has regained enough strength to hold her hand up to the crack in the wall, feeling the breeze through it.

It's terrible, but even now, she feels a sense of hope at being someplace other than the Outskirts. She never thought she would make it this far from the Ordinem again. In Trellis, she is only a few hours from Jakara. The thought makes her ache for the place, even if she hardly remembers it and knows there is nothing left of it.

"We're getting close to the Facility," Rosemaries says, her voice quieter than it was before. "That's where they're taking me, so I imagine we'll stop soon."

Zahra imagined they were getting close. There have been more lights these last few miles, and the buildings have grown taller.

She hasn't ever seen buildings like this. They're not nearly as interesting as the ones in the Ordinem's capital, all square and wood and steel, but they make up for it in size.

"We won't see each other again, so I want to say goodbye now, before we lose the chance. I'm really happy to have met you, Zahra."

Zahra looks over at Rosemarie with sad eyes, shaking her head.

"You don't know we won't see each other again," she insists.

"If we do, I won't remember you," Rosemarie reminds her.

She shrugs, folding her hands together.

"We'll start over," she says. "We can get to know each other in better circumstances."

Rosemarie smiles a little at that, looking away.

"That sounds nice."

It is not long before the carriage pulls to a stop. When it does, Zahra lets her hands fall to her sides, pretending she is unable to move. She has no plan, but she does not want to receive another dose of the paralytic.

She can't imagine Rosemarie does either, because she too has fallen completely still. She is looking outside without turning her head, and Zahra can't help but notice the fear that has returned to her eyes.

"Stay safe," Rosemarie whispers, anyway. "If you can hear the Wind here, tell it to give me a break, please."

"I will," Zahra promises. "If we meet again, I'll remind you—"

"Don't remind me of any of this," the girl interrupts.

Zahra doesn't argue.

"I hope you get out of here one day," she says, instead. "I hope this next life is the best one you've had, and that you make it somewhere that doesn't feel like prison."

"I hope you make it somewhere you don't have to try so hard," Rosemarie mutters, and the words make Zahra's chest ache.

She doesn't want what happens next.

CHAPTER TWENTY-FIVE

The back door of the transport is pulled open, and Jack climbs in, helping Rosemarie off the floor as carefully as he can.

"Thank you," she whispers.

He meets her eyes for only a second, and then looks away, his chest tight.

"You have her?" Ursula asks, standing uneasily at the door. He looks back at her quickly. He is uncertain, but he nods anyway, keeping a loose hold on one of the girl's arms.

"Can you walk?" he asks her.

"I don't know," Rosemarie replies.

He sits her feet on the ground and watches as she attempts to stand, her legs unsteady.

"Is that alright?"

"I... I think so," she says, already out of breath. "If you can just support me..."

He drapes her right arm around his shoulder, wraps his arm around her back, and she takes his hand with her left.

"Is this okay?" he asks.

"Yes, thank you."

Ursula watches them and bites the inside of her cheek. She is barely breathing when Aliya walks over to her, brushing her own hair out of her face, in visible discomfort.

"Would you like me to pull that back for you?" Ursula asks. "I don't want you to pull the stitches."

"Would you?" Aliya asks.

Ursula nods and steps behind her, but keeps her eyes on Jack.

"You shouldn't be touching her," she reminds him. "It's first thing you learn about dealing with E.D.T.s—"

"How would you like me to handle her, Ursula?" Jack snaps. "Drag her in in chains? She can't walk."

"Don't be sharp with me," she says calmly. "I'm only trying to help you."

The man looks at Rosemarie, ignoring Ursula, and finds her with her eyes tightly shut.

"Are you okay?" he asks, and she nods, quiet.

"I hate this place," is all she says.

As Jack helps Rosemarie regain her footing, he watches the Guide. He is standing at the gate to the Facility, speaking with a short blonde woman. He looks exhausted.

When Charles explained what he planned to do, Jack could hardly believe him. He shouldn't be surprised that the Ordinem's Guide is willing to go against himself for a cause he deems higher, but he never thought Charles capable of bargaining with a life. All these years, he has hoped that the man he once considered a close friend still might still hold the gentleness he used to. He has hoped the man might be a helpless bystander to the cruelty around him, not knowing how to stop it.

Now, he is forced to confront that that is not the case. Charles is the Guide, fighting tooth and nail for the Code— willing to do whatever it takes to fill the streets with Grim blood.

After a few minutes, he returns to them, flexing his hands at his sides.

"We're free to go through," Charles says. "They'll meet you at the door and take you to speak with their Commander."

"Us?" Aliya asks. "Where will you be?"

"I'll join you before he does," he responds. "Don't worry about that. I'm just going to deal with the Deviation. I don't want anything holding us here if this talk goes poorly."

"Understood," Aliya says. "Anything more to know?"

He casts a glance at Rosemarie, but hesitates before approaching her, his jaw clenched.

"Are you stable?" he asks.

She looks at him with dark eyes, holding Jack's hand a little tighter.

"Yes, Myon."

"Are you sure?"

"Yes," she forces. "I'm sure."

He looks at her another moment before nodding, and turns away.

"No," he says. "That's all. Be on your way."

The moment they step into the Facility, Rosemarie begins to cling to Jack more desperately, and the feeling makes his stomach twist.

It is familiar, too.

"Are you okay?" he asks again, low enough that only she can hear.

She can feel the cool tile floor through her shoes. She thinks that maybe if she had not been here before it would be comforting; instead, she can only feel herself breaking against it. The sharp, fluorescent lights seem to bounce off the gray walls, blinding her.

Bile rises in the back of her throat.

"I'm okay," she says.

"Have you been in this building before?" he asks.

"Mm—" Something clatters against the floor in another room, and she flinches, too weak to jump back. "Y-yes..."

"I've got you," he says softly. "Just try to breathe."

Fear builds in her chest, and her head starts to spin.

"I'm not sure," she whispers.

"Not sure of what?"

"That I'm stable." She starts to cry, and he pauses, holding her tighter. "Oh, no. No, I don't want to hurt you. I don't want to hurt anyone."

"You aren't going to hurt me," he says calmly. "You're going to be okay—"

"You don't understand." The words are cold as ice, pleading. "It's not going to be okay. I'm not going to be okay."

"You've got to stay calm—"

"Jack." Aliya's voice rips him away. He looks up at her, anxiety making his head spin. "Look at her. Look at her face."

"I'm disgusting, I know." Rosemarie mocks her, a sob rattling through her body.

But Aliya is right in her observation: The girl's face has changed, once again white as a sheet, dark veins like rivers under her skin. Her eyes are nearly black.

Jack doesn't want to give her more paralytic, but he isn't sure how much longer he can deny the risk he is taking by leaving her mobile. If the darkness of Assecula gained complete control, there is no telling what would happen.

"This is dangerous," Aliya continues. "It's not worth it. She's no more comfortable like this than she will be if you give it to her—"

"What if we take your body away from you?" Rosemarie laughs. "Does that sound comfortable?"

Jack shuts his eyes tight, gritting his teeth. There is no way around it. There is nothing he can do. He might kill the ones he loves to take her somewhere safer, if he thought they could escape the city, but he knows better.

There is *nothing* he can do.

But just as he goes to take the syringe from his pocket, Ursula raises her hand between them, indicating for him to stop. He freezes, gripping the paralytic tightly.

"If she's completely paralyzed, the Commander might not take her," she suggests. Jack hardly thinks it's true, but he hesitates anyway, listening. "I deal with demons like this all the time; Reapers, the like. I can handle her. It won't be difficult. And then Commander Hawkins won't think we've harmed his property."

Rosemarie is tugging away now, trying to get free, but Ursula does not falter. She only pulls a pair of gloves over her hands and steps forward, grabbing the girl's arm and wrapping it around her neck.

"I hate you," Rosemarie growls, tears streaming from her eyes. "I *hate you—*"

"I don't care," Ursula says, not even bothering to look at her.

With the words, she continues further down the hall, carrying the E.D.T. with her. Everyone follows her silently, watching as Rosemarie writhes and tugs against her.

Only Jack notices the way the darkness in the girl's eyes recedes.

Chapter Twenty-Six

Zahra is drowning in an ocean of dread when the back of the carriage opens again. She jerks her head up, clasping her hands together to keep from moving more.

Her eyes meet the Guide's, and her heart jumps into her throat.

Burn them and get out, Rosemarie said. She isn't sure if she's able to use her power yet, but when she thinks of it, her hands warm.

"I would have appreciated more of a warning about all this," she says, turning away.

"Are you alright?" the Guide asks, and she bites her tongue.

"All things considered, I suppose I'm doing pretty damn well, sir."

He laughs at her, and her stomach twists.

"Can you stand?" he asks, and she doesn't reply. "If you don't answer I'm going to carry you, but I have a feeling you'd rather use your legs, so please speak now."

"Where are you taking me?"

"Not to your execution," he says, and she inhales sharply, letting her eyes fall shut. She won't die today, then, if he is telling the truth. But she still doesn't know how to answer his question. She has no reason to trust him, and she does not want to be paralyzed again.

"I might be able to stand, but there's no chance of me walking," she lies. In an instant, he has pulled himself into the carriage and crouched over her, gesturing toward her back.

"May I?" he asks, and reluctantly, she leans forward.

He scoops her up like a child, and her stomach tightens as she braces; actually, it lurches. She thinks she might be sick.

"I might vomit on you," she states, and he shakes his head, sliding out of the carriage and shutting it behind them.

"I've been through worse."

She tucks her head into her chest, pressing her hands against her face. The wind blows wildly, rustling in the trees. It makes her wonder if a storm is coming here, too.

Despite her curiosity, she cannot bring herself to look up at the sky. She can't even bring herself to open her eyes.

"Where are you taking me?" she repeats, her voice fragile is a way that disgusts her.

"I'm taking you to the military base," the Guide says, and her stomach sinks deeper.

"Why?"

"Because they might take you," he replies.

Her hands are warm, but not warm enough. Her body is not all her own yet, but her jaw clenches.

Anxiety fills her chest at the thought of being pulled into war again, hot as fire. It drives tears to her eyes.

She wants to go home. She wants anything but this. She can't remember crossing the warzone with her parents, but sometimes she thinks her body can; now is one of those times.

"I hate you for bringing me here." The words escape her mouth before she can stop them, a pitiful gasp.

"I know," he responds.

There is no apology. There is not even an attempt to justify what has happened— and if there were, she would still be angry, but the lack of response makes her even angrier.

"You're no saint," she mutters, sweat gathering on her temples. "You're barely even a man—"

He stops sharply, jerking away and dropping her to the ground. She stumbles, but to both of their surprise, she lands on her feet. It is harder than she expected it would be to keep her balance, but after a few seconds, she finds her footing, slumping over in pain.

She watches as the man in front of her looks at his burned hands in disbelief, and wonders if he will retaliate.

There isn't a chance he'll believe she didn't mean to do it.

"Have you no sense of self-preservation?" he asks, angry. "You're alive because *I* am letting you live, and you insult me, and harm me—"

"Do you want me to worship you, Guide?" The words are rough, caught in her throat. She wonders why she can't stop, even when she knows she should. "You take two girls and sell them off and expect thanks?"

"I've sold no one. I risk my crown to *free* you."

"I was free before you captured me," she shouts. "If you cared for me, you would let me go home. Instead, you take me to the country that destroyed my parents' homeland

and expect me to serve there. You want to feel like a hero, Charles. You want to be able to sleep at night. You don't give a *shit* about me."

The Guide stares at her. His eyes are dark with something like anger, but she cannot make herself fear them enough to falter. Perhaps she has no self-preservation after all.

"If that's how you feel," he says. "I won't insult you by offering any more help. Just know that, without identification, you'll most likely be taken into custody, if not killed by someone with a quick gun."

"Maybe I'd rather die than be in your debt."

"Maybe Deviations are as rash as they're stereotyped—"

It is the last thing he says before she lunges at him, shoving him backward with force he could not have imagined. He struggles to catch his breath as she starts to hit him, her fists like stones as they collide with his skin.

Despite how well she fought in the University, there is none of that now. Her attacks are force and very little else— blow after blow upon his chest and his arms. She swings with anger that is not calculated, taking all of her grief out on his body. It is *all* his fault, she thinks. Every minute she suffered in Karneji and the Outskirts; the fact that it was so unbearable she risked *this*. The fact that this is what she gets for trying to join them. She doesn't even pause to notice how little he fights back until she is too tired to continue, her breath heavy and strained.

Damn the paralytic, she thinks, stumbling away.

Maybe he was going to free her, but what does that matter, when he is responsible for her captivity? Maybe he is hesitant to retaliate, but he is still *wrong*.

She can't even bear to look at him, much less have him carry her to her fate. Still, she turns back to face him, her throat hot as fire.

"*I* am rash and hot-tempered because I was made that way, not because I was born that way," she says. "Your words are thoughtless."

"You judge me for how I was born," he counters. "Yours are no better."

"If you mean to tell me you're cruel without reason, I hate you even more. You're not helpless, and I don't pity you."

"I pity you," he says, and she falls still.

Part of her wants to ask what for, but truthfully, she doesn't have the energy to care. She doesn't care about anything the man thinks anymore.

A drop of rain falls on her skin and she looks down at it, watching as it evaporates. She looks up at the sky when it is gone and finds dark clouds, reflecting a shadow of the city lights back in her direction.

Home is so far away.

"It looks different here, doesn't it?" the Guide says.

Zahra closes her eyes, her pulse ringing in her ears.

"It's going to rain. You're going to need shelter. I can get you that. I can help you, if you'll let me."

Another drop hits her face, and her heart sinks deeper. She has done this before. She can do it again.

"I'm walking," she mutters. "I'll follow you, but I'm walking."

Hesitantly, the Guide nods and steps past her.

Soon, the rain is coming down steadily, making Charles' clothes stick to the burns on his arms. The noise of the wind washes out the sound of Zahra's steps behind him.

He glances back to make sure she is there, but does a double take when he finds that the space behind him is vacant.

"Zahra?" he calls; then, louder: "Zahra!"

Anxious, his hand travels to rest on his dagger, but finds the sheath as empty as the space she left.

CHAPTER TWENTY-SEVEN

Rosemarie is taken to a small room in a quiet part of the Facility, where she sits in a cold metal chair. Jack is beside her again, now that the whites of her eyes have returned.

He has tried to comfort her, but tears still stream down her face.

"You're doing good," he says, and she nods, not looking up from the floor.

The room is awful. Sterile, with white walls and a white floor. The lights are too bright, humming in a way that makes her even more anxious.

They are in it for a long time before the door opens again and Charles steps through it. He appears just as they are starting to worry, but doesn't say a word about what has taken so long.

"The Deviation?" Ursula asks, when a moment passed.

He shakes his head, casting a sideways glance at Rosemarie.

"Dealt with," he says.

There are burn marks on his hands. There is a terrible hollow feeling in Rosemarie's chest. She can't help but imagine Zahra struggling, fighting to get free before finally succumbing to the paralytic and this man twice her size.

Her face is raw from all the crying.

"How long until the Commander is here?" Charles continues.

"He'll be here any minute," Aliya says. "Are you alright, Myon?"

Charles looks up at her and nods.

"Why wouldn't I be?" he asks. "Are you?"

Aliya goes to respond, but before she can, the door opens a third time.

Commander Hawkins steps into the room. He is nearly a decade older than the lot of them, with thick, graying brown hair and hard eyes.

He looks at Rosemarie before he looks at anything else, and a sick smile spreads across his face.

"Hello again," he says. The words send a shiver up her spine.

Charles shakes the man's hand, not acknowledging them, and bows slightly in a false act of respect.

"It's been a while," the Commander says, and Charles nods, grimacing.

"It has."

It feels as if Rosemarie's skin is tightening around her bones.

She tightens her grip on Jack's hand without meaning to, and watches the two men carefully, her stomach turning.

"Why have you come?" Commander Hawkins asks.

The question lingers in the air. The man does not release Charles' hand.

"I believe she belongs to you, doesn't she?" Charles responds.

"And you belong to the Code." The Commander's eyes burn. Rosemarie can hardly believe the Guide doesn't flinch away from them.

"You speak of the Mercy Clause," Charles says calmly. "We swear mercy upon our enemies, yes, but life is often more complex than the text. We have many enemies, and there is potential for an outpouring of mercy greater than one E.D.T.'s execution."

Commander Hawkins squints and releases Charles' hand, circling to the desk in the corner and sitting beside it.

"Very well, then. I imagine you mean to make a proposal. What will you be requesting, in exchange for the girl?"

Rosemarie laughs under her breath, stifling a sob.

She will never be a person. Not really. She is only a prisoner to be returned. An experiment. A soldier.

"Word is you've found a way to enter Morta." The Guide's words interrupt her thoughts, drawing her eyes up. *Morta.* The land of the Grim; the land of the dead. "How?"

There is a long moment of silence, only broken by the Commander drumming his fingers against the surface beside him.

"We've discovered nothing new," he says finally. "You can't enter Morta unless a Reaper takes you."

"And yet?" The Commander narrows his eyes, considering, and Charles leans back against the wall, wearing an expression of nonchalance. "We want the information, and we want in," he says. "That's our price."

"Let you in?" the Commander asks. "And give you the power you need to wage war on us?"

"We don't want war," Charles says. "We never have."

"Why would you want passage to Morta, then?"

"If we can reach Morta— The Grim, and the Mortum— we can study them more effectively. It's much easier to protect yourself against an enemy you understand, yes?"

The Commander nods, suspicious.

"I suppose."

"It's in our Code," Charles continues. "We can't use the Malemortum for warfare. The founders saw that potential even before you did, and they prohibited it."

"Does your Code prohibit the use of Reapers?" the Commander asks.

Charles pauses a second, blinking, and then shakes his head.

"Not explicitly, no. But you can hardly... *use* a Reaper."

"And E.D.T.s?"

Jack shudders, feeling the hands of the girl beside him grow colder.

"For warfare," Charles says.

"We would be traveling with one of each."

Rosemarie straightens, her heart in her throat.

"Have you found another?" she asks.

The Commander looks at her, a small smile tugging at his lips, but does not respond. Her breath grows shallow.

"An E.D.T. and a Reaper?" Charles asks. "Together?"

"Yes," the Commander responds. "They've been neutralized. It's not without risks, obviously. We've not tested it yet, I'm surprised you caught word at all. But I'd be more than happy to do our first experiment in Ordinem territory, Charles."

Jack shoots the Guide a look that tells him to think twice, but he nods anyway, extending a hand as he pulls himself from the wall.

"It's a deal, then?" he asks. "We give you the girl, and you provide us transport—"

"What will you do with the girl?" Jack interrupts.

Charles glares at the man, but the Commander only shrugs, eyebrows furrowed.

"Study her, the same as we've always done. Though I hardly see why it matters."

"It doesn't," Charles says. "It's none of our business."

Rosemarie watches as their hands meet, and shake in agreement. She feels sick— sold.

To her surprise, though, she does not feel at risk of losing control. It is anger that burns in her chest, more than fear.

The only true fear she feels is for the E.D.T. they will be traveling with.

"I'll show you how we've subdued the Reaper," the Commander says. "I want Rosemarie here for that. She's weak. It'd be easy for the thing to take control of her."

"I understand," Charles replies.

"We'll have to bring her to the E.D.T., however," he continues. "He won't agree to help you until he's seen her."

"Agree to help us?" Ursula asks, stepping in front of Charles as the Commander moves to the door.

Hawkins laughs under his breath, but doesn't reply.

"Just two of you," he says instead. "The other two need to remain with her. If she gets out of hand, don't hesitate to—"

"I'll stay," Jack interrupts, and Aliya nods in agreement; though she hasn't much choice. Ursula is already halfway out the door, and Charles is not far behind her.

He *is* behind her though.

He hesitates a moment before following them into the hall, and takes one last glance back at them before proceeding. When his eyes find Rosemarie's, a terrible guilt settles in his chest.

CHAPTER TWENTY-EIGHT

The Guide only keeps his legs steady until he exits the room where the Reaper is being kept. The second he steps into the hall his knees begin to tremble, and soon he is crouched over the nearest wastebasket he can find, unable to breathe.

His eyes burn, and his hands move unsteadily to his hair, catching it before it falls into his face. He pulls himself up from the ground, empty, and leans back against the wall, fighting the urge to sob.

"Charles—"

"*Charlie?*"

The voice stabs through him like a blade, and he shakes his head, swallowing hard.

"Away from me," he mutters, his eyes closed.

"Charles." Ursula is closer now. His heart feels like it might explode. "What's the matter?"

The Reaper knelt in front of him with hollow eyes, reached forward, and wiped the tears from his face.

"Why are you crying?" he asked. "What do you have to be afraid of?"

Charles began to sob, struggling to breathe, and the Reaper tilted his head to the side.

"Do you think yourself innocent, Charlie?"

"Don't touch me," he forces, only half there as Ursula places her hand on his shoulder. "I said not to touch me."

"I'm sorry, I was only trying to comfort you—"

"Comfort me?" he asks, a pang of familiar guilt filling his chest. "Ursula, are you *mad?*"

"Are you?" she asks. "I don't know what I've done."

"Stop," he pleads. "This isn't about you. I don't want to fight with you. It's not you."

"What is it, then?" she asks. "I can't understand if you don't explain—"

"You need me to *explain what's going on*?" His voice comes out harsher than he expects, and she freezes in response, her eyes cold. "Did you not see..." His voice cracks, and he turns away, a hand to his lips. "Did you not see what I saw?"

"It was a *Reaper,*" Ursula says, confused. "It was just a Reaper, Charles."

"I don't *care* if it was a Reaper," he says, not even thinking before he speaks.

The words feel foreign in his mouth; wrong.

Ursula's eyes harden.

"Well aren't you compassionate," she says quietly. "You don't care, Charles?"

He looks down at the ground, his chest tight.

"They destroyed us," she mutters, angry tears spilling from her eyes. "They destroyed *everything*. What you saw in there was not a man. They are not *men*. You do know that?"

He stops, shakes his head, and puts his hands over his face, trying to push away the images of the room behind him.

It *looked* like a man, just like the Reaper he encountered so many years ago. He was not supposed to suggest such a thing then, either.

Of course he wasn't. It was a monster, just as this one is; even if it put on an act of suffering.

"Of course I know," he says, but there is uncertainty in his voice.

She hears it; he knows she does.

"Did you convince him to take us?" he asks, anyway, fighting off another wave of nausea.

"Yes," she forces, looking at him with disbelief in her eyes. "I did convince *it*, Charles."

"How?"

"I told it that we wanted peace," she says. "That is still what you want?"

"Yes, it's what I want," he breathes, hoarse. "I just... What if this isn't—"

"Finish that sentence, and you will lose your throne the moment we return. You know that."

"A whole *realm*, Ursula," he whispers. "Tell me, honestly, that you have never doubted once. You've *never* questioned what we're called to do?"

"Not once," she says. "It's not my place to doubt. It's not my plan. The moment I took the vow I gave up my right to question this, just as you did."

"Ursula..."

"The founders are why we are here, are they not?"

Charles stops, his chest tight. "Yes."

"And they were wise, yes? Wiser than us?"

"Yes," he says, not daring to hesitate.

"Then who are we to question?" she asks. "We have been fools before. Our minds are weak. If this plan has kept us alive till now, it stands to reason we should not abandon it."

"Even with the plan," Charles says. "The degree of suffering we just witnessed—"

"You and your sympathies," Ursula breathes, shaking. "If we do what needs to be done, their suffering will end."

He stays silent, hardly acknowledging her words, and she straightens, reaching toward him again.

He does not even look at her as she brushes the hair from his face, her fingers grazing his skin.

"You will be free from them," she whispers. "Finally, *finally* free from the bondage they have placed on you and so many others."

He meets her eyes with hesitation, hating himself for still being as comforted by her voice as he is.

"Isn't that enough, love?"

When they meet Jack and Aliya back in the small room they first came from, they find Rosemarie half hysterical, curled up on the floor with Jack still by her side.

Charles forces himself not to look at her.

"Alright," the Commander says, ignoring the sobbing girl. "One down, one to go."

"*Charles,*" Aliya forces.

Charles turns to face her, and she glances toward the girl, her eyes pleading for him to do something.

He bites his bottom lip so hard that he tastes blood and crosses the room, kneeling beside the girl with shaking hands.

"Rosemarie?" he asks. "Can I help you, somehow?"

She looks up at him, shaking so badly that he can hear her teeth chatter, but doesn't respond.

"What's wrong?" he asks softly. "What's the matter?"

"What's *wrong?*" she cries, clenching her jaw. "You have no soul, Guide."

The words are like ice in his chest. The only thing colder is the realization that he has no defense against them.

He has earned them. He is working for them now.

"We need to go," the Commander interrupts. "I'm afraid I don't have time for this."

Jack sighs, only loud enough for Charles to hear him, and shakes his head in frustration.

"Do you need me to carry you?" he asks.

A breathy sob escapes Rosemarie's lips.

"I'm too heavy. I can manage."

"You aren't heavy, child. I'll be alright."

Hesitantly, she nods and reaches out, wrapping her arms around his neck.

Jack scoops her up and cradles her in his arms, letting her cry into his chest. When he stands, he stares at the Commander with a look that frightens everyone who knows him.

The Commander pushes the door open anyway, and the rest of them follow him out into the hall.

Much like in Karneji, this E.D.T. is not held in the main Facility. He is held further away than even the Reaper, in a large room under the building, accessible only by one steel lift.

They pile into it now, cramped as it is, and Rosemarie's cries grow louder.

"She needs to be tranquilized," the Commander says, hesitating over the button that will close the elevator doors. "If she lets go of control—"

"We aren't tranquilizing her," Jack says firmly, and Charles does not dare contradict him.

Commander Hawkins swallows hard, trying to hide his fear.

"Very well," he says. "But you know what will happen—"

"We're going to be fine, Commander," Jack interrupts.

He is the only one who believes it, but no one debates him.

The doors close, and they descend into darkness.

CHAPTER TWENTY-NINE

The chain rattles above the lift as it moves down, and Charles looks up at the ceiling, his eyes dark.

For a government that they claim to stand against, Trellis' means are eerily similar. This is so like Karneji, he feels like he has been here before.

Ursula slides her hand into his, and he looks down at her, his chest tight.

The redness of her eyes stands out in the dim elevator light, the circles around them heavy and dark.

This isn't how he expected it would feel, being so close to victory. He expected to feel something like hope. He expected to find the eyes across from him gleaming. It isn't supposed to feel as wrong as it does.

With this thought, the lift hits the floor.

Even before the doors open, Charles can feel the silence beyond them; they all can. It's like they've left the world behind. The air has grown cold, and Rosemarie has fallen quiet.

The doors open, and it grows colder.

In front of them is a long, steel halfway. It stretches out hundreds of feet, the walls lined with dim yellow lights that end at one single door.

"Very inviting," Aliya whispers, and Charles swallows hard, following the Commander out of the lift.

Their shoes clatter against the metal floor, but the space is too small for the noise to bounce, so even that provides little relief from the quiet.

What it must be like to be confined here, Charles thinks. He would lose his mind quickly, and he would lose his patience much faster.

"Is it very powerful?" he asks, his voice quiet.

Rosemarie tucks her chest deeper into the crook of Jack's neck.

"Extremely," the Commander answers.

"Are we safe?" Charles asks.

"He is subdued," he responds, "but I would try not to anger him, anyway. Err on the side of caution."

"Does this not anger him?" Aliya asks. The Commander ignores the question.

"It's of extreme importance that none of you do anything to hurt the girl while we're here," he says instead, stopping at the door and turning back to face them. "Understand?"

"Yes, sir," Aliya says, and the rest nod in agreement. Jack holds the girl a little tighter.

With that, the Commander twists three large bolts, and the door swings open.

In front of them lies a large, stone room. One by one, they step into it and feel their stomachs sink.

When Charles sees the man— not fifty feet away— he closes his eyes tightly, fighting the nausea that grips him.

He listens as Jack, Aliya and Ursula shuffle in behind him, just to fall still.

Rosemarie stirs at the silence and tries to lift her head, but Jack quickly presses it back against his shoulder, his chest cramping.

"What is this?" he asks, his voice heavy with breath.

The Commander turns back, flashing something reminiscent of a smile.

"This is Kieran," he says.

From where they stand, they cannot tell whether the E.D.T. is standing or hanging. His wrists are clasped in chains that connect to a large bar not far from the ceiling, stretched too wide, and pulled too far back. His shoulders twist unnaturally and his body hangs forward. The tops of his feet barely touch the metal step beneath him, leaving most of the weight on his arms.

He should be writhing— should be fighting for comfort, somehow, in the position he's in. But he is completely still. At first glance, everyone but the Commander thinks he must be dead.

His eyes hang open, empty, and do not move to acknowledge the new presence in the room. Instead, they stare ahead at the wall in front of him.

"Is he alive?" Aliya asks, unable to hide the trembling in her voice. "Does he know that we're here?"

Blood is caked thickly all over his body, soaking through every article of his clothes. Charles thinks, at first, that all of his skin must be gone.

"Kieran," the Commander says. "Do you know we're here?"

The E.D.T. does not respond or move, but his eyes make their way over the lot of them— the only sign of life in his seemingly breathless body.

"What have you done to him?" Charles asks, hushed.

The E.D.T. looks away, his eyes resuming their place on the wall.

"Oh, don't worry, he'll be fine," the Commander says, leading them closer to him. When he finally arrives beside him, he reaches out a hand and places it against the young man's neck— still inspiring no movement. "You'll be fine, won't you Kieran?"

This time, he does not even move his eyes.

"He'll heal," the Commander continues. He turns back to them, and when he does, Kieran's eyes move to Rosemarie. "He always heals."

"This slowly?" Charles asks.

"The process has been inhibited," he responds. "But that's information you don't need—"

"Anthony," Kieran interrupts. His voice is quiet, but the sound of it sends a shudder down Charles' spine. "Get these chains off of me."

There is something rough in his voice, something dark, and it causes all of them to feel afraid, for a moment.

To their surprise, the Commander reaches into his pocket and pulls out a key, unlocking the cuffs around the E.D.T.s wrists a few seconds later.

When his hands are free, Kieran pulls them slowly to his chest, taking one long, shaking breath as his feet land flat on the floor.

"What do you all want from me?" he asks. "Why are you here?"

Rosemarie pulls against Jack's arms, her breaths shallow.

"Let me see him," she whispers. "Please."

Hesitantly, he sits her on the ground, watching carefully as she turns to face him.

There is sadness in her eyes, but no shock.

"They're hoping to enter Morta," the Commander says. "Seeing as they would be traveling with you—"

"You want to be sure I'll defend them," Kieran interrupts, his voice slow. "Your enemies?"

"They have bargained—"

"They brought her back," he says. "How long did they keep her?"

"We had it less than a week," Ursula says, and his eyes move to her, heavy.

"You," he whispers, "are *despicable.* Do not speak to me."

She stills, her chest hot with rage, and falls silent.

"What a group you are," Kieran says, glancing at all of them, and then looking back at the wall. "I want to speak with him." He points at Charles. "Alone."

The Commander looks over at Charles, who stands motionless, waiting for him to say something.

"I'd rather not have him alone," Ursula says. "Seeing as—"

"I'm not talking to you," Kieran interrupts. "If you want my help, I'm willing to speak with your Guide."

"Can you not command it?" Ursula asks, frustration barely hiding in her voice.

"*Him,*" Rosemarie forces, and Ursula looks over at her, her eyes sharp.

"I'm not commanding him to work for an opposing side," the Commander says, disregarding the girl's comment. "If you want my help, you'll need to convince him that you're worth our time."

"This is ridiculous," Ursula scoffs. "How can you—"

"It's fine," Charles interrupts. "We don't need to fight. I'll speak with him."

They all turn toward him, and he nods, his chest tight.

"I'll be fine, go on." Everyone hesitates a minute, and then the Commander turns, gesturing for them to follow him away.

Kieran watches as they go, and then turns back to Charles, his shoulders falling.

"Would you sit, please?" he asks. "I would prefer if you would sit."

Charles glances down at the floor uneasily— concrete, sticky with blood— and Kieran clears his throat.

"You don't have to," he says.

"Oh, no." Charles shakes his head. "I don't... I don't mind."

He sits down on the floor, and Kieran watches him with careful eyes.

"Give me just a minute," he says, and with the words he walks— slowly, unevenly— across the room to a small metal table, covered in shining, sharp tools.

He opens one of the drawers below it, rummages, and returns a few seconds later, a cigarette between his fingers.

He lights it with nothing but his bare hands, takes a long drag off of it, and sits down, his throat burning.

"Alright," he says slowly. "Charles. You did say your name was Charles?"

"I didn't," the older man says, visibly uncomfortable. "No one did."

"Mm," Kieran shrugs, shakily exhaling smoke. "Well, it is, isn't it?"

Charles only looks at him, his heart in his throat.

"Why do you want to enter Morta?" Kieran asks, not needing a reply.

"The goal has always been to understand the enemy," Charles forces, his voice slow. "If we understand it, it will be easier to live a life with some kind of peace—"

"You'll study them, then?" Kieran asks. "Like they're studying me?"

Charles falls silent and shakes his head, but before he can reply—

"Charles, look at who you're speaking with, please," Kieran says, still not looking at him. "I am the Exercitum De Tenebris himself. You have no reason to lie. Have you forgotten that I was their enemy before you were?"

For a moment, it seems that Charles can see all of the darkness surrounding the young man: the shadows holding to his shoulders, hanging thick in the air around him.

"All I have ever wanted," Charles says, "is peace."

"I believe you," Kieran breathes. "But how will you attain it? Peacefully?"

Charles glances at the floor, and Kieran shakes his head.

"You should give more credit to your doubt," he says. "You're so *close*—"

"I don't know what you're talking about," Charles interrupts.

"Sure you do." Kieran coughs. "You know that they're lying to you; about us, about the Grim—"

"Any doubts I have will be paid no mind," Charles says. "I have to trust the—"

"The Code," he interrupts, shaking his head. "I know."

He stands up, crushes the cigarette under his foot, and crosses the room again. This time, he brings the whole pack back with him.

"I can't convince you of anything," he says, lighting another. "I'm not going to waste my time trying. Only two things matter to me, presently. One is that I need to communicate with the Reaper. I'm entirely uncomfortable traveling with him, having not..." He pauses, shakes his head. "Established my place, if you understand."

"I understand."

"Convince the Commander to let me speak with the Reaper, and I will offer you the same protection I offer him. Understood?"

"Understood."

"Secondly," Kieran says. "I need you to give him a message for me, since you've inspired i t."

Charles opens the door, and the Commander raises both eyebrows.

"So quickly?" he asks.

"He wants to see the Reaper alone ," Charles responds. "That's the only way he'll allow either of us protection."

"See the Reaper?" the Commander responds. "He'll kill it."

"He's given me his word that he won't."

Anthony looks up at the ceiling, letting out a long sigh.

"Anything else?"

"Yes," Charles says, casting a glance at Rosemarie. "He said to tell you to enlist the girl, and that if she isn't gone by the end of the day, you'll have nothing from him."

"He's in no place to threaten me," the Commander says. "I'll do what I want—"

"Given what the boy's told me," Charles interrupts. "If you don't agree to enlist her, she will be coming back with us."

Ursula's eyes widen, but Charles does not look at her; he does not look at anyone but the Commander.

The words could start a war.

"If you don't want her serving, we'll find another way to enter Morta."

Rosemarie keeps her eyes on him, pale, as the Commander begins to laugh. It is a slow, unsteady sound. It makes Charles feel sick.

"What did he tell you?" he asks, and Charles shakes his head.

"You know what he told me."

"You realize I have no reason to help you, now," Hawkins snaps. "I gain nothing."

"We'll take the girl back, then," Charles replies, and the other man's eyes darken.

"Take her and you'll find the other E.D.T. at your doorstep."

"Or yours," Jack suggests.

Commander Hawkins grits his teeth.

"We should keep this peaceful," Aliya interjects, her voice quiet. "It will cost you very little to aid us, and much more to engage in another conflict. You can study her from a distance, can you not?"

Charles looks at Rosemarie and finds her hands shaking wildly.

For a second, he pities her, but he swallows his guilt and looks back at the Commander.

"You're gaining a testing ground, aren't you?" he asks. "You're gaining subjects. And if you truly wouldn't benefit from having her here, you wouldn't be considering it."

"What do you care what I do with her?" the Commander asks, beet red. "Do you think I've missed the rope scars on her wrists? You act holy now, but she shudders when she looks at you."

Charles wants to lower his gaze but keeps it steady, his voice even. "I won't engage you in a debate of morals, Hawkins. These are *your* E.D.T.s demands. My words only matter if you would be able to force his hand without enlisting her, and I don't really believe that's an option for you, anyway."

The words strike a nerve. The Commander's shoulders fall.

"If the thing has no other demands," he says, when a moment has passed. "We'll proceed."

"There's one more," Charles forces.

For a second, he thinks the Commander might kill him.

"And what is that?" he replies, tight-lipped.

"He wants you to let him see her."

Charles gestures to Rosemarie, and the Commander nods, angry, but visibly relieved.

"Five minutes," he says.

CHAPTER THIRTY

Rosemarie steps into the cold stone room and shuts the door behind her, struggling to breathe with the smell of iron in the air.

Kieran looks up at her instantly, his eyes heavy, and stands as she walks over to him.

"Hey," she mutters, her throat hot.

"Hey," he replies. "Are you..."

She wraps her arms around his waist, not minding the blood, and buries her face in his chest.

He rests his chin on her head, rubbing her back as she starts to cry.

"I'm sorry," he whispers. "I'm so sorry, Ro."

"I wish I never left," she confesses, struggling to breathe between sobs. "I've missed you. I hate it here, but I've been so alone, Kieran."

"I've got you," he says softly. "You didn't find him?"

"My brother's gone," she cries. "It's hopeless. It's just desert, and—"

"Did they hurt you?" Rosemarie holds him tighter, his blood staining her face, and feels his breath grow heavier. "I'm sorry," he whispers, and she pulls back, meeting his gaze for the first time in weeks.

She places her hand against his face, brushing his dark hair out of his eyes.

"*I'm* sorry," she forces. "I'm so sorry they did this to you. Is it because of me? Because you helped me?"

"No." He shakes his head, his voice catching. "It's because of them, it has nothing to do with you. Don't worry for me, love..." He pauses, cringing at his words. "I'm sorry, is that okay?"

"Is what okay?" she asks, pulling her sleeve over her hand and trying to wipe the blood from his face.

"Love," he repeats. "Maybe once, but I suppose I'm less to you, now."

Her eyes dart back and forth between his— brown and blue, red with exhaustion.

"Kieran," she whispers. "So many people have called me love carelessly—"

"I don't say it carelessly," he forces, and she stops, letting her hand fall to his shoulder; she runs it down his arm until their fingers are intertwined, and brings his hand to her lips, placing three kisses across the back of it. The action is so gentle that the darkness recoils within them both.

"I forgot someone like me could be loved," she says, letting his hand rest on her face.

His eyes fill with tears, and he shakes his head again.

"You've always been loved," he says, brushing the hair from her eyes. "Always."

The room is so *cold,* so dark. A shiver runs down the girl's spine, and she wishes she was in his arms again. There is so much fear inside of her that needs silencing.

"And now," he continues, "you're going to be safe, too. Safer than you are here—"

"I don't know if I can start over again," she whispers.

Kieran smiles unevenly, sad.

"You can do anything, Ro. You're stronger than you remember. I've seen it. You're resilient."

"I don't feel resilient," she says. "I started wondering, in Karneji... Maybe you can only fight so long, Kieran. I'm tired. I'm ready for it to be over."

"Hey," he whispers, taking her chin in his hand. "Look at me."

She looks up at him, trembling, and he wipes the tears from her face.

"It's almost over," he says, his voice so soft she can barely hear it. "I promise. When it's done, no one will ever hurt you again. You're never going to see these stone walls, or smell blood, or feel the sting of that man's hands again. You're going to see the ocean, and the stars, and run in green fields... and pick wildflowers for your hair."

She closes her eyes, trying to believe him.

"It's going to be over and you're going to be free, Ro. I swear it on my life, and the moon, and the whole sky. I just need you to hold on a little bit longer."

CHAPTER THIRTY-ONE

I t's started to rain.

Zahra stumbles through the streets of Trellis with her jaw and fists clenched, looking for any place she thinks might offer shelter for the night.

So far, the best places she has found have been bars, but those have been packed with soldiers, police, and government officials.

It isn't the best crowd for a refugee.

Now, despite trying to blend in, she stands out more than ever. If her Ordinem uniform wasn't a red flag on its own, the fact that she is limping down the middle of the road soaking wet certainly is.

"*Fuck,*" she mutters, wringing out her shirt. "Fuck this fucking bullshit. Fuck all of it. I should have stayed on the fucking Outskirts."

There's a sign on her right pointing to the military base, and she curses it too; then she follows it, sick to her stomach.

The irony is almost humorous. All of this because she didn't want to spend the rest of her life fighting, and it is leading her to the center of a war not even the most ruthless are able to stomach. She wishes she saw a better option. She wishes she didn't agree with Charles. But besides getting drunk and getting herself killed, what can she do?

Zahra can't imagine she'll make a very good soldier, but maybe she can be good enough to earn a little bit of food and a place to sleep. Then, maybe—

"There's no point!" she exclaims. "There's no point to any of this shit. I'm better off dying in the wastes—"

"Excuse me, lady?"

Zahra turns sharply to look at the man behind her, and when she does, flames burn around her hands.

The man takes a step back, shaking his head.

"I'm sorry." She forces the fires to die. "It's not intentional."

"Whatever, hothead."

He continues to back away, but she follows him, water dripping from her hair into her eyes.

"Wait," she pleads. "Do you know if there's a shelter nearby? Any place to get help? I'm not from here, and I don't know where to go—"

"Any shelter's gonna need to see an I.D.. We're in the middle of a war. Trellis is struggling, it's hard enough for it to support *us*. I suggest you just go back to wherever you came from."

"Don't you think I would do that if I could? You fucking asshole."

"There's probably a place for you on the streets, if you don't mind whoring yourself out—"

Her fist collides with his mouth, and he stumbles away, spitting blood.

"Go to hell," he mutters. "Take a joke."

"I'm going to die here," she says. "I need help, and you—"

"Oh, eat lead, Waste."

The words burn all over her skin. She thinks she could kill him, if she weren't too tired to follow him down the road.

She looks down at her hand, then wipes it on her shirt, staining it with the man's blood.

A flare gun, she thinks. She's a fucking flare gun, trying not to stand out.

She can see the military base in the distance, but she turns away from it. They will not take her, soaking wet, bloody, and volatile— clothed in the garb of an opposing country. She knows that. She can't humiliate herself more by trying anyway.

At best, it will get her pity, and that is a thing worse than death.

For better or for worse, all she wants now is a pint of vodka. So she stumbles back toward the bars. She pulls open the door to the first one she finds and ignores the feeling of the handle heating and flexing beneath her touch.

It is dark enough inside that she doesn't draw much attention, but when she approaches the bar the tender looks at her with his eyebrows furrowed.

"Are you okay, Miss?" he asks.

She pulls herself up onto a stool and leans forward on her elbows.

"I'm fine," she says. "Give me the strongest thing you have."

"Anything to eat?"

"Surprise me."

The man nods, apprehensive, and steps away. Zahra looks around when he is gone. She finds the place busier than she would expect, given the hour. No one seems like they are enjoying themself. Perhaps she fits in better than she thought she would. The bar is either poorly maintained or very old, maybe both. The stools are worn metal, the wallpaper is chipped, and the ceiling is showing a good amount of water damage: A feat, considering there is another floor above it.

In the corner is a man with a snake tattooed on his neck. It makes her think of Ghost, and her eyes grow heavier.

"Here you go, Miss," the bartender says, and she turns back to him. There is a shot glass between them, filled to the brim with something dark. She takes it and shoots it down, grimacing at the flavor. It burns her throat and hits her stomach like poison. For a second, she thinks she might vomit it back up, but the feeling mostly subsides.

"I'm going to need more than one," she says.

The bartender sits a plate in front of her, shaking his head.

"Eat," he suggests.

She looks down at the food, and catches a whiff of it: grilled meat and a warm slice of bread. Her stomach growls, even though her appetite is gone.

Food like this was scarce back home. She feels guilty that she's having to steal it, here, but imagines letting it go to waste would be worse.

Reluctantly, she takes a bite.

Another shot glass is sat in front of her, and she eyes it with shaking hands, struggling to chew her food.

"Zahra?"

The boy's voice startles her so badly she drops her fork. Her throat tightens.

"Icarus?" she asks. *"Are you okay?"*

"I am. I made it. I moved into the Compounds this morning." Zahra takes a sip from the little glass with her eyes closed, trying to collect herself. *"I don't think I would have made it alone. Thank you for being there."*

She can't remember another time she was as tired as she is now, but the words do bring her some comfort. At least it wasn't *all* for nothing. Still, she struggles to open her eyes, tears collecting behind them.

"You're welcome, Icarus."

"I think I've been selfish, though," he says. *"You're going through something, too. If you need anything..."*

She hates the way her anger softens when people are kind to her. She doesn't want to feel what's beneath it.

"You have enough on your mind," she says.

"The Outskirts aren't far. I can come to you. I don't know what's going on, or what kind of strength you need, but I'll do what I can to lend you some of mine."

She swirls the alcohol in her cup, her chest empty. She has no idea what to say to that.

"I know I'm not from the Outskirts," he continues. *"But I'm from Jakara, and I know how lonely it can be. Our country is gone—our families. Nowhere really feels like home, right? I was thinking about you trying to join, and I was trying to understand why you did it. Then I realized it's probably the same reason I'm here. And the thought of you looking for home and being cast away again... hurts."*

If he was with her, this is the part of the conversation where she would dismiss his concern and try to get rid of him. It is harder when his voice is in her head.

"I think we're kind of... the same. Different. But we both have Jakara, and we both have this, and that's not nothing. I've never been good with words, so I apologize, but what I'm trying to say is... If you need something safe to come home to... I'm a little dysfunctional, and it won't be perfect, but I'll try to be that, as much as I can."

The rim of the shot glass is cool against her lips. She tries to focus on the feeling, and not the shaking of her hands.

"Are you there?" Icarus asks. *"Can you hear me?"*

"I lied to you." She forces the words across the space between them, sick. *"They didn't send me back. They took me outside the wall. I got away from them, but I don't know what to do now."*

There is a long moment of silence, then:

"Where are you?" he asks. A radio kicks on across the room, and Zahra leans forward on the counter, covering her ears to block out the sound.

"Trellis. They brought me here with another girl, but I'm alone now. I'm scared. I'm in a bar and I don't have money to pay for the drinks they're giving me. It's storming. It's dark. The streets are full of men, and I can't keep my power under control so most of them hate me. I have someone's blood on my shirt, and my clothes are torn, and the paralytic they gave me hasn't worn off. I'm tired. I'm scared—"

"There's got to be someone that can help you," he says. *"Trellis is no different from any other place. There has to be someone there that will help you."*

"I'm an outsider. There's a war... I can't force my way into a place that doesn't want me again, Icarus."

"I know. I know how you feel. But you have to make it."

"Why?"

"Because you're worth too much to end like this."

She swallows down the rest of her drink, unable to control the silent sobs that shake her chest.

"Sometimes I think I was supposed to end a long time ago. Maybe with the rest of Jakara, or with my parents... Maybe that's why I struggle so much. Because I wasn't supposed to make it this far."

"I know. I feel that, too."

"You shouldn't."

"I know," he says. *"That's why I keep moving."*

"Miss." The bartender interrupts the conversation, and Zahra opens her eyes, scooting back into her seat. "Are you sure you're okay?"

"No," she mutters. "I'm sorry, I have to go."

"Ma'am..."

She slides off the stool, shaking her head.

"I'm sorry," she repeats. "I don't have any money. I won't take anything else from you—"

"You've already been paid for." The words catch her off guard, and she stops, her hands trembling at her sides. "Stay. Please."

She really looks at the bartender for the first time. He is much older than her, with graying hair and deep creases around his eyes. He has kind eyes.

"I know a refugee when I see one," he continues. "I don't know how you made it across the wastes. It's not my business. But I've called someone for you— a good friend of mine. She can help you, if you're willing to stop running."

It could be a lie. He might've called the police, or a trader.

He might have seen the way she melted his door handle.

But hesitantly, she returns to her seat.

"Sit, finish your food, have some water with your liquor," he suggests. "She's not far. She'll be here any minute, and she'll get you taken care of."

He steps away, and she stays, staring at the bar with hollow eyes.

"I've been praying for you," Icarus says. She swallows hard, picking at the wood on the bar's underbelly. *"I've barely prayed at all these past few years, but Zahra... I promise, I haven't stopped."*

It is a little under half an hour before the woman arrives at the bar. It's just enough time for Zahra to finish eating and stop crying. She has just finished talking to Icarus when the woman sits down beside her, putting a hand on her shoulder.

"Hey," she says. Her voice is gritty in a way that makes Zahra think she must smoke. "I believe you're who my dear friend called me for?"

Zahra looks at her for a long moment. The first thing she notices is her uniform: Military. She should have guessed as much, but it still makes her stomach sink.

"What makes you think that?" she jokes, forcing something just shy of a smile.

The woman returns it, holding out her hand.

"Sergeant Bellamy," she says. "It's nice to meet you."

Her hands are as rough as her voice, but there is something comforting in her grip. In a way, the woman reminds Zahra of her mother. She holds herself with the same dignity, her eyes heavy with compassion and strength.

"Zahra," she replies, returning her hands to her pockets. "I'm sorry he called you out here on my account."

"I'm not." The bartender brings Sergeant Bellamy a glass of beer, and Zahra watches as she takes a long drink. "This place can be hard for us women, especially when we're not ourselves. You look lost. I don't like the thought of you wandering alone."

Zahra sips her water, her mouth dry.

"I notice you've got blood on your shirt. Are you injured?" the Sergeant asks.

"I hit someone," she says. "It's his blood, not mine."

"And your uniform. That's Ordinem, isn't it?"

Zahra can't believe the woman didn't question her harder on the blood. Somewhat relieved, she nods.

"It is, but I'm not."

"Tell me about that. What's your story? Why are you here?"

She stares ahead at the wall, exhaustion lowering her shoulders.

"I don't even know where to start."

"Anywhere," Sergeant Bellamy says, and Zahra rests her hands on her chin.

"I'm from the Outskirts," she mutters. "And Karneji, and Jakara. We crossed the wall when I was two, my parents raised me in the desert until it took them. When I was six, a boy— a Deviation— escaped his execution and stumbled into my home. I took care of him while he got better, and then we took care of each other. We found our way to the Outskirts, and that's where I've spent the rest of my life. Up until yesterday."

"How long were you by yourself before he found you?"

"I don't know. Maybe a year, maybe less. It feels like a lifetime when you're five."

"Yeah," Bellamy nods. "*Yeah*. And how old was the boy? Old enough to take care of you?"

"Ghost was sixteen."

"You were both just kids, then—"

"Please don't pity me," Zahra interrupts. "It's over. It is what it is, and I did what I had to do."

Sergeant Bellamy stares at her, baffled, then shakes her head.

"I don't pity you," she says. "What happened yesterday?"

Slowly, Zahra recounts the story of how she came to be a traitor against her government, abandoned in the streets of Trellis.

She tells the Sergeant about her deviation, and life on the Outskirts, and even Anemos. When she mentions him, the Sergeant's eyes go wide. It's strange to remember the whole world has eyes on the boy she considers her little brother.

Then she continues to the trials— how she was almost caught at the beginning but lied her way into the Guide's good graces. She tells Sergeant Bellamy how she melted the handle of her sword and wound up drugged in a carriage with the woman in charge of Karneji's Facility.

"I don't know how you can handle someone the way they handled me," she says, her eyes glassy. "Like I wasn't even a person. But they did, and then they threw me in the back of a carriage, and now I'm here."

Bellamy blinks slowly, shaking her head.

"Why here?"

"Because that's where they were bringing Rosemarie," Zahra breathes. "Back here. Back to the Commander. And I guess because the Guide thought I might escape execution here, though I don't know why he cared. I'm not even sure he did."

Bellamy leans back in her seat, sighing heavily.

"When I first met your Guide, I met him as Charles," she says. "He traveled here with the old Guide, his father, who was a dreadful man outside of the peoples' eye. I've encountered him twice since then, and he's struck me the same every time."

"How is that?" Zahra asks, surprised to hear the woman ever knew him.

Sergeant Bellamy smiles sadly, shaking her head again.

"As a man doing what he thinks is right, and hating every minute of it."

"You think he's a good man?" Zahra asks.

"No," she replies. "But I think he'd like to be, and I think your execution is something he couldn't justify to himself."

They are both quiet then, listening to the radio blasting across the room.

Music, too, was hard to come by on the Outskirts, so Zahra tries to enjoy it, but her mind is a thousand other places.

"Let's talk about what comes next," Sergeant Bellamy says, sitting down her empty glass. "I can get you back on your feet, Zahra. I'm happy to do it. I can provide you with shelter, food, and whatever else you need. The only problem is, there are some serious legal issues with you being here."

"I imagined there would be."

The woman smiles gently, tapping her shoulder.

"I can get it straightened out for you. Albeit, not in the most legal way, but that hardly matters. In the meantime, we'll work on building your strength, bulking you up, and getting you to a place where your abilities are less volatile."

Zahra runs her burned hands over her thin arms, her cheeks warm.

"Yes, Ma'am."

"After that, the best place for you *will* be in the military. And I know that's unfortunate, but Trellis can be a tough place. Everyone your age is required to register, and Deviations are drafted in as soon as they're identified, so you're going to end up there one way or the other."

"I'm no soldier, Ms. Bellamy." Zahra says it like an apology, but the woman doesn't take it.

"I beg to differ, Zahra. Everything you've told me about your life implicates otherwise, but we'll argue that tomorrow. Tonight, you need rest." She stands up, holding out her hand. "Come on, let's get you cleaned up."

She follows the Sergeant outside, and finds that the rain has stopped.

INTERLUDE: BEFORE THE STORM

A large metal door grinds open, and Kieran lifts his head. He is clean now, dressed in the same green-gray military attire that Zahra will be handed an hour later.

The Commander walks him through the Facility with a tight grip on his arm.

"If you kill him..." he begins.

"I understand," Kieran says, calm. "I'm not going to kill it."

They are silent most of the walk, and Kieran keeps his eyes on the wall.

No clocks here. He wonders what time it is. He wonders why it matters.

The Commander's nails dig into his shoulder, but he does not mind the pain; only the hand. He imagines it cold— still— and a shudder passes through his body.

They stop in front of a door in the middle of a dark hallway, and the Commander turns a key.

"Hopefully you're less squeamish than their Guide," he says.

Kieran lowers his head as the door is opened, and he steps into the room slowly, letting it close and lock behind him.

He stands in the dimly lit room silently for a minute, letting his eyes adjust to the darkness, and watches as the Reaper in the center of the room begins to wake.

It lifts its head slowly and turns toward Kieran as if it can still see him through the gaping holes in its marred face.

"Is someone there?" it groans, its voice heavy and sick.

Kieran swallows hard, takes a step forward, and the man jerks back instinctively, crying out in pain.

The younger man looks down at the Reaper's hands— swollen, bleeding, mutilated like the rest of his body, nailed into the ground beneath him, and grimaces.

"I'm here," he whispers, his voice hardly audible over the groaning of the man in front of him.

"An E.D.T.," the Reaper breathes, in between gasps. "Dear God, please, no—"

"I'm not here to hurt you," Kieran says, kneeling beside him. "I'm here to help."

"We're enemies," the Reaper groans. "Enemies by birth..."

"I don't believe that," he says. "What's your name, sir?"

The Reaper falls quiet, weakly shaking his head.

"My name is William," he breathes. "No one has asked me that in years."

"William," Kieran repeats. "I'm afraid we don't have much time. Did you speak with a man and woman earlier today?"

"From The Ordinem?" the Reaper asks, hesitant.

"Yes, about crossing into Morta."

"Yes," William cries. "They said... They said they wanted peace—"

"They plan to kill them," Kieran interrupts. "All of them, all of the Grim living there. They've lied to the Commander, and they've lied to you."

A wave of pain comes from the man on the floor, so strong that Kieran worries he might suffocate under the weight of it.

"Is that possible?" he asks.

"We will cross from The Ordinem's territory. They will have as many men as they need, and the attack will be completely unexpected," Kieran whispers. "If they don't kill them all, they will kill most."

William turns to face the floor, his body breaking more with each strangled sob.

"I can't refuse them any longer," he cries. "They won't stop. They won't let me *die*. Even if I resist now—"

"Don't resist, then," Kieran says. "Take them across. Take them to an army." Darkness rushes through the boy's veins, causing his chest to cramp, but he remains steady. "Just don't take them to Morta."

"Are you suggesting—"

"I am suggesting," he breathes, "That we do whatever is necessary, sir."

William falls silent a moment, still writhing, and then, quietly:

"You understand that your life would also hang in the balance?"

"Yes," Kieran whispers. "But one life is a much easier loss to carry than a thousand."

PART THREE: THE BETRAYAL

"Life, although it may only be an accumulation of anguish,
is dear to me, and I will defend it."
—— Mary Shelley, Frankenstein

Chapter Thirty-Two

I carus is sitting at his kitchen table when he first hears what the Ordinem has planned. It is confidential, of course. He is not even supposed to be hearing it. But his Mother is one of his best friends. She tells him everything.

"I don't think it would be fair not to tell you," she says. "It's a dangerous thing we're walking into, and if something happens, I don't want you caught off guard."

He stares down at his fork, unable to breathe.

"Th... this could start a war," he mutters. It is the least of his concerns, but it's still present. "You're lying to the Commander."

"It'll be worth it if we succeed," Aliya insists. "If we don't, he'll never know."

Icarus' body feels heavy as stone. Today was the first day since the ceremony that he thought he might get some relief from the anxiety that's plagued him at the Compounds. He was looking forward to something safe: a dinner with his family. That hope has been shot to hell.

He rubs his hand over his face, careful not to catch the scab where the Guide cut him, and shakes his head.

"I don't know what to say."

"I don't like it," Jack mutters, his arms crossed. "The plan is grotesque; gassing them so they can't fight? Slaughtering them while they sleep? That's the work of cowards."

"Grim are a difficult enemy," Aliya says. "We're doing what we have to do."

"We're committing a war crime."

"It's what we swore ourselves to," Icarus interrupts, distant. "They don't deserve to live. They're abominations, and you're treating them as such."

Jack stares at him long and hard, a brokenness in his eyes, but Icarus watches his mother.

He wonders if she is proud of the filth he has spewed.

Instead of responding, she moves the conversation on to other things. She discusses Trellis, and the Ceremony, and asks Icarus how his first week at the Compounds has been. He lies and insists it has been fine. He doesn't tell them he hasn't slept since Karneji, or the way he has been harming himself to cope with the guilt he feels; guilt for being Ordinem, but even more for continuing when he knows his death would benefit the Code more than his life.

He has been carrying that burden for a long time, but now, never able to escape the reminders, it is becoming unbearable.

He is back to wearing something under his uniform so that no one sees what he has inflicted upon himself if his shirt comes up during his exercises. But he can't think about that. Not on top of the news he has received.

The news makes him question whether it is even worth fighting.

"How's the bird doing?" he asks, changing the subject again.

His father forces a weak smile, grief in every line of his face.

"Took the bandage off yesterday," he says. "Little guy's made a remarkable recovery. We'll need more seeds for him, with how much he's been eating."

"I'll go to the market when I get a chance," Icarus mutters, still picking at his food. He wants to see the little creature but doesn't have the heart for it tonight. "It's been good seeing you guys. I've missed you."

"We've missed you too," his mother says.

He walks back to the Compounds in silence, not even turning to glance at the shadows that stalk him down the streets. He thinks of talking with Zahra but can't bring himself to do it. He thinks of praying, but he only prays for others these days, only when he is most desperate. He can't trust himself to know the voice of the Wind from the groans of Assecula. That's one thing they always emphasized in school: that some Reapers die still claiming to have seen Inanis. But demons can't pray to the light; they can only be fooled by the darkness.

Being what he is, it isn't worth praying.

There is one place left that might offer him guidance, but he can't tell the Counselor of the true conflict inside him.

He will go soon, anyway. He will think of a lie close enough to the truth to help but far enough from it to leave him alive.

He'll think of something.

Icarus walks through the door of the Compounds with his hands in his pockets. The air is different inside, cool enough to make him shiver. On the other hand, the light is warm and dim— soaked up by the deep red of the floors.

One of the men he trains with tips his head in greeting as he walks past, and Icarus responds with a small smile that shows none of his grief. It's strange how much more civilly they treat him now that he has taken the vow. He knows from how they look at him that nothing fundamental has changed, but they have started to treat him like he is one of them. He supposes he *is* one of them.

Now, past the exams, with their mark carved into his skin, they have no right to question him. He is safe in the midst of those that are hunting his kind.

It causes him no relief.

Walking down the arched hall, he looks at the art decorating the walls and the story it tells:

The Reaper that hid in Ordinem garb for years, waiting for its moment to strike— the journey it took to become the one known as the Oracamatis. It gathered four others of its kind and one Deviation in Morta under the cover of twilight.

The painting of what happened next gives Icarus chills every time he sees it: A woman, eyes to heaven, bombarded by shadows. Her expression is hopeless, and those of the five around her are triumphant. The Reapers used their power to merge the woman's soul with the spirit of Assecula, creating a weapon like nothing seen before: The first E.D.T.

He stops in front of the next painting for a long moment, staring at the depiction of the veil between realms being torn open— darkness descending upon Terra, killing nearly everyone it touched.

He knows what comes next; the forming of the Ordinem's territory —the killing of the Reapers and the protection of what life remained.

The call to end the war once and for all, and not to stop until every agent of darkness in the realms of Terra and Morta has been sent back to the place that birthed it.

That is what his parents, his teachers, and everyone else are working toward. That is what he should be working toward. He resents himself for wanting so badly to live.

"Icarus."

Zahra's voice startles him, and he looks at the floor to hide it. He should have known better than to try and avoid her. It never works. At least, it hasn't this past week.

It would be easier if he wanted to.

"Zahra," he replies. *"Isn't it late in Trellis?"*

"Early," she corrects. *"Bellamy's making me rise hours before the sun. I hate it."*

Icarus lets out a heavy sigh, a smile tugging at his lips as he lifts his face, turning away from the paintings and back toward the hall.

"Training?"

"Push-ups, crunches, squats... Jogging in one place, for Inanis' sake," Zahra says. *"In the Outskirts, we built muscle from actually doing things. I hate this. It's only the one thing that gets me through it."*

"And what is that?" Icarus asks.

"The thought of kicking your ass in our next spar, Leech."

He laughs despite himself, folding his hands behind his back. *"Good luck."*

"I won't need it."

"You know, I've been training a good deal myself," he reminds her.

The words are a vast understatement.

Since the ceremony, Icarus has trained day and night almost without ceasing; he has only stopped when his friends have made him, or his body has refused to keep going.

It's better than thinking.

"Prove it," she challenges, and he shakes his head, keeping his eyes low.

"What do you mean, prove it?"

"You've shifted before, haven't you?" The words send chills over his shoulders. He swallows hard. *"Not here. I imagine that would be too challenging. Of course, I don't know, you are Grim."*

"You assumed correctly," he affirms.

"But we could meet in Inanis, couldn't we?" He can almost hear her hesitating. He's fidgeting with the hems of his sleeves. *"I know I'm not the only one that's thought about it."*

She isn't.

He thought of it the instant she told him what had happened to her. He even wondered, briefly, if he might be able to bring her back from the place with him.

Then he remembered what he was and buried the idea along with many others.

Icarus isn't even confident he has seen Inanis anymore.

"It's too dangerous," he insists. "Even if it wasn't, I have no idea how I'd find you in a void that vast. There's so much space between us."

"You can't feel me, then?" she asks.

He exhales heavily, his lips pressed together.

"I never said that."

CHAPTER THIRTY-THREE

Icarus pulls back the arrow in his hand, stretching the string of his bow, and squints through tired eyes. Three arrows stick out of the target in front of him, all at various points on the edge, and two lie on the ground behind it, but none lie even remotely near the center.

He steadies his hands and lets out a long sigh, but just as he goes to shoot, Cole bursts into laughter behind him.

Icarus jumps, and the arrow flies free, sticking into the wall behind the target. He turns sharply and finds Anemos hanging by his knees from the pull-up bar across the room.

"My word," he mutters. "What are you—"

"He's being a fool, is what he's doing," Cole interrupts, his arms crossed over his chest. Anemos doesn't argue. His face is red with laughter, his hair hanging wildly.

"Please help me," he pleads. "I didn't think it through, I admit it, but I'm stuck."

"And it serves you right." Cole laughs uncontrollably, still dismissing his struggling friend. "I don't know what you were thinking."

"Does the Code not call us to mercy, Cole?" Anemos snaps, and it breaks what little composure Icarus has. He sets his bow and arrows on the floor and sprints to where they stand, pulling his stranded friend from the bar and letting him fall.

"You know how smart I think you are," he says, watching as Anemos continues to laugh, gripping his sides in pain. "But you're so stupid."

"You're all so mean to me," Anemos groans, wiping tears from his eyes. "You hang from your hands and set a record; I do it from my knees, and I'm stupid? That's some bullshit."

Icarus puts his face in his hands, laughing so hard it makes his chest hurt. He only looks up again when Cole wraps an arm around him, giving his shoulder an almost aggressive squeeze.

"Finally," he remarks. "The stoic Icarus cracks a smile. I'll have to hold on killing the imbecile after all. He's done good work."

"You all messed up my shot," Icarus responds, and Anemos cackles, pulling himself up from the floor.

"I think you did as well as you were going to," he teases. "You've hit everything but the target."

"Hey," Icarus frowns in mock offense. "Come on."

"You're good at lots of things, Icarus. It's okay to admit this one isn't your strong suit," Cole remarks. "I mean, it's *really* not your strong suit, but that's okay."

"You guys are so m...mean—"

"You're the one that makes us train at these ungodly hours if we ever want to see you," Anemos counters, and Icarus' shoulders fall.

It's all in good spirits, but he knows there is truth to the statement.

"You're telling m...me this isn't how you want to spend your every night?" he jokes, and Anemos shakes his head, picking the bow and arrows up from the floor.

"No, not even close. I'd like to be sleeping. I'm tired."

"I'd be tired too, if I had to listen to my whining as much as you have to listen to yours," Cole says, and then he snaps around, startled by the sound of an arrow striking the target across the room. Icarus turns and finds that Anemos has hit just right of the bullseye.

They make eye contact, and Icarus hisses, walking away.

"Alright, that's it. I'm going to bed. I'm done."

"I'm sorry, I don't mean to be so funny and talented," Anemos shouts, running to catch up with them. "It just comes naturally to me."

Soon, they are back in their shared room, Anemos and Cole sitting together, splitting a plate of food they took from the Compounds' kitchen.

Icarus didn't get anything. He is reading a book of Code-reliant philosophy, curled up on his bed with his back against the wall.

Cole holds out a dinner roll in his direction— having already buttered it, and Icarus looks up, shaking his head.

"Come on," Cole insists. "You're working out twenty hours a day. You have to eat."

Reluctantly, he reaches out and takes it, even though he isn't hungry. He sets his book on the bed and takes a bite, folding his arms over his chest.

"Thank you," he says, and Cole nods, watching as Anemos scarfs down his half of the plate.

"How's your book?" Cole asks, and Icarus nods, chewing slowly.

"Good."

"What's it about?"

"Oh, it's just more philosophy. About the same thing as the rest: how to be a better follower of the Code, how we ought to see the world around us according to it."

"So, spit some wisdom," Anemos says, his mouth full. "Give us a word."

Icarus glances at the window, watching the leaves blow behind it.

"I don't have any wisdom," he mutters. "That's why I'm reading it."

Both of Icarus' friends look at him in a way that makes him feel like the iron-red walls might swallow him.

"I think life is a better teacher than books are," Anemos says, finally. "You've lived a lot of life. You probably have more wisdom than that book already."

"Someone wrote it, though. It's not just words on paper. They lived, too."

"Well, sure," Cole nods.

"And it's not just anyone either," Icarus says. "It's an Ordinem man. He's a hero to a lot of people. He served on one of the first Councils—"

"That doesn't really mean anything, though," Anemos remarks, and Icarus shrugs.

"I don't know," he says.

They finish the rest of their meal without much conversation, but Icarus doesn't bother opening the book again. It was making him sick anyway.

Instead, he uses the quiet moment to take in the room, something he hasn't really done since he moved into it. One single bed and one bunk. Carpeted floors— which seems senseless, considering they are training to be soldiers. However, Ordinem warriors tend to live in luxury. There is only one window, and one table next to it with two chairs. Icarus is the only one that has used it so far.

It isn't homey, but it is starting to feel lived in. Anemos and Cole have stopped bothering to make their beds in the morning, and Icarus has books strewn about everywhere.

He keeps finding crumbs but tries not to mind them— or the dirty uniforms thrown over the curtain rod.

"I think we should bring the bird here," Cole says. "No one would ever know."

"I told you already; he has a name," Anemos says, and Cole rolls his eyes, fighting a grin.

"I think we smuggle Chip in, then. Did you see him tonight, Icarus?"

"I actually didn't get a chance, but m...my dad said he's doing really well."

"You didn't get a chance to see our son?" Anemos asks, and the words are the final straw. Cole chuckles, patting him on the shoulder.

"Okay, it's too late to keep talking. We're going to bed."

Icarus stands, holding out his hand.

"Give me the plate. I'll take it downstairs."

"We are capable of cleaning up after ourselves, you know," Cole says, but Anemos hands him the plate anyway, collapsing back on the bed.

"It's fine," Icarus laughs. "I'm going anyway. I need to get my laundry, which was hung on a line, like it's supposed to be. You know, instead of a curtain rod."

"If my clothes needed to dry, I would've hung them on a line, but they just need some air. Some Higher-class Ordinem bullshit washing jeans after every wear."

Icarus lowers his face, trying to keep it straight, and shakes his head in mock judgment.

"Whatever. I don't want to fold my clothes tonight, so keep the top bunk open."

"You expect me to sleep with this rascal?" Anemos remarks, and Icarus nods sarcastically.

"I think you guys will be fine."

"What is that supposed to mean?"

"I'm going now," he says, opening the door. "You guys can p-put it tog...gether while I'm gone, I'm sure."

CHAPTER THIRTY-FOUR

The Compounds' kitchen is vacant at this hour. Icarus stands alone at the sink, washing his friends' plate and a few other dishes left behind.

The walls in the kitchen remind him of the University— light brown stone in large, decorative arches— so he doesn't mind lingering. The smell of soap makes him think of nights in his kitchen with his father. Even here, though, the comfort only goes so far.

Words are carved into the wall before him: *Remember your nature.*

He has studied enough to know what it refers to, but it hardly matters. The words are part of a larger thought. You should remember your nature as a member of the Ordinem. You are a servant of others, never to place yourself above the men beside you, and never to expect service from anyone else.

Wash your own dishes, cook your own food, take a little but give more. Icarus doesn't mind the sentiment, but he isn't sure of his nature anymore. Even if he wants to be a servant, he is also a Jakaran, and a Reaper. He has spent his whole life trying to *forget* his nature.

He dries the dishes and puts them away as quietly as possible, every sound echoing in the space around him. Then he moves from the kitchen to one of the building's many doors, stepping outside. The air is cool enough that the breeze gives him chills, but he doesn't mind that either. He hates heat like he hates sand. It all reminds him of home.

The clothesline creaks in the otherwise silent night, and he walks over to it, grabbing one of the baskets stacked by the door on his way. It is a *strangely* silent night. He can hear the grass crushing under his feet. He can hear his clothes beating in the wind. It makes him uneasy, so he begins collecting it, eager to get back inside.

There is a field behind the Compounds, the same field that stretches to the cliffs and drops off into the ocean. Staring out at it, he often feels like he is at the edge of the world— like if he ran far enough, he could fall off. Tonight, though, his mind is on everything it could hide. It makes him think of the high grass in Morta, the way it blows and blurs in the wind, becoming one with the horizon. Sometimes it is almost as beautiful, but now, the horizon is an eerie pool of blackness.

By the time Icarus gets to his last article of clothing, he has thoroughly convinced himself that something is watching him, blending into that darkness. He pauses and watches the shadows for a long moment before pulling his shirt from the line and throwing it in the basket, backing away from the field without ever moving his eyes.

In the end, his effort doesn't matter much. When he returns to the building, he feels for the door and finds it hanging open. His stomach sinks, his pulse quickening as he turns to face it.

He doesn't see anything in the kitchen. He doesn't hear anything in the adjacent halls. He attempts to close the door behind him as he steps through it, but it catches. Whispering a silent prayer, Icarus turns back around.

The Malemortum's eyes are the first thing he notices; they are the same inky black as the horizon. They stare past the cracked door, just above where the thing's pale gray hand holds it open.

Its hand looks burnt. Icarus thinks he is going to be sick.

"Let me in—"

He slams the door, overpowering the thing, and bolts it shut, stumbling away. Even with the ringing in his ears and the vertigo that has suddenly overtaken him, Icarus can hear the thing groaning outside, banging its bloodied fists against the door.

He drops the laundry basket and runs, locking himself in the nearest bathroom and gripping the sink in terror.

He runs the water to block out the sounds he is convinced he can still hear and splashes it on his face, unable to breathe. His vision is going in and out, the corners all blurry and dark, and the pressure in his ears makes him want to put his head down between his knees.

"P-pull yourself together," he whispers to himself. "Come on, you've gotta breathe."

He clears his throat and tries to steady himself, but when he looks into the mirror, his reflection takes what little strength he has left.

He can't meet his own eyes as it happens. He can only stare into the sink as the room darkens. That wasn't him in the mirror. He tries to rid the image from his mind but to little avail. The room keeps growing darker.

"Please," he cries. "P-p-please make it stop. If anything is listening..."

The shadows solidify and wrap around his throat, choking him. Icarus reaches up and tries to pull them away, but despite being able to feel them— warm, slick, and *living*— he cannot grab hold of them.

They lift him off the floor by his neck, and he kicks his legs to get free until his eyes find their way back to the mirror, and he falls entirely still.

The room is gone, except for the mirror and the sink, and the light is gone, but he can still see clearly.

His eyes have gone black in his reflection, and blood runs from them— from his nose, from his ears, from his mouth— His skin has turned a pale gray, and purple veins stand out on his neck and his arms.

He is too afraid to scream.

The shadows pull him toward the mirror so quickly that it jars his spine, and suddenly, what sounds like a hundred voices fill the space around him.

"This is what you are."

"No..." His voice comes out strained and breathless; he has no belief in his own words.

The darkness senses it.

The sink disappears, and the image in the mirror dims, the darkness growing stronger. Wind begins to blow from every direction, so cold that it burns his skin.

"Is this your Inanis, Reaper?"

"No," he whispers.

The darkness holds him more tightly. He thinks it might crush him.

"You are deceived."

"N...No..."

"They don't want you here."

He falls silent, his body beginning to lose its fight.

"You are not welcome in the Ordinem. You are not welcome in your home."

He thinks of his mother, and his chest becomes impossibly tighter.

"You are not welcome in Inanis..."

His hands return to his neck, and this time, he manages to grab the thing but still can't pull it away.

"Let m...me go. In the name of—"

All of the wind is knocked out of him, and he is thrown back against the wall. The mirror grows until it covers the whole space in front of him, and his reflection stares him in the eyes.

The darkness forms a hand and clamps his mouth shut as his reflection steps forward.

It opens its hands, revealing a bleeding red line down the center of each, and smiles obscenely, its liquid eyes blinking open wider.

"We are cursed—"

"Icarus?"

Zahra's voice breaks through the shadows, and Icarus shuts his eyes tight, sobs wracking his chest.

"Icarus, can you hear me? Is something wrong?"

"I can hear you."

"Is something wrong?" she repeats.

He can hear the sink again, running on the other side of the room. He doesn't feel the thing's grip around his throat. He opens his eyes and finds himself curled up on the floor, his back against the bathroom wall.

"I was asleep, and this dream woke me up," Zahra continues. *"I saw you. You were being held by something dark, and I woke up with this heavy feeling in my chest."*

Icarus rests his face against his arms, struggling to pull air into his lungs.

"I'm okay," he lies. *"It was just a dream."*

He is shaking so violently that his teeth are chattering.

"Don't worry about me, Zahra." The words are a plea. *"Don't dream of me."*

"I can't help it if I dream of you."

"You dream because you worry," he states. *"Don't. Please. I don't want to wake you up."*

"Something's wrong. I feel it. Talk to me."

Icarus ignores her, only curling deeper into himself.

"You said you'd be some type of home for me," she reminds him. *"Let me be the same for you. Tell me what's happening."*

He pulls in a heavy breath, and chills spill down his arms, enveloping him.

"I can't," he says, his face sticky with tears. He rubs his eyes and checks to make sure he doesn't have another nosebleed. *"There's nothing to tell you. It's the same thing it's always been."*

"Icarus..."

She doesn't say anything else in response, and Icarus doesn't blame her. There is nothing she could say that would make it better. There is no way to help him.

He is starting to think there is only one way for his story to end.

"I'm okay," he says again. *"I'm going to speak to someone tomorrow..."*

Warmth spreads over Icarus' shoulders, and he falls quiet, his breath the only thing breaching the room's silence. At first, he thinks he imagines the sensation, but then it grows heavier, wrapping around his back and shoulders like a blanket.

It is not unlike the feeling in his chest whenever he hears Zahra's voice.

He closes his eyes, swallowing hard.

"Zahra?"

"Can you feel me?" she asks, and he nods, weak.

"Yes." He doesn't question how, even though he wonders. All he can do is lean into the distant embrace, collapsing into its safety.

"Just rest, then," she says. *"You don't have to say anything."*

His breath comes heavy, his heartbeat slowing.

"I see you, in Inanis. You're like a pale shadow. Whatever darkness is plaguing you doesn't make it this far."

CHAPTER THIRTY-FIVE

Icarus wakes up at six in the morning, still curled up on the bathroom floor. He opens his eyes and squints against the harsh white light.

He is calm, but he is heavy.

The feeling of Zahra's arms around him is gone, and the feeling in his chest has grown lighter. She must have fallen back asleep.

He will not allow himself to do the same, but he will try to stay calm enough not to wake her again.

Everything hurts, but he pulls himself from the floor and back into the hallway, glancing at the mirror on his way out and finding it unchanged.

The clothes he dropped are still scattered, and he isn't surprised. Cole and Anemos have no reason to suspect something went wrong when he has vanished *every* night. They probably went to sleep, thinking that he went to do more training.

He gathers his clothes, sits the basket in a corner of the room where he believes it will be left alone, and then abandons it, making his way back through the main building.

There is no plan besides his destination, but he walks toward it anyway, not paying any mind to the shadows that have slithered into the building with nightfall. He keeps his eyes on the floor— blood red like the cut on his hand.

There is no other place to go, seeing what he saw. *This* is his duty, even if he doesn't understand it.

Soon, he is stepping out into the city, leaving the Compounds behind. It is still too early for the sun to have risen, and with the heavily polluted sky, he has no starlight to light his path. It wouldn't make sense if he did. The path to the tall gray building in the distance allows for very little wonder— it is all cast in the shadow of its destination.

Icarus arrives with shaking hands. He climbs the stairs to the door even though he isn't confident his legs will carry him.

The Temple of the Counselor was the first building built in the Ordinem territory. Its walls are engraved with the movement's history, and the windows are all red stained-glass. The place is always open and always guarded.

The Counselor never leaves it. He is the holiest man in the city— above even the Guide. To be in his presence is to touch Inanis, and maybe that is why Icarus seeks him now. If he burns up under the saint's gaze, at least he will no longer suffer.

He steps forward hesitantly, his eyes on the guard: A woman with hair as dark and gray as soot. She is wearing a red robe and standing beside a silver altar.

She looks at him without sympathy. "You've come to see the Counselor?"

The wind blows steadily, chasing his hair into his face.

"The most gracious of all," he responds, and she lowers her head. She holds a dagger in his direction.

"Atone," she insists.

He looks at the blade for a second and then takes it from her, dragging it across his palm, reopening the mark before it has even healed. He lets his blood fall upon the altar, but never moves his eyes from the woman, who steps aside without offering him a bandage. This is sin, too. And maybe that's why he does it.

Grim blood is cursed, but here he is, spilling it in the holiest place he can.

He has no idea what his motivation is anymore, but he steps past her anyway, pushing open the heavy wooden door to the Counselor's dwelling.

Icarus has only been brought to this place three times— as a seven-, eight-, and nine-year-old child. He had to be brought here and blessed if he was to stay in Ordinem territory. He had to come back and confess. It looks just like he remembers it looking:

All white marble, the floor scattered with dull red stains. There is nothing else, save a stone table in the center of the room and a large silver statue at the far end. It is a sculpture of Nathaniel Warnock, their now-dead saint. He stands with his eyes to the heavens, crushing underfoot a thing that Icarus knows is not human.

It is *him*.

A shuffling to the side of it pulls his eyes and thoughts away, toward the Most Gracious Counselor, who enters the room without expression.

Icarus falls to his knees as soon as he sees him, bowing his head in a show of respect. He clutches his bleeding hand to his chest.

"Your honor," he mutters. "I rep...pent." There is no reply, but he can hear the man approaching him. He can feel it as the man stops in front of him—his heart pounds.

There is risk, being here. Maybe that is why he has come. Some say the Counselor is all-knowing, and being known is Icarus' worst fear.

"I repent," he repeats, shaking under the Counselor's gaze. "I repent of everything."

"I've not seen you in eleven years," the Counselor says, his voice blank. The words are like a spear through Icarus' chest. "Lift your face. Look at me."

Hesitant, Icarus looks up into the man's pale gray eyes.

The Counselor, too, looks just as Icarus remembers. He looks *ancient,* white as snow with hair that matches.

"You've been gone too long," the Counselor says. "A boy of your nature should have come frequently. I've thought of you often, and wondered about your fate. Do you know why your parents kept you away?"

"You frightened me," Icarus confesses. "I begged them to keep me away."

"They should have brought you anyway. Then you might not be suffering," the Counselor states. "Alas, some things have to be learned. You're here now. Tell me what's driven you back."

"I had a vision—"

"Of what?" Icarus attempts to lower his face, but the Counselor shakes his head. "No. Keep your eyes on me."

"It was of m...me," he forces, struggling not to flinch under the Counselor's eyes, which seem to bore into his very soul. "My eyes were dark, and both of my hands were marked. The world around me was just... blackness."

The Counselor only looks at him for a long moment, considering.

"Your allegiance is split," he says, finally. "You've only just taken your vows. Did you mean them?"

"With all of my heart."

"What about your mind?" the Counselor asks. "Your body? Your soul?"

"...I don't know," Icarus mutters.

"Your heart might be with the Code, Icarus. But perhaps the rest of you is elsewhere."

"Where?"

"I suspect you know where." The man takes several steps away and sits down at the stone table, still holding eye contact. "You repented thrice. You can't repent without confession. What are you apologizing for?"

Icarus hesitates, and the Counselor continues, unaffected.

"Have you brought it before your god?" he asks, and Icarus shakes his head.

"Sometimes I worry God doesn't hear me. It f...feels like there's a wall up between me and Inanis and everything that dwells there."

"And that's why you've come to me." The man nods, beckoning him forward. "Rise. Join me here."

Icarus pulls himself up and over to where the Counselor sits, taking the seat across from him. He wants to read the words inscribed on the table, but forces himself to keep his gaze steady.

"You're a sinner," the man says. "Your sin serves as a veil between you and the holy. You know this, and that's why you've come."

"Yes, Myon," Icarus nods.

"You haven't told me what you seek. Is it someone to take your words to that holy place? Intercede for you? Or are you ready to leave your sin behind?"

"I've never wanted it," Icarus mutters. "I've been trying to abandon it my whole life. I need prayer, and I need my prayers heard. So I suppose... I suppose I seek everything, Myon. I'm desperate, and I'm tired."

The Counselor watches him, considering, and then reaches forward, his carved palm facing the ceiling.

His eyes are compassionate, Icarus thinks. There is some crack in his expressionlessness.

"Take my hand," he says, and Icarus shakes his head.

"I'm bleeding."

"There is no atonement without some shedding of blood. Take my hand."

Icarus reaches forward, trembling, and grips the holy man's hand. The second he does, a cry breaks from his lips, and he doesn't understand why.

"I'm sorry," he whimpers, and the Counselor nods.

"Cry as long as you need," he says. "Release your pain, and then we'll speak of your sin."

"There's so much of it," Icarus mutters, his chest tight. "Sometimes I think it's all I am... S-sin and pain."

"That must be exhausting."

"It is." He breathes deeply, trying to steady himself. "It *is*. It's like... It's like I'm being ripped apart. Like... everything I am, and everything I want to be... I don't know."

It is silent in the Counselor's temple. The pale light and white walls make the silence feel cold.

Icarus' cries are the only thing to break it for several minutes, and the only thing that keeps Icarus from noticing how chilled the room is making him is the Counselor's hand.

When the holy man releases his grip, he shivers. He pulls back his wounded hand and tries not to look at it, nauseated by the smell of his blood.

He feels so sick, but this is helping. He is talking. There is someone with him who cares—

"Confess your sins," the Counselor says. "I will take them to Inanis. I will bring word of your forgiveness, and we will work together to purge the darkness from your soul."

Icarus watches him with pleading eyes, his stomach twisting.

"The words of our prophet offer life, child. Receive them, follow them, and break free from this hell you exist in."

He has never wanted anything as much as he has wanted freedom.

"I m...m-miss the person I was... before," he mutters. "Before here. Sometimes I think... M...maybe that's me, and not this. I feel like I have two souls, and they're killing each other—"

"Tell me about before," the Counselor interrupts, and Icarus nods, weak.

"Before, I was a Jakaran. I *was* my homeland. I believed in magic, and I saw the world as a big... *Wonderful* place, full of stories, and I wanted to read all of them."

"You romanticize that period of your life."

"N...no. It was miserable, but I was... I had hope. I didn't see what you all have shown me. I didn't know how *awful* this world was."

"And that ignorance was bliss for you."

It was ignorance, Icarus thinks. It had to be. A beautiful world would not have taken his home.

"Me and my sister used to look at the stars and talk about the places we would go, and the people we would be, and it was none of this. I didn't dream of fighting the whole world, and fighting most of myself—"

"Your problem is that you see who you were before as who you are now, Icarus. You're still that boy from Jakara. That's the narrative you're choosing."

"Maybe—"

"You say you're ready to leave your sin behind, but you're clinging to it. You're telling me of stars, and stories and dreams, as if you weren't a doomed child born in a land of hedonism."

Shame settles in Icarus' chest, making his cheeks flush.

"You were thin as paper when you were brought here, Icarus," the Counselor continues. "You were starving, covered with bruises and scars. You didn't speak a word the day you were blessed, and you flinched away when I stepped toward you. Tell me, were your parents people of stars, stories, and dreams?"

It is a fight not to sob. He shakes his head.

"They hit me," he says.

The Counselor does not offer him any sympathy.

"Has it occurred to you that perhaps you cling to your past because you grieve it? You make your country a place of wonder because you can't accept that it wasn't. Have you ever considered that you cling to something that never existed? This boy from Jakara that you still think you are... It has never been something *worth* being. And it is easier to cling to what it wasn't than to accept the tragedy that it was."

"What if that *is* what I am?" Icarus asks, and the Counselor shakes his head.

"Then you repent," he says. "And you keep repenting until your nature is replaced with a better one."

Finally, Icarus lets his eyes fall. He feels the heaviness returning, but tries to swallow the words anyway. Maybe there is truth to them.

He has never felt like he has been worth anything.

"But... M...my sister..." he mutters. "I had a sister, and if I let go of all of it..."

"You let go of her," the Counselor finishes. "But holding onto her is holding onto everything else. Holding onto a boy abused by his own parents."

Icarus doesn't respond to that. He only continues to stare at the table, his eyes too full of tears to read the words written upon it.

"I still grieve her, even though I shouldn't," he whispers. "I dream of finding her alive, and sometimes I wish I could take her place."

"That's senseless," the Counselor says, and Icarus tries to imagine some gentleness in the words, his chest aching.

"I know."

"It's over, Icarus. She's gone, and she's not coming back. At this point, grief is just an indulgence. You've got to see the truth of the situation. If she had lived through the raid, you would have both been left to the streets. Jack might not have saved you if he had been required to take you both. It's better for one to be saved than for two to be lost."

Icarus can't help but think that the Counselor is wrong about what his father would have done, but there might be some truth in the rest: They might have never found Jack and gone elsewhere. They would have died in the rubble—

"In Jakara, you were both as good as dead. You would have become reprehensible people. Just like your parents."

His heart plummets into his stomach, and he closes his eyes, barely able to breathe.

How can he respond to a thing like that?

"Some truths are hard," the Counselor says, when a moment has passed. "Especially when you have become accustomed to lies. I *will* pray for you, that your eyes will be opened, but the next steps are yours to take. I cannot bring you forgiveness for sins you want to hold on to."

"Tell me what to do, and I'll do it," Icarus pleads. "Tell me how to let go, and I will."

"Repent," the Counselor repeats. "Pray. Fast. Return to me and let me aid you. If we don't find a path to your freedom through acts of the mind, seek physical atonement. Kill the person you once were and become new. *Honor* the words of the prophet—"

"I repent," Icarus forces. "I repent *every day...*"

There is no reply, and Icarus shudders at the absence of the man's voice.

He leans his head forward on the table, his eyes closed.

"I *scorn* the boy from Jakara, and everything he was. I'll do whatever I have to do—"

A hand is placed on his shoulder, and he jerks away, panicked. When he opens his eyes, he sees it is only the guard that offered him the dagger. He looks around and finds that the Counselor has vanished.

"He's finished with you," the woman says coldly, and Icarus nods.

He stands with his voice still caught in his throat.

CHAPTER THIRTY-SIX

Icarus makes it back to his room just before sunrise and finds Anemos and Cole curled up together, just as he expected they would be.

He shuts the door quietly so as not to wake them, but Cole opens his eyes anyway, outstretching his hand as Icarus walks by.

"Hey," he drawls, his voice tired. "Where'd you go?"

Icarus takes his hand and gives it a tight squeeze before letting it go and climbing into bed.

"Training," he whispers. "Reading, in the library."

"Were we bothering you that much?"

Icarus forces a small smile, shaking his head. "No."

"You know you have to sleep sometime."

"I know. That's why I'm here."

"Have you been crying?" Cole pulls himself up slightly, careful not to wake the boy beside him. "You're hoarse, and your face is red."

"I'm just tired," Icarus forces, but Cole does not believe him.

He watches him for a long moment before lying back down, closing his eyes.

"I'm here for you, whenever you're ready to talk. Don't worry about waking me."

Anemos shifts in his sleep, wrapping his arms around Cole's waist and tucking his face into his neck, and Icarus watches, laughing under his breath.

"It looks like you have your hands full," he whispers.

Cole would be okay without him, he thinks. Anemos might miss some sleep, but he would recover, too.

"My hands are never too full," Cole insists. "You're my friend, I'm here for you."

"I know you are," Icarus says. "It means a lot. Thank you for caring."

Cole nods, brushing Anemos' hair away from his eyes.

"Thank *you* for caring, Icarus. Thank you for letting things like this happen."

Icarus lies down, his chest heavy. "You don't need to thank m...me for that."

"If anyone else saw me holding him like this, they'd—"

"You're friends m...making do with only one available bed," Icarus interrupts. "That's not forbidden anywhere."

Cole hesitates a long moment and then lets out a weary sigh.

"I wish I could hold him every night. I wish this place was less cruel."

Icarus stares at the ceiling, rubbing his wounded palm. "Me too."

Chapter Thirty-Seven

The days stretch on with the weight of months. Icarus drags himself through them like a dead man. He laughs with his friends, but when the night comes and the distraction ceases, he sinks deep into darkness and depression. He never sleeps. He never prays. Only the shadows keep him company.

This is life in the Ordinem. This is life for the Grim. This is all that life will ever have for him.

"Come to dinner," Cole begs, tugging on his arm. "The training room will still be there. You need to eat."

"I'll be sick if I do," Icarus says. "I don't have any appetite."

"Maybe you should see the nurse. I don't remember the last time you did."

"I ate this afternoon," he lies. "I'm okay. Don't worry."

The fasting is leaving him with ringing in his ears and stars in his vision.

CHAPTER THIRTY-EIGHT

"Tell me about Trellis," Icarus says. He is in the city market, searching for seeds. *"Is it like home?"*

"I don't remember home very well," Zahra admits. *"From what my parents told me, though... It's pretty different. It's not desert. It's full of trees, and plants, and fucking mosquitoes."*

Icarus laughs quietly, pulling several bags from the shelf in front of him.

"Not fucking mosquitoes."

"I'm always covered in bites," she says. *"I think the humidity draws them here."*

"What else is there?" he asks.

"Birds. Lots of birds."

This should be enough feed to keep Chip for months, Icarus thinks. He'll be fine. He'll be taken care of by Cole and Anemos, if not by his parents.

"I'd like to see that," he says. *"This bird, here... It sings in the afternoon. I'd love to hear more than one. I think it'd be beautiful."*

"It is," Zahra replies. *"There's a lot of beauty here, even with the war. I'm starting to think they lied to me on the Outskirts. I'm starting to see life here."*

"You think you could be happy there?"

"Maybe. I miss my family, but... God, Icarus. There's music here. Everywhere. It was so hard to find music on the Outskirts. I had one cassette."

"Music is one of the things I miss the most," Icarus says. *"Sing me something. Anything worth sharing."*

"My baby's coming home tonight." Her voice floats in his mind, painting a soft smile across his features. *"Gonna make love till it's all alright. Gonna stay up, sing the moon a song. Going to drink till the whiskey's gone... Ta-da. That's all you get."*

"You don't see me, but I assure you, I'm clapping."

"Sure you are."

He buys the bird feed, shoves it in a large bag, and leaves the market, walking towards his home with slow steps.

"How long till you're enlisted?" he asks.

"Sergeant Bellamy says she thinks I'll be ready within a month," Zahra says. *"But I don't know about that."*

"It'll be good for you, being around other people... Not being cooped up in Bellamy's house."

"I'm bad at making friends. It'll be just like this, but with people beating me up all the time."

"You're going to be fine, Zahra," he laughs. *"If anyone tries anything, set them on fire."*

CHAPTER THIRTY-NINE

Again, Icarus sits at the table with his family. This time, though, his demeanor has lightened.

"I'm doing good," he says. "Starting to adjust to things. I've gotten in a lot of good training."

"That's great, Icarus," his mother says. "I told you it would get easier, see?"

Jack watches his son with doubtful eyes.

"You've lost weight," he says, and Icarus nods, taking a bite.

"It's been hard to keep up with how much I've been doing, but I'll get it straightened out. Hey, that reminds me— I've got food for Chip, in the bag by the door."

"Oh, we got some," Aliya says. "You didn't need to."

"Always good to have backups," he shrugs. "Actually, I'm gonna go see him. Is he still in my room?"

"Mhm," Aliya nods, and he stands up, dusting his hands on his pants.

When he leaves the room, Jack turns to his wife with worried eyes, shaking his head.

"He's not eating," he whispers. "He's not well. He's barely made it through half of his food."

"This is the happiest he's seemed in months," Aliya insists. "He's probably just tired."

Icarus reaches his fingers between the bars of the birdcage and runs them carefully over Chip's wings.

The little bird blinks as it watches him, chirping contentedly.

"You're the only good thing that's happened this year," he whispers. "You can't understand me. I know. But you're a miracle here, and I wish I could tell you that."

Chip flies away from him and up to a bar a few inches away, pecking at it aimlessly. Icarus watches and laughs, tugging nervously at his sleeves.

He turns away and looks back at his room, a heavy feeling in his stomach.

He misses it, even though sometimes he thinks that the walls have absorbed all of the grief they have seen.

His room has always felt very heavy.

He walks over to the shelf in the corner and shuffles through his notebooks, looking for a story he has finished.

Most of his stories will go unfinished. This one, though, will work. He takes it and pins it under his arm, taking one last glance at Chip before he goes back to the kitchen.

"Dad," he says, holding out his story with a tight throat. "I've been thinking about it, lately. I want you to read this one. It seems like something you might enjoy. It's not Ordinem, but..."

Jack turns around and takes the book, uneasy.

"Is this one of yours?" he asks. "It doesn't need to be Ordinem."

"It's set—"

"I didn't think you would ever let me read this," Jack interrupts, and Icarus folds his arms over his chest. He forces a quiet laugh.

"Well... I know you've got to miss me terribly," he jokes. "This way you'll have me, even when I'm gone. We can talk about it next time I come over—"

"Icarus."

The boy stops, quiet. The room is too warm. He can hardly breathe.

"Yes?"

"Don't be gone long," his father says, and he nods, a soft smile on his face.

"Of course not."

CHAPTER FORTY

He is going. He is sure of it. His whole life, he has fought against the shadows, and now he is done. Icarus is finally going to do what the world has always wanted.

Some peace comes with the resolve that has settled over him since he visited the Counselor. He has gotten confirmation of what he has always known: No part of him is worth keeping around.

His interests are perverse, his worldview is distorted... His nature is bad. No amount of repentance will ever change that, and even if it could, he can't bear to keep doing it. The guilt has exhausted him.

He has taken up a last notebook, and he's written in it every night this week: An explanation for those that will be left in the wake of his death. He hopes they'll understand his choice. It is the only way left for him to follow the Code he has sworn himself to, and that is all they have ever wanted him to do. He won't mention the grief driving his decision, or the way that the coming war has influenced it. He won't mention the way he is torn about what side to take. If he cannot live as an Ordinem warrior, he will die as one.

He doesn't want to be the Jakaran boy anymore.

There is a date set in his mind, and it is approaching rapidly. He knows how he will do it, and where he won't be stopped. He doesn't want his parents or friends to find him. He doesn't want to cause them more grief than he has to.

He will just fade away, and everyone around him will be better for it.

"I miss school," Cole groans. "This is worse."

He is tying his shoes, getting ready for a consultation about a station he might be getting assigned to. Icarus isn't sure what station. He hasn't been able to pay attention, lately.

Anemos sighs loudly, rummaging through the closet.

"Has anyone seen my staff?"

"How did you manage to lose something five feet long?" Cole retorts, and Anemos groans a little louder.

"I don't know."

"Do they not have a staff for you to use?"

"No." Anemos is preparing for a similar meeting. He is being considered for an active position in battle. It isn't a surprise. "They want me to have my own."

"Your meeting isn't until tomorrow morning. Don't worry about it tonight."

"I'm not very good at not worrying about things."

Icarus laughs at the truth of the statement, holding the book he's reading a little tighter.

"You can take mine," he offers. "I don't mind."

Anemos trips on his way back from the closet, shaking his head.

"It has to be *mine*. I can't imagine why, but that's the way they do it."

Icarus shrugs, glancing over at the staff leaning against the wall beside his bed.

"I don't have a consultation. I can get another one later. It's yours."

Anemos freezes. Even Cole looks over in surprise.

"Didn't your dad give you that staff?" the latter asks, and Icarus shrugs, closing his book.

"It's just a staff. I don't need it. I ca...c...can get another one."

Neither of them reply quickly, but after a minute Anemos lets out a heavy sigh, crossing the room to the table by the window.

"Didn't you just give Cole your jacket the other day?" he asks, and Icarus shrugs again.

"It's a jacket. It's not a huge deal."

"Yeah, okay. I think I probably just left my staff at home, so I'll just go get it and bring it back."

"You're going to go home?" Cole asks. "Tonight?"

"I need a staff."

"Don't go *home* for it," Icarus says, his chest heavy at even the thought. It's a Tuesday, so it will likely only be his mother, but he knows going home makes Anemos anxious.

"Frankly, Icarus... I'd much rather go home than take yours."

The words sting, pulling Icarus from his worries. He doesn't understand what's happened, but it is enough to make him retreat behind the wall he has started to build.

"Don't want to be seen with a Waste's staff?" he asks.

The air in the room changes. Anemos folds his arms over his chest, furrowing his brows in disgust. It was only a joke, but it isn't one Icarus should have made.

"What the hell, Icarus?"

He lowers his head, his chest burning.

"Whatever, it was just a joke. I didn't mean to start anything."

Anemos only continues to look at him, his face hard.

"Do what you want with what people have called you," he says, when a moment has passed. "I get it. Humor. But don't suggest that's how I feel about you *ever* again."

"I'm sorry. I didn't mean anything by it."

"You know that's not how I see you," he clarifies, and Icarus nods; his throat too tight to respond with anything else. "I don't want to take your staff because I'm *worried* about you. I never see you. You never sleep, you barely eat... You've not been the same since ceremony night. Now you're giving away your things, and I'm worried. It's like you don't care anymore. Have I done something to make you think that's how I feel about you?"

"No," Icarus forces. "You haven't done anything, I'm sorry. I'm just focused. I care about the Code. That's... w...what I'm *supposed* to do. That's what I swore to do.."

Anemos' shoulders fall, his eyes heavy. He reaches for the keys on the table and shoves them in his pocket.

"I respect that. I respect you. But I took an oath before this." He gestures at his scarred hand and shakes his head. "You're my brother, and if there's a*ny* chance that taking your staff will harm you in *any* way, I'm not doing it. That's my reasoning, and as paranoid as it might seem, you're not going to talk me out of it."

"You don't need to worry about me," Icarus says.

Anemos crosses the room, opening the door. "I'm always going to worry about you. We can talk more when I get back, I don't want it to get dark."

The door slams shut, and Icarus looks down, his stomach sick.

He wants to disappear. That is *all* he wants. It feels like his skin is burning with shame, and he can feel Cole's eyes on him, which makes it worse.

He doesn't want to be worried about. He wants to disappear.

"It's Tuesday, will it be his Mom at home?" he mutters, and Cole shakes his head.

"It should be, but it's never a hundred percent who will be there..."

Icarus pulls himself up, visibly exhausted.

"I'll go with him," he says. "Go to your consultation."

"Hey, hold on—"

"I don't know what he's on about. I don't kn...know why he didn't just take the-the fucking staff, and we have to go through all of this."

"Because something's wrong, Icarus," Cole snaps. "He's *scared* for you, just like I am, and he'd rather go home than take your staff and find out that's the last thing you had to give away. I felt the same way with your jacket, I just didn't want to make anything worse by saying it—"

The door slams again, and Icarus is gone.

He walks as fast as he can to catch up with Anemos, and even though Cole's words are weighing him down, he finds him before he leaves the building.

Anemos turns at the sound of his footsteps and looks at him with tired eyes.

"What are you doing?" he asks, and Icarus shakes his head, red with frustration.

"I'm coming with you," he says. "Don't argue. You're not changing my mind. Let's just... g...go before it gets any darker."

CHAPTER FORTY-ONE

Anemos stands in front of his home, his hands tucked into his pockets. The wind blows his hair around his eyes, and as he looks back behind him at the setting sun, he thinks that things almost seem okay. Just like Icarus has *almost* seemed okay.

It's a beautiful night, and he is going back to his home— a place he should miss— with one of his best friends at his side. And yet, he feels as if he's watching from somewhere else as he knocks on the pale wooden door in front of him. He hates the sound. But he does not hate it as much as when the door swings open a minute later, his father behind it.

It always seems to be his father, and that is evidence that he is a luckless individual.

Alastor looks over the two of them with little expression, but the way his eyes scan over Icarus is enough to reaffirm the sentiment they both already know.

The Jakaran boy is not supposed to be here.

"Anemos," Alastor says blankly. "What are you doing here?"

"I forgot my staff," Anemos responds. "I have an analysis tomorrow, and I have to have it."

His father sighs, the sound almost a groan.

"Very well," he says. "I'm afraid your friend will have to stay outside. The place is unfit for company."

"I think I'll be fine," Icarus mutters, but Anemos shakes his head.

The floorboards creak under their feet. He can smell the alcohol on Alastor's breath already, but he tries to ignore it.

"It's alright," he says quietly. "I'll just be a minute."

"One?" Icarus asks, and Anemos furrows his brows, staring blankly for a minute before understanding his question.

"Five," he mutters. "I should be out in five minutes. Max."

"Alright," Icarus says. "I'll see you then."

Anemos nods and crosses into the house without another word.

He makes it only five steps before the door closes behind him, and he walks quicker, his chest tight. He is stopped anyway, before he even makes it to the stairs. His father grabs his shoulder just a bit too tightly.

"Anemos," Alastor says. "Don't be so rushed. It's the first time you've visited since you left."

Anemos freezes. He clenches his fists in his pockets and turns around with a bitter smile.

"He's waiting for me," he forces. "Maybe we can talk some other time. Or you can let him in."

"You're fucking ridiculous."

He's drunk. Anemos tries to think of it as an explanation, so that the blow might be softened, but the words set off alarm bells inside of him.

"Okay," he responds blankly.

Alastor laughs unhappily and lets him go.

"You never come home, you ungrateful shit. I don't even see you, the second you're given somewhere else to go. I don't know why it surprises me—"

"I don't know why it surprises you either," Anemos mutters, turning away. "I'm sure I'll make it back sometime."

"Now that you can live with your people, you've got no need for us, huh? Do the *wastes* listen to your bullshit?"

Anemos keeps walking, but he only makes it halfway up the stairs before he's caught again, grabbed by the collar of his shirt, and yanked backward.

He tumbles down the stairs and hits the ground, pain shooting up through his spine, jarring his neck and spreading through his arms and legs.

He only barely manages to catch himself on his wrist, keeping his head from hitting the floor.

"Now I didn't pull you *that* hard," Alastor says. "Is all that really..."

Anemos doesn't hear what happens next; he only feels himself being pulled from the ground and back up the stairs he has just been pulled down.

"Don't walk away when I'm speaking," Alastor says. "Your little bitch can wait a few minutes."

"I'm sorry. I thought—"

"Speak up."

"I thought we were finished," he forces, his voice trembling. "Could you let me—"

"I'll let you go when you answer me."

"What did you even ask?"

He is pushed into his room so aggressively that it makes his vision shake.

"Why are you *so* intent on ruining this family's reputation? With your lies, and your behavior, and now, still, by associating with people like *him?*"

The door is slammed shut, and Anemos shudders, sick. He wants to defend his friend but is too afraid to speak.

"Haven't I told you not to bring anyone by without asking?" Alastor hisses, continuing without the answer he previously demanded.

Anemos moves slowly toward the staff in the corner of his room, trembling.

"I'm sorry, I didn't—"

"You never think."

"I'm sorry." He shakes his head rapidly, battling a wave of dizziness, and takes the staff in his hands.

"What is that?" Alastor asks. "Are you all twitchy now?"

He tries to reply, but the words get stuck in his throat. He's so dizzy he has to grip the windowsill to keep from falling over.

"I don't want them back here again," Alastor restates. "I don't want them getting any ideas. It is *my* house."

"I understand—" Anemos flinches away from the older man when he steps forward, then clears his throat. He tries to keep his voice level. "I'm sorry, I'm... I need to go."

"You'll go when I say you can go."

"I'm going now," he snaps, and it feels like he's watching himself say it. "I'm sorry, I don't mean to snap—"

Alastor puts a hand on his shoulder again, but this time, Anemos is too afraid to move.

The man looks at him with eyes that hold no affection— bloodshot and angry and wasted. He is close enough that Anemos can feel his breath, and he wants to shrink away from it. Before he realizes what is happening, a hard slap lands on his face.

The feeling brings tears to his eyes, but they don't fall. He stares at Alastor with grief heavy in his chest.

"You never learn anything," the man says. "You'll do anything to upset me. Anything to get attention. Fucking whore is what you are. All you ever want is to have someone looking at you, you'll do anything."

The words burn like fire in his throat. He thinks he might be sick.

"You want attention?" Alastor asks, his speech slurred.

He places a hand on Anemos' chest, letting it fall toward his stomach, and Anemos jerks away. He forces the staff between them, but Alastor rips it from his hands, throwing it to the floor.

"Don't touch me." Anemos can barely get the words out. "You're drunk."

"You wish I'd touch you."

"Icarus is outside. I'll yell. He'll hear."

"Threaten someone who doesn't know you. You won't make a fucking sound."

"I'll—"

Anemos is slammed against the wall before he can finish, a hand pressed over his mouth.

————

He is only inside for four minutes before Icarus lets himself in.

The Jakaran boy walks through the door with no attempt to quiet the action, shuts it behind him, and takes a step up the staircase.

"Anemos?" he calls, hesitant in a way his voice doesn't show. "Are you ready to go?"

There is nothing to be hesitant about, he thinks. He doubts he can make things worse— certainly not for himself, when he has never been allowed to set foot in the house before. He cannot make Alastor hate him much more than he already does.

"Anemos?" he repeats, raising his voice, but there is no response.

He takes a quiet, steadying breath before pulling himself further up the staircase, but before he can make it far, a door opens, and Alastor steps out into the hall.

They meet eyes, and the man's gaze takes Icarus somewhere else.

Back home.

"I told you to stay outside," Alastor says, seemingly stunned by his presence.

Icarus nods, swallowing hard. "I know."

"What are you doing, then?"

"He said he would b...be out in five minutes, and he's still in here. I wanted to m-m-make sure everything was okay—"

"It doesn't really matter what you want," Alastor interrupts, and when he does, Icarus can hear the slur in his voice. "It's my house."

He doesn't know how to respond, instantly; but sometime between when he begins questioning his next move and when he speaks, he realizes how quiet it is. He realizes that

Anemos did not step into the hall with his father, and that he cannot hear him moving in his bedroom. It is enough to turn one fear into another, and he clears his throat, picking nervously at the skin around his fingers.

"I don't care whose house it is," he says. "You're drunk, and I'm not leaving without him."

Alastor stares at the boy a moment, unblinking, and then speaks again, his voice like gravel. "You'll leave if I tell you to, you dirty fucking waste."

Waste.

Icarus cannot remember the first time he heard the word used as the slur it has become. Only the first time he realized what it meant.

No one ever had to tell him it meant he would always be less. The word was enough of an insult before it became synonymous with *other*.

He pulls himself up to the top of the stairs without another word, only stopping when he meets Alastor in the hallway. He lowers his voice, burying his shaking hands in his pockets.

"Get out of my way, or I'll move you," he says. "Call someone to arrest me if you want. I don't care."

He waits only a few seconds for the man to move before shoving past him, walking to his friend's door without asking twice.

"Anem...mos?" Icarus asks, tapping on the wall outside Anemos' room. As he does, he hears the stairs creak behind him.

The door slams a minute later, and Alastor is gone.

"An," Icarus repeats, cracking his door open but keeping his head turned away. "Are you okay?"

There is a quiet sob, and the sound makes his stomach turn. He closes his eyes in response, his breath shallow.

"I'm coming in, okay?"

"Oh..." A quiet, sharp inhale interrupts the word, and Icarus steps into the room. "Okay..."

"Anemos..."

The boy sits on his bed, his hands folded in his lap with his head lowered. Tears stream steadily from his eyes, and his shoulders shake so violently that at first Icarus wonders if something else is wrong.

No one should shake so violently from fear of anything.

"What happened?" Icarus asks gently. He sits down beside him, but doesn't touch him, afraid he'll make things worse. "Are you okay?"

"No," Anemos replies. His voice is so different from how it usually is. It is like all of the life has gone out of it. "No, I'm not... Go, Icarus. This isn't your problem. It's my life."

"Do you want me to go?" Icarus asks, and Anemos hesitates, struggling to breathe.

Then, with a voice like broken glass: "I don't know," he weeps. "I feel bad asking you to stay..."

Icarus reaches over and takes Anemos' hand while he is still speaking, pulling his fingernails from his palms and grimacing at the blood left in their wake.

"Don't," he mutters, his own voice weighted. "Never. Not with m...me."

Anemos nods, silent, and Icarus stands, shaking his head.

"I'm going to go get a bandage," he says. "Are they—"

"In the kitchen," Anemos whispers, and Icarus nods.

"You'll be okay till I get back?"

Anemos nods in response, tucking his hands under his elbows, and Icarus leaves the room without another word, stepping over Anemos' discarded jacket on the way out.

When he returns, he sits back beside Anemos and takes his hand, wrapping it as gently as he can. He tries not to look at the boy's arms as he does, despite the heat that rises in his chest upon catching a glimpse of the scars that litter them.

"I'm sorry," Anemos whispers, his voice trembling, and Icarus shakes his head.

"You don't have to be."

"There's something wrong with me..." Icarus stops, setting his hand down. "I don't know when it happened, I don't know what I did..."

"Anemos—"

"Why would anyone harm a child?"

The words drive cold through Icarus' bones. He can't force a response.

"I keep playing it through my head," Anemos says, his voice empty. "Trying to figure out... What I could have done to deserve it; his hatred, or his anger, or any of it. But I just... I don't understand. I don't understand what I could have done. I can't think of a single thing a kid could do..."

"It's nothing you've done," Icarus says, and Anemos shakes his head again.

"I know I'm not a kid anymore. I know that."

"But you're his."

"I'm his," Anemos mutters. "I've... I've spent so long trying to make excuses, and find explanations, because I'm his. But he's not... He's never been a parent. He's never treated me like a kid should be treated. I mean, he read me stories, and... he tucked me in and fed me and tried his best to take care of me, but... *I'm* the one that raised myself, and protected myself, while all of these grown-ups took all of their issues out on me. They took their illnesses and instead of healing themselves they made *me* sick, just like them. Now *I'm* broken, and wrong, and—"

"You're not broken, An."

"I *feel* broken," he says. "I feel disgusting, and stupid, and... I mean, I thought I could last five minutes. I thought I'd be safe that long. I feel so trapped."

Anemos' voice comes out as broken as his words— shards, sharp around the edges. Icarus knows the feeling.

He almost goes to tell the boy that he isn't trapped anymore. That he isn't a child, and he is free to go. He almost reminds him that he has moved into the Compounds, and that Alastor will not follow him there, but he knows it is not all true.

Alastor is family. He may not be a father, or a parent in any sense of the word, but he will always be there. It will always have happened, and Anemos will always wonder why. At least, that is how it seems now.

There will come times when Anemos wants to come home to see his mother and will have to choose between seeing her and avoiding him. There will be days when he wants to see his father and will have no one to turn to. There will be undeserved chances he is tempted to give, still, through all of the anger.

If Icarus could try again, he would, and he doesn't understand that. He doesn't understand why parents are as much as they are: why they are so hard to cut from ourselves. Anemos is not trapped; not really. But that does not make it any easier.

"What did he do to you?" Icarus asks, and Anemos looks away, his eyes heavy. "Just now, what... what did he do?"

There is silence a long moment before Anemos responds, fidgeting with the bandage on his hand.

"I can't," he says. "I can't talk about it. I just want to forget any of it ever happened, and not... freak out. I don't want to have another episode. And if I try to talk about it—"

"What kind of episode?"

"Seizures," Anemos says. "I've been having them since I was fourteen. It's fine, I just can't take anymore tonight."

"You don't have to s..." Icarus pauses, clears his throat. "*Say* it's fine. It doesn't have to be."

"Yes I do," Anemos mutters, wiping his eyes. "I don't have time to stop and think about how not fine it is. I can't deal with it, so it has to be... God, my clothes are so tight. I can't breathe. I feel like this shirt is glued to me."

Icarus pulls off his jacket and casts it around Anemos' shoulders. He watches as his friend begins to still, his breath slowing.

He does not dare interrupt his silence.

The past few weeks, he has been so in his head that he forgot to worry about his friends. He has convinced himself time and time again that they are well, and don't need him.

He has justified dying to himself, over and over again.

Right now, though, Anemos does not seem strong. The Ordinem's Higher-class does not seem holy.

As tired as he is, he thinks the boy beside him might carry a weight just as heavy. And he can't justify the hurt it would cause to make him carry it alone.

He's embarrassed that he even thought about abandoning him.

"Icarus?" Anemos mutters.

Icarus looks up, grief suffocating him.

"Yeah, An?"

"You really mean what you said?"

"Which thing... sp-s...specifically?"

"That I'm not broken," Anemos whispers. "Honestly, do you think... You really think I'm worth something?"

The question breaks Icarus' heart.

"Of course I think you're worth something, An."

He lets his eyes fall even lower, his breath and voice growing shallower.

"And if... If I were damaged..." His voice trails off, his eyes falling shut with the anxiety he feels. "If someone did something to me, and I let them, because I didn't know any better.... If I was too afraid to stop them even when I did... Would that be enough to change your mind? If you knew I still lied for him, and tried to talk to him, and kept letting myself get hurt—"

Icarus takes the boy's hand, his throat tight, and gives it a gentle squeeze, willing himself not to tremble.

"Look at m...me," he says, and Anemos does, only meeting his eyes for a moment before letting his own fall again, a quiet sob escaping his lips. "You haven't done anything wrong."

"I feel wrong," he breathes, and Icarus nods.

"I know," he says. "I know you do, and I'm sorry you have to, but you haven't d-done... done- done...." He grimaces at his own voice, shakes his head. "It is-is-isn't your fault, An. Anything he's done is on him."

Anemos meets his gaze again, his eyes darting back and forth, and Icarus swallows hard, the grief on the boy's face draining every bit of peace from his chest.

"You're not him," he whispers. "You never will be."

CHAPTER FORTY-TWO

It has been over a week since Icarus held Anemos' hand and walked with him back to the Compounds in the dark. They didn't make it back till almost one in the morning, because Anemos was shaking too badly to walk home.

He hasn't been the same since. None of them have, but a few days ago, Icarus asked Anemos to join him in training just to get him out of his bed.

Now, they avoid their troubles together, rising early and staying up late.

Icarus knows it is far from a solution, but he hasn't found a better one yet.

"You've got to make sure you're eating enough," he says, and Anemos nods, wiping sweat from his face. "Your body needs fuel when you're w...w-working this much, or you're going to feel like shit."

"I already feel like shit," Anemos mutters, and Icarus sighs, letting his staff fall to the floor.

His hands are horribly blistered, but sparring seems to be what is helping Anemos most, so he has just bandaged them and continued.

"Maybe we need to do something other than train, then," he suggests. Anemos glances at him for a second, and then looks back away. "We could go out like we used to. All three of us?"

"Cole works through the afternoon."

"Tonight, then," Icarus says. "I'm sure he could use a break, too."

He can't believe he is initiating something with his friends when he was supposed to be dead four days ago. He can't believe he is still trying to be a person when he had already given up.

But Anemos nods, and soon they have plans to sneak back to the University and look for starlight— even though it never makes it through the clouds.

"Do you think it'll kill you to miss a night of training?" Cole asks, elbowing Icarus in the side without much force.

"M-m-maybe," he laughs. "I can't i...magine fresh air at night."

"You're gonna drop to the ground and start doing push ups in the middle of a conversation," Anemos sighs. "I'm prepared."

"I'm pretty sure we'll get our asses busted if we're caught," Cole whispers. "So, I don't know, maybe wait to do that until we've actually made it to the roof."

"Okay," Icarus whispers back, laughing under his breath.

It's a cold night, and the temperature is still dropping. The sun has only just set.

"B-by the dragon," Icarus says, shivering. "My hair isn't even dry."

"Do you need to go back?" Anemos asks. "We'll wait."

"I'll be fine," he breathes, shaking his head. "J-just... just cold. Being cold never killed anyone."

"Being cold has killed lots of people, actually. You could get pneumonia."

"Good grief, Anemos," Cole laughs. "You're such a smart ass."

"Oh, screw me for caring, yeah?" He takes off his jacket, handing it to Icarus without thinking twice. "Here, take this. The cold doesn't bother me."

Icarus forces a small smile, nods in thanks, and pulls the jacket over his shoulders, following his friends down the street.

He never walks the streets at night, but tonight the shadows do not bother him. The Mortum which roam the street— calling his name every few minutes— pale in comparison to the voices he has heard at the Compounds. Those dead and living; human and other.

When they arrive at the University, his eyes begin to burn.

"It f-feels like it's b...been so long," he sighs. "I don't even feel like the same pers.. Pers...son."

Cole stops in place, waits for him to catch up, and then drapes an arm around his shoulders.

"I think you're the same person," he says, and his voice is so soft that the boy almost believes it. He *wants* to believe it.

"Do you miss it?" Anemos asks.

He doesn't miss school, but he has missed his friends. He misses the time they used to have, and his family, and his house. He misses being able to get away from it all for even a few minutes.

"A little," he says. "It was easier."

"*Hell* yeah," Anemos laughs, taking the lead. "A walk in the park."

He leads them around the building, through locked doors and up several flights of stairs, until finally they reach the small hatch that takes them to the roof.

Icarus is the last to go through it, and he closes it quietly behind him.

"I freaking knew it would be better at night," Cole says. "I *told* you."

"Yeah, yeah, you did," Anemos shivers. "We're still not at the top."

"Well, lead the way, sergeant."

Icarus smiles a little, laughing under his breath as he looks past the ledge, out over the city.

He follows his friends to the top in silence, not fighting as Cole takes his hand.

Cole who, for all of the healing power he possesses, hasn't the slightest idea how to take the pain away from either of his friends, but tries anyway; who prays into the early hours of the morning for the end of suffering he does not understand.

"This is beautiful," Icarus says softly. "I bet you can see everything from the top."

Anemos grins, despite everything, and takes a step up onto the ledge, holding his arms out beside him.

"I'm on the top of the world!" he yells, and Cole jumps at him, grabbing his arm in an attempt to pull him down.

"Get down, asshole. You're gonna get us caught."

Anemos looks back for only a second as he points to the sky.

"The pollution is so close I can almost touch it!"

Icarus laughs, *really* laughs, his face breaking into a wide smile as he watches them.

"You're gonna fall," Cole says, laughing as much as he's panicking. "Or give me a heart attack. Please, get down—"

Anemos kicks himself back off the wall and falls right into Cole, clinging to him to keep from tripping over.

"Just kiss him," Icarus mutters, squinting up at the sky. "I'm not looking."

"*Excuse* me?" Anemos retorts, straightening. "You're making some pretty serious implications there—"

"M...my word," Icarus laughs, interrupting. "*Stars*, guys."

Anemos' face falls slightly in disbelief, and he rushes over to Icarus' side, looking up.

"Where?" he asks.

"Right there," Icarus says, pointing up at them. "Peeking through the clouds, see?"

Sure enough, a small cluster of stars shine down through the heavily polluted atmosphere; the first any of them have seen in years.

"Alright," Cole says. "Which one of you Deviations worked this magic?"

Anemos reaches back behind himself, grabbing Cole's hand, and then falls silent.

They *all* fall silent, staring up at the little miracle like it might be the only one they will ever see.

CHAPTER FORTY-THREE

"We could just stay here," Anemos breathes. "All night. I could get us out in the morning without them seeing us."

"You'd freeze to death," Icarus says. "And-and I would too."

"Just a bit longer then?" he asks, his teeth chattering.

Cole removes his jacket and drapes it around his friend's shoulders. "Sure, Annie."

"That name needs to die out before it grows on me," he says. Then, more quietly: "Thank you."

Cole nods, pressing his lips together, and pats Anemos' back.

"Yeah, you're welcome. You'll keep me warm enough."

Soon, they are curled up on one corner of the rooftop, their backs pressed against the ledge. Icarus' arms are folded, and he is hugging himself as Cole holds to Anemos, pulled in under his jacket.

Cole has already nodded off to sleep.

"The sky really is beautiful," Anemos yawns. "Even with all the clouds."

"It is," Icarus whispers. "I wonder if there are still places you can really see it."

He thinks of the sky in Morta, and chills spill over his arms.

"Have you ever seen it?" Anemos asks. "Clear, I mean."

"Not clear," he lies, "but it was better in Jakara, twelve years ago. You could still see the moon."

"You remember that?" Anemos asks, turning to face him.

"Y-yeah, yeah. I... Me and my sister used to sneak out of the house at night. Not the safest thing to do, but..."

"You were kids." Anemos nods. "I get it."

"It was fun." Icarus laughs softly. "I don't think we gave a *shit* about the monsters, then. I... I really m-m...miss it, sometimes."

"I bet," Anemos breathes, his eyes heavy. "I'm sorry. Sometimes I forget you haven't always been here. I mean, I don't forget, but... I've never known how much you remember, and how you feel about what you do. I've wanted to ask, but I didn't know if you'd want to talk about it."

The Counselor's words replay through Icarus' head, and he falters under the weight of them, but only for a minute.

"I do. I didn't think anyone would want to listen. The Ordinem looks down on Jakara, you know?"

"I'm barely Ordinem, Icarus," Anemos confesses. "I don't care what they think. You're my friend, and that was your home."

Icarus clenches his fists, cold, and lets his face fall.

"You have no idea how m...much that means to me."

"You might—"

Anemos' words are interrupted by a low rumble in the distance, and both of them look up, eyes wide.

"What was that?" Anemos asks.

Icarus' chest tightens, and he pulls himself up from the ground, walking to the edge of the roof, his hair blowing like ice against his face.

His heart plummets.

"It's the wall," he says. "It's open."

"Why would it be open?" Anemos asks.

War. Massacre.

"It l...looks like the train is coming through."

"Why..."

Icarus doesn't hear him—he only stares ahead with vacant eyes, a dozen nightmares replaying in his mind. This is how they begin: With the Commander coming in, the E.D.T. at his mercy.

"I'm gonna go investigate," he says, and he isn't sure if he's lying as he says it.

"Do you want me to come with you?" Anemos asks.

"No, that's alright. I'll meet you guys back at the Compounds. I'm sure it's just a test or something."

He begins to walk away, but stops at the sound of Anemos' voice behind him.

"Be safe," he says.

Icarus turns around and flashes a quick, guilty smile.

"I will be."

The University is different now, in the middle of the night. It is almost empty— lit only by the dim chandeliers hanging from the ceiling, but it is not asleep.

Icarus retraces his steps back through the building as quietly as he can, staying close to the wall, and only stops when he hears footsteps.

He is on the second floor, near the balcony that looks down on the first— one of the only places on the route where he will not be hidden— so he freezes in place, standing stiffly behind a large pillar.

The footsteps are from below, but they are getting closer.

He peeks around the corner as Ursula walks into the room with Elise and two men he doesn't recognize at her side.

"And they've just crossed?" Ursula asks.

"Yes, Myon," Elise responds. "A bit behind schedule, but you know how it can be."

Ursula stops in the middle of the room, her hands clasped together in front of her.

"I do."

She looks so much like him, Icarus thinks. He has never been able to see any similarity between Anemos and Alastor, but he can see it in Ursula. They have the same dark hair, the same olive brown skin, and the same button nose, but the similarity goes deeper than that. It is in the way she holds herself, the controlled movement of her eyes— her tendency to tug at the gloves on her hands when she's nervous.

"Will you be coming into Morta with us?" she asks.

"If that's what the Guide commands," Elise says. "I believe that only a few of us will be allowed to cross, given that the E.D.T. is meant to protect us all."

Ursula nods, and one of the men speaks.

It is only upon hearing his voice that Icarus recognizes him from the examination, and when he does, his skin crawls.

"Isn't it a bit strange," he asks, "that their prisoner has such a large sway on their missions? He practically seems to be in control."

"Well," Ursula breathes. "Kieran is a very special prisoner, Ralph."

"I've never heard of an E.D.T. willing to step before a Reaper," the other man remarks. "Not since The Six—"

"Hold," Ursula interrupts, raising one hand in the air.

The other three stop cold, watching as her eyes run over the space around them, and Icarus presses his back against the marble, swearing under his breath.

"We're being listened to," Ursula says calmly. "There's someone here."

Elise glances up at the place she caught sight of Icarus moments before, and then lets her eyes wander.

"Would you like me to search the place?" she asks. "I'll be fast."

"Only what's within our vicinity, please."

There are a dozen ways Icarus could escape being found. He has followed Anemos through the University enough times to know his way around, and he has eavesdropped enough in his life to be fast and stealthy in his retreat.

He could get away without doing what he is going to do.

But for a second, he feels he has very little choice. The feeling of being hunted makes his skin crawl. He can't help but imagine if there was gas in the air to keep him from moving, and he was an unprepared victim instead of a spy.

They've always told him his imagination might be the death of him.

The truth, though, is that even if his pulse was not racing, he would still be going to Morta. The truth is that he has known he would have to go to the realm of the dead from the instant his mother told him the Ordinem's plans, and he knew where he would end his night the second he heard the wall groaning open.

Even now, as he watches the world fade around him, he tells himself that he hasn't decided.

The voices in his head tell him there is time to change his mind, and fall into the arms of the darkness that has offered him escape the past month; he can still choose to be a hero instead of a traitor. He can still let the Grim die, and decide that the scar on his hand stands for something.

When Elise comes to search the deck— prepared to look away from whatever she finds— he is already gone.

CHAPTER FORTY-FOUR

In Morta, Cyrus sits silently.

The night is loud with rain, but his home is quiet. A fire burns in the center of the room, and he sits beside the window, pressing his fingers against the glass, tracing the paths that the rain makes across it.

He fights the familiar urge to think of his family, standing to pull a box of matches from the door beside him. He makes his way into the dining room, places them in a small wooden box beside several candles, and then closes it, walking over to the door.

He opens it before the boy has a chance to knock, and looks him up and down with weary eyes.

"I've been expecting you," he says softly. "Please, leave your jacket on the hook, there's a coat for you in the dining room."

Icarus— silent, pale as a ghost, and confused beyond measure— only nods in response, and peels away his wet jacket as he steps into the home.

CHAPTER FORTY-FIVE

Icarus pulls Cyrus' heavy black cloak over his shoulders and stands awkwardly beside the kitchen table, watching as Cyrus continues moving through the house.

He grips the back of a chair, picks absentmindedly at the wood, and swallows nervously as the man approaches him, holding out a small wooden box.

He takes it without speaking, unsure of what to say.

"Thank you," Cyrus breathes, extinguishing the candles around his home with the tips of his fingers, leaving them with only the dim light of the lamp on the table. "I apologize for the mess."

Icarus looks around the house uneasily. Books are stacked on nearly every surface, and on the floor along the walls. Papers lie strewn across the room, and there is a large ink stain on the table.

"Y-you're fine—"

"I had a bit of a writing incident earlier, and... Well, you see."

"What were you writing?" Icarus asks. He doesn't know *why* he asks the pointless question, being almost too anxious to speak.

"A speech," Cyrus breathes. "I don't write them, usually, but my thoughts have been all over the place this last month, so..."

He pulls something from behind the wall which, at first glance, Icarus thinks is a staff; but the long, curved blade on the end of it catches the light just before it is turned out.

"Is... is that..."

"A scythe?" Cyrus asks, his voice smooth— light in the dark of the room. "Yes. Only a precaution. Come now."

He pushes the front door open, and the sound of rain fills the house; then the creaking of the porch as Cyrus steps out onto it.

"Where are we going?" Icarus asks, following him out into the storm, pulling the hood of the cloak over his head.

"Visitation."

"Wh-what is—"

"You'll see soon enough. I apologize for dragging you along like this, but the day's nearly gone, and I was already on my way out. You're welcome to stay back."

"In your home?" Icarus asks, flinching at the sound of thunder in the distance. "You don't even know why I'm here."

"Why are you here?"

He stops, biting down on his bottom lip, but before he can say that he isn't sure—

"We're on the same page then," Cyrus nods. "Perhaps the walk will clear your mind. Stay close."

They walk down a long, stone path, the sides overgrown with weeds and the same high grass that covers most of the place. It blows in the wind tonight, seeming to blur in the darkness.

Icarus looks out over the fields anxiously, his heart in his throat as thunder lights up the space around them. It is a struggle to keep up with Cyrus, especially when his knees are this unsteady.

The walk feels much longer than it is, and when they finally arrive at a small, gray building, Icarus is dizzy with exhaustion.

"No door?" he asks quietly, eyeing the stone archway in front of them.

"No," Cyrus breathes. "You must stay quiet inside, understand?"

Icarus nods, gripping the box in his hands more tightly, and Cyrus leads him in.

The hall they enter is dark and cold, the only light being that of the candles which burn on the walls.

Not more than fifty feet back, they turn into a small, empty room, and a wave of chills spills over Icarus' shoulders.

"The box," Cyrus says quietly, and Icarus hands it to him, hoping the man does not notice the trembling of his hands. "You may remove your coat."

He takes it off, sits it on a chair in the corner of the room, and stands uneasily beside it until Cyrus looks back at him, his eyes gentle.

"Come," he says. "Sit."

Icarus crosses the room, kneels beside the older man, and looks over the space around them cautiously.

The air seems to whisper.

"Visitation," he mutters. "To... For the dead?"

"Mm," Cyrus hums, nodding slowly. "More for the living."

He pulls three useless candles from their place on the wall, among many others, and replaces them with three from the box, striking a match when he has.

"I come here most nights," he says. "It keeps me steady. I've found it's harder to act when you're weighed down by grief you haven't let yourself feel."

He holds the flame out to Icarus, who looks at it with heavy eyes.

"Why?" he asks, his voice shaking

"To remember them. The Grim that passed on ceremony day."

Icarus' brows furrow, the corners of his mouth twitching. He has no idea what he expected the man to say, but he knows nothing that would have hurt as badly as this.

"It isn't m-my loss—"

"You're grieving," Cyrus interrupts. "It is, as much as it is mine."

Icarus looks at him a moment, his chest aching, and then takes the long match from him with trembling hands.

The fire makes him think of them.

He holds the light up and leans forward, lighting four candles before the match runs out. He closes his eyes tightly, the sound of the rain drowning him, but Cyrus quickly offers him another. The dim glow seems to burn his eyes.

"I can't..."

"Please," he says. "You have too much sorrow not to mourn."

Icarus takes the flame again, and something in the air changes; something that both of them feel.

"There..." he tries to speak, but his voice catches in his throat. He doesn't even realize his eyes are watering until tears are streaming down his face. "There are s-so m-m-many..."

"I know," Cyrus whispers.

Images flash through Icarus' mind: The Train. The fire. The guard standing above him.

He lights a few more candles but stops when the light catches his palm. The scar down the center burns, almost like it's still bleeding, and a quiet cry breaks free from his lips upon seeing it.

The match falls to the floor, and he draws his hands to his chest, unable to restrain the pain inside of him any longer.

"I'm sorry," he whispers. "I'm so sorry. I shouldn't be here."

"Why shouldn't you?"

"Because I... I've *hated* you," he breathes. "I've hated all of you, m-my entire life, and I've cursed you—"

His breath catches, and he shakes his head, guilt suffocating him. Guilt for what he's done against them, and what he will do for them.

He presses his nails into his palm, and Cyrus takes his hand, pulling them away.

"Don't hurt yourself."

"I want to," Icarus says, and he doesn't mean to. The words come forth of their own volition, and the shadows in the corners seem to grow darker with them. "I'm so... I can't do this anym-more, you don't understand. You don't understand the v...vows I've taken... The things I've s-said, and done-done—"

"Don't I?" Cyrus asks. He opens his own right hand, revealing the same thin white line across it.

For some reason, seeing it only breaks Icarus more.

"You're so stupid," he whispers, "thinking they could want you."

"You aren't stupid."

"I can't d-do this." He rips his arm free from the man's grip. "I can't be... I'm not evil. I'm not you. I'm not this—"

"What are you?" Cyrus' voice is gentle, and Icarus hates it. "What are you, Michael?"

"I'm *nothing,*" he yells, his voice breaking. "I am... n-nothing. I have no one I can trust, I have no b...beliefs, no purpose—"

"Do you care about anything but yourself, Michael?"

His skin goes cold, and his face runs pale, but he keeps speaking over the darkness, even as it begins to suffocate him.

"I'm so tired."

The candles behind him blow cold, and smoke rises steadily around him. Cyrus casts a glance at them and slowly, carefully, rises from his seat on the floor.

"Michael—"

"That isn't my name."

"Isn't it?"

The word echoes in his ears, but it is drowned out by other voices— distorted, tainted. He hears the voice of his mother, his father—

"I'm-I'm... I'm..."

"Oh, here we go again," the man scoffed, his pale face red with anger. "Yes or no, Michael. Is that simple enough for you?"

The boy stood frozen and tried to speak, but couldn't muster a word.

A hard slap landed on his face, and the girl in the corner flinched, her hands in front of her eyes.

"I want an answer now," the man reiterated. "Did you take your mother's food, or didn't you?"

"I did," the boy said softly. "I... I'm sorry, she..." He looked at his sister and corrected himself. "I was starving."

"We're all starving."

"But you g-get ever-everything... It's b-been... It's been days—"

Another slap, and the girl began to cry.

"You brats care about anyone but yourselves?" he asked. "Anything?"

The boy tasted blood. He didn't respond.

The man scoffed again and walked across the room, rubbing his jaw.

"You're monsters," he said, his voice heavy. "You're a fucking monster. Look what you've done. Look at your sister."

The words repeat in his mind, and the darkness closes in around him.

"Look at what you've done. Look at what you are."

The sound of sick, dark laughter fills his ears, and he presses his hands over them, his whole body shaking.

"Help m-me," he cries. "Please... please... just..."

"What do you want, Michael?"

"I want to be *free* from this."

The words have barely left his mouth when they are choked away from him, a cold hand closing around his throat.

Cyrus staggers backward, his eyes wide at the sight of the thing that has appeared behind him— A body nearly twice his size, with large, sharp, bloody wings. Its mouth hangs open, overflowing with the same black liquid as its eyes.

Icarus reaches up, instinctively gripping at its claws, and it leans closer to him, its breath hot on the side of his face.

"You will."

It would be a lie to say a part of him is not relieved at the words, even spoken so cruelly, but it doesn't matter. His friends need him. This man in front of him *needs* him.

He wants to die—he hopes to fail—but pulls helplessly at the things wrists anyway, struggling to breathe.

The beast jerks suddenly backward, its claws ripping long gashes across his neck and shoulders, pulling him down onto his back before releasing him.

He looks up at it with wide, scared eyes, his head spinning.

"Mine," the thing hisses, pressed back against the wall by something he cannot see. *"He's mine—"*

"No," Cyrus interrupts. "He's not."

Icarus grips his throat, choking on his own blood, and Cyrus pulls him back, practically slinging him to the other side of the room.

"Is it not his choice, Oracamatis?" the thing growls, its words a strangled gurgle. *"Is it not—"*

"I am not your puppet," Cyrus snaps, his voice firm. "I am not your Oracamatis, and this is a child. He has *never* been given a choice."

"And yet he chooses me."

"On the basis of a lie?"

"I've..." Icarus coughs, and the action sends pain through his throat. "I've not... I've not chosen you... I just want it to stop. I want to *escape* you."

"Nothing escapes me, Oraca—"

Cyrus lifts one hand in the air, as if he is gripping the thing from across the room, and it howls in pain, shrinking back against the wall.

"No more lies!" he says. "Not here."

"Do not command—"

"You have no power here," he interrupts. "None."

"You think you can—"

Cyrus pulls the scythe into his hand and swings it down upon the beast in one movement, slicing the head clean off its shoulders.

Its limp body falls to the ground, and thick black blood spills across the floor. Icarus pushes himself back against the wall with his feet and clasps his hands over his mouth, his stomach twisting.

He is hardly in his body as Cyrus approaches him, pulling him from the floor.

"You're bleeding..." The words blur, the smell of iron drowning his senses. "...to a healer."

He looks down at himself, sees only red, and looks back away.

"Can you stand?"

"I d-don't... I can't..."

One arm finds its way around his back, and another under his legs, and then he is pulled from the ground, whimpering in pain.

"You're going to be okay," he says. "Hold onto me."

"Leave m-me," Icarus breathes, his mind too fuzzy to think the words over before he says them. "Just *leave me*, Cyrus."

"No," the man replies, already moving back along the path they walked on minutes before. "*No.*"

Icarus manages to pry himself from the man's arms, stumbling across the road and falling back into the field, too hysterical to think clearly.

"I cursed them," he cries, rain pounding down on his face. "I cursed all of them. I don't deserve your help. I don't even *want* it."

"It doesn't matter what you've done. You're safe here. Please, give me your hand—"

"I want it to be over!" he screams. He watches the sky above him— the shadows circling like vultures, and his vision blurs. "My God, I can't take another minute of it! I can't hate myself any more. I can't..."

"Why did you come here?" Cyrus asks, trying to hide the concern in his voice. "To die?"

Icarus buries his face in his hands and shakes his head, the thunder booming in a way that rattles his spine.

"I *can't,*" he cries. "I can't betray them. I can't betray this damn—"

"Your *life* betrays the Code," Cyrus yells over the rain. "Your whole existence."

"I'll die then. I'm not... afraid to."

"In your state?" he asks. "You should be. Your soul would not last one moment out of your body before it was taken."

"Am I th-that wicked?" Icarus breathes, his words blending into hyperventilation. "You think the darkness would c...claim me that easily?"

"Wicked?" Cyrus asks, broken. "No. Afraid, attached... Young. Too young to die. Michael please, you're bleeding more than you know."

He glances up again, and finds the darkness closing in around them. It's like a wall. Like the city—

"If I go with you, then I betray everything I've ever..." Icarus' breaths shorten, his vision red. "Everyone I... The Ordinem..."

"My God," Cyrus mutters, his eyes burning. "Child, is your life not worth more than the words on that scroll? Please. Let me help you. Michael..."

Icarus digs his hands into the dirt, his fingers tangling with the grass, and closes his eyes, his hearing muffled.

Grass, he thinks, barely managing to hold himself up.

Of course there would be grass here; life in a place of death. Of course the simplest good he has ever loved would be in a place like this.

"Tell me something good," his father asked him, and he did not respond with the Code. He did not respond with the Order. His chest caves under the weight of the simple realization: The words on the scroll have never been what he has clinged to.

He collapses back onto the ground, grief breaking his fragile body.

"I want my dad," he whimpers. "I just want my dad."

"I'll take you to him, but you have to let me help you."

Icarus nods, but cannot pull himself from the ground; he cannot move, speak, or do anything but sob and gasp and claw at the dirt around him.

Cyrus collects him once more, and this time, he clings on as tightly as he can, his hands like ice.

His eyes are open, but they are vacant, dim.

"Can you look at me?" the man asks. "Look at me, please, Michael..."

Shock, he thinks, looks too much like death.

But this boy is still breathing, even as his blood drips down onto the ground, staining his face as his head falls over onto his shoulder.

Chapter Forty-Six

"*R ight,*" the Wind speaks.

Cyrus turns off the road without thinking twice, stumbling through the high grass.

There is a little house not far off. He sees it just as the hands grasping his shoulders lose their grip.

"Michael," he whispers, his legs heavy. "Come on, I need you to breathe."

His cries are growing weaker; they have almost ceased entirely when Cyrus opens the door of the home, not bothering to knock.

Two women sit in the room across from him.

Cyrus turns to the freckled girl on the right, and his face breaks with the relief he feels.

"Shannon," he says, his voice trembling. "*Please.*"

The young girl springs up from her seat, eyes wide with concern, and nods.

"Bring him over," she says. "What happened?"

The other girl pushes every item off of the table and onto the floor, her face red with worry.

"An Oracath," Cyrus says. "At visitation."

"At visitation?" the second girl asks, pushing her blonde hair out of her face. "So close?"

"It's dead, Emmy." Cyrus peels off the boy's shirt as carefully as he can, placing him on the table, and Shannon flinches at the sight of him.

"That looks bad," she whispers. "I've barely trained. The healer is just in town."

"I need you to try," Cyrus insists. "I don't think he'll make it to town."

Shannon bites her lip, and thunder shakes the light above them, but Icarus does not notice it.

"Okay," she whispers. "Okay, I need... Can you both go into the other room, for just a moment?"

Cyrus nods, and Emmy follows suit, moving quickly to his side and following him down the hall.

Shannon looks down at the boy on the table, her throat tight, and forces a gentle smile, moving his face until his eyes meet hers.

"Hey," she breathes, placing her hand over one of the long gashes on his neck. "I need you to stay awake for me, can you do that?"

His breaths come fast and shallow, and gentle cries continue to fall from his lips.

"It might hurt a little, I'm sorry. You can hold my hand, if that would…"

She moves her other hand over to his, and he takes it hesitantly, squeezing it more tightly than he means to.

Too cold, she thinks.

She moves her other hand slowly, touching his wounds as lightly as she can, and his body tightens against the pain. Blood seeps between his lips as he coughs, and he groans under his breath.

"You're okay," she whispers. "Just hold on to me."

Soon, Icarus is awake, and Cyrus is sitting in a chair across from him, watching as Shannon takes a warm rag to his shoulder.

He is shivering, pale as snow, and almost too weak to move but he's alive.

He's still alive.

"I can do it," he mutters, lifting his hand to stop Shannon's. "You don't… don't h-have to…"

Shannon shakes her head, brushing the hair from his face.

"You need to rest."

"I'm…" He wants to fight, but he can't. Not anymore. He clears his throat and shakes his head. "Th-thank… you…"

"Shannon," she finishes. "What's your name?"

He hesitates, his voice caught in his throat. When he speaks, his voice is broken.

"My… My name is… M-Michael," he says, "but Icarus is… Easier, for me… For now."

"Icarus, then," she says. "Yeah?"

Cyrus catches his eyes for just a moment, and he lowers his head, his heart in his throat.

"Yeah," he whispers.

Shannon draws away the cloth and forces a small smile.

"I'm going to clean this off," she says, and he nods, the action taking more energy than he has. "Emmy's checking to see if she has something you can wear. Your shirt is... *really* stained."

"Thank you," he forces.

As soon as she is gone, he turns to Cyrus, his head lowered in shame.

He should thank the man, he thinks, but he cannot muster the words; he cannot mean them yet, under the weight of what he still has to do.

"I'm sorry," he says, instead. "I'm sorry for what I said. I'm sorry that I brought... darkness, to one of your sanctuaries."

Cyrus looks at him steadily, his face giving away very little of the emotion he feels.

"Icarus," he says.

"Yes?" the boy breathes, his voice barely a whisper.

"You are not evil."

Shannon returns to wipe away more blood, and Icarus keeps his eyes on the floor, trying to find rest in the silence until she leaves once more.

"I know how real it all feels right now," the man continues, "but you've been fed lies since the day you were born."

Icarus laughs weakly, wetting his lips.

"What's the truth, then?" he asks. "Where do I find it?"

"You already know it," Cyrus responds. "You've always known it."

"I know nothing," he utters, pain heavy in his voice.

"You trust nothing," Cyrus forces. "There is a difference."

A moment later, Shannon comes back with Emmy at her side. The latter holds out a soft, wool sweater, a sad smile on her lips.

"It's mine," she says. "But it's big, so, I think it'll fit."

Icarus's body strains as he pulls himself to standing, taking the garment with careful hands.

He smiles as lightly as he can.

"Thank you. This... Y-your kindness m...means the world to me. Thank you."

Emmy smiles, nods, and squeezes her hands together in front of her, watching as he pulls the sweater over his head.

"It fits well," she says. "Good. Um, while we have you here..."

He looks up, meeting her eyes hesitantly, and her face softens.

"You're welcome to come back," she says. "Anytime. Anytime at all, if you need a friend, or... Or anything like that; really. I know Cyrus said he's taking you home tonight, but... If you need somewhere to go."

"Thank you," he says. "I w-wouldn't want to... Intrude..."

"Intrude?" Shannon laughs, sad. "Icarus, you're blood. You can't intrude. We're here for you."

"I've not been..." He stops himself, shakes his head. "Thank you."

Icarus' arm is draped around Cyrus' shoulders, and he is led outside, leaving the warmth of the house and the girls' kindness behind.

Instantly, his skin grows colder.

As soon as they're alone, he stops, turning to the older man with tired eyes and an empty chest.

"I need to tell you something," he says. "But I n-need you to promise m-me... that you won't hurt my father, because he's... He's the only thing I really have, and I can't lose h im."

"You have my word," Cyrus breathes, confused.

Icarus looks back at the house, clenches his fists, and thinks of the Ordinem.

The Ordinem, which once seemed like something good and safe.

He holds the stories, the heroes, the lessons, and everything he ever wanted to be in his hands for just a moment before speaking, his words a betrayal he did not think himself capable of.

"They're coming," he whispers. "The Ordinem, they're... They're coming. They're coming with an E.D.T. from Trellis, and gas bombs, and..."

Cyrus' face pales, but otherwise, his calm demeanor remains.

"When?" he asks.

"Tomorrow evening. They're planning to... to-to catch you off guard. I should have warned you sooner—"

"How many?"

"Not... many," he breathes, "but..."

"I understand," Cyrus says, falling silent for a long moment. Then, as if the words had never been spoken: "Right, let's get you home, then."

Chapter Forty-Seven

Jack is sitting in his living room with tired eyes and a glass of wine in his hand when the Reaper knocks on his door.

He lifts his head, takes a deep breath, and pulls himself up from his chair.

It is too late for anyone to knock, he thinks— anyone but Icarus, or perhaps one of his friends, but even they would come with trouble at a time like this.

He is not sure that he can look his son in the face, but when he opens the door, he does.

For what might be the first time, he cannot read him; cannot distinguish anything but pain in his eyes.

"I'm sorry to bother you so late," the man standing beside him says, "but your son..."

Jack meets Cyrus' eyes, and both men fall completely silent.

Fear washes over the latter, a familiar thing.

He clears his throat and shakes his head.

"Your son—"

"Come inside," Jack interrupts. "Please... We can talk in..." His voice breaks slightly. "My word, I'm sorry. You look like someone I used to know."

"I've been told I have a familiar face," Cyrus forces. "I don't want to intrude—"

"You aren't intruding. Come in, please, it's beginning to... Well, you look like you've been through a storm already, but..." His throat tightens. "Icarus, are you alright?"

"I'm f-fine," he says softly. "I was..."

The Wind whispers something that makes Cyrus' skin crawl, and it takes everything in him not to disobey the command.

"He was injured," Cyrus finishes. "Very severely. He would have died had there not been a healer."

"A healer?" Jack asks, his heart picking up as he looks at the two of them, trying to process the words. "Was this on the Outskirts, then?"

Icarus eyes the floor below him, and Cyrus shakes his head, forcing the words from his throat as quietly as possible.

"It was in Morta, sir. An Oracath manifested— you know they appear much more easily, there— and it…"

Icarus shifts uneasily and reaches up to the neck of his shirt, pulling it aside to show the long, reddish scarring left across his shoulders, neck, and throat.

Jack pales, looking from his son to the man and back again.

"He was too weak to shift back on his own," Cyrus continues. "Too weak to walk, really; hence why I've brought him to you."

"From Morta," Jack repeats.

"Yes, sir."

"Then you're…"

"Yes."

He holds out his hand, fighting back the anxiety that claws at his stomach, and Jack looks down at it, his eyes catching the narrow white scar across it.

He shakes it without remark.

"Would you come in, please? There are things I would feel more comfortable saying behind closed doors."

"I understand, sir."

The following conversation is unnecessary, but not unimportant; it is not unimportant to the boy who sits listening to his father's betrayal with shaking hands.

They have a Reaper, he says, and Cyrus knows his name without a moment's thought: William, lost in Trellis seven years prior.

Seven years to break him, Icarus thinks. Of course, he has not been broken; not really, but they do not know that yet.

Cyrus' face pales at the mention of the E.D.T. — Icarus can see that now, in the light. And it is not because he buys into the dogma of hatred the world has sold, the lie that the two groups are enemies by nature, but because he knows that there is reason behind the hatred so many of them feel.

Because he knows that any E.D.T. Trellis trusts in Morta must have the power to exact as much vengeance as he sees fit.

"I'm sorry there's so little time," Jack says. "If I could have told you, I would've. The only way I could think to give you word was through Icarus, and… I couldn't ask him t o—"

"I wouldn't have asked you to," Cyrus says. "He's a child. I wouldn't have asked you to involve him."

"I app-pre-preciate the sentiment," Icarus mutters, his head full, "but I'm already involved, just by-by... b-being here."

"I understand," Jack nods. "But I know you have ties to both sides. I couldn't ask you to choose."

"I chose." The words are lonely, and he is too tired to force any warmth into them. "I thought you would be angry. Just, because of Mom..."

"She won't be harmed," Cyrus says. "I don't plan to fight. Evacuation will be difficult to do quickly, but... Better than bloodshed."

Jack nods and looks at Icarus.

"You did the right thing," he breathes. "I love Aliya more than... Almost anything, but she's wrong."

"She doesn't know?" Cyrus asks.

"No." Jack shakes his head. "She would turn him over if she did."

Icarus stifles a sob, sinking further back into himself.

He does not hear the rest of the conversation; he cannot hear anything but the dull rhythm of his own heart, the ringing in his ears, and—

"Michael."

His eyes wander aimlessly over the wall, over photos and chips in the paint. Home, he thinks, as if he might be seeing it for the last time.

"She doesn't want you here. She'll turn you in. She'll leave you."

He looks down at his hands, picks at the skin around his fingernails.

"I will never leave you."

"They'll recognize the scarring," Cyrus says, sometime later. "You'll need to stay covered."

Icarus nods, sighing deeply, but not responding.

"How are you feeling?"

"Better," he lies. "Less pain."

"You may still be sore for a few days."

"That's f-fine."

"You need to make sure you rest. There's likely venom in your bloodstream."

"Venom?"

"Its claws... You'll be fine. Just weak, for a few days."

"They'll be locked down tomorrow," Jack says. "It shouldn't be difficult to rest. Nothing to do. You could stay here."

"With me."

"That's alright," he breathes. "My friends... An will need m...me, there. He's... really.. Claustrophobic."

Anemos needs him, he thinks. He is needed. Someone—

"If he knew..."

"An?" Cyrus asks.

"Anem...mos," Icarus nods. "The Guide's nephew."

"Right," he says. "Is he... Is he *safe,* do you think? For you, I mean."

"No," Icarus states. "But I love him, and he'll n-need m-m-me, so..."

"Be careful," Cyrus forces, as gently as he can. "Love is a dangerous thing. Beautiful, but not... Don't confuse loving him with being able to trust him."

"Either of them," Jack adds, his voice tired. "They're good kids, but—"

"I understand," Icarus breathes, closing his eyes. "I don't trust anyone."

CHAPTER FORTY-EIGHT

The front door opens again, and Cyrus steps out onto the patio, his hands in his pockets and his cloak cast over his head.

"Thank you for your kindness," he says, nodding in Jack's direction. "Please know that my home is always open to you, Icarus, if you need a place to go."

Icarus nods, his face pale.

"Thank you," he says. "I'm sorry that..."

Cyrus shakes his head, holding one hand in the air between them.

"No apologies needed. Please, keep yourself safe, and know that you are worthy and good. I want nothing else."

Icarus nods, his eyes burning.

"Thank you," he whispers.

The Reaper bows and leaves, disappearing as quickly as he came. He turns the corner and vanishes into the fog.

Jack turns to his son as soon as they're alone and opens his arms, his eyes red.

"Can I hug you?" he asks, exhaustion straining his voice.

Icarus nods, his eyes still on the door, and a moment later, he is pulled into his father's embrace.

He collapses into it, his breath heavy, and does not make a sound as his tears spill onto his father's shoulder; he barely moves at all.

"I'm so sorry," Jack whispers. "I'm sorry I can't do more."

"More?" Icarus asks. "You've already betrayed them. You've... Will they come for you? Will you b-be suspect—"

"Don't worry about that, love," Jack interrupts. "You've got enough on your mind. I'll be alright."

"You have to be, you know. You're... You're really... You're all I have."

"You have yourself," Jack says. "You have the Wind."

"Is that enough?"

"It doesn't always feel that way, but, yes, it is. It kept me long enough." He pauses, moving his hand over his son's back in an effort to comfort him. "*You're* enough. I'll be fine. I love you."

"I love you too," Icarus cries. Then, his voice a broken plea: "Pray for me, Dad. Please. I'm...m so afraid."

"I always pray for you," Jack whispers, brushing the hair back out of his face. "Every day. Every hour."

"Why is the darkness so *loud?*" the boy asks. "Why can't I... Wh-where is the light? I've heard n-nothing of... of the Wind in *years.* "

"Of course you have, Icarus. Just... Listen to me, alright?" he pulls back away from him, wipes the tears from his eyes, and looks at him, holding his face in his hands. "Close your eyes. Listen to my voice. Just my voice."

Icarus closes his eyes, and the darkness behind his eyelids seems to shift. He is almost somewhere else; impossibly close, just as he always is.

"Can you hear me?" Jack asks.

"Mm," Icarus nods, still in tears. "I can hear you."

"When I'm afraid, and the Wind is still, and the darkness is so loud I don't know where to find the light, do you know where I look?" he asks. "I look at you."

Icarus stills slightly, shaking his head.

"Me?"

"We call the spirit the Wind," Jack whispers. "Yes?"

"Mhm."

"Well," he says. "How do you experience the wind? How do you know it's there? Sometimes, when it's strong enough, close enough, you hear it. Other times you can only feel it, but sometimes you're separated, yes? By a wall, or a window, or maybe it's just above your head, out of reach; but still, you know it's there. How?"

"You can... You can see it... blowing through the trees—"

"And so I see the Wind in you," he says. "And so you can hear it through me."

Icarus leaves his home an hour later, his soul a little lighter, even under the weight of the burden he has taken.

"You're beautiful," his father said. *"You're full of light, and love…"*

Every word he said stays with him, quieting the darkness just enough that he can hear his own mind, lonely and afraid as it is.

He walks along the pavement slowly, tracing the trail back to his school, not yet ready to face his friends.

He should rest, he thinks, but he can't.

A few dozen more steps, and he collapses back against the University wall, sliding down to the ground.

He looks up at the sky— looks for stars, and her name finds his lips almost as if of its own volition.

"Zahra?" he asks, whispering the word out loud as well. *"Are you awake?"*

"Icarus?" Her voice is worried, tired. *"No, I was asleep. I only just fell asleep, I've been so panicked over you."*

"Panicked over me?" he asks. *"Why?"*

"I kept calling for you, and you didn't answer. I tried for hours."

Icarus' brows furrow in confusion. He folds his arms over his chest.

"I didn't hear any of that."

"I thought maybe you were gone. I couldn't feel you anymore, I looked for you and I couldn't find you—"

"You thought I was gone?" he repeats.

"It was like when my parents passed. That same empty spot in my chest. It was just like death."

Death. She didn't feel his panic, or his pain. She felt *death*.

Oh.

"Are you okay?" she asks, starting to wake up.

"I'm… fine," he says. *"I wasn't fine, but… I don't think that's what you felt. I went to Morta. Could that have felt like death? Is that why I couldn't hear you?"*

"You went to Morta?" she asks. *"Why weren't you fine?"*

Icarus looks up at the sky, watching the clouds.

"I have a lot I have to tell you. I've not been honest."

She is quiet, and he takes the silence as an opportunity to continue.

"I was attacked by an Oracath, and I think it was my fault. I think I brought it to me."

"Why would you bring it to you?" she asks, and he hesitates.

"I was overwhelmed to the point of wanting to die. I panicked. I know I shouldn't have, but... They're going to invade Morta. That's what we've not talked about. It's been killing me. Commander Hawkins is going to help the Ordinem invade Morta, and they're going to slaughter the Grim."

"Did you warn them?"

He wonders if she will hate him for it. He has endangered everyone she knows with his actions, too. The Outskirts are even less protected than the city.

"Yes," he admits, anyway. *"I'm sorry. I didn't have a choice."*

"You did, and you made the right one. Don't apologize."

"Okay." They are both quiet a long time, feeling the weight of all of it, but then Icarus speaks again, hesitant. *"I'm afraid. I'm afraid of the choice I made, and what it's going to mean tomorrow."*

In Trellis, Zahra sits in darkness, staring at the wall of her basement room.

She has no idea what time it is. Her heart is pounding in her chest, and her eyes burn.

"Me too," she whispers. *"It means war, doesn't it?"*

"Cyrus, the man I spoke with, said he was going to evacuate everyone to a safer realm. He said there won't have to be."

"But what about us?" Zahra asks. *"Between the Ordinem and Trellis. If Commander Hawkins suspects he's been lied to about something, or one of your men did something to warn the Grim..."*

"Why would he suspect that when we hate them so much?"

"To keep them out of Trellis' hands?" she suggests.

"It's better than the conflict we would have otherwise," Icarus says. *"They've not disclosed their whole plan to the Commander. That would have brought war, undeniably."*

"Okay, okay." Zahra nods. *"What about you? Doesn't this endanger you?"*

"It does," is all he says.

It was a stupid question, she thinks. Of course it endangers him. Of course he knows that.

"If they find Morta empty, I worry it will make them think they've miscalculated. I don't want them thinking there are more of us in Terra than they thought. I don't want them looking any harder than they already are, or becoming even more grotesque in an effort to drive them out. I don't want them to put more pressure on my friends, and force them into violence they don't want."

Zahra's heart aches at the thought of that. She shakes her head.

"I don't want that either. Actually, Icarus, I've not been entirely honest myself. I wasn't sure I could trust you, at first—"

"I did hold a sword to your throat."

She stops, laughing in spite of both of them.

"That you did, Leech."

"You can trust me," he says. *"I'm done lying to you. What is it?"*

It feels like her throat might close from the anxiety she feels. She's glad she doesn't have to speak to him in person, out loud.

"I know your friends," she admits. *"Cole, Anemos... I knew about you, before I came to the Ordinem. I used to live in the same sector as Cole, whether he remembers me or not, and Anemos and I have known each other almost a decade. I went to the Ordinem for all the reasons I told you, but mostly, I went because I wanted to protect him."*

There is no response at first. The quiet makes her stomach twist.

She should have said something sooner, she knows that, but the time has never seemed right.

"Say something," she pleads.

"He's struggling," Icarus says. *"But he's okay. I wish you would have told me sooner so I could have told you he was okay."*

"I wish I'd have told you sooner. I've been worried sick." She breathes a sigh of relief, a silent prayer of thanks on her lips. *"Thank you for not being angry."*

"I don't think I'm in any place to judge someone for secrets, Zahra."

She stands, knowing she won't find her way back to sleep anytime soon, and walks to the corner of the room where she trains the most. She shoves the punching bag hanging from the ceiling nonchalantly, her eyes starting to adjust to the darkness.

"You were attacked by an Oracath?" she asks. *"Are you okay?"*

"I'm okay."

"The worst of it will hit tomorrow when the venom sets in. I realize that's not a helpful thing to say, but you just woke me up, and I'm not helpful at the best of times."

"You're fine, Zahra."

"Take anti-inflammatories. They help more than you might think." She stretches, rubbing a sore spot on her neck, and sits on a box of supplies.

"Personal experience?" Icarus asks, and she chuckles, wrapping her right hand in cotton.

"Karneji is a terrible place."

"I can imagine. How did you and Anemos meet, anyway? At the wall?"

"He used to come across the wall," she says. *"If you tell anyone that, I'll find you and kill you."*

"I'd die before doing anything to hurt him, so I'd fully expect you to," he responds, and she smiles a little, clenching her fists. *"I feel like we have so much to talk about, Zahra."*

"I agree," she says, standing again. She pulls the chain on the light above her, squinting a little as it switches on. *"I'm glad you're still here."*

"Me too."

"I'm here. Don't summon any more monsters without talking to me first—"

"I'm not planning on going anywhere," he interrupts, and she pauses, her eyes closing in relief. *"I was. But... I'm not, anymore. I promise."*

He is the *only* friend she has.

His promise is so important that she can't find words to respond to it. They've not known each other more than a month. She will not be so vulnerable as to say just how much he has come to mean to her in that time. She doesn't want to frighten him.

"No more monsters," he says, and she nods, swallowing hard.

"No more monsters."

INTERLUDE: THE MARIONETTE

Ursula, the lady in black, walks through the Facility with her hands clasped in front of her, two soldiers leading the way.

She is not easily frightened, but the closer she gets to the room waiting for her, the more her skin begins to crawl.

She tries to reason with herself— to remind herself it is only a child. She tries to coax the anxiety from her veins, but her eyes burn.

"Assecula has no children."

A strange one— that's what the Commander called him; a pain in the neck, but worth the effort.

"He'll only speak with you," he said, pointing at the cloaked woman. *"He demands it be tonight."*

For once, Ursula wanted to cower, but she nodded before she had time to consider, her face stoic, careless.

"Very well," she said. *"I'll speak with him now, if we're finished."*

She watched as Aliya and the two men at her side left the room, and she tried not to feel like a prisoner as the soldiers appeared to escort her.

She figured, then, that she would be led down; down to where Rosemarie was kept, down to where the Reapers sat in silence— where they had put William, but it is occurring to her now that she was wrong.

"Is he not being kept with the prisoners?" she asks, her voice giving away nothing but vague curiosity.

"Was this not discussed with you?" one of the soldiers asks.

"No, it wasn't."

The man hesitates and then looks ahead, avoiding her eyes.

"He's been given his own chamber in the private quarter, Myon. He can't leave the room, but he's free otherwise."

"Lovely."

She returns to silence, her lips tight as they walk down the corridor, and does not speak again until they reach the wooden door to his room. She takes her gloves from her pocket, pulls them over her hands, and stares ahead at the door blankly.

"If I don't return to you in half an hour, it's killed me," she says; then, seeing the concerned expressions of the men beside her, she turns with a smirk playing on her lips. "I'm only kidding."

One man forces a weak, frightened laugh, but the other only watches her, his face pale.

"Myon," he says. "You understand that his powers are uninhibited now? He's hardly a benign threat—"

"I think you forget me," she interrupts.

"And I think it's best you are not blinded by your hubris. The E.D.T. is... *extremely* gifted."

"Gifted?" she asks, a laugh behind the word. "Oh, my apologies."

"You know what I—"

"Watch your language, Sergeant," she breathes, grabbing the door handle and twisting it slowly, her voice light. "It doesn't take much to warrant a report these days, and I'd hate to see you on the lower floor..."

In the room behind the door, Kieran sits on a windowsill, listening to the conversation in the hall and smiling around the cigarette between his lips, laughing as he exhales.

"Magnificent," he mutters, pushing his dark hair out of his face.

He looks over his shoulder, out the window, and leans against the glass, letting the cold soothe him.

The glass is several inches thick, strong enough to keep out anything that might find its way into Karneji. He watches little cracks explode through the window as he drums his fingers against it.

The door opens behind him and shuts, but he does not turn around; he continues to smile at the glass as he speaks, his voice smooth.

"Hello, Changeling," he says.

Ursula blinks once, the fear in her chest turning to a kind of vacant calm.

"You needed to speak with me?" she asks, ignoring the comment.

"*Needed?*" he asks, shrugging as he turns to face her. He looks her up and down and smiles, even as anger tugs his lips. "God," he whispers. "The *fashion.*"

Her brows draw together, and she tips her head to the side.

"Excuse me?"

He takes a drag, nodding as he cracks his neck.

"You're really a beautiful woman, you know that? Stunning. You'd never guess..." He stops, shakes his head. "Would you like a cigarette? I'll trade you for one of the gloves. I'm feeling very underdressed, here."

"I thought I was despicable."

"You are," he affirms, "but even despicable women can need a smoke, no?"

Ursula laughs under her breath, peels the silk glove from her left hand and holds it out to him.

"Come, then."

Kieran stands, and when he does, she feels pain unfurl in her chest.

He is taller than she realized in Trellis, but still small: fragile in appearance, but not in the way he holds himself. His shoulders are relaxed, his arms scarred, and his body thin. Hungry, she thinks, and the thought— although only an observation— seems to strain h er soul.

She swallows hard, and Kieran's eyes soften.

He takes the glove from her hand, replaces it with a lit cigarette between her fingers, and places a hand on her shoulder, for just a moment.

"Some conflict, then," he says.

She avoids his eyes, clenching her teeth.

"Don't touch me," she says.

He nods, stepping away from her and walking over to the bed in the center of the room.

"I apologize," he breathes, and she holds the cigarette up to her lips; she savors the burn in her throat.

"It's terrible," she coughs. "For your health."

"You're kidding," he laughs. "My lungs have taken worse, *Myon*."

"Have they?"

"Cigarette smoke is the breath of heaven, Ursula."

"If they have—" She clears her throat, the question coming too fast, too easy. "If they've put you through so much pain, why do you serve them so readily?"

Kieran smiles as he leans back in the bed, his face pale.

"Do you really not know?"

"I know nothing," Ursula says. "I'm not like you."

The words seem to hover in the air, and they almost hurt, but he doesn't let them.

"Some things are better left unsaid, don't you think?"

The dim lighting of the room, the darkness beyond the window, and the smoke clinging to the air hit her with the words.

She almost forgets that she is in Ordinem territory, drawn for just a moment into the feeling of a time long past.

"Why did you want to speak with me?" she asks, the words cold.

"Because I'm lonely," he groans, "and *terribly* bored."

"You could have spoken with Charles."

"I already know Charles, the man is an open book. Some other time, maybe, but... You. I don't understand you, Ursula. Not entirely. Not yet."

"And yet you so confidently call me wicked."

"You *are* wicked."

She smiles like she might laugh, her face hot.

"Is that what you think?"

"What I think?" he asks.

"You know everyone so well." She says the words like a challenge. "What do you think of me?"

Silence hangs heavy over them.

The boy sits up slowly, his hands on the bed beside him, and looks her dead in the eyes, his own impossibly tired.

"I think you're a hypocrite," he says. "A liar, and a coward."

She looks straight ahead at him, her face giving up no emotion.

"Is that—"

"I think you hurt those weaker than you because it puts you in control, and I think you hurt those you care about because you're afraid. I think you're motivated by vengeance, even if you claim to be an agent of justice. I think you take the disgust you have for yourself and you take it out on everyone else. I think you tied Rosemarie's wrists so tightly that the ropes dug down to her bones, and that you're blinded by hatred."

"Well," she whispers, a smile on her lips. "I do sound wicked, don't I?"

"Mm," he nods. "Quite. To be fair, I also think you're quite intelligent and extremely driven; very respectable qualities."

He pulls the one silk glove over his left hand, setting another of the cigarettes alight between his fingers.

"What do you think of *me?*" he asks. "Since we're discussing."

"I don't think much of you."

The statement is so short, so simple, and yet it causes a bright smile to spread across his face, and a soft laugh to emerge from his lips.

"You will." The words drive cold through her bones, but before she can respond—"What are we?" Kieran asks. "What do you believe we are, Ursula? The *E.D.T.s*."

Laughter dances around the last word; laughter and anger, but Ursula's face is unchanging, her hands steady.

"Puppets," she says calmly. "Play things for the darkness. Nothing more, nothing less."

"Hm," he breathes. "Well, I appreciate your honesty. I must wonder, then, why you are so willing to entertain the devil."

"Curiosity," she answers. "You think I'm the devil, no?"

"No," he laughs. "I've seen the devil. You're just a woman, pouring him a glass of wine despite the poison you've tasted at his hand."

Smoke is still leaving his lips as he takes another drag.

"A servant, if not a slave. Is this your payment? Or only another command?"

"I have no master. I serve the Order, I receive no pay."

"You serve the words of men," he interrupts, and then, tilting his head to the side: "Good men?"

"Are any men truly good?"

"And we've stumbled upon the issue! You'd make a lovely cynic. Why do you trust them, your founders? There are a hundred rulers, a hundred leaders in this world—"

"These were men of Inanis."

"Are you a woman of Inanis?"

Ursula bites her tongue, nodding, but not letting the words pass her lips.

"Is Alastor a man of Inanis?"

"Yes," she replies, but the word is forced.

"Mm." The air around him changes. "Damn the place, then; let it burn with your Code."

"You're a blasphemer."

"I..." he says weakly, "I am tired. And *you* are a liar. Does the Order not forbid lies?"

"It does."

"Then you're a hypocrite. We're back to the beginning."

Ursula falls still. Then, after a moment of uneasy silence:

"What do you know of my husband?"

"I don't want to discuss your husband."

"I didn't ask what you wanted."

There is a threat in the words— one Kieran recognizes instantly. It is one he might've expected.

His hands fall to his lap, and his face loses the little color it had.

It is a long moment before he speaks again.

"Rosemarie," he starts, and the name throws her off; it rattles her bones. "She doesn't remember much, these days. It's... In Trellis, they have wondered if the lack of a past would make a more... efficient, soldier. If you lack your own motive... If you forget the crimes that have been committed against you."

He laughs sadly, shakes his head.

"They want her to be a weapon. Like me, yes? She makes a terrible weapon; won't fight, won't kill... Anyway, she's worthless to them, otherwise— as she's worthless to you— so she's made a wonderful candidate for testing the theory. Only issue is, their methods are faulty, so she's never forgotten everything, not really. Some memories gone, most repressed— there, just out of reach. But she has a few she keeps... *really* close."

He clenches his fists once, shakes his head again, and Ursula grows uneasy. It is for no reason she can realize, but it comes with the sudden carefulness in the man's voice; his hesitation.

"One of these memories," he says softly, "is that when Rosemarie was little, she wanted to be an artist. She used to paint with her brother. Of course, there is very little paint in Trellis, but she... She has very little of herself, so she does what she can to keep that part of her alive. She's taken to drawing. She's been drawing as long as I've known her, with stolen pencils on stolen scraps of paper. I've seen her make art with ash, spread against the backs of bandages, and walls..."

He looks up at Ursula, and his eyes seem to burn through her soul.

"The issue is, these last few years, she's been having a really, really hard time drawing. It started about... Thirteen, maybe fourteen, where she just... Her hands started shaking, and she didn't think I noticed, but I always notice things like that..."

He pauses, shakes his head once more, as if he is lost, and extinguishes the rest of his cigarette in the palm of his hand, not flinching at the pain.

"She can't even hold a pencil anymore, much less draw. She tried a few months ago and just... Broke down crying, because, I mean, it's all she had, you know?"

Ursula's face does not change, but her stomach twists inside of her.

"I don't understand what this has to do with—"

"*That*," Kieran interrupts. "Is what men like your husband— Men who think of people smaller than themselves as... Playthings, did you say?" He pauses, biting the inside of his cheek. "That is what they do to people they have power over. Do you need me to say more?"

Blood pools in her left hand, dripping on the carpet.

"I think that will suffice."

"You should go," he says suddenly. "For your own safety. I'm in a great deal of pain, and that usually means nothing positive."

"I didn't—"

"No, I'm sorry, you didn't, but you know now. Please, if you could grab me that syringe from the table, there..."

Ursula turns to her side, eyeing the needle only a second before placing it in his hand and stepping away.

Her eyes catch the dark, black veins emerging around his eyes.

"A holy land..." he says softly, pressing the serum into his arm. "A holy land would spit him out. But instead, you tell me that *she* is damned, for *this;* for pain she did not choose."

He pulls the syringe from his flesh, empty, and swallows hard, gripping the mattress.

"Your Code can rot in hell, Ursula."

The woman stares at him as he speaks, her chest empty.

"I promised to speak with you, so I'm speaking with you," he says. "Tell your people I'll protect a small group of them, no more than four or five. I imagine that should be plenty to collect information, or accomplish a great deal of killing, or whatever your current narrative id. I hate the Grim, and I hate Morta, so don't expect to stay long."

"Kieran—"

"I have nothing else to say. Depart from me, in the name of everything you claim to stand for."

Ursula steps out through the Facility doors just as Alastor is stepping back in. She does not stop to acknowledge him on her way out.

Instead, she scans the place around her quickly, and approaches Charles, her hands gripping the inside of her pockets.

He turns to her with tired eyes.

"Anything worth mentioning?" he asks.

"No," she says. "It's all just as we assumed."

Her voice cracks, and his brows furrow in concern.

"Is there something wrong?" he asks.

Ursula shakes her head and rubs the gloved hand across her face, keeping the bloodied one to her side.

"I do not delight in torment," she says. "You said you believed I delight in torment. I don't."

"Okay," he breathes. "That's—"

"Can I come home with you?" she asks. "I know I've forfeited my right to, but..."

"Yes," he whispers. "That's fine."

She nods, turning her face from the wind, and falls silent again, unable to thank him, unable to breathe past the sick feeling in her chest.

Hesitantly, he puts a hand on her shoulder, and she struggles not to flinch away from the touch.

Part Four: The War

"Let us fear ourselves."
— Victor Hugo, Les Miserables

CHAPTER FORTY-NINE

Icarus wakes up at seven in the morning to the feeling of a hand on his shoulder and the realization that he has slept through the night. He opens his eyes to find Cole smiling at him with tired eyes.

"Hey," he whispers. "Good morning. I'm sorry to wake you up, but…"

Thunder rumbles quietly in the distance, and Icarus rubs the sleep from his eyes.

Already, he can tell that Cyrus and Zahra were right about the effects of the Oracath's venom. His head is throbbing.

"What's going on?" he yawns.

"Training's all canceled today, they're putting the place on lockdown. Anemos said you saw the wall open last night?" The events of the night before flash through his mind, leaving him dizzy. He nods without speaking. "Yeah, well… It's something. Anemos is downstairs waiting, I told him I'd wait to talk anymore about it. Come on."

Icarus sits up, pushing the hair back out of his face, and Cole squints at him, despite the morning light pouring through the curtains.

"What?" Icarus asks.

"You're flushed," he says.

Icarus takes a deep breath, rubbing his face groggily.

"I'm warm, but I'm sure I'm fine."

Cole presses his hand to Icarus' forehead, and concern paints itself over his features.

"You're *hot*," he says. "Do you feel okay?"

Icarus sighs, noting the dryness of his mouth, the pulsing of his head, and the dark spots in his vision before nodding. "I f-feel f-fine."

Cole squints at him a minute longer, and then nods, unconvinced.

"Alright, well, you should eat, either way. Get some water."

Icarus pulls himself up, but sways so badly that Cole reaches to steady him, nervous. "I really think you might need—"

"I'm alright," he forces. "I... Time is of the essence, I can m-m-manage a f... f... Oh m-my *word*, I can't s-s-s..."

He stops, looks up at the ceiling, and groans in frustration.

"I can... manage," he repeats, slowly. "A *fever*, without the nurse."

"A fever is usually a symptom of something else, though."

"M-my body is committing arson because I have-haven't been letting it sleep, or giving it water, or... Anything. But I'm *fine.*"

"Nothing you just said is fine." Cole's eyes are wide, insistent. "You need to take care of yourself."

"I am, I promise; I'm trying. Just... not the nurse. Not today."

His friend watches him for a minute, debating on whether or not to argue. Icarus shrugs away from him, not giving him a chance.

"Come on, I'm sure An is in a state. We need to all talk together."

"You might have trouble reaching the nurse once the lockdown starts. It could be some kind of infection. Have your injuries healed okay?"

"*Cole.*" Icarus puts a hand on his shoulder, shaking his head. "I'm okay. Thank you for worrying. Thank you for caring, but I'm okay. I promise. I'm going to get dressed and I'll meet you downstairs."

Reluctantly, Cole concedes, nodding as Icarus walks to the other side of the room, rummaging through his drawers.

A second later the door clicks shut behind him, and Icarus falls still, groaning at the ceiling.

"*Zahra?*" he says. He closes his eyes and rubs his temples, fighting a wave of nausea.

"*Icarus?*"

"*I feel like absolute shit. Will vomiting help?*"

"*Nope. Been there, tried that.*"

He opens his eyes and tries to steady himself. He feels like he imagines it would feel on a ship— like the ground is moving beneath him.

"*Food. Lots of water—*"

"*Talk to me about something,*" he asks. "*Anything.*"

"*Something good?*" Zahra asks. "*I slept in this morning. Sergeant Bellamy didn't wake me. She says she might let me get out of here this afternoon, if I want to run to the market for her.*"

"And get out of that musty basement? That's not good. That's excellent." He grabs a jacket— he wishes he had hung it in the closet, but he is too tired to worry about the wrinkles. *"Are you jumping with joy? I would be."*

"I've done a few dances this morning, for sure. I have something better to tell you, though."

"Shoot."

"I shifted to Inanis yesterday morning. I was going to tell you last night, but... It didn't feel like the right time."

His chest hurts at the mention of the place, but his heart still speeds up with excitement. Every mention she's made of it has felt like rain in a desert: Someone who really knows him talking to him about something holy.

He misses it more every time she says its name.

"And?" he asks, eager to hear more.

"I'm learning a lot," she says. *"I've been able to bring things out of the void— not just simple things, but... Stars. I envisioned them, and a moment later they were there. You wouldn't believe how brightly they glowed, in all that darkness."*

"I want to see them."

"Come with me, then," she insists. *"I'll show you."*

A smile tugs at his lips. The thought makes his stomach fill with butterflies, but there is still enough fear at his throat to pull him back.

He isn't welcome there. He can't possibly be welcome there.

"Last night I was too weak to shift back from Morta. It could be a long day. I need to save my strength."

"Soon, then," she says. *"Promise."*

He pulls the jacket over his shoulders, wiping sweat from his forehead.

"I have to go. We'll talk soon."

"You're ignoring the question, Leech."

"Bye now."

When Icarus finds his friends in the dining area, he finds Cole with wide eyes and Anemos with wildly bouncing knees. The latter practically jumps from his seat when he sees Icarus, fidgeting nervously with his hands.

"You went and investigated," he states, stopping him before he can reach the table where Cole is waiting. "What's going on? What did you figure out?"

"Good morning to you, too. You were right. The... cold can kill people." Icarus brushes Anemos' hand from his shoulder, sniffing. "I wouldn't get too close if I were you."

"Sick?" Anemos asks, but he doesn't stay on the topic long. "Come on, you had to find something. Where did you go?"

"I went to my parents' house."

"*And?*"

"And I talked to m...m–my dad, and pretty much everything he told me was confidential."

"Okay," Anemos nods. "And?"

Icarus blinks slowly, looking around him at the packed dining area. It looks like everyone from their segment of the Compounds is in the small room, and everyone is talking over each other. The anxiety is palpable.

"Confidential means I can't tell you," he says.

Anemos' shoulders fall, his eyes widening with disbelief.

"You're kidding."

"I'm sorry—" Anemos turns away, walking back to the table and sitting with his face in his hands. Icarus makes his way over slowly, sitting beside Cole.

His whole body floods with relief at the feeling of *resting*, but his stomach still turns. He can't imagine eating. Even the smell of food is making him nauseous.

Anemos' frustration is making him dizzy.

"If you're not going to tell me," Anemos says, finally. "I'm going to go find out."

"From who?" Cole challenges, and he shakes his head.

"From my mom, if she's home. If the bane of my existence opens the door, I'll go to the Palace and find out from Charles."

"It's an *hour* till lockdown—" Anemos is already standing to exit the room, cutting him off without meaning to. Icarus and Cole instinctually stand up and follow him. "Anemos, come on. Think about this."

It still surprises Icarus how fast the two of them walk, when they get going; dizzy as he is, he can hardly keep up. His breaths are short gasps.

He can hardly argue when he can't *breathe*.

To make it worse, it turns out everyone isn't in the dining hall. In fact, it seems that there are even more of them out here. It's a struggle not to trip as he weaves his way around them, muttering apologies as he goes.

When he's finally able to stop, it brings him no comfort, having to watch Anemos approach the guards at the door.

He was hoping to spare his friend some anxiety, but it's apparent that plan has failed.

"I'm the Guide's nephew," he is saying. "I need to see my mother. It's crucial that I'm able to speak with her—"

"Lockdown is in less than an hour, Myon. I'm afraid I'm not permitted to let you through," the guard says, and Anemos scoffs, baffled.

"It's in an hour, it isn't now."

"In an hour, you're not meant to leave your rooms," the guard corrects. "I suggest you eat while you can. It's bound to be a long evening."

Anemos paces back and forth in front of the door anxiously, and the Icarus watches in exhausted acceptance.

Anemos is not going to let this go.

"You understand my mother works in Karneji?" he says, and the words make the guard pale a little, moving a hand to the sword on his waist.

"Yes, and that's one of many reasons I'm not going to open this door—"

"Anemos," Icarus interrupts, and the boy turns around, his face red.

"Yes?"

"Come on, we'll talk."

Cole breathes a heavy sigh of relief, and Anemos nods, dropping his fight and walking back toward the dining hall.

"Nope," Icarus says. "Not in there, and I'm not walking anywhere that fast again. Let's go somewhere quiet."

Anemos leads them— slowly— out of the main halls and to somewhere quieter.

They end up in a room they haven't been in before; one with crates stacked in the corners and cobwebs decorating the chandelier swinging above them.

There must be a draft, Icarus thinks. There are no windows for the Wind to slip through, and no Mortum to disturb it—

"Quiet enough? "Anemos asks, clearly impatient.

Icarus nods, his chest tight.

"Yeah," he mutters. There's no easy way to say what he needs to. He takes a heavy breath as he prepares to rip off the bandage. "Yeah, Okay. Um... So, there's an attack planned, tonight. Trellis is...s... aiding us because we returned something that they'd lost. He didn't tell me what it was, but it seemed significant."

"An attack where?" Cole asks, anxious. "Why are we working with Trellis ?"

The chandelier hasn't stilled. The creaking sound resulting doesn't make Icarus feel any better.

"Because Trellis can get them into Morta," he says. Cole's face runs pale, but Anemos' turns angry. "The attack is on Morta, tonight. They're shifting in from Karneji. They've locked us down because they're concerned something will be drawn in by the activity; Oracaths, or blood dogs—"

"Or Saenks," Anemos continues, bitter. "Or Grim."

"They haven't done anything like this so they have no idea what could come from it. Anything could attack us." Cole's voice is so icy with fear that hearing it sends chills over Icarus' arms. "My God."

"How are they doing it?" Anemos asks. "Have any defensive measures been taken beyond the city?"

"How do they plan to attack *Grim*?"

"With weapons we pledged not to use," Icarus states. "Gas bombs, white Phosphorous—"

"It's not human warfare, so there aren't any rules," Anemos mutters, almost to himself. " *God*."

"It's only a few of them going," Icarus continues. "The plan is to kill them while they're down. Gas first, slaughter them while they're defenseless, then bomb the shit out of whatever's left. He didn't tell me what kind of defense they've prepared in the Outskirts, but I'm willing to bet it's the usual."

Cole's eyes grow dark, no doubt reminding him of the things he experienced before coming to the city.

"Very little, then," he says.

Anemos glares at the floor.

"Very little," Icarus confirms. A wave of dizziness rolls over him, and he stifles the urge to gag. "They know the risks, but they think it's worth it."

"Who?" Anemos demands, "I know damn well my mother wouldn't have agreed to this."

"She was its third biggest supporter, next to M... my mother, and Charles."

"You're telling me she pushed it more than Alastor?"

"She fought dad on it pretty hard." Icarus says the words like an apology. "Though she didn't like the idea of putting a weapon back in Trellis' hands."

"There's got to be a misunderstanding," Anemos exclaims. "She's from the Outskirts. She knows what will happen... My best friend is out there, I have to stop this."

Anemos goes to leave the room, but Cole grabs him sternly by the shoulder, shaking his head.

"There's nothing you can do, An."

"Don't tell me what I can and can't do. I'll talk to Charles, or I'll get to Zahra and warn her..."

Zahra.

Anemos is worried about Zahra.

He doesn't know, and Icarus can't tell him without endangering himself.

"You won't make it back in time," Cole says. "It's less than an hour. You'll be stuck—"

"So will she," Anemos snaps. "Fucking Damn it. This government. They care about nothing and no one. That's my sister out there."

The words make Icarus' head spin. He knows it's different— that Anemos just loves her as a sister— but if there is one thing life has taught him, it's that blood is not all that can make someone family.

He knows this pain.

"What am I supposed to do? Just sit here waiting and let her die in this war? Watch as Saenks and Assecula burn through her home?"

"Sometimes there's nothing you can do, An. " Icarus' voice cracks. "It's war. It takes and it kills, and it's out of our hands. You're right— they care about nothing. They love nothing as much as they hate the Grim. And that does put the Outskirts in danger, but it's not something you can stop, right now." Anemos stares at him, his fists clenched, so he continues: "Zahra lives out there. She's survived... Probably more than we know, and she may very well survive this. But you? Alone out there? You won't. You won't have time to get sheltered, and you certainly won't have time to bring her back here."

Anemos jaw tightens. Cole's hand remains on his shoulder, trying to steady him.

"Icarus is right, " he whispers. "She's better off fighting for herself. It's not like she's defenseless."

"I don't want this war," Anemos says. "I don't want to be a part of this, I don't want her to be a part of this. It isn't fucking fair."

"I know," Icarus forces. "Trust me, I know, An."

Anemos falls quiet then. He stands still, his eyes closed, for a long second before he looks up again, holding his hand out in front of him. It trembles wildly, like it did at his home. It trembles in a way that makes Icarus worry it might mean more.

He knows by the look in Cole's eyes that he is thinking the same, but neither of them dare say it.

Anemos swallows hard, letting his hand fall, and shakes his head.

"I hate this," he says. "I hate being fucking useless. I can't even think of all of it without my body turning against me. You're right that she's better off fighting alone than with me. You're right..."

Icarus goes to comfort him, but before he can, the boy's voice breaks.

"I hope they're right about what they're doing," he says. "I hope they're right about the Grim. I hope their death is worth what they think it is."

The words turn Icarus' stomach to stone, but he reaches out anyway, taking Anemos' hands as gently as he can

"If they're wrong," he mutters." "I'll tear the whole thing down myself, I swear. I'll burn it to the ground."

CHAPTER FIFTY

Ursula sits waiting, Alastor beside her. The sun is just beginning to set, casting shadows across the room, and her throat is tight.

"It'll be within the hour," she mutters. "Everything we've worked for will be within our grasp."

"Yes," Alastor replies, "I suppose it will."

She keeps her eyes on the window in front of her. It is thick enough it distorts the horizon, but she still tries to make sense of it.

"I feel no joy," she states, and he looks over at her, disdain painted across his face.

"You should," he snarls. "It is *your* vengeance, after all."

She is so still it frightens her. Her hands do not tremble, despite the fear she feels. She wants to argue that it has nothing to do with her— to deny that she has any idea what he speaks of, but she doesn't have the stomach for it.

"How much is my vengeance going to cost?" she asks. "What are we sacrificing, here?"

"It's a bit late to be asking that."

"I've not been in my right mind," she breathes, digging her fingernails into the skin above her knee.

Alastor doesn't respond. He doesn't even look at her.

"Are you... Do you feel confident?" she asks. "*Really* con—"

"Did the E.D.T. say something to sway you?" he interrupts, his voice cold.

The woman falls silent, and he laughs under his breath.

"I thought you were braver than this," he says. "Perhaps you should stay back."

"My doubt has nothing to do with my bravery," she mutters. Her eyes are dark. "I'm concerned with the measures we've taken. They're hardly comprehensive."

"Aren't you the one that insisted this was worth the risks?"

"If done *properly,* but—"

"There are plenty of guards in the city." Alastor's voice is an annoyed groan. "You question what your precious Guide has approved?"

She looks away, staring at the blank wall in front of her.

"You know as well as I do that Charles is barely here, Alastor. He's acting in haste, and even if he were capable of carrying this out, the Council has handled it carelessly. The Outskirts are almost entirely without protection—"

"Perhaps the population will decrease and we can use less of our resources on Wastes."

She hasn't any idea how to respond to that, so she doesn't. Silence wraps itself around her throat.

A moment later, the door opens, and Charles walks into the large, dark room— Kieran, Jack, Aliya, Ralph, and Elise trailing behind him.

"Good," he says calmly, "You're already here."

Each of them sits down at the table, and Ursula watches with heavy eyes, ringing in her ears.

They begin to go over the same plan they've discussed a hundred times, but this time, her mind is elsewhere.

She meets Charles' eyes across the table, and Kieran watches, gripping the hem of his shirt tightly.

"It will take twenty minutes for the sedative to dissipate," Ralph says. "If you enter the area before that, you've ruined it."

"How long will they be debilitated?" Alastor asks.

"Hours," he responds. "Plenty of time."

"And they have no other defense method?" Jack asks, actively stripping the emotion from his voice. "No automatic—"

"Nothing," he says. "They'll be helpless."

Helpless. The word is spoken so casually, thrown into the room like nothing but a simple fact. Kieran thinks back on his own life, hearing it; he thinks of Rosemarie. He thinks of how much worse the pain seemed to feel, sedated, out of control, and unable to fight back.

Jack thinks of his son— crying to him the night before, and abandoned in Jakara by almost every man that looked upon him.

Ursula and Charles think only of the task ahead, but for a moment the word makes both of them sick. It settles in Charles' chest just as it is pulled from Ursula's— held in front of her.

"You were helpless," the darkness whispers.

"I can take four of you," Kieran says, his voice blank. "Not including the Reaper. So, that will be..."

"I'm weapons," Ralph says. "Useless otherwise."

"Right," he responds. "Just my old Trellis friends, then. Which one of you will be staying?"

"I'll be staying back," Charles says.

Ursula thinks him a coward; always making other people dirty their hands, never stepping into the line of fire. If she didn't love him, she might hate him.

"You?" Aliya asks. "Charles, you're our best—"

"I think that's the point," Kieran interrupts. "If something breaks through here, whoever stays will have to fight it alone, whereas, as you've so wonderfully stated, there won't be much of a *fight* in Morta. Carnage, yes. Massacre? Sure, but not a fight; not unless something manifests, and that is equally likely here."

Charles watches the young man carefully, and then nods, his head spinning.

"You'll be alright here?" Ursula asks, and the question turns every head toward her. "On your own?"

He opens his mouth to speak, but before he can, a quiet beeping sound rings through the room, and Elise glances down at the pager on her waist, her face pale.

"The Reaper has been stabilized," she says softly, urgency edging her voice. "We need to go now."

CHAPTER FIFTY-ONE

"How are you feeling?" Cole asks, placing a hand against Icarus' forehead. It burns like fire, sticky with sweat. "Any better?"

"N...no, not-not... n-not really."

"Give him something else," Anemos breathes, pale. "His fever's too high."

"I don't *have* anything else to give him. The nurse is on site, Icarus. It wouldn't be any trouble."

"I'm not g-going to the nurse," Icarus says, his voice just a little too sharp. "I don't need t o."

Anemos recognizes the fear in his tone, even if he can't understand it. He isn't going to force the issue, and he won't let Cole— even if he knows his heart is in the right place.

"I'll just go talk to him," he says. "Ian is pretty lenient, I think he'll take my word and give me the medicine without seeing him."

"I'll be okay, An," Icarus groans, and Anemos nods, tapping the bed as he walks by.

"You will," he says. "Because I'm going to get you *drugs.*"

"What if it's something serious?" Cole insists. "It could be some kind of infection. *Sepsis.*"

Anemos laughs under his breath, running his hand up to the side of Cole's face, pulling it toward him so their eyes meet.

"You need to calm down."

"You were the one saying the cold has killed people—"

"Argue all you want." Icarus' voice is an exhausted snap. "I'm not going to the nurse. You c...can tie me up and drag me by my-my feet, I'll shift to Inanis. By the power vested in me—"

"I can see if they have any mood medication, while I'm at it," Anemos interrupts, walking away. "I'll be back in twenty."

"Fifteen," Cole says, and Anemos squints, swinging the door open and stepping out into the hall.

"Seventeen," he says. "No more, no less."

The door closes, and silence falls over the room. Silence, except for the ringing of Icarus' ears and the chaos in his head.

Cole sits down on the edge of the bed, and Icarus roles over to face him, a chill running through his body.

"Are you going to tell me what's going on?" Cole asks.

Icarus looks at him long and hard, his chest heavy.

"There's nothing going on."

"There's *something* going on," he says. "Please, Icarus, I've known you since you were fourteen years old. I know when something's up."

Icarus lets out a long sigh and shakes his head, but doesn't respond.

"You know you can trust me," he says. "Whatever it is. I'm not going to repeat it, or... Whatever you're worried about. I mean, you could rat on me and Anemos right now. You have blackmail."

"I'm not going to blackmail you," Icarus groans, pulling himself up to a sitting position despite the throbbing headache that results.

"I know," Cole breathes. "I'm just... What I'm trying to say is that if it's something, *you know,* difficult, I'm not going to tell anyone."

Icarus wishes that his friends would stop being so kind. It would make lying to them easier.

He takes Cole's hand, his heart in his throat, and shakes his head again.

"I promise," he says. "There's *nothing,* Cole. Nothing you need to worry about. I've told you before, yeah?"

"Yeah."

"Then it stands to reason I would tell you now, if there was anything... You know?"

Cole lets out a long sigh, shaking his head in disbelief.

"You promise?" he asks.

His voice is so gentle, so trusting, that Icarus almost considers telling him the whole truth, right there.

"I promise," he says. "I have missed you, though. I think... I think m-maybe I need to spend less time training?"

"Maybe?" Cole laughs. "You think?"

"Shut up," Icarus laughs, pushing the hair out of his face. "I kn-know—"

A quiet beeping sound rings through the room, suddenly, and both boys look over at the red light on the wall as it flashes on— once, twice, three times— and then goes dark.

"Just a test," Cole says, his voice nervous. "I guess that means..."

"They're crossing," Icarus mutters, his voice hollow. "Any minute."

The hall is too dim tonight; too quiet. Anemos walks down it as quickly as he can, trying not to let the silence disconcert him.

The beeping from every room rings into the hallway, and he pauses, counting three.

It does not ease him. He picks up speed.

A guard meets him by the doors at the end of the hall, and he stops, listening as rain pounds on the roof.

"You can't be out," the man says, nervousness seeping into his otherwise firm voice. "Everyone is meant to stay in their quarters, now—"

"I need to see the nurse," Anemos interrupts. "My friend is sick."

The guard pauses, visibly uneasy.

"Where is he?"

"He's back in our room. It's just a fever, Myon, but I'm meant to get him some medicine—"

Thunder booms outside, and both of them jump a little at the sound. The guard lets out a shaking sigh, and Anemos cracks his knuckles.

"Please," he says. "I don't want him to get any worse."

The man grabs the radio transceiver from his waist and clicks it on, scratching the back of his neck.

"Private," he says. "Can you cover this hall? I've got a boy needing to see the nurse."

The radio goes static a moment, silent, and Anemos swallows hard.

"That's fine," a voice responds, seconds later. "Be quick."

"Copy that," the guard says, returning the radio to its place. He opens the doors and gestures for Anemos to follow him. "Come on."

Chapter Fifty-Two

Kieran is the first to enter the large, gray room that Elise ushers them all into, and he is the only one brave enough to look upon The Reaper in its center. Even the dim light of this room makes the gore in front of him more obvious than it was in Trellis. It seems to hollow his chest, even though his expression is entirely unaltered.

They have taken a man— his government— and turned him into nothing but a tool. A living, suffering, tool.

William's body lies mangled in the middle of the floor, upon an otherwise empty sheet of metal. He hardly looks like a man now; hardly looks like anything capable of speaking, or thinking. But still, Kieran does not turn away, because it *is* a man in front of him, and he cannot look away from a man's suffering. He cannot let the injustice go unseen. He will not leave him alone, even if the image burns his eyes.

He whispers words of comfort through the Wind, beyond the ears of anyone but William. He promises him, with all earnestness, that it will be over soon; that death will offer rest, and that he will pray for his soul as long as he lives— even if he is unsure, in moments like this, that anything could possibly be listening.

Strips of metal lie implanted inside William's chest, making up a second set of ribs, staking his body and keeping him from moving. Each one of them attaches to the chains that lie beside him, a metal clasp on each end.

Elise approaches him, picks them up with trembling hands, and fights down the bile rising in her throat.

"You'll need to attach these to your wrists," she says, avoiding the eyes of those piling into the room. "You..."

"What the *hell* is this?" Aliya asks, her voice breaking.

Jack catches only a moment's glimpse of the man, and his entire body runs cold, but he stays silent, for fear that any discomfort at the sight of his suffering might reflect back on his son. He takes Aliya's hand and shakes his head, pleading silently for her to stop, but she doesn't; she can't.

"Is all of this necessary?" she asks. "Is all of that—"

"Perhaps you should stay behind," Kieran interrupts, "if the thought of a Grim's suffering bothers you."

It shouldn't, she thinks, and yet her stomach twists inside of her.

Ursula watches, pale.

"Look at the pity it draws," the darkness whispers. *"So deceived, your people are, by a human form."*

"Do you need to go?" she asks, her voice weak. "I understand that some people can't stomach torture. No one will judge you."

Aliya looks at her husband, her eyes frightened, and he looks at the floor, avoiding them.

"Just make up your damn mind," Alastor says, jerking his hand back as Elise adjusts the clasp around his wrist. A quiet cry breaks free from William's lips, and it seems to spear through the chests of almost every person in the room. "We need to—"

"Aliya," Ursula interrupts. "Whatever you need to do, love. Don't mind him."

Aliya looks away from the man on the floor, her stomach sick, but holds her wrist out in front of her. Elise clasps the metal around it without speaking, and then does the same to every wrist in the room.

The cold sting is familiar on Kieran's skin, and it sends a chill through his body.

"It can't leave us behind, with this?" Alastor asks.

"No," Kieran responds. "Is everyone ready, then?"

A collective nod of agreement works its way through the room, and Elise steps out of it, bolting the door shut behind her.

The sudden quiet makes the space grow colder. The smell of blood in the air is too thick.

Ursula cannot help but think that it looks like a man.

Kieran walks to the center of the room and kneels beside William, every motion he makes sending waves through the silence of the room.

He places one hand on the man's bruised, swollen flesh, and speaks with a cold voice, despite the sadness behind it.

"Reaper," he forces. "Take us to Morta."

All of the warmth leaves the room with the words, and the walls begin to shake around them. The lights flicker before going out completely, leaving them with pitch darkness and a cold that seems to burn.

They should come out of it, they think. They should move past the darkness and into something reminiscent of a world, but the darkness only seems to deepen, the space around them vibrating.

Heat comes next, dancing with the cold without ever mixing with it. And then the movement stops, the air going still, even with its variety; piercingly silent.

It is wrong, they think, but no one is brave enough to say it. Shock weaves its way through their bodies as the realization of their failure sets in; an eternity in seconds.

"Morta," Kieran forces, holding the hand of the man on the ground as tightly as he can. "Take us to... Damn you, Reaper. Take us to *Morta—*"

It takes only *seconds* for them to be found.

Something runs past them, close enough that it throws muck from the wet ground onto their legs as it does, and before anyone can react, a tearing sound and a subsequent pained scream split the air.

William's hand is ripped from Kieran's, and the E.D.T. falls back against the ground, the impact jarring his spine.

Alastor stumbles backward, the third voice to break the silence as he curses under his breath.

"Where the hell—"

The screaming continues, but before Aliya can reach for the light on her waist, a flash lights up the space around them. A hand clamps down over her mouth.

"Quiet," Kieran whispers, his breath warm against the side of her face. "Aliya, please." Another flash, and his words do matter.

The clasps rattle and pull on each of their wrists as the rest of William is ripped from the metal encasing him, choked down by the creature standing in front of them— fifteen feet tall, shaped almost like a man, but with arms far too long, and hands far too large. The arms look loose in a way that reminds Kieran of tentacles, but then the appendages straighten, slicing down deep into the dark earth as the thing tosses its bleeding, skull-like face back at the sky, letting out a high-pitched cry.

A similar cry comes from their right, and by the time they turn toward it, its hands have already closed around Ursula's neck, tearing a deep line across her throat.

Jack pulls Aliya into his chest, silencing her as Kieran raises one hand in the air, ripping the Saenk away from the woman who does not scream as she falls to the ground.

The other one, finished with William, runs toward them, cutting a long slash across Jack's side before it is stopped.

Kieran's body shakes as he holds them apart, trying to focus on the both of them at once. Blood rises behind his eyes, blackening the veins underneath them, and he lets out a long, hateful scream as the two of them twist, tearing into pieces as they fall to the ground.

His head spins and his vision blackens, but he pulls control back from the place around him, stumbling toward the woman on the ground as Aliya throws herself at her.

"Ursula," she cries, grabbing at her cold hands. "Ursula... Ursula please... Please don't... Look at me..."

"We need to go," Alastor yells. "Before more of them come. She can't shift back like this."

Ursula chokes, too weak to hold the hand in hers, and tears spill down her face as blood spills from her mouth.

Kieran pulls her toward him, his hands shaking. "I can help."

"We don't have *time* for you to—"

Aliya stands, her knees shaking, and presses a knife against Alastor's throat before he can say another word.

"You're a monster!" she cries. "I should have killed you the first time she came to me—" Jack pulls her away with one hand, and she falls into him, blood staining her clothes. "Oh... *No, no...* not you..."

"Will you make it back?" Kieran asks, yelling over the inhuman cries that saturate the air around them.

"I'll be fine," Jack forces.

"Take her with you," he says. "Take her, and take *him.*"

"But you can't—"

"*She* will bring me back," Kieran says, draping Ursula's almost lifeless form over his legs. Another of the beasts runs toward them, and then falls backward a few feet away, its chest ripping open. "Go," he says. "*Now.*"

A moment later, the young man sits alone, the woman's still choking body held in his arms.

"Look at me," he says. "Just... Just look at me..."

His hands close around her throat, and she cries out in pain, blood spilling down her chest.

"You're going to be okay," he whispers. "You're..."

Another Saenk splits into the scene in front of them, letting out a loud cry as it opens its mouth, blackness dripping from its teeth.

Ursula shuts her eyes tightly, her body trembling more violently with each passing second, and he softens his voice as much as he can.

"I've got you," he breathes. "You don't have to be afraid..."

Ian places three pills in Anemos' hand and forces a small smile, even as the thunder continues to roll.

"There you go," he says softly. "I hope he feels better."

The radio on the guard's waist beeps, and he picks it up, holding it to his face.

"What's the matter?" he asks.

The static returns, and then a voice takes its place, so afraid that the trembling in it can be heard even over the fuzz of the transceiver.

"There's been an incident in Karneji," it says quickly. *"Code red. Please, act quickly."*

The guard's face pales, and he takes Anemos by the shoulder, nodding with his heart in his throat.

"How much time?" he asks.

"A Saenk has already been spotted in the fifth cluster, Myon."

His breath quickens, and he shakes his head.

"What's happened, Private?"

The room goes suddenly dark, a dull hum filling the space around them as the indoor lights power off, and the outdoor emergency lights power on.

Every red light in the building begins to flash, and the siren sends a shudder down Anemos' spine.

"It seems..." The man replies, his voice broken by the static. *"...Assecula."*

"Any casualties?" Anemos asks, his body suddenly numb.

The guard hesitates, then lifts the radio back to his lips.

"How many..." He clears his throat. "Casualties, Myon?"

The words on the other side of the line are garbled, broken.

"*Ah, yes— Myon— there are... The prisoners—*" The static takes him for a moment, and Anemos shakes his head, choking. "*Several of the Higher class are injured... It's really— It's bad... We don't know—*"

"The fifth cluster?"

"*There's no...*" The man's voice breaks. "*Get them to shelter, now, there's no time. You need to—*"

The line cuts and Ian turns to Anemos as the guard tries to reconnect, unable to hide the fear in his eyes.

"Go to your friends," he says. "Get to the lower floor."

Anemos nods before the man can even finish his sentence, and Ian pulls earplugs out of the drawer beside him, pressing them into the boy's hand.

"The noise will be worse when you get lower," he says. "Hopefully this will help."

Anemos nods, pulls the man into a quick, tight hug, and then steps away.

"Stay safe," he pleads, his voice breaking. "Please. Be safe."

"I will," Ian forces. "Go, now."

CHAPTER FIFTY-THREE

The moment William tore into Assecula, Assecula tore into the Facility. It was not a single Saenk manifesting, like they had feared; not a gateway letting in monsters like they might meet near the wall. This was a tragedy before they even realized they were in danger; the wall to the room was torn away before Elise had even returned from bolting the door.

Six Saenks. Their bodies ripped up through the ceiling, tearing down through the floor.

Two broke through the wall, running, instantly, toward the Outskirts; one tore further up into the Facility, two further down, and one directly into the hall, running at the figures beyond the room with sharp hands and open mouths.

When Aliya, Jack, and Alastor return to the Facility, a third of it has gone up in flames.

"By the dragon," Alastor mutters, looking at it. "What's *happened?*"

Jack ignores him, his head swimming as he turns to Aliya, keeping one hand pressed tightly against the wound in his side.

"Get to the train," he says, flinching at the sound of one of the beasts, obviously inside the building. "You'll be safer there, hide under the—"

"No," she cries. "No, you can't... Come with me. Please."

"Aliya," he forces, his voice breaking. "I need to go find Charles. He's in there."

"Then let me fight!" she yells. "I can *fight,* Jack, I'm not..."

An image of Ursula forces itself into her mind, and she chokes, her hands trembling too violently to even attempt holding a weapon.

"Please," he begs. "I need you safe."

"I'll take her," Alastor says dryly. "It won't be an issue. I'm going anyway."

"Going?" Jack scoffs. "But you're—"

"I agreed to fight Grim," he snaps. "Not Saenks."

"Take her, then." The response is cold, tired, but Alastor does not seem to notice. He only grabs her by the wrist, a guilty look filling his eyes as he abandons Jack to fight alone.

The latter man walks into the building nearly doubled over in pain, shielding his lungs from the smoke with only the fabric of his shirt. He fights the urge to close his eyes at the sight of it all— burning, littered with the mutilated bodies of prisoners and guards that were alive only moments before.

His stomach twists, and tears fill his eyes long before he spots the man he is looking for, lying twisted and broken amongst the debris.

Jack falls to Charles' side with his heart in his throat, removing as many of the stones strewn across his chest as he can, and the man begins to gasp for air instantly, grabbing onto Jack's free hand before he can even process where he is.

"What's happened?" he pleads, his voice breaking. "What's—"

"The Reaper pulled us into Assecula," Jack says. "It's hardly been any time at all."

"Your side," he interrupts, his eyes dazed. "You're... Are you..."

"I'll be fine," Jack whispers, and as he does, Charles begins to cough, blood splattering across his lips.

Jack pulls up his shirt with one hand and winces, all of the blood leaving his face as he looks at the man's crushed chest; dark purple bruising covering almost his entire left side.

"Can you breathe?" he asks. "Charles?"

Charles shakes his head, his chest spasming as he tries to pull himself from the ground. He catches a glimpse of the bodies around him, and falls back onto his elbows, his teeth chattering.

"Where is she?" he asks, trying not to sob, trying to breathe, even as it becomes increasingly more difficult. "Where is she, Jack?"

"Charles..."

He coughs again, continuing his struggle against gravity, and squeezes Jack's hand so tightly that Jack worries he might break it.

"Where is... Is she alright?"

Jack bites the inside of his bottom lip, shaking his head.

"I need you to breathe right now, Charles. Can you tell what's wrong?"

A Saenk cries out nearby, and Charles sinks back against the floor, trying to think past the pain and the dizziness and the cold, even in the midst of a fire.

"My chest..." he cries. "It feels wrong. I can't—" He coughs again, and Jack closes his eyes, unable to see any more of the man's blood without breaking. "I need to get to the city," he gasps. "I need to get to Anemos, Jack. I need to... I can't breathe."

The shrieking becomes louder, and suddenly, Jack can see the shadows of the things: two of them, coming closer.

Thinking as quickly as he can, he grabs the largest piece of wall he can find and slides down next to Charles, pulling it over them.

"I need to get to them, Jack," Charles continues, the taste of iron filling his mouth, seeming to slur his speech. "I... God, what have we done? What have we done?"

"A foolish thing," Jack forces, his stomach sick. "A foolish, terrible thing—"

"It's what we were supposed to do." The words are sharp with pain and anger, laced with poison. "I can't die here. *Look* what they've done to us. I can't die and leave it unfinished—"

A Saenk roars behind them, and the scared man falls silent.

Jack watches him with heavy eyes, hardly able to breathe.

He should leave him, he thinks. He should leave him to die here for all the crimes he has committed: For trading a child and starting a war and for all of the blood on his hands. He *would* leave him, no matter how much he has come to think of him like a brother, if it were not for the man that would step into his place.

Alastor would be worse. He *knows* Alastor would be worse.

So he holds the wall to shield the man dying on the floor beside him, praying for his life to be spared.

The creature moves away from their hiding place, and Charles lets out a shaking exhale, tears still flooding his eyes.

"My son is in the city, Jack," he says.

"Oh, God," Kieran mutters.

Ursula holds tightly to him, so weak that she fears she might fall, unable to raise her voice above a whisper.

Her eyes scan the broken Facility— the floor that breaks off not more than thirty feet away, collapsing into the space and fire below it. The bit of the hall that still stands is torn apart as if it was made of cardboard, the walls stained with blood.

Her gaze lands on a form lying up against the wall a few feet away, and she taps Kieran's shoulder, pointing in its direction.

"Elise," she breathes, tears still forming in her eyes.

Kieran looks over, pale, and pulls loose from her.

"Can you stand?" he asks.

Ursula nods, uncertain, and trails behind him on willpower alone.

Elise lies, eyes hazy, with both of her arms pulled into her lap; one is torn and mangled— twisted— with long, bone-deep slashes running over nearly every inch of it.

Still, she breathes a sigh of relief upon seeing them, and Kieran takes her shoulder into his hand as gently as he can.

"I'm going to help," he breathes. "Can you tell me what's—"

"A Saenk broke through some of the electrical," she says, her voice strained with pain. "Caused an explosion, fell through the floor. Only reason I'm alive—"

She winces, and Kieran shakes his head.

"I'm sorry," he says. "I know it hurts."

"Holy *shit,*" she groans. "Who knew healing was such a bitch?"

Ursula takes her other hand, letting her squeeze it tightly, and looks around, uneasy.

"The others?" she whispers.

"Ralph is gone," Elise says, her voice trembling. "It got him first. Charles was there when it collapsed. I haven't seen him."

Ursula's eyes go impossibly darker, and Kieran turns back to her.

"Can you fight?" he asks. " Are you strong enough for that?"

She does not note the fact that he has read the thought in her mind before she can speak it; only shakes her head, her eyes burning.

"Alastor won't fight," she whispers. "Aliya is traumatized, Jack was wounded, Charles..." A quiet sob escapes her lips, and she wipes her mouth. "Charles might be dead. *Someone* has to fight. Our son is in the city."

"Go, then," he says. "I can handle this. I'll find him, Ursula. I won't leave without him."

She wants to plead with him, beg for a promise she knows is unrealistic— tell him to swear he'll bring Charles back to her *alive,* but instead, she only nods, giving Elise's hand one more tight squeeze.

"You stay with him," she forces. "You can trust him."

The younger girl nods, biting down hard on her bottom lip.

"I know," she cries. "Go, now. Be safe."

Ursula nods, lets her go, and leaves without another word, her legs trembling as she walks, her mouth still metallic with the taste of blood.

She drops herself down through the rubble, fighting not to stumble as she lands outside, clutching the hilt of the sword on her waist as she walks around the back of the burning building. If things were less pressing, she would have felt some sort of relief at finding the horses alive, but as things are, she does not even think as she cuts one loose from a carriage. She pulls herself up onto the back of it and holds onto the reins tightly, her vision going in and out with the dizziness in her head as she kicks its side.

She does not look back as she rides away, and does not note any fear that she feels as she sets off into the wilderness, towards the Outskirts, and then the city.

She pushes away the thoughts that try to penetrate her mind— that remind her there will be no one to protect her when she gets there, that tell her she will be unable to battle darkness without losing control to it, and scream Charles' name as if he is already gone.

She silences all of it, as she silences everything else, and moves forward.

CHAPTER FIFTY-FOUR

When Anemos, Icarus, and Cole reach the lower floor, it is already fuller than it should be. Too full, and too loud, and far too stressful for any of them to handle. Anemos struggles to breathe.

A young man is yelling at one of the guards, and as they walk past he grabs him by his throat, pushing him back against the wall.

"How can you not fucking know anything?" he spits. "How do you not know if—"

Icarus catches a glimpse of the man's face and squirms, remembering their last interaction, and the broken leg which resulted.

His leg is still cast.

"Hey," Cole says, pulling Regis back from the guard. "What the hell is going on here?"

Regis turns around to look at Cole, then at Icarus, and springs forward at him, even on his crutches.

"Not *you,*" he says, his voice rough. "Damn it, we don't have any *space*. Why are we wasting it on Jakara *scum* like you?"

"You need to shut your damn mouth, Regis," Anemos interrupts, but Icarus waves him off, shaking his head.

"I don't care," he breathes. "There's t-too much going on."

"Ralph," Regis continues, yelling the name into the guard's face. "He's on the Council. Weapons."

"We're not getting many specific reports from Karneji," the guard says, feigning calm. "All we know is that the damage is substantial. I can't tell you anything about your father."

"Your father?" Icarus asks, pale. Guilt settles in his chest. "Is he there?"

"Do you have any idea what happened?" Cole asks, turning his attention to the guard. "Or what we're dealing with?"

"I'm afraid most of the information around it is classified, for now. All I can tell you is that four Saenks were spotted moving toward the city."

"Four Saenks?" Cole breathes, and with the words, he looks back at the place around them. "Shouldn't more people be taking shelter?"

"Capacity is limited, Myon."

"But there are hardly *any* of the Lower-class here," he laughs, frustrated. "You... They have to be bringing more?"

"The safety of the young is our priority. Many of the younger students are taking shelter at the University. We have guards stationed with defense outside, we're taking the precautions we can."

"Is anyone guarding the shelter?" he asks. "Not the crisis shelter, the live in. The home. For the outskirts kids? Are they all at the University?"

The man's face reddens, and he shakes his head, reluctant.

"No, I... I don't believe... That's not priority. "

"Are you kidding me?"

"You understand my frustration now?" Regis asks, pulling at his hair. "*We* are sitting down here, safe in our shelter, leaving *untrained* civilians with little to no defense. I mean that's—"

"Bullshit," Cole interrupts. "That's bullshit."

"Cole," Anemos breathes, his hands shaking. "Maybe we should—"

"We can fit more people in here," he says. "There's space. There aren't more than fifty or sixty kids in that home. There's *plenty* of room."

"We are already at capacity—"

"Damn the capacity," Regis says. "There are *Saenks*. This isn't a storm, or a pack of blood dogs. People are going to *die,* and you expect us to just sit down here, comfortable? I didn't take that vow."

"Put enough of us down there and we might stand a chance," Cole starts, and the guard shakes his head.

"You've not been trained to combat Saenks. You've only been in advanced training for a month, don't be naive."

They're all quiet a minute, but anger simmers between them— Cole's quickly rising to a boiling point.

"Icarus," Regis says. "Screw you, but you're the best fighter here. If I get some people on board, are you in?"

He doesn't imagine he has much choice. They are dying at his hands. *He* warned the Grim, and brought this upon them.

He nods, clenching his fists.

"An-anything I can do to help—"

"Okay, guys," Anemos says, his voice quiet. "I hate this, but... The guard isn't... He isn't completely wrong, we're not really trained for—"

"Then stay back," Regis snaps. "Cole?"

Cole thinks for only a few seconds, glancing at Anemos out of the corner of his eyes before lowering his head, guilt filling his stomach.

"I'll go," he says. "If you can get a plan quickly."

"You can't be serious," Anemos says, his chest cramping. "Cole, you'll die."

"Well, I don't know what I'm supposed to do," he forces, exasperated. "I know those kids, An, I can't just leave them."

Anemos looks away, shaking his head.

He can feel his hands beginning to tremble at his sides. His pulse is wild and his stomach is sick.

"I need to sit down."

"Anemos—"

"No," he interrupts. "I... I understand, but I can't... I need to sit down."

"There's n...no way we can bring them in?" Icarus asks. "Are you s-sure we've reached capacity?"

"I'm sure," the guard responds.

"Go to hell," Anemos snaps, and with the words, he walks away; he walks halfway back to the other side of the shelter before sitting down and putting his face in his hands, struggling to breathe.

He can't even breathe when he is needed most. He can't even be sure his body will stay his own, if the anxiety of the night continues.

He imagines following his friends into battle and sees nothing but his ability to hold them back, seizing in a moment of crisis, dissociating when he needs to strike. His hands are already shaking. His legs don't feel capable of holding him.

The next few minutes are too long. He keeps his head low, stares at the floor, and covers his ears in an attempt to quiet the noise around him, forgetting the earplugs shoved into his pockets.

The night is moving too quickly, he thinks. It is all too sudden. He can't process things at the speed they are moving.

Not more than five minutes between the first test sirens and the real ones. Only one call to strip any sense of safety he thought he had away.

And now, he is powerless. Panic burns in his stomach, bad enough that he does not want to be alone.

When Cole sits down beside him, it is too soon. The boy puts a hand on his shoulder and he flinches away without meaning to.

He looks over at him and finds his eyes guilty.

"Where's Icarus?" he asks, unable to muster anything else.

"With Regis," Cole says, and then, more softly: "Are you angry?"

"I don't know," he says, wiping his nose. "Are you going?"

Cole hesitates, biting the inside of his bottom lip, and Anemos shakes his head.

"Please don't."

Cole straightens, pushes his hair back out of his face, and laughs shakily.

"I think I'll hate myself if I don't, though."

Anemos watches him, notices his trembling hands, and pulls them into his, shaking his head once more.

"You don't have to, Cole," he says. "It isn't your fight. You don't need to die for it."

"No one else is going to help them," Cole whispers. "I don't know what else to do. I mean... Shit. It's all happening so fast, I... Tell me that I shouldn't go, and I won't. Tell me why my life is any more important than theirs—"

"It isn't," Anemos says. "Of course it isn't, but their lives aren't more important than yours, either."

"But I have a choice," he says, his voice breaking. "There's no one protecting them. No one at all. I mean, I could help. Isn't it worth trying?"

Anemos lets out a long sigh, his eyes filling with tears.

"I can't tell you to do this," he says. "I can't. I would risk the whole world to protect you, right or wrong. You know that."

"But that's selfish."

"I know it is, but you mean more to me than everything, Cole." He chokes slightly, trying to stifle a sob, and pulls Cole into a tight, trembling embrace. He presses a kiss to the side of his face. "You're my whole world."

Cole runs one hand through his hair, staring vacantly into the distance, and when he finally speaks again, the words are broken.

"You won't be mad?" he breathes. "Please, promise me you won't be angry with me, I can't bear the thought of that. I can't bear the thought of something happening and you hating me for it."

"I could never hate you," Anemos whispers. "Never, I promise."

"Thank you," he whispers. And then, fighting back a sob: "I'm sorry."

Anemos nods against his shoulder, his vision fading.

"Promise me you'll come back," he pleads. "Even if it's... Just promise me, please."

Cole pulls away, giving his hand a final tight squeeze.

"I promise."

When Cole walks away, Anemos' eyes return to the floor. He doesn't watch him as he rejoins the group standing by the exit. He doesn't stand with him, encourage him, pray for him, or tell him to be safe. He doesn't tell him that he's proud of him for doing the right thing, or that he thinks he's braver than he will ever be, or hug him on his way out. He doesn't tell him that he loves him.

Of course, Cole expects none of these things, but nonetheless, Anemos will regret not having done each of them; all of them.

He stares at the floor so intently, looking at all of the cracks, stains, and seams, that after a while he can't even tell how much time has passed. He only realizes it hasn't been long when Icarus stops in front of him, holding out one hand in his direction.

He takes it without thinking, and the blond boy kneels down in front of him, forcing a sad smile.

"Hey," he says softly. "We're going."

Anemos nods, hating himself for feeling as numb as he does.

"I'll try to protect him," he continues. "I s-s...swear, I'll do everything I can."

"I know," Anemos says. He forces his voice to soften: "Thank you."

"Will you be okay here?" Icarus asks, rubbing his thumb over the back of the other boy's hand.

"I'll be fine," he breathes, his throat tightening. "Stay safe."

A cry erupts, in the distance, and Anemos' eyes darken.

"I'll try," Icarus says, his voice shaking. "Pray for me, will you?"

"Sure, Icarus."

"Alright! Chop chop, lads," Regis yells. "Places to be."

"Can I hug you?" Icarus asks, and Anemos embraces him without a second thought, holding him so tightly that all of the fear leaves him, for a moment.

It is only a moment.

Then Icarus pulls away, and squeezes his hand tightly, and goes. Anemos realizes how warm he still was once he's gone and looks down at his hands, his heart speeding up.

He would hold them back if he went. He knows that. He is too prone to panic— to seizures, and stumbling, and trembling...

And yet, he feels the urge to run out the door after them, because suddenly, he is alone.

The ceiling above them creaks, the lights flicker, and everyone falls quiet, as if the fear steals the breath from all of them at once.

He is not sure when the numbness goes and he begins to think. He only realizes, suddenly, that he could lose everything by the end of the night. It is morbid, he thinks— and selfish, worrying about the way all of *their* suffering could hurt *him,* but his mother is in Karneji.

His mother is in Karneji, Charles is in Karneji, Jack is in Karneji, Zahra— to his knowledge— is on the Outskirts, and the only other two people he has ever trusted are in the city, and none of their lives feel like a guaranteed thing, and suddenly the rain is too l oud.

They could all be dead before sunrise; everyone. Everyone he knows, everyone who has ever tried to protect him from anything.

Alastor could live, the Compounds could be destroyed, he might have to go home and he might have nowhere else to run to, nowhere else to hide.

He tugs at his clothes and closes his eyes; his breath catching, his legs curling toward him, and his arms starting to twitch. Alone, in a room full of people he does not know and does not trust.

It feels as if his whole world is already gone.

CHAPTER FIFTY-FIVE

Regis is talking, but Icarus doesn't hear him. It seems, for a moment, that he cannot hear anything but the rain.

Chills work their way over his feverish body, and he shivers slightly, letting his head hang back, looking up into the starless sky.

They're all so casual, he thinks, considering what is coming.

Discussing their plans like they're still in class, joking about Regis' leg, which Cole tore out of its cast ten minutes earlier, swearing that four weeks was plenty of time to heal. Shockingly enough, it was.

Icarus might have noticed it was strange, if the circumstances were different, but he hardly even registers the event now; only the laughter.

Only the pretending.

It is strange how little he wants to die *tonight*, thinking clearly. It is stranger that he is questioning it, he imagines, but he still does.

Tonight, when he thinks of his death, he thinks of Anemos asking him to be safe, his father looking for some sign of light and finding his son gone, and Cole fighting alone, and her.

He thinks of her, and it is like ice in his veins.

"Aye, firefly?"

Zahra lifts her head slightly, mostly asleep, and smiles as she lets her face fall back against the pillow.

"Firefly?" she asks. *"I like that one."*

He smiles a little, despite everything, and the action sends pain through his chest.

"Me too."

"How are you feeling?" she asks.

"Much better," he lies. *"Things are actually pretty scary right now, though."*

"Are you safe?"

Cole places a hand on his arm, and when he looks over, the other four— former classmates, people he has known since childhood, even if he has not known them well— are already walking away.

He wonders if he will ever see them again.

"Yeah, well, that's why I wanted to talk to you. I hope I didn't wake you."

"I hope we're not too late," Cole says, his voice heavy in a way Icarus has not heard before. "They sound close."

"I hope th-th-there's something we can do—"

There's another cry, closer, and both of them start to walk, quickly, hardly noticing the r ain.

"You can wake me."

"Zahra, I might need to go to Morta for a little while," he lies.

"Oh, okay."

"I just thought I should tell you," he says, his hands trembling. *"I don't want you to think I've done something, if I disappear. I don't want you to worry."*

Her face falls a little, and she pulls the thin blanket more tightly around her, her sore body seeming to ache even worse upon hearing the words.

"Will you be gone long, do you think?"

"I can't really be sure," he says. *"I'll try not to be."*

"You'll be safe?"

Something falls nearby; something big.

They both freeze in place, and Icarus places one hand on the sword strapped to his waist.

"I'll be safe," he says. *"Try not to worry, okay? Try not to miss me too much."*

"Did that sound..." Cole's voice trembles. He clears his throat. "Did it sound like it came from the left or the right?"

"Left, I think," Icarus says, having to yell over the rain. "W-which way to the shelter?"

"Straight, then right," he breathes, and then, laughing nervously: "My word. I'm so glad that Anemos stayed back, and that he'll be safe, but..." He laughs again, shaking his head. "I think I've overestimated my ability to handle literally anything at all without h im."

Icarus smiles, sad, and squeezes his shoulder.

"Well, we'll be-be-be-b-back to him soon, yeah?"

"Yeah," he sighs. "Yeah, definitely."

They turn the corner slowly, swords gripped tightly in both of their hands, and their eyes land on the shelter, still untouched, undamaged.

"I almost wonder if they'd be safer in a place that's already been hit," Cole says. "This feels like such an easy target."

"Is there any shelter inside?"

"There's a basement, but it's hardly—"

Another cry, and they both shudder at the sound.

"I'm thinking a b-basement is better than nothing."

"Yeah," Cole nods. "Okay. Should we both go in? Or?"

"I'd rather not separate." His chest cramps, and he blinks tears away from his eyes.

"You're afraid," he says. *"Don't be afraid, I promise, I'm safe. I'm going to be fine."*

"It feels like you're saying goodbye."

Cole pulls open the door to the shelter, and the cold air from inside seems to sting.

Icarus twists his neck slightly, wincing against the cold, afraid of the darkness of the hall ahead of him.

Like Karneji, he thinks, and he does not even mean to grab Cole's hand as he does.

"I'm not," he says, wondering if it is really kinder to lie to her. *"I might not even go. I just didn't want to scare you."*

"I don't know if I believe you."

Cole flicks a switch on the wall, and the lights on the ceiling come on, warm and dull.

"It's so quiet," he says. "It feels empty. I bet they've gone down already."

"You check," Icarus breathes. "I'll s...stay here, watch out."

"Okay," he nods, and with the word, he walks out of the room, leaving Icarus alone.

There is dirt on the floor, Icarus notices; cobwebs hanging along the ceiling, chips in the paint and the wood of the floor.

Not a priority.

"Icarus?"

"I just didn't want to scare you, since you thought I had died last time. A bit dramatic though, Zahra, if we're being honest."

"Oh, stop it."

He smiles a little at her voice, tears flooding his eyes, and thunder rattles the window panes, making the lights flicker and his body tremble.

"I have to go now," he forces, and the words seem to tear something from him. *"I'll talk to you soon."*

She hesitates, her hands balled into tight fists, and tells herself that he is not lying to her, despite the feeling of dread in her chest.

"Okay," she forces. *"Stay safe, Reaper."*

It's as if he can feel her leave, feel himself shutting her out, cutting himself away so the pain misses her if it comes.

When he does, his chest seems to cave in on itself, forcing the tears from his eyes.

"Look at yourself, Oracamatis," Assecula whispers.

"No," he says, out loud, and he wipes his face with the word, unsure of where it comes from. "I'm not yours."

The moments pass slowly, but after what feels like hours, Cole turns the corner and nods, pale.

"They're... Yeah, they're down there."

"What's wrong?" Icarus asks, burning with fever.

"It's nothing. Nothing's wrong, it's just that..." He lets out a long sigh, blinks rapidly. "Icarus, they're twice as crowded down there, in the basement, as we would all be at the Compounds if they came." He shakes his head. "I'm just so damn tired of all of it. Sixty kids and not one single guard—"

There is a loud thump above them, so loud it shakes the ceiling, and then a cry erupts from the roof, seeming to split them both to their core.

The lights die.

Icarus looks over at his friend, in the darkness, and can barely see him. Still, he knows that he is afraid. He can feel the shortness of his breath, the shaking of his shoulders.

Too soon, he thinks. Too sudden.

"What do we do?" Cole asks, his voice broken. "What do we—"

The roof caves in.

Time seems to stop.

Both of them remain still, listening to the thing walk, tear, and destroy, only a few floors above them.

An eerie calm sets in, and Cole turns to Icarus, much of the fear in his eyes drowned by a familiar grief; the same grief that Icarus has felt almost every day— even as a child, in Jakara.

"It's inside," he whispers. "Should we... The doorway, we can lead it out."

"Okay," Icarus nods.

They move to the door, and when they open it the thing shrieks, as if in response, but it doesn't matter long.

It is a strange thing, tragedy.

In all of the stories told to the children in the Ordinem, it is a crescendo. Its destruction is expected, final— beautiful, in a way. Usually, it is with purpose. The Oracamatis, splitting the veil. Some Higher-class man dying with a scythe to his throat, sacrificing his life for a higher cause, helping to bring darkness to its knees.

In the Ordinem, tragedy is a romance, a ballad, and a lullaby; but the Ordinem, as always, is a distortion.

There is nothing beautiful here. There is no preparation. There is no fight, no struggle, and certainly no hero.

The Saenk on the upper floor is so loud that Icarus does not hear it happen. He only feels it, as a wave of red sprays against his skin.

At first, he thinks that it is his, but there is no pain, and the realization stuns him— it knocks the air out of his lungs.

The Saenk waiting behind the door is not as loud and animalistic as the one upstairs. It waited quietly, patiently. It listened, waiting for the door to open instead of breaking it down, and now, when Icarus turns around, it seems to smile.

Icarus does not even notice it as his eyes fall to Cole, who looks down at the sharp hand run through him vacantly, silently, as if it is nothing at all.

Icarus stares at it in shock, and then looks back at his friend, broken and bent around it, his head hanging limp on his shoulders and blood running from his mouth; not quite dead, but not alive, either.

"Icar—" The boy chokes, realizing, unable to lift his head. "Icarus, don't... Don't look—"

The thing jerks, and Icarus falls toward him, grabbing his hands.

"No..." he whispers. "No, n-not... Not you—"

The thing jerks Cole again, and a weak cry escapes his lips at the pain it sends through him.

"Stop," Icarus cries. "Stop, please..."

He fumbles for the sword on his waist only to realize that he's already dropped it, and his body is suddenly too numb to let him bend and retrieve it, so he only stares ahead in horror as the thing opens its mouth, almost as if it's laughing.

Cole tries to hold Icarus back, tries to hold onto anything at all, even if it is only his breath, but fails, too weak to move even his hands.

"I'm sorry," he chokes, unable to breathe, and Icarus squeezes his hands, trying to warm them even as the other Saenk breaks through the ceiling behind him.

"It's... It's going to be oka—"

The one in front of him jerks its hand to the side, violently slamming Cole's already broken body against the doorframe, watching as everything in Icarus breaks in the same instant.

He does not even notice as a long slash is cut across his back.

"Stop!" he yells, sobbing. "P-p-please— Please stop—"

It jerks Cole to the right, smashing his face against the wood, and the living boy falls back against the floor in horror, unable to think, much less fight.

The thing moves, behind him, and the Saenk in front of him tosses Cole across the room like a ragdoll, bending down toward Icarus as the other one claws the crumbled boy up from the ground.

Icarus scrambles backward, his hands slipping in all of the blood, and the Saenk lifts one hand in the air, straightening it back into the same blade-like appendage that ran through his friend.

He slips from his elbows, his back hitting the floor, and lets out a loud cry of pain as the cut tears deeper.

The hand thrusts toward his chest, but just as it is about to make contact with him, the Saenk lets out a long, strangled cry and stumbles backward, hitting the floor in two botched pieces.

The world falls quiet.

Someone kneels beside him, trying as best they can to pull him from the ground.

"Icarus," she says, her voice shaking. "Icarus, I need you to look at me."

He jerks away, struggling to breathe, and shakes his head.

"There-there's another one," he cries. "Behind m-m-me, there's... It has him."

"There's nothing there, Icarus," she breathes. "It's gone."

"No," he cries. "No, he... He can't b-b-be—"

"We need to go," she whispers, as gently as she can. "I need you to hold onto me."

"But the... People..."

"There are only two more Saenks," she says. "Both at the Compounds, they'll be—"

"Josh," he cries. "Regis, M-mara, Halley?"

"They're safe," she says. "Icarus, I need you to—"

"I c-can't move," he gasps. "I can't..."

Another figure appears at his side, this one younger, unfamiliar.

"He's injured," the man says, and when he reaches forward, Icarus flinches back away from him. "I'll take care of him, you go to the Compounds."

Ursula nods, casting a last, sickened glance at Icarus before pulling herself from the ground.

"Th-there's another one," Icarus says again. "Just, right behind me."

"There's nothing there," Kieran says, pulling him up by his wrists. "There's nothing there— hey."

Icarus pulls back away from him, and he puts a hand on his shoulder.

"Hey," he whispers. "There's nothing there, you're safe."

"It cut me... It h-had him... It was right there."

"I believe you," he says. "I believe you, but it's gone now. It's gone back."

"He's gone," he sobs. "Cole, he's... He's.... W-we have to find him."

Kieran clenches his jaw, shakes his head, and opens his arms, letting Icarus cling to him like they are not strangers.

He moves a hand around to his back, pressing it over the cuts as gently as he can, trying not to startle him.

"It's okay," he whispers. "You're going to be okay... What's your name? Can you tell me your name?"

"M-m-michael," the boy cries, and he doesn't even mean to say it; the name is the only one his lips manage to find. "My name is..."

Kieran pales, his chest hollowing out.

"Michael?" he asks. "Your name is Michael?"

"I go by Icarus," he corrects himself, and then he winces in pain, tears coming faster.

"I know," Kieran whispers. "I'm sorry, it won't hurt long."

"How are you..."

"I'm a Deviation," he says, and as he does, his eyes catch the long, dark scars running over Icarus' shoulder. "Icarus?"

"Y-y-yes?"

Fear runs through Kieran's body, but he speaks anyway, as slowly and carefully as he can.

"I need you to listen to me, alright? I know... I know you're in shock, but..." He pulls back away from him, not minding the blood on his hands as he takes him by the side of the face. "Things are going to get worse before they get better. I'm sorry, I know that's not what you want to hear."

"Wh-what?"

"William was warned of their plans, he took them to Assecula to hold them back... God, I'm so sorry about your friend, I didn't think they would come through here."

"What are you—"

"Are these scars from Terra?" he asks, and Icarus' body becomes impossibly tighter, paler. "It's okay, I'm on your side, you don't have to be... Take this."

He unbuttons his shirt and pulls it off, pressing it into the other boy's hands, leaving him with only the thin black shirt underneath it.

The scarring peeking around the edges makes Icarus flinch.

"You need to stay low if you're going to survive. Things will only remain calm for the grieving period, and that won't be long. They'll suspect treason from someone with access to the Higher-class, but they'll likely interrogate all of you. If you can shift into Morta—"

"I'm too weak," he breathes. "And I can't leave—"

"Then you need to be careful," Kieran forces. "Extremely careful. Hatred for your kind will likely become much stronger here, in these following days."

There is a cry, in the distance, and Icarus pulls the shirt around his shoulders, dazed.

"Things are not what they seem, do you understand?" Kieran asks. "I know you're in shock, I know you've just lost... But I need you to hear me. Life, death, Inanis... None of it. None of these people. *Nothing* the darkness tells you... You are so much less alone than you think you are. I need you to hear that, especially in the light of *this*. Do you understand me?" Icarus nods, unable to speak, and Kieran takes his hands again. "Can you stand?"

Icarus digs his heels into the floor and pushes himself up, trembling so violently that he nearly falls again before Kieran presses his sword back into his hand.

"Can you fight?" he asks, his voice loud over the rain.

Despite the uncertainty Icarus feels, he nods, sobs still wracking his chest.

"Have you ever been trained?" Kieran continues. "By one of the Grim?"

"N-no..."

"But you know your capability?"

"I have heard only of the-the-the *harm* I can bring."

"What else?"

"Wh-what do you m-m-mean what else?"

"That you're darkness?" he asks. "That your mind is easily won?"

"I…"

"Throw it all away," he says. "All of it. You have already lost too much to that lie, and to the other."

"The other?"

"That you must sacrifice your power to be good. They will *not* take control of you if you use it, not like—" He shakes his head. "Deviations like me, *we* have to worry about that. Our power is of Terra; it is neutral, gray. Yours?"

He shakes his head and walks to the open door, taking Icarus by the hand. The latter looks the former over with tired, darkened eyes.

Too thin, he thinks, dizzily. The man's collarbones stick out sharply, and his elbows stand out like two knots in his arms, bruised, all the way up his neck.

Veins surface, dark, under his eyes. It is the only real sign of life in the man's pale, ashen s kin.

"You are Assecula's antithesis, Michael. It has no power over you."

"But… but… Th-the Oracam-m-matis."

"Angels fall, yes? You can give up your control, but it can not *take* it," he says, stepping out into the rain. "I need you to use the power you hold, Icarus. I need you to use it *now.*"

"I'm too weak."

"This isn't realm shifting. This will come naturally to you. You're Grim, it's in your nature. *I* need help. It's too much, tonight. Too many of them."

"If I do anything," Icarus says, "They will *kill* me."

"Stay with me," he nods. "I'll play the part, but I *need* you. Everyone at the Compounds needs you."

Icarus shakes his head and looks down at the ground, his blue eyes red with fear, and grief, and fever.

"I *can't.*"

"Do you believe in all of it?" Kieran asks. "Do you believe that the Wind speaks?"

"Y-yes."

"Then listen to it now."

Icarus chokes, wipes his face, smearing the blood across it, and closes his eyes.

He can almost feel it, almost.

He looks back up, unsure, and nods anyway, letting the man lead him away.

He thinks, deep inside, that he is returning to the Compounds as less than half of himself, his hands numb, his stomach sick, and his chest hollow.

He is still seeing it, and yet he is walking, as if on autopilot. His mind is back at the shelter, dying again and again.

"If I fail..." Icarus cries.

"You won't."

When they arrive back at the Compounds, this building, too, is burning; everything, all of it, turning to ash.

One Saenk pulls itself up through what is left of the roof, howling as if in greeting, and Icarus flinches back.

"I'm right here," Kieran says. "I won't let it—"

It leaps down from the roof, landing on the ground in front of him, and Icarus' nose starts to bleed; pushing the thing's voice out of his head.

Blood, spraying across his face—

It is with nothing but a tired, broken sob, that he throws the thing back against the building, writhing and shrieking in pain, blood vessels popping open across its arms and l egs.

"Kill it," he says, through gritted teeth. "Take the sword."

Kieran pries the sword from Icarus' grip uneasily, and steps toward it, his eyes dark.

"Fuck you," he mutters, jamming the sword into the middle of its throat and yanking the blade back and forth artlessly until the head falls from its body, rolling lifelessly across the ground.

Kieran turns around, wipes his nose.

"Are you okay?" he asks.

"No," Icarus breathes, trembling. "Where's the other one?"

The other side of the building begins to move, to groan, caving in like the rest of it, and they both look over at it uneasily.

They don't talk as they head toward it.

"It's inside," Kieran says, after a moment. "I'd say we wait it out, but I don't know the strength of your shelter."

"M-me neither. I don't... don't know if I want to risk it."

He pulls open the still intact door and a cloud of smoke pours out into the street, but there is no immediate light behind it.

He coughs, choking on it, and turns to Icarus with his eyebrows raised.

"If that's what you think is best," he says, "I'm with you."

Icarus stares into the building for a moment, noting the quiet inside.

Like the Saenk behind the door.

"I don't want anyone else to get hurt," he says. "But I don't want to get cor...ornered."

"What if I take out the wall?" Kieran asks, pulling his wet hair away from his mouth. "Will that help?"

"Can you *do* that?"

"I can try. Structures aren't as—"

A shriek comes from inside, and then several loud bangs.

Fighting.

"Try," Icarus says, and Kieran turns back to the building, his chest heavy.

He closes his eyes, tries to focus through the shadows in his head, and Icarus watches as the walls begin to crack.

Pain burns through every inch of the young man's body, as if the blood in his veins is poison, and his mind begins to slip, darkness closing in around his vision.

"Michael," he whimpers, his voice strained. "Take my hand, please."

Icarus steps forward without question, grabs his hand tightly, and puts one hand on his upper back.

"I'm sorry," Kieran says. "I promise, I'm not going to—"

"You're an E.D.T.," Icarus breathes, watching as he winces in pain.

"Yes," he says. "But I'm not going to lose control. I'm in control."

A loud crunching sound fills the space around them, and the walls crumble— several of them, back through the building, leaving the Saenk and Ursula in plain sight.

It is above her, rearing back, preparing to attack, but when it jumps forward, it is thrown nearly to the other side of the building, catching fire before standing again, shrieking at the lot of them.

"Was that... y...you?" Icarus asks.

Kieran coughs, blood staining his lips, and grips the sword in his hand.

"Hold him down," he says. "I'll kill him, just... hold him there."

"In the fire?"

"I'll be fine," he breathes, his voice rough. "Just hold him."

Icarus hesitates, watching the man in front of him with fearful eyes, but then the thing collapses to the ground, as if being pushed, and Kieran nods in thanks.

He approaches it quickly, not minding the flames, not stopping as the heat burns his arms, and drives the sword directly through its heart— more than once.

Dark blood sprays out from the thing's body— into the fire, onto his face— but he continues long after it is dead.

When he is finished, he stares down at it vacantly and does not move.

"And yet I am still with you," it whispers. *"We are still one."*

"Hey," Icarus calls, stumbling toward him, through the fire. "Hey, come on."

"And look what we've done together. Think of what we'll—"

A hand is placed on his bicep and he is pulled back from the decay, his lips trembling.

"Look at me," Icarus says. "Look at m-m-me, hey."

His eyes drift away, but Icarus still searches for them, holding the side of his face with one hand.

"What's your name?" he asks. "Can-can...can you tell m-me your name?"

"Kieran," he says, his voice airy, dissociated. "My name is Kieran."

"Nothing the darkness says," Icarus breathes. "You're Kieran. You're n-not... H-hold on..."

Ursula arrives at their side a moment later, out of breath, and Kieran looks up at her with dark eyes.

"I don't blame you," he says shakily. "I really... c-can't blame you..."

She steps forward, drapes one of his arms over her shoulders and holds him up, wiping the blood from his face, but she does not respond to him. She does not even acknowledge his words.

"Icarus," she says, her voice strained. "Are you alright?"

"I'm... I'm n-n-not harmed, but... M...Myon, Cole..."

Her eyes become impossibly darker, her shoulders tense.

"It was Cole," she mutters, disbelieving. "It was *Cole,* who was with you?"

"I thought you knew."

"No, I didn't..." Her voice breaks. Icarus has never heard it break before. "I'm sorry. I'm so sorry, but we have to go. I've been given word to head to the Palace."

"But An—"

"Charles will collect him," she interrupts. "It's best we... We get the both of you safe. Icarus... I don't want you there, when he finds out."

Icarus nods, his hands shaking. He is too terrified to argue.

"Okay," he whispers.

Kieran lifts his head, blinking slowly.

"Back to the Palace?" he asks. "You're taking me back to the Palace? Did anyone find the Commander?"

"He'll come in later this evening, he's instructed us to keep you in the prison here tonight. You'll be leaving tomorrow."

"Prison?" Icarus asks, his voice shaking.

No one responds to him. Kieran nods in Ursula's direction, chewing on his lips.

"Very well, Myon."

"Is... Is m-my... Are my parents..."

"They'll be fine," Ursula nods. "Your father's with a medic now, but he'll be okay. They both will. I promise."

Icarus nods, his weary body breathing a sigh of relief. It is the last thing any of them say before Ursula leads them away, too troubled to say anything else.

Chapter Fifty-Six

It is almost an hour before Charles makes it back to what is left of the Compounds. He walks into the shelter with still bloody clothes and his hands clenched into tight fists.

The guard bows to him, steps aside, and the respect revolts him.

When he steps into the main area, the sight of them all dizzies him. He can barely manage well enough to look for his son among all of the pale, tear stained faces.

"Anemos," he says to the guard. "Where is Anemos?"

"The back," the guard responds. "He had... A bit of an incident."

"An incident?"

"A seizure, Myon, but he seemed to recover quickly—"

Charles does not wait for the man to finish before he moves past him, pushing through the crowded room until he sees Anemos, up against the wall in the corner of the room, his knees curled up to his chest.

The boy lifts his head to see him, and then lets his eyes fall shut, his heart hammering against his ribcage.

"Why are you here?" he asks, when Charles is closer. "Why are you... Where are they?"

Charles hesitates, and Anemos straightens his legs slightly, pulling himself up.

"Where are—"

"Anemos," he interrupts. "Can we go outside?"

Anemos' eyes darken with fear, but he nods, too tired to panic instantly.

"Yeah, we can..." He looks Charles up and down, swallows hard. "What happened to you?"

"You don't need to worry," Charles says calmly. "The Facility collapsed, and I got caught on the lower floor. I'm fine now."

"The Facility collapsed?" Anemos asks. "Is Mom okay?"

"Your mother is fine."

"Jack?" he asks. "Aliya?"

Charles' chest tightens, but he forces himself to nod, turning away.

"They're alright," he says. "Come, now."

He starts to walk away before Anemos can debate him, before he can ask any more questions.

"The guard says you had a seizure," he asks. "Are you alright, now?"

"I'm exhausted," Anemos responds, trailing behind him, "and terrified, but otherwise... I guess. Charles?"

They step through the door, out into the cold, smoky air, and come to a pause beside the building.

Anemos looks up at the Compounds, and his throat tightens.

"It's all... Where will we stay?"

"At home," Charles says, resuming his pace, trying to get Anemos as far away from onlookers as he can; trying to protect him, even if it is futile.

"At home," Anemos repeats. "Well, that's... Where will Cole stay? He was at the shelter before."

The older man lowers his head slightly, his eyes burning, and continues walking without a word.

"Charles?" Anemos asks.

He turns around, nods.

"Are they alright? Cole and Icarus? You've not said anything."

"I want to talk to you alone," he says. "The shelter isn't—"

"We're alone now." Anemos stops in the middle of the street. "There's no one..." He shakes his head, cracks his knuckles. "I mean, are they... Are they hurt?"

The words sit in Charles' throat, but they do not come, no matter how hard he tries to force them out.

Dread fills the boy's chest, his stomach, cold and sharp.

"Charles?"

"Icarus is back at the Palace," Charles says. "Where we're going. He was injured, but he'll be alright."

"And Cole?"

He hesitates a long moment, and then shakes his head, his hands trembling.

"What?" Anemos breathes. "What's happened?"

"Anemos..." Charles softens his voice, fighting the urge to look away from the boy's eyes as they begin to understand. "Cole didn't..."

"Stop," he says, his voice breaking. "Stop. You're... Is he hurt?"

"Anemos—"

"Did something happen to him?" he asks, tears already forming in his eyes. "Did something... Where is he? Can I—"

"Anemos," Charles interrupts, his own voice choked.

"What?"

"...Cole is gone."

Anemos freezes, all of the air leaving him in the same instant. Charles can see it— the change in his very being that takes place upon hearing the words.

"Gone?" he asks, his voice a broken whisper. "He's *gone?*"

"Anemos, I'm so sorry—"

"Stop," he says. "You're... You're lying."

"I'm not—"

"Why the hell are you... Why are you saying this? Josh, and Mara, and... The rest of them made it back."

"I know."

"So why the hell are you telling me that he didn't?" he asks, his breath catching in his throat, turning into a sob. "Why are you... You're wrong. He's... Did you even see it?"

"Icarus saw it happen," Charles says. "He told Ursula."

"Saw *what* happen?" Anemos cries. "What happened?"

"I... I don't know everything, but, it was a Saenk—"

"A Saenk?" he asks. "It was a..." He chokes on the words, his whole body vibrating with fear, unable to process any of the other man's words. "Did they find him?"

"He was gone by the time Ursula got there."

"But his body?" He grabs at the hem of his shirt, his fists clenched so tightly that his palms begin to bleed onto the fabric. "I mean, they found something. They had to find *something.*"

"He was gone—"

"He can't just be *gone,* "Anemos yells. "He's not... No. That isn't... He can't be..."

He sways, gags, stumbles forward, and Charles reaches forward to catch him on instinct, taking his hands.

"Hey, hey..."

"He can't be... Please, tell me you might be wrong. Please. He can't be."

"Anemos..."

"It's *Cole,*" he cries, unsure of whether to hold on to Charles' hands or let them go. "He was just here, just a few hours ago."

"I know."

"And he said he'd be back, and I mean... He wouldn't lie to me. He wouldn't... No. I mean, he's Cole. He can't be..." His cries grow louder, more violent. "He's my best friend. He's all I have."

"I understand—"

"No you don't," he cries, and the words are not meant to be cruel. "You don't. You can't. I mean... You wouldn't be telling me he was gone if you..."

He falls silent, his eyes moving back and forth rapidly, and does not even breathe as panic sets into him.

"Anemos," Charles says. "I am so... *so* sorry."

He falls forward into Charles' chest, sobbing, clinging to him like he might be the only thing left in the world, and Charles holds him as carefully as he can.

"Breathe," he whispers. "I need you to—"

"I love him," Anemos cries. "I love him more than anything, he can't be... I *need* him."

Charles rubs one hand slowly over his upper back, nodding against the top of his head. "I know."

"I *love* him. Please... We have to... There has to be some way to bring him back. There has to be..."

"If there was any way... Anyway at all—"

"I never even *told* him," he gasps. "I love him so much. I have to find him, I have to—"

"He knew, Anemos."

They stop talking after that. They stop moving. They only stand, in the middle of the street, Anemos seeming to break more with every moment that passes— Charles becoming gradually more resentful of himself and of everyone around him.

It is strange and horrific, but as he holds the war torn boy, his rage does not point at the Reaper. The Reaper, who committed a far less deadly crime than the one the Ordinem would have committed in Morta.

He is too tired to fight his own mind as it leads him toward the truth; the fact that the Reaper might possibly be a man, much like himself. The fact that he sought even *more* destruction than this, to protect his own people. The fact that the crisis at hand could have been averted, if those that claimed to be righteous had not been so blinded by their fear, and their hatred, and held back the unstable attack.

This is their fault, he thinks; the Ordinem's.

And through the grief wracking Anemos' body— through the pain, the loss, and the loneliness crippling his mind— he thinks so, too.

Anger seeps into the grief like acid, burning what is left of the hope inside of him away.

"I can't stand anymore," he whispers, sometime later. "I can't... I need to sit."

"Okay," Charles says, and he guides him to an un-burnt wall sitting on the cold, wet ground beside him.

"I need..." Anemos says, barely able to speak through the sobs which have not stopped. "Can I talk to you, please?"

"Yes, of course you can."

"P-please don't make me go home," he cries. "Not right now, not... I can't..."

"I wasn't going to send you back tonight."

"I need you to not send me back," Anemos weeps. "I can't go back. I can't explain, b ut... I can't take anymore. I know you said no, before, but I... I think it'll kill me. I know it will— "

"Okay," Charles responds, concern evident in his voice. "You can stay with me, if that's..."

Anemos nods, and Charles follows suit, his chest aching.

"Okay," Charles says. "I'll talk with your parents tomorrow. You don't need to worry about any of that."

"What if he—"

"If he tries to talk to you, come and find me."

Anemos nods, pulling his knees back up to his chest, fighting the nausea in his stomach, and after what feels like hours he moves a little closer to the man beside him, resting his head against his shoulder.

He stays there, held, long after the tears stop, long after sleep takes him, and Charles does not move.

Charles stays awake, his breath heavy, and prays for wisdom, in a world where almost everything he has ever been taught has been wrong, where he has been told so many lies that he does not even know where to *look* for truth; he prays, and as he does, he looks at his son curled up against him.

After eighteen years of failure, he thinks, wearily, that he is sure of something.

INTERLUDE: A GOODBYE

A *nemos met Cole when he was thirteen years old.*

It was a cool day, right at the end of summer, near the beginning of their first year at the University. Anemos was sitting alone, far off from the others, and Cole was curious.

He had been watching Anemos since the beginning of the year— wondering, questioning— but unlike many of the other children, his curiosity was untainted by the jealousy and intimidation that so frequently surrounded children of those in the Ordinem's Higher-class. He saw only a boy; a lonely one.

He exited the cafeteria and went out into the hall, opening the door with his feet and carrying his food and drink with both hands.

Anemos was sitting by one of the windows when Cole found him, his feet propped up on the ledge.

"Hey," Cole said, trying not to sound shy. "Why do you always sit out here?"

Anemos turned around, nervously cracking his knuckles, surprised by the boy's presence but trying not to show it.

"I like being alone," he said.

"You can't like being alone all of the time."

"Sure I can," he laughed, confused. "I don't like the other kids very much, anyway."

"How are you supposed to like people you don't know?"

"I'm not, but..." He stopped, picking up a piece of food. "Look, I just like being alone, okay? I'm not good with people."

"Neither am I," Cole sighed. "You're lucky you don't care. Being alone is awful when you do."

"You're never alone," Anemos said. "You're always talking to someone."

"I guess."

"What do you mean you guess? You're the most social person here. Always talking, always being loud and—"

"*Annoying?*" *Cole interrupted.*

Anemos pressed his lips together and shook his head. "Funny. I was going to say funny. I mean, you make me laugh, with all the stuff you say."

"*Yeah, no, people laugh sometimes,*" *Cole said lightly. "But you know, as much as I talk, no one really cares. I think that's being alone, too."*

Anemos looked down at his hands.

He understood, even if he didn't say it then.

"*I'm sorry, I shouldn't be bothering you. I just thought maybe..." Cole stopped, realizing that he had said too much again, and shook his head. "I'll leave you alone."*

He turned to go, but Anemos stopped him, resenting himself a little for doing it.

"*If..." he started, and the boy turned around. "If you're really that lonely with them, I wouldn't mind you sitting out here. I'm not looking for a friend, but... I don't know. I don't mind you."*

A smile tugged at the edges of Cole's lips, but he tried to hold them down.

"*Don't expect me to talk much, though," Anemos said. "Or like, hang out. I don't do that... stuff."*

"*Yeah, sure, that's... That'll be fine."*

"*I'm cold," Cole said softly, his teeth chattering.*

"*You're always cold," Anemos said, pulling a blanket around his shoulders anyway.*

"*But it's really... really cold here. The ocean makes it colder." He wiped his nose, looking over at his newfound friend with bright eyes. "What time is it?"*

"*Eleven fifty-eight," Anemos said, kicking his legs out over the edge of the cliff they sat on. "Two more minutes as a thirteen year old, any final thoughts?"*

"*Hm," he sniffed. "Let me think, uh..."*

"*Eleven fifty-nine."*

"*Okay, okay. Sure, here's something: I think thirteen's been my favorite."*

"*Really?" Anemos asked.*

"*Really, I mean—"*

"*It's 'cause you've had me here," he joked, and Cole laughed, despite the truth of the statement.*

Anemos just watched him, his heart in his throat.

"You know, I've not celebrated my birthday in... I don't even remember the last time. This is nice. All of this is nice. You, too."

"Me? Nice? You're the only one who thinks so."

"No one else knows you, then." He shivered once more. "You're wonderful."

"Shh," Anemos scolded. "It's your birthday, you can't ring it in complimenting me."

"But I—"

"Midnight," he said. "You're so freaking old."

Cole laughed, pulling the blanket tighter around his shoulders, scooting closer to him. "So freaking old."

"Old man."

They both looked out at the sea, falling quiet a moment, happy, together, and then Anemos took Cole's hand— careful, like it was something precious.

Cole turned back to him with a light smile on his face, and Anemos let out a heavy sigh.

"I hope we always have each other," he said softly. "I'm sorry, that's weird."

"We will," Cole said, anyway.

"Yeah?"

"Yeah, Anemos."

"Do you want me to come with you?" Anemos asked, the cold biting at his face.

"No, that's alright," Icarus said. "I'll meet you guys back at the Compounds."

He began to walk away, but stopped at the sound of Anemos' voice behind him.

"Be safe."

Icarus turned around, flashed a quick smile.

"I will be."

When he was gone, Anemos stayed at the edge of the rooftop, staring out beyond the city with a knot in his chest.

Cole shifted slightly behind him, stretching as he opened his eyes.

"What are you looking at?" he asked, sleepy.

Anemos turned around and shook his head.

"There's a train coming in," he said, walking back toward him. "Icarus went to investigate. I'm sure it's nothing to worry about."

He sat back down beside him, and took Cole's hand the same way he always had.

"Should we go back?" he asked. "You're freezing."

"I'm always cold," Cole said, his breath like fog on the air.

"You can have your jacket back if you want."

He laughed softly, shook his head.

"I'm fine, Anemos. I..." He looked at him for a second, then leaned his head back against the wall. "My word, it's been so long since we were alone, hasn't it? Without the noise of that place, and the chance of someone barging in."

"Mhm," Anemos nodded. He went quiet, the way he did when he was thinking, keeping his eyes on the other boy's.

"What?" Cole asked.

"Hm?"

"What are you thinking?"

"Nothing," he said.

"Something," Cole responded, squeezing his hand. "Come on, share."

"It's really nothing. It's just... I don't know. I like it. I like being alone with you."

"Oh," he said, almost laughing. "I like being alone with you too."

Anemos could have told him the rest. He could have told him he didn't ever consider the possibility of enjoying being alone with someone— didn't ever even think he would be comfortable alone with someone, but instead he just smiled, looking away and up at the sky.

"Anemos?"

"Mhm?"

"I want to ask you something, but I'm worried it might... I don't know."

He looked back down, eyes starry, and laughed under his breath.

"Just ask," he said.

Cole looked at him a moment, his heart beating too fast, and then spoke softly.

"I know you're... Different, about these things. We've not talked about it much, about what you... I'm stumbling, I'm sorry."

"Cole, it's me. What is it? What things?"

Cole looked up, swallowed hard, and then looked back at him, his face flushed with embarrassment and cold.

"I want to kiss you," he said, his voice careful. "Can I kiss you?"

"Oh." Anemos paused, caught a little off guard, and then shook his head. "Why are you so nervous? That's not a hard question."

"It isn't?"

"No." He laughed softly, giving the boy's hand a tight squeeze. "Yes. The answer is yes."

"Yes?" Cole asked, and he nodded, even as his heart rose into his throat. "Do you want me to?"

One hand moved up to find his curls, pushing them out of his face, and Anemos nodded again, swallowing hard.

"I want you to."

He was kissed once, hesitantly, and his hands fell open, losing their grip on everything.

Their lips parted a second, their foreheads still together, and Anemos' hand moved up over Cole's arm, caressing his neck.

"Are you—"

He nodded before Cole could finish, pulling him back in, letting his lips fall open slightly as they met his, soft and warm despite the cold around them.

He breathed him in, then. Felt his breath on his lips, the beating of his heart, and let his hands fall to his stomach, resting there between them a moment, unfocused, reveling in the feeling of gentle hands weaving through his hair.

It took only seconds for the hesitation between them to die, giving way to the same safety they always felt with each other, and in the end, Cole smiled against his lips, breaking away with laughter.

He let his head fall forward onto Anemos' chest, and let his hands fall to his shoulders, shaking his head.

"I'm fucking freezing, An," he said, and somehow it was the right thing to say, because Anemos laughed too, pressing a kiss onto his forehead.

"Okay," he breathed, pulling him up from the ground. "Let's go home."

A loud sound filled the space around them, startling them both, as the wall separating the Ordinem from the Wastes creaked closed.

Cole looked over at it, his eyes remaining there long after Anemos' moved on, fear rattling around in his chest.

So much like a cage, he thought, despite knowing the thought was foolish.

He looked out over the space in front of him, looked all the way out of the city, and only looked away when Anemos squeezed his hand, his voice low.

"What are you looking at?" he asked.

"Everything," Cole said. "It's such a beautiful night," he said, but there was something sad in his tone. "Might never see it this way again. I want to remember it."

Anemos looked out at it too, and wrapped his arms around Cole's waist, burying his chin in the crook of his neck, pressing a kiss onto his shoulder.

Cole smiled, telling himself to ignore his own anxiety, telling himself that having a good thing did not mean he would lose it, and looked up at the starless sky, letting the cold air fill his lungs. He took Anemos' hand once more.

"Let's go home."

PART FIVE: THE FUNERAL

"And you'll always love me, won't you?"

"Yes."

"And the rain won't make any difference?"

—Ernest Hemingway, Farewell to Arms

CHAPTER FIFTY-SEVEN

Kieran sits in a dining area near the entrance of the Palace. He has been forbidden to move, but his hands are not bound.

Ursula didn't bother with chains or alert the guards to watch over him, even though he wouldn't have judged her for doing so. He's sure that's what the Commander would want. He's sure that Ursula wasn't supposed to leave him in the main area, with this Higher-class boy she's supposed to be protecting.

He watches as Icarus— *Michael*— sits staring at the floor. His face is red with fever, and his whole body is trembling with grief and fear.

"I can't believe he's gone," he says, almost as if he's talking to himself. "He could have b...been my brother. He's the closest I've had to one."

Kieran can't help but feel guilty for his suffering, guilty in a way that burns.

"I'm sorry, Icarus."

"I didn't protect him." Icarus' voice is blank; hollow. He doesn't bother to push his blond hair from his eyes. "I was supposed to protect him... Anemos will never forgive me. I'll never forgive myself. I might as well have killed him."

Kieran's stomach aches. Bile rises in his throat.

"It's not your fault. There's nothing you could have done."

Icarus looks up, eyes like glass, and lets out a shaking breath. His teeth chatter.

"I didn't know I could still feel like this," he says. "I've seen so much. I've gotten so desensitized. I didn't know I could still hurt this bad."

Images flash behind Kieran's eyes: The Facility in ruins, bodies strewn about in the desert sand, Ursula's slit throat and Elise's mangled arm.

He swallows hard, pale.

"I understand."

Icarus nods, picking anxiously at the skin on his forearms. "I know you do, Kieran."

Kieran watches the floor, not moving until Icarus speaks again, his voice quiet.

"I'm not going to leave you alone. You shouldn't have to be alone, after everything that's happened."

"Prison's cold," Kieran states. "You're ill. You'll stay with your friend, and stay warm."

"But wh...what about you?" he asks. "I know how m...m-much worse it is, when you're afraid. It's dark around your eyes, even now."

The E.D.T. already knew, but having Icarus notice makes him feel a little sicker.

"You're the only person that's ever cared," he mutters, his voice catching. "I've dealt with it alone for a long time, I can handle one more night—"

"M...my sister was like you," Icarus interrupts. "I've seen what it's like. You'd have to be a monster to know and not care."

The words are more confirmation than Kieran needs. Still, they send a fresh wave of pain through him.

He can't believe how *close* Rosemarie was to finding him. He can't believe he is sitting here now and can't tell him she's alive.

If Icarus tried to go to his sister, he wouldn't make it out; Kieran can't shake the feeling that he would go for her *immediately.*

He clears his throat, shoving his trembling hands beneath his legs.

"I'll be okay," he forces. "You need to worry about yourself, right now. Things are going to get bad. They're going to be looking for a traitor, probably before the sun rises. They're going to be looking for Grim."

Icarus' eyes are distant. He looks away, leaving the words sitting between them.

"I don't care as much as I should," he mutters, finally. "I can't. Whether I live or die... It's nothing to me, right now. I'm worried about Anemos. I miss my friend."

Kieran grows cold. He feels horrible for even bringing up what's to come, tonight; trying to plan.

Sometimes he forgets people are meant to grieve. He doesn't remember the last time he had a chance to, but that doesn't matter. Icarus should get better than that.

Icarus shouldn't have to be afraid of anything else.

"When did you meet him?" he asks, toying nervously with the chair beneath him. "Cole?"

Icarus looks back up, tears falling in a steady stream down his face.

"I was fourteen. I started studying at University late, for... a lot of reasons. I was terrified."

A lot of reasons. Kieran can only imagine the anxiety the boy has suffered here, being what he is. He knows well the damage he suffered in Jakara, losing his family and his home.

He shouldn't have to suffer anything else. He shouldn't be suffering this.

"I think Cole knew," Icarus continues. "As soon as he saw me, I think he knew. He told me he was going to be my friend, and I didn't understand why. Him and An spent... A lot of time protecting m...me from the-the-the other kids. They really... They saved my life, completely."

Kieran thinks he might be sick.

"He sounds like an amazing friend," he says.

"He was. He was the best friend anyone could ask for, and I..." Icarus stops himself, but it is too late. Kieran knows as soon as he thinks it.

He killed him. That's what he thinks. He thinks this is all because *he* warned them.

Kieran shakes his head, trembling.

"It's not your fault," he says again. "Icarus, I mean it. It had nothing to do with you."

Icarus nods, unbelieving. His eyes are somewhere else.

Kieran glances back at the closed door to the dining area, looking for a crack someone could be listening through, and then speaks again, choosing his words carefully.

"William knew," he says. "The Reaper, from Trellis. He knew of the Ordinem's plan, and he took them to Assecula. *That's* why the Saenks entered the city. Not because of you."

"And who told William?" Icarus asks, his fists clenched. The tone of his voice implies guilt he does not deserve to feel. "Some Grim. Someone from Morta?"

It's the most reckless thing Kieran could possibly do: confess his crime to a boy that could so easily rip his soul from his tired frame, but he doesn't care.

He imagines the guilt Icarus feels could grow into something deadly, and he isn't going to let it. Not when Rosemarie is still looking for him.

He is never rash, but this isn't something he knew to prepare for. This isn't something he can decide on rationally. Michael is sitting across from him with the darkest eyes he has seen since entering the Ordinem's territory.

He can't allow that. He won't.

"*I* told William," he whispers, and Icarus's face twists in confusion that makes him a little afraid. "Whatever you did or didn't do, William knew because I told him."

It feels like the dark, stone walls are watching; listening.

"*You* told him?" Icarus asks. And then, no doubt seeing the darkening of the Changeling's features: "You don't have to be afraid. I'm not... I don't understand. You told him? *You* warned him?"

"It's my fault," Kieran affirms. "All of it. Your friend, your city—"

"*Why?*"

"Because I didn't want..." His voice cracks, a wave of heat passing through him. "I'm sorry, Icarus. I didn't want this, but I couldn't watch it. I couldn't be a part of it. It was going to be an act of evil unlike anything we've seen since the Six. *Children*, slaughtered in their sleep. Grim being exterminated in the one place that should be safe for them. And I know you're Ordinem, I know you have some loyalty to these people— "

"I've always been told you're my greatest enemy," Icarus interrupts, and Kieran falls quiet. "Grim and E.D.T.. You're meant to hate us— you blame us as responsible for your suffering. I thought it might be true. I wouldn't have blamed you if it was."

The words are the last thing Kieran expected. He shakes his head.

"You should've. Children shouldn't have to die for a war between men they've never met. I'd be no better than any of the Six if I stood and watched it happen." He swallows nervously, rubbing his knees. "Do you think I'm your enemy? Do you think of me as a puppet, like they've told me you do?"

"Of course not." Icarus exhales shakily. "I would do anything in the world to undo what they did. I would *die* if you told me I could free you from the darkness the Six put on you."

"Your death is the last thing I want. Your friend's death is the last thing I wanted. *Daia, Lord,* I don't want any more blood."

He can *feel* the veins around his eyes darkening, his vision blurred.

It scares him, as it always does, even if he knows he can resist Assecula's pull. He closes his eyes to hide them, forcing himself to keep breathing.

"It's not your fault he died," Icarus says. "This was our war."

"But he's my casualty." Kieran whispers. "No matter what you did or didn't do, it was *my* move on the game board that pushed him off of it. I won't let you walk around with blood on your hands when you had no part in shedding it."

The words make Icarus' shoulders fall. He stares at Kieran in disbelief.

A long moment passes in that silence, only ending when Kieran opens his eyes again, having regained himself enough.

Icarus must know how hard things are getting, because he changes his tone— making it impossible softer.

"*Daia*," he repeats. "*Lord.*"

Kieran nods, suddenly still, but doesn't move his eyes from the floor.

Icarus leans forward in his chair.

"You're Rustikan."

"My faith is all I have left," Kieran mutters. "It's the only thing they can't take from me; not to say they haven't tried."

Even with all of Kieran's knowing, he has no idea how deep those words run.

Icarus' breath slows.

"Do you need my forgiveness?" The words are spoken softly, but they sink Kieran's stomach all the same. "That's one thing I remember from my classes. Rustikans needing the forgiveness of those they've sinned against or their pain will... It w-w..will make-make itself like a... chain around them. That image always stuck with me."

"It's a powerful image."

"You think Cole's blood's on your hands, and you haven't asked my forgiveness."

Kieran inhales sharply, his hands folded together.

"I'm more worried with making things right than I am freeing myself. If I've made you suffer, I'll suffer with you—"

"I forgive you anyway," Icarus says, and Kieran falters.

It isn't a thing he thinks he deserves, but he is not permitted to reject it.

"You've done nothing more than me," Icarus says. "Your hands are clean too."

But Kieran's hands aren't clean at all.

They're covered in blood: Ursula's, Cole's, Elise's, and Icarus'. He's not had a chance to wash them. And now, he can't stop them from shaking, no matter how hard he tries.

Icarus sees him looking at them and moves closer, taking the only clean corner of his shirt and gathering it in his hands. It is damp from how many tears he has wiped on it, but that should help more than it will hinder.

He cleans Kieran's hands in silence— the cracks around his knuckles, and the blood under his fingernails. Then he takes them, holding them while he can.

It is forbidden to touch an E.D.T. in the Ordinem, and in Trellis. It is forbidden among most.

The simple touch brings tears to the Changeling's eyes, but he fights them back.

"You're forgiven," Icarus repeats. "Forgive m...me, for being a part of this. For bringing this war to you."

"Of course you're forgiven," Kieran mutters. "Icarus—"

Movement at the door interrupts him, and on instinct, he tries to pull his hands away. But Icarus doesn't release them so quickly.

He holds them long enough for Ursula to see, and it freezes her in place, stopping her in the middle of the doorway. Still, Anemos manages to stumble past her.

This is Anemos, Kieran thinks. The future Guide, if he manages to follow in his family's footsteps; though most of the talk he has heard about him has suggested he will fail to.

It only takes a second in his presence to realize most of the talk he's heard has been wrong.

Anemos walks like a man half dead, his clothes stained and his eyes swollen. He shakes like he is still crying, even though his tears have ceased. He is coming apart, but his mind is still full.

Kieran wonders if anyone else can sense the rage simmering under his grief. He wonders if they're as afraid of him as they should be.

"An..." Icarus says, pulling himself up.

Anemos steps around in front of him, and Icarus' eyes grow impossibly heavier.

"I'm so sorry," he continues. "It happened so fast, I couldn't..."

Anemos pulls him into a tight embrace before he can finish, even though the blood on Icarus' shirt sinks his stomach.

Cole's blood, Kieran realizes.

"It's not on you," Anemos forces, his voice hoarse. "It wasn't your responsibility, okay? It wasn't your duty or your fault, and I don't blame you."

"I'd do anything to bring him back."

"Me too." Anemos nods against his shoulder, his voice trembling. "I'm so glad you're okay. I thought I'd lost you both. I wouldn't have been able to live with that."

"I wish it was him here with you, now, An. If I could trade places with him, I would—"

"Don't," Anemos whispers. "I don't wish it was you. Don't think like that—"

"Kieran," Ursula says, and he snaps his head in her direction, startled out of the conversation. He knows what she is going to say before she speaks, judging by nothing but her eyes. "It's time. The Council will be making their way in at any moment."

"I understand," he nods.

He stands as quietly as he can, so as not to disturb either of the grieving boys across from him. He shuffles out of the room, following close behind the woman in black, and doesn't fight when a guard binds his hands behind his back.

Of course, the guard's hands are gloved, as if he is a specimen. Contagious. Disgusting.

A cloth sack is placed over his head, and Ursula is scolded for failing to imprison him sooner; scolded by a man with a much lower rank than her.

This is the life he will be returned to. This is life as he knows it.

It is all dark, save for the uneven slits in his mask.

He takes a final glance back into the other room, trying to remember the way it felt for his hands to be held, and lets his eyes fall shut.

"Don't speak," the guard says. "Try anything, and you'll be sedated..."

The door to the Palace is opened again, and he is pushed out into the night.

There is smoke in the air, but it is still fresh in comparison to his place in Trellis— still living. Unstale. Unsaturated with blood, and chemicals, and acid.

There should be some way to keep his mind from wandering back, and yet, every step he takes in the present only seems to reflect his past. He can almost feel the Commander's brutal hands on his skin.

But then, there is dirt under his feet instead of concrete, and a gentle breeze in the air, and the ropes on his wrists are not so tight that he will bleed.

He tries to savor the good, but it is thin ice, and the weight on his shoulders is heavy enough to break through it.

He throws his head back and squints at the sky, hoping to see stars and finding only darkness.

"One day, Kieran," Rosemarie said, her voice trembling. "One day, when we're free, we'll go. I'll take you somewhere you can still see the stars."

"Home, to Alaheim," he whispered. "They say the skies are still clear there."

"Alaheim, then," she said. "And we'll steal the finest clothes the streets have to offer, and drink wine made for kings."

"I'll take you to the ocean. You can paint the moon, rising over the cliffs—"

He is pushed down into the prison beneath the castle: A cold place that smells of mildew, silent except for the occasionally dripping from the ceiling.

A cell is opened in front of him: Empty, with nothing to eat and nothing to warm him. The guard doesn't take the mask off before he shoves him inside, slamming the door shut behind him.

"Waste," he mutters, and Kieran doesn't respond, only watching as the man walks away, leaving him in darkness.

CHAPTER FIFTY-EIGHT

"I'd do anything to bring him back," Icarus whispers.

Anemos nods against his shoulder, and when he speaks, his voice is frail. "Me too. I'm so glad you're okay. I thought I'd lost you both... I wouldn't have been able to live with that."

Icarus knows he means it. He *knows* he does, but he can't help but think that this is the next worst outcome. Anemos would have been able to cope had *he* not returned. He wouldn't be as broken as he is now.

Cole was Anemos' everything. He has lost *everything*.

"I wish it was him here with you, now, An," he whispers. "If I could trade places with him, I would—"

"Don't," Anemos scolds. "I don't wish it was you. Don't think like that..."

There is movement across from them, and it pulls Icarus' eyes away.

Kieran is being called away, taken from the room by Ursula and two men that he doesn't recognize.

It makes his stomach twist inside of him.

"No one should have died tonight," Anemos says. "Not Cole. Not you. None of the people on the Outskirts and none of us in the city. Don't carry what *they've* done. Don't think like they want you to and fantasize about the tragic sacrifice you could have been. You should both be here, but this horrible place killed him, just like he feared it would."

Kieran's hands are bound behind him, and a sack is pulled over his head.

Icarus thinks he might be sick.

"Did you see it happen?" Anemos asks, and he nods silently, the memory burning inside him. "I'm so sorry. I'm sorry I wasn't there with you—"

"I don't wish you were," Icarus says quickly. He watches as the Changeling is taken away, and waits until every guard has gone with him; then, he pulls back, flinching as he meets his friend's helpless eyes. "I'm sorry we didn't stay."

Anemos clenches his jaw, swallowing hard.

He is as angry as he is grieved. Icarus can feel it radiating from him.

"I'm sorry we made you go," he says.

"You begged us *not* to go, An."

"I begged you, but I didn't beg my family to rethink their plans. I didn't fight the Council, or warn the Lower-class areas, or—"

"You didn't have time."

"I should have," Anemos whispers. "I should have been more involved from the beginning. I should have started pressing them the moment they returned from Trellis, right after Ceremony night. I should have known something was wrong— that they were planning something— but I was hiding. I was hiding from all of it: The Council, and my parents, and the Guide. Because I don't want any of it. I hate this government, Icarus. But now this has happened, and I swear, the blood's on my hands as much as it's on theirs. I could have done something. I know I could've. And I will. This won't happen again."

"It's not all your responsibility."

"Of course it is," he says, a sob breaking the words. "Of *course* it is. It's my family. It's my country, and these are *my* people, suffering at its hands."

"We were just kids last month." The words escape Icarus' mouth as something like a laugh, and Anemos shakes his head in response.

"We're not anymore. We never will be again. Maybe we weren't allowed to be in the first place. I don't know." His hands are shaking violently, and Icarus can't steady them, but he tries, holding them tight. "We never got to be children, and Cole's never gonna get to grow up. Imagine the person he would've grown into. Imagine the kids we could have been."

"Anemos, you're barely breathing."

"I'm never going to let this happen again," he mutters. "I *can't.*"

"You have to calm down, An."

The room grows quiet around them, the air as heavy as stone. Anemos struggles to regain control of his breath, all the light gone from his eyes.

He turns around cautiously, glances at the couch behind them, and shakes his head.

"Was that him?" he asks. "The E.D.T.? He was wearing prisoner's clothes."

Icarus nods, and Anemos swallows hard, looking sick.

"Where did they take him?"

"They've taken him back to prison," Icarus says. "The prison below the Palace."

"He looked our age."

"He's just like us," he whispers, and Anemos shakes his head again.

"I need to speak with him. He'll know more about what's happened than I do. Will he talk to me?"

Icarus hesitates, wanting his friend to slow down and rest, but knowing there's no chance of it.

Even if there was, he can't bear the thought of Kieran alone in the dark.

They wait until the Palace has gone quiet.

It is just enough time for them to get cleaned— for Icarus to change his bloodstained shirt and Anemos to gain some semblance of calm.

Then, when the Council has gathered in the east wing, far from where the boys sit awake, they emerge from their room and move about the Palace in silence.

Icarus is led through a series of halls and rooms he has never visited, following Anemos without question.

The main entrance to the prison is guarded, so they are taking another way in.

"I have no idea how you remember where everything is," Icarus whispers, and Anemos lets out a restrained sigh. He yanks open the door of an old dusty closet and steps inside.

His hands are still shaking.

"I spent most of my time here, when I was little," he mutters. "You can memorize a place quickly when you have nothing else to do."

He feels along the wall of the closet blindly until his fingers catch a snag in the wood. It wiggles loose, and he glances back at Icarus with heavy eyes.

"Help me pull it," he says, and Icarus steps forward, feeling for the seam.

It takes a minute of considerable effort, but then a large portion of the wall comes loose, releasing a cloud of dust that makes both of them cough.

Beyond it is a dark tunnel, small enough that they'll both have to crouch to enter it, and illuminated by nothing.

Icarus' stomach sinks.

"You're sure this is it?" he asks, and Anemos nods.

"It's not far to the prison, and there's light near the end. It's a straight path, so we won't get lost."

"It's dark the whole way?"

"I'll give you my hand and lead the way." Anemos pulls the closet door shut behind him, leaving them in pitch darkness. "If we bring a light, we're going to be making ourselves obvious."

"Anemos?"

"What?"

"Don't let go of m...me, okay?" The words make him feel pathetic, but all he can see in this darkness is the darkness of the shelter— the Saenk behind the door.

Anemos takes his hand and squeezes it tightly, leading him into the cold of the tunnel.

"I would never leave you in a place like this."

The tunnel gets smaller as it goes, and Icarus finds himself curling up in an effort not to feel it. He keeps one hand in Anemos' and the other on the wall— cold and damp, coated in dirt.

After a few minutes Anemos trips, barely catching himself, and takes a shaky breath.

"Stairs," he says. "We're getting close. It's a few stories down. Be careful."

Icarus nods, slowing his steps as he follows him down.

It gets colder as they go, making goosebumps rise on his arms and the heat of his skin feel more vivid.

Still, he can only be so worried for himself; Kieran is being kept here. Kieran is alone, with no hand to hold.

He thinks of his sister, when his parents would lock them in their room as children; her quiet cries as she struggled to keep control of herself in the face of being trapped.

Of course, the Changeling isn't a child. But this is not a bedroom, either. He can't imagine it's an easy place to fight off the darkness, or that Kieran does not cry for freedom just like she did.

"What's he like?" Anemos whispers, his voice bouncing off the walls. "They talk about E.D.T.s like they're myths— especially this one. A legend, or... a ghost story. Never someone I expected to meet."

"He's just like us," Icarus reiterates, and Anemos lets out a heavy sigh, giving his hand another tight squeeze.

"Okay."

"Are you afraid of him?"

The darkness is beginning to lift, soft light in the distance. Icarus can see his friend's silhouette.

"I don't know," Anemos whispers. "I don't know anything anymore."

A few minutes pass in silence, and then they turn a corner, and the tunnel comes to an abrupt end. It opens into a much larger passageway— one built with stone and lit scarcely.

It's dead quiet, and cold as ice.

"Which way do we go?" Icarus whispers, thinking aloud. They are in the middle of the passageway, and both directions lead to darkness.

Anemos looks uncertain, and that frightens him.

He closes his eyes while his friend considers, and tries to imagine the place fading around him. He tries to find the E.D.T. in the void— feels for the pull of his spirit and the darkness that plagues it.

"They hardly use this place at all anymore," Anemos says. "It's completely abandoned toward the center of the Palace. He would be near the entrance, but we've taken so many turns, I don't—"

"I think we should go right," Icarus says, and Anemos looks back at him, uncertain, but he doesn't argue.

"Okay," he says.

"Okay," Icarus repeats.

With the word, he takes the lead, pulling Anemos along with him. The hall is long, with so many twists and turns they start to worry they will never find the exit. It is as much a maze as a prison, but Icarus continues forward with only the feeling in his chest to guide him.

There are still lights on their path, and it is confirmation enough that they are moving in the right direction. It *has* to be.

And surely enough, after what feels like an eternity of wandering, they turn their final corner, a prisoner coming into view.

At first it is too dark to make out the figure that sits behind the rusted bars of the prison cell, leaning against the cold stone wall. But when the light from a distant lantern catches the boy's face, Icarus nearly runs for him.

"Kieran," he calls, his voice no louder than a whisper. "Kieran?"

The prisoner opens his eyes, looks up, and scrambles to his knees, crawling toward the edge of the cell— which is far too small to stand in.

"Icarus?" he asks, his voice frail. "What are you doing here?"

Icarus lets go of Anemos' hand and kneels down beside the bars, reaching between them. He takes Kieran's hand and finds it cold as ice.

"I told you I wouldn't leave you alone, didn't I?"

"Yes, but I didn't think you'd be crazy enough to actually..." Kieran glances up past him and falls a little paler. "Anemos?"

Anemos kneels down beside his friend, a stunned look in his eyes, and nods in Kieran's direction, but before he can speak—

"You've just lost your friend. Why would you come here? You should be grieving... Safely, I mean. Not in a prison. Not with a person that bears any responsibility."

"I need to speak with you," Anemos admits, his voice hushed. "But that seems beside the point, now."

Kieran shakes his head, shivering violently. "No. Of course. I'll tell you whatever you need to know. It's entirely the point..."

There is a burlap bag in the corner of the cell with two slits in it. It lies beside an abandoned rope that Anemos imagines once bound the boy in front of him.

He pulls off his jacket and presses it between the bars, a chill running down his spine.

"You're freezing," he says. "Put this on."

"Oh, Myon... Please. You don't have to—"

"I've done nothing to be deserving of your respect," Anemos interrupts. "Just call me by my name, and take the jacket."

Hesitantly, Kieran lets go of Icarus' hand and reaches forward, taking the jacket and pulling it over his shaking shoulders. He tugs it tightly around him, chilling at the warmth it provides.

"Thank you," he mutters, and Anemos nods, looking away.

He is trying not to look at the dark veins that run under Kieran's eyes.

"I'm sorry it took us so long," Icarus says. "The main entrance to the prison was guarded—"

"The fact that you came at all is... More than I ever would've asked for," Kieran says. "I feel horrible that you've gone to the trouble. I would've been okay. I would've made it to the morning. This place is..." His teeth chatter. "It's not so bad. It's not as dark as I was expecting."

"You don't have to do that," Anemos says, and Kieran shakes his head.

"If I don't, I'll lose my mind. It's taking everything in me to keep it off of... *Everything.* It's easier if I focus on... The light, and... I've been able to rest a little bit, here. I'm rambling. I'm sorry. I don't get much conversation."

"Do you want to talk about it?" Anemos asks. "*Everything?*"

"You've had a long enough night, I think—"

"It might help me understand," he says, and Kieran pauses, hesitant.

For a second, Icarus thinks he can see the whole night playing out behind his eyes. There is terror, there, no matter how carefully it is subdued.

"Okay," Kieran whispers. "Okay. What do... What do you know, Anemos?"

"I know that Saenks got into the Outskirts, and the city. I know they devastated the Facility, and injured many of the Higher-class. No one's said a word of what happened in Morta—"

"Nothing happened in Morta," Kieran says quickly. "We never made it to Morta."

Anemos looks at him a long moment then, baffled.

"What do you mean, you never made it to Morta?"

"The Reaper took us to Assecula," he says. "Have you spoken with your mother? Has she told you any of what happened?"

"No one's told me *anything,*" Anemos breathes. "I only learned of the plan this morning, and no more than the most major details of it."

"How long do you have?"

"I have all night."

"And how much do you *want* to know?"

"Everything. I want to know every last word that came from the mouth of the Council, every step they took, and every drop of blood they shed."

Kieran's eyes are heavy, but he nods, his arms folded tightly around him.

"Luckily for you, I don't think I'll ever forget a second of it."

He relays every moment of the night, only leaving out the goriest details, and those that implicate himself or Icarus. He tells Anemos that his mother almost died and watches the light leave his eyes as he says it.

He tells him Alastor wanted to leave her, and the boy is not surprised.

"She was the first to make it back to the city, and the first to see the damage done in the Outskirts. I would speak with her, as she can give insight to that and what was said on the Council when I wasn't present—"

"I didn't even speak to her tonight," Anemos mutters. "She said my name and I just turned away, I was so angry with her."

"You have every right to be angry," Kieran says, finally starting to still. "She's far from guiltless, but... I will say, Anemos... She's terrified, and she has a great deal of reason for that. That's where many of her choices are stemming from. The Council stands against her, and she's only one woman. No matter how grieved their choices make her, there's only so much she can do. And they *do* grieve her."

Anemos looks at his hands, his hair hanging in his face.

"I know they do."

"You were all she thought of when it happened, though. I think you should know that. In Assecula, all she thought of was getting back to you."

The words hang heavy in the air. Anemos isn't sure how to respond to them, but he hears them.

He needs them now, feeling a kind of lonely he hasn't felt since thirteen. He wants to believe it— that he is cared for— but it isn't easy.

"I don't mean to overstep," Kieran says softly. "I apologize if I have."

"You haven't," Anemos assures him. "If you don't mind my asking... What did you hear when the Council met with you? Anything on defense measures?"

"I'm sure it's as you'd imagine. All defense was split between Karneji and the city, with the majority in the city. The Outskirts were spoken of mainly as a barrier between the two— something to slow down anything that might escape the Facility. They spoke mostly in terms of religion, when it came to the city, saying that the safety of the High-Class Ordinem had to be prioritized for the wellbeing of the world at large. The Lower-Class— the workers and common teachers, the very young or very elderly— unable to fight or serve, not deemed as well educated as the children of the Council..."

"Expendable," Icarus mutters, and Kieran nods, quiet.

"Replaceable."

A soft cry falls from Anemos' lips, and they both look toward him with concern, only to find his steady facade breaking apart.

"He wasn't replaceable," he whispers. "There was nothing replaceable about him, or any of them. I'm sorry, I don't mean to lose control of myself, I just..." Another sob ripples through the air around them, and Icarus wraps an arm around his shoulders. "It makes me so sick. I'm *sick*. How could they think of people like my Cole as nothing but a barrier? How could any of them have let this happen?"

Kieran watches with sad eyes as the prince across from him unravels, and Icarus holds him tightly, unsure of what else to do.

"What god lets a thing like this happen?" Anemos cries. "What religion commands it? What the hell have I sworn myself to? Cole is gone, and I'm here with this damned mark on my hand. I'm going back to sleep in their Palace, and eat their food... What am I doing here, pretending like it's of any use? You said it, Kieran. You said my mother is one woman, and they're all against her. I'm *one* person, and I'm a damn useless one. I sat in *their* shelter while Cole went to fight. I'm as damned as they are, and I'm here, pretending like I'm some kind of soldier—"

"Anemos," Kieran interrupts, holding his hand out between the bars. Anemos shakes his head, his eyes bloodshot, but grasps it anyway, holding it tightly. "Your words aren't your own. You can't believe them."

"I'm sitting here taking the reassurance of a man my family put in chains," he says. "I'm no better than Charles. I'm no better than any of them."

"You can be," Kieran insists. "You *are*. Listen to me. You're right that you shouldn't be here; you shouldn't have to be. You're fighting when you should be grieving."

Icarus watches them both, his eyes heavy, but doesn't say a word.

"What was the plan if they succeeded?" Anemos asks, disregarding any suggestion that he should slow down. "The Commander would have been outraged."

"There would have been a war," Kieran says plainly, and the words take the little energy Anemos has left. "They were prepared for that."

He covers his face with his free hand, gritting his teeth to keep from sobbing.

"Were they?"

"They were prepared to throw us into the line of fire," Icarus murmurs, and Kieran nods in affirmation.

No one says anything else for a long time.

It seems, to each of them, that there is little left to say. There is little to do, in the middle of the night.

The information Anemos holds does him no good, now, while the Council is meeting without him. Even if it did, he is too sick to do anything with it.

Useless, as usual.

Useless.

Cole is dead and there is nothing he can do. There is no way to avenge him. There is no *justice* within reach.

He's not been dead more than a few hours, and the world seems irrevocably changed—

"Anemos?" Kieran asks, and Anemos looks up. His hand is still held. He hadn't even noticed. "I'm sorry you lost him."

Anemos slips his hand away, wiping his eyes.

"I'm sorry for everything you had to see. I'm sorry you're here, now. I wish there was anything we could do—"

"I'm where I need to be," the prisoner says softly, and Anemos shakes his head.

"No. You don't deserve this."

"I didn't mean to suggest that I did, but thank you for saying that." He folds his arms over his chest, letting out a heavy sigh. "Do you... Are you both intending to stay long? Because I'd never expect such a thing, and I don't need it. I'd prefer you take care of yourselves."

"No one should be alone tonight," Anemos says, and Kieran tilts his head, uncertain.

"Won't they be looking for you?"

"They will." Icarus answers for him. "Charles will, won't he, An?"

"I don't know."

"But your Mother will, after the Council meeting concludes." Kieran says the words not a second after Anemos thinks them, and that makes his stomach turn.

He had forgotten that the boy reading his mind was a possibility, but now he wonders.

"I'm sorry, I don't mean to do that. It's habit," Kieran says, and Icarus' brows furrow.

"Do *what?*"

"It's fine," Anemos says, shifting nervously anyway. "You're right. She will. She always does. But that doesn't make me feel any better about you here alone."

"I can s...s-stay," Icarus says. "It was an easier walk than I thought, I'll be able to find my way back."

"You're sick."

"By the dragon. I have a fever, you all act like it'll be the end of me." Icarus settles in, obviously unwilling to debate. "I'll be fine. My parents won't look for me because they think I'm with you."

Kieran shuffles a little in the small prison, clearing his throat.

"Let me give you your jacket, before you go."

"You can just wait and give it to Icarus. You need it more than I do."

"You'll be okay, back at the Palace?" Icarus asks, and Anemos nods, pulling himself to standing.

"As okay as I'll be here."

"You promise?"

Anemos puts his hand on Icarus' shoulder and nods, exhausted.

"I promise. Stay with him, and then go home to your family. I'll be here whenever you find your way back."

A minute later, he has disappeared around the corner, and Kieran and Icarus are alone again.

"You don't have to do this," the former says. "You can go with him. I'll be okay."

Icarus looks at him with tired eyes but doesn't bother arguing.

He takes his hand through the bars of the cell and leans against the wall, fighting a yawn.

"Is it h...hard to rest, when no one is watching out for you?" he asks. "It was for me, when I was back in Jakara. Of course, I was young then."

"Very," Kieran whispers. "I worry, falling asleep here... Someone might have *mercy* on me and run a blade through my heart."

"I could never sleep in a place like this. It's too dark. I don't... I don't like the dark. I know it's silly."

Keiran holds up a hand, and little sparks appear between his fingers before fading into the air.

"It's not silly, but it wouldn't make much sense for me."

"One of my best friends has fire in her hands." Icarus smiles a little at the words, but his chest aches. "I told her I was going to Morta, when the Saenks hit the city; just in case something happened. I need to let her know I've made it."

"Have you thought about *actually* going to Morta?" Kieran asks. "You'd be much safer there than you are here."

Icarus considers the words for a few seconds, looking at the ground, and then moves on, shaking his head.

"Enough about me. You— rest. As long as you can. I won't leave without waking you."

"You'd stay and just watch me sleep?"

"I'll count the spiders on the walls," Icarus says, and Kieran nods, lying back against the same wall, forcing his eyes to fall closed.

It's a strange thing, this moment of safety. Keiran hasn't felt anything like it in longer than he can remember. He doesn't know what to do with it.

He doesn't know how he'll manage when it ends.

CHAPTER FIFTY-NINE

Icarus can barely keep his eyes open.

He doesn't know how long it's been, but Kieran's breathing slowed a long time ago. His grip on Icarus' hand has eased.

Hours, he has been silent, and Icarus has sat beside him.

He has thought of everything there is to think of: Of Cole, mostly, and Anemos, and Zahra— who he knows is waiting to hear from him. He's considered opening himself up again, talking to her, but he can't bear the thought of recounting the evening again. Not y et.

That, and he isn't sure how long he will be *out* of Morta.

It is calling him to it, even if he doesn't want to admit it.

"Michael?"

Icarus flinches at the name, then looks over at the mostly-asleep boy that uttered it.

"What is it?" he asks, and Kieran groans a little, opening his eyes a crack. "Are you okay?"

"I thought I heard something. Like a door opening. Did you hear it?"

"No, I didn't..." A quiet thump in the distance interrupts him, and he straightens, listening.

Before he can say anything else, Kieran has scrambled up and pulled his hand away, shrugging Anemos' jacket off.

"Hide," he whispers. "If someone sees you... I don't know. Thank you for staying with me. Thank you, Icarus. But you have to go."

"Why would anyone be coming down here this late? She said the Commander wouldn't be-be...be in until morning—"

"It doesn't matter what it is, Icarus. You need to go. You need to go *now.*"

"But I don't want—"

A man rounds the corner, startling them both to silence. Before either of them can see who he is, he is frozen in place by the boy in the cell, his arms raised haphazardly beside his head.

Only then, when the threat is gone, do Icarus' eyes adjust to the darkness. Instantly, his breath fails him.

"Dad?" he asks, and when the otherwise motionless man nods, he scrambles to his feet. "Wh...what are you doing here? Kieran, let him go. He's safe."

Instantly, Jack's hands fall to his sides, and a heavy exhale escapes his lips.

"Lord," he mutters, and Kieran shakes his head, his face reddening.

"Sorry, sir— Myon."

"It's a disarming feeling, kid. I won't lie to you, but I appreciate the intent." Jack turns to Icarus with heavy eyes, his face cast in shadows. "They told me you were with Anemos."

Darkness settles over Icarus' shoulders, the conversation he knows is coming already stealing his breath.

"I was," he says. "He just left. He said his mom would be looking for him."

"Is he okay? Are you okay?"

"No, and no," Icarus replies. "You heard?"

Jack nods reluctantly, his eyes full of sorrow.

"Charles told me. I don't think anything I say will help much, but I'd give anything to bring him back, Icarus. I thought I'd be sick when I heard."

"Kieran got there right after it happened." It is a desperate attempt to change the subject. He sees his mangled friend every time he is brought up. "I don't think I would have m...m-made it out, if he hadn't."

Jack steps toward the Kieran's cell in response, kneeling beside him with an out-stretched hand.

"I owe you my life, then," he says. "And all of my thanks."

Kieran shakes his hand hesitantly, a sad smile painted across his features.

"I don't need that. I only wish I'd gotten there earlier."

Jack pulls his hand back and digs in his coat pocket, retrieving a small paper bag and pushing it between the bars.

"That's not your burden to carry. Please, take and eat. I brought what I could."

Kieran takes the bag, reaches in, and pulls out a piece of bread. His stomach growls at the sight of it.

"Thank you, sir."

"I apologize for every part of the role I've played in your suffering," Jack continues, softening his voice. "I apologize I didn't stand up for you... Icarus? Come here, would you?"

Arms folded over his chest, Icarus kneels beside them, searching his father's eyes.

"I have things I need to say to both of you," Jack continues. "*Apologies* for both of you."

"You owe me nothing, sir," Kieran mutters, taking a small bite; but Jack shakes his head in disagreement.

"I owe you both a great deal," he says.

There are cuts and bruises littering Jack's body— things that will one day become scars, if they are lucky. He should be resting too, Icarus thinks; but instead he is here, offering apologies.

He can't imagine what his father could need to apologize to him for. All the guilt is *his*. *He* is the burden and vice.

"There's much I've wanted to do," the man continues anyway. "Much I've wanted to say. There are times I've wished to defend you, and I haven't. In Trellis, Kieran. I wanted to rebuke them all for the way you were treated. I wanted to protect the girl, too. Tonight, I wanted to tell them all to cease, and not involve a sick child in their wars, but I felt it would've been useless. I feared I would do more damage than good—"

"I heard all this strife inside of you," Kieran says. "I bear you no ill will for any of what's happened here."

"Nevertheless, for whatever purpose, I didn't stop evil from happening. I didn't stop you from seeing it. And I apologize seriously for that."

Keiran nods in acceptance, taking another bite of food, and Jack turns to Icarus.

"Son," he says, and Icarus swallows hard, still unable to feel entirely deserving of the word. "I offer you the same. For every word I've failed to quiet, and every arrow I've not shielded you from. I realized last night... That perhaps you didn't know where I stood on this, before. And Love, I assure you, it is with you. Before your mother, or this Code, or anything else. More than that, I need you to know I don't see you as an exception, or love you despite anything. If I was more powerful than I am, I would smother every fire the Ordinem has set, and bring back every life they've taken."

"I know you would," Icarus whispers.

"My failure has been vast, toward both of you. But I will help when I can." The words have an urgency to them. Kieran swallows hard, nervously folding his hands together, and Icarus slouches with exhaustion, afraid of what will come next. "Now, it seems apparent that what you both need is to *escape*. The morning is coming fast, and it carries great threat for both of you. Icarus, you need to go. You know you need to go—"

"I can't just *go*, " Icarus says. "Not now, with everything that's happened."

"Precisely with everything that's happened," Kieran mutters, and Jack nods in agreement.

"They're going to be looking for a traitor," he says. "You know you'll be targeted, just as you always have been. With the scars on your shoulders, you have little defense—"

"I'm n-not leaving him." The words are firm, but they choke him all the same. "You can't expect me to."

"I'm not," Jack says. "I'm *asking* you to. As your father. It's not safe here."

"It's not safe for *anyone*— "

"*Icarus.*"

He lets out a heavy sigh, looking at his hands.

He's losing this fight. He knows that, but he isn't ready to leave. If Anemos was *well,* he wouldn't be ready to leave.

This is his home.

"If you won't go forever," Jack forces, "go for a moment. Go long enough to speak with the man who brought you back to me, and see what he tells you."

"He'll tell me to stay," Icarus groans.

"Maybe you can find Cole?" Kieran suggests, and the words silence him.

He has thought about it, even before the suggestion, but the possibility of that terrifies him too.

"People are going to be hostile, when tomorrow comes," his father says. "Blame will be placed everywhere but where it should be. The hatred for your kind is going to come to a boiling point when the city discovers what happened, and you should not have to be here when it does."

He keeps his eyes low, but nods in response, quiet.

"Okay. I'll go for a moment. Tomorrow, but not tonight. I need to just... Go home, tonight. I need to see Mom, and see if our house is still standing, and just... Have a fucking *night* to process what's happening. My best friend died tonight. I can't think about fleeing. I can't think about losing anything else right now."

It is cold as ice in this prison, and it is growing colder. Icarus hugs himself as he speaks, but it isn't enough to hide the way he is trembling.

He isn't even going to mention how afraid he still is of the place they're both insisting is a refuge for him. *This* was supposed to be his refuge.

He has been told his whole life to fear Morta, and now they're begging him to flee to it. He would laugh if he wasn't so sick. He would cry if he were alone.

Luckily, the conversation shifts away from him, his father knowing not to push him any further. Instead, his gaze shifts to Kieran.

"You're in just as much danger," he says, keeping his voice soft. "You know that."

Kieran shifts uneasily, but shakes his head in disagreement.

"They need me. I doubt I'll have a *pleasant* return to Trellis, but I'll survive it."

"I suspect you've already survived a great deal more than anyone should have to."

Kieran nods, just barely, watching as Jack reaches back into his pocket.

"Perhaps," he mutters, his eyes following his hand. "But that does seem to be a burden I was built for, sir..."

A small, bronze key is held out in his direction, and the sight alone silences him.

Icarus, too, grows still in response.

It doesn't feel real to Kieran, who reaches a shaking hand forward to retrieve it. It's a miracle, and he will cherish it as long as he lives. He will remember the cool feeling of it in his hand, even when his palms are full of fire.

But he won't hold it for more than a moment.

"Freedom," he whispers. "You offer me freedom."

"The train goes all the way to Jakara," Jack says, and Icarus flinches at the mention of the place. "No one will see you if you go now. Wait in an unused cart until the Commander gives up on finding you—"

"Sir." Kieran's voice is sad, but nonetheless firm. He shakes his head and pushes the key back between the bars of the cell. "You've given me a great deal of hope with your actions, and I can't thank you enough, but that lock isn't what holds me here, and I'm afraid I can't take that key as my escape. God forgive me for rejecting such a noble action..."

"Both of you," Jack says. "I know freedom feels out of reach, but *both* of you have it within your grasp. You speak of this being your burden to bear— You deserve safety, not this. You weren't born to spend your whole lives at war."

Kieran swallows hard, searching for Icarus eyes' but finding them pointed away.

"I want to believe that, sir. Maybe one day, by the grace of God, I will. But my war isn't over yet. I might not be safe, but I'm where I need to be. I'm not the puppet they've told you, and I'm no one's slave. If I were, I would take your offer of freedom without a second thought, I assure you."

Slowly, Icarus looks up from the floor, his eyes red.

"Is this how you feel about me staying here?" he asks. "I would break the bars and drag you to the train myself, if I thought I could best you."

"You certainly could, but I appreciate your apprehension, friend. Yes. I'd have you safe in Morta in a second, if I could."

Icarus forces something like a smile and looks away again, his chest aching in a way that makes Kieran feel a little sicker.

"Win your war," he insists, and Kieran nods, still tracing the place the key rested in his hand.

"I'll come find you when I have. We'll go somewhere safe then. You too, sir." He looks at Jack, fidgeting nervously. "Somewhere you won't have to lie anymore, or worry for him. I imagine you're in just as much need of rest."

Icarus has never seen his father's calm demeanor break, but he thinks he can see the cracks in it, now.

There are tears in his eyes, even if he won't let them fall. His hands are unsteady.

He fumbles through his coat and pulls out a pack of cigarettes, giving up his fight as he sits them on the ground between them.

"Ursula wanted me to give these to you, if you insisted on staying."

Kieran presses his lips together tightly, nodding in appreciation.

"Thank her for me, would you?"

"Ursula?" Icarus asks; then, when Jack does not respond: "Could you light one for m...me as well, Kieran?"

He grabs the pack, pulls out two smokes, and nods in the older man's direction, his eyebrows furrowed.

"You too?"

Reluctantly, Jack nods, and soon he is pulling smoke into his lungs— putting a hand on Icarus' back as he coughs it out of his.

CHAPTER SIXTY

They leave the prison no more than an hour after Jack's arrival, a heaviness in both of their hearts that cannot be measured.

Icarus doesn't see Anemos on his way out, but when he tries to stay and look for him, his father pulls him along. The Palace isn't any safer for him tonight than it has been any other time, and Jack has seen too much to leave him.

They step outside and the air hits them like poison, so full of smoke it is difficult to breathe.

"It's been hours," Icarus whispers. "I thought it would've cleared out some."

"I wouldn't be surprised if there are still fires burning. Especially beyond the city. And there's no wind tonight."

Icarus squints, his eyes watering, and shakes his head.

"There should be wind," he says. "There should be rain. Why isn't there rain?"

Jack looks at him with tired eyes, keeping a hand on his side.

"What do you mean, love?"

"W...w-we call the spirit the Wind. It's not putting out any fires. It's gone, now that we need it. There's no rain, or *help.*"

They make it to the base of the Palace stairs and pause, Jack considering the words carefully. He isn't sure how to respond, and that scares Icarus even more.

"If God's real, maybe he's abandoned us," he whispers. "That's all I can think, Dad. That there's no good here at all."

Jack lets out a heavy sigh and wraps an arm around his son's shoulders, sad.

"There's *some* good here," he says. "But I can't answer those questions, Icarus. I wish I could, but I've seen things tonight that... Would make any man doubt. Just like you. Hideous cruelty. Evil. I've never felt further from God than I did in Karneji."

"I feel alone," Icarus mutters. "Like I've... All... *Always* been alone."

"I still don't believe that. I *know* differently."

"How?"

"I'm having a hard time understanding tonight," Jack says again. "But I *know,* Icarus. Whatever's out there, it's not abandoned you; or Anemos, or Kieran. I have to believe it will make sense, in the end."

"My friend is dead," Icarus breathes.

There is muck on the road they walk; a mix of water, dirt, and ash. Icarus steps over it carefully. He doesn't know what it used to be: His room at the Compounds? Someone's home? Someone else's friend?

Before his father can respond, a loud noise startles him out of his thoughts.

"What was that?" he asks, and Jack pushes him along, shaking his head.

"I don't know."

"It s...sounded like a-a-a gun. There aren't guns here, are there?"

"There shouldn't be, no."

After a moment, the sidewalk opens up to a wider street, and the smell of smoke grows stronger. Icarus hides his hands in his pockets, clenching his jaw.

They're passing the University. They're on the same path Icarus has walked a thousand times. He isn't on a train through Karneji, and he isn't back home in Jakara. He tries to remember that when another crash rings through the air, and the explosion that follows sets the corner of their school alight.

Flames lick the window of a class he took his first year.

Three guards run past, nearly knocking into him, and attempt to stop the fire. Another two run behind the building, shouting words he can't make out. A minute later, the flames are dying down and a young man is being pulled out into the road.

A guard punches him squarely in the jaw, and Icarus flinches, looking back at the building instead.

In the dying light of the fire, he can make out something scrawled across the walls. Letters. Words. *Scripture,* in paint as red as blood.

"Cursed one, cast from Inanis, cast from the spirit, cast from grace. Bathed in darkness and left to death. There is no life here, no goodness. No gentleness has ever touched this spirit, for darkness begets only darkness."

The words, having followed him all of his life, twist his stomach in knots.

"May he be damned," it reads— the words of their prophet, encountering the devil he is.

"How could they know what happened already?" Icarus mutters, trembling wildly, and the man on the ground starts to shout.

"Damn you all!" he yells. "You brought devils into our midst. You've done this to us!"

Jack takes Icarus by the shoulder again, shielding him like the fugitive he is, and guides him toward home.

CHAPTER SIXTY-ONE

The next morning, Charles stands beside the train to Trellis with several of the Higher-class, staring at the doors of the Palace's west wing with hollow eyes.

There are guards stationed on every corner, keeping the city quiet long enough for the Commander to exit the territory, but tensions within the Council have not eased in the slightest.

"They're lucky we aren't declaring war," a woman says, her voice sharp. "It was—"

"It wasn't their attack," Charles interrupts. "The Reaper was their most valuable asset. They wouldn't have thrown him away."

"I'm not so sure, Myon, " Cindy interrupts. "If they broke one, they could have broken another."

"We're lucky *they* aren't declaring war," Elise suggests, leaning back against a gray brick wall. "Considering... You know, the Reaper's sudden change of mind *does* implicate our ulterior motives."

"It *implicates* that someone warned him of them," Alastor says coolly. "Don't you think, brother?"

"I think that this will be discussed behind closed doors, and dealt with *professionally,* in due time. If you could all please—"

"In due time? What is due time, when there is a traitor in our midst?"

"Perhaps once the grieving period has ended," Jack breathes, his hand closed tightly around Aliya's— still cold and trembling, like it has been since Assecula.

Aliya clears her throat and looks up at Alastor, her eyes careful.

"I'm sure Charles is... He's the Guide. I think he can handle figuring out the best approach."

Charles watches her with sad eyes, but before he can respond, the Palace doors open behind him.

The crowd falls silent.

Each one of them watches, motionless, as Kieran and Commander Hawkins approach the train. The younger man's hands are bound behind him, and yet he walks with no less dignity or confidence than the Commander. He holds his head evenly, his lips pressed tightly together and his eyes moving casually over his surroundings, finding each of their eyes for a second as he does.

The sight of him stuns them all for a moment, but not for long. There is no warmth toward the man from anyone in the crowd. There is no more gratitude for him than one might have for a gun, or a blade.

A puppet. Something to be wielded and used, with little intent of its own.

And so, naturally, their eyes linger on him only a moment before moving to the much more provocative picture of the woman beside him.

Ursula walks forward without looking at any of them, one gloved hand balled into a tight fist at her side, and the other— ungloved— placed upon Kieran's shoulder. It could be considered a simple gesture, but in The Ordinem, no gesture is *simple.*

Charles pales instantly, and the woman behind him speaks again, her voice lower than before.

"What is she..." Her voice is strained, nauseous. "Is she *touching* it?"

Kieran hears the words, even from across the lot, and a light smile paints itself across his face.

"She shouldn't be touching it."

"Perhaps we've found our traitor," Alastor says. "If that isn't a show of disrespect—"

"Silence," Charles interrupts, his voice sharp, and Ursula's eyes find his, hesitant in a way he does not understand.

She stops in front of them, does not look at them, and keeps her hand in place as the Commander turns to Charles, his eyes harsh and cold as stone.

"I can only hope this does not stain your opinion of my people," he says. "I'm sure you can understand that occasionally there are mishappenings, with things of this nature."

"Of course."

"It's a risk you take, working with devils."

Charles meets Kieran's eyes, and the young man looks at him knowingly, the anger in his chest almost pity as he nods, unable to do anything else.

"Yes," he says. "Well, it's a mistake we won't make again."

"Risk you take with poor security measures, too," Elise mutters, and Kieran snorts, unable to stifle the laugh that rises in his chest.

Charles closes his eyes tightly, rubbing his forehead, and the Commander holds out his hand, forcing a bitter smile.

"We leave as friends," he says, and Charles looks down at the man's hand with tired eyes, but does not raise his own to shake it.

Seconds pass in silence, and then Kieran clears his throat, licking his lips.

"Well," he says, his voice laced with laughter. "Aren't we lucky that you can have neutrality without friendship?"

The Commander drops his hand, nods, and places it on the side of Kieran's neck.

"Very well," he says, and he turns with the words, guiding Kieran to the train by the space between his shoulders.

Ursula watches them go, and doesn't turn back until the train begins to move, not flinching as a dozen eyes stab through her chest.

It isn't new.

She doesn't lower her head as she pulls a notepad from her pocket, scribbling on it for a moment before tearing off a sheet of paper, folding it neatly, and walking forward.

She passes Charles, avoiding his eyes, and does not acknowledge anyone but Alastor until she stops in front of Aliya. She takes the message and presses it into her hand, pulling her into a tight hug once she has.

There are tears in both of their eyes when she pulls away, but neither of them lets any fall, and after a moment Ursula walks away, never speaking.

Aliya unfolds the paper with trembling hands, looks down at it, and reads it with tight lips.

"Care to share?" Charles asks.

She looks up, folds the paper again, and places it in her pocket.

"The doctor's put her on vocal rest. She apologizes for the inconvenience, and requests the right to withdraw participation until the grieving period has ended."

Cindy laughs, shakes her head, and Aliya looks over at her blankly.

"They never change, do they?"

"Pardon me, Myon?"

"These damn—"

"*Enough,*" Charles says. "By the dragon, you're like a lot of bickering children."

Jack pulls his hand loose from Aliya's grip, lets out a long sigh, and begins to walk away. Charles shakes his head.

"Where are you going?" he asks.

"She saved my son's life," Jack says. "I'm going to thank her."

"Your *son?*" Alastor asks, and Jack meets his eyes with such anger and disgust that he flinches away from the gaze.

He does not offer any other response before he goes.

Jack walks as quickly as he can, his hands squeezed into tight fists, and catches the silent woman just inside the Palace door, calling her name and being met with raised eyebrows.

Ursula stands with her hands interwoven in front of her, her shoulders tight, and her eyes dark.

He has already thanked her. He thanked her immediately, upon returning. Now, the words in his throat do not come as easily.

"You're alright?" he asks, and she only looks at him, knowing he can deduce the answer. "Can I help?"

She bites down on her bottom lip, squeezes her hands, and shakes her head, clearing her throat.

"Pray," she says simply. "Pray and... Well..." She laughs weakly, looking at the floor. "You know they'll come for us first?"

He hesitates a moment, pale, and then nods.

"Of course."

"It wasn't you, was it?" she asks. "You didn't... You didn't warn it?"

"I can't imagine I'd tell you if I had."

"Mm," she nods. "Fair point."

"I didn't," he says, and she stops, her shoulders falling. "I know you don't *like* me, Ursula, but I can only hope you know that I would never... You're very important to me. I wouldn't put you in that kind of danger. Any of you."

"I do like you," she says, her face still stoic, and he laughs in response. The action lights up his whole face, and she smiles in spite of herself. "I mean, you're a bloody bastard..."

"Ah, there she is," he says, and the words break her a little.

She looks up at the ceiling, trying to make out the patterns carved into it, and lets out a short, sharp breath, the smile falling from her lips.

"Stay safe," she whispers. "Won't you?"

CHAPTER SIXTY-TWO

The first place Anemos goes, when he gathers the strength to leave the Palace, is the place where Cole died.

Condemned, like he expected, tied off with pale ropes that have been stained with ash. There were no casualties beside his friend, but the building will not be repaired for months, if it ever is.

Anemos can't imagine it's a priority.

He stares into it from a distance, just out of view of the guards that circle it. There is red staining the floor and the door frame, and he is tempted to go and sit in its midst, just to prove to himself it is real.

That blood is all that is left of Cole. There isn't even a body to bury, much less to hold.

He can't help but think of the way he would hold Cole now, if he was still here. The thought has been making him sick all night, but it will not leave him.

His friend was supposed to make it home.

Next, he goes to the Compounds, his hands trembling at his sides.

The plan for eighteen years— shot to hell.

He steps through the charred space that used to be a door and breathes in the smell of ash. *Their* floor is gone, he realizes, and he is not sure if he cares; he doesn't want it without him.

He walks to the right side of the building anyway, scanning the floor for anything that might look familiar, and finds nothing. He doesn't know whether or not that's okay.

He paces a moment, dizzy, and then bends to the floor, picking up a photo of a family he doesn't recognize. He is still wiping the filth from it when someone approaches from behind him, calling his name. He turns around, eyes tired, and fails to force a smile.

"Josh," he says. "Hey man, how are you doing?"

Josh stops in front of him, his brown, coily hair pulled back away from his face so that Anemos can see the red around his eyes.

"Fine," he lies. "I've been looking for you, actually."

"Oh."

"I wasn't sure if you'd make it over, given... everything, so I went over the debris from your side of the building and tried to pull out your stuff. I didn't get much, but there was some. I went ahead and put Cole's stuff in with yours, since..." He clears his throat, looking sick. "I don't really think he had anyone else. I hope that's okay."

"Yeah." Anemos nods. "That's fine. Thank you, you didn't have to."

"I had to do something," he says, his dark eyes cloudy.

Anemos nods again, unable to speak, and Josh gestures for him to follow him across the building.

They don't speak as they go.

Soon, Josh presses a medium-sized box into Anemos' hands, wiping his eyes when he has.

"That's all," he says. "I'm sorry there isn't more."

"Don't be," Anemos whispers, avoiding the items inside. "Thank you, again. I really appreciate it."

"Mhm." Josh nods, looking at the ground. "Well, I thought I should do something, since... You know, I wasn't... I wasn't *incredibly* close to him, but I always considered him a friend, whether or not I was a shitty one. I've been so busy."

"He always tried to make everyone feel like a friend." The past tense turns his stomach. He omits the fact of how lonely he felt, anyway, and instead only says: "He loved all of you, at the shelter."

"We all come from the same place. That gives us something."

"Where are you going?" Anemos asks. "Now that the Compounds and the shelter are gone."

"I'm staying with Regis' family— Shit. Did you hear about Regis?"

"I don't think so."

"His father died last night."

Anemos picks at the edges of the cardboard box, thinking back to the panicked look in Regis' eyes as he questioned the guard.

"Give him my condolences, please. Let him know I'm here if he needs anything—"

"You have enough, Anemos," Josh interrupts. "We all do. You know my brother? Zedd?"

Anemos pales.

"He didn't—"

"No, he's alive. But he's got to go back, before the week's end."

"Back?" Anemos asks. "Back where?"

"Back to the Outskirts."

His eyebrows furrow.

"What?"

"All of them, under sixteen," Josh says. "They've all gotta go back. Worried about Deviations, Grim... Paranoia's a nasty drug."

"I'm going to—" Anemos cuts himself off, clears his throat. "Before the grieving period is over?"

"Before the grieving period is over."

"That violates—"

"I know," Josh mutters. "Might as well just write over the parts of the Code that concern us Outskirts kids, huh?"

He carries the box back to the Palace when Josh goes and sits it down on the dining room table, staring at it vacantly.

He cannot make himself touch any of it, so he only looks down at it, gripping the table. Gone. Gone. *Gone.*

"Anemos?"

His eyes rise to meet Charles', and the older man almost flinches under his gaze.

"Yes, Myon?"

"Are you alright?"

"No," he answers. "Is there something I can help you with?"

"There's going to be an address this afternoon, four o'clock, focusing on your friend. I thought you should know."

"Why?" Anemos asks. "Why him? Plenty of others died."

"Because he was... You know why."

"Because when someone the Ordinem doesn't deem useful dies, they're a number and not a name," he says. "Yes, I understand."

"Many are uncomfortable with the idea that a child training for battle has passed, they're worried about the competence—"

"As they should be."

Charles nods, squeezing his hands into fists, and Anemos reaches into the box, too angry to care about the tears that fall from his eyes as he does.

He pulls out a jacket— the same one that was draped around his shoulders not two days earlier— and stares at it, his throat tight as he attempts to speak.

"He didn't have to die," he says, and the words are the nail in some unspoken coffin, and the jacket still smells like him. "You know that? If they'd put one damn guard by that shelter, he'd be here."

"I know," Charles responds. "Anemos, I'm not permitted to do much, during the grieving period."

"The Council is moving without you."

"We are moving together, on emergency response alone."

"Is that what you call it? Sending *children* back to a bloody wasteland. There comes a time when you just override the damn vote—"

"And then the public is unaware of the vote," he says, quietly. "If I override, *I* will be questioned, and the Council will be entirely in the clear. The people won't hear the negotiation, only the result."

"I don't understand."

"The public won't be happy with this decision. It could be enough to spark an uprising."

"It's being done out of lawful timing, they'll never even notice."

"Not unless someone points it out."

Anemos freezes a moment, trying to process the words, but before he can speak—

"The funeral is in five days," Charles says, a bit louder. "For all of them. Quite the event, most everyone in the city will be obligated to attend."

"Who will speak?"

"Many. I've had four of the Higher-class ask for permission to speak on your friend *today.*"

"May I have permission?" Anemos asks.

"You may," he says. "You can find any additional information you may need on how these *ceremonies* work in the bottom drawer of the dresser in your room. I recommend looking over it, even if you think you're well versed."

"Comprehensive?"

"Entirely." He stops, nods at the floor. "On another note, I talked with your mother and... Alastor."

"And?" Anemos asks, his heart still pounding in his chest.

"I'd avoid him."

Anemos sighs, laughs sadly, and looks down.

"Eh, I've got a head start. Mom?"

A look crosses Charles' face, brief, but so full of pain that if Anemos had been looking, the lie might have been spoiled.

The relief in her eyes, her tears staining his shirt, the unspoken desire between the both of them that she could stay as well, and not be left with *him*.

"She asked me not to let you come home," he says.

Anemos looks up, gripping the jacket in his hands more tightly.

"Hm?"

Charles steps forward, pulls a folded sheet of paper from his pocket, and hands it to him, shaking his head slowly.

"Read it in your own time," he says softly. "She wanted me to give it to you, but doesn't want you to rush. She understands you need... Space, time, she understands. She loves y ou."

"Did she say that?" Anemos asks, taking the paper carefully. "Did she say she loves me?"

"She didn't have to."

He nods, sticks it into his pocket, and takes the box back in his hands, walking away.

When he reaches his room, he leaves the light off. He sits the box on top of the dresser, and pulls the jacket on, breathing it all in and failing in his attempt not to think about it.

He sits the letter beside the box and then turns to face the bed, climbing up onto it and pulling a blanket around himself.

Cole is gone.

He pulls himself up, not wanting the lonely warmth of the bed, restless, and kneels down beside the bottom drawer.

It feels like if he stops moving too long it might kill him.

He tugs it open, eyebrows furrowed, and pulls out three of the heavy files inside, flipping through them each.

"Well, shit," he mutters, standing up, locking the door before sitting back down and looking through the rest. No time to read them all now, so he grabs the smallest one, eyes the date it was written, and flinches.

All of the details of the night before, and the days ahead, right in front of him.

His head spins in the way only anger, grief, and lack of rest can make it, but he does not bother with calming down or mourning, eating or sleeping.

He goes to move into a corner, to at least lean back against something, but the corner with his jacket makes him think of Cole as much as the bed. So he stays, legs crossed, in the middle of the floor, not taking time to note the trembling of his own hands.

CHAPTER SIXTY-THREE

"You really shouldn't be shifting this soon after everything. It's a lot on you, especially considering you've barely trained." Shannon's voice is quiet. She sits across from Icarus with one arm folded around her, like she might be fighting a chill. "Are you sure you're okay?"

"I'm okay," Icarus whispers, uneasy. "It wasn't easy, but... I didn't have m...m-much of a choice. My dad..." He takes a sharp breath, watching as the girl in front of him runs her hand lightly over his arms. You don't have to do that."

"Sure I do," she says softly. "You shouldn't have to keep hurting if I can fix it."

He lowers his head slightly, his eyes tired, and she shakes hers, letting her hand rest against his skin.

"Hey," she says. "No shame here. You're safe."

"I'm afraid," he whispers, "and I don't even know why."

"So am I. It comes with being what we are, I think." She tucks a stray strand of hair back behind her ear and smiles sadly. "I'm sorry, though. I know it has to have been worse for you, there alone."

He nods, quiet.

"What we are," he repeats, trying to make the words fit in his mouth.

"It isn't a bad thing," she says. "I promise, it isn't. No matter how hard they try to turn it into one."

Icarus is not completely sure why he went to Emmy and Shannon's. He didn't really even think about it, as he turned toward their home instead of Cyrus'. It scared him less, somehow. Maybe because they are younger, maybe because they look less like what he has been taught to fear. No matter what the reason, he was right to go, and Shannon welcomed him in like an old friend— like family.

He doesn't understand, but he is thankful anyway.

"Is Emmy here?"

"She's already at the gathering," Shannon says. "Same place I'm going, same place everyone is going. You should come. You're welcome to stay back here, but..."

"Oh, I don't... I don't know... I..."

"You're shy, aren't you?" she asks. "So is Emmy."

"M...m-more than that," he says softly, and he isn't sure how to elaborate, so he doesn't.

She stands up, walks across the room and over to the kitchen, returning a minute later with two glasses of water, pushing one into his face.

"You're dehydrated," she says simply, and he takes it from her, surprised by the trembling of his hands.

She notices but does not comment as she sits down across from him, keeping her face light.

He clears his throat, takes a drink, and lifts his head, looking at her hesitantly.

"The... the gathering," he says slowly. "What is it, exactly?"

"Mm." She sits her glass down on the table, shakes her head. "It's just what it sounds like. It's just creating a space where we can be together, grieve together... It was a long night, it's easier to process when you have people with you."

"Grieving?" Icarus asks. "B-b-but the Ordinem never made it here, why..."

"We're grieving for your people, Icarus."

The words catch him completely off guard. He shakes his head.

"Why would you grieve *us*?" His voice falters. "We... We're..."

"They're just people," she breathes. "War is always something that should be mourned. Last night, when it happened... People poured into this place so fast that Cyrus felt it. He knew something was wrong and came back— found them terrified and confused. They didn't have any idea what had happened to them..."

Icarus cannot help but think of Cole. It makes his stomach turn.

"And many of them were lost," she continues. "Because of their fear. Because of what the Ordinem did to them... Some were Grim."

"Sometimes I forget I'm not the only one," he mutters.

"That's the whole point of tonight. You should come, trust me. It'll make more sense than me trying to explain. You can stick with me and Emmy, or I can take you to Cyrus, if you'd prefer that..."

A gathering of Grim hardly sounds comforting, but it is exactly what his father suggested: That he grieve with people like himself.

"Will it be loud?" he asks, hesitant.

"Not at all. "

"And they're not... They won't want m...me to leave? Or... I don't know."

"You're not the only Ordinem kid in Morta," she says. "I know it's complicated. Nobody is going to hate you for what you were born into. *Most* of us wouldn't even ask you to choose. I swear. Nothing to worry about."

He looks at her a minute, hesitant, and then nods.

"Okay..."

"Thank you, thank you. Thank you for trusting me. Now, I have to get ready, so... Make yourself comfortable." She stands up, walks to the edge of the room, and then turns back around, a sort of sad smile on her lips. "I'll only be a minute, but if you need anything at all, just holler."

He smiles at her, even though it hurts, and nods in thanks, not letting his expression fall until she turns away.

When she does, he almost expects the darkness to speak to him, but it doesn't.

There is sunlight coming in the window.

When he notices, he walks over to it, peeking between the blinds.

"Shannon?" he calls, after a minute.

"Yeah?" Her voice echoes from the back of the house.

"Do you m...m-mind if I go outside for a... minute?"

"That's fine!"

"Okay," he says, too quietly for her to hear him. He turns the handle like it might burn him, stepping back outside slowly, and turns his face toward the sky: light purple and pink in the daylight, the moon already rising— a different moon, he realizes. Bigger.

He wonders for the first time where *exactly* he is. He wonders if it is like Inanis, or like Terra. He wonders if he is on a planet, and if there are others.

He wonders for just a moment if it could ever be home, but the reason for the thought makes him sad enough that he pushes it away.

His family is home, he thinks, and his family cannot come here. His family would never... Not all of them.

He wonders if Zahra would, and he doesn't even know why. He almost says her name just to tell her the sky is clear somewhere before remembering she can't hear him.

He lets his hands fall to his sides and steps into the high grass. It is soft on his hands, almost like cotton. He keeps walking almost without thinking, so close to where he fought death not two days earlier, and yet the tragedy does not linger in the cool air. Icarus cannot, for the life of him, feel anything but peace outside himself. Peace, and then wind, blowing steadily, mussing his hair, sending goosebumps down his arms.

There is something else, in the breeze; something he stopped feeling in the Ordinem a long time ago. He folds his arms over his chest, lets a long sigh pass his lips, and rubs the tears away from his eyes.

"Why?" he whispers, to whatever is listening. The question is muttered desperately, for fear that the spirit will leave if he does not ask quickly enough. It is only after asking that he realizes he is not sure he wants an answer. And so, there is no response. No response but a whisper deep in his chest, and he is not sure if it is his voice or another.

Stay.

He runs his hands over his arms, trembling, careful to keep them soft, to keep his nails from his skin.

"I can't... I have to go home,"

Too much, Michael.

His breath catches in his throat, and he hesitates, heavy.

"I can handle it."

You shouldn't have to.

He looks back up at the sky. The clouds are tinted blue in the west. The clouds are separate here: they do not blanket the sky. They are water, fog, and ice, unpolluted by smoke, untouched by the chemicals that burn Terra's skies.

There is salt in the air. He wonders if the ocean is clear, blue, or green. He wonders if there is an ocean at all— if there could *possibly* be a sea he could *touch* without stepping into thin air, hitting it and turning it into concrete.

He wonders, then, how many things that mean death in The Ordinem could mean life in Morta.

Life in Morta. Life amongst death. *In* death.

Or perhaps, it is not really death at all.

Michael stepped into *death* at six years old, sitting at the edge of a bed he did not know, in a home that wasn't his, in a place that did not want him. And then he stepped into it again with every day that passed. It held his hand before then, in Jakara, had already become familiar before it ever invited him in.

Left to death, the Code said, and he felt the words.

❖

Michael wanted to kick his heels against the bed frame— wanted to move, nervously, but was too afraid that it would upset someone. He thought then that the fidgeting and the noise might be enough to make them regret bringing him back, and the mindset has still not left him.

Aliya stepped into the room with her hands clasped tightly behind her back, and he looked up at her, frightened and pale.

She closed the door and sat down on the floor, exhaustion showing in her young features.

"It's been two weeks," she said softly, making her voice as gentle as she could manage. "Two weeks, sweetie. We just... It would be wonderful, if you would say something— anything."

He looked at her hesitantly, did not even move as tears threatened to burn his eyes.

"Can you tell me what happened?" she asked. "You can tell me. You're safe."

Fire, he thought. Soldiers. Guns. Noise.

He couldn't explain. He couldn't even think—

"Can you tell me your name?"

She had asked before, they both had, and still he did not answer; not at first. He did not even consider answering until an exasperated sigh escaped her chest, and frustration tugged at her mouth, and he worried what might happen if he didn't.

He tried to form the word in his mouth, while she continued on, asking questions and saying things that he did not really hear. He had almost gathered enough strength to force it out when the doorbell rang through the house, and Aliya dropped her head, standing up to leave.

"M-m-m..." His voice was so quiet she almost didn't hear it, but she did, and she turned around, her face a little lighter.

"Yes?" she asked. "What is it?"

"M-m-mi... Mi..." His breath caught, and he started to panic, the word seemingly stuck in his throat. Michael. Michael. Michael.

His face turned bright red, and he clenched his fists, picking at his knees.

Always stuck on his Ms. Always stuck on Michael.

Rosemarie let him say it, always. All the way through, never impatient. The rest would interrupt, cut him off, or lose interest.

It occurred to him suddenly, harshly, that he did not want to be Michael; of course, he did, but not as much as he wanted to be wanted. Not as much as he wanted to be loved, and no one wanted Michael. No one wanted anything he was.

No one wanted too curious, or too many questions, or too loud, or too opinionated, or too needy—

"Icarus," he said, his voice timid. "N-n-name... Icarus."

His name was the first of many deaths.

"Icarus," she repeated, and he nodded, his chest tight. "Thank you for telling me."

He nodded again, the lie burning in his stomach, and she took a step back toward him.

"Can you tell me what happened—" *She was cut off by the second ring, and swallowed hard, opening the door.* "Hold on just a minute, I've got someone else who wants to see you."

He nodded, and she left without another word. It was hardly a crime, having spent so much of the past two weeks comforting the boy, and coaxing him to speak. So far, he had only spoken when waking from dreams, and very little of what he had said made much sense; still, he felt lonelier with her gone.

He listened for her voice beyond the door, and found it blending with the voice of another; a voice like music, he thought, but he could not hear much.

"Name."

"Icarus."

"Alone?"

"Are you sure?"

Fragments. Nothing worth much. And then the door opened, and a woman he did not recognize stepped into it, smiling at him with such pure care that his hands relaxed instantly upon seeing her, his shoulders falling.

Her hair fell in long black ribbons down her shoulders, across her black clothes— a dress which covered all but her feet, and an inch below her chin.

She tugged off her gloves as she sat down across from him on the floor, her dark eyes shining with as much light as she could pull into them for the boy in front of her.

"Hello," *she said, her voice light despite the heaviness in her chest.* "Your name is Icarus, yes?"

He nodded, his light blond hair falling into his eyes.

She reached up and tucked it back behind his ear, her touch gentle enough that he found some comfort in it.

"Ursula," *she said softly, and she held her hand out in front of her.* "It's so nice to meet you."

He placed one thin, trembling hand in hers, and she smiled as she shook it.

"Would it be okay if I asked you a couple of questions?" she asked. "Just so I can understand a little better? Help Jack and Aliya understand a little better?"

He looked at the floor, shook his head.

"B-bad..." he whispered. "B-b-bad at t-talking."

"You?" she asked, her eyes widening a little. "I don't think—"

"S-s-slow..." He stopped, cleared his throat. "S...sorry for... in-in-in-interrup..ting you, I d-didn't m-m-m-m-m-mean—"

"Hey," she whispered, running her thumb along the back of his hand. "It's okay, love. You're okay. You're safe here."

He didn't look at her, didn't believe her, and a little light fell from her eyes.

"Were you not safe in Jakara?" she asked, her voice careful.

He shook his head, starting to cry, silently.

"Were you in a shelter? Or..." He shook his head again. "With your parents?"

A weak nod, and when he opened his mouth to speak, she fell silent.

"They-they-they did-didn't l-like m..." He dropped his head a little further, struggled another second before giving up, a quiet sob escaping his lips. "Gone. They're... They're gone..." She rubbed his shoulder lightly, trying to console him, and he dropped his voice to a trembling whisper. "I w-wish I was gone..."

"Well I'm certainly glad you're not," she said. Her eyes were burning, but her voice was still gentle. "You know, Icarus, you're very young. Too young to be gone."

"Then why did everyone want to leave m-m..."

Her throat tightened. She shook her head.

"I don't know," she whispered. "The truth is, Icarus, that people can be very foolish, and very afraid, and very cruel, but that doesn't mean there's anything wrong with us."

He looked at her then, desperately, and she let her shoulders fall.

"I was left too," she whispered, and his eyes widened a little at the words.

"You?"

"Mhm," she nodded. "Before I came here, I didn't have anybody at all. Nobody wanted me. Not like a child should be wanted."

"Why not?" he asked, and the question was pure, but her heart fell a little anyway; the question was too familiar, then, as it would be now.

"I don't know," she said sadly. "But, you know, I have to try and believe that it isn't... It isn't our fault, when we're left behind."

His eyes searched her face, trying to believe the words, and then they stopped just below her right eye, darkening slightly upon seeing the small, purplish brown blotch that lay there.

He pointed to it, sniffed.

"Hurt?" he asked.

She reached up, grazed it with her fingers, and then shook her head.

"Just makeup," she lied, letting her hair fall forward to cover it. "Nothing to worry about, and you," she said, "You have nothing to worry about, Icarus."

He let his face fall, and she squeezed his shoulder gently.

"These are good people," she said. "Good, safe people. I promise you that. You can trust them. They will take care of you, and love you very much, if you let them."

"How do I..."

"Just be, Icarus. You just let yourself be. You don't have to do anything..." Her voice trailed off, and she shook her head. "Sometimes people leave," she whispered, "but sometimes people stay. Hm?"

He nodded, even though he wasn't sure, and she followed suit, opening her arms.

"You want a hug?"

The fragile boy nodded, and she pulled him into her arms, as gently as she could.

He held on tightly, wishing someone had offered the token of kindness sooner.

"So you'll talk to them when I go?" she asked, pulling away. "You promise?"

He nodded, hesitant, and she smiled, just as brightly as before.

When Icarus steps back inside, Shannon is standing in front of a mirror, struggling to put her hair back into a braid. She groans loudly, pulling it free again.

"Emmy's left me in my hour of need," she says. "Okay, I'm sorry, it's her hour of need and I'm being overdramatic but oh my *god*."

"Do you need..." He laughs softly, stepping toward her. "I can help."

"Would you?"

He nods, finishes pulling the messy braid apart, and separates it into three strands.

"One?" he asks.

"Yeah." He nods, starting to interweave them, and she smiles a little, even as sadness plants itself in her chest. "So, you're coming?"

"Mhm."

"I should probably tell you about Emmy before we get there, just in case... You know what happened in Karneji?"

"Mhm."

"Okay, so... The Reaper who did it, his name was William..."

"I don't understand why he did it, if you were going to evacuate."

"Because they'd use him again," she sighs. "Him, or some other Grim, and they'd come back when we *weren't* evacuated. I hate it, but... They had him in Trellis for ten years, Icarus. Even if there was another way, I'm not sure I can... I don't know if I can blame h im."

"I do, a little," Icarus sighs. "But... I think I lost too m-much not to."

"No, no. I understand. That's the thing is, Emmy does too, but..."

Her words trail off, and Icarus pauses.

"What?" he asks.

"She's his daughter," she says, her voice quiet. "That's why she's here, she's not even Grim. I just thought I should warn you, so you know why she's..."

"Oh," he breathes, and with all of the thoughts that swarm his mind in the same instant, he only speaks one. "Is she okay?"

"I don't really know. She will have seen him by the time we—"

"*Seen* him?" he asks, resuming the braid. "I thought you s-s-s..." He clears his throat. "I thought you s...said she wasn't Grim."

"She doesn't need to be Grim, we're in Morta. The dead are as present as anyone else."

"Oh," he says again. "That s-seems obvious, n-now that you've said it. Hair-tie?"

She nods, hands him a small rubber band, and then looks back at him, tipping her head in thanks.

"You're good at that," she says.

"I appreciate it."

She nods again, smiles, takes his hand, and soon they are out the door, walking along the pale dirt road that leads to town.

Peaceful, he thinks again.

"It's beautiful here," he says, just as he is starting to hear voices in the distance. "I m-mean, it's amazing."

"You should see the sunrise," she says. "*That's* amazing."

"Shannon?" a voice calls, and then, more surprised, "Icarus?"

They both turn, and Cyrus walks toward them, his face light, but his blue eyes heavier than before.

Grieved, Icarus thinks.

"It's good to see you both," he says, his voice tired. "I was just going to come looking for you, Shan. Emmy's back, and she was looking for you."

"Is she okay?" she asks.

"She's doing remarkably well, considering." He stops, turns to Icarus. "How are you doing?"

"Well," he says. "Considering..."

"You lost someone." Cyrus says it more as a fact than a question. "I'm so sorry. What was their name? They might still be here, if you want to..."

His heart speeds up, jumps into his throat, and he sees it all again, Cyrus' words fading into the background.

Blood, spraying across his—

He clears his throat, blinking slowly as he attempts to speak.

"The... The darkness keeps telling m...me that he'll blame m...me, if he knows what I am," he says. "Do you think... Do you think I would m-make it harder, for him?"

"I don't," Cyrus breathes. "I can't say for certain, of course, but I think you should try. I think you'll regret not trying, and I can stay with you both, help..."

"Cole," Icarus says. "His name was Cole. The Ordinem doesn't do last..." He shakes his head. "I don't need to tell you this."

Cyrus nods.

"Okay, I'll see what I can find. You'll stick together? It'll be getting dark in a few hours, I don't know when I'll be back."

"We'll stick together," Shannon says, and Icarus nods hesitantly.

"Okay," Cyrus says, gripping nervously at the cloak around his shoulders. "I'll see you both then. I'll be as quick as I can."

"Are you okay?" Icarus asks, suddenly, and the older man turns to him with an expression that says enough on its own.

"I don't know," he responds, and then, shaking his head, "Yes, I will be. I'm glad to see you're safe. I was worried." He pauses, clears his throat. "Hey, is... You said you were Anemos' friend, yes?"

"Yes."

"Is he alright, do you know?"

"He's trying to be."

"His mother?"

"Ursula?" Icarus asks. "Ursula's... I don't know. She m-made it back, she's stable."

"Charles?" he asks, and then, more softly, "I'm sorry, I'm barraging you, aren't I?"

"N-no, you're fine... Charles is alright, why do you—"

"Alright," he says, his voice quieting with relief. "Thank you. I'll be back as quickly as I can be. Did I interrupt you? I'm sorry, my mind is everywhere this evening."

"You didn't," Icarus lies. "Are you sure you're okay?"

"Mhm," he nods, his eyes saying differently. "Just in a rush, is all. I need to be going, now, unless there's something either of you need?"

"We're okay," Shannon says, putting a hand on his shoulder. "Deep breaths?"

"Trying," he says, letting out a shaky sigh. "Thank you. You'll keep an eye on Emmy?"

"Mhm."

"Okay," he breathes, and he repeats the word once, nods, and goes, his head turned toward the ground.

Icarus turns to Shannon, confused, and she answers his question before he can ask it.

"They're family," she says softly. "The Guide is his brother."

His face pales slightly, and he turns to look back at Cyrus, but he is already gone, out of sight.

"You're... you're sure?" he asks.

"They're not allowed to talk about him, in The Ordinem. They've practically erased him."

She resumes walking, and Icarus follows suit.

"Why n-not?"

"Because he... Well, they think he's dead, and they don't grieve past the deadline, no? His *death* almost broke the entire..." She clears her throat, shakes her head. "It was a tragedy. You should ask him."

"Do you... Do you think it would upset him?"

"No, he's open about it. Just, maybe not tonight."

"Oh, of course n-not..." They turn the corner into a crowd, and before Icarus can register that he's surrounded by Grim, his eyes fall on the sad, blonde haired girl sitting not fifteen feet away, a cloak pulled up over her head. *His* cloak, he thinks, looking at the size of it, and for some reason the thought chokes him. "Hey, there's Emmy."

She looks up at her name, makes eye contact with the both of them, and pulls herself up from the bench she sits on, walking slowly through the crowd until she reaches them, pulling Shannon into a hug first, and then turning to Icarus, her eyes filled with tears.

"I'm so sorry," she whispers, and he shakes his head, dusting his hands nervously on his pant legs before embracing her, careful. "Are you okay?"

"I'm okay," he says, and for a minute, it feels like the truth. "Are you?"

"I'm okay," she answers, pulling away. "Just really, terribly sad, and I've got this... This guilt, in my chest... I'm so sorry, Icarus."

"You've not done anything," he says, and he is not sure where the words come from, but he knows she doesn't believe him. "Hey, I'm Ordinem, yeah?"

She nods, wiping her eyes, and he forces a sad smile.

"It wasn't you," he says, and then, as if compelled. "It was-wasn't really *him,* either."

"You don't think?"

He looks at her for a moment, the grief in her eyes, and shakes his head.

"No. He... I m-mean, they would have come back, I think. They would've seen M...morta, and then..." His chest hurts, as he says it. "Who knows what could have happened?"

Shannon watches him as he speaks, nods in agreement.

"He was just trying to protect you, Emmy; trying to protect all of us. You know he wouldn't have done it otherwise."

"He was a *pacifist,*" she says. "I can't imagine what they must have done to him, to convince him that *that* was the way. I don't know whether to be angry with him or grieve for him."

"Grieve for him," Icarus says. "Did you speak with him?"

"Mm, briefly," she nods. "Not briefly, it was hours, but it was hardly enough. Sometimes I think it's easier, the way everyone else... The way *I* would experience death, outside of this place. Like, maybe losing something is easier than letting it go; especially when things are this... complicated."

They both nod, quiet, and a minute later Shannon speaks, careful.

"Did it help, though, do you think?"

"A little," she says. "It was good seeing him."

"That's good."

"He was different. I guess I am, too, but... His eyes were different. He didn't tell me what they did to him. Just that..." Her voice breaks, she wipes her eyes again. "Just that he was alone, for a long while."

CHAPTER SIXTY-FOUR

U rsula stands with her hands clenched into fists, trying not to grimace at the growing crowd, trying not to tremble in fear.

The space around her seems to twist, pulse, and ring, beating against her chest and filling her lungs, but then, someone stands beside her.

A hand finds hers, prying her fingernails from her palm, and then holds onto it firmly.

It pulls her mind away, too, and when she looks over at him, her heart is in her throat.

Anemos looks at her with tired eyes, Cole's jacket still cast around his shoulders, and gives her hand a tight squeeze.

"Breathe," he pleads, and she tries, looking back away from him, silent. "I'm glad you're okay," he says. "I should have said that last night."

"You didn't need to," she forces.

"Yes I did," he nods. "I was... It was cruel, not to... I heard what happened, once you were gone."

"Which part?"

"All of it, I think."

She nods, and he watches her, in awe of how little emotion touches her face.

"Are you okay?" he asks. "That's... Horribly traumatic, just to hear—"

"Anemos," she interrupts, her breath catching in her throat. "I can't... I'm not going to ask for your sympathy. I know I deserved it."

"Deserved it?" he asks, his eyes widening. "Mom..."

"I was late," she whispers, her jaw clenched. "I was just *seconds* late, Anemos, and if Kieran had left me behind, he could have gotten here in time to..." She stops, shakes her head. "I should have—"

"No."

"If my mind hadn't been so clouded with hatred, we wouldn't be in this situation."

"Yes we would. You think the whole rest of the Council would have shifted their vote for..." He stops himself, shakes his head. "You don't really think I would rather Kieran have left you behind?"

"No." She shakes her head. "Not consciously, but... Cole took better care of you than *I* ever have."

Anemos shakes his head, his breath heavy.

"Yeah, well, he didn't live with Alastor either, did he?" She falls silent. "I'm not going to lie to you, Mom. You've screwed up a *lot*, and I'm not going to tell you there isn't some resentment because of that."

She looks at the ground as he continues talking, her throat tight.

"But I'm also not oblivious to..." He clears his throat, shakes his head. "I read the letter, before coming. I think you should know that you haven't failed, not entirely. I know that you've borne the brunt of it, okay? I didn't use to understand, and I used to be really angry with you, and I'm still angry but... You *have* protected me, more than I care to think about."

"I've tried," she whispers, her face low.

"I know," he says. "I know you have, and whenever you want to tell me the rest, whatever it is, whenever you want to explain how we got here, I'll listen, okay? I'm not so angry I won't hear you out."

She nods, and a low ring shakes the space around them, a microphone clicking on.

"In the meantime, though, I need you to be honest with me about something else."

"Yes?"

"You're from the Outskirts," he says, keeping his voice low. "I know it's been a long time, but I need to know if you're as outraged as I am."

"*More* outraged," she mutters. "I'm sick over it. The kids from the shelter, the lack of security, the bullshit we're about to—" She stops, clears her throat. "Excuse me. The *drivel* we're about to listen to."

"What will they say, do you think?"

"Oh, they'll call him a hero for trying to defend the same children they'd leave for the birds. Won't take any responsibility. The usual."

"I could hate them for it," he says, and she nods.

"I wouldn't blame you. Don't repeat that." She pauses, shakes her head. "Don't repeat anything, actually. I'm not supposed to be speaking."

"Not a problem," he responds, and as he does, a woman steps up to the podium on the stage in the distance.

Ursula lets out a long sigh, rubbing her forehead.

"Everytime this woman speaks," she says. "My will to live dwindles."

"She visited the shelter once, when Cole was there, and he overheard her calling them all *miserable wretches.*"

She turns to him, eyebrows furrowed.

"You can't be serious?"

"Jack was with her. Cindy spent the next five minutes trying to convince him she didn't mean it how it sounded."

"My word," she says, not listening as the woman begins to speak. "Almost as bad as Ralph, may his soul find peace."

"Any idea who will fill his position?"

"Probably her, on Outskirts matters. She was his second."

"Of course she was. Weapons?"

"Alastor, unless I challenge him."

"Challenge him."

"I might." Cindy says Cole's name, and both of them flinch, simultaneously tightening their grip on each other's hands. "You know, you could challenge *her.*"

"Me?" He almost laughs, shaking his head. "No."

"You're smarter than her."

"No, I'm..." He stops. "No."

"You came in second in the exams, Cindy came in thirty-seventh."

"Twenty years ago."

"She's losing intelligence over time, love." He laughs, but it's strained, and she looks over at him, worried. "Are you alright?"

"No," he says, reddening. "Every word she's said has been a damn lie, and we're a minute in..." His breath catches. "It doesn't fucking matter. He's gone."

"It matters. You don't have to stay, if you don't think you can handle it."

"He's not at home, either." He wets his lips, lets out a shaking sigh. "I don't know how to do this. Have you ever... How do you deal with losing someone you love this much? How do you *live?*"

"You assume that they would want you to. You live for whoever else is left behind..." She shakes her head. "I lost someone, once; a young man I considered my brother."

He looks over at her, eyes red, and she lowers her voice.

"I know it's... different, but it was one of the worst things I've ever been through, so—to some degree— I know how much it hurts."

"Who?" he asks.

CHAPTER SIXTY-FIVE

It is long past dark, and Cyrus has still not returned.

Icarus sits cross legged on the ground in the field where the gathering began and has slowly begun to disperse.

The pain of those around him seemed to fade with the sun— his own pain, even, and he is still not sure exactly what has happened.

It was nothing more than a gathering.

A few hundred people, coming and going, eating and drinking, talking, laughing, and crying, but it is safe, and he has never been safe before.

When the sun started to set, they started to light the candles; dozens, making the night seem to glow. And now he sits among them, in a small group of people he doesn't really know, feeling as if he is with family.

He laughs, running his hands along his arms, and the man across from him— Elazar, a few years older with brown skin, a short black beard, and thick locks pulled back behind his head— looks over at him, taking a drink from the small glass of wine in his hand.

"So," he says, his voice smooth. "You're Ordinem?"

Everyone falls silent, looking at the blue eyed boy patiently as he shrugs, shaking his head.

"I don't know," he says. "They-they-they don't... Don't seem to want *me.*"

"I could never," a woman— Olive— says, her brown hair falling into her pale face, hiding her gray eyes for only a moment. "Too much of a romantic."

"Oh, that's right," Shannon breathes. "What is it you all do about relationships?"

Icarus takes a drink, savors the alcohol on his tongue, and shakes his head once more.

"Practically banned," he says. "No dating, no... No intimacy, really."

"Abstinence?"

"You can have kids. Beyond that is..." He shakes his head. "You've got m...marriage, but it's a business deal. They pick who you're going with, they pick everything... It's a partnership... V-very rarely has anything to do with love, and when it is, you're violating the Code."

"Why?" Emmy asks, and he turns toward her, his hands still tracing paths across his wrists.

"Because they serve the Code," he says simply. "Serve only the Code, love only the Code."

"Would you live like that?" Elazar asks. "If they wanted you?"

Icarus lets out a long sigh, shakes his head.

"I don't know. I've never really been given... They-they're all about choice, right? But you choose between... O-ordinem, or Outskirts, and the... the Outskirts are... I m-mean, it isn't... They keep it bad, out there."

"Think it's a tactic?" Olive says. "Trying to get more kids? Drive up the desperation?"

"It could be."

"That's fucked," another man says, brushing his short blond hair from his face, smoking something that smells like pine.

"Language, Kane," Olive says, and he rolls his eyes.

"Sorry, sorry, sorry."

He looks at the ground, and Icarus looks into the fire in front of him, running the glass across his lips absentmindedly.

"You know," Elazar says, tossing a stick into the fire. "You do have a choice now, kid. We've just given you one."

He looks up, takes a deep breath, and the other man continues, looking him dead in the eyes.

"You will be welcome here," he says. "You know that. Whenever you're ready."

"Hell yeah," Kane coughs. "You can sleep on the top bunk in my house. Loaded with books right now, but I'll clear it out for you, my man. Take you on a couple dates, let you get a contact high, it'll be like the Ordinem never happened."

"*Kane,*" Olive hisses, obviously fighting back laughter that Icarus doesn't bother with, leaning forward and looking to the left, trying to meet the other man's eyes.

"Watch it, I might take you up on that," he says, and Kane smiles.

"I think you should."

"Very Grim of you to flirt at a funeral, Icarus," Shannon sighs, putting a hand on his shoulder. "You're adapting."

"Shh," Emmy laughs softly. "Tell him the agenda and we'll have to kill him."

Icarus laughs, and then, after a minute, shakes his head.

"I don't know, though," he says. "I don't... Sometimes, I hear the Code and want to... How do I put this lightly?"

"Stab yourself?" Kane asks.

"Thank you, that works well."

Kane laughs, takes a drink, and Icarus pushes the hair back out of his face.

"It's just that... The Order. There's s-so... So much that I don't want to let go of..."

"Why would you have to let it go?" Elazar asks. "The Order predates the Ordinem, the Code..."

"The modifications," Kane mumbles, and Elazar nods, seemingly disappointed in himself for agreeing with the man.

"He's not wrong," he says simply. "Why don't you just follow the old religion?"

"Follow the Order?" Icarus asks. "Without the Ordinem?"

"I do," he answers. "There's a lot of wisdom there. First group of people to shift. Explains a lot about the Wind, about Inanis..."

"It works for him," Olive says. "I could see it for you. You seem the type."

"I didn't think people still—"

A twig snaps nearby, and all of them look up, look over, as Cyrus approaches the group, his cloak pulled up over his head.

He nods at them, a little warily, and a few strands of his black hair fall into his eyes, shining in the light of the fire.

"He returns," Kane says, raising his blunt in the air.

Cyrus looks over at him, forces a smile, and then turns back to Icarus, his eyes tired.

"Icarus," he says roughly. "I'm sorry for the delay."

"Oh, that's fine, don't worry."

"If I could speak with you alone," he says, an odd tone in his voice. "In regards to your friend?"

"Of course." Icarus stands up, nods to the group, a little awkwardly, and Elazar takes his hand as he passes him, squeezing it tightly.

"Come find me, next time you're in Morta," he says. "We'll talk more."

Icarus nods, and Olive takes a deep breath.

"Better see you again, kid."

"You will," he says, and Kane looks away, clearing his throat as his eyes meet the ground.

Before Icarus can go any further, Shannon runs up to him, pulling him into a hug like he might be an older brother, and Cyrus smiles a little, even through his exhaustion.

"Stay safe," Emmy says, and he only nods in response, a little too choked to speak.

Chosen, he thinks, and when he goes, five prayers follow him, one riddled with obscenities, and tossed to the ground with the butt of a joint.

When they are just out of earshot, Cyrus takes Emmy's suggestion one step further.

"You should stay here," he says, his voice light and sad. "It'd be safer than going back."

"My friend s-said the s-same," Icarus responds.

"But you're not going to listen to either of us." He lets out a long sigh, rubs his face. "You're Grim, alright. Bullheaded."

"M-maybe," Icarus breathes. "No, n-not bullheaded, just... I can't abandon them all now. You understand."

"I understand." He kicks a rock in the path. "Better have a plan though, if things go south. Getting worse everyday, and I think my girls are getting attached."

"Your girls?"

"Well, I've gotten attached. Been taking care of them a while now. Not so much anymore, but, when they were younger... We're getting off on a tangent, and we were already on a tangent, back to that later." He stops, shakes his head. "Actually, hold on, *other* tangent: You seem okay, kid. A lot of trauma for you to seem this okay."

"I *feel* okay," he sighs. "I don't know. I don't f-freaking understand myself. I feel okay now, I'll probably have a breakdown because I like, drop a pen later... I think something's wrong with m...me, m-maybe."

"Kane's like that," Cyrus says. "Don't get me wrong, always angry, but... Tangent, again. I'm sorry. Your friend."

"My friend," Icarus repeats, and Cyrus stops in the middle of the path, shaking his head before placing a hand on the boy's shoulder.

"Sit down," he says.

"S-sit down?"

"Sit down."

Icarus glances down at the ground briefly, a little uneased, and then sits down in the middle of the path.

"Okay," he says. "A little nervous *now.*"

"Don't be," Cyrus yawns, shaking his head.

"Bad news?"

"I don't really..." He shakes his head. "No, no. Not *bad*. Just... odd. But you," He points to him, his voice a little slurred, "Are going to stay *calm.*"

"M-more nervous, not making it better."

"It's really not necessarily terrible, just.. A pen? Maybe."

"Not *necessarily* terrible."

"On first glance it's actually excellent news."

"Are you going to tell m...me?" he asks, a nervous laugh escaping his lips.

"I'm trying to ease you in."

"You're literally just giving m-me anxiety. I m-m-mean, I don't understand... I don't m...mean to be blunt, but he's *dead.* I'm not really seeing what you could possibly tell me—"

"He isn't."

Icarus pauses, blinks a few times before speaking.

"Isn't here?"

"Isn't dead," Cyrus says. "We have a record of who enters Morta, who leaves. He's never been here."

"You took *four* freaking tangents, Cyrus. *Four.*"

"I have not slept in over sixty hours, *Icarus.* Both times I've seen you? All one day for me. A bit of slack—"

"Okay," Icarus breathes, standing up from the ground with shaking legs. "Okay. But like, where the *hell* is he?"

"Well, see, that's the disconcerting bit, is that all *I* know is that he isn't here."

"But he's alive?"

Cyrus looks at the younger man, his voice calm, but his eyes showing something else, red and frightened and full of hope and dread.

"He's alive," he says.

"Then we can find him, right? I m-mean..." Icarus stops, rubs his face. "It's setting in now, I think."

"Breathe."

He nods, his hands trembling, and looks back in the direction of the fire. He can still hear laughter in the distance.

His heart drops deep into his stomach.

"You're *sure?*" he asks.

"Completely."

"But I *saw* him. I was-was-was there when he..." Cyrus can see his eyes watering in the darkness and places a gentle hand on his shoulder in an effort to calm him. "It's impossible. No one... No one could live through that."

"What happened?"

"Saenks. They-they attacked the shelter, and..." He shakes his head, seeing it all again. "There was one on the roof, and it was t-tearing its way down so we... We went for the door..."

The Saenk behind the door was waiting, patiently, as the one on the upper floor frightened them toward it, and when it opened, it ran him through before it could even see him, as if expecting him to be there.

It did not rip him apart, there, and the Saenk behind Icarus only watched, waiting to catch the broken boy in its hands.

"It-it-it... It stabbed him from behind, all the way through, and then... slammed him into the wall, and then threw him across the room—"

"You witnessed this?" Cyrus asks, his eyes widening. When Icarus nods, he shakes his head. "I'm so sorry."

He has seen worse, he thinks, but he doesn't say it.

"It's... it's okay... But... There's... The one from upstairs grabbed him, and I didn't see... He was gone before anyone saw what happened."

"With the Saenk?" Cyrus asks.

"With the Saenk."

"To Assecula then, more likely than not."

Icarus falls silent a moment, eyes wide, and pulls his hair back out of his face, trying to process.

"You think *Cole* is in..." He almost laughs, fear weaving through his veins. "Is that worse?"

"No," Cyrus breathes, his voice unsure. "No, I mean... No."

"But why would he be..." He cringes. "I m-mean, unless they're stocking up for winter—"

"They would have killed him by now if they just wanted to... There's no delicate way to say that. Unless he's managed to escape somehow, they're keeping him alive."

"Is that *worse?*"

"Not necessarily." He pauses, shakes his head. "No, he's alive. That means there's hope. It isn't worse."

"Do you think he's still... I have to t-t..."

Icarus stops, his lips pressed tightly together, and Cyrus raises his eyebrows.

"You have to *what?*"

"Nothing."

"Icarus, if you attempt to enter Assecula—"

"What?" he asks. "No, I wouldn't... I wouldn't even know where to look if I... I have to go home. I have to... What the hell do I do?"

"Nothing," Cyrus says. "Do nothing, not until we know what we're dealing with."

"B-b-but how will we know what we're dealing with unless I *do* something?"

"*I'll* do something," he says, the shadows under his eyes seeming to grow darker with the words. "I'll... I'll handle it, Icarus. You need to focus on keeping yourself safe, right n ow."

"But I want to help."

"If I need your help," Cyrus breathes, "I will come find you. Whether you're perceiving it or not, you have just suffered a great trauma and should be *resting.*"

"I don't *want* to rest."

"But you need to."

"So does he."

"That is not your responsibility—"

"Yes it is," he breathes, frustration now evident in his voice. "I was s...supposed to protect him... *I* was supposed to—"

"No." Cyrus' voice is firm, and the word is angry. "The Ordinem was supposed to protect him. The grown persons in power should have protected *both* of you, and they failed on both counts, but *I* am not comfortable with letting an unprepared child risk their life when they do not have to."

Icarus clenches his fists, grits his teeth, and breathes slowly, glaring at the man.

"I am not," he says, "a *child.*"

"You're eighteen years old. You're a *teenager.*"

"I'm—"

"It isn't an insult, Icarus."

"It feels like one."

"I know it does, but it isn't," Cyrus breathes. "You're allowed to be a child, just as you're allowed to need help, and training, and *rest.*"

"I'm r...really not sure that... *any* of those things are true," Icarus says, and as Cyrus watches him, his chest aches with familiarity and grief.

There is an irony in the words being spoken by a man like him, sworn to the Ordinem at fifteen years, having been denied help for so long, having refused training for so many years, having never rested.

"Cyrus?" The younger man asks, pulling his mind back to the present.

"Hm?"

"I just need to know I'm... *We* are doing everything we can, I don't... He's family, and I don't h...have m-much."

He blinks a few times, nods.

"I understand. I promise you, I will do everything I can, and I'll let you know as soon as I know anything... You don't trust me," he says, his voice gentling. "I understand that, too, but you can, I promise, I'm not like them."

"But they're a-all I've ever known, Cyrus."

There is pain in every word.

"I know."

Icarus falls silent a moment, shakes his head.

"You know I'm trying," he asks, and Cyrus nods.

"I know," he repeats. "You know you don't always have to?"

Icarus looks at the ground a moment, thinking before speaking.

"I can't leave them, can I?" he asks. "I can't stay?"

"You can. You can stay."

"He told m-m-me I... I should."

"You should."

"I want to," he breathes, his eyes watering. "I really, really want to. You know I've n-never... never in m-m-my life felt as safe as I've f-felt today, and I don't know why that scares me so..." He clears his throat. "If we aren't *bad*, why do they hate us?"

"Because they're afraid."

"Is that enough of a reason to do—"

"No."

"Sometimes," he says, "I think that if I didn't hate m...myself so m-much, I'd be so angry at them that it might kill me. I m-mean, how do you *live* with it? What do I do with it?"

"I don't know."

"I wish you had all the answers."

"So do I," Cyrus says.

"I'm sorry, I know you're tired,"

"I like talking to you," he says. "It's like talking to myself at your age."

"You were a f-freaking mess, then."

He laughs a little, and Icarus smiles, pain in the lines of his face.

He holds out his hand, a little shakily, and nods at the scythe held in Cyrus' hand.

"Can I hold that for a second?" he asks, and Cyrus nods, handing it over without asking why.

Icarus takes it in his hands hesitantly, and lowers it to below eye level, running his fingers along the blade a minute before letting his eyes wander to the staff, squinting to read the words carved along the side in the darkness.

His own heart chokes him.

"What is this?" he breathes.

"Words of the Order's wise man," Cyrus says. "From the original text. Read it in the Code, first, back when I was there. Always took comfort in it, even before I got the rest worked out... Are you okay?"

Icarus nods, even as tears run down his face.

"Yes," he forces. "Yes, I'm okay, could you... I'm sorry, could you write this down for me, before I go?"

"You're going?" Cyrus asks.

"I have to," Icarus says, a sob breaking through his voice, and Cyrus only nods, not arguing.

"I have paper back at the house, if you don't mind the walk."

"I don't."

They walk back to Cyrus' quickly, and talk very little along the way. When they arrive, Cyrus writes the same passage twice, in two languages, and then folds the paper tight, handing it to Icarus with eyes half open.

"Don't let anyone see this," he says. "Stay safe."

"I'll try," Icarus says, and Cyrus pulls him into a tight hug, squeezing his arms as he pulls away.

"May the spirit be with you," he says. "You and your friend, wherever he is."

"Mazzi zon es extraen," Icarus breathes. "He may be damned..."

"*Affi,*" Cyrus says, the old language easy on his tongue. "But he will find his way out of hell."

CHAPTER SIXTY-SIX

Icarus goes to the Palace first.

It is nearly an hour after dark when he arrives, and when he reaches the entrance, the guards look at him with suspicion written plainly across their faces.

They step in front of the gate as if he might force his way in.

"What's your business here?" one of them asks, and Icarus hesitates a moment, picking at the skin on his wrists.

"I'm here to see Anemos," he says. "My name's Icarus, he'll know me."

"Only the Higher-class are allowed visitation past sundown."

"I'm from the Higher-class, Myon."

"You *live* with the Higher-class," the other says. "I believe your blood says differently."

Icarus pauses a second, almost caught off guard, and then forces an understanding smile onto his face.

"Yes, well, I'll need accompanied, then, I believe my father should still be—"

"I believe your *father* lies in the dust of Jakara, same as you would, if not for the Ordinem's apparently unstinting hospitality," the first guard says, unflinching. "Perhaps you should learn to follow its rules."

Icarus clenches his jaw, the words forcing the air from his lungs.

"The Guide himself inv-vited me to stay here, j-just last night."

"The Guide, all respect to him, is not here to verify that."

"Can't you—"

"What's going on here?" a voice says, behind him, and his shoulders tighten instantly upon hearing it.

"The boy wants to see your son," one of them says, and Icarus does not turn around. "Do you have an opinion on the matter?"

"Oh..." Alastor stops beside Icarus, looks him over as one might look at a leper. "Yes, I have an opinion."

Icarus bites down on his bottom lip, silent, and looks over at the man with disdain.

"You missed the event," Alastor says, his voice smooth, quiet, cold. "Where *were* you?"

"I was..." He clears his throat. "I was resting."

"Resting," the older man scoffs, and the woman behind him closes her eyes, her throat tight.

"Alastor," she forces, her voice frail. "Please, he's a child."

Icarus turns toward Ursula, not noticing her previously, and shakes his head.

"Myon," he whispers. "You don't need to... to..."

"I do," she says. "Let him in—"

"I'll go," he says, speaking over her, in the hopes that Alastor will not hear her. "It's okay, I'll... I'll just come d-during v...visiting hours, it's fine. I'm sorry for the trouble."

"*No,*" Ursula says. "My word, do you all forget that this boy nearly suffered the same fate as the one you claimed to grieve not three hours ago?"

Both of the guards drop their heads, and she shakes hers, taking Icarus by the shoulder.

Alastor watches with violence in his eyes and does not move as they walk past him, through the gate. He only stares, not speaking, until they are long out of earshot.

Once they are gone, he turns to the guards with his teeth gritted.

"I want him flagged," he says. "I want them both flagged for investigation, when the grieving period is over."

"Your wife, Myon?" one of them asks. "You understand that they may be... *severely* interrogated, until the traitor is found."

"Are you implying that I should *not* implicate my wife if I suspect her?"

"No. No, Myon, of course not,"

"Good," he says. "His father too, and the boy."

"The boy?"

"Anemos."

"Why?" The second guard asks, a little pale. "On what grounds?"

"I'm not going to argue with you. Do as you're told."

Hesitation, and then:

"Yes, Myon. "

"You'll handle it?"

"Yes, Myon."

"Very well," Alastor nods. "If Ursula is not back out in half an hour, please remind her that I am waiting."

When Ursula and Icarus step through the Palace doors, she takes his hand and squeezes it tightly.

Her hand is so cold he flinches at the touch.

"I'm sorry," she whispers, her eyes darting aimlessly around the space around them. "He's a bitter... Cruel man. He doesn't know a thing about compassion. I apologize for his behavior."

"It's not your fault," he says, and she nods, wiping at her eyes as she moves toward the stairs.

"I appreciate you saying that—"

"Myon?"

Icarus' voice takes a tone it usually doesn't with most of the Higher-class. There is a vulnerability in his tone that reminds her of the way his father speaks. It stops her in her tracks. She almost expects to see Jack standing beside him when she turns around, but she finds the Jakaran boy alone.

It is not right that he should be so grown up already. It feels like he was a child just yesterday.

"Yes, Icarus?"

"I spoke with Kieran yesterday. He told m...me... Mm." He struggles with the words a second before shaking his head, nervous. "He told m...me what happened in Assecula, what happened with Alastor."

Ursula has no idea how to respond. She folds her hands in front of her, silent.

"I'm sorry," he continues. "I'm so... so sorry. I know how it feels when someone tries to leave you be...behind, but it's not... It's not your fault what happened. You know that, don't you?"

Her heart is like a hammer, beating against her ribcage. She swallows hard before shaking her head, forcing a sad smile.

"You're remarkably kind, Icarus," she says. "But I don't want you worrying about me. That's not your job. The Council, the *adults*, we're meant to be taking care of you. Not the other way around."

"I appreciate that, Myon, but I'm not a child anymore. I can't help but worry..."

She looks down at her hands while he speaks, and her stomach twists. They are stained blood red, along with her clothes.

She closes her eyes and tells herself it isn't real, but when she opens them again it is still there.

She tries to focus on what Icarus is saying, but she can barely hear him over the ringing in her ears.

"I want to help," he says, and she watches the blood spread from her wrists, up her arms, to her neck. "How can I—"

There is a loud pop, and the lights in the Palace die. Ursula jumps at the sound, and Icarus falls silent, taking a step toward her on instinct.

He is so startled that his hands shake.

"What was that?" he asks, but Ursula only shakes her head, struggling to catch her breath. "There's no weather, why would—"

"Take care of Anemos."

Icarus quiets, his heart pounding in his chest.

"I have no right to ask anything of you, but I..." Ursula shakes her head again, wiping her tears before they fall. "I worry for him, and I'm not well enough to give him the support he needs. If you *want* to help—"

A door opens upstairs, interrupting them, and they both turn toward the sound, watching the dim glow coming from the hall grow brighter as the lantern moves toward the corner.

Anemos stops briefly at the top of the stairs, noting them both, and then continues down.

"Fancy seeing the both of you here," he says, his voice rough. "What the fuck happened?"

Ursula looks down, her breath shallow, and Icarus watches her with heavy eyes. He clears his throat as he turns back to Anemos, burying his emotions deep in his chest.

"I just came to apologize for this m-morning, and for m-m-missing the ceremony."

"You're better off for it." The lantern flickers, and Anemos jams his fist into the side of it once, making it steady. "All is forgiven; except for you walking over here in the middle of the night in the dark like a damn fool, but I'll get over that."

Anemos puts a hand on his shoulder, a little unsteady, and Ursula watches without speaking.

"I'll walk you back home, if that's all," he says. "I want to see how far this black out goes, anyway."

"Then... then y-you're walking home alone."

"I'll be *fine*," he says, twisting the handle and swinging the door open. "Or maybe someone will fucking kill me, whatever Inanis wills. "

"Anemos," Ursula says, her voice firm even in its hesitance. "Have you been drinking?"

He laughs, the sound cracking with pain.

"Would I do something like that?" he asks. "Come on, Icarus, let's go."

Icarus looks over at Ursula, a little hesitant to follow Anemos— a little hesitant to leave her— but she nods, speaking in a voice so quiet that only he can hear her.

"I'll be fine," she says. "Go on."

As soon as they step outside, they know that it's bad. It is so dark that they can hardly see a few feet in front of them— can only see the small gas lamps at the gate.

They walk toward it without speaking, and when they reach it, Anemos' stomach tightens.

He does not even acknowledge Alastor, who turned back to the gate, unable to see his path in the darkness.

"Leaving so soon?" one of the guards says. Then, seeing Anemos, his tone changes. "You shouldn't go out now. We aren't sure how much of the electricity is out, it won't be s afe."

"Is the wall down?"

"We don't know," the guard says. "You should stay here until we do."

"Will he be here?" Anemos asks, gesturing to Alastor.

"Until the power returns."

"I'll risk it, then. Icarus?"

"I'll... I'll follow you, either way."

"Hold on," Anemos says, and with the words he turns, walking quickly back up to the Palace and returning not five minutes later with a sword held in each hand. He hands one to Icarus and nods. "Let's be on our way then."

They step toward the gate, and one of the guards steps in front of it, lowering his head.

"We have to strongly advise—"

"You have advised," Anemos snaps. "Thank you, I appreciate your time."

"If the lights are down—"

"I don't know what you're so damn worried about," he laughs. "Something gets in, we die, you all get two more martyrs, yeah? You can pretend you liked Icarus, *you*—" He points at Alastor— "can pretend you liked *me,* and everyone can move on like one big happy family."

He grabs Icarus's wrist, tugs him along as he shoves the gate open himself.

"Valias," he says. "Too-da-loo."

"Anemos," Alastor says, grabbing his shoulder as he walks past him. "You need to—"

"Get your fucking hands off of me," he snaps, his voice cold. Both of the guards flinch hearing it.

Alastor grits his teeth.

"You disrespectful—"

"Oh, yes. Scold me like a child. I don't give a shit." Anemos looks at him, his eyes hard, and does not tug away. "Get your hands off of me, *now.*"

Alastor pulls his hand back and rubs his forehead, exasperated.

"You act like I've *abused* you."

"Do I?" he laughs. "I wonder why that is."

"My word," Alastor sighs. "Not this. Not again. Not here."

"What the hell are you talking about?" Anemos asks. "Not *what?*"

"I appreciate that you're grieving, but—"

"I'm not listening to this."

"This attention seeking behavior has got to *stop.* I have been *more* than compassionate. Perhaps more compassionate than I should have been, considering you've obviously not changed."

Anemos grips the sword on his waist a little too tightly, scoffs.

"Unbelievable."

"Anemos," Icarus says softly. "We should go—"

"What the hell have I done for attention?" Anemos asks. "What have I ever done for attention?"

"I'm not doing this here," Alastor says.

"*You're* not doing this here?"

"I'm not giving your delusions another audience," he says. "You want to talk to me, you want to talk about this? Come home. Talk to me in private. But you're not going to do that, are you? Because there's no one to *pity* you there."

"No one even knows I'm here!" Anemos says. "If I wanted attention, I would get attention, but I haven't done anything... I haven't *said* anything. No one has *ever* pitied me."

"I've pitied you."

"Name one *fucking* thing I have done for attention," he shouts. "*One.* One lie I have told."

"I'm not doing this here."

"Because you have nothing to say."

"Because I don't want to *humiliate* you any more than you're already humiliating yourself, Anemos. Because I don't want to air your dirty laundry in front of your friend—"

"Didn't care about that when you had me pinned to a wall last month, did you?"

"An," Icarus says, his voice trembling. "*Please.*"

Anemos stops, tasting iron, and nods, taking one step toward the man before leaving.

"I'm not a little kid anymore," he says, his voice quiet enough that only Icarus and Alastor can hear him. "I don't keep your fucking secrets."

Alastor laughs quietly, angrily, and shakes his head.

"You're right," he says. "You're not a little kid. You tell one more *damn* lie, and I'll report you as an adult, yeah?"

"*Anemos,* please, come on—"

"Go ahead," he says, the jacket seeming to tighten around his shoulders. "I don't care anymore."

"Then you're a fool," Alastor says.

"No," he steps back, grabs Icarus' bicep, and tugs him away. "You are."

They barely talk as they go, walking quickly, quietly, through the darkness. Neither of them speak a word until they reach town, and it is Anemos who breaks the silence.

"I wonder what blew it out," he says. "There's not even wind."

"Anemos?" Icarus asks.

The lantern flickers out again, leaving them in blackness, and Icarus' chest tightens.

No wind, he thinks, and yet, suddenly, something like breath blows against the back of his neck, sending chills down his spine.

He flinches away, and Anemos punches the light again, three times before it rattles back to life.

"I'm fine," he says, answering a question Icarus has not yet asked. "Don't worry about it
."

Icarus looks behind himself, lets out a long, shaky breath, and then looks up as thunder
rolls through the space above them.

"I h-have-have to worry," he starts to say, but when he turns back around, he freezes,
his hand flying up in front of his mouth.

"What?" Anemos asks, turning and looking behind him, not seeing the thing that
stands a few inches from him. "Did you see something?"

The Malemortum turns toward Icarus, its caved, bloodied face forming a hollow,
wicked smile.

"In his state," it says, its voice a heavy, husky breath. *"His soul would not last a moment—"*

The thing flies backward before it can say another word, its body breaking against the
wall of the building behind it, falling to the ground with a loud cry of pain.

"I don't know," he says, as the thing continues to writhe on the ground. "The dark
m-m-makes m-me see crap, I don't like it."

"Okay," Anemos nods. "Yeah, I'm sorry, I shouldn't have you out here. We should be
back at the Palace."

"No," Icarus breathes, trying not to watch the thing. "No, it's fine. I want to go home.
I just wanted to see you first—"

Something touches his neck, again, and he twists around without thinking, his hands
trembling.

Anemos watches with troubled eyes, shakes his head.

"Icarus," he says, his voice not holding the same suspicion of his face. "What's happening?"

"You would even consider telling him?" the voice is smooth, concerned. *"Your own
mother would turn you in."*

"Do you have him?" Icarus asks, and the darkness falls silent.

"I want to go home," he says. "That's all. The thunder has me skittish. I'm sorry."

"You're fine," Anemos says, his voice softening. "I'm really sorry, I shouldn't have
brought you out here."

"I would've walked home alone," Icarus says. "You're j-just come-coming with me, you
haven't done anything."

"I have you all."

"If you're sure," Anemos says, and the lantern flickers again. "Let's go, before it dies."

"Look at him," the darkness says. *"Can you see it? Can you see me, with him?"*

"Take my hand," Icarus says, and Anemos does, not questioning why, as they begin to walk toward the house.

"Do you see me?" Icarus asks.

"You speak boldly," it says. *"As if you could frighten me."*

"I've frightened you before."

Anemos pulls him up a step, balancing him when he reaches the top.

"You good?" he asks, and Icarus nods, looking at him carefully; his hair— his curls flat, pushed back away from his face and sticky with gel he ran through it when he was too tired to brush it— the shadows under his blue eyes darker than they were in Karneji.

The damn jacket he still hasn't taken off.

"You don't really believe that."

Icarus bites the inside of his cheek, squeezing the hand in his a bit tighter.

"You know nothing of my power, Oracamatis. I have orchestrated your whole life. Every success, every failure, every word."

"I don't believe you."

"You will. And when you see... When you see what I have done, Icarus... You will kneel, just as those who came before you knelt."

They step up onto his front porch, and Anemos gives Icarus a quick hug before heading back down the patio stairs.

"Hey," Icarus starts, and Anemos turns around, starting to sober up. "If you want to stay here, tonight... No one will mind—"

"I have too much to do," he mutters. "But thank you, for offering."

Icarus can't bear the thought of him walking away, but he nods anyway, having very little choice.

"Stay safe, please," he says, and the dark haired boy nods, raising the lantern slightly— as if in a toast— before disappearing into the darkness.

CHAPTER SIXTY-SEVEN

I carus steps inside, and finds himself alone. It is quiet, allowing his mind to race, and pitch black save a dim glow in the kitchen. As he approaches it, his mother turns the co rner.

"Icarus?" He pulls his sleeves over his hands, anxious, and nods in response. "Where were you?"

"I was with An."

"Before that, during the ceremony."

Thunder booms again, cutting them both off, and Icarus shakes his head. "I don't really know. I started walking, and... It's... It's all a blur. Can grief do that?"

"Grief can do many things." Thunder. He cannot help but squirm at the sound. "Is the storm what knocked the power?"

"I don't know," he says.

"Is the wall down?"

"I don't know."

She nods, drops her head.

"Did you see your father?"

"I was-wasn't at the Palace long."

"I'm glad you're here," she breathes, her voice trembling. "Silly as it is, this darkness, it just makes me think of..."

"Assecula?" he finishes.

She nods, quiet, and then takes a deep, unsteady breath.

"I'll make coffee."

Aliya brings two cups of coffee to the table, and Icarus takes one of them from her, noting the shaking of her hands.

"You okay?" he asks, and she hesitates a moment before answering.

"No," she says. "Not really. Are you?"

He holds the warm cup to his lips, breathes in the earthy smell.

"No," he says. "Not completely, b-but... I m-mean, you can talk to me. You should, to someone."

She smiles softly, a sadness in her eyes that Icarus has not yet seen, and shakes her head.

"I'm not going to burden you."

"You're not going to burden m...me, I don't mind listening, I..." His breath catches in his throat, his eyes avoiding the form that passes through the space behind her, shadowy, out of her eyes' reach. "You've listened to m...me plenty..."

She looks down at the table, her face falling a little, and stirs her coffee absentmindedly.

"It's just... I'm... I'm feeling a little out of control, I think."

"That seems natural, after..." The dead girl steps around the corner, her face pale, faded, but he keeps his eyes on his mother, clearing his throat. "After everything, I mean."

"He wanted to leave Ursula," she says. "Alastor. She was on the ground, just... Just bleeding out, terrified, and even *then* he could not spare an *ounce* of compassion for her. I mean..."

The girl, no older than fifteen, sits down beside him, watching him with careful, gray eyes.

"*Can you hear me?*" she asks, and he nods, still not turning to face her.

"I almost lost my best friend," Aliya says, her eyes welling with tears. "I mean, before Jack, she was... She was my best friend." She stops, her voice strained, and shakes her head. "I'm so sorry about Cole, Icarus. I shouldn't be... I'm in no place to complain."

"No," he whispers. "No. You're hurting too—"

"*I need help,*" the girl says. "*Please, I want to move on, but I can't.*"

He takes her hand under the table, too tired to be afraid.

"It's a lot. It's all... It's all a lot."

"That damned Reaper," Aliya breathes, and Icarus feels his chest tighten. "You know, I can't even regret it, the choice we made. I regret... Some of the technicalities, but..."

The girl beside him weeps, silently, and he squeezes her hand a little tighter.

"I don't understand," she continues, "how there can be such *cruelty,* such *evil*... I had the audacity to be repulsed by its suffering, when I saw it."

"*Your mother?*" the girl asks.

"Perhaps this is my punishment," Aliya scoffs. "Pitying something like that, for even a second."

"It's only natural to look away from a m...man who's suffering."

"A man," she repeats. "Yes, but this was not a man, this was... Do you know what it means, for something to be an abomination?"

"Yes."

She taps her nails against the table, biting the inside of her cheek.

"I can't regret my decision, because in my heart, I know that if I had another chance... Even with all of the risks, if I had another chance to kill those hateful... hateful things, I would take it this instant."

Icarus is quiet, his face unchanging.

"And *that,*" she says, "is what I have not told your father; because he is so loving, and so gentle, that I think it might break him, but... The grief is nowhere near as *heavy,* nowhere near as paralyzing, as the hatred."

"I worry about that often," he says, and her brows furrow.

"What?" she asks. "What do you mean?"

The front door opens again, and Jack steps through it, drenched in the rain that Icarus did not even notice as it began to pour down, moments before.

Aliya looks over at him, and Icarus takes the opportunity to steal a glance at the girl beside him, her pale brown hair falling like silk over her milky white shoulders.

"I need help," she says again, and Icarus' eyes fall away, staring, heavy, into the distance.

Jack and Aliya begin to talk, but their voices are muffled. The room seems to move around him, the space swelling, shrinking, and the air becoming too thick and too thin and too heavy all at once.

A hand is placed on his shoulder— his father's hand, and he looks up, unsteady.

"Are you feeling better?" the man asks.

"Mm," Icarus nods. "Better."

His mother's voice kicks in again, and the sounds all blur into the falling rain.

Blackout to the edge of the city, he says.

No idea what caused it.

No idea what happened.

All the boy can think of is the look in Ursula's eyes as it happened.

"Icarus?" the girl asks, as the conversation stretches on.

He does not even know how long it's been when he shakes his head, breathing deeply for what feels like the first time in hours.

"Is that your name?"

"No," he mutters.

His parents look over at him, apparently having both been talking, and he bites his bottom lip, staring at the floor another moment before looking up, into the corner of the ro om.

"What?" Aliya asks, and he shakes his head, his throat tight.

It is a moment before he speaks, and when he does, the words are strained.

"My name is Michael," he says, and when they both fall silent, obviously confused, he continues, his heart pounding in his chest. "My name," he repeats, his voice dazed. "It's not Icarus. It's Michael. I lied to you. I've been lying to you since I was six years old. I'm s orry."

They are staring at him, stunned. He wants them to look away, but can think of no way to lessen their shock.

Truth be told, he doesn't care to.

"Why?" Aliya asks, and he shakes his head.

"I don't know..." He stops—laughs under his breath. "No that's... That's another lie. I'm s-sorry. I lied because I hated it, because I hated m-myself... And I kept lying b-because I never... I never stopped."

They're both quiet another second, and then Aliya's voice cuts through the silence, hushed and surprised and sad.

"You hate yourself?" she asks, and he nods, his eyes still unfocused.

"Yeah. No, not as much as I used to, but..."

"Why?"

He closes his eyes, struggling to gather his thoughts, and a cold hand finds his shoulder.

"Well," he breathes, unsure of why he is saying any of it. "I hated myself when I was six because my parents didn't take care of m...me, and you... You know, when you're a kid, you don't understand why. You don't know what to blame, or... The psychology behind it, you just... B-blame yourself. *I* blamed myself, because I thought... I m-mean, I thought parents were supposed to take care of you, and I thought I must have done something, that there must have been s-something wrong with me, for them not to..." His voice catches, and he clears his throat, shaking his head. "Then I hated m-myself after that, for coming h ere..."

He looks up at them both, his eyes tired, and wets his lips.

"Children are aware when people don't want them, you know. Especially children that have been left behind before... And I knew... I *knew* how little I was wanted here. I was acutely aware of the fact that... That you... and you, and Charles and Ursula, were the *only* ones that didn't m-m-mind m-my being here. I heard the conversations, I saw... I knew.

And then when I was... eight or nine? It was the nightmares, and the-the terror, and the w-waking you up, so frequently, and why couldn't I j-just be a *normal* child, and why couldn't I stop being a burden, and then I hurt myself, b-because..." A quiet cry escapes his lips, but he pushes past it, not bothering with the tears forming in his eyes. "Because of *all* of it, and because I was alive, and I didn't want to be, and because of the guilt over... Over everything in Jakara, the guilt of *surviving*, when m-my family, when my *sister* didn't... God," He whispers, even though he is not supposed to. "It was too much for a child, and I took it out on my...myself, because I didn't know... Who else to blame... And then I hated myself for that, too..."

The room seems to become darker, his parents seeming closer and further away, and he looks away from them, staring into the candle instead, drumming his fingers against the table.

"And then I was eleven, and twelve, and thirteen and I was so... so far behind, because..." He takes a shaky breath. "Because *living* was so hard, and... Then *school*, and they taught me all of the reasons I couldn't trust myself, and all of the... the things that were wrong with m...me that I n-never even thought about before. They taught me to b e *selfless*, and I already was, but I really leaned into it then. And they taught me that I was wrong for having questions, and for... For having *needs*, because other people's needs mattered more, and they taught me that wanting to be *close* with people was wrong, and that *touching* people was an indulgence, and *loving* people was blasphemy... And I just loved it, all of it, because it told me I was right, hating myself, and it told me how to fix it. They told m...me exactly what to do to be good, and I... I really did it, didn't I?"

Neither of them argue, and he shakes his head again, pale.

"And then I hated myself even more, and *then...*" He almost laughs. "Then I realized that it was all *bullshit*, because no m-matter what I did, no m...matter how much of myself I ripped away, and replaced, and how many rules I followed, I still wasn't good enough, because I was from *Jakara*, and be...because, I had trouble speaking, and because I was too small, and too..." He clears his throat. "So I made m-myself quiet, and I worked, and I got bigger, and then that m-made them angry too, because they don't want someone from outside to be *too* good."

"Icarus—" Aliya starts, and he shakes his head.

"It was you too, Mom, " he says. "You made me... So... so angry, talking a-ab-b-bout people, out there, like that wasn't *me*—"

"It *wasn't* you."

"It's *always* been me," he says. "It doesn't m-matter how h...hard I try to pretend otherwise, I am from *Jakara. I* am an outlier— worse than an outlier, and you called them *dirty,* and lazy, and perverse... And I don't even think you m-meant half of it, but I believed all of it, and I hated myself for it so... so much, and I heard it *everywhere,* because even if you weren't saying it directly to me, everyone else was... And I just realized with time that it didn't matter what I did. It didn't matter if I spoke up, or silenced myself, or cut myself and *bled* onto their Code, it would never, ever be enough, and I didn't know who else... Who else to blame... So..."

A sob breaks free from his chest, and he rubs his face, trying to breathe.

" called myself Icarus because... My parents— my birth parents: Alan and Elizabeth Cothran... They made really, really shitty parents, not because they were lazy, or dirty, or perverse... Just because they were terrified, and probably too young to be parents, and... Anyway, they... Despite all of it, they still told us stories, sometimes, because they liked stories. And not Ordinem stories, you know? Stories from other countries, and other realms, that-that weren't all the same, and they didn't come with a freaking *key* to tell you what you were supposed to think of them. They collected stories, in Jakara. That was one of m...my favorite things about it, before..."

Another sob, heavier, and Jack moves across the room, putting a careful arm around him, rubbing his shoulder.

"I really liked this one story about this stupid... *stupid* boy that tried to fly into the sun. He was trapped, and his father made them wings, so they could escape... But he warned him that-that... That he shouldn't go too high because... They were made of wax, and if he went too high, they would melt. But Icarus... Icarus started flying and just... He tried anyway, be-because... It was the *sun*, right? Who doesn't want to touch the... the sun... Right?"

He leaned into his father's embrace without meaning to, still holding the hand under the table.

"I used to think he was so *brave,* for trying... But now I just think... Maybe he knew. He had to know, didn't he? He had to know he couldn't touch the sun, and I'm not sure he was brave for trying. I just think it's *sad,* because... Even if he had, it would have killed him, and I think he probably had to be so... so cold, to need its warmth that badly, and...

God, I don't m-m-make any sense, but I just... He tried so hard that he fell into the sea, because the tools he was given were never *meant* to take him that far, and..." He cries, and the sound seems louder than the thunder. "I've tried so hard... And I just... I didn't even realize how w-well it *fit*, before... But..."

His breaths come in gasps, suddenly, and he pulls himself up from the table, pulling away from his father, pulling the girl with him.

"Icarus," Aliya says again, but he only shakes his head, walking away.

"I need air," he says. "I just... I need to be alone, just a m-minute—"

The moment he shuts the door behind him, the moment he steps outside, thunder lights up the space around the two of them, and he turns to the girl, still struggling to breathe, trying not to shout over the rain.

"H-how can I help?" he asks.

She looks at him with sad, frightened eyes.

"I have to tell someone," she says. *"Before I go, I have to. The Ordinem are lying, and they're going to tell more lies."*

"What?" he asks. "Tell me."

"They need help, Michael. I wanted to help, but I can't anymore, they're lying about so many things, but they... I'm from the fifth cluster. I've seen so much."

"So much..?"

"Not enough living to bury the dead," she says. *"No help. No aid. No food. No sleep. Bodies, lying in the streets. Injured, left to die."*

"Because of the Saenks?" he asks.

"No shelter. No food. No help—"

"Hey," he whispers, and her eyes find his, somewhere else.

"I'm like you," she says suddenly. *"I was alone, until just now. I didn't think anyone... I wish I'd known you while I was alive."* She stops, trembling, and grabs his hand tighter. *"What's waiting for me?"*

"I don't—"

"Darkness?"

"No. No, not darkness."

"I thought I should hold on here," she says. *"Just in case... I'm so scared to let go."*

"Everyone is," he says. "But whatever's next... You'll rest there."

"I've never rested," she whispers, and the thunder rolls on.

She looks out at the street, looks out over the trees, looks at him, and begins to cry, but no tears fall from her eyes.

"Pray for me," she pleads, *"Before I go."*

She is already gone when Jack opens the door, finding Icarus alone, staring out into the darkness with grief heavy on his shoulders.

He steps out onto the patio, shuts the door behind him, and walks slowly to the edge of it, beside his son, who holds one hand out into the rain.

"Michael?" he asks, gentle. "Is that what you want me to call you?"

"I'm not going to m-make... you."

"You're not making me," he says. "It suits you, you know. Michael Cothran. It fits."

Icarus takes a deep breath, looks over at his father, and sets it free.

"I worry I m-might have killed him," he says. "I certainly tried."

"No," Jack says. "Not killed; lost, maybe, but lost things can always be..." He stops, shakes his head, and ignores the sound of something shattering inside. "What is it?"

"Cole is alive," Icarus says, suddenly, and Jack falls silent a long moment before speaking.

"What?"

"He's alive," he repeats. "He's alive, and he's lost, and I... I don't know where..." He stops, chews the inside of his bottom lip, and exhales, tears streaming from his eyes. "I have to tell him," he says. "I *have* to tell Anemos, Dad. I'm worried this is going to kill him, and if it does... If it does, and I knew something that could have saved him, I'm not going to be able to live with myself."

Jack takes his hand and squeezes it tight, his face unchanging, even as his heart seems to break inside of him.

"I know you know the risk you'd be taking," he says, and Icarus nods, his chest tight.

"I know."

"And you're prepared?"

"Of course not, but it doesn't matter. I can't lose him, Dad. I can't lose them both. Nothing would be worse than that. *Death* wouldn't be."

"I understand," Jack says.

He holds his hand a little tighter, fights back the fear in his chest like he has done everyday for the last eight years, and forces some fragment of peace onto his face.

"Michael?" he asks.

"Yeah?"

"You know I couldn't be any more proud of you than I am?" His voice breaks slightly with the words, his eyes red. "You're the best person I've ever known, the best son I ever could've ever dreamed of."

"You're the best father I could've p...possibly asked for," Icarus says. "I know."

Jack nods, wrapping an arm back around his shoulders.

"You know I'm from out there, too," he says, "So... I mean, you know I understand— not everything, of course, but... Your mother doesn't understand. She can't. She's never been anywhere else."

"I know," Icarus breathes.

"I don't know how much it matters, but..."

"It matters," he says. "You should go check on her."

"Oh, she's not talking to me right now. Gave her the input of an outsider. It frustrated her. Sometimes I think she forgets I'm from Brekka."

"Sometimes *I* forget you're from Brekka. You never talk about it."

"They don't want me to talk about it."

"What was it like, there?" Icarus asks.

His father laughs, shaking his head.

"Take all of the stereotypes, combine them, and then make it worse. A bunch of scamps."

"Yourself?"

"Oh, absolutely. The worst of them." Icarus smiles past the fear in his chest, looking over as Jack continues to speak. "You can take the boy from Brekka, but can't take Brekka from the boy, eh?"

"You're not a *scamp.*"

"Only at heart," he breathes. "You're following in my footsteps."

"I hope so," Icarus says, and Jack looks over at him with heavy eyes.

"Thanks, kid," he says.

"I m-mean it—"

Jack pulls him in and hugs him tight. He prays with every breath, trying not to show his fear, trying to reassure his son even though he is too tired to reassure himself.

"I love you, Michael," he says softly, and the boy smiles, his eyes red. "More than—"

"Everything," he whispers. "I love you too."

Chapter Sixty-Eight

A week passes in silence.

It is the silence of a goodbye no one dares to utter.

Icarus sleeps as little as he can, only admitting his fear of the coming days in split second glances, and Jack hardly ever leaves his side.

Grasping to every moment— both of them, for fear it may be their last, for fear it may be *his* last, but his mother barely leaves her room.

Icarus does not say how much he needs her, because he doesn't know how.

Every child from the shelter is moved swiftly through the gate in the dead of night, even without the lights to guide them.

Josh hugs his brother at the line, and slams his fists against the marble when he is alone.

Regis stays awake with him, tries to subdue the jokes he used to hear his father make, and tries to help even though he doesn't know how.

There is too much grief to banish in a week.

The nights are too long without power.

Icarus walks to the University every day, but never makes it all the way to the Palace, and Anemos never makes it all the way to his house.

Anemos hardly makes it out of his room.

He drifts like an apparition from the floor beside his bed to the kitchen and the bathroom, but he never eats, never showers.

Somehow, he wakes to the same realization every morning, as if it is new, and worse. The smell of *him* slowly fades from the jacket, and moments of rest become few and far between. Seizures wrack his body, twice, and he goes to no one.

He goes to no one, and he asks for no help, fearing the accusations that might be made against him if he did.

He does not want attention— has not wanted attention since he was a child, experiencing it in all the wrong ways, and lacking it in most of the others.

No, he does not go for help, but he needs it.

Anemos wakes up the day before the funeral with stars in his vision, and he damns them. He thinks, as he opens his eyes, that death feels too close. That his body feels too weak, and his mind too broken, and that he cares too little.

He pours whiskey into his mouth and forces it down his throat like poison, knowing he cannot stomach it.

He smashes the bottle against the bathroom floor, and does not bother to clean it up.

He is afraid of himself, and instead of going for help, he locks the door. He lies on the ground, pain splintering through his fragile frame, and lets his eyes linger on the half open blinds. They stay there for hours. They stare until long after the sun has set, and still, he does not move.

Cole told him not to do this, he thinks. He told him not to drink, told him not to give up, told him to eat, told him to rest, told him not to hurt himself, told him not to isolate himself, told him to ask for help when he needed it—

He pulls himself from the ground at one in the morning and drifts back to the bathroom, his vision spotted by black. He opens the medicine cabinet, pulling a bottle of pills from the second shelf.

Two pills for a migraine, he shakes the bottle and five fall into his palm.

Not enough to kill him, probably. He takes them, and then pours five more, only looking at them.

He wonders if you can do a thing like that for attention, when no one is watching, and pours ten.

Ursula pulls herself up in bed, that same hour, and looks down at the form next to her with sad eyes.

She puts one hand on Alastor's shoulder, and he jerks awake, jerks back away from her, hardly breathing as he does.

"It's me," she says, her voice level, unstained by the emotion she feels, the fear that causes her hands to tremble. "It's... It's just me, Alastor."

"Damn it," he mutters, harsh. "You can't—"

"I'm sorry," she says. "I'm sorry, I... We have to be there early."

"You can't just *touch* me when I'm not awake."

She stops, falls silent, barely able to see him in the darkness, and shakes her head.

"I'm sorry—"

"Then stop fucking up."

Her face turns toward her hands, and she lets out a long sigh, closing her eyes.

"I'm *trying,*" she says. "I am trying, Alastor, but I... By the dragon, it's hard sometimes, I'm sorry—"

"Try harder," he snaps. "Try *harder.*"

"I *can't,*" she whispers, her throat tight. "I can't try any harder. You could sleep in another—"

"I don't want to."

"But I... *I* want you too."

"Do you?" he asks. "Well, that's all that matters."

"That isn't fair."

"I know," he says, and then, more quietly. "Shit. I know. I'm sorry, I'll... I don't know, maybe..."

"Alastor," she whispers. "Take my hand."

"I don't—"

"Please."

His hand finds hers two minutes later, and she squeezes it tight, her stomach sick.

"I'm sorry," she says, and then, again: "I'm *sorry.*"

He pulls away, shakes his head.

"I need a drink."

"Please, Alastor."

"I need a—"

"*—drink,*" he said, rubbing his face with his hands. "*I need...*"

"*Alastor,*" Charles said. "*It's not—*"

"*Not what?*" he snapped. "*It's a disaster, damn it. It's... You should have...*"

Ursula sat silently, her face in her hands and her legs crossed, listening with her heart in her throat.

"*I don't give a shit what I should have done,*" Charles said. "*It's done now, and I... Nothing I do is an excuse for you to drink. Not after—*"

"*Compare me to him,*" Alastor snapped, "*and I will cut out your tongue.*"

"*Please...*" Ursula whispered, her eyes watering. "*Please, don't fight.*"

"*Stop it,*" Charles said. "*Stop being aggressive. Stop being this. This isn't you, and I'm sick of it. I'm sick of the way you've been treating everyone since he—*"

"*Stop,*" Alastor forced. "*Stop it, now.*"

"No, I'm not going to stop. It's been two years, and you've been so— You're not the only one who's broken over it. You can't just throw yourself away because you couldn't—"

"Couldn't what?" he asked, his teeth gritted, his face pale. "Couldn't save him? Couldn't stop him? You were there, Charles. Not me."

The younger man's eyes turned gray, his vision blurring.

"I wasn't blaming you."

"Well, I don't know what you want me to..." Alastor stopped, looked at Ursula, and let his hands fall to his sides. "Is she okay?"

Charles turned back, paled, shook his head, and then moved quickly to kneel beside her, taking her hands.

"Ursula," he said, his voice losing any harshness it had with his brother. "Ursula, love, look at me, please..."

Ursula's eyes wandered the room, panicked, her breath coming fast and shallow, and Alastor watched with heavy eyes.

He watched Charles speak to her, watched him keep hold of her, even as her nails unintentionally dug into his skin, and felt his chest tighten.

"Is she okay?" he asked again, and Charles nodded, his eyes saying differently.

"She'll be fine," he breathed.

"What's happening to her?"

She took a sharp breath, a sob shaking her chest, and he stopped, watching his brother put a hand on her shoulder.

"It's okay," Charles whispered, pushing her hair back out of her face. "You're here, I'm here, you're... Alastor, if you could get some cold water, please."

Alastor nodded, walking quickly out of the room, and Ursula squeezed Charles' hand impossibly tighter, starting to cry.

"No," she whispered. "No..."

"Shh," he breathed. "It's alright, I'm here, I'm not going anywhere."

"Closer, please."

He pulled himself up onto the bed beside her, wrapping an arm around her shoulders, and she leaned into his chest, hugging tightly to his waist.

"I'm sorry," she cried, and Alastor walked back into the room, a glass of water in one hand. He handed it to Charles, who thanked him with tired eyes, and Ursula's cries grew heavier. "I'm sorry, Alastor," she said. "I'm so sorry."

He shook his head, silent, and sat down across from them with his chin resting on his hands.

"I know it isn't fair," she said. "I know it isn't... This isn't fair to you, and I'm so... so sorry."

"Breathe," Charles said, and Alastor felt his heart in his throat.

They were silent for a long time, then.

"It's against the Code," Alastor said, once she had started to calm. "You both... You know that."

He was met with silence, but continued anyway.

"I can't knowingly let you both continue like this, you know that."

"I know," Charles answered, and she held to him tighter. "I'm not asking you to. I would never ask that of you, I just... I want her safe, now. That's all. That's all I want."

He looked at them both a minute, uneasy, before nodding.

"Okay," he said.

"Okay?"

"We'll do it soon, yes? The marriage? That will cover it? You pretend it's mine, and then we go on like nothing ever... Like nothing ever happened."

A quiet cry escaped her lips, and he held onto her, not letting his facade break for even a moment.

"Like nothing ever—"

The bedroom door slams shut, and she is alone.

She listens to his footsteps, all the way down the stairs, into the kitchen, and slides out of bed, unsure of whether or not she should lock the door.

She is not even angry as she hesitates over the bolt; she is too tired to be angry, but not too tired to be afraid.

Her skin burns, suddenly, and she swallows hard, her hands trembling.

She can feel the disagreement of another in her chest as she swings the door open, walks down the stairs a bit too quickly, steps into the kitchen and pulls the bottle from Alastor's hand.

He whips around, startled, and looks at her with angry eyes.

"What are you *doing*?" he asks, following her around the counter.

She tips the bottle over, pouring the alcohol down the sink.

"What are *you* doing?" she responds, letting it fall from her hand.

He steps toward her, too close, and she does not move.

"You know better than this," she says. "You have *always* known better—"

"Stop!" he yells, and she does not flinch enough for him to see. "On Inanis, you never learn. Your help is not wanted here, Ursula. I don't care what you—"

"You're lying," she snaps, "but it doesn't matter. I don't care what you want. I'm not going to sit upstairs waiting for you to get blackout drunk and come looking for me. I'm not doing it tonight. I'm not."

"By the dragon, I'm not going to—"

"You always come looking for me, Alastor; everytime, and I'm too tired to... Unclench your fists, calm down."

"You come down here like *this,* and tell *me* to calm down."

"Yes."

"I wouldn't even be like this if you hadn't—"

"*Stop.*"

"Just let me have it."

"No," she says. "No. Talk to me. I'm right here. Just *talk* to me."

"Do you never give up, woman?" he sighs, exasperated. "I don't want to—"

"You don't deserve to," she interrupts, and he stops, his chest tight. "You want to, you just don't think you deserve to, and you're right, damn it, but I'm here."

"You shouldn't be."

"But I am," she says, "and as long as I'm alive, as long as *you're* alive, we are *stuck* together, so talk to me."

"No."

"*Please.*" He looks at her a little too long, not speaking, and she reaches forward, taking his hand. "Please, Alastor. I can't do another day of this."

"I *can't,*" he says. "I can't... I can't even *look* at you, Ursula, I need you to please... Just leave me alone, okay?"

"But—"

"I've done too much," he says, and she freezes, unable to process the words.

"So have I."

"No," he laughs bitterly. "No, Ursula."

"Yes," she says. "I've hurt you, too, and I've hurt... I hurt *him,* and—"

"*No,*" he says. "Stop trying to... We aren't the same. We aren't... You fuck up, Ursula. That's all you ever—" His voice catches in his throat. "I am *wrong.*"

"But people aren't just *wrong.*"

"I don't want your mercy," he says, pulling his hand away. "I want you to leave me alone, and I want a drink."

"Stop—"

He looks at her so sharply that she falls completely silent, her hands knitted together in front of her, and when he speaks, his voice has changed, again.

"You are going to be quiet," he says, "and let me drink, or I am going to hurt you. Is that clear enough?"

Ten minutes pass in darkness before she turns the knob on the bathtub faucet, letting it fill as she sits with her eyes closed.

Almost twenty years, and is not any easier. It is almost the first betrayal, again, but then, he was a good man doing a bad thing to another good person.

She tried to be a good person.

A good man, broken as he was, she told herself as she forgave him the first time; and he was a good man, once. She had known him as a good man for years— as a friend.

It was hard to blame the bad man when he was not always bad, when he apologized afterward, when he had so many excuses, when she knew he was afraid, and when it was just the alcohol, and he just wasn't thinking, and God, he was so lonely, and it wouldn't happen again. He swore it wouldn't happen again.

But it would, and it did, again and again, and then the apologies stopped being believable, and they turned to accusations, and then suddenly she couldn't forgive herself, even though she wasn't sure what she had done, how she had offended, why she wasn't enough—

And then it got worse, and she stopped caring, and very quickly, she stopped thinking of either of them as good people.

She is not a good person, not when she's wanted to cause him pain, not when she's said the things she's said, not when she's hurt him so badly.

She turns the water off, sinks down into it, and rubs her face with her hands, begging the heat to take *any* of the stress, any of the pain, but it doesn't; not really, not enough.

And then the water changes.

She moves her hands through it, not sure of what she is feeling. She feels the thickness of it— the stickiness, and opens her eyes before remembering it is too dark to see.

She breathes once, sharply, and nearly gags on the smell of iron that now permeates the air, floods everything. It's as if she can taste it.

She reaches up to her throat on instinct, and starts to scream, to choke, pulling herself from the water and stumbling into the floor, back against the wall, trying to wipe the blood from her face, trying to claw the skin on her throat back together with her bare hands.

She does not stop to wonder how it's happened, does not even wonder how she is lasting so long, staying alive as her own blood pours down her body, thick and warm and suffocating.

The door creaks open, and she looks up at it, gasping his name like he might help her, but when she does, the shadowy silhouette standing in the doorframe does not reply, does not even move.

"Alastor," she cries again, "Please... Please..."

The figure moves toward her, but she does not hear his feet on the ground. She does not hear or feel anything as it bends to meet her, and she almost cowers away until it places one cold hand on her shoulder.

"Ursula," It says softly, and she recognizes the voice, even though it is not his. *"It isn't real. You know it isn't real."*

"Then make it stop," she cries. "Please... please make it—"

"Do you want me to?"

She sobs loudly, still tasting blood that is not there as she shakes her head.

"No... no..."

"I won't hurt you," It says. *"I would never hurt you."*

She stays silent, gasping, and it places one hand over hers.

"Just until it's over, Ursula. Just so it doesn't hurt so much."

"Just until it's—" her voice breaks. "Just until it's over?"

"Yes."

"Oh...*okay*—"

She opens her eyes, and the darkness is gone.

The air is crisp, and there are voices in it. Hundreds of voices. Thousands.

"Ursula."

She turns, her heart racing, and meets Charles' eyes with panic in her own, but does not respond.

She looks around her, trying to get a bearing on where she is, trying to remember.

Flowers, white, everywhere. Black clothing. Grief in the air.

He puts a hand on her arm and she flinches away.

"Hey," he says softly. "Where've you been? Are you—"

"I'm fine," she says, too quickly. "I'm... I've just been..."

A voice fills the space around them, and she looks toward the stage, the podium, her head in a fog.

"I've been trying to reach you."

"I'm sorry."

"It's fine, it's just that I didn't know where you'd... Are you sure you're alright?"

"I didn't realize you always needed to know where I am, Charles," she says, and her voice is harsher than she expects, colder. "I'm *fine.*"

She looks away from the hurt in his eyes, her nails sharp against her palms, and when he speaks again, his voice is hollow.

"Please," he says. "Please listen to me..."

So much noise, so many sounds, too many, and she cannot even hear him, does not even know she is interrupting.

"I can't."

"You... can't."

"I don't..." She swallows hard, trying to rid the ringing from her ears, and clears her throat. "I'm not sure... I can't..." *Breathe.* "...do this, right now."

"It's Anemos, Ursula."

CHAPTER SIXTY-NINE

Icarus slides through the crowd nervously, excusing himself with every step he takes, an extra time for every shoulder he bumps. He is wearing the same clothes he wore to the ceremony— all black, covering almost every inch of his body— and yet, somehow, he looks different.

The cut that the Guide made on his face then has healed now, leaving only a faint red line under his eye. It is nothing compared to the ones which line his shoulders.

Perhaps a man holds himself differently, hiding a thing like that.

His hair is not quite dry, damp in the cold of the morning, and he pushes it away from his ears every few minutes, the air like ice in his lungs.

He stops next to his parents, exhales a cloud.

"I can't find him," he says. "I didn't s...see him with Ursula, either."

Jack presses his lips together, his eyebrows furrowed.

"I'll go look for him," he sighs. "I'll look for Charles, anyway. He'll know."

"I can look for Charles, if that would be—"

"No," Jack says. "You stay here, you've looked enough."

"Are you sure?"

"I'm sure, Icarus."

Icarus nods, and Jack begins to move through the crowd, just as another speaker steps to the stage.

Aliya turns to Icarus, her eyes faded.

"Only calling you Michael at home, then," she whispers.

He turns toward her, takes a deep, shaky breath, and shakes his head. It is the first thing she has said to him in days, but he cannot make himself angry. Not now.

"Oh, yeah, well... I'm... I'm-m just trying it out, so, I don't really want everyone... I'm not ready for that. I don't know if that makes sense."

"It does," she says, and then, more quietly, "I'm having a hard time trying it out."

"Yeah."

"It's just... You've just always been Icarus."

"I understand."

"And, more than that, I don't... I don't know how I feel about what it means to you. Does that make sense?"

Clapping. They join in without listening.

"Not... N-not really," Icarus says. "If you want to... elaborate?"

"It's just that... I don't want to offend you."

"You're not going to," he says, folding his arms over his chest. "The Code com...mands honesty, yes?"

She bites down on her bottom lip, mimicking his posture.

"You were given that name in Jakara," she says, and he thinks, deep inside, that that is the heart of her complaint, but does not say it, "by two people that didn't... By two people who thought of you as less than you are. I should have said that the other night, by the way— that they were wrong about you, that I'm... I'm sorry."

"It's alright," he says, and she nods, her eyes heavy.

"I'm trying so hard to understand, Icarus, but... You came here wanting to be more than you were; more than you were told you had to be. You knew at six years old that you wanted to be more than what you were born into, more than what you were given, and I've always been so proud of you for that. For knowing that you were better... That you *could* be better, and for working at it so hard... All of this, you did as *Icarus.* Your last name didn't fit, so you picked one that did, one you took pride in..."

He breathes deeply and forces himself to nod, listening carefully as his eyes continue to move over the crowd.

"Beyond that, Icarus... Icarus is the name that you... *Icarus* is of the Ordinem, yes? If you start going by Michael... I've never known a single person to change their name here, in forty years. I'm not sure how that will be..." She sighs, letting her arms fall. "You're struggling right now, I see that. You said you don't feel like you'll ever be enough, and now you want to revert back to the name you had when you were... I worry that, perhaps, you are lowering yourself. I worry that so many people have told you that you are where you come from that you've started to believe it."

He tucks his hair back behind his ear.

"You are *not* that little boy from Jakara, Icarus. You aren't. You've changed. I told you, when you were little, remember? I told you you were born for more, that you weren't born to be conquered. I told you that you would have to work and fight, and you have, and you have done it beautifully. Don't throw that away for what they told you you have to be. I know it's difficult now, but—"

"I didn't want to be better," he says softly, and she stops, her face falling.

"What?" she asks. "What do you mean?"

"You said I wanted to be... b-better than what I was; that I wanted to be more," he repeats, shaking his head. "I just wanted to be loved."

"Icarus..."

"I m-mean, I tried to be *better,* sure, but... It was out of... necessity, I..." He shakes his head. "I *wanted* to be loved, and taken care of. I mean... I got obsessive when I got a little older, sure. I wanted to be good. I'm not saying I didn't want to better myself, but... I was a little kid. I wanted to be loved."

She falls silent again, looking at the stage, and Icarus looks over at her, his eyes heavy, clouded.

"You can—"

"Did I make you feel unloved?" she asks, her voice barely a whisper.

"No," he says, not even stopping to think. "You made me feel like I could do anything."

"You can," she says, and he smiles a little, his chest tight. "I swear, I'm trying."

"I know," he nods. "Call me whatever you want, okay? Don't stress. You w-want m...me to be Icarus, I'll be Icarus."

"Because you want to be loved?" she asks, and he shakes his head, but before he can think of a response, the clapping begins again, and someone else walks onto the stage.

All of the blood drains from his face as Anemos steps up to the podium, clearing his throat as his eyes search the crowd for his friend's, breathing a sigh of relief when he finds them, and then looking back away from him, out into the sea of strangers.

He looks different, too.

One-thirty in the morning, Anemos poured a handful of pills back into their bottle and turned on the shower instead. He stood under the water until it ran cold, and tried not to think.

Two-thirty, he looked in the mirror and thought that he looked almost as weak as he felt, his face pallid and his eyes red and his body thinner than he thought it could become in such a small amount of time.

Too thin before, he thought, and he pulled out a razor and shaved.

Three, he returned to his room, gave the files in the drawer one last glance, and then unlocked his door, opening it with hesitation that even he could not understand.

Three-thirty, and this time, Charles was already in the kitchen.

He lifted his head and let a sad, tired smile find his face.

"Hey," he said softly. "Early or late?"

Anemos let out a long sigh, shaking his hands.

"I don't really know anymore," he said. "How about you?"

"Early, I guess. I don't think I'll sleep again."

Anemos nodded, letting his face fall.

"What woke you up?"

"Dream," Charles said, taking a drink from the mug in front of him. "There's still hot water, if you want some."

"My stomach is fucked right now. I'm sorry, that was vulgar—"

"It's Chamomile," Charles interrupted. "It might help. I can make it for you, if that would be—"

"Okay," he says. "If you wouldn't mind."

"Mind?" Charles asks. "Why would I... I don't mind. Do you want anything to eat?"

"You don't need to worry about that, I can take care of myself."

Charles' brows drew together. He opened a small box on the counter.

"Of course you can, but you're grieving. That's a lot of hard work on its own. Figure you could use some help where I can lend it."

Anemos kept his eyes on the ground, cracking his knuckles as Charles spoke.

"I know... I'm sorry if this is overstepping, I know you've struggled with eating some, in the past, when things have gotten to be too much." He poured leaves into a small strainer, pulled the water from the stove. "My brother used to deal with that, sometimes; not Alastor, my other... Anyway, it seemed easier for him, when someone was offering. And I know grief makes it hard, even without the rest; harder for me, anyway."

"You're not overstepping," Anemos said. "I am struggling, I just don't want... I'd rather not burden anyone else with it."

"Anemos," Charles breathed, sitting the mug in front of him. "Paperwork is a burden. Being forced to sit through twelve meetings a day is a burden. You are a person."

He forced another laugh, ran his hand along the rim of his cup, and Charles watched him with sad eyes.

"Something bland?" he asked. "It'll help."

Anemos swallowed hard, nodded hesitantly.

"...Okay."

"I lost someone," Anemos says, skipping the introductions that the other speakers offered. "I know that's an obvious statement, where we are, but... I lost someone, and I need to say it, because I haven't. Because I don't want to admit he's..." He rubs his face, shakes his head. "Cole was eighteen, which you... You probably already know, given the address, last week, but..."

Alastor turns around where he's standing, pale, in the same instant as Cindy, who stands beside him.

"Son of a—"

"He was my best friend in this whole world, and he's... Gone, that's what they told me. Gone, just like that, in a night, and I am supposed to work through the grief in a *week*." He looks up at the crowd, shakes his head again. "It doesn't feel like enough, does it? It seems ridiculous, if I'm being honest with you— thinking it's possible to pick yourself up from something like that so quickly; but we will, because that's what we do."

Someone in the audience claps, mistaking it for a statement of confidence, inspiration, and the rest of the crowd joins.

He steps back a moment, only looking at them, before continuing.

"It's what we do because we have to, because mourning too long would be an unspeakable indulgence, when there is so much else to do—" More applause, and he looks at the crowd with disgust, deciding to speak over them. "But the grieving period... The grieving period is sacred, yes? Not an indulgence, but a necessity; an act of respect, for those fallen."

His eyes lift, meeting Cindy's just as the crowd begins to quiet.

"Somehow," he says, "the Higher-class thought it appropriate to violate this *decades* old tradition, transporting every single child from the shelter back to the Outskirts— discreetly, privately— this last week. Of course, prohibitions can be set aside in an emergency, but this wasn't an emergency, given the amount of homes that could have taken them; the amount of space in the emergency shelter, for Inanis' sake. The emergency shelter which, in truth, could have taken all of them in on the night that it happened; a detail they have conveniently omitted, at their addresses."

"What is he *doing?*" Josh whispers, tugging nervously on his sleeves.

Regis sniffs, his arms folded over his chest.

"What needs to be done."

"So many ceremonies," Anemos laughs cooly. "Hundreds of you, all of you, claiming that my sweet friend, this boy I've known since I was thirteen, was a *hero.*" He lowers his head, blinking as slowly as he is speaking. "He *was,* but not because of this. There was nothing *heroic* about the way my friend died. His death was pathetic, and sad, and you are— all of you— *liars.*"

The air changes, suddenly, and everyone feels it, as if the grief— the anger— that was previously subdued becomes too heavy, all at once.

"The *truth* is that my friend, my Cole, was as Lower-class as you can be, another detail you all leave in the dust. The *truth* is that if this had happened three months ago, not one of you would know his name. Miley, Andre, Michelle... All three Lower-class, all three aspiring to serve, all three dead. All three younger than *him,* and left to fend for themselves, because there were hardly any guards in the Lower-class sector, when it happened."

He looks out with fire in his eyes, anger previously quieted, and when he speaks again, his voice is hard.

"Don't you *dare,* make a martyr out of my friend," he spits. "Cole was eighteen, and he died because *you*—" He points to the majority of the Council, his hand trembling. "Because *you* failed him. Because you did not think a shelter full of *children* was worth protecting."

He lets his gaze fall back to the rest of the crowd, but continues to point.

"They tell you that this man, this *child,* was a hero because he died trying to save a group of people that our government, our *Higher-class,* was too full of cowardice to protect; cowardice, and laziness, and prejudice." He grips the podium. "He is only a hero to you because he is dead, because if you call him a hero, you think you can pretend he was not a victim. You all claim to grieve him? I see through your grief, I see through it because n ot *one* of you was there for him while he was living; because he came to *me,* cried to *me,* asking why he was not enough. Because he told *me* how cruel you all were, and he never once blamed any of you for it; never once hated any of you, but... You didn't care then. You didn't care then because Outskirts kids are only good when they are silent, and only heroes when they're dead."

He lets the words sit a minute, shuffling through the papers in front of him, and the crowd stays silent, the Higher-class watching the Lower-class carefully, and the Lower-class standing with white knuckles.

"My mother is from the Outskirts," he says, his speech slow. "I've spoken to her a little, this last week, more before. I try to talk to her because... I'm just her son, and Cole's friend, I don't... I don't understand how they've suffered the way they do. Notice that *she* isn't speaking; no one from the Outskirts is speaking. If you're from out there, let me confirm your beliefs: They *want* your silence. They only want your words when they're a regurgitation of their own, or when it is something for them to use. You are not people to most of them, only bodies to be posed, and played with, and thrown into duty protecting the people they do see."

He finds Ursula's eyes, in the distance, looking for permission, and she nods him on, her chest tight.

"Some twenty years ago, The Ordinem commanded my mother to be married into the Higher-class. They told her, then, that having someone from outside at the top would inspire more trust from you; that she would make you believe it was attainable. Of course, it should be attainable, but in twenty years, only she has managed, and she hasn't managed; she has not done anything but play a role, in the end. Pretend to be respected... Pretend... Let me tell you what you are fighting for.

My mother was married in one year early, pulled from the training she had pursued, and forced into service she did not want— service no one else would take. Hours, days, *years* in the dark, suffocating in the smell of blood, hearing dulled by constant screams. They told her that the men and women she was forced to harm deserved the torment, the isolation, the execution, but it provided very little comfort. Many days, she would come home too frightened to be near *me*.

She requested, repeatedly, to be moved to a different division, and not once was her plea so much as acknowledged until she was threatened, told that she was *lucky* being allowed to continue at all, told that she could be removed, if she was unhappy. Better yet, she could undergo a sort of reparative punishment, on her way out; the same *reparative* punishment I was subjected to as a child— some highlights being forced fasting, solitary confinement, drugging, forced self mutilation, and electric shock."

He swallows hard, his throat too tight, his mouth too dry.

"Understandably, she did not request removal again."

Quiet murmuring moves through the crowd below him, around him, above him; the eyes of the Higher-class seem to burn through his skin.

"Now," he says, "despite doing the Ordinem's worst work, without a single complaint in almost two decades, she is still told to silence herself in Council meetings. She is barred from making any decisions regarding the Outskirts, because they suggest she may have some lingering, unspoken bias... She is silenced, as you are silenced, as Cole was silenced, until they saw some way to use him; even if it is painted to look like respect.

They call him a hero for attempting to save a group of children that, without intervention, are now likely to die. Children left alone in the Outskirts have no higher than a twenty-three percent rate of survival, sixty percent dying of starvation, because our government provides them with so little food, thirty at the hands of demons we have not sheltered them from, and ten from disease we are able to treat. Since what happened in Karneji, the Ordinem has not done a single address on the state of any of the five clusters; luckily, their motions and laws— and who voted for them— are public, or we would never hear a word." He lifts several sheets of paper into the air. "You have a right to request these at any time, by the way, despite any resistance they may try to give you."

"Alastor," Cindy says, her voice sharp. "Perhaps..."

The man stares ahead at Anemos with dark eyes and nods.

"Go," he says. "Have Elise collect everyone needed for interrogation, get the rest to safety, just in case."

"Yes, Myon."

"See how many guards they like in the Lower-class sector, hm?"

She stops, her face pale, and tilts her head to the side.

"I believe that is beyond the scope of your authority—"

"And I believe that when the sun dies, five hours from now, it will not matter. Cast a vote if you'd like."

"That won't be necessary."

"From these documents," Anemos says, "we can see that the damage is listed as catastrophic. We can also see that every motion introduced to render aid has been overturned by a nearly unanimous Council; the most commonly stated reason that it will have to wait until the grieving period has ended."

Regis laughs, loudly enough that the Council can hear, just as the rest of the crowd begins to speak louder, less discreetly.

"We're *screwed,*" he breathes. "Didn't think he had this in him."

"Gonna pick sides?" Josh asks.

"Your side," he says. "Be a damn fool not to pick his side, now."

"So, just to be clear," Anemos sighs. "We could break the Code in order to force a bunch of kids back into a warzone, but not to assist thousands of people, lacking shelter and nutrition, mauled by Saenks— Saenks that got loose because of kinks in a plan that I, an eighteen year old boy, managed to pick out in fifteen minutes; risks that they were *fully* aware of, and fully prepared for..." He shrugs, sighs. "In the Higher-class sector, anyway. No casualties there, but that's all that really matters, to them, yeah? Praise the Code, but I don't see any proof that these people have ever read it."

Icarus stands with his fingers pressed against his lips, his eyes red and his face pale. Everyone is angry, all at once, and he thinks that he should find comfort in the solidarity, but he doesn't.

He thinks that maybe, *maybe* this could spark some justice, thinks that he is proud of the man on the stage, thinks that all of it is necessary, and he should feel ready to fight.

He looks at Regis, in the distance, and thinks that he can see fire in his eyes, but he does not feel it.

He looks at Anemos, and his chest aches with grief and fear— more for his friend than himself. He thinks of the terror on his face, in Karneji, and the way his hands shook around his father. He thinks of his body seeming to cave in on itself every time he sobbed, the way it felt trying to hold him tightly enough to keep him from falling apart.

He thinks of all the years spent in such close proximity to each other— spent as friends— but too shy to go beneath the surface. He wonders if he could have helped.

He realizes how quickly he would take Anemos' suffering upon himself, if he could; all of it, all of the horrors, all of the anger, all of the pain—

"Myon," Elise says, placing a hand on Aliya's shoulder. "I need you to come with me, actually just... Head on over with the rest of the Higher-class."

"Where's my husband?" Icarus hears his mother say.

"Myon, I don't have time to..."

Anemos steps away from the podium, a roar of different opinions coming from the crowd, but it is all muffled to Icarus.

He pulls away from them without even thinking, dropping all niceties as he pushes his way through the crowd, practically running, hardly breathing, and still, he is far behind him when finally reaches the edge of the crowd.

He *actually* runs to him, then, and only catches up to him *inside* of the University—closed today, but that has never been an issue for Anemos, and Icarus has known him long enough to follow him without much trouble.

Inside, he spots him just about to turn a corner at the end of a hall, and calls his name breathlessly, gasping for air.

Anemos stops, turns around wide eyed, and retraces his steps at an even quicker pace than he took them before.

"Anem...mos," he says again, and Anemos stops in front of him, placing one hand on his shoulder, and holding tightly to Icarus' hand with the other. "I need to... I have to—"

"You're trembling," he breathes, and Icarus shakes his head, his eyes watering.

"I'm fine," he says. "You... Are you..."

Anemos nods, and Icarus' breathing slows, just enough that he can speak, crying as he does.

"I'm s-so sorry, An. I'm so... I wish I could have helped."

"No," Anemos whispers. "No, Icarus. You have. You've—"

They hear a door open, in the distance, and Icarus flinches at the sound.

"I need to talk to you," he says, and Anemos shakes his head.

"I don't think there's time for that—"

"He's alive, An," Icarus cries. "I... I thought he was... But I didn't know..."

"What?" Anemos asks, frozen. His voice is all breath. "What do you mean?"

"The Saenk b-behind me, I thought it killed him, but it only *took* him. They-they were... looking for him, An. It was waiting at the door and... They took him."

"Why would they—"

"I don't..." Icarus cries, and another door opens. "I don't know."

"Even if they were looking for him, even if they took him, that doesn't mean... He couldn't have survived in Assecula. He couldn't have lived through that, even if he didn't die here."

"But he *did* live through it," Icarus says, and Anemos pulls away, covering his hands with his face. "That's what I'm trying to—"

"No," Anemos says. "No, he couldn't have..."

"Anemos—"

"How?" he asks. "How could—"

"I don't know—"

"But how do you *know?*" his voice is louder now; pained, and angry, and desperate. "How could you possibly know?"

"I can't—"

"You have to," Anemos says. "*Please,* Icarus."

Icarus lowers his head, runs his hands nervously through his hair, over his face, and Anemos breaks, unable to contain the sobs breaking free from his lips.

"*Please,*" he repeats, and Icarus nods, unable to breathe.

"I... I'm..."

"Please," he cries. "Please, I need him to be-"

"Because I'm Grim," Icarus says, and the words silence the room, turning the air to poison. "I know because I'm..."

Chapter Seventy

"**I**'m Grim."

The words leave Icarus' mouth like a curse, stealing all of the air in his lungs away.

Twelve years of careful secrecy wasted in a moment. Pointless. And Anemos only stares at him, terrified.

Something inside of Icarus breaks.

"I'm s-so s...sorry," he forces. "But I went to Morta looking for him, the day after it happened, and he wasn't there. He was *never* there, An. I'm so—"

The door opens before he can finish, and Elise steps into the room, red eyed and pale.

"Boys," she says, struggling to keep her voice calm. "I need you to come with me."

"Why?" Icarus asks, and the sound of his voice makes Anemos flinch. "What's... What's happening?"

"I can't explain until we are with the others. Quickly now, please."

Anemos lets Icarus walk first, but says nothing at all.

Soon, they are ushered into a small gray room, with fifteen black chairs and one small desk.

They are the last people to enter the room, but not the most frightened.

The *most* frightened woman in the room meets Anemos' eyes with dread, and stands to look at her husband with pure, unconcealed hatred.

"No," she says, pointing at him. "*No.*"

"Ursula," Cindy says, sighing as Elise presses Icarus and Anemos down into two chairs beside each other. "Honey, you need to sit down."

"Fuck you, Cindy," she snaps. "Alastor, you..."

He lowers his face, rubs his forehead.

"I think you should sit, love."

"I think you should sit. You're not going to do this again—"

"Behave," he says, "or you will be made to behave. We are prepared to deal with you, any of you, however we must."

"He hasn't *done* anything."

"Oh?" Alastor laughs, and she grits her teeth.

"Where is Charles?" she asks. "Does he know?"

Anemos looks up from the ground without meaning to, afraid of the answer.

"I do not have to disclose that to you."

"Perhaps I should disclose it to him."

"Perhaps," he says, and she tries, but her words never reach him.

Darkness floods her vision, suddenly, and the blood drains from her face.

She cannot feel him, she realizes; cannot find him, and a quiet cry escapes her lips.

"What have you done?"

"Sit," he says. "Now."

She only looks at him, not moving, and Elise steps closer to her, slowly, putting a hand on her shoulder.

"Ursula," she whispers, hesitant. "Please, there's nothing you can do. I understand how you're feeling…"

Icarus listens to her voice, and the world around him seems to blur; to fade away.

It feels like death, somehow.

Alastor begins to explain what's happening— carefully, but it provides no comfort.

"A brief examination, in Karneji, mental and physical…"

He watches the way Anemos' eyes darken, finding the floor and resting there, petrified. He watches the way his hands start to tremble, the way he grips the chair in an attempt to stop them.

He watches Ursula, who fails to fight back the tears in her eyes, and can hardly breathe as realization sets in.

He can not explain away the scars of an Oracath; not easily, probably not at all.

He could shift to Morta, but, if he went now, he could never return.

Icarus looks at the faces in the room around him. Twelve that he hardly knows. He wonders what secrets they might be hiding. He wonders what secrets will be uncovered, or acquired, in Karneji.

He thinks of Alastor interrogating Anemos alone and fights the urge to be sick then and there.

"If we do not find our traitor in the first phase, more extreme measures will be taken with those who raise any considerable suspicion. Understood?"

"We're not an hour away from the funeral," Ursula cries. "We're not... My son has done nothing to warrant this."

"Mom," Anemos pleads, his voice fragile, and she falls silent, her bones seeming to shake.

Icarus wonders what secrets *she* might be hiding, and realizes he has made a sympathizer out of his best friend.

"This will only go until we find our traitor," Alastor says. "So, if any of you know *anything*—"

"It... It'll stop?" Icarus asks.

"Stop?" Alastor laughs. "It will take quite a bit of information to avoid interrogation, child. Perhaps if you give us the traitor's name."

"Will *you* be handling the interrogation?" he asks, and Alastor stops and nods.

"It is *my* division," he says, and Anemos flinches, cracking his neck nervously. "Now, as I was saying..."

Too many faces, he thinks. Too much in this room to be lost.

He wonders if Anemos has the strength for another trip to Karneji, and his throat tightens.

"How do you even know the traitor is here?" someone says, and there is familiar fear in the voice.

"We don't," Cindy says. "There are six other groups this size we will be interrogating as well."

"And how do you know the traitor is *there*?" someone else asks. "You will torture us on the basis of nothing but *suspicion?*"

"We can only pray that it does not come to that."

He wonders if he is the only Reaper here— wonders if there are Deviations.

He thinks of Zahra.

He realizes, again, that Anemos has not spoken when he could.

He thinks of the last time he hid— really hid— in Jakara, and thinks that he will not be able to forgive himself again.

"Torture?" someone asks, and the boy next to him closes his eyes.

Icarus moves his hand slightly, letting his fingers brush his friend's for just a second before Anemos jerks away, quietly enough that no one else notices, but it does not matter.

"Excuse m...me," he says, his voice trembling. He does not mean to interrupt, but he does not care. "M-maybe... Could I speak with you alone, Myon? For just a m-moment?"

Everyone falls silent.

Cindy looks at him a second, confused, before nodding.

"Elise will have to supervise... It's pressing?"

"Mm... Y-yes, it's..."

She looks over at Alastor, moves toward the door, and he stands up, his hands trembling.

The door shuts.

Fourteen faces are left in silence, and Icarus steps out into the hall, unable to breathe.

The wall he had pushed around his mind falls away, and suddenly, there is another.

Zahra looks up from the plate of food in front of her, swallows hard, and sits down her fork, Sergeant Bellamy's voice muffling into the background.

"Icarus?" she asks, her heart sinking deep into her stomach. *"What's wrong?"*

"I'm sorry, Firefly. Something's happened, and I can't... I shouldn't involve you. I shouldn't burden you, but you're the only person I have—"

"Sergeant," Zahra says, and she does not mean to interrupt, but she doesn't care. "May I be excused, please?"

"If you tell us who it is, we'll wave the sentence," Cindy says. "You'll need to do a bit of... therapy, just to straighten yourself out, but..."

"B-but they won't have to..." His voice trembles. "It's just that none of them... None of them know, and I hate to think they'll be tortured, endlessly, for not giving a confession."

"They'll be released, yes."

"I have your word?"

Cindy hesitates a moment, then nods, holding out her hand.

"I swear on the Code."

He places his hand in hers, pulls it back away, and lowers his face, picking at the skin on his wrists.

Fifteen minutes later, Charles steps into another small gray room with vacant eyes and trembling hands.

"Jack," he says, his voice hoarse. "If you could come with me, please. The rest of you are free to go."

"What's happened?" Jack asks, his face already pale. "Is everything okay?"

"No," he says. "It isn't..."

Aliya steps in beside him, her face tired, sick, and Jack stands, already knowing, wishing he didn't.

"Where is he?" he asks, stepping toward them. "What's happened?"

"Jack," Charles pleads. "Please. Please stay calm."

"Stay *calm?*"

"He's not..." Aliya's voice is cold, numb. "Jack, love, we've been lied to."

"Lied to?"

She folds her hands in front of her and stares at the floor, tears spilling silently from her eyes.

"He's... Icarus is Grim, he's just... They've just discovered it—"

"Where *is* he?" Jack repeats, his voice strained.

Aliya freezes, her whole body shaking with something like terror.

"It's with Cindy, now," she says. "They'll be headed for Karneji before nightfall."

"*It* is our child," he cries, and she shakes her head.

"No, no, Jack, it isn't..." He tries to shove past her, and she struggles to hold him back. "It wasn't *real.* It wasn't... *Stop.*"

"Let me see him!" he yells. "God, you're going to burn him alive, can I not see him while he's still my—"

"It is *pretend,* Jack," she cries. "You have been deceived, just as we all have."

"Yes, you have," he snaps, choking on his own tears. "Let me—"

"Let him pass," Charles says, his voice heavy, and Aliya looks at him, but does not respond. "Jack," he says. "It will be handled discreetly; swiftly. He won't... The Council understands your pain—"

"They understand *nothing.*"

"He won't suffer," Charles says, his voice breaking. "He won't burn—"

"You're going to *kill* him," he cries. "That's my *baby,* and you're going to—"

"He's Grim, Jack," Charles snaps, fighting back the sobs building in his own chest. "He isn't... Listen to your wife. He warned them. For Inanis' sake, Ursula nearly died; we *all* nearly died, and he didn't—"

"Let me pass!" he yells, and Aliya stumbles backward, too broken to fight.

He is stopped again as soon as he reaches the hall by a man who cares less.

"Did you know?" Alastor asks, his voice like ice, void of any feeling but hatred.

Jack hesitates only a second— not enough to be found guilty— and Alastor pulls the blade from his side, sinking it deep into the man's chest, up between his ribs.

By the time Charles turns around, Aliya's hands are already up in front of her face, and she has already started to scream, and he does not even know what has happened when he sees Ursula at the end of the hall, eyes wide with terror.

"It's as if you all forget how we deal with sympathizers," Alastor says, jerking the dagger back, wiping the blade clean on his sleeve. "He's as guilty as his son."

Jack falls to the floor, blood pooling around his body, and Ursula walks directly past her husband, not even hearing him, kneeling beside the limp form on the floor with tears spilling from her eyes.

She presses two fingers to the side of his throat and stands, blood staining her clothes.

"Aliya," she whispers, moving to stand in front of her, putting one hand on each of her shoulders in an attempt to hold her back. "I need you to... Don't look, okay? Don't look at... Please... Charles?"

Charles stands paralyzed, looking at Jack with trembling hands, unable to breathe.

"Charles," Ursula repeats, trying to get help, but Aliya has already broken free from her grip by the time he responds, starting to cling to the bloody, cold shell of the man that stood in front of her only seconds earlier, lifting his face to hers, crying out as if in pain. "I need..."

"No," Aliya repeats, again and again, so many times that the word stops sounding like a word. "No... No... Look at me," she cries. "Don't... N-no... No."

She can feel the lack of breath in his body, and it paralyzes her; it nails her to the floor.

Charles drops down beside her, pulling her hands away, pulling her into his chest, and when he looks up from the body of his friend, Alastor is already gone.

"Help him," Aliya cries. "You have to..."

"He's gone, love," he whispers, trying not to look, unable to stop his own tears from falling. "He's not... He's gone."

"He can't be..." He holds her steady, holds her as she begins to still, grief overtaking her usually strong frame, making it seem fragile. "I can't lose them both..."

"Charles," Ursula says, her voice broken. "We don't have time to—"

A scream breaks loose, outside, and he lifts his head wearily.

"People are angry, and the Council needs—"

"Where's Anemos?" he asks, his voice all breath.

"I don't know," she whispers. "He left when it happened."

Charles nods, pulling Aliya up with him, as carefully as he can.

"Get her somewhere safe," he says, "and stay with her, please."

She nods, and he casts one final glance down at the man he knows he will not see again; the man that will haunt him while he is awake, and in his dreams.

One of the only men he has ever really known to be good.

"If Alastor comes near either of you," he says, "do not hesitate a second."

Another nod, and Ursula pulls Aliya into her arms, barely able to hold her up.

"I won't," she whispers, and he nods, taking her hand for as long as he can, and then slipping into the shadows.

Interlude: The Sea

"Cyrus," an older woman said, nearly two decades earlier. "What a lovely name, son. Do you know what Cyrus means?"

"No, Myon," Cyrus said, sixteen, his face light despite the darkness in his eyes. "I'm afraid not."

"I do believe it means... One who bestows care," she said, and he raised his eyebrows with interest, as if she had not told him this a hundred times. "It was my father's name, you know."

"Oh?" he asked, smiling. "What are the chances of that?"

"And look at you," she put one withered hand on his shoulder. "Taking care of me. Such a sweet boy. It's been lovely meeting you."

"Lovelier meeting you, surely," he said, his grin wide enough that he looked happy, his eyes sparkling in the way they always did. "Enjoy that bread, now, and..."

"Is it very cold?" she asked, and his face fell slightly.

"Hm?"

"Why, your hands are shaking, child."

"Oh," he said, shoving them into his pockets. "No, I'm... Could I give you a hug, actually? Just this once?"

"Of course!" his grandmother said, opening her arms, pulling the young man into a hug that was surprisingly firm, considering her frail frame. "You're sure you're not cold, love?"

"I'm sure, Myon. It's spring, see? You can tell because it's all green again."

She peeked past him, smiled brightly.

"It is! Isn't it? My, I remember the fun we used to have outside in the spring, before it happened. Do you remember? Oh, no, you're too young."

"Can you tell me about it?" he asked, pulling away, surprised that she remembered anything at all. "I'd love to..."

"Well, now that I think of it, I just remember the flowers."

He smiled, shook his head.

"There are flowers here, Myon."

"Flowers here?" she asked. "Where?"

"Out in the field," he said. "Little purple ones, usually... I'll take you sometime."

"That would be lovely," she said, taking his hand; and then, sadly: "Oh my dear, what's happened here?"

He pulled his hand away, as if on instinct, and shook his head, wishing he could burn the scar from his skin.

"Just the ceremony scar," he said. "Nothing at all. You have one, too."

The woman looked down at her own hand, blinked several times, as if trying to remember, and then shook her head.

"But you're too young for that, aren't you? You're a child."

"Too young for what?" he asked.

"I'm not quite... I'm sorry, I've forgotten your name."

"Cyrus," he said, the light smile on his face unchanging.

"Oh, that's a lovely name."

"Could I talk to you?" he asked suddenly. "I've been really... really needing someone to talk to."

"Of course," she said. "Of course, come in, I'll make some tea..." A promise that used to mean something, an echo now. "What was your name?"

She was the only one he ever told, and he only told her once, sitting cross legged in the center of her couch, his hands together in front of him.

He knew that she would not remember long.

"Grim?" she asked, and his heart was in his throat, anyway.

"Yes, Myon."

She paused, serious, and he returned his hands to his pockets, eyes burning.

"Well," she whispered, finally, "that's very sad, Cyrus."

"Hm?" he asked, nervously cracking his neck.

"You seem a very kind young man," she said, and it was a kinder response than anything he could have ever imagined— a kinder response than most others in the Ordinem would have given him. There was no threat, no implication that his well mannered, careful demeanor was a guise, and to her he was— apparently, still human. Her voice had no hostility, and no fear, as she said it. Only genuine, tragic, grief. "I hate to think of you as damned."

"Cyrus," Charles said, his voice heavy and strained as he tried to wake the boy, again. "Cyrus, please. Come on, wake—"

Cyrus sat bolt upright in his bed, gasping for air, his body drenched in sweat, and Charles took his hands, trying to calm him.

"It's okay," he whispered, brushing the boy's hair back out of his face and letting him collapse into his chest, his body wracked with sobs. "It's okay..."

"No it's not," he cried. "I can't do this any more, Charlie... I can't..."

"What was it?" Charles asked, and Cyrus held him tighter, his whole body shaking so violently that his older brother nearly panicked himself.

"Fire," he said. "Burning... All burning... I can't make it go away, Charles. I can't... How do I make it stop? How do I..."

"I don't know." The boy's cries cut him off, and he swallowed hard, fear tightening his chest. "How can I help?"

"I don't know," Cyrus cried. "I don't..."

"It's just the dream?" he asked. "There's nothing else?"

"No, no."

"You know you can tell me, if there is. If it's something with Dad, or... anything, Cyrus. Anything at all. You know you're safe with me."

"It's just the dream, Charles."

"Should we go get some air, then?"

"I don't want air," he cried. "I don't want..."

"We could go to the sea," Charles whispered, a little desperately. "Would that help?"

The sea.

A horrific thought planted itself in Cyrus' head, upon hearing the words, and he knew, somehow, that this time he might not be able to push it away. It was as if he could feel the darkness in his very bones, pushing him there, promising a despicable kind of rest. The kind of rest that killed stars, and silenced song.

The kind of rest that haunts everyone it touches.

"Just stay with me," Cyrus said. "Please, just..."

"Okay," Charles said, his voice sad, frightened. "Cyrus—"

"Just promise you'll stay tonight. Promise me you won't leave me," he cried, more terrified than he had ever been. "I can't be alone anymore."

PART SIX: THE END

"No one ever told me that grief felt so like fear."
—C.S. Lewis, A Grief Observed

CHAPTER SEVENTY-ONE

The boy was seven the first time he entered Inanis.

He was sitting on the floor in his room, behind a closed door, with his knees to his chest and his hands over his ears.

He didn't know if he believed the stories, but he was a child, and children don't always have to know.

Icarus was desperate, and in his desperation, it was the only hope he had, so he closed his eyes, and prayed to anything listening that he could go somewhere else—

Anywhere else.

And he did.

When he opened his eyes, he was alone. It was only him, and the void, and the wind.

"Hel...hello?" he asked the nothingness. "Is there an-n-anyone there?"

The noise was gone, but the wind still blew, and it wrapped itself all around him, lifting him up.

The boy's eyes widened as his feet left the ground, but he did not feel afraid. There was no malice in the darkness, and as he continued to rise, the void began to come to life.

He could not understand how, but it was as if he could feel the place's breath, it's heartbeat.

When the girl first shifted, she was four.

"*They know,*" Icarus says, and she slams shut the bathroom door, her back against the wall.

"*How do they know?*"

"*Dear little Icarus,*" Aliya said gently. "*You look as if you've seen a ghost.*"

"*A M-Mortum,*" he said. "*They... they aren't called ghosts, they're the Mortum.*"

She sat on the bed and offered a small smile. "*Right, the Mortum. Too many stories for me.*"

She leaned back against the wall and folded her arms, sighing deeply.

"*I say you're ready to join the Ordinem now.*"

The boy's eyes were dark; too dark for a child.

"I'll never be ready to join the Ordinem," he said. "N-not like this."

"Like what, dear? Don't tell me you think a little trouble with your words will hold you back."

He sighed and put his chin on his hands.

"They won't want me like this."

"Why?" Cindy asks, pale. "Why would you—"

"Because I'm Grim," he says, and she takes a step away, horror in her eyes. "Because..."

"You're *what?*"

He unzips the top of his shirt with trembling hands, pulling it aside to show his torn shoulder.

"I'm Grim," he repeats. "I got these scars in M-morta, and I... I told William— his name was William... I told him, be-because you were going to *kill* us—"

"Elise," Cindy says, still as a statue. "Please... Get... Get the serum."

Elise fights to pry her own nails from her palms.

"Yes, Myon."

"You don't have to..." He chokes slightly, his lips trembling. "I'm... I'm turning myself in, I'm not going to... I'm not going to hurt you."

"The serum," Cindy says. "*Now.*"

"I told them," he says. *"They were going to interrogate so many people, Zahra. They were going to hurt Anemos."*

Her eyes well with tears, and she presses them shut, pressing her hand against them, and starting to cry, her whole chest shaking.

"I think he hates me."

"He doesn't hate you," she says.

"He was so... so scared."

"He could never hate you for something like this."

Elise pulls a small, clear shot from her pocket; she reaches for Icarus' wrist, and he offers it willingly, his hands trembling.

"It's not going to hurt," she whispers. "It'll just... It's just a paralytic, so, you won't be able to move—"

"Elise," Cindy says, and she sticks the needle into his wrist, fighting back tears as she does.

"You should sit," she says. "You don't want to fall."

He nods silently and lowers himself to the ground, his body already heavy.

"Paralytic," he says, and Zahra nods to herself, trying not to stay calm.

"Make sure you can see all of them," she says. *"You won't be able to move your head. I couldn't speak, either. That's the scariest part, so don't try."*

"It hurt," he says, and she opens her eyes, staring ahead vacantly.

"What did?"

"The needle," he replies. *"Just the needle, Zahra. It was just a needle, and it hurt."*

Her heart breaks.

"I know," she says, wishing she had any more comfort to offer. *"It hurt me too, just... keep breathing, remember you can breathe, and don't stop... You're going to be okay."*

Alastor steps into the room. He looks down at him with something dark behind his eyes, and Icarus presses himself further back against the wall, just as he begins to lose control of his legs.

"What if I'm not?" he asks, and Zahra clenches her fists together in front of her.

"You will be."

"But if I'm not?"

His voice is petrified, she realizes, and— worse than that— knowing.

"Then I'll be with you," she says, and somehow, the words soothe him.

"One paralytic?" Alastor asks. "It's a Reaper, not a damned Deviation."

"Well..." Elise sighs, running her hands through her hair. "I only have one, Myon. I wasn't instructed to bring more than that."

"You wouldn't lie to me," he says. "Would you?"

"By the dragon," she breathes. "I'll check again, give me just a moment."

"What was the dosage?"

"The highest," she says. "We hardly need two."

"Give it three."

"You promise?" he asks, his hands falling, limp at his sides.

"I promise," she whispers. *"Until the very end."*

Elise grimaces, cringing at the sight of the serum she knows she can't pretend not to see, feeling her chest tighten with confusion as she realizes that one is *actually* missing.

She kneels at the boy's side, avoiding his eyes as he watches her force more of the drug into his veins.

"Can you tell me where you are?"

Icarus' eyes become suddenly heavier, along with the rest of his body, and his throat tightens.

He is almost too weak to breathe.

"The University," he says, and then, more softly: *"Zahra, I feel wrong. I think they gave me too much."*

"Where in the University?"

"I'm in a hallway, outside one of the smaller classrooms..."

"Can you see anything specific?"

Alastor takes a step closer— takes a step directly onto the boy's hand, not even acknowledging it, and Icarus realizes, much too quickly, that even though he cannot move, he is not numb; not numb in the slightest.

"I don't—"

"I don't assume you carry the sedative for their kind?"

"Which sedative is that?"

"Enthroproxan."

Elise freezes, shakes her head.

"No, Myon. I don't think anyone carries that out of Karneji."

"There's a reserve at the Palace, isn't there?" Cindy asks, and Alastor nods, shifting just enough to send fresh pain through the boy's hand, up into his arm.

It is the least of his concerns, as the second dose of the paralytic works its way through his blood, leaving his mouth hanging open, drool running down the side of his face, and silencing his tears.

"Yes," Alastor says. "Do you think you could retrieve that? I have some business to—" He shifts again, the sharp steel of his boot breaking skin, "—attend to. Namely informing the Guide, and—"

"You want to leave it with *Elise?*" she asks. "She'll probably lose it."

"Hey, Cindy, remember when Ursula told you to go fuck yourself earlier?" Elise asks, and the woman falls silent, her face red. "I'll be fine. I think I can handle *this.*"

She gestures to the boy on the floor as if he is nothing, and Alastor nods, addressing the older woman instead.

"It is young," he says. "Untrained, it seems. I don't think it will be much of a threat." He turns to Elise. "Bloodlet it, before you kill it. The less cursed blood spilt on these grounds the better."

"I understand," she says, and when Alastor steps away, Icarus' eyes fall on the wall behind him, avoiding his hand.

"One-zero-seven," he says, and Zahra's hands loosen.

"One-zero-seven?" she asks.

"I'm outside of room One-zero-seven. That's on the third floor. I used to take class next door."

Zahra opens the bathroom door again, yelling out into the living room.

"Bellamy, ma'am?"

"Yes, Zahra?"

"I'm alive," she says, turning the faucet on the bathtub as cold as it will go, clogging the drain, and then returning to the door as it begins to fill, turning on the sink and turning off the lights. "Leave the water running."

"Are you safe for now?" she asks. *"I need just a minute, love."*

Alastor and Cindy step out of the room, slamming the door behind them, and Icarus catches Anemos' eyes through the crack— cold, void of anything at all.

"I'm alright," he says, listening as closely as he can to the words being spoken beyond the door, not even noticing as Elise pulls another shot from her pocket, pressing the needle through his shirt and into his shoulder without ever speaking.

The blood of those behind the door runs cold, but Alastor's expression does not falter as he speaks, his voice the epitome of calm.

"It attempted to..." He clears his throat, shakes his head. "Well, it feared it might be caught and overestimated its capability for escape, but it's been neutralized, now."

"Icarus?" Ursula asks. Her voice sounds sad, from behind the door. "That's impossible."

"They're lying," he says. *"I don't understand why they need to lie."*

"Because you did something good," Zahra says, peeling the shoes from her feet, shivering as she steps into the cold water, trying not to slip. *"The truth means nothing to them, Icarus. They want them to be terrified. If the truth doesn't reflect their Code, the truth is a lie. Any distortion can be justified with a mindset like that."*

Icarus blinks once, slowly, and a loud cry breaks behind the door, followed by Ursula's voice, pleading for her son to calm down.

"I stayed in its *room*," Anemos cries. "I ate at its table... I..."

"Anemos, please."

"No..." He pulls loose from his mother and takes a step toward his father— toward the door.

"Anemos—"

"I want to *kill* it," he yells. "Let me—"

"Zahra," Icarus cries, his chest heaving with sobs, even with the paralytic—a soft whimpering sound between his lips. *"Zahra I can't do this. I can't."*

"He *killed* him," Anemos screams. "He killed my..."

Zahra turns the faucet off, water moving gently around her knees, and places her hands down into it, closing her eyes. The sink continues to run, and the sound drowns out everything else; everything but him.

"Spirit," she whispers, her voice trembling. "Please, don't give me more than I can bear."

The air around her changes, almost too quickly, and she begs her own hands not to scald her, her whole body trembling at the grief that washes over her as suddenly as the wind.

"Give me strength... *Icarus?*"

No.

She stops, listens, and lets her shoulders fall.

"Michael?" she asks, and then, more softly: *"Michael, okay. Another thing to talk about, when this is all over."*

Icarus sniffs once, quietly, wishing he could wipe his face, or close his eyes.

"How do you do that?" he asks.

"I don't—"

"Not the knowing," he says. *"I understand the knowing."*

"What, then?" she asks, opening her eyes slowly, trying to bring color to the darkness around her, trying to clear her vision, trying to see *through*, and around, and over.

"You speak all my curses as if they're blessings," he whispers.

"Who told you your name was a curse?" she asks, and the void around her seems to shake, sadness thick in the air.

"Everyone, Zahra."

CHAPTER SEVENTY-TWO

"*R* *each for me,*" Zahra says, and Icarus lets his eyes fall shut, unable to swallow. "*I don't know how, anymore.*"

"*You do,*" she says. "*You're doing it now. You can hear me. You found me after the ceremony.*"

"*I'm too weak, Zahra, I'm too...*"

"*No,*" she says, and her voice is too firm for him to argue. "*Listen to me. The weakness of your body has no control of your spirit. I am with you now, just as the Wind is with you. You just have to let go, Michael. Just... You're afraid. You don't need to be.*"

"*I don't trust it anymore.*"

"*You don't have to,*" she breathes. "*Trust me. I'm not asking you to shift into Inanis, only to see. I know you can... Just, pull me to you.*"

Icarus feels something like a hand on his shoulder, something like wind brush his arm, and he does not have to look to know that she is there.

If not in body, in spirit.

The touch he feels is faint, closer to that of a Mortum, stuck in Terra; she is pressure, warmth, breath, but she is there, her image a little faded, a little like a mirage, but enough.

She steps around him, kneels in front of him, and pushes the hair from his face.

To his surprise, it moves.

"*I told you,*" she says, her voice almost playful, despite the tears in her eyes— the tears pouring down her face, tightening her throat in Trellis. "*Like a leech, Michael. A fucking leech.*"

A soft, breathy laugh escapes his weak frame, and she pulls one of his hands into his lap. She takes it into both of hers, intertwining their fingers.

"*That's not how it works, Zahra. I don't think you know what a leech is.*"

"*Shut up, love.*"

He closes his eyes, groans slightly in pain, and does not instantly open them again.

"How can you touch me?" he asks. *"How is that possible?"*

"Because we're both here, both there, both—"

"Between two worlds," he finishes. *"Hm?"*

She nods, rubbing her thumb across the back of his hand.

"Between two worlds," she says, and then, more softly: *"Hey."*

"Hm?"

"You're going to be okay."

He opens his eyes slowly, letting them run over her face.

"Okay," he nods.

"Okay."

"You know, I say that to Mortum, too, Zahra."

"Stop it."

"I'm sorry," he says. *"I don't—"*

Footsteps, just outside the door. They both hear them, both flinch at the sound, and she holds his hand a little tighter.

"Did they say what they're going to—"

"Enthroproxan," he says, and in Trellis, she begins to cry harder. *"Do you know what that does? I know it's bad—"*

"Hold on to me," she says quickly. *"Even if you can't feel me, you hold on. Do you understand?"*

"I—"

The door opens, and Alastor steps into the room, stepping on the boy's arm as he does, and not hesitating a moment before grabbing him by the hair, pulling him from the ground in a position so unnatural that Zahra has to look away, even as she feels his hand twitch with pain.

There is blood on Alastor's hands, his sleeves.

"What happened?" Elise asks, her pale, and Zahra looks over at her with wide eyes, not having noticed her before.

Alastor grunts slightly with the effort it takes to pull him up, pulls his hand away from hers and ties it with his other behind his back, dropping him back against the floor as he does. Icarus' face is starting to bleed.

"That bastard knew," Alastor says, pulling an injection from his pocket, pulling Icarus back up again, and stabbing it— gracelessly— into the side of his neck. "Had to..."

Zahra drifts from Icarus and over to Alastor, pressing a hand to his shoulder that he can not feel, closing her eyes.

She is in the man's mind only a moment before falling back to the floor, trying to reach around his jagged movements to find the one who needs her.

"Don't listen," she pleads, catching his wrist. *"Don't listen to him, Michael, please..."*

But the boy's face has already changed, pale, veins standing out on his throat, blood and foam spilling between his lips as his entire body begins to tighten, and she realizes, suddenly, that he has not heard a thing; that he cannot even hear *her*, as the new drug takes hold of him.

Alastor pulls another syringe from his coat, and Elise stands a little straighter, shaking her head.

"Alastor—" He jerks him back again, sticks the needle into his throat, and a wave of pain spreads out from him, seeming to suffocate Zahra— to push her away. "You're going to kill it *here.*"

"It will only wish it were dead," he says, and he drops Icarus to the floor again, where he begins to cry out in pain without even moving its lips. "Can you handle it, or do I need to ?"

Elise looks down at the boy, wonders how gentle she can be safely, and nods.

"Yes, I can handle it."

"Good," he says, opening the door once more. "Elise?"

Zahra stops at the name, turning and glancing back at her.

Elise. *This* is Elise.

"Michael," she whispers. *"I don't know if you can hear me, but this is a friend. She is a friend. You can trust her."*

"Time is of the essence—"

CHAPTER SEVENTY-THREE

"Five minutes," Charles snaps, turning away from Cindy with his hands in his hair. "Give me five damn minutes to think."

"I'm meant to be with Alastor," Cindy stresses, her eyes dark. "They'll be heading to Karneji any minute."

"Go, then," he says. "You're useless *here.*"

"Hardly, Myon, when I'm the *only* one to do anything in regards to—"

"In regards to what?" he asks. "Defense? You think this is *defense* you've ordered? Turning the Lower-class sector into a military state?"

"What did you want me to do?"

"Your job. I wanted you to do your job, your *service,* and leave unselected divisions up to me, the way the Code commands." His voice is cold. She flinches in its presence. "You know better."

A door opens, down the hall, and they both look over.

"Did you hear—"

Charles stands, walks over to the door and opens it with a hand on the dagger at his waist.

The hall is dark and windowless, the power still not returned, and he sees nothing as he walks down it— not until the very end, where one door has swung wide open. He steps through it, looks at the open window across from it, and lets out a relieved sigh.

He approaches it slowly, noting the smell of smoke permeating the air, but doesn't close it.

Cindy closes in beside him, and he buries his trembling hands in his pockets.

"You understand," he says, "that your order only proved the boy's point further, yes? Reacting to a speech given by a Higher-class man with too many guards in the Lower sector."

She is silent, not pushing her blonde hair from her face.

"Answer me."

"Yes," she says. "I understand."

"Then what, I pray, were you thinking?"

"I was fulfilling orders given to me by your brother."

"Knowing he did not have the authority to issue them. I cannot accuse him when it was only a suggestion, at his rank, just as you cannot blame him for your own foolishness." He pauses, rubs his face. "Perhaps I have been too lenient."

"I repent of my error, Myon."

"As you should," he says, "but you will not have mercy without some consequence. I relieve you of your duty. Go."

"You *what?*"

"Go, Cindy. Go home."

"You can't—"

"Can't I?" he turns around, his lips tight. "Leave and go home, before I send you elsewhere."

He is alone not a minute later.

He looks out the window only another second before turning and going, hesitating in the hall, his head spinning. He leaves the Palace in seconds, the air crisp, and his eyes dry, and his throat tight, and his mind full of blood, and death, and his ears still ringing with s creams.

Two hours have passed, and the sun is already low, the hour golden by the time he reaches the train that has still not left for Karneji.

"Where is he?" he asks a guard, not bothering to modify his speech. "Where have you put him?"

A large steel door gives way to the dimly lit train car they've put him in, and then closes behind Charles as he steps inside, looking down at the body on the floor with burning eyes.

Just Grim, he thinks, and the thought does not make it easier.

He cannot make himself fear the thing in front of him— the thing he has feared his entire life.

Icarus lies crumpled on the floor, unable to move, really, but still trembling; twitching and writhing like a man might do in his sleep, having a nightmare. His hands and arms are covered in cuts and bruises along with his face, his mouth no longer open but clenched tightly shut with pain, his teeth gritted.

This boy they found in Jakara and promised to protect.

Charles' stomach is sick.

He kneels down on the floor beside him, and Zahra watches with heavy eyes, almost unable to breathe.

Of course, he cannot see her, so any mask he wore outside the train, knowing he was in the presence of others, falls away.

His breath becomes suddenly heavy, his hands shaking violently as he presses them against his lips.

It is too much, too much for anyone, and she feels it, as she watches him: The turmoil of a man who's whole world was ripped from his hands by something he couldn't understand, his mind poisoned by lies for which he had never been offered an alternative, his hands stained with blood he did not even know he was shedding.

Demons, masquerading as souls; that's what he was told. Masters of mimicry. Tears shed in manipulation, smiles to deceive, nothing real, nothing good; but this boy in front of him was never anything but good, never anything but careful.

But what then? If he was good, if *they* were capable of good... To admit such a thing would be to admit that his own soul was damned, and what then? He could not help. To save this life would be to crucify himself, and then the next Grim would be subjected to tyranny far worse than his own.

This is what they want, he thinks. This destruction in his spirit, this hatred in his bones. This tangled web the darkness has spun around him, masking as a boy, masking as something good.

And still, he reaches toward him, puts a gentle hand on his arm, and flinches at the heat of his skin.

Enthroproxan. A drug created when Charles was just a child. A feared form of torture before it was used as a sedative, because it is not a sedative so much as a poison, reaching to the victim's mind, clouding it with pain, telling every nerve in every inch of their body to burn at once, as if on fire.

One dose has killed before, two is a death sentence.

He wonders if you still feel human, in pain like that, and then reminds himself that it *never* felt human, and pulls his hand away, but another finds his shoulder— a touch so light he does not even recognize it as touch, only feels his spirit break in response.

"Charles?" Zahra asks, and he starts to cry, heavy sobs, like those he cried two decades earlier. *"Charles, can you hear me?"*

His spirit can, somehow, but his mind is too clouded; even so, he reaches forward once more, wiping the blood and spit from Icarus' face with the cloak cast round his own shoulders, only to find that the mild pressure causes more blood to spill from between his lips.

"Please," Zahra cries. *"Please, he's dying."*

The man stands up, sick, and she clings to his wrist as he turns back to the door, opening it before she can say another word.

"He's good, Charles. He isn't—"

The door slams in her face, and she turns back to Icarus, sitting beside him, pulling his head into her lap, and running her hands through his hair as gently as she can.

"Shh," she whispers, her hands trembling as another pained whimper escapes his lips. *"I'm here, it's going to be okay..."*

"Elise," Charles says, and the girl turns around, her face tired.

"Yes, Myon?"

"How much Enthroproxan did you give him?"

"Alastor administered two doses, Myon," she says. "And another two doses of the paralytic. He tried for three."

"In your opinion, how much should it take to subdue him?"

"In my opinion?" she asks. "One dose of the paralytic, a quarter dose of Enthroproxan."

"A quarter?" he asks, his voice breathless. "Then why—"

"I've never seen two doses used on one of them, Myon. A boy of his size, it's a miracle his heart hasn't..." She stops, clears her throat. "It's a risk. You know the Code prohibits killing them in the city."

"Do you have the combatant?"

"Yes, Myon. I already spiked him with Larmoxin to fight the paralytic, but I didn't know... I'm sorry, that's beyond my authority."

"Administer a dose of Cactun as well," Charles says. "Neither of you are permitted to torture him. I do not want his suffering, do you understand?"

"Yes, I..." She pauses, tears in her eyes. "I'm sorry, I'll be right on that."

"Elise," he says softly.

"Yes, Myon."

"Take a moment, please. Try to breathe."

Her lips form a tight line, her throat tight as she stifles her sobs.

"I'm not sure that's possible, now, Myon."

CHAPTER SEVENTY-FOUR

"*B*reathe," Zahra pleads, holding Icarus in her arms. *"Please, keep breathing."*

His muscles contract again, the pain stronger than the paralytic, and she pulls his fingers from his palms— the action taking almost more effort than she has.

She can hear his teeth chattering. She can feel his spirit begging for the pain to end, and almost feels guilty for praying it will continue.

Two hours she has been holding him, knowing that he can't feel her. Two hours she has spoken, knowing that he can't hear her.

Two hours dreading the moment she might stop feeling him.

"Michael," she starts, and the train door opens again.

Elise steps inside with the back of her wrist pressed over her mouth, trying and failing to muffle her cries.

She gives up, once the door closes, kneeling down beside Icarus with trembling lips, trembling hands.

She presses one needle into his wrist, and another into his neck, handling him as gently as she can.

"Why didn't you go?" she whispers, wetting a cloth and using it on his mouth, his arms, and his throat. "Why didn't you go, baby?"

He does not move to answer. He doesn't move at all, and she leans closer, pressing one cool hand to his forehead.

"Fight," she whispers, the smell of his blood choking her. "You've got to fight, Icarus."

She gasps for air once more, whispers a short, pain stricken prayer in a language Zahra barely understands, and then stands and leaves.

The sky darkens, and thunder shakes the air.

In Trellis, the thunder shakes the walls.

Rosemarie sits up from her bed on the floor, pushing her hair from her eyes, and rests her weary face in her hands, trying not to be bothered by the noise as she pulls the thin blanket up around her shoulders.

She doesn't know why she is awake, so she assumes it must have been the thunder that startled her. Still, she can not make herself lie back down.

She scoots forward a little, stretches one leg out to the boy across the room, and kicks his foot lightly; once, twice...

"Elio," she whispers, and he lifts his head, his hazel eyes still mostly closed. "Are you awake?"

"It's just thunder," he whispers back, his voice rough from sleep. "You're okay, kid."

"I'm not a kid," she says, and he laughs, even in his sleep, brushing his brown hair away from his eyes. "And I *know* it's thunder."

Another bolt flashes through the windows, and he opens his eyes a little wider, pushing himself up on his elbows.

"What is it then, Rosemarie?"

"I don't know."

"Then *I* think," he lies back down, pulling the blanket up to his face. "You should try to sleep."

"But it's *something*—" He sighs, tired, and she shakes her head. "I'm sorry."

"No, no, don't..." Another sigh. "Don't be sorry. I'm here if you need anything, okay? But if you don't know what it is, it might be nothing, or it might be... Maybe it's the storm messing with you."

"Maybe." She pauses a minute, trying to relax, trying to let him sleep, but her heart is speeding up, and she cannot always tell what kind of attack she is having, so she stands, just in case. "I'm going to get some air."

"Do you want me to come with you?" She hesitates just a second, and he stands, taking her hand. "Alright, come on,"

"Actually?" She pulls her hand back, suddenly worried she might hurt him. "Could you go get some of the serum? I... I don't feel... I feel bad."

"Hey," he says, tired. "Yes, I will, but you need to breathe."

"I'm breathing."

"Are you?"

"I'm trying."

"Okay," he breathes. "Do you want to come with me?"

"No. I just want to get some..." Her heart skips a beat, and the sensation makes her chest start to ache. "I want air. I'm gonna go find the cat."

"The cat?"

"I don't know. I'll be just outside, okay?"

"Stay close."

"Yeah."

Two minutes later she is standing outside of the sleeping quarter, walking to the edge of the porch, stretching her hand out into the rain.

She likes the rain, even if she doesn't like the thunder, but it doesn't soothe her tonight.

She's telling herself to breathe, but she's starting to cry.

She sits, traces patterns into the puddle on the wood with trembling fingers, and only averts her eyes when she hears the sound of small steps behind her.

"Hey, Crow," she says, making her voice soft, and the black cat crawls into her lap, rolling onto its back and swatting at her hand like it might be a moth.

She smiles a little, sniffs, and runs her hand over the top of its head, taking a long, heavy breath.

"I'm so scared," she whispers, as if it might be understand. "It feels like I'm dying, and I don't even... Maybe it's the storm. Maybe it's nothing."

Crow blinks slowly, purrs against her hand, and she wipes her face, pressure building in her chest.

"I don't know why... I don't remember enough to know why, but it feels like it felt when I was five, when..." She flinches at the thunder, and Elio sits down beside her, rubbing his eyes.

"When what?" he asks, surprised to hear she remembers anything at all.

"It's so stupid."

"No," he interrupts. "It isn't."

"But it doesn't make any s-sense..." She stops, pushes her hair out of her face, and picks nervously at the skin around her fingernails, staring out into the night with red eyes.

"Rosemarie," Elio says, and she shakes her head, silent. "Talk to me."

"It feels like losing my brother," she says, and the words feel too real, once she's said them. "And that's ridiculous, because he isn't here, and he hasn't been... It's been twelve years, you know? I'm not losing him *now*."

"But he's all you remember, yeah?"

She chews the inside of her bottom lip, nods.

"Yeah."

"So you remember him, and you've got all this grief from all of this... From the rest of your life, that you *can't* name. It makes sense for you to connect it to something you can."

She doesn't know how to respond, so she doesn't; she only stares down at Crow, tears streaming from her eyes, and digs her fingernails into the wood beneath her.

"That isn't ridiculous, Moon."

"But it feels like I'm losing him *now*," she whimpers. "Right now, tonight. It's like... There's this place in my chest that's hollowing out, right now. I can't explain it, but it's not what it always is. It's like I can feel him slipping away all over again."

Elio watches her with sad eyes, wrapping an arm around her back in an attempt to soothe her.

"Like my memories," she cries. "Like everything else. I just can't hold on."

"Come here," Elio says, and she does, leaning into his chest like a frightened child. "It's going to be okay. I promise. Nothing's slipping away—"

"I want my brother, Elio." Her voice is like broken glass. "I want him back."

CHAPTER SEVENTY-FIVE

There is chaos in the city; such chaos that three hours into trying to clear the tracks peacefully, Icarus is moved to the back of a carriage, much like his sister, and much like the girl that is with him now.

He doesn't even know it is happening. He doesn't realize as they begin to move toward his death, and doesn't feel himself being held.

Zahra knows this, and still, she does not move.

It is hours until his body begins to still.

It's only when she can see the distant light of the Facility that his body begins to cool, and his hand loosens in hers, squeezing it once, as if making sure she is there.

"I'm with you," she whispers, and a moment later, the transport pulls to a stop.

He does not fall out onto the ground like she did, but he is pulled, and no soldiers are called to pick him up.

He opens his red eyes and stares up at the black sky, the Facility lights nearly blinding him. He can't see her now, his mind poisoned and hazy— he can't hear her, and can barely feel her as his back hits the gravel, his head scraping against the stone.

It is too easy for them, he thinks past the fog.

Alastor grabs his wrists, re-ties them together— too tight, and Icarus swallows hard against the pain.

He is left there in the rain for what feels like hours, and then he is pulled, stones tearing across the skin on his back, tearing his clothes and bruising his bones.

"...Execution?"

"Quickly."

"Tonight?"

"...Three... morning."

He chokes, and can barely cough the blood from his windpipe.

Elise pushes him onto his side, as discreetly as she can, and glass tears his arm.

He coughs red onto the ground, takes short, strangled breaths, and blinks slowly, his eyes unable to focus.

"...hurts," he manages.

"I—"

Her voice is only there a second, and then it is gone again, but it is different now.

He hears it: the grief, even in the one word, and it makes him shudder. It makes him want to push her away, and she feels it.

"No," she says.

"It's not fair to you—" His face scrapes against the pavement, and he shuts his eyes, fighting the urge to scream. *"Go."*

"No."

"Zahra, please."

A stone tears across his throat.

"You asked me to stay."

"I shouldn't have. I don't want you to."

Large metal doors open, and he is yanked from the ground, pulled over a bump, and thrown back onto it, his head colliding with the concrete floor, leaving red behind it.

The girl's heart nearly stops.

"I'm not leaving you."

"Please, Zahra," he cries. *"You've already done more than I ever should have asked."*

"No."

"I don't want you at the very end. I want you safe. I want you to remember me while I was alive."

"Michael—"

"Don't make me push you away. Don't let that be how this ends."

"It isn't going to end—"

"Zahra."

Time slows for both of them, and when he opens his eyes he can see her again, nearly doubled over with the pain she feels in her chest.

"It's okay, Zahra."

"No, it isn't," she says. *"But I can... I can—"*

"You shouldn't have to." Elevator doors open, close, and they are headed down, in pitch darkness. His head pulses. *"I can't handle being something that breaks you, Zahra. I can't. That'd be a thing so much worse than death."*

"You're not going to…"

His hand finds hers— light, and delicate, and warm— and she realizes she is lying.

She stops, takes a broken breath, and clenches her other fist, a sob breaking from her lips.

"Just a little longer. Please. Just until…"

"He'll need another dose," Alastor says. "Get him through the next five hours without coming out of it."

"Paralytic, Myon?"

"Yes."

Another needle, and Icarus thinks that death might be better.

"Just until it's time," Zahra pleads. *"If you want me to go then, I will. But not yet. Don't make me leave you yet."*

"That's fine," he whispers, and the doors open again, giving way to more darkness, and he is going to die.

He is going to die alone.

He is going to die with everyone who he was supposed to trust pinning him to the ground, and he always knew it could happen, always suspected it would, but now he is here, and the cold ground does not soothe him, and there is no grass, and he wonders why he ever wanted any of it, and then realizes that it doesn't matter; that in five hours, electricity or poison or fire will take what is left of him, and he is terrified.

A steel door opens, and he is placed behind it.

They do not bother to tie him in place, when they go, and they do not need to. His broken body is long past the point of fighting back now.

Zahra moves toward him when they are gone, unable to see, and hesitates, her hands hovering over his tired form.

"Can I help?" she asks, and he swallows hard.

"Yes."

She puts her hands on him lightly, rolling him off of his face, unfolding him. She lies him on his back, bends his knees a little, and rests his head in her lap, brushing his hair from his eyes.

Her touch is so gentle that it makes his stomach ache.

"Is this okay?" she asks, and he moves his head a little in response, chills spilling over his spine as she takes his hand again.

"Zahra?" he asks.

"Hm?"

His eyes search for her, pointlessly, in the darkness, and light breaks behind them. Colors, patterns— he used to trace them as a child, in the darkness of his bedroom; a distraction from the blackness.

"Can we pretend, just a little while?" he asks, a strangled breath escaping his lips. *"Just a few minutes?"*

"Pretend?" she asks, her voice frail.

"That we're okay," he says. *"That you're just here, and we're just... I don't know—"*

"We're okay," she whispers, running one hand over the side of his face. *"You're okay."*

He eases at her touch, lets his eyes fall shut, and— hesitantly— opens his mouth to speak.

"C...can you..." He clears his throat, fighting hard against the drugs pulsing through him. "Can you... hear... m-m-me, like this?"

Zahra nods, tears streaming from her eyes at the sound of his voice; his *real* voice, tired and frail as it is now.

"I can hear you, love."

"Love," he repeats, wetting his cracked lips and tasting iron. "Why?"

"Because that's what you are," she says and the words sit for a moment, in his mind, and his stomach, and his chest, before becoming too much.

The only response he can manage is to move his thumb across the back of her hand, and it takes almost more strength than he has.

"You have a beautiful voice," she adds. *"I missed hearing it."*

"I... I m-missed you, this last week. M...missed talking to you, I..."

"I missed you too." She tries not to think of the weeks to come, tries not to think of the silence. *"You weren't in Morta, were you?"*

"N-no, not... Not the whole time... I... There were Saenks in the city, it was bad."

"I heard a bit about it in Trellis, from Bellamy, I..." She pauses, clears her throat.

She was worried, but she cannot say that now. Not here. Not when she is supposed to be okay.

"It's so dark in here," she breathes, changing the subject. *"You know I was afraid of the dark until I was fifteen?"*

"Sixteen," he counters.

"We're pathetic," she says, and he laughs— really laughs, despite how quiet it is, despite the pain that it causes him, and the tears in his eyes.

"I kn-know," he says, coughing. "How did-did you get over it?"

She raises one hand in the air between them, sparks a small fire, and forces a smile across her lips.

Such a worthless skill here, she thinks, but the boy looking up at her disagrees.

He looks at her like a miracle; like she might have the whole world in her hand, smiling, studying her eyes as if he is trying to memorize them, not bothering to fight the tears in his own.

"Firefly," he whispers, and something between a laugh and a sob breaks from her chest.

"Leech."

"Traitor."

She laughs again, and he watches her with a smile, gripping her hand as tightly as he can manage.

"Spooky ghost boy."

"M-my word, no—"

The light dies, a dreadful laugh escapes her lips, and she presses his hand to them, kissing it once, gently.

"I can't pretend," she whispers.

"I know."

"I'm going to miss you."

"Want me to haunt you?" he asks, and she shakes her head, not having the strength to laugh.

"I want you to rest."

"I don't w...want to rest anymore."

Her breath is heavy, strained with the same cries that choke his voice.

"You're Grim," she whispers, as if it is a plea. *"Tell me what comes next. Tell me if... Will I see you again? Is there another life, past this one? Can I find you there?"*

"I don't..." He clears his throat, not having the heart to tell her how little he knows. "I think... I think we can find each other anywhere."

"Yeah?"

"I could stay in the inbetween," he whispers. "In M-morta... I could wait for you."

"I want you to rest."

"And I want *you,*" he whispers. "I want... I want to know I'm going to talk to you again... And... Wander this place, that place, just... just a little while, I... There are worse things than that. The sky is clear in Morta, I'll watch the stars till then, if that's what it comes to."

"*Michael*—"

"It'd be *fine*, Zahra—"

"*Michael.*"

He stops, his body shaking, becoming more weighted and less useful with every moment, and too suddenly, he cannot speak for the pain in his throat.

"*I don't want that for you.*"

It shouldn't be like this, he thinks; it shouldn't be off and on, and it shouldn't set in all at once. Too many drugs fighting inside of him. Too much.

He never once valued his voice until it was stolen.

"*It's getting bad again,*" he whispers. "*It's...*"

He winces, tightening his grip on her hand without meaning to, and Zahra looks down at it, her eyes heavy.

"*I thought she gave you the... If she gave you another dose of the paralytic, you wouldn't...*"

A cry of pain, quiet whimpering, and suddenly her mind is elsewhere, the familiarity aching in her bones.

"*Shh,*" she whispers, holding him close. "*Shh, I've got you.*"

She lies down beside him, wraps an arm around his torso, and holds him close, her face nuzzled beside his, resting on one of her hands.

It hurts so badly that his teeth chatter, but she is safe, and so he relaxes, revelling in the pain while he still has it, trying to feel all the life inside of him; trying to feel her, trying to feel held.

He moves one hand slowly up to his chest, feeling his heartbeat: too fast, too out of rhythm, but alive. He feels his own chest rising, falling, breathing, and then he moves his hand to her shoulder, rests it there, and closes his eyes.

Time drains away in silence.

He thinks of William here; he thinks of all the Grim that have been left in the dark, drugged, awaiting their death month after month with no one beside them, and thinks that maybe there is nothing else.

He thinks he might see the symphony, and that the conductor might be wickedness afterall. That the void might be nothing more than a void, that the spirit he felt there might have never been anything but his own, and that he should have cursed it less.

He thinks that maybe the voice of the Wind has never been anything more than the voice of his father, but he prays for his father anyway, not knowing.

He wants him now, thinks that somehow he could make it less scary, just like he always did with everything else.

He tries to reach for him, and finds nothing. Then he thinks that maybe his mind is broken. He realizes he has not seen a single Mortum in all of Karneji, and wonders what they have done to him— why they couldn't do it sooner—

No, he does not want that.

Icarus, his mother said. He thinks now, that that is who he is, that that is all he will ever be. He wonders how he lost everything, and the loneliness of the question eats into his b ones.

"Zahra?" he whispers, and he is met with silence. *"Zahra, are you..."*

He moves his head slightly, lifts it from the floor, and stares into the darkness around him with trembling hands.

It couldn't have been five hours already. It couldn't have gone so fast.

Surely she would not leave without saying goodbye. *Surely.*

"Zahra..." he says again, but he is alone, and he is still alone when the elevator doors open down the hall, when the footsteps are moving toward him, when there is already a noose around his—

Elise kneels beside him with her heart in her throat, touches the back of his head and feels blood.

There is hardly any movement in his body, now; hardly any warmth. The pain is dull, his nerves unable to continue firing at the rate they have been, and he does not even realize he is dying; only that suddenly, everything is less, and he is tired.

She tilts his head up slightly and pours water into his mouth, but he doesn't swallow it.

"Please," she whispers. "Come on, wake up, *please.*"

CHAPTER SEVENTY-SIX

I carus opens his eyes, and he is clean.

There is light in his eyes, and breath in his lungs, and a book in his hands. A thin blanket is tugged up over his legs. He runs one trembling hand over it, recognizing it from all the years before, and then looks up to see a hand on his shoulder.

"Icarus," his mother says. "Are you okay?"

He blinks a few times, looks around at his living room, and sees Anemos and Cole asleep on the floor.

"Why... Why wouldn't I be?"

He glances out the window, sees that the sun has already set, and realizes there are tears in his eyes.

He doesn't remember, at first.

"You were crying," she says, her voice soft.

"Oh," he responds. "I'm... I'm sorry."

"You don't need to be—"

"I was just... I was having the worst dream. I..." He blinks a few times, swallows back tears, and Aliya places a hand on his shoulder.

"What was it about?"

He looks down at his palm, and there is no scar.

Looks at his friends, and they are still there.

He sees his father in the dining room, drinking coffee too late in the night, reading, trying not to look too concerned.

"Nothing," he said. "Nothing... Nothing important."

"Well, if you need to talk, you know I'm here."

"Thank you," he said, his voice still tired from sleep. "Thank... Thank you, I—"

"Should I turn this out?" she interrupts.

She gestures at the lamp in the corner of the room, casting dim, warm light over all of them, and he shakes his head.

"No, no, I..."

Sixteen.

"Okay," she walked over to him, wrapped her arms around his shoulders, and hugged him tight, kissing his temple. "I love you, kiddo."

"I love you too."

"Are you sure about the lamp?" she asked, and he looked over at it, watching it flicker with the wind outside the house.

"Yes, I'm sure."

"But you're going to sleep, aren't you?"

His unconscious body is placed in a firm leather chair, strapped against it, and he does not even feel it.

The room is cold, and Elise watches, sick.

Another strap. Desperate attempts to keep his fragile frame from breaking when the energy meets it.

He stares at the dim lamp in front of him with tears in his eyes.

"N-no," he says softly. "No... I... I'm not..." He chokes on the words, swallows hard. "I'm not ready to..."

"It's almost three a.m.," she says, and the words, spoken with such care, make his stomach start to twist.

"But I'm not ready."

"You could just try tonight," Aliya said softly. "Since your friends are over."

Icarus breathed slowly, still tired, and held tightly to the book in his hands.

"And if you get scared, you can just turn it back on."

He looked back at the window and nodded, even though he was not comfortable.

"Okay."

"Okay?"

A thick piece of wood between his teeth, metal clamped on around his head, and his eyes do not open, his hands do not move.

The metal door swings open again, and Alastor steps into the room, several files and a key in his hand.

He inserts it into the machine at the edge of the room and turns it on nonchalantly, as if it might be an old car.

Icarus' breath caught in his throat.

Too embarrassed to say no, he nodded again.

"Okay—"

His mother turned out the light, and the words died on his lips; died with a sharp breath of fear that *she* did not hear.

She walked back over to him, kissed the top of his head, whispered— once more— that she loved him, and then left the room.

Anemos stood and clicked the light back on not twenty seconds later.

Charles steps back into his office at two-thirty-seven, sits a lantern down on the table, and walks over to the window, looking out at the city with heavy eyes.

The guards have only started to quiet the people; have only started to regain peace—

The light dies.

He turns around quickly and takes a step back toward the lantern but before he reaches it, he is stopped. A hand grabs his wrist and twists it around behind his back so quickly that he does not even feel the needle sink into his skin. He is shoved to the ground, spilling the alcohol he held across the floor.

He coughs, the air knocked out of him, and rolls over, but when he does, a dagger meets his throat.

"Move," a voice says, "and I won't hesitate to cut it."

All of the blood drains from Charles' face as realization sets in, and a heavy breath passes his lips.

"Anemos?" he asks. "What are you doing?"

"When is the execution?" Anemos asks, pressing the blade just close enough to break skin, a thin line of blood left in its wake. "*Swiftly?* I imagine that's electrocution?"

Charles falls silent, and Anemos deepens the cut, raising his voice.

"Answer me!"

"Three," Charles gasps. "It's... Yes, electrocution."

"And you can cut the power from here, yes?"

"Yes."

"Do they have a backup supply?"

"Yes, but we have override—"

"Tell me how to do it," he says. "Quickly, tell me how to do it."

"Anemos, he's *Grim*."

"And he's taken better care of me than you *ever* have."

Icarus opens his eyes slowly, tries to swallow, and gags on the wood between his teeth. He is barely present, but he is aware enough to realize where he is, and when he does, he panics, jerking back against the seat.

Jerking back against the seat.

Moving.

He stills, glancing over at Alastor and Elise— their backs turned away from him— without moving anything but his eyes.

He moves his hand slightly, and tears flood his vision, just as Alastor shuts the door and looks back at him, eyes sick with anger and pleasure.

"He wakes," he says, and Icarus bites down on the wood. "I worried you'd already died."

The man pulls a chair up across from the boy, closer than is comfortable, and puts a hand on his knee.

"I wanted to talk to you first, and look, we've got..." He glances up at the clock on the wall, eyebrows raised. "Ten minutes, before I'm authorized to..."

Icarus looks at the man with disdain, fights the urge to jerk his leg away, and stays silent, despite the fact that he feels he probably does not *have* to.

"Do you know how many executions I've performed, Icarus?" Alastor pauses, as if waiting for a reply, and then shakes his head. "Neither do I. Although, I've actually not done many electrocutions on your kind. The last one was... I don't know when. A girl, about your age, maybe younger."

Through the pain, he thinks of Shannon.

"Turned it up high that day, because I wanted to go home, and she was dead in a minute flat, right where you sit."

His stomach twists, and Alastor watches, unflinching.

"Her eyes popped out about forty-five seconds in, and she managed to break her spine, but that... That was swift, Icarus." He moves his hand slightly, just enough to frighten the younger man— taught, for years, that even a gentle touch could mean the death of a soul.

"This will not be, and I want to warn you of that, because they've all told you it will be fast, and Charles told your father you wouldn't suffer, but you're going to. And do you want to know why?"

A quiet cry escapes his mouth, his whole body trembling, and Alastor's lips tighten.

"It's because you're a man to me, Icarus."

He reaches forward, grabs Icarus hard by his jaw, and he does not fight.

"All these years," he says, "and I've never understood their hatred for Grim. You know that? I mean, I see you for what you are, but... You don't hate a Saenk for being evil. It's a Saenk. I can't judge a thing for its nature any more than I judge myself."

Fingernails dig into the side of his face, and the red of his eyes grows deeper.

"But you, Icarus. You're so fucking special, you know that?"

His chest starts to shake, hard, and soft whimpers escape between his teeth, tears streaming down his face.

A scared child, still, begging wordlessly for the man to stop.

"I hated you without knowing, because I didn't need to know *this* to know you were fucking... God, Icarus. You tried so hard to convince us all you were worth something, it was *pathetic*. I mean, there comes a time when you have to realize you're not wanted, but you just never did."

Alastor looks at him for a long moment, and then laughs.

"Was it worth it, kid?"

Icarus digs his fingernails into the leather.

"You convinced the Outskirts boy, but he's gone. You convinced Anemos, my wife, your mother, and none of them are here for you now. You convinced your father, and that killed him."

Icarus' eyes widen— change— as soon as the words are spoken, and Alastor stops, laughs under his breath.

"Oh, I'm sorry. You missed that," he says, and Icarus begins to sob, loud, heavy, out of control. "That's what he gets, loving an abomination like you."

Some words are too cruel to be uttered, too cruel to be heard; some events too dreadful to ever be repeated.

In Karneji, Alastor's words, said so casually, become a barrage so great that everything they touch burns away.

The light in Icarus' eyes dies away before he has even started.

"You know what they tell us about your kind, Icarus?" Alastor asks. "They tell us not to kill you in the city, because your blood— even your *blood* is cursed. They say it will bring harm to any place it touches."

The boy barely listens, his chest— the heart inside of it— breaking.

His father is gone. His father is *gone.*

"I've always believed that to be superstition, but now, seeing *you.*" Alastor lets his face go, walks across the room, and runs his hands over the machine, looking up at the clock. " *Two* families, Icarus?"

He twists the dial, barely, for no more than a second, and Icarus' body jerks back against the chair, shock running through it like fire, before being let free, still spasming.

"That was one," he says, "We'll get it to ten, but we're going to take our time. Let's go through this, for a minute. You lost *two* families. *Two* sets of parents. Your sister... Had a bit of fun with her earlier this year, as well. Gone, now. Came here looking for you... I'm assuming. Reminded me of you, and, given that you told Ralph you picked your name... What name did she use for her brother? Michael?"

Another shock, level one, and he starts to scream, gripping the chair.

"Dead, now. Traded her for access to Morta." Icarus' cries grow louder, his spirit breaking. "Should have stayed in Trellis, but she came looking for *you.*"

Shock.

"So, I think you see why I hate you, yes? I think you see the..."

Icarus blinks rapidly, unable to think, unable to breathe.

"...Hypocrisy, yes? Pretending you're better than me when you kill everything you touch? Pretending to be virtuous when you knew the best thing you could do for this world would be to drive a knife through your own..."

"You'll be mine," the darkness whispers, and he does not care; he does not even acknowledge the voice, although he believes it.

"You really thought you could protect him?"

The words bring him back into focus, unfurling a fire in his veins.

Another shock, worse this time, and the wood splinters in his gums.

"That's three. Same setting we used on Anemos, last time he was here... God, I don't know what you see in that boy, he's more pitiful than *you.* I mean, do whatever you want to him, he's *silent.*"

Another shock, and suddenly, it does not matter that Icarus has never had an ounce of malice— an ounce of violence— in his veins.

He does not even notice the searing pain that shoots through his mind as it battles against the drugs; only thinks anger, only hears himself screaming, only sees the man slam back against the wall behind him, and feels the leather around his wrists tear.

His mind is broken, by then.

Nothing to live for, he thinks; nothing left, and yet, he does not care.

Alastor tries to stand, and cannot, held to the ground much like the Saenk in the city.

When Icarus pulls the wood from between his teeth, he tastes blood. He claws at the braces around his torso, and busts the ones around his legs.

The power dies, leaving only one dim red emergency light.

He pulls himself up from the chair.

Icarus staggers, unsteady, spitting on the floor as he catches himself on the machine. He stares at the man with heavy, spotted eyes, sick long before he makes it over to him.

The devil is alive, he thinks, and it is all he thinks as he pulls the dagger from the older man's waist, the small object almost too heavy to lift.

It is all he thinks as he drives it into his chest, and rips it free, more times than he should, more times than he needs to or means to.

In truth, the boy hardly knows what he is doing; he only realizes, when he is finished, that he has held the door shut— that he is covered in the other man's blood, his knees resting in a puddle of gore; but the realization is that of a nightmare, too much to take.

And still, he does not feel safe, staring down at the corpse like it might move, or resurrect, just to cause another moment of pain.

He looks over at the chair behind him, and peels the body from the floor.

Not in his right mind, barely able to think.

The man's head falls forward, resting against his chest, and he shudders, dropping him out of panic.

Alastor, he manages to think. Alastor. A man he's known since he was just a child.

A man, dead by his hands.

There is too much blood.

He pulls the man up again— pulls Alastor up again, and he does not even realize he is screaming.

He is still somewhere between his living room and the cell, and Cole is still dead at his feet, and his parents lie dead in front of him, and his sister is dead and gone and dead again and Anemos wants to kill him, and they *all* want to kill him, and it is too much and he killed the only man that ever really cared, and there is too much blood, too much fire, and he is not sure he remembers doing it, but he is terrified—

And there is still thunder, loud, in the distance.

He still flinches, hearing it, and it makes sense, because his head has not ached like this in twelve years.

It has *never* ached like this.

And soon he is on the ground, his back pressed against the wall, and he is desperate, but too afraid to pray.

"I d-didn't mean to," he cries. "I didn't..."

"I have never blamed you, Icarus."

Ten minutes pass, and Elise stands alone in the east wing of the Facility, staring at the electric chair in front of her with one hand pressed in front of her mouth and nose, trying to block out the smell of blood that permeates the air.

Alastor sits upright, strapped in, his head hanging limply on his shoulders, and his clothes stained a deep red.

Blood drains onto the seat underneath him, dripping down to the floor, almost black in the dim red light of the room.

She takes the radio from her hip and clicks it on with one shaking hand.

"Elise, here," she mutters. "Copy?"

Anemos holds the radio up to Charles, hesitant, and he swallows hard before responding.

"Copy," he says. "Is something wrong?"

"The Reaper is..." Static breaks the line, and Anemos leans forward, eyebrows furrowed.

"Elise?"

"He's not here, Myon. He... I'm sorry, something's happened..."

"He's not there?" Charles asks, static breaking his voice.

She lifts the radio back up to her lips with trembling hands, tears falling from her eyes.

"No, sir. He..." Her breath catches. "Alastor is dead."

Anemos' features darken, and Charles looks up at him with concerned eyes, struggling past half a paralytic to reach up and take the radio from his hand.

"The Reaper's escaped, Myon."

"Did you see where he went?"

She hesitates a moment, thinking back to the door, nearly torn from its hinges. Icarus' eyes met hers for only one short moment before they turned away, heavy and guilty and dark.

"No, Myon. I was in the west wing, when it... I'm sorry."

"Come home," Charles says. "I need you to come home."

"And what of Alastor?" she asks.

"Alastor will be dealt with. Come back to the city, now."

"Yes, Myon."

The static cuts, and Charles sits the radio down, looking back at his son with heavy eyes.

"Go to your mother," he says, and Anemos looks up from the floor, his eyes red.

"What?"

"Go to your mother," he repeats, his voice breaking. "Please. Just..."

"But I—"

"You're forgiven," Charles says, and Anemos freezes, too confused to speak. "God, did you think I'd execute you Anemos? You're my..." He stops, sick, and shakes his head. "Just go."

Half an hour later, Anemos knocks on the door to Icarus' home, and it is almost enough to break him.

Jack is gone, Icarus is gone.

Ursula opens the door and meets his eyes with a haze over her own.

"Anemos?" she asks, her voice strained. "What's the matter?"

"It's Alastor, Mom."

He relays the information as well as he can, and as he does, she changes.

"Gone?" she asks. "He's gone?"

Anemos nods, fighting back tears in his own eyes as he watches hers.

"Yes, he's gone." A sob breaks free from her lips, so sudden that it almost startles him, and he takes her hands. "Are you... Hey, hey, you're okay..."

Her cries are too heavy to subdue, so he holds onto her instead, running one hand carefully over her back.

"Mom..."

"Come home," she cries. "Please."

The words are all it takes for him to know that her shoulders fall with relief, just as his did, upon hearing the news.

He swallows hard, nodding against her neck.

"I will," he whispers. "I will. It's okay."

"I'm so sorry, Anemos. For every day, for your friends—"

"It's okay," he repeats. "You're safe now. We're safe."

"No one else," she says. "I promise, no one else will ever... I'll be better."

"Mom," he cries, pulling back just enough to see her. "It's *okay.*"

"I know," she whispers. "I know, I just... What happened? How did he die?"

"Icarus killed him," Anemos states, and the words silence her.

She stares at him, her hands shaking, and only speaks when rain begins to pour around them.

"Come inside," she says, and he nods, stepping through the door. "Come in... You're okay?"

"I'm okay," he says, and then, more softly: "I'm coming home."

CHAPTER SEVENTY-SEVEN

"*I*t's just a spill, Cy, It's nothing to worry about."

"We're going to be late," Alastor said, starting to pale. "If we're late—"

"Well, that isn't Cyrus' fault, is it?" Charles snapped, and the younger boy in the corner of the room lowered his face.

"Just go without me," he said. "I think I can handle a bit of glass."

"Apparently not."

"Alastor," Charles forced, and the addressed clenched his fists. "Just go."

"Know your place."

"Please," Cyrus begged, his voice fragile. "Please don't fight."

"We aren't—"

"Alastor," Charles repeated, and his brother stopped, his lips tight.

"What, Charles?"

"I spilt it, I'm late, you just take Cyrus and I'll handle whatever wrath incurs, okay? It's fine."

"That's not fair," Cyrus whispered, and Charles looked at him with pained eyes. "You both go, this is my mess, I'll... I'll deal with it. I have to change anyway, see? I've gotten it on my clothes."

"Cyrus—"

"Father will be mad? I don't care."

"I'm not going to leave you here alone. Not after last night—" The words came too fast, and he did not even realize he had said them until he regretted it.

Cyrus paled.

"What the hell is that supposed to mean?" Alastor asked. "You're saying he's not safe alone, now?"

"No, no, I'm fine—"

"I don't think I can handle another psych case in the family."

Charles looked up, at that, his eyes cold, and shook his head.

"Don't," he said, but Alastor rattled on anyway, too afraid not to.

And the fighting grew louder, and Cyrus' chest hollowed out, and before either of them had a chance to realize, the boy stood and walked away, slamming the door behind him.

They did not even suspect it was a last, but Charles ran after him anyway, and when he was gone, Alastor cleaned up the wine, and broke down on the living room floor.

The air is cold, the morning after the Reaper's capture, and the Higher-class sector is quiet. There is rain pouring down over Karneji, a light mist in the city.

Fog on the Palace windows.

Charles picks glass from his office floor.

He tosses the shards in an old waste basket, rolls his neck in an attempt to stretch it, still stiff from the night before, and glances back at the window behind him.

It reminds him of Cyrus.

It reminds him of them.

He does not avert his eyes until he hears the Palace doors creak open in the distance, the noise barely audible, even in the quiet of the building.

Not Anemos, he thinks, not Ursula.

He steps out of the office with his hand clasped tightly around the hilt of the blade on his waist, and makes it to the top of the stairs before the door shuts again.

When he does, he freezes in place, his heart like a stone in his chest.

"I'm not going to leave him here," Jack said. "He's just a child. I'll stay before I leave him, if you think that will be necessary."

"Of course not," Charles said, glancing at the frightened boy, sitting— nearly paralyzed with fear— on the wall behind them. Six years old, so thin Charles could see his bones through his shirt. "No, just... Ignore them. I'll handle them."

"I don't want to let them around him, either."

"Well, no. Can't imagine he'd do well in the defense transport, either way." Charles paused, watching him with careful eyes. "You want him to travel back with me."

"I wasn't going to ask."

"That'll be fine," he said, rubbing his face. "I... That'll be fine."

A minute later, he knelt down in front of the boy, who would not meet his eyes.

About Anemos' age, he thought, and too petrified to meet a man's eyes.

"Hey," he said softly. "We're gonna get you out of here, okay? Get you somewhere safe?"

The boy looked up hesitantly, trying to catch a glimpse of the man, but never letting his eyes rest anywhere.

Charles held out a hand, and Michael jerked away, trembling violently.

"Hey," the older man said. "Hey, you're safe."

It took nearly an hour to coax the child to the carriage, but Charles never forced him, never pulled him or grabbed him, only spoke— ever so gently— until the boy agreed to follow him. When they got to the transport, though, he still refused to get in, silent and hesitant, gripping the hem of his shirt so tightly his hands bled.

Jack turned the corner, sent from the defense transport— which was growing highly impatient— and sat down in front of the child, pushing his shoulder length hair back out of his face.

"Having trouble?" he asked, his voice not showing any sign of stress.

"Oh, just a bit. Got him here, so... At this rate, in six hours or so, we might leave."

Jack laughed softly, folding his arms.

"Six hours?" he asked. "My word, child, you sound almost as stubborn as me."

"Well, I never said that."

"You scared, kid?" Jack asked, and the boy looked up at him for only a second. "I understand. I wouldn't want to get in a transport with this big tall cape man either." He glanced back at Charles just in time to catch him rolling his eyes, and then turned back to the boy, resting his hands on his knees. "But I'm going to ride with you, too, and I'm your friend, so you know you can trust me."

Michael shifted slightly, looking over at the carriage behind them with nervous eyes.

"And you know, you can see a lot from inside, when it gets moving. It's a big world, and a long journey home, so... Lots to see. We can just watch it, and then you don't have to worry about talking to us anymore. Just climb in, and we'll get you... Here, see?"

He pulled the jacket from his own back, draped it around the boy's shoulders, and watched as he tugged it tighter around himself.

"More comfortable, yeah? Yeah. You know, keep it, you'll grow into it."

The boy looked up a little more steadily, and Jack smiled at him brightly, pushing his hair back again.

"So," he said, "Here's the deal, kid, is that I told Big Spooky back here that I'm not leaving you behind."

"Charles," he said. "My name is Charles."

"And Big Spooky's friends make fun of him when he's late, but he's too in love with me to leave me behind here."

"By the dragon—"

The boy laughed once, quietly, and Charles stopped, sticking his hands in his pockets.

"So," Jack repeated. "We need to be going, if that's okay with you. I'll stay with you, either way, but... You know, I swear that the transport doesn't bite, if you want to try."

"Ei...eith-th-ther w-way?" Michael asked, and Jack stopped and nodded, his eyebrows raised.

"Well you didn't think I would just leave you here? With my jacket?"

Five minutes later, and they piled into the carriage, Charles at one window, Jack in the middle, and the boy at the other.

He pressed his small hands against the glass, and his father put a hand on his shoulder, pointing out things they passed that might be of interest.

They stayed that way, and Charles stayed quiet, watching with an ache in his chest.

Now, Icarus stands in the middle of the Palace with bruised, vacant eyes. His shirt is stained with blood, even though the rest of his body has been washed clean by the rain. His left hand is clenched into a fist, and there is a dagger in his right, but both hands are trembling.

He looks up the stairs, looks at the man in front of him, and grips the blade a little tighter, twisting the fist at his side and watching as Charles staggers backward into the wall, suddenly dizzy, barely able to move.

He approaches him silently, not even looking at him as he slowly scales the Palace steps, his breath heavy and pained, his body and mind still drugged and uneasy.

When he reaches the top, the Guide has been pressed to his knees.

"Charles," he says, and the man flinches at the sound of his voice— the same, but different, harder, and strained. "Charles?"

He does not— cannot— respond, and Icarus bites down on his bottom lip, not wanting any more of it as he raises the dagger to his throat with no intention of violence.

"Will you answer m...me now?"

"What?" Charles forces. "What do you want?"

"I want my father," he says, his eyes burning. "I want m...my... Tell me where he is."

"Go to Morta," the older man says. "You're Grim, go look for him there."

"I can't," Icarus says. "I... I can't..." He releases him, the dagger still to his throat, and Charles falls back onto the floor, gasping for air. "Just take m..me to him, please, I... I just need to see him."

"He's *dead,* Icarus."

"Then what harm will I do?" he laughs, tears streaming from his eyes. "Please, Charles, I... I'll go away after that, I... I promise you won't... You w-won't see me back here ag-g-gain, just—"

"I *can't—*"

His voice is cut off by a scream— so loud, so angry, and so grieved that he almost thinks he's imagined it, but the sound knocks him back further, terrified, pulling his sword from its holster.

"Oh," Icarus laughs, his face breaking, his nose bleeding. "Oh, you're going to fight me now? You're going to... Look at me! Look me in the eyes."

Charles looks up, and another wave of wrongness moves through him; nausea, dizziness, and pain down to his core.

"Twelve years," Icarus cries. "Twelve *years* you've known me."

"I've never known you." He stands, at the boy's allowance, and holds the blade out by his side, trying to steady himself. "You're *Grim.*"

"And?" he cries. "What else have I ever done, Charles? I d-didn't decide to be *born,* I didn't... Is existence a crime deserving of what you have done to me? Just b-being here? I can't... I tried so hard, for so long... And this thing that I can't even *help... That* is what you judge me on?"

"You would rather me judge your character on a disguise?" Charles asks, his voice strained. "On an act? A mask?"

"What are you—"

"A being of darkness can take many forms, Icarus; even light, but you are not..." He closes his eyes tight, presses his hand to his forehead. "What are you *doing* to me?"

"I know your worthless Code," Icarus spits, his voice cold. "I don't want to hear any more of it."

"And yet you try to convince me you are good."

"Better than that rotten thing."

"It isn't—"

"Do you not see how grotesque you are?" he asks, and a cry chokes the words. "Def-f-fending ink and... and papyrus, and opinion, as if it is a *man*, while living things die at your feet? Defending a *lie*."

"It isn't a lie."

"You took m...my faith and turned it into a guillotine."

"You have never had any faith, Icarus." The words are a dull ache in his chest, heat behind his eyes. "Not in anything good."

"I..." He shakes his head, clenches his fist. "You're right, Charles. You've never known m...me."

"Perhaps you really believed the mirage presented to you, but that doesn't change anything, Reaper. Darkness is darkness, no matter how it may masquerade."

"It is," he says. "It is, and you... you are still wrong."

A cry escapes his lips with the words, some semblance of who he was yesterday, and he lowers his face, taking a strained breath through the sobs that shake him.

"You are *wrong*," he repeats. "Wrong to th-think we... deserve this, wrong to teach children hatred, and *fear*, before they can ev-even..."

The cries grow heavier with every passing moment, and Charles' spirit grows wearier, his hands weak.

"You m-made my mother hate me, you took my home, and m-my friends and... Just b-because I was *born*, just because I was... And I don't even hate you for it, because I could have been you. I *have* been you, but you... You are *killing* people, Charles; with fire, yes, but with so m-m-much more than that. You've killed m...me, even as I stand before you, and The Ordinem is... You're better than this. You can see it, I kn-know you..."

"I see a demon," the man says, "desperate to believe he can be something else."

"And I s...see a man, so controlled by f-fear... that he does not even *see* the shadows to which he clings."

The words sink into his chest, grip his stomach, but his face does not change, not until he is released from whatever grasp the boy previously had on his spirit.

Icarus steps back, standing on the tips of his toes to wrestle a sword down from its place on the wall, and casting the dagger aside.

"You want to fight?" he asks, his voice rough, tired. "Fight. You did so well last time."

"I didn't try last time. It was a *test*."

"A test?" he asks. "I thought it was a *learning* opportunity."

"For the rest of them," Charles says. "It hardly matters, now."

"You were trying to trigger a response," Icarus breathes. "M-my word, you... You were trying to catch me then, too."

"I had nothing to do with it. A few members of the Higher-class were suspicious... It doesn't matter."

"Did you expect me to m...melt the hilt of my sword, Charles?" he asks. His voice is cold, stained with pain Charles cannot understand. "Or did you think my eyes would go dark, like my sister's?"

Charles stops, pale.

"What are you talking about?"

"S-surely you didn't ex...pect me to rip your soul from your body by *accident.*"

"Rosemarie?" he asks, his chest aching. "Rosemarie was your sister?"

"You've taken... *everything,* from m...me," Icarus says, gripping the sword in his hand a little tighter, tears still streaming from his eyes. "*Everything.*"

"I didn't—"

"I wasn't trying, either," he says. "I f-figured, you know? Figured it'd get turned back around on m...me, somehow."

He closes his eyes, suddenly, and Charles' body goes rigid.

"M-my god, I d-don't..." He winces, pressing the palm of his hand to his forehead. "Let's just get it over with."

Charles' body is released, and he stumbles forward slightly, sick, but he only dodges as Icarus stabs in his direction, suddenly unsure of the weapon in his hand.

Icarus swings around behind him, fully aware that he could plant a foot in the center of his back and knock him to the ground, just as easily as he can still him with nothing besides his mind, but he does not do either; only watches, pain tearing through his body and grief holding his throat.

"You're slow," he says, and Charles jabs in his direction, meeting the boy's blade with a loud clang.

"Paralytic," he says simply, aware that he should be losing this battle, his body too heavy to fight back. "Hardly Enthroproxan."

Icarus slides both swords around quickly, jamming the hilt of his own into the other man's rib hard before pulling it back, swinging it nonchalantly.

"Hardly."

Their swords meet again, three times, between them, before Icarus twists Charles' loose from his hand, letting it fall to the floor.

He looks at it only a moment before kicking it back toward the man, pacing as if he might be training him.

"And what of the Wind?" he asks. "W-what of Inanis? Can it lend you no aid in a cause so n-noble as killing the devil? No strength?"

The Guide's face burns with humiliation, his chest tight, and Icarus laughs, but there is no humor in the sound.

"Do you w...worship nothing, man?"

"Some faith you have."

Another wave of dizziness, and the man is knocked to the ground again, gasping for air. His vision is so blurred that for a moment he cannot even see what is happening, but then a hand grabs the collar of his shirt, pulls him from the ground, and presses the sword back into his hands, pointed down.

"I don't... claim to have faith any...more."

"Then you never did."

"I want m-my father," Icarus says. "Not to argue, not to harm you... I just want to see him, and then I'll go. Is that... r...really, t-too m...much to ask?"

Charles hesitates, staring at the boy with burning eyes.

"We both know this isn't a f-fair fight—"

He makes an uneven stab at the boy's waist and misses terribly, but still leaves a long slash across his side— leaves Icarus staggering backward, one hand over the wound. But then the boy steps forward again, swinging, leaving a cut under the other man's eye.

"I almost feel sorry for you," he cries, laughing painfully with the words. "You don't even know what you're doing."

Another slash, and Icarus' mind leaves him once more, giving way to spite.

He does not really care to live anymore, but he does not want to die *here;* not by the hands of someone he used to consider a friend.

And so the two swords collide again, over and over, only of them ever really trying for a hit at the other man's body, and it never manages to land one, but it does twist the other blade up and out of Icarus' hand, leaving him watching as it clatters to the floor.

He does not even have time to think before Charles raises the blade to his throat, trembling and out of breath.

Another wave, and Charles' vision goes black.

His back hits the ground, and Icarus takes the sword from his hand, raising it up above him without even thinking—

And then he stops.

Bent to his knees in front of the man on the floor, the ring in his ears is interrupted by the sound of footsteps— two sets, one further than the other.

He looks down at the man below him, who he has released without meaning to, and finds that his eyes are afraid, exhausted.

He thinks of the woman who would take his place— thinks of any of them losing someone else.

He thinks of Cyrus' concern, and thinks that this action will cement the Guide as a hero, cementing the Grim as villains, and he is already retreating when the other boy picks his dagger from the floor.

The blade finds his throat only seconds later.

"Icarus," Anemos says from behind him. "Drop your—"

His sword hits the floor, and his hands rise beside his head in an act of surrender.

"Stand up," he says. "Slowly."

And Icarus obeys, more willing to die than he is to defend himself against *him*.

"I wasn't..." His voice comes out a strangled, frightened whisper, and Anemos' heart sinks into his stomach. "I wasn't going to hurt him—"

"You need to go," he says, trying to make the words harsh instead of desperate. "You need to..."

He is close enough to feel his friend crying, shaking with pain and fear, his body too warm, and he wishes they were alone; he wishes he could pull him close and comfort him, somehow.

He swallows hard, brings his face close, and drops his voice to a hesitant whisper.

"My mom is right behind me, and I need you to go."

"What?"

"Please, Icarus."

The Reaper closes his eyes, his heart in his throat, and takes a sobbing gasp of air.

The world slows to a stop.

"You can't let me go" he whimpers, and Anemos shakes his head.

"I'll be fine," he whispers. "I'll be fine, Icarus."

"No, you... You need to make it look like an accident, at least. Take your aim and strike me somewhere you think I'll recover, if you have to, but you can't just let me go."

"I'm not going to—"

"Anemos," he says, and his voice is firm, despite the chaos; warm, and desperate, and pleading. "You're m-more... m-m-more important to me than... I will *not* live in a world that has taken you. Don't put your blood on m-my hands, please."

The footsteps are closer, now. They both realize.

"I'm going to push you," Anemos whispers. "Tuck your chin."

Ursula turns the corner, and in the same moment, Anemos draws the knife away from Icarus' throat, pushing him— hard— in the center of his back, sending him tumbling down the staircase, unable to catch himself, unable to protect his ribs from the harsh marble underneath them.

It is the distance he needs, but when he lands, he finds himself unable to stand, unable to run, hardly able to breathe for the pain in his body.

"Charles?" Ursula asks, and then, turning: "Anemos?"

Not enough time, he thinks, watching Icarus at the base of the steps. Not enough time to escape; not from her.

He doesn't have any other choice.

He takes one shaky, tearful breath before stabbing the dagger into his own abdomen, and the feeling is a wrong he has not felt before. Death and dread, wrapping themselves around his chest.

He turns back to his mother with his hands still clasped around the hilt, as if he doesn't know whether to leave it in or take it out, as if he is shocked.

"Help..." he chokes, his lips trembling. "Help... Help me..."

Ursula's hands fly up in front of her mouth, and suddenly, the boy on the floor below them does not matter. Vengeance does not matter. Justice does not matter.

Charles' eyes widen, and he pulls himself up from the ground, just in time to keep Anemos from falling onto it.

"Go," he says to Ursula. "Go get a doctor, I'll stay with him."

She nods, still hesitant to turn away, and he swallows hard, watching as blood pools in his son's hands.

"He'll be fine," he says, unsure. "Go."

Icarus does not hear them. He can not hear anything, over the ringing in his ears. Not until he is yanked from the ground by his shirt and pushed to the door, barely able to stand.

"I don't want to see you again," Charles says, opening it and pushing him through the frame. "Do you understand?"

Icarus takes a hold of the door frame, trying to steady himself, and only swallows, unable to speak.

"Y-yes."

"If I found out you've come near him, I'll kill you."

"I under—"

"I hope you're pleased with what you've done to him."

"You kill everything you touch."

"I didn't—"

"I don't want to hear it," he snaps. "I'd kill you here if I didn't think it would kill him, but it's apparent you've deceived him beyond that point, now."

"Stop," Anemos cries, in the distance. "Stop it, Charles."

"What did he—"

"You need to go," Charles says, his voice firm. "He'll be lucky if he lives."

"What did he *do?*" Icarus cries. "What did he—"

The door slams in his face, and the sound is an echo of twenty years earlier so clear that for a second, even Charles feels it.

Of course, Icarus does not, and so, like Cyrus, his mind panics.

His breath comes heavy, and his sobs come fast, out of control.

He has the realization, on the other side of that door, that there is no one there to save him; that he is truly alone, for the first time in years, and that he does not feel safe with anyone— not even himself.

And so, like the other boy, he turns right off the Palace steps, not bothering to walk the path, not bothering to think through where he is going.

Away from town, he thinks; away from anyone else who can make the pain worse, or god forbid, anyone else he might harm.

"He's not safe," Anemos cries, inside. "He isn't..."

His body quakes with the sobbing, and it sends more pain through him, makes the blood come faster.

"Anemos," Charles says. "You need to stop."

"I need to go after him," he cries, trying to pull himself from the ground. "I need to... He's fragile, Charles. He can't... He shouldn't be alone. He shouldn't be by himself."

"Stop, Anemos."

"He would've shifted if he could, he doesn't have anywhere to go, he doesn't—"

Icarus' feet meet the grass, and he folds his arms tightly over his chest, trying, for what it is worth, not to tear at his skin, not to shed any more blood, lest it be cursed.

He looks up at the sky, and it is gray, as it always is. There is a breeze in the air, salt and ice and mist.

It's beautiful, he thinks. He should have come here more often. He should have come here with his father. He should have come with his mother, while she still cared. He should have come with his friends.

"Everything you touch dies."

There are small, purple flowers littering the ground, and he thinks that he'll die, too.

He thinks that there is probably nothing else; thinks that even Morta, even Grim cannot rid him of the guilt, and rage, and grief in his chest.

"They're better off without you."

He thinks that his head hurts, and that he is tired.

He thinks that the ocean will be cold enough to offer him some relief.

He thinks that it could all stop, and that he wouldn't have to hurt anymore, and that somewhere, his father's body is lying, rotting, and so is his sister's, and both—

"Because of you."

He stops, his feet on the edge of a decision. He doesn't know how he made it so far so fast.

A mile, or two, or three, and the ocean is beneath him, and it looks like something that will accept him, like something that might catch him.

It looks like an escape from the hellscape behind him. It looks like the only thing he has, now, so he stares down over the edge.

He tries to imagine how it will feel, if it will hurt, if the impact will kill him, or if he will drown, and he doesn't know, but he isn't sure he cares.

He looks up from the sea, looks at the sun, rising in the east, and closes his eyes, trying to feel the heat on his skin; trying to feel alive, for a moment. He knows he loves it— being alive— just not like this. Not when—

"You kill everything you touch."

And the darkness never seems to quiet down anymore, which is, of course, how it feels every time it speaks.

He lets his hands fall to his sides and thinks it's probably true. He probably is cursed, and abandoned. An abomination, an error, something to be corrected. Something to be hated, and then purged.

Maybe they all are, and he is too bathed in darkness to see it.

Maybe he is too blinded to see the truth.

Maybe he has had this argument with himself every day for six years, and he is ready to stop; ready to be damned, if he's going to be.

Ready to be anything but this.

He opens his eyes, and they are full of tears; tries to swallow, and his throat is too tight.

He wishes they had just left him in Jakara. He wishes he had never been born, so he would not have to have lived, and would not have to die.

He thinks of Cole and Anemos, thinks of the roof, and the stars—

Thinks, mostly, that he could have been happy, but that is a lie.

He thinks of all the nights spent up too long, and all of the studying, and the way he used to love all of it. He thinks of climbing into a bigger bed, and listening to stories, and walking back and forth from school, and his father reading in the corner, and every damn thunderstorm they stayed awake through.

He thinks of his mother saying he was not born to be conquered, and thinks that life may never go lightly on anyone, but it did not have to hurt this much.

He thinks of Inanis, and his stomach twists.

He thinks of Zahra— the fact that she thought he was good without having a reason, even knowing what he was, and he hopes it does not hurt too much.

His absence will hurt less than his presence.

"Everything you touch dies."

And he cannot decide whether he deserves this or not. Maybe not for being Grim— or maybe that is enough.

Regardless, the hatred he feels in his chest pushes him further; slow, hesitant feet, stepping toward something he should not be chasing.

Rest. Bad rest. The kind of rest that haunts everything it touches.

He looks down at the water with every single memory held in his hand, and takes one step forward, one foot landing in open space, when—

"Icarus."

He stops, his breath caught in his throat, and a hand closes around his wrist— one on his shoulder, hesitant.

"Don't touch me," he cries. "Please... P-please don't."

"Step back."

"I don't want to."

"I know," the voice says— gentle, frightened, quiet. "I know you don't, but, if you'd please just talk to me a moment—"

"I don't want to." His breath catches in his throat, and a sob breaks free from his lips. "Please, leave m...me."

"No," he says, and then, after a second of silence: "No, Icarus."

"Please."

"No." Cyrus steps to his side, as carefully as he can, and glances down at the water, his stomach sick. "I'm not going to leave you."

"I can m-m...make you."

"Maybe," he says. "That's... you might, but I'm not going to leave otherwise. Icarus—"

"I killed him," Icarus says. "Alastor. Your brother. I... I killed him."

"I know."

"I don't think I was thinking clearly, I... I didn't think of you, or Charles."

"I'm not sure you had a choice."

"There's always a choice." Icarus' voice is heavy, pained, his feet still gripping the edge of the cliff. "I can't *do* this anymore, Cyrus. I can't... I don't want to."

"I understand how you—"

"If you understood how I felt you wouldn't b...be asking me to stay."

Ursula is sitting on the floor beside her son, watching as the doctor pulls the blade from his skin, when Charles goes suddenly pale, all of the blood draining from his face, and his hands beginning to tremble.

"What is it?" she asks, and he does not even hear her. "Charles?"

He stands, shakes his head, and grabs the rail beside him.

"I'll be back," he says.

"Where are you going?"

"Just a moment, I have to check on something."

"Right now?" she asks, and Anemos winces, gritting his teeth.

"I'll be fine," he says. "Let him go."

"Just a moment," Charles repeats, and when he says it, he is already halfway down the stairs, skipping every other step. "I just... I just need a moment—"

"We're a lot alike," Cyrus says, his voice trembling. "You know that? I really... I couldn't understand you much more than I do."

"And yet you're s-standing here."

"Only by the grace of God," he breathes. "I shouldn't be, love. I didn't want to be either."

"You didn't?"

"Same cliff, a few miles down," he says. "Stepped off at sixteen... I tried."

"But you're still... You're still here."

"And I'm happy," he says, and the words do not sound real. "I mean, by God, not right now, not seeing you like this, and not always, but... I'm okay now, Icarus. The pain doesn't last forever, and you're... I mean, you're only a child. There's so much ahead of you."

"I don't want it," Icarus cries. "I'm sorry, but... We're not all the-the same, Cyrus, I'm... M-maybe I'm just not as strong as you."

"Oh, bullshit," he breathes, a sob escaping his lips. "You're stronger than I ever was, kid. You're talking to me. That's better than I... You know, Charles came calling after me and I just... I didn't even turn around."

"But you're still here," he repeats, breathless. "How... how are you still here?"

"I don't know," Cyrus responds, honestly. "I mean, beyond the surviving... I got help, I found people that wanted to love me— all of me... I realized I was worth something, but I survived that fall..."

"By the grace of God," Icarus repeats.

"Came out of it in Inanis," he says. "I've no idea what pulled me there. I might've done it myself, at the last second, or... Maybe the Wind... I don't know, but... I was there a long time, Icarus. I was too terrified to even think of entering Morta."

"I'm terrified now," Icarus whispers. "I've been there, I've... I've been there, and I'm still so afraid, I don't... There's something wrong with me."

"No," Cyrus says, shaking his head. "No, there's nothing wrong with you."

"I don't know how to do this."

"You don't have to," he says. "I'll help you."

Icarus turns around, his face red, his eyes hazy, and shakes his head, his voice no more than a whisper.

"Are we cursed?" he asks, and the older man shakes his head, pushing the hair from the younger's face.

"No," he whispers, and for some reason, after it all, the word is enough.

Chapter Seventy-Eight

Charles crosses the field in under half the time it took Icarus— horseback, needing an answer, needing to check the place once more, and unable to deny the feeling in his gut.

Pushed, perhaps, by something beyond himself, to the place he has spent two decades avoiding.

When his feet hit the ground, he can barely stand.

He ties the horse to a tree like he used to do on nightmare ridden nights, and walks the rest of the way, not wanting to bring anything else living too close to the edge.

It is strange how a place can suffocate you; how it can hold an event, or a time, or a feeling in the air. It is almost as if it is still happening— like Anemos in Karneji, like Cyrus, here at all.

His feet carry him slowly, weighed down by more than any man should have to carry, and when they crest the top of the hill, they stop.

A heavy black cloak, in the distance. The boy he threatened standing beside it, at the edge of the cliff, like his brother did so many years earlier.

And suddenly, he wants to pull him back.

He wants to beg the boy from Jakara to stop, because in this moment, he cannot see anything but a child, and the cloak beside him, trying to pull him away.

This time, though, the boy turns around.

He says something brief, something Charles cannot hear, looking tired as he does.

So tired, too tired, and then his eyes fall past the cloaked man, and meet his, and do not move.

"Cyrus," Icarus says, the wind blowing like ice against his tear stained face. "Cyrus, it's—"

The cloaked man turns around, twenty years late, already knowing, and his eyes soften on the figure before him— soften even as he pushes Icarus into line behind him, using his body as a shield.

But there is no hatred in the man's eyes, looking at them, no anger— only pain, cold, and deep, and alive.

Charles can't breathe.

He doesn't know what to say— if he should say anything, after everything, but it is Cyrus who breaks the silence, his voice heavy and broken.

"I'm sorry," he says, keeping one hand in Icarus', "for all of the suffering I've caused you, Charles. But if you..." His voice cracks, and he pauses, struggling to breathe. "If you take one more step toward him, I will not hesitate."

Charles only looks at his brother, tears streaming from his eyes, and brings one hand to his face, trying to stifle the sob that breaks free from his lips when his body forces him to breathe.

There is nothing to say, no apology that could possibly be enough, and he only wants to run to him, to hold him like he would have that day, if he had come home.

But he does not deserve even that. He deserves nothing.

He drops his sword and falls to his knees in surrender.

There is a moment of hesitance, and then— driven by a force beyond himself—

Cyrus steps forward, and Icarus watches with heavy eyes as he does.

The man kneels in front of his brother with unsteady hands, and fights the urge to be sick as he flinches in response.

"I'm not going to hurt you," he says, and Charles shakes his head, his spirit breaking.

He is silent for a long moment, and then, with a voice like broken glass:

"I didn't know," he cries, and the words are not an excuse. "I didn't... I swear, I didn't know. If I had known—"

"No more," Cyrus says, and the man stops, all of the oxygen leaving his lungs. "No more, Charles."

Charles looks up, meets his brother's eyes, and finds them full of tears.

"I can't end it," he says, pleading. "But you can."

"I can't—"

"I can't lose anyone else," Cyrus continues.

Charles' eyes fall to the boy behind him, who stands with his hands knotted together, unable to control the cries falling from his lips, and something in his soul dies.

"I'm sorry," he cries, and Cyrus takes his face in his hands, pressing a kiss to his forehead. "I'm so sorry, I didn't—"

"The Wind has been speaking to you since the day you were born, Charles," he says, his voice strained. "Please, stop calling it darkness."

Cyrus leaves the Guide behind, kneeling in the dirt, and returns to the boy at the edge, taking his hands and holding them tightly.

"We should go," he says. "He's waiting for you."

"Waiting for me?" Icarus asks. "Who?"

"Who do you think told me you were in trouble?" Cyrus asks, wiping Icarus' eyes. "He wasn't going to cross without seeing you, one way or the other. He was insistent on that. He didn't want you alone, if you didn't make it, and he didn't want to leave without saying goodbye if you did."

"My father?"

"Your father," he affirms. "Come on, I'll take you to him."

Icarus hesitates, staring out at the beckoning sea beside him, and then turns back, shaking his head.

"Just a m...minute," he says. "I need..."

Cyrus nods, and Icarus steps back, walking unevenly toward the man on the ground.

A man he used to consider a friend, and will never trust again.

"Charles," he says, and the Guide looks up at him, shame in every line of his face. "Anemos will be okay, won't he?"

The man nods, hardly able to breathe, and Icarus takes a step closer.

"Promise me you'll protect him," he says. "You owe me that, if nothing else."

"I promise," Charles forces, and Icarus nods, turning away again. Before he can make it back to Cyrus, though, the man stops him. "Icarus?"

He turns back, his eyes dark.

"Yes?"

"I don't know what Alastor told you, but as far as any of us know, your sister is alive." The words make Icarus' chest ache, even if he doesn't believe them. "We took her to Trellis. She's safe. Kieran made them promise to keep her safe."

His eyes dart over Charles erratically, searching for truth, until finally he turns away.

He returns to Cyrus' side with his hands in fists.

"I'm ready," he whispers.

They are gone a moment later, and Charles walks back alone.

He moves as quickly as he can, buries the confusion he feels as deep as he can, and returns to the Palace with a heavy spirit.

"Did you see him?" Ursula asks, when he makes it back, pale and red. "Icarus. Did you see him?"

"Yes," he says, his voice strained. "He's... He went to the cliff."

Her eyes change slightly, but nothing else.

"The cliff?" she asks. "Did he—"

"Yes," he lies. "He's dead. Icarus is dead."

CHAPTER SEVENTY-NINE

Michael opens his eyes, and Cyrus still has his hand held tightly.

"Are you okay?" he asks, and the boy looks around with heavy eyes.

The skies are clear.

"Dizzy," he mutters. "Kind of nauseous... And my head hurts, and I think m...my ribs are broken."

"We'll get you to a healer," Cyrus says, patting him gently on the shoulder. "Did they give you anything?"

He is pushed along with urgency, despite the calmness of the man's voice.

"They g-gave m...me a lot of Enthroproxan, and some paralytic... Cyrus?"

"Yes?"

"I have a friend, in Trellis, and... I d-don't kn...know how to explain, but I... It's like... She's with m...me, usually, somehow, and I can't... I can't feel her now."

"That's completely normal after what you've been through. All your... sensitivities, will be off for a little while—"

"But she's okay?"

"I think it's a safe assumption."

"And I'll... I'll be back to normal—"

"A few days to a few weeks. The Enthroproxan needs to wear off."

"And will the pain go away with that?"

"Most of it, yes," he says. "Just, with time. It's going to take time."

"I have blood on m...my shirt," Michael whimpers, and Cyrus nods, a bit out of breath.

"I know." He pulls off his cloak and wraps it around Michael's shoulders. "I know, love. I'll get you a new one. Just try to stay as calm as you can. The more adrenaline you have, the stronger the Enthroproxan left in your blood will become."

Michael nods, but he thinks the words are pointless. It is impossible to be calm. It's almost impossible to breathe.

He grips the hem of his bloodstained shirt, trying to steady his hands, and stifles a sob, following the man down the long dirt road before them.

It's a familiar path: through the fields with the high grass. Michael remembers it, the further they go.

"Visitation?" he whispers.

Cyrus nods.

"It's where he wanted to be," he says. "It's where he found me. He wanted a quiet place so he could pray without distraction, and said it would do well."

"He always liked the quiet," Michael murmurs. "Cyrus?"

Cyrus turns around again, his eyes soft.

"Yes?"

"I don't know how to face him. I'm not the kid he loved anymore. Th...there's blood all over m...my hands. He knew Alastor. *I* knew Alastor, and I... I'm not innocent, not now. There's no denying that. What if he thinks I'm what they say I am? What if he's afraid of me?"

"Your father loves you," he says. "Don't be afraid. He's just ahead."

They continue to walk in silence, but Michael's mind is loud enough for both of them. He tugs the cloak around him in an effort to calm himself like he has been told to do, but his tears have not ceased since Karneji.

He still tastes blood.

Soon, the small stone visitation building comes into view, and his heartbeat quickens. He wants to run to *and* away from it.

"Cyrus?" he asks again.

"Michael?"

"I'm not ready to say goodbye."

Cyrus turns back, forcing a sad smile.

"We rarely are." He steps toward him and takes his hand, continuing down the path more slowly. "I've been here more than a decade, and I've hardly met anyone that's ready to say goodbye. I've never been ready to say goodbye myself, and I've had more practice than most. But Michael... Look at me."

He does, his eyes burning.

"Goodbyes are a blessing. And you have as much time as you need."

"I need a lifetime," Michael cries. "I need him to read my stories, and teach me how to be. I need mornings with him, and thunderstorms on the porch. But I can't ask for that, c an I?"

Cyrus gives his hand a tight squeeze, and Michael nods.

"It has to be today. It has to be quick, so he doesn't fade like the rest. I know."

"I'll be with you," Cyrus says. "I promise."

It's not enough, but Michael knows there's nothing else the man can offer. Grim may be able to see the dead, but they can't bring them back.

Michael can't bring him back, even if he'd give his life to do it.

Soon, they enter the little building, passing through the doorless arch. The cool of the stone walls wraps itself around them, silencing the breeze and darkening the sky.

Michael runs his fingers along them, imagining everyone else that has walked this path. Most have walked it only to remember— to light candles, as he will do, in the months to co me.

This is a blessing, he tells himself; even if it feels like a curse.

It is easy to find the room where his father waits for him: Lit like a beacon for his son to follow. The warm candlelight travels far out into the hall.

When Michael reaches the doorway, his heart plummets into his stomach, and he drops Cyrus' hand, closing his eyes.

A blessing. It is a blessing, but he can't make himself enter the room.

"Michael?" a voice asks from inside, and he shudders, a sob forcing itself from his lips. "Are you there?"

He never thought he would hear his father's voice again.

"Come on," Cyrus whispers, guiding him forward. "Come on, you don't have to be afraid—"

"Michael, love, why would you be afraid?"

Jack's voice breaks through the darkness of his fear, and Michael forces his eyes open, just as he is pulled into his father's embrace.

"Dad?" he asks, and Jack nods against his shoulder, his voice rough.

"I'm here, kiddo. I'm here."

He is embraced so tightly that he falls apart, sobbing into his father's chest, clinging to his shirt, unable to breathe.

"You have him?" Cyrus asks, and Jack nods, tears in his eyes.

"Yeah," he whispers, pushing the hair back out of his son's face. "I've got him."

"I'll be right back, then. Don't leave till I've returned, please."

Jack nods again, and as Cyrus leaves, Michael holds on tighter— so tight that his knuckles turn white.

"I've got you,," he says, and Michael gasps for air, burying his face in his father's chest.

"I'm so sorry, Dad," he cries. "I'm so sorry."

"Sorry?" Jack asks. "Sorry for what?"

"I d...don't... want you to be gone. Not because of me. Not because of anything—"

"Gone?" he asks, his own voice wracked with tears. "I'm right here."

Michael's sobs grow louder, and Jack holds him closer, running his hands through his hair like he did when he was ten.

"It's okay," he whispers. "It's okay... Hey, look at me."

He pulls back a little, wiping his son's eyes, and shakes his head.

"I don't regret anything. Not one minute. This isn't because of you, and if it was, I still wouldn't change it. Loving you is the best thing I've ever done."

Michael shakes his head, crumbling.

"Your love's the only thing I've ever been sure of," he says. "I don't know what I'm going to do without it."

"You're never going to be without it."

"You're going—"

"It doesn't matter where I go," his father says firmly. "It doesn't matter how far I am, or how different things are. You're always going to have my love, and you're always going to have me. You think I won't be listening, wherever I am? You think I won't be watching you ?"

"We don't know," Michael whispers, and Jack shakes his head.

"The same thing that's carried me here will carry me there, and it'll never carry me so far I can't find you. If I don't know anything else, I know that. You just have to promise to keep talking to me, okay? Keep looking for me. You know all the places to look for me, don't you?"

Michael nods, and Jack takes his hands, trying to memorize the feeling one more time.

"I'm sorry I couldn't protect you," he whispers. "But you're safe now. You're with good people, Michael. *Safe* people. And you're going to be okay." Michael's hands loosen, his face softening. "You know that?"

"No," he admits. "Nothing feels okay, right now."

"I know, but it will. I promise, one day you'll look back at all this and know it can't hurt you anymore. You're going to have to fight..." The words are gentle, but still firm enough to leave no room for argument. "You're going to have to fight *hard*. But remember that I'm proud of you and keep fighting, and keep loving, and never give up on it all, do you understand me?"

"I understand."

"And if it gets to be too much," he whispers. "If it *ever* gets to be too much, you just look up at the sky, wherever you are, and you remember that I'm with you, okay? And that I love you— all of you, and I always have, and I always will, okay?"

"Yeah, Dad," Michael cries. "I love you too."

"More than everything," Jack continues. "You'll remember that, won't you?"

Michael nods, and he holds on tight— memorizing the rhythm of his father's breath, and the feeling of his arms, and the sound of his voice.

"Everything?" he whispers, and Jack pulls him in tight, once more, just like he did when he found him in Jakara.

A goodbye. A blessing. A reminder that he can grow out of the ashes again.

"*Everything*, Michael."

EPILOGUE

"Zahra," Bellamy says, her voice raised. "Zahra, you need to wake up"

The girl opens her eyes, but they are heavy. She looks ahead of her for a moment, not moving, remembering, and her stomach tightens.

She takes a shaky breath, wipes her nose, and pulls herself up. "Awake, ma'am."

"Did you not sleep?" the woman asks, and she rubs her face, shaking her head.

"I slept fine, ma'am—"

"Zahra."

The girl stops, her hands lying limp in front of her, and lowers her face.

"Yes?"

"You can talk to me, if you need to. You can tell me what's wrong."

Gone. He's gone, and she felt him fade. She can still feel it— can still feel the dying, but can't feel him. She can't feel anything but absence.

"I'm fine," she says. "Thank you."

Half an hour later, she is sitting at a table, poking at the eggs on her plate with the tip of her fork, too nauseous to eat.

She tries, anyway.

"A lot of paperwork?" she asks, and the question feels like nonsense.

"I did most of it for you," Bellamy responds. "You'll just need to fill in some basic information."

"Great," she says. "Thank you. And which way is it, to check in?"

"My son will take you," the Sergeant says. "We discussed this previously."

"Right." Zahra nods, forcing a bite down her throat. "Chaperone, yes. Sorry. And you said his name was..?"

"Elio, but you will refer to him as Private Bellamy, unless stated otherwise."

"Right," she says again. "Copy that. *Private Bellamy.* Should be easy enough—"

There's a knock at the door, and she jerks, startled, spilling coffee across the table.

"Sorry," she says. "Sorry. I'm sorry, let me just—"

"*Zahra.*"

"I'm fine," she snaps, but her voice is too sharp, and her hands are too hot.

"It's been two weeks of this, and still—"

"Well, I'm sorry not all of us can move on in two fucking weeks," she says, not meaning to, and Bellamy's face falls. "I'm sorry for swearing."

"Move on from *what*, Zahra? My God, you'd lost everything when you came here and you weren't acting like this. What *happened?*"

"Not everything," Zahra says, but before she can be questioned again there is another knock on the door.

They both fall silent.

"Zahra," Bellamy whispers, gentle. But the girl only shakes her head.

"Please," she pleads. "Please, ma'am, drop this subject."

"We can move your enlistment off a day. You need to talk about this to someone."

"No," she interrupts. "Talking isn't going to help."

"Zahra—"

"I appreciate your concern, but please, stop asking."

Bellamy watches her, the lines on her forehead showing her worry, but Zahra turns away.

She opens the door with unsteady hands.

The man that stands behind it is hardly more than a boy– her age, with dirty brown hair, tan skin, and forest green eyes.

He smiles at her, but it's forced, and she can tell.

"Private Bellamy," she says, and he holds a hand out to her, shaking his head.

"Elio." He corrects her, looking at the red of her eyes and hesitating. "Are you ready to go?"

She glances back at Bellamy, bites the inside of her cheek, and nods, shaking his hand.

"Yeah, I think so."

A few miles away, Rosemarie steps through the door of the military compound they're heading for with a roll of gauze in one hand, and a thick leather ball in the other.

"I'm sorry," she says, tremors still running through her hands. "I'll do better."

"You're fine," the man beside her says. "You just keep working on it. Keep practicing... You're sure you don't remember the cause?"

"My file says they're psychogenic, sir."

He lets out a long sigh, nods.

"Just the same, practice your focus. It isn't uncommon for a man's hands to tremble in battle. As long as you can work past it, there won't be an issue."

She knows the words aren't a threat, but her heart still seems to pause inside of her, as if bracing.

"I understand, sir."

"You all have a few days to get adjusted, though. Remember, training isn't mandatory until two days from now."

"I understand," she repeats. "Thank you, but a head start never hurt anyone."

"Very well," he nods.

She starts to walk away, but he stops her, calling after her before she can get more than a yard from him.

"Rosemarie."

She turns around, eyebrows raised.

"Yes, sir?"

"I want you to know that I respect you for it. The... pacifism."

"Oh." She stands awkwardly, unsure of what to say in response. "...Okay."

"I just want to make sure you understand that standing against violence in any way is an act of bravery, because there are some here who might ridicule you for it—"

"Thank you, sir. I appreciate that, but I'm sure I can handle it." She turns again, waving as she goes. "Have a good evening."

"Have a good evening, Rosemarie."

She walks quickly, her steps light on the ground, and soon she is in the barracks, listening to the creaking sound the floor makes when her boots meet it. She doesn't bother to take them off as she reaches her bunk, climbing up onto the ladder.

She stops, reaches forward, and grabs a small box from the center of the bed, studying it curiously for only a moment before starting to smile, jumping back down.

Elio steps into the room at the exact same moment, Zahra trailing a few feet behind him.

"Elio," Rosemarie says, holding the box in front of her. "Do you have any idea where this came from?"

Elio takes the box from her hands, raises an eyebrow.

"Charcoal sticks?" he asks. "Shit, no. We moved to lead a while ago."

"Yeah, see, that's what I thought. I've been wanting to get some cause... It's easier for me, with the tremors, I can kind of smudge it around, and... Anyway, it was just sitting on my bed..."

Zahra steps into the room, still looking elsewhere, and Rosemarie stops.

Her eyes freeze on the girl, trying to remember and drawing a blank; still, she shakes her head, muttering that she looks familiar.

Zahra tugs her gaze away from what she was looking at previously and looks at the girl across from her, her eyes widening.

"Rosemarie?" she asks, and Rosemarie's eyebrows lift, surprised.

"Oh, you... You are familiar then—"

Zahra steps forward and hugs her tightly, before she can even finish speaking, and Rosemarie feels her heart fall into her stomach.

The stranger is crying, she realizes— her body shaking, her eyes blinking tears onto her shoulder, her hands warm— balled into fists so that the heat does not spread.

And Rosemarie, for all her good intentions, can not really understand the emotion. She does not remember, of course, but even if she did...

Zahra is clinging to her like she might be the last good thing in the world, and she is doing it because for all her time in Trellis, she has had nothing to cling to; no familiar face, no real friend besides Michael, and Michael is gone.

Her cries grow heavier, suddenly, and she feels sorry for it; sorry for making this girl the outlet for her grief, but this girl, she knows, is strong enough to hold it.

Hard enough not to be surprised, even if she cannot remember why.

And so, Zahra falls apart, there, clinging to someone who is almost a stranger— clinging without realizing why Rosemarie's eyes seem to make the pain so much heavier.

Rosemarie wraps her arms around the girl without knowing her, buries her chin in the crook of her shoulder, and holds her tight, not needing to.

Author's Note

If you're reading this, I want to say thank you. Thank you so, so much for listening.

I want to tell you about how we got here, if you'll give me a bit more of your time.

If you haven't finished Icarus yet, please go back and finish before continuing: this will contain spoilers.

My first attempt at writing this story was when I was thirteen years old, and it looked very different. The Grim were not yet even a part of it, and it was set in a world that looked much more similar to ours. Originally, it was focused on a group of Deviations living in what has now become Brekka, struggling to survive under the constant threat of a wicked Commander.

It also featured two E.D.T.s: a dark-haired boy with immense power who worked under the Commander's hand, and a blonde girl that didn't know her power or her past.

Then, at fifteen, it became a very different story in a very similar climate. This time, it followed a group of four friends: A girl with fire in her hands, a boy named Michael who was cast out of his church for possessing deviations, and two best friends-to-lovers that would, undoubtedly, seem a little familiar to most of you.

Over the years there were many different attempts, but none of them were ever complete. None of them worked. Something was missing.

So, I started working on something else.

An entirely different story about realm shifters, and a mystical void called Inanis. A girl who didn't know who she was (again) and a man named Anemos living in the shadow of tragedy: A tragedy in Terra, where a dark force known as Assecula took the man he loved— Cole— away from him.

I only made it about forty pages into this one, because again, I felt like something was missing. But it never left my mind, and I knew, eventually, I would return.

It was early 2021 when I decided it was time.

I was at a particularly turbulent point in my life when I first dreamt up the other boy who visited the void: The boy who disappeared from Anemos' life following the tragedy, and was dead to the kingdom he came from. He was like a phantom in the background of *Void* every time I tried to write it, and slowly, he became what I was most curious to explore.

It was winter when his character started to come through to me: I remember the day. I saw an image of him in the kingdom he loved, striving to make it love him back, only to end up on the edge of a cliff, betrayed by all of it.

Why? Why was he betrayed by his home?

Because of what he was.

For those who don't know: My life has always been heavily touched by religion. I can't remember a time when it wasn't. And my faith was something I clung to very tightly, growing up. (It's something I cling to even tighter, now.)

Icarus found me at a time when I had ceased to pray, due to being told, over and over and over again, that my nature was wrong.

There was something wicked in me that I couldn't purge. It wasn't worth praying, when I could not trust myself to know whether the Spirit responded to me or the devil.

You are good, you are loved, you are okay. Those are the words I felt in my soul, when I prayed for guidance. But how could I trust that, with such a deceitful heart?

I started writing Icarus to show what it felt like to live like that. I started writing a tragedy about a child told that he deserved fire; a child crushed under the weight of his own religion.

Luckily, that is not all this story ended up being. It grew, rapidly, almost as if of its own volition. It became a story about war, about friendship, about love, betrayal, ghosts, family, and so much more. But most importantly, it became about a boy that *was* good and loved, even if he was told otherwise.

In the end, all my stories came together to tell that one, just as they were always meant to. So, I think it would be wrong to end this book without speaking that message as clearly as I can: You are good. You are loved. You are okay.

Michael's story does not end with him being claimed by the sea, mine didn't, and yours doesn't have to, either.

Acknowledgments

Writing this book was truly a marathon, and it took a whole bunch of people to get me to the finish line.

But first, I want to thank my God: the source of my inspiration and hope. None of this would be possible without him.

I want to thank my sister, who told me to abandon my other WIP for this one after reading four extremely messy chapters of the very first draft. Thank you for seeing something special in my story before I did, Sam. Without the late night book-talks, there's no chance I would have gotten this far.

Thank you to my family for encouraging me: For never telling me to do something more practical with my time, and keeping me sane while I abused my sleep schedule for this. Thank you for believing in me and just generally being such an awesome group of people. I love you always.

Thank you to my brother, David, for always being there, and to my friends, who taught me the importance of found-family and make all of this life stuff worth it. You all mean more to me than you know.

To everyone who helped get this book ready to publish— to the people that read it before it was edited, and helped me fix things I didn't even realize were there; to my editor and friend, Brittany— I don't know what I would have done without you.

And lastly, to the reader. Thank you for caring about this book and its characters. Thank you for listening. You make this all possible, and it means more than I will ever be able to express. I thank you endlessly.

CHARACTER GUIDE

Charles (Ch-ah-rls): The Guide, Head of the Council. Brother of Alastor and son of the Original Guide.

Ursula (Uhr-suh-lah): Anemos' mother, wife of Alastor, Council member and overseer of the Karneji Facility.

Alastor (Al-uh-stur): Brother of the Guide, Husband to Ursula, and Father of Anemos. Council member and Overseer of the Karneji Facility.

Anemos (An-neh-muss): Nephew of the Guide, son of Ursula and Alastor. Student of the Ordinem.

Jack (Jak): Adoptive father of Icarus, husband to Aliya. Council member and right hand of the Guide.

Aliya (Uh-Lie-ah): Adoptive mother of Icarus, wife to Jack. Council member. Next in line for the position of the Guide.

Icarus (Ih-kr-uhs): Adopted son of Jack and Aliya. Top student of the Ordinem. Born in Jakara.

Cole (Kohl): Close friend to Icarus and Anemos. Transfer student from the Outskirts. Family status unknown.

Zahra Shah (Zah-rah Sh-ah): Close friend of Anemos. Has lived on the Outskirts most of her life. Elemental Deviation and Realm Shifter.

Elise (Eh-lees): The Guide's assistant. Member of the Higher-Class Ordinem. Background unknown.

Cindy (Sin-dee): Council member. Head of security within the capital city.

Ralph (Ral-f): Council member. In charge of weapons and defense.

Regis (Ree-jis): Ordinem Student. Son of Ralph. Friend of Josh.

Josh (Jaash): Transfer student from the Outskirts. Friend of Regis.

Ian (Ee-uhn): Medic in the Capital city.

Athena (Uh-thee-nah): Close friend to Zahra and Ghost.

Ghost (Gohs-t): Close friend to Zahra and Athena. Unspecified Deviation.

Kieran Atherton (Keer-uhn Ath-er-ton): An E.D.T. under possession of the Trellisian government. Born in Alaheim. Top soldier of Commander Anthony Hawkins. Close friend of Rosemarie. Known internationally as the Changeling.

Rosemarie Cothran (Rose-merry Koth-ren): An E.D.T. under the possession of the Trellisian government. Born in Jakara. Family status unknown. Close friend of Kieran.

Anthony Hawkins (An-thuh-nee Hah-kins): Commander of Trellis.

Elio Bellamy (Eh-lee-oh Bell-uh-mee): Son of Sergeant Bellamy. Soldier of Trellis.

Sergeant Bellamy (Bell-uh-mee): Soldier of Trellis.

William (Will-ee-um): Grim. Prisoner of Trellis.

Cyrus (Sai-ruhs): Grim. Realm Shifter. Former Ordinem student.

Shannon (Shan-nuhn): Grim. Deviation. Background unknown.

Emmy (Em-mee): From Terra, lives in Morta. Daughter of William.

Kane (Kae-n): Grim. Background unknown.

Olive (Ah-liv): Grim. Background unknown.

Elazar (El-uh-zahr): Grim. Follower of the Order. Background unknown.

Nathaniel Warnock (Nuh-than-yuhl War-nok): Credited with writing the majority of the Code. The Ordinem's most revered prophet.

LOCATION GUIDE

The Ordinem (Ore-dih-nem) Territory: Theocratic. Encompasses the Capital City, the Outskirts, and Karneji (Kar-neh-jee).

Brekka (Breh-kah): Southwest of the Ordinem Territory. Formerly a part of Trellis until it seceded over political differences. Governed by its Military.

Trellis (Treh-lis): East of Brekka. Formerly Democratic. Dictatorship. Known for the heavy military presence within its capital.

Jakara (Juh-kar-uh): South of Trellis and Brekka. A casualty of the war between them. Little remains but ash, but some survivors still live on the Jakaran islands.

Alaheim (Al-ah-hime): An Aristocracy across the sea from the Ordinem's Territory, bordered by the Deadlands.

Sciana (See-an-ah): A country southeast of the Deadlands with heavy ties to the Ordinem. Home of many creatures that have died off in the rest of the world.

Arquis (Ahr-quihs): A small, Democratic Island system between the Ordinem's Territory and Alaheim. Most well known for its trading ports.

The Deadlands (Ded-lan-d-s): A large mass of land destroyed in the tearing of the veil. Overrun by beings from Assecula. Desolate.

Realms

Terra (Tare-uh): The earthly realm.

Morta (Mor-tuh): Parallel to Terra. The realm of the dead.

Inanis (In-ahn-is): Parallel to all realms. Worshipped by some. Can offer great power and wisdom to those connected to it.

Assecula (As-sec-yul-ah): Parallel to all realms. A place of darkness and desolation. Capable of possessing the living and the dead.

Important Terms+Roles

Guide: The Ordinem's political leader. The Head of the Council.

Counselor: The Ordinem's spiritual leader. He holds more authority than the Guide, but is largely unknown by those outside of the Council.

Deviation: (1) A person with abilities deemed supernatural. (2) An ability deemed supernatural.

Grim: Those with the ability to see and control souls, before and after death. These are often casually referred to as Reapers.

Myon (M-yon): A term of respect used primarily in reference to the Ordinem's Higher-class.

E.D.T.: A Deviation (1) that is host to the spirit of Assecula.

Veil: That which separates one realm from another. Most commonly used in reference to the veil between Terra and Assecula.

The Six: The five Reapers and one Deviation involved in the tearing of the veil between Terra and Assecula.

Oracamatis (Or-ah-cah-mah-tis): Another name for the first of the five Reapers to fall. His name is not spoken within the Ordinem's walls.

CREATURES

Acthen: Commonly known as "blood dogs", Acthens are wolf-sized, four legged beasts with leathery skin and pale, bony faces.

Oracath: A large creature with bat-like wings, taloned hands and razor sharp teeth. Venomous.

Saenk: Often exceeding ten feet in height, Saenks bear a shape similar to man's, but with arm-like appendages almost the length of their body. Due to their make-up, they are able to straighten these into sharp stakes, as well as use them for climbing, running, and grabbing.

About the Author

Jessica Jeannine is a writer, reader, and all around lover of stories based just out of Atlanta, GA. She lives with her parents, siblings, and two dogs.
When not writing, she can usually be found listening to music, making people coffee, and haunting the library.
The Ballad of Six: Icarus is her debut novel.